PRODUCT OF
THE STREET

UNION CITY BOOK FOUR

E. BOWSER

CONTENTS

ACKNOWLEDGEMENTS

I would love to hear from you, so please consider joining the Product Of the street book group on Facebook!

I want to thank God for letting me be able to write the stories that I love. I also want to thank my mother and the love of my life for putting up with me.

I would like to thank Sallie for staying up with me and encouraging me to write something different. I would also like to thank my editor, Blossom Reigns, for helping to make my book the best it can be! Big thank you to my ARC Reading Team! Also, thank you to Sinful Secrets with a Deadly Bite Group, who always has my back whenever I release, even

WHEN IT ISN'T PARANORMAL. TO ALL OF YOU WHO HAVE SUPPORTED ME THROUGH MY WRITING CAREER, JUST KNOW THAT I APPRECIATE IT. THAT IS WHAT KEEPS ME WRITING.

SIDENOTE THANK YOU FOR ALWAYS BEING IN MY CORNER!

HTTPS://WWW.FACEBOOK.COM/GROUP

MEET THE CHARACTERS

<u>Protagonist</u>

Hendrix 'Henny' Pharma (Black Market Pharmacy, Dr. Sexy)

Malcolm Pharma (Henny's Brother, deceased)

Malikita 'Mala' Samuels (Vanessa's Daughter, Henny's 1st cousin)

Vanessa Samuels (Henny's Aunt, Mala's mother)

Stephanie Jenson (Vanessa's Best friend and Shantel's mother)

Shantel Jenson Waters (Business Manager over all Oz's businesses, Dominatrix)

Rizyn Jose Waters (Shantel's Younger half-brother)

TALI SAUNDERS (TRAVEL NURSE SHANDEA'S YOUNGER SISTER)

SHANDEA 'DEA' SAUNDERS (TALI'S OLDER SISTER, TRAVEL SOCIAL WORKER)

NAOMI SAUNDERS (TALI AND SHANDEA'S MOTHER)

CRESCENT 'CENT' JOHNSON 'WELLINGTON' (C.N.A. FLOAT/ COLLEGE STUDENT)

LENNOX 'OZ' ANDERSON (ESCORT SERVICE, OWNER OF MYTH AND OTHER BUSINESSES)

IAN MORGAN 'LAWE'/ NEVIN 'ROUGE' LAWE (CIA/CEO, OZ'S HALF-BROTHER)

LAKYN KYTE 'LINK' MOORE (COUNTERFEIT/ OWNER OF BLACKBAY CASINO)

LAKINA 'KINA' MOORE (LINK'S YOUNGER SISTER)

LAVERNE AND ELIJAH MOORE (LINK'S PARENTS)

FRANSISCO 'FAXX' WELLINGTON (ARMS DEALER) (TEAM: ACE, ECHO, WHISPER)

FRANCESCA 'CECE' LAKEN WELLINGTON (FAXX'S DAUGHTER)

SANTINO 'STAX' WELLINGTON (FAXX'S OLDER BROTHER/DOCTOR)

SANTINA 'DESIRE' WELLINGTON (STAX'S DAUGHTER, FAXX'S NIECE)

SANTARA 'PASSION' WELLINGTON (STAX'S DAUGHTER, FAXX'S NIECE)

SANTINO 'S.J. /SLAUGHTER' WELLINGTON (STAX'S SON, FAXX'S NEPHEW)

SANCHEZ BUTLER (ARCHITECT/FRIEND OF U.C.K)

NIA 'NIKA' BAILEY (MYTH MANAGER)

DR. SEYRA McQUEEN (OBGYN/ U.C.K. MEMBER, DOMINATRIX)

CRESSIDA 'CRESS' GRANT (CRESCENT'S CHILDHOOD BEST FRIEND)

GABRIEL PARKER (VETERINARIAN/ U.C.K MEMBER)

BRYSON PARKER (GABRIEL HUSBAND X-RAY TECH)

ELIAS KREED (A.O.K., INTERNATIONAL SHIPPING COMPANY, HENNY'S COUSIN)

Kalvary 'Khaos' Danvers (A.O.K member affiliate of U.C.K.)

Kalamity 'Khaotic' Danvers (A.O.K member affiliate of U.C.K.)

Horizon 'Karma' Kalm (A.O.K member affiliate of U.C.K., Link's God brother)

Meridian & Noelani Kalm (Karma's parents, Link's Godparents)

Kodey 'Konceited' Kreu (A.O.K member affiliate of U.C.K.)

Krimson 'Havoc' Green (A.O.K. member affiliate of U.C.K.)

Travis Cortez (Cece's boyfriend)

Adriàn Cortez (Interim police Chief, Travis's father)

Antagonist

Jakobe 'Ja' Howard (U.C.K. enemy)

Xavier 'X' Anderson (Lennox's Brother, Chop-Shop/Smuggler)

Sincere 'King' Kingston (Del Mar)

Princeton 'Yung D-Mar Rapper' (Pusha P) (Del Mar)

Rodney 'Roe' Gates (Shandea's ex, D.E.A. Agent)

Katrice James (Tali/Dea's cousin, Boutique Clothing Store Owner)

Yasmin James (Tali/Dea Cousin, Finance Officer)

Danita James (Yasmin & Katrice Mother)

KENNETH MORGAN (SENATOR/OZ FATHER)

CHARLES MORGAN (MALA'S FIANCÉ, DEPUTY MAYOR/RUNNING FOR MAYOR)

CARMELO ROJAS (CARTEL)

ALEJANDRO ROJAS (CARTEL)

IGNACIO 'TRE' TREMONT (TALI'S EX) (DOCTOR)

ROMAN SHARPE (HUMANITARIAN 'AGAINST GUN VIOLENCE/MUSIC PRODUCER, CRESCENT EX)

MARVIN HOWARD (JAKOBE'S FATHER, CARTEL)

TYENIKA GLOVER (FAXX & SANCHEZ CHILDREN'S MOTHER)

TRIGGER/CONTENT WARNING

EXHIBITIONIST- an exhibitionist is a person who becomes sexually aroused by being observed naked or engaging in sexual acts. This thrill can be achieved through fantasy or by performing these acts in front of people or in public.

VOYEURISM- the practice of gaining sexual pleasure from watching others naked or engaged in sexual activity.

HOPLOPHILE- someone with an irrational love of, or fetish for, weaponry (especially firearms).

GUNPLAY- is used to refer to the practice of including actual or sometimes simulated firearms in a scene. The motivations for this vary significantly among participants, with some using it as another method to experience/control fear. In contrast, others see the power of a weapon as a symbol of dominance since it has often meant just that in history. The weapon is rarely loaded during a gunplay scene, though a minority of gunplayers do, in fact, use loaded weapons for this activity. More commonly, the gun is part of a mindfuck where the sub is led to believe that there is a real risk of injury or death when no such risk from discharge exists.

EDGEPLAY- is a subjective term for types of sexual play that are considered to be pushing on the edge of the traditional safe, sane, and consensual creed. It is nearly universally held that these forms of BDSM activity should not be attempted without proper supervision, safety precautions, etc., as appropriate.

AUTASSASSINOPHILIA- is in which a person is sexually aroused by the risk of being killed. Examples include drowning or choking. This does not necessarily mean the person must actually be in a life-threatening situation.

EROTIC ASPHYXIATION (EA)/BREATH PLAY- is a type of sexual activity that involves intentionally cutting off the air supply for you or your partner. Although it may heighten arousal for some people, it may have **life-threatening implications**.

ROPE BONDAGE- also referred to as rope play, kinbaku, shibari, or fesselspiele, is bondage involving the use of rope to restrict movement, wrap, suspend, or restrain a person as part of BDSM activities. Japanese bondage is the most publicly visible style of rope bondage. An alternative style, "Western bondage," is about achieving restraint.

ORGY- is a sex party where guests freely engage in open and unrestrained sexual activity or group sex.

COLLARING- a symbolic gesture that signifies a committed D/s (Dominant/submissive) relationship. It can be analogous to a vanilla relationship's engagement or marriage.

PRIMAL HUNTER PLAY- Hunters are the Dominant primals. They will hunt down their prey and try everything they can to control the prey. This can involve all kinds of actions, from biting and scratching to kicking and hitting. Also, primal hunters can use mental tricks to subdue their prey. This is known as a mind fuck. Although most primal play is physical, a proportion of it can be mental.

MASK FETISHISM- is persons who want to see another person wearing a mask or taking off a mask. The mask may be a Halloween mask, a surgical mask, a ski mask, a ninja mask, a gas mask, a latex mask, or any other mask.

FINANCIAL DOMINATION (ALSO KNOWN AS 'FINDOM')- is a fetish lifestyle activity in which a submissive is required to give gifts or money to a dominant.

STALKING- is a course of conduct directed at a specific person that would cause a reasonable person to feel fear. Unlike other crimes that involve a single incident, stalking is a pattern of behavior. Stalking is about power and control.

ANTISOCIAL PERSONALITY DISORDER- A personality disorder characterized by a persistent disregard for the rights of other people. Failing to comply with laws and social customs, and irresponsible and reckless behavior.

PSYCHOPATH- A person affected by a chronic mental disorder with abnormal or violent social behavior.

SOCIOPATH- A person with a personality disorder manifests in extreme antisocial attitudes and behavior and a lack of conscience.

SHARED PSYCHOTIC DISORDER- is a rare disorder characterized by sharing a delusion among two or more people in a close relationship.

·

PROLOGUE

SHANTEL JENSON WATERS

Erotica- literary or artistic works having an erotic theme or quality.

"*LET ME PLAY WITH THE PUSSY THAT BELONGS TO ME.*"

I looked down at my phone once more, and up again quickly, before I got called out a second time for being on my phone at the table. I swallowed hard and forced myself to leave Ian's message on read.

> **Lawe: I can still feel the diamond weave rope technique you used on me. I can still feel the burn around my shoulders and arms, but most of all,**

I can still feel your lips wrapped around my dick. You will come to me, Shantel, and then you will cum for me.

I took a deep breath, and squeezed my thighs together, trying not to let his words affect me. It didn't matter because I was already slick between my folds, and I knew if he demanded, I would go to him tonight. I didn't know what it was about him, or maybe I did. It was possibly the fact that he knew that I was stalking him, but I did not know that he had been stalking me first. I blinked twice when Mala came out of the kitchen, looking like who had done it and why. I didn't know what purpose Charles was here for, but I could tell it was a bunch of bullshit. I've known for years that Mala was keeping things from me, hell, from us all, but I understood. I understood that she wanted to handle it on her own, but I couldn't understand her walking away from Link. Mala looked at me, and I tilted my glass from side to side, letting her know that if she was smooth with it she could get by without Charles noticing that she was just thoroughly fucked. I almost smiled at the thought because I knew nothing else would matter when she and Link connected. I bit down on my tongue to keep my mouth shut as Charles spoke, until he noticed that the big ass rock wasn't on Mala's finger. My eyes darted from side to side, trying to figure out what to say to get the attention off of her when Link walked into the room.

I looked around, taking in everyone's posture and demeanor. I could tell Oz and Henny were confused about Link's attitude, but when I looked at Faxx, I could read in his eyes that there was more going on between Link and Mala than sex.

I pushed away from the table, and Henny's eyes landed on me, asking a question without words. I didn't know what the fuck was happening, but whatever it was, it must have come to a head the night that she went to MYTH.

"Mala!" Link shouted. I snapped out of my thoughts, looking away from Henny. I stood up, and it was like shit went down in slow motion. I tried reaching out for Link as Charles pulled Mala toward the door, but it was too late. Link maneuvered away from me and around the table behind his father. Charles opened the door as Vanessa stood up, gripping the table. I looked at Mala, but she was staring at her mother before she glanced in my direction.

"Sorry, everyone. I will see you at work, Link, and everyone else next week. We need to let his parents know as well," she smiled.

"What the fuck is happening?" I whispered. My eyes widened as Link grabbed the platter from the table and launched it at Charles. I pushed his shoulder, causing it to slam into the wall next to his head. We didn't need a concussed or dead deputy Mayor at his parents' home. I was panting hard with my heart slamming into my rib cage.

"What the fuck is your problem, Lakyn?"

"Nigga—" Link seethed as he started forward. Faxx was already out of his seat and grabbed Link under his arms as Oz and Henny approached him.

"What the fuck is going on with you, Lakyn?" Mr. Elijah shouted as the door slammed. I couldn't tell what Faxx said to Link as he gritted his teeth together.

"Naw, fuck that! She's not walking away again. I don't give a fuc—"

"Chill, chill. Whatever it is, we'll deal with it, my nigga. I need you to chill the fuck out," Henny gritted.

My heart pounded as I watched the anger, confusion, and betrayal travel across Link's face while Faxx and Henny spoke to him. His hands clenched into tight fists, and I knew if my mind was swirling, so was everyone else's.

"It's business. It isn't something I can talk about here," Link snapped. Henny put a hand on Link's chest, pushing him backward as Mr. Elijah stepped forward, still not understanding what the fuck was happening. I moved to intercept, because whatever was going on, I knew it had to do with Mala. There was more to the story than I may have initially thought for Link to respond that way. I knew Mala was in love with Link, so her playing this role with Charles after what went down between them made no sense. I stepped in front of Mr. Elijah, causing him to stop before he got closer.

"Lakyn, I'm going to need you to check your tone and actions. It would be best if you had a clear head, and acting this way isn't going to solve whatever problem this is, son. I don't know what is happening, but this seems personal and not business. We should discuss it like a family and figure it out like we do everythin—"

"With all due respect, Father, this is U.C.K. business regardless of personal involvement. I apologize for my outburst, Mother, but I need to handle some shit that y'all cannot and will not be involved in," Link stated. Faxx released him as he pushed past Henny and Oz. I swallowed, looking back at the door and the mess on the floor. My mind swirled with thoughts of confusion, wanting revenge for the look on Link's face as Mala walked out with Charles, and wanting to storm outside to find out what the fuck was happening. I wanted to demand an explanation from Link, and I was about to when my phone buzzed. I looked down, seeing the name that had been consuming my thoughts just a few minutes ago, and I read the message quickly. *Fuck.*

> **Lawe: I won't return like I thought I would, but you can come crawling to me. I'll even let you use that little knife you keep between your breasts, Sweet Angel.**

I sucked in a breath as my nipples hardened, and my brain temporarily went blank as the image of me doing that flashed through my mind. I couldn't figure out how Ian could get to me like this. I didn't fuck with niggas, and I definitely wasn't the type to crawl to nobody. I snapped out of my thoughts when a heavy arm landed on my shoulder and lips pressed to my ear. I hit the button on the side of my phone, blanking out my screen, as I let out a slow measured breath. Oz always had a uniquely intoxicating smell that I knew was specially made for him.

"I don't know where your mind has been lately, Shantel, but if I need to stretch you out over my knee, I will," Oz threatened. The low baritone of his voice mixed with the threat had my body tight.

"Oz—" I started, but the arm over my shoulder tightened, and he pulled me closer.

"Naw, you've missed a total of eight sessions, and we both know that is unlike you. After we deal with what the fuck just happened here, we need to talk. And it will not be like Oz and Shantel. Do you understand me?" Oz demanded.

Everyone who needed to know already knew about me and Oz's situation. Although it wasn't sexual, he was still my Dom. He had been the only person to put order into the chaos of my mind after I was taken. But, that was until Ian Lawe walked into *MYTH* that day and shifted something inside of me that I didn't know existed anymore. I was getting a reprieve because of what was going on, and I was going to take full advantage. I did not know how the fuck I would explain to Oz the entanglement I found myself in. Especially now, after finding out who Ian was to Oz.

"Yes, Sir," I whispered. I felt him pull away as everything else snapped back into focus. Henny was gone after Link, and I saw Faxx on his phone with a frown. Dea sat with a hand over her belly and her light brown eyes on me while Tali helped Mrs. Laverne clean up Link's mess. Oz was already stalking down the hallway, and I knew I needed to follow. They would all be in their emotions and need me to balance their craziness. Whatever it was, I could tell Henny had already felt something off, and Faxx already knew the deal. I turned back to Dea and smiled, letting her know I was good. I thought she would have had a problem with the dynamic Oz and I shared, but Dea actually picked up on our situation before I spoke to her about it. When I brought it up to Oz, I shouldn't have been surprised that he put it all on the table after the Nia incident, but apparently, she had already suspected it. I didn't know how I felt that she easily assessed me and what I needed, but we were similar regarding feeling secure in some ways. They all did that for me in certain ways, but Oz could reach me when no one else could.

I followed in the direction that Oz moved, and as I passed by Faxx, I gripped his arm to pull him with me. He was distracted, and I got the reason since he had basically just gotten married a few hours ago.

"What the hell is going on, Faxx?" I asked. Something told me deep down that there had to be a reason for Mala's actions, something beyond what my eyes could see. I knew Mala loved Link like he was the air she breathed, but when she was leaving, the look in her eyes said she was taking her last breath. What would make her turn away from him again?

"I'll let Link lead with this one. This is definitely more about business, but it has everything to do with family. Eli would not have been able to think levelly if he knew this information right now," he gritted. We made our way through the kitchen and out of the back door. I pushed through the screen door that led into the sunroom, where I saw Link pacing.

"Link, what the fuck is going on? I know you and Mala had history, but there's more to it than that. What the fuck does our business have to do with Charles?" Henny questioned. Oz leaned against the large windows, staring at Link before he shifted his gaze to Faxx.

"Faxx? Does any of this have anything to do with what's going on with you and Crescent's situation?" Oz deduced.

I watched Link's rage build, and I moved slowly toward Link to get in his way. His pacing halted because he didn't want to run me over, but the look of concern etched across my face had him blinking. I could tell his mind was running down so many pathways that he all but zoned out, not realizing he was being asked questions.

"It has some of the same elements as my situation with Crescent, but this is on another scale of shit. Give him a minute because that shit back there was all kinds of fucked up, and the reasons behind it aren't going to be anything none of you are going to want to hear," Faxx stressed. Faxx looked down at his phone again before sticking it into his pocket. I turned back to Link, reaching out to touch his forearm so he would focus on me.

"Link, what's going on? You look like you're about to explode if you don't release the information you know. You understand that if we all know the problem, it will be easier and faster to solve. Maybe at the beginning, your calculations might have said you could handle it without us, but what is the percentage of that chance now?" I urged.

Getting Link to focus on percentages and facts helped the disorder of his thoughts when random factors were at play.

"This nigga got a whole handler over here," Oz mumbled. Henny leaned his head to the side, studying Link. I waited for Link's black gaze to meet mine, telling me he was present. Link took a deep breath, struggling to calm himself. He flicked his gaze to Faxx, and I saw Faxx raise his brows.

"It's Mala," he muttered through gritted teeth.

"We all gathered that. She walked out on dinner with Charles and you're not feeling that because—"

Link cut off my sentence with words that hit me like a splash of cold water, momentarily stunning us all except for Faxx. I had been so consumed by my own hurt, rage, and self-pity that I hadn't even considered there might be something else going on with Mala all these years ago. I just wouldn't have believed it would be to this extent.

Get the fuck out of your head, Shantel.

I hadn't had to scream those words in my mind in weeks, but the stress was mounting as the tension in the air grew thick as fuck. Oz's eyes seemed to dim, and I could see Henny's muscles tighten under his shirt as he held himself rigid. We all quickly realized the gravity of the situation and what Mala had done for over eight years.

"I'm going to kill this nigga! This nigga knows exactly who and what we are, and he still trying to play in our faces?" Henny snapped.

"Then we need to get this nigga to find the original copy and body this mutha fucka tonight. This entire time she was being blackmailed on some bitch shit? Naw, fuck that shit. I don't give a fuck if we related or not. This nigga is about to find himself at the fucking *BUTCHER SHOP* tonight," Oz grumbled. My heart sank at the word blackmailed. How the fuck had I not seen that shit or known it was that fucking deep? The weight of the revelation hit me like a ton of bricks. It suddenly made sense why she had acted so out of character and left Link, me, and her mother the day she turned eighteen without any explanation. I felt a surge of anger toward that bitch nigga Charles for tormenting her all of those years. I could tell Link was on the same wavelength as the others, but I knew Mala and how she thought about things from her point of view.

"Fuck! Y'all do understand that she did this because of this very reaction. We can roll up over there with no plan to take this nigga, but we don't know what else he has planned. He's had eight years to hide his hand and set shit up in case we ever came after him. Regardless of what y'all niggas believe, Charles isn't stupid, but he is calculated in his movements," I clarified.

We all knew that Mala was U.C.K. for life. More importantly, she was family, which made all of this so much worse. But she saw what they wouldn't see and that was if they went down for the murder of the old Mayor, none of what we'd accomplished would have come to fruition. It wasn't only us that we took care of, but a network of people from family to friends that depended on us. Link breathed a long sigh and closed his eyes before they opened again. I could see the makings of a plan forming in his eyes. I saw Faxx step away as he brought the phone up to his ear. Whatever it was, I was going to have to wait because we needed to secure Mala and deal with Charles by peeling the skin from his body while still alive. I smirked to myself because if I knew Mala, she would have imagined doing just that and probably would once we got what we needed.

"It's time for Seyra to do what she returned home to do. I didn't know it would be for this, but Kenny's bitch ass may be the only nigga that could get the location from Charles without his backup plans being alerted. If I get the original, I will be able to tell how many copies have been made and make them disappear, but Mala ain't staying with that nigga, not another—"

Link stopped mid-sentence as Faxx shouted into the phone.

"Bet, Link and I are on the way. Probably like ten minutes behind y'all," Faxx grunted. "Cent, do whatever Milo tells you to do until I get there. If he says to stay in the fucking truck, stay in there. If he tells you to run—"

Henny, Oz, and Link went on full alert. The conversation we were discussing faded to the background at the tone of Faxx's voice.

"Ten minutes," Faxx replied before turning to face us. Link was already approaching Faxx on instinct, and I was on his heels.

"The fuck is going on now?" Oz questioned.

"This chick Gigi from her past just hit Cent talking about she has her sister. Cent and Milo were already out, but the feelin' I'm getting right now is telling me we need to move," Faxx gritted.

"Me and Faxx will handle this. I need an outlet before I snap this nigga's neck and say fuck the consequences. Somebody get Seyra up to speed. We need a meeting with Rodney's boss. He has something to do with this Charles shit," Link stated.

"I'll find out more about his mother's side of the family," Oz said, taking out his cell.

"I'll talk to Seyra and smooth this shit over with your parents," Henny said as Faxx and Link walked back into the house.

ONE WEEK LATER

I slammed my fist into the wall over and over until my knuckles bled, and the pain started to clear my mind. Cent had been missing seven days, six hours, and twenty-three minutes. Faxx was slipping further and further away, and Cece wouldn't leave Shandea's side for a second. We couldn't even lay Milo to rest until this situation was cleared up, and that was also another thing fucking with Faxx. How the fuck had we not predicted this? Why hadn't we put two and two together when Ian handed us those files? It took four days to get a complete timeline of when Crescent and Milo left the house, went to her apartment, and then to the chicken spot. Seeing Pamela slam the butt of a gun in Crescent temple sent all of us on a fucking rampage, but seeing Rodney step out of an alley to drag Cent's body away moments before Faxx and Link showed up gutted all of us. That bitch Pamela was the one handing over information about the hospital to Rodney, but what would've made her go this far? What did Rodney want with Crescent? He doesn't know shit about her. The replay of her breaking Crescent's finger to remove her wedding ring bothered the fuck out of me. What would've been her motive to go to that extent? Why would Rodney want Crescent in the first place? The sound of the footage was taking longer to isolate, but Link assured us that it would be done tomorrow. I really wanted to know what the fuck they were saying because Rodney didn't look happy, but he still helped Pam kidnap Crescent. My phone beeped twice, but I ignored it while I tried and failed to see the connection.

My phone beeped again, and I pushed from the wall of Faxx's in-home gym and moved over to my bag. My body shook, and my hands were no better as I tried to fumble through my bag to get the fucking phone. It was my job to find out all the information about Pamela, but everything I got on that bitch told me nothing of why she held so much hatred toward

Cent. As for Pamela and Rodney, the connection was clear because she was also a part of another hospital takedown in Clapton. She was the witness that sealed the deal, but then she went under the name Patricia Manning. I was just provided that information this morning and needed to run that down. We were only about to get that information because of Ian. It was buried deep and not information that was stored electronically, so Link wouldn't have been able to find that. No wonder it was missed in the initial reports on her. The last name played at the edges of my mind, but I was so fucking tired I couldn't connect all of the pieces. I could barely think straight, but I knew I had to find out more about that bitch before tomorrow. I already had Damari heading to the hospital where she used to work to see what else he could find out. As for this bitch Pam, I was also hoping that with her real name, Link could pull some shit out of his ass. Ian and his team were good as fuck, but I know Link. I knew how he would dig until there was nothing left to uncover. I pulled out my phone to see I had several missed calls from Ian and three text messages. I blew out a breath and opened the messages. I knew I couldn't ignore him for long, but I had to correct my wrongs. I rejected the thought that Crescent was going through what I did years ago, but how would we know that? We didn't know what those two were capable of, and they had been off the grid since their car disappeared in the chaos.

> **Lawe: If you do not answer my next call, I will come to you, Shantel.**

> **Lawe: I will come to you, and I don't give a shit who knows about us.**

> **Lawe: It's been a week, Shantel. Answer me in the next ten minutes, or I will see you in thirty minutes. The chopper is on standby.**

I looked at the time and had one minute to respond to his threat. I hit his number as I panted, waiting for the call to connect.

"Come to me tonight, or I am coming to you," Ian said without greeting. I bit down on my instant reply of *fuck you.'* I knew that anywhere outside of the bedroom, I would fucking fold for him. I closed my eyes and sucked in a breath so I could make him understand that I couldn't.

"Lawe, I can't leave right now. I have to figure out where—"

"You've been going non-stop for seven days on less than two hours asleep a day," he interjected.

"Have you found out anything?" I sighed.

"Even with my access, someone did a good job of erasing Pamela's past. As for Rodney, you know as well as I do, he's protected to a certain extent right now. But as for Pamela a.k.a. Patricia, I will figure out who buried her records. But right now, you need to decompress. Come to me tonight, Shantel, or I'm coming for you," Ian commanded before ending the call. I pulled the phone away from my ear just as a text came through with an address to a hotel in Del Mar.

"Fuck!" I shouted because he was right, and my body was breaking down. I closed my eyes as the feeling of exhaustion, anger, sadness, and need traveled through my body. I felt myself relent, knowing damn well he wasn't lying, he would come for me and find me. I wasn't ready for that or the questions that would come with it. I grabbed my bag and headed for the shower while I texted that I would be there tonight after I got a few hours of sleep.

Once I woke up, it didn't take long to get on the road heading for Del Mar and to the hotel where Ian was staying. Del Mar was a few hours away, but I should make it there in less than three hours with light traffic. While driving, I let my mind wander about everything and what I missed about that bitch. I knew Crescent and Pam disliked each other, but all this, and for what? If she didn't know who she was fucking with, she had to know it now. I let my mind run with all the shit I was going to do when I got that bitch, so much so I had arrived at the hotel, and I did not know it had been two and a half hours of driving.

"Maybe Lawe ass is right. I need to decompress and sleep," I whispered. I pulled up to the front and waited for the Valet attendant to come to the door before stepping out. Lawe's last text informed me that a key was at the desk for me.

"Welcome to *The Royal Meridian Fornices*. Here is your ticket. Please let the concierge know when you are ready for your vehicle, and we will have it waiting for you," the young man smiled. I looked at the name stitched on his shirt and smiled while taking the card.

"Thank you, Abel. Can you have my bags sent to the Presidential Suite, please?"

Abel agreed with a nod, as I reached for my purse and stepped out of my Range Rover. I walked straight to the ivory desk, where a tall woman stood looking at her computer. Her braids were pulled and tied into a tight bun at the back of her neck. Her dark brown skin set off the blond of the braids while also highlighting the gold undertones of her skin. My heels clicked against the marble floors, causing her to look up with a bright smile.

"May I help you?"

"I should have a key waiting for me. Under the name Waters," I said. With a few clicks, I had the card that would give me access to the suite Ian was occupying. After sliding the card through the reader of the private elevator, it shot straight up without stopping until it opened to a large entrance leading into the penthouse. The lights were dim, but my adrenaline ran high as I moved further into the suite. I crossed the penthouse, heading toward the large double doors that I suspected led to the room. I slipped out of my heels, leaving them next to the royal blue sofa facing massive floor-to-ceiling windows that showed the lights of Del Mar. It wasn't Union City, but I saw its appeal and how we would make our mark on this city. Either they bow down to U.C.K., or end up like Sincere, without a head. I sat my purse on the sofa and removed the needed rope.

Ian demanded that I come, and I would demand his submission. The cold marble nipped at my bare feet as I approached the room. I pulled the silk rope between my hands so tightly that the slick fiber bit against my bruised fingers. I pushed open the door and sucked in a breath as I caught sight of Ian. He watched me standing in the doorway while he sat in the middle of the room in a large black leather chair. The him and the chair were only highlighted because the huge row of windows let in the lights of downtown Del Mar. The room overlooked the city, and the only source of bright light was the moonlight washing in, pouring over his naked, tatted body.

His head was tipped back, but I knew his hazel green eye and his brown one, was focused on me. The cords of his muscular frame were highlighted by the pale light showing off his light-brown caramel skin. His salt and pepper tapered fade, and his goatee and beard were freshly shaped up. Ian licked his thick lips as his eyes traveled over my body. His gaze and flesh called to me, almost begging for my touch, and I could tell he felt the same way by how hard his dick was the moment the door opened. It pointed upward but curved slightly toward the right. I sucked in a breath as my clit pulsated, and I became slick just watching him.

"Not sure where to start, Shantel?" Ian chuckled while curling a finger, beckoning me closer like he was still in charge. A grin bloomed across his lips at the way my brow raised while my gaze roamed his body. I hated how, with just a simple gesture or a few words, he could drag me by an invisible red thread leading directly to him. I moved as I gripped the silk rope tightly in my hands and came to stand between his parted legs. I stared down into his light and dark eyes, licking my lips as his dick jumped at my nearness. His grin remained as he held my gaze defiantly from his seat.

"That's *Mastress* Shantel, remember? I'm in control, Lawe," I reminded. I had to know I had this control every single time. That was the only way it could be, and he knew this. Ian bristled and shivered at the sharp tip of my nail under his chin so I could look into his eyes. I had to see into his soul, so I knew he could give me this. Ian was used to being in control, but so was I. I never hid my aversion to submission to him in the bedroom while, at the same time, I didn't really need to voice it.

It was why my heart pounded with fear, affection, and lust when he submitted to me without me saying a word. Knowing how much he trusted and knew me meant so much to me. I craved control, but I also craved his ecstasy and his dominant personality outside of the bedroom. I wanted to hear him beg to cum and melt as I teased him and marked the most sensitive parts of his body as mine. He was just as crazy as I was because he liked what I did to him. I was hungry to be pleased but hungrier to leave Ian delirious with desire.

"You know the drill, Lawe. What's your safe word?" I leaned down to whisper the words against his lips. I let the tip of my tongue trace his lips, just wanting to taste him. He always tasted good as fuck because of the spiced teas he liked to drink. I instantly felt the shift in him as his breath became shaky and hot against my mouth. His body tightened, and I knew he was fighting himself not to touch me. I loved his control, but I loved to cause it to snap more. I hated the fact that he was right, and I needed this.

"Same as always, *Mastress. Awol*," he stated, in a voice so low that it rumbled against my skin, causing my nipples to harden.

"Good," I praised him while running my fingers through the soft hairs of his beard. He moaned and strained not to lean toward me. I saw the struggle in his eyes, but he leaned back into the chair, awaiting my next words. I smiled, loving the feeling of power and knowing he wanted and needed me just as badly as I did him. It was tonight I needed more from him, and I knew he wanted more from me, but he never pressed the issue of sex. I knew once I did this shit, everything would change, and this secret little game was ready to be thrown wide open. Just seeing him sitting and waiting for me shifted something in my mind and soul. Knowing that he didn't expect shit from me while giving me what I needed had me questioning if I *wanted* something more. My heart slammed against my chest because I knew the answer. I knew it the moment he called, worried about my sanity and well-being enough that he would stop everything he was doing just to come to me.

"Just relax," I panted, pulling the rope taut in my hands. Ian's half-lidded eyes met mine and flared like he knew shit was about to change tonight.

"You do this, *Mastress*, and not you or anyone will keep me from you. You know that, right?"

"I'll take good care of you, baby. Hands behind your back, and sit up straight for me, Lawe," I said before I thought twice about his words. They were said deadpan, but I knew it for what it was, and he was serious as fuck.

The way his gaze stayed on me and how he followed my directions without a word made it clear I was about to slide my pussy onto his dick tonight. I flushed hot but pulled up my gunmetal gray mid-length pencil skirt so I could straddle the throne of his lap. My body purred at the sensation of him between my legs. The head of his dick bumped my clit, causing a moan to leave my lips and for him to bite his. Our gazes locked fiercely together while I threaded the rope around his muscled chest. The hair of his beard tickled my neck as I tangled him in pretty knots. I pulled the rope tight.

"Mmmm. You know I like it when you pull a little tighter, Mastress," he grunted against my ear. I knew he could feel my hard nipples through the thin fabric of my blouse. I swallowed as I leaned back to drink him in. I admired the countless tattoos inked across his body, covering his chest, arms, and legs. The ink stopped before it hit his neck and before it reached his wrist, making it easier to cover up. Seeing Ian outside, he was always in suits that covered him from neck to wrist, but it never diminished the dangerous vibe he gave off. I stared at him and saw the threat he could pose in his eyes, yet he gave me the power.

I anchored him to the chair securely, but in the back of my mind, I knew if he wanted to, he could free himself no matter how tight I made his bonds. I pulled the last knot tight and leaned down to kiss medium-thick soft lips.

Even though I had him where I wanted, he took control of my mouth, sucking my tongue into his. I moaned into his kiss, loving the sucking sensation on my tongue, reminding me how he let me sit on his face. He sucked my clit with his hands tied above him and my thighs on either side of his head. I pulled back, panting and feeling the wetness soak through the thin material of my panties. I smoothed a palm down my skirt as I watched Ian watch me.

"Remember, Awol," I reminded him sharply. The thought that he could be slightly in danger excited him. Probably because the first day he ran up on me, I stabbed him in the shoulder for getting too close. The nigga just smirked at me, and my nipples got harder. I knew my craziness always seemed to excite him because it showed in his eyes. The way they lit up and burned when I came around him. I was told repeatedly that I would come crawling toward him once his thick dick branded me. I looked down at his hard length pulsating between my thighs, begging for more attention. The baseball bat he referred to as his dick called to me so teasingly that I dragged the smooth skin of my thighs along the pulsing length. Then I rose from his lap, and a needy hiss escaped his lips as I stood a few feet in front of him. My eyes lingered on him, commanding his attention as I turned my back toward him and began to shed my high-neck white silk blouse, letting the fabric roll off my chestnut brown skin like water pooling to the floor.

My nipples ached to be sucked, and I was glad I wasn't wearing a bra. I did the same with my skirt and panties, not bothering to face him as his groans and deep breathing was enough to have my pussy aching. I heard his breath hitch when I stood up to my five foot-seven height. I could feel his eyes roaming every inch of my naked body. I looked over my shoulder and caught his gaze lingering over Union City's skyline with the four horses of the apocalypse under the letter's U.C.K tattooed across my back. It was somewhat similar to the city just outside the window beside us. Goose bumps rose along my skin in the cool air, but I could feel the heat of Ian's eyes on me, and I knew if he could touch me, he would burn me because of the heat scorching between us.

The only thing left on my body was the strap around my thigh that held my knives. His eyes roamed down until he saw it, and a bead of pre-cum leaked from his tip.

"Fuck," he gritted.

"Not fuck. Beg," I said, undoing the strap and pulling out the knife I wanted to use. I wanted him to beg for it—to worship me. And I knew just how to get his heart pounding harder in his chest like mine did whenever I was in his presence.

"I need you, Shantel. I need to feel your pussy clamp onto my dick while your blade is at my throat," he moaned. His words were heavy, and I could feel the anticipation in the air between us. I saw the question in his eyes that he wasn't sure if I would give him what he'd requested.

"What did you call me?"

"Mastress Shantel," he gritted. His teeth were clenched tightly as I approached him. I sank my teeth into my bottom lip, knowing my eyes radiated nothing but carnal promises and pleasure. I invaded his space like he did to me in public and began to kiss down his neck, trailing my tongue over his collarbone and tracing each tattoo with the blade in my hand. I pressed harder on the fleshiest parts of his chest and arms. I grazed along the bulges of his biceps and over his pecks. I placed the flat of the blade on his nipple. I felt him tremble, and I could taste the mix of adrenaline and musk in the air as I moved the blade over his abs, lowering myself to see his dick. The Jacobs ladder that ran up the underside of his length had me pressing my thighs together as I imagined the sensation of it rubbing against my soaked walls.

"Sssssss," he hissed as I licked the head, slurping his precum into my mouth. While I tasted his him, Ian groaned and hissed as his bonds creaked while he tensed in his seated position. I swept my tongue through the trail of essence sliding down his length, and he groaned, trying and failing to rise from the chair. The taste of him was driving my senses wild. The feeling of the piercing on my tongue only had his hips moving and his length sliding to the back of my throat. The sensuous torture continued as I sank between his legs, trying to take every thick inch I could. His toned inner thighs twitched and jumped at every touch, alive with electricity, as I ran the cold blade over him while I continued to suck.

"Mmmm," I moaned. I kept my eyes on him, and saw when his head fell back when I dragged my tongue from his balls to the tip of his length. I swept my tongue over the tip again, but this time, I hummed deliciously in response to his groans of aroused pleasure. My tongue teased his head while the knife in my hand pressed into his thigh.

"Fuck! Shantel. *Mastress*, I need you to sit my pussy on this dick," he grunted.

The wild look in his eyes as I pressed the blade harder had me wondering if he wanted the cut. I smirked as I cupped his balls with my other hand and then used my hand with the knife to stroke him without applying the amount of pressure needed that would cut myself.

"Fuck!"

I fed his length further into the cavern of my throat, swallowing around him while my senses blurred—my mind awash in lust. I was on autopilot, teasing and punishing him for thinking he could order me here. I was becoming intoxicated by power. I relished in his every tiny reaction to his overstimulated body.

"You want more, baby?" My whispered question sounded slurred while I licked a trail up his body to his neck. I pressed my lips against the shell of his ear.

"Do you?" I asked again.

"Yes," he hissed with impatient need.

"What was that?" I asked, bringing the tip of the blade to his throat.

"Yes, Mastress," he answered, licking his thick lips. I could feel the strain in his body, and I knew if I let him go he would pin me down to the bed to fuck the shit out of me. I just didn't think my mind could handle that. But the more it played in my head, the more I craved it. The more I needed it. The more I just needed all things him. I hated my obsessive thoughts, but my obsession with Ian Lawe was quickly getting out of my control, and he knew it.

"This will mean nothing, Lawe," I whispered. His deep chuckle against my skin lit it on fire, causing me to pull back slightly.

"The fact that you believe that shit is hilarious, Shantel. Once I brand my name on those walls, you are not going any fucking where, and I dare a nigga to check me on it," he warned. His dominant personality had my clit throbbing, but I still had to have this. I had to be in control.

"Beg," I commanded, pressing the blade harder into his neck. Only enough to excite him but not hard enough to break the skin. He winced but moaned my name while trying to rock his hips.

"Fuck me, Shantel. You know you want to sit that pussy on me, grind on this dick, and fuck me so you can feel the drag of my Jacob's ladder against those tight-ass walls," he growled with a dangerous look on his face. A boundary within us was blurring because I wanted to feel that, and I wanted him to hold me down on his length while I took what he could give. I moved, not thinking twice about what I was doing, and heard the snap of the rope. Ian wasted no time yanking at the knot at his wrists. My heart pounded in my chest as his hands gripped my waist, and he rose from the chair. Instinctively, my legs wrapped around his waist while his wide eyes stared at me intensely as he glared possessively at me. What the fuck was I doing? One hand stayed securely around me as the other powerful hand came up to close around my neck like an iron collar. He moved until I hovered over the California King-sized bed.

This was the first time since the night I was taken that I found myself in a weakened position. But, what shocked me more was that my mind didn't black out while he pinned me beneath him. Ian stretched me out on the bed as my knife fell from my hand. I felt my need for control being replaced by a different type of need. I needed him more than I needed to feel in control, and that scared the fuck out of me.

"The knife," he ordered. I instinctively reached for it and then placed it in his hand.

"I told you that you would come to me, Shantel. All I had to do was let you set the pace, and you came crawling like a good girl for me," he smirked.

"Lawe," I moaned as the head of his dick slid between my folds, getting coated in my juices.

"Now, let me play with the pussy that belongs to me," he commanded.

Ian's body blanketed mine while his fist balled around the knife handle. His hand never left my throat, so I knew he felt my pulse slamming against his fingers. The blade sank into the mattress beside my head as he squeezed my neck. The sudden, violent thrust of the blade into the mattress caught me off guard, but it had my legs wrapping around his waist, trying to pull him closer. I could feel the glide of the cold steel against the skin of my cheek as he moved the blade like he was fucking me.

"Oh my God," I moaned as my walls clenched for something to grip on. Ian's grasp tightened further while his teeth grazed my flesh like he was ready to take a bite out of me. I felt his teeth pulling at my hard nipple, and his tongue circling as he sucked each of them into his mouth. His hot tongue seemed to brand my flesh while he pinned me down. I clung to him, my fingers trailing overheated cords of muscle. His dick sat at my entrance, pushing in slightly, and pulling back out. I tried to move to take in more, but he pressed me down harder into the mattress.

"You want it?" he asked as his hips rocked slightly, edging me. Ian dragged his hot length between my slick folds, causing my pussy to tingle and throb, internally screaming to feel him deep inside. I couldn't think straight enough to form words as I began to get light-headed. He eased his grip while leaning down to bite my lips till they stung, and I nodded helplessly, trying to beg for him to fill me. I needed him to claim me, and make me remember what it felt like to truly be wanted.

"Beg for it, Shantel. Let me hear you," he demanded. I trembled with need and lust as my juices slid over my thighs and covered his dick. I was leaking for this man, and I never thought this shit would happen to me.

His hips paused, punishing me, leaving my sensitive folds yearning for more stimulation.

"Annh! Please fuck me, Lawe! Fuck me, m-master—"

My eyes were wide at my words while my heart damn near leaped out of my throat. I couldn't believe I said that word not after—not after—

"That's my good girl. Eyes on me, Shantel, and I'll give you what you want," Ian grunted. His focus stayed on my eyes until all I saw was him. It was almost like he knew to wait until I was fully present in the moment. Ian bit his lip as his attention drifted to my sopping core. My hands gripped onto the sheets as he hooked his forearm under my back and around my waist, pinning me in place as he reared back. I looked down at his long thick dick as the metal in it glistened. His head fell in line with my entrance, but before he moved, he placed his hand around my neck and pulled me down forcibly. Ian slid in so deep I couldn't help the scream that tore out of me.

"Fuck! Ian! Oh God," I cried as he backed out slowly, tormenting me salaciously with his languid pace. Then his hips bucked, and I raised to meet his thrust, but his large hand subdued me, and the other massaged my neck while he pulled out then slid back inside. The Jacobs ladder caused a sensation like a ribbed condom making my pussy walls clutch him tightly as he slammed back in. My body trembled from the sensations of it as it dragged along my walls, touching spots that lit my soul on fire. If my pussy could cry, it would have wept at how good his slow, deep thrust felt as he licked at my lips while staring into my eyes.

"Fuck Shantel. I want you to say my name and bend all your rules for me. I want you to break for me, and know I will always put you back together," he gritted against my lips. My mind went blank under the tender, yet possessive thrust of his hips, and words. Ian took his time dismantling me with every stroke of his length. All my worries and thoughts evaporated under his touch, caresses, kisses, and possessiveness. The way he filled me drove me mad with ecstasy as I melted for him. His fingers slid up my jawline, gripping my face and forcing me to look at him as he licked his way into my mouth. Each push moved my body across the bed. I lay beneath him as my body moved over the satin sheets, and his muscled body flexed over me, driving his dick faster and deeper into my core. I would swear time crawled to a halt as he fucked me so hard, fast, and then slow as tears rolled out of my eyes. I felt his tongue follow the trail of tears along the side of my face. Our bodies were built to a fever-pitched climax, causing us both to moan.

"You like playing with knives, but this is the only sheath mine will slide into. You're mine, Shantel, so you might as well accept it. It's been this way since the day you stabbed me," he grumbled against my lips. His words ripped the coil of pleasure in my gut that was twisted tightly, causing it to snap finally. The dam broke, and I went right with it.

"Ian! Fuck, shit, fuck! Oh Jes—oh my God," I cried out. My pussy convulsed around his girth—milking him, trying to take all the seed he had out of his body.

"Ian! Fuck, yes, Ian," I screamed louder as my orgasm came so hard that when he squeezed my neck, I thought I would black out. My walls gripped him and pulled a low, deep groan from Ian's chest that vibrated through my body. I could feel his length throbbing as he sped up, roughly pounding his cum inside of me. His long wide dick stretched me open, making my walls form to his length. He consumed me, and I wasn't afraid.

"Take all of it, Shantel. No going back, understand me?" He whispered against my lips. Ian pumped wave after wave of his thick essence into my depths, coating me, and branding me at the same time. Ian's hand squeezed me tighter as he pulled out to the tip and slammed back inside, grinding his thick cum covered dick into my core, causing my body to shake uncontrollably.

"If you think your thoughts about me are obsessive, then wait until you understand how it feels to be possessed by your obsession," he whispered against my skin, marking me with his words. How the fuck is he reading my mind?

Shit. I am so fucked!

My eyes opened to sunlight beaming down on me. My entire body was sore, but I waited for the panic and fear to kick in as Ian held me around the waist. I held my breath, but nothing happened. I slowly let out the air from my lungs and swallowed.

"Angel, when will you tell me what you are so afraid of? I think I've shown you that whatever it is or whoever it is, it isn't me," Ian said in a low husky tone. I opened my mouth, but closed it, not ready to bring up that time as memories assaulted me. I gently moved his hand, so I could sit on the side of the bed.

"Shantel—"

"I'm going to jump in the shower and then find a gym," I smiled, turning to face him.

"We will talk, Shantel, but I'll give you what you need," Ian conceded. I leaned over, kissing his chest before I stood. I could feel his eyes watching me, knowing he wanted to ask more questions. He probably would tell me about the state-of-the-art gym in this hotel, but Ian Lawe wasn't a stupid man. He knew I needed a little space.

After handling my business and quickly showering, I returned to the room to see Ian sitting at a large desk on the opposite side of the room. His laptop was open, and he had his phone to his head, but he heard me. He didn't stop speaking as he pointed to my luggage. I grabbed a pair of black sweatpants and a large tee shirt from my bag. I put it on, smelling like Henny, and when I looked up, I saw a frown on Ian's face. I grabbed my sneakers and threw them on before he could finish his call. I moved through the room quickly then went out of the door to grab my purse and phone. I headed for the elevator and called the concierge to bring my SUV.

I did lie because I wasn't going to the gym. I would find the first convenience store around to get a Plan B. I knew better than to have unprotected sex because I didn't want children. I was too damaged to raise a child, and I knew if I were to get pregnant, Ian wouldn't bat a fucking eye. He would expect me to keep it, and for us to raise it together. How could I bring a child into this world knowing full well the horrors of this place? I closed my eyes briefly, still trying to reconcile that fact I called him...shit. I last used that word when I was forced to say it repeatedly. And I swore I would never call someone else that even though I knew the world I frequented. It never happened, not until today. I was the fucking *Master*, but now—

I stepped outside into the cool air just as my SUV was brought to the front. The young lady got out smiling, and I handed her my ticket. I tried to push the intruding thoughts out of my mind and focus on something else, but it was beginning to get harder.

"Good morning. I hope you have a wonderful day," she smiled. I looked at her name while taking my keys and handing her a tip.

"Thank you, Beth. I hope I will as well," I said, sliding into the driver's seat. I pulled out and stopped at the stop sign, pulling out my phone. I typed in the nearest convenience store to the hotel, hit the navigation, and pulled out into traffic. I took slow, measured breaths, trying not to freak the fuck out about Oz learning about this situation. I think I feared he might keep me at arm's length and our close relationship would suffer. I pushed past those thoughts as well.

Crescent. Crescent. Crescent. She should be my only focus at this moment.

I made a right at the light and pulled into the parking lot of *Wayward Goods and Pharmacy*. I backed into the parking space and cut the ignition. Reaching for my purse, I saw a few customers leaving the store. And that's when I saw that bitch, Pamela.

"Son of a bitch," I whispered, restarting my engine to follow her.

CHAPTER ONE

FRANSISCO 'FAXX' WELLINGTON

I hopped out of the truck and looked up at the matte gray of the large box-shaped building that Alex's family-owned. I didn't have time for bullshit, but them niggas thought it was a good idea to keep fucking with us. Alex made a move on my business, stopping a shipment of weapons needed to fill a contract I had with a few agencies. Roman thought it was a good idea to make a move on our docks, and that shit wasn't about to happen. Not only did I need to find Crescent, but we had to ensure our city stayed intact. This nigga thought it was a good idea to touch my shit, and I needed him to understand U.C.K. didn't give a fuck about them, nor their people. I couldn't wait until it all came crumbling to the fucking ground. I heard the other vehicles pull up as I moved towards the building that should have been empty. I was sure Alex didn't have shit to do with Crescent's kidnapping, but she wouldn't even be in this position if it weren't his fault somewhere down the line. We knew that Roman had nothing, or almost nothing to do with Cent being taken, but in my eyes the shooting made it possible for this shit to happen.

Everyone connected to Crescent's kidnapping was going to feel it, and I didn't give a fuck what anyone had to say. At first, looking at the footage once it was put together, I didn't understand why the fuck Rodney was helping Pamela. We knew their connection about the hospital, but her hatred toward Cent made no sense. A work fight wouldn't constitute someone going to the extent of kidnapping. Then there was the look of 'what the fuck' on Rodney's face when he stepped out of the alley and saw Pamela dragging Crescent. I couldn't make this shit connect in my head, but Link gave his word by the time we finished here, he should have the audio of that night so I could plan my kill list out accordingly. Next on the list was running up in Roman's shit. No matter how far removed from the situation, his actions that night made this shit possible. With that at the forefront of my mind, all I could think about was dismantling everything until I got the information that I needed to find my fucking wife. The first place we went to was Pamela's home, leaving a trail of evidence heavily connecting Rodney to her and her accounts as a payoff for her lies. Then I allowed Cece to push the detonator button to watch that bitch go up in flames. Cece's mental health was important, but I wasn't stupid, and I knew she needed an outlet for the rage she felt at losing Cent. My daughter was fighting for her sanity, and could barely be away from me, or any of the others. She was attached to the hip with Shandea and Tali after asking to burn Pamela's house down. But today, Shandea and Tali had an appointment about their mother that couldn't be missed. After that, Dea had an appointment with Seyra, so I knew we had to get this shit done soon so Oz could be with her. So, since Dea and Tali had stuff to do today, Cece was with her Papi and Uncles. My daughter's eyes were beginning to match my own, and the increasing whispers she was having with her "*dolls*" were getting darker and darker. Since Dea learned about Cent, we've collectively worried Dea would enter preterm labor. I knew Oz wanted to return as soon as possible because we had been worried that she'd been gaining weight too fast. We knew Dea was beginning to panic, but when Cece was around, it seemed to calm them both down. I shifted my gaze as Henny sucked his teeth before swinging open the large steel door. I knew that Alex thought no one knew this was his little stash spot for illegal weapons, and he thought placing the shipment into a family-owned building would hide what it actually was. An auction house for untraceable weapons. *Fuck him.*

I could feel Henny's agitation and rage as if it were a living, breathing thing as he walked beside me. I was fighting hard to stay present, to keep my mind clear enough to function. I knew that was the reason none of them would leave me to do what I needed to do. Maybe blowing up a residential home had gained a lot of attention, but fuck it. Each day that Cent was missing, I would blow up something until someone started talking. People were there, and someone saw something. Niggas would talk if they were afraid their shit was next. Pamela's little nurse friends understood what the fuck was going on when their shit got ran-up in as well. Some people wouldn't be showing up for work, but that's neither here nor there. At least Oz left a cleaver at random times to throw some shit off. The same with some of Rodney's little spies. He might as well had called their families because none of them niggas were going the fuck back home. I would run these streets red until I get the necessary answers.

"If you're worried about more heat coming to us, then you should have stayed at the hospital," I stated. We passed the large desk where a security guard normally sat. Today it was empty after I dropped in on them niggas. Alex probably didn't realize that his small security force to guard this place had all been taken the fuck out. Slit throats and headshots to each bitch who thought to pick up a weapon. The ones that surrendered got taken to the *RANGE*. I knew they could have some useful information, but it was really for a nightcap. I couldn't sleep, and I needed...distractions. Target practice helped me to hold back the blackness that was trying to consume me. No one said anything about it, or the extra time I took blowing off limb by limb, making my brother or Henny patch them back up so I could continue.

"Nigga, fuck you. I don't give a shit about the heat. I know that's coming. I need to make sure your bitch ass is still around once we get Cent back," he grunted. I side-eyed him, and I could tell I wasn't the only one trying not to burn this city the fuck down. At least not yet.

"Stop fucking blaming yourself for shit you didn't know. No one knew Pamela would do some shit like this. Why would we?" I asked. None of us would have pegged Pamela for this bullshit. I was for sure it was all fucking Roman behind this shit or even the Cartel. I was sure Gigi was a setup to get Crescent, but we were wrong. The only thing to come out of any of this was that we got Dylan, but even that was a touch-and-go situation. Luckily, Jacinda was needed because of Dylan's rare blood type. Otherwise, I would've blown her neck off when she blamed Cent for what happened to her sister. The bitch was madder at the fact that she could lose out on her payday than her child's safety. I knew this building held four underground levels, so I hit the button for the elevator as I leaned my neck from side to side, trying to release the tension. I watched as Henny dropped one of the small duffle bags next to a trash can before he came to stand next to me. It was early as fuck, but the people who ran this spot would be here soon. Alex will be aware of the downfall of his security in the next twenty minutes when he called. I need to see his face when close to sixty million dollars' worth of weapons crumbled to the ground causing a sandstorm around this bitch. I wanted it so hard to see that once it cleared, the entire area was leveled to the fucking ground.

"I should've slit her fucking throat when we were in that meeting. The fact that I thought about it after she touched Cent should have been my warning. I didn't see this happening, and I should've. Just like that nigga Eric. When we find him, I'm chopping off his fucking hand for thinking he could touch my work wife. That treatment needs to be a fucking standard from here on out. No grace to none of these niggas, and I don't give a fuck if they are U.C.K., they touch, they die. Then maybe mother fuckas will understand," Henny fumed.

"You do know Cent is my wife, right?"

"Semantics, my nigga," he retorted. Henny cracked his neck while clenching and unclenching his hands. The only time I've seen Hendrix this mad was when Malcolm died. Maybe the streets would run red again. I smirked as the door to the elevator opened. We stepped inside, and I hit the button for the lowest sublevel.

"Henny, it's impossible to do it all or see it all, no matter how powerful we are. Sometimes shit goes Fubar. At least now we have a way to prevent shit like this from happening again," I said, as he nodded. Link finally finished a project he had been working on since the Dea situation. If only it were ready before all of this shit happened. As soon as I got Crescent back, she would be tatted and then cuffed to my fucking wrist.

"That's true, but we should have anticipated this. We knew shit would change, and they were our weaknesses once they came into the picture. This is why I wanted more time, but as you say, we can't control everything, and I don't like that. But, at least Tali will be getting hers tomorrow once Link finishes the last round of testing," he stated. I could feel Henny's dark gaze on me, and I smirked slightly because I knew what he was thinking.

"You sound and are acting entirely too calm," Henny observed. The chime of the elevator sounded. I stuck my hand into my hoodie pocket, pulling out a small black box that looked like one of the buttons belonging to the elevator. I slammed it next to the other numbers and smiled wider. I knew my smile looked unhinged, but I couldn't help it. It was going on eight days without Crescent, and I know I hadn't slept more than six hours out of those days.

"You will understand that sense of peace once you feel the blast. It's cathartic," I said, stepping out to see rows and rows of weaponry. My shipment that was stolen hadn't been this much, but interest was a bitch. I looked to each side, calculating how much we would get before my phone call. I raised my wrist and typed in commands for the team to come and take what they could while we placed the charges.

"I can understand what you mean. It's the same way I feel during surgery," Henny chuckled.

"Surgery as in slitting a niggas throat?" I asked.

"Exactly. To be honest, I hate the fact that we are here dealing with this bullshit because niggas think they can attack us. We have better shit we could be doing," he swore. No one was at the desk toward the back of the basement, but the large office doors were open, and I could hear two voices speaking. I was told two people would be here because of the large shipment that had just been dropped off. Lucky for them. Messages had to be sent since niggas thought they could come at us. People just kept trying to test U.C.K., and I was done with it. I had no more fucks to give. I wanted things quiet, so it could be easily swept under the rug when it came to Alex and Roman, but fuck it.

"Do you think this may be too much for Francesca?"

Henny stopped next to me, looking down at his phone. I received an alert on my watch telling me that our team was entering, and the countdown had begun.

"My niece is one of a kind. As much as we want her to be a normal child, she isn't, and that's okay because we know exactly how to handle her. If we don't manage her need for revenge about her mom being taken, her mind will split further to handle the trauma. Seeing something being done to fix the problem will keep her in the here and now," Henny stated. Quiet as kept, I knew he knew exactly what he was talking about because of Malcolm. His brother broke when they lost their father, and the only thing that held his mind together was tracking down those involved until they got to the right person. Henny never told anyone that. I only knew because Malcolm told me himself one drunken night.

I sighed as I stopped in the doorway to see two men pointing to a clipboard.

"It may have been better if y'all would've called out sick. I could've even given you a doctor's note," Henny smirked. I reached for my Glock in my holster and pulled it out. I shot one of the men in the kneecap as Henny shot the other in both shoulders. The taller man holding the clipboard was thrown over the desk by Henny's shots while the man I shot fell to the ground holding his leg.

"Ahh! Ahh! Who...who the...do you know where you are—"

"Nigga shut the fuck up. The question should be, what can you do to make it out of here alive," I chuckled. Moving forward quickly, I kicked the man on the ground in his blown-out knee before leaning over and shoving my Glock under his chin.

"Do you know who the fuck I am?" I gritted through clenched teeth.

"Fifteen minutes," Henny said. I felt him move by me, and I heard the other man scream as Henny dragged him from behind the desk.

"What do you want? What do you want? Money? Gu—"

I pulled my Glock away and slammed it across the man's face twice until I heard teeth crack.

"I want to watch every last thing your boss owns burn to the fucking ground. Now get the fuck up and walk that shit off. We have a call to get ready for," I grinned. I stood up while gripping the collar of his polo shirt and dragged the rotund man to his feet. His rutty cheeks grew redder from the pain as I got him to his feet.

I felt someone at the door and could sense who it was before he spoke. I was sure Gabriel had already put the other bombs on the upper levels. I knew he was going to be pissed about the time limit I put on gathering these weapons, but it was what it was.

"Faxx, stop playing with these niggas, and let's go. We have their vest for them to wear, although it looks like it may be a little snug on kneecap over there," he stated flatly.

"We're ready. How much did you get?" I answered. The brown-skinned older man Henny shot was still screaming but screamed louder as Gabe shoved the vest over his blown-out shoulders.

"What do you want? What do you want?" he screamed until Henny placed a scalpel on the side of his neck.

"All we want is for you to shut the fuck up and go down with the nigga you work for. You know this is Union City, and your boss touched our shit, so you will pay for his crimes. Take that shit and man the fuck up," Henny seethed. Gabe moved over toward me, handing the vest to the other man to put on.

"My fucking leg, I...I can't—"

"Fuck it," I gritted and put the Glock to his head, pulling the trigger.

"Oh, my God! We don't know anything! I don't want to die. I don't wanna die, I don't wanna die," he cried as Gabe shrugged and turned to push that crying ass nigga out of the door. I looked at my watch, and time was just about up. I followed Henny out of the door and was surprised at how much was taken in such a short amount of time. I honestly didn't give a shit about it, but it was to prove a point. No matter what the fuck was happening with U.C.K., business would always be handled.

"Let's move unless y'all want to dig your way out," I shouted as people moved to the large industrial elevators after loading the last of the pallets of weapons.

We stepped outside just as Gabriel finished slamming the last Centaur forge railroad rail track spike into the collarbone of the man, pinning him to the outside of the building.

"Ahh! Ahh! Please, plea—"

Bang!

The last swing of the sledgehammer sounded against the concrete of the building. I didn't even look over as I approached the truck where Oz, Link, and Cece stood. Link held Cece in his arms as he rubbed her back while she lay on his shoulder.

"Gabe, inventory all this shit and put it in storage," I shouted back at him. The vehicles and trucks were loaded with two minutes to spare. Cece raised her head at my voice, and red-rimmed eyes looked at me.

"Papi, was Cent in there?" Cece asked. Oz rubbed a hand over Cece's two French braids while she played with Link's locs. That was always Cece's go-to when she was upset. Cece dropped Link's hair, and leaned over, so Oz could take her.

"No, baby. She wasn't," I said, pulling out my phone. Francesca buried her face in Oz's shoulder, and Link stared at me before looking back at his laptop on the truck's hood.

"Just blow it up, Papi," she cried. Henny raised a brow, and my phone rang right on time. Oz sucked his teeth and opened the back door, putting Cece inside before climbing in. Link closed his laptop and slid inside to the driver's side.

"Alex!"

"What the fuck do you think—"

"Hold up. Let's make this a video call," I chuckled. We moved closer to the truck to be sure we were far enough away from the blast. Everyone else was pulling away, leaving us the last to go.

"Where are the rest of my people, you son of a bitch! My brother-in-law may lose his fucking right lung trying to deliver your fuckin—"

"There we go. Look familiar?" I asked as his tirade came to a stop. The man nailed to the building wailed out in pain as blood pooled at his feet. I was surprised the pain didn't knock his ass out.

"This is a bad move, Fransisco. You will not be able to get away with—"

His words were cut off as the building exploded from the inside like a planned demolition. The concrete began to crumble as each of the C4 exploded. I waited a few more minutes before returning the camera to face me.

"Don't get too comfortable, my nigga. No one is untouchable in my fucking city, and I don't give a fuck who your family is," I threatened before ending the call. I turned to look at Henny as he ran his hand over his goatee. His platinum grills flashed in a sneer before he exhaled.

"Where do you need to go next? Clapton?"

"Exactly," I agreed.

The footage Link had put together finally had sound. While he drove, I listened to the short but informative conversation Pamela and Rodney had before they dragged Cent away. I already knew Pamela was the one to hit Cent, but was she the mastermind behind the kidnapping or what?

"I didn't call you here to just fucking stand there," Pamela shouted.

"What the fuck are you doing, Pam! I am not getting involved in your little vendetta," Rodney gritted.

"If you want more shit on Hendrix, then we need to get her out of the way. I can't get close if she is in the way! She is fucking up two things in my life. You need me to win this case, Rodney. Who else is left? Who else do you have?" Pamela shouted.

"Help me, and I will do whatever you need me to do. No questions asked," Pamela finished.

She pulled Cent's motionless body away from Dylan. Pamela stopped dragging Cent, dropped her like trash, and reached for her ring. She twisted it so hard I heard the snap and knew for certain her finger was broken. Pamela threw the ring on the street, which was filled with so much chaos that no one watched them. Pamela was spotted sitting outside Cent's house earlier that evening. She sat staring at the apartment building for hours without blinking and had a look of pure hate on her face. Why? All this couldn't be just because she thought Crescent and Henny were together. This bitch was crazy as fuck.

"You better have a fucking plan on how to get the information we need out of her, Pam. You have a week before I make this call. I know people who might want this one, and it will be less I'll have to clean up," Rodney grunted.

I watched as Rodney pushed Pamela out of the way and began to drag Crescent toward the alley, where he'd stepped out. I saw the headlights of a vehicle, but that was all I could see as he dragged her into the darkness. That shit didn't do a damn thing but added fuel to my rage.

We had moved from business to business that Roman owned under the table, blowing each of them up in relation to Milo. At the same time, in search of answers, we tried to find Cent. I got a text message this morning from Shantel letting me know she had some information on Pamela, but she was waiting for a few more things. I saw we had at least four hours before the meeting, so I let the adrenaline course through my veins.

The last stop was the residence where Crescent lived with Roman until she got the fuck out. The gated driveway didn't mean shit, and neither did the small guard shack in front of it. A dark-skinned nigga leaned out, revealing a dark green shirt with a security logo of a company we just blew up. I guess he didn't know he no longer had a job.

"This is private—"

Link let the window down, pointing his DWX 9mm out of the window, shooting the man in the forehead. Before he could hit the ground, I opened the gate while typing a few commands on my watch.

"Uncle Oz, can I sleep with you and Dea again tonight?" Cece asked. I looked in the rearview mirror at her on her tablet. She pushed the large black and pink headphones off her ears to look at Oz.

"Of course, princess. You don't have to keep asking," he answered.

"When Auntie Dea has the babies, and it's girls, I can't be your princess anymore," she frowned. Oz raised his brows as he looked down at Cece. Oz stared at me, and I waited to see how he would handle it. Oz might as well get practice in now. Link pulled up the long driveway and saw at least six vehicles lined up. We parked away from the house to watch the fun safely when it happened. We already knew Roman bitch ass had been in hiding since the country club, but still trying to call shots.

"If we have a girl, then I will have two princesses, but that means you will be a big sister," Oz said, removing her headphones. He hadn't acknowledged Cece's use of girls in plural, knowing the other baby was already deceased. I looked up as Cece's eyes widened at this announcement.

"Would that mean I have to babysit them? I can babysit," she said, staring at Oz.

"Yup, it's a big job. Can you handle it?" Oz asked. Cece scrunched up her face as she looked in my direction.

"Will Cent be mad if I'm a big sister to Dea's baby first?" she asked me.

"No, baby. She will be happy about it," I answered.

"Is she at this house?" Cece asked. I took a breath, but Link answered instead.

"I don't think she is, baby girl, but some of these people were there when she went missing," he said.

"Can I blow this house up if she's not? I don't like how it feels," she asked as Link parked further away from the other vehicles.

"We'll see. If you can finish all of your work while we ask some questions, I'll let you push the button," I bargained.

"Uncle Stax told me that pushing the button is a really important job, and it tells everyone not to press my buttons," she smiled.

What the fuck?

"Finish your classwork, and then I will see. Uncle Henny is going to make sure you finish all your work," I insisted, gripping my Glock tightly in my hand.

"Okay! Uncle Oz, I think I can help you out and babysit sometimes," she answered, switching subjects.

"Thank God because I didn't know what to do without your help. Now, be good and finish your work, or no reward. Uncle Henny will know if you're cheating," Oz warned.

"Francesca is too smart to cheat, right?" Henny asked.

"Yup, plus Travis would be mad if I did. He says doing your own work is best because no one is smarter than me," she smiled. No one said a word about that damn doll because it was the first time she talked about it since Cent had been taken. I took it as a good sign and opened the door. I stepped out of the SUV, gripping my Glock tightly, my fingers wrapped around the cold metal. I kept circling back on Pamela and Rodney, imagining breaking their bodies into pieces. Even though this didn't seem like Rodney's plan, he was still part of it. It wasn't like he could use his law enforcement connections for this mess, so would he reach out to our enemies? We made our way to the door, and I tested the knob to find it unlocked. Dumb ass niggas get lax thinking a gate and security would stop a threat. They should've been on high alert with all those businesses going up in flames and crumbling to the fucking ground. We stormed inside, and the element of surprise had niggas inside caught off guard. Their expressions were a mix of fear, confusion, and defiance when they realized they fucked up. I wasted no time getting to the point with my voice low and threatening.

"Y'all niggas think you can run up in Union like shit sweet?" I smirked.

The first dumbass moved. I took the shot, hitting him in the neck, causing him to drop the gun he'd pulled out to cover his neck.

"These niggas don't know shit," Oz chuckled as he pulled out a cleaver and played with the edge. The gurgling noises became more pronounced as they looked at us stunned.

"Where the fuck is Roman?" I demanded.

"Fuck you! Fuck y'all Union niggas. Ain't nobody—"

Another body hit the floor with a fucking cleaver to the forehead. My senses sharpened as the smell of gunpowder hung in the air when shots started to ring out.

"Butcher! Butcher!" someone shouted as niggas moved, dodging left and right. I tightened my grip on my Glock, catching one nigga on the stairs, and another running toward the back of the house.

"That's all these niggas know is the fucking Butcher. This nigga got people believing he's the nigga from the Silence of the Lambs," Link laughed. I could hear the muffled commotion coming from deeper within the house as I moved to kick the man running. I kicked him so hard that his body flipped over, and I gave him a headshot before leaning against the wall.

"I might have a *BUTCHER SHOP*, but I ain't eating people my nigga. I do feed the body parts to my gator," Oz divulged. I approached a narrow staircase leading to the upper floor, knowing that nigga Rico was probably hiding up there. After looking over the footage, we saw him twice around Cent's spot, and everything about him led back to Clapton and one of Roman's right-hand men. I took a deep breath, steeling myself for the battle ahead. Until what Oz said registered in my head. I looked back slowly as Link shot a nigga twice in the head while placing a small flat device by the busted TV.

"I thought Betsy died," I said. I watched Oz step on the chest of the man he hit with the cleaver and began to pull it free.

"Naw, that bitch up in age, but she still has a few miles left on her," Oz chuckled. I glanced up the stairs and then looked at Link to be sure he was ready.

"You're wild as fuck, Oz," I chuckled. I looked toward Link and raised my brows.

"Police?" I questioned Link.

"They are all tied up with the last explosion, but we need to make this shit quick and get back to Union. From what I can tell, Union City is hot as fuck, but Briggs is making it out to be random acts of violence," Link gritted. I took a deep breath at another complication when the Chief of Police Donald Briggs retired. It's like starting over from the bottom, but hopefully, we can fill the position quickly, but that shit was on Henny to figure out.

"Bet. Three niggas, one of them being Rico, went upstairs and probably headed for that panic room. Is the feed down?" I asked.

"Don't play me like a bitch nigga. Shit has been down, so let's move," Link said, coming up beside me. I looked at Oz, but he was checking over the bodies making sure niggas weren't playing dead.

I turned away and looked back toward the stairs. I ascended them stealthily, my training kicking in as I moved with calculated precision. I felt Link behind me, but I couldn't hear his movements at all. At the top, I peered around the corner, scanning the hallway for any signs of movement. Suddenly, the door to a bedroom swung open, and one of the niggas that ran was armed with two guns at the ready.

I reacted swiftly, and I dove to the side, narrowly avoiding a barrage of bullets. Link went the other way, our training with each other helping the situation play out perfectly. I returned fire and rolled to an open doorway, using it as a makeshift cover. The deafening sound of gunfire echoed through the house.

Link leaned out, taking calculated shots. The adrenaline surged through my veins. I plotted my next move by taking advantage of Link's distraction and capitalizing on it. With a burst of energy, I sprang from my spot, firing my weapon in quick succession.

"Oh shit! Oh shit! Close the door! Rico hit the button and close—"

The air filled with smoke and the acrid smell of burning gunpowder sifted as their bullets whizzed past me, shattering nearby windows. I ducked and weaved while raising my Glock to shoot the nigga screaming in the head. I raised my leg and slammed it into the door, making it slap the falling man in the face, pushing his body back as the door broke off the hinges. The room was an office, and in the midst of the chaos, I glimpsed Rico slamming his hand against the button to try to get the panic-room door to close. Out of the corner of my eye, I saw the other nigga raising his pistol, but I turned slightly and throat-punched him. Then I grabbed the back of his neck and slammed him face-first into the wall four times. Link was already moving by me, laughing at Rico's expression. Rico's eyes burned with a mix of fury, desperation, and fear.

"No matter how hard you hit that shit, it's not going to close my nigga. Step the fuck out, and don't even think about trying to grab that shotgun. Better yet, do it so I can blow your fucking hand off," Link ordered. Rico's eyes widened in disbelief when I stepped around his two dead friends and trained my gun on him, my voice dripping with determination.

"Gerico Brown, I need two things from you."

"Fuc—"

I moved to slammed my Glock into his face and then gripped his jaw before slamming him down onto the large oak desk.

"Nigga this ain't no mutha fucking conversation. I tell you what the fuck I need, and you do what the fuck I say. You came into my city, stalked my fucking wife, and you believe you are allowed to speak to me?"

"Five minutes," Link said while looking over the computer on the desk.

"All I need is for you to contact Roman and then for you to tell me everything you know about him."

"I—I ain't ssss—"

I squeezed tighter and laughed at the way blood began to fill his mouth. I shoved my Glock to his temple and leaned down.

"The fact you think you will have a choice is fucking hilarious," I grunted.

"You know about U.C.K., and that means you know we got ways to make niggas talk," I chuckled. His eyes grew wider, and I could tell he'd heard some stories. I wondered how true they were. Link hit a key and then stood up to his full height.

"Done. We need to move," Link said as he placed another small black box next to the computer. I grabbed Rico and pulled him to his feet, pushing him in front of me while holding my Glock to the back of his head.

We made our way down the steps, and Oz stood at the bottom with his Desert Eagle pointing toward us until he noticed we were coming down.

"No one else is here, and if they are, they're hiding good as fuck," Oz stated, looking at his watch. If they are hiding, that sucks for them. They wouldn't make it out this bitch today. I knew Oz finished placing the devices around downstairs, so everything was a go. He turned, and we followed him out the front door over to where we parked the truck. I pushed Rico, and he tripped over his feet, slamming into the truck's passenger side. I saw another dark SUV pulling up, but I knew it was Ace.

"Ahh! Fuck! Fuck you niggas! Y'all just don't fucking know what—"

I slammed my Glock into his mouth while Link dug into Rico's pocket, pulling out his phone. He held it to the untraceable phone and cloned it. It took less than two seconds for Link to find what we wanted. He hit the call button, handing me the phone. Link dropped Rico's phone to the ground and slammed his booted foot down until it was crushed into pieces. I held the phone up so Roman would see Rico's face first as blood slid from his lips. I looked over his shoulder, but Cece was engrossed in her tablet. I caught Henny's eyes. He tapped his watch, and I knew it meant time was up. We needed to be ghosts.

"Now is not the time, Ri—what the fuck?" Roman shouted. I turned the phone to face me and smirked.

"You think attacking my city didn't warrant any payback, my nigga? Coming after my WIFE is another story," I started.

"Wife? Nigga ain't—"

"I want you to see how close we can get Roman. Just because you're hiding right now doesn't mean we won't find you," I interrupted. I turned the phone around so the camera could face his house and knocked on the back passenger window. I waited a second, and it came down.

"Was Cent in there, Papi?" she asked, knowing the answer. I could read it in her eyes.

"No, baby," I answered.

"Then I don't want to see the house anymore," Cece sighed. I held out my wrist and looked down at her dark brown eyes.

"You can hit the button," I said as she reached out. A smile flickered and touched her lips as she pressed in the middle of my watch. The house was sat further back from the driveway, and we parked far enough, but close enough to feel the heat as each part of the house began to explode.

"You are fucking bitch! I'll kill you, you bitch ass nigg—"

I ended the call and grabbed Rico by the collar as his swollen eyes stared in horror as flames covered the mansion. Ace was standing beside Oz, waiting for me to hand this nigga over. I pushed Rico in his direction, anticipating the torture tonight because I knew I wouldn't be sleeping.

"Take him to the *RANGE*. String him up with the others for target practice," I ordered as I opened the door. Cece stared at the fire for a second longer before making room.

"I finished all my work, Papi," she whispered. I closed the door as Oz and Link jumped inside.

"I knew you would, Cece. Now we—"

My phone buzzed, and I frowned because the only people who would dare to call me right now were sitting here. As Link reversed out of the long driveway, I pulled my phone out, frowning.

"What have you found?" I asked Shantel without a greeting.

"That fucking bitch, Pamela! And I swear I'm going to cut her open from her head to her fucking toes," Shantel yelled. I sat forward, and I could feel eyes on me, but—

"Where the fuck are you? Do you see Crescent?"

"Naw, naw, but I followed that bitch. I'm in Del Mar, but I have this handled. You do not need to be out here," she stated.

"Fuck you! Got damn right I do. You can't run up in that bitch alone, Shantel," I insisted. I felt Cece's small hand on my leg where my Glock rested, prompting me to place it in my holster. I was trying to calculate how fast we could get there.

"I've called in the calvary. By the time you get here, we will have her. Just—"

I was already typing on my watch to Whisper so she could get airborne.

"I will be there in thirty-five minutes! Send me the fucking location Shantel," I ordered.

"Already done, but you need to stay on the border of Del Mar, and you know that. Y'all do not need to be seen here after this goes down. She will be there when you land," Shantel said before ending the call.

"Where the fuck is she?" Henny asked. I stared at the location before looking up at Henny.

"Del Mar. Those bitches took her to Del Mar, and apparently, Shantel has called in the '*Kalvary*' to help," I said while sending Whisper to the location where I needed to meet her for pick up. I sent the coordinates to Link's watch, and he looked down, causing us to make an immediate left to go in a different direction.

"Jesus. The fucking twins! Fuck," Oz grunted. Henny rubbed at his goatee with a shake of his head. Cece stared at me with hope I didn't want to give her until we had Cent. I wouldn't say a word to her until I could be sure she would see her face to face.

"Let's just hope they don't burn down the entire fucking city," Henny said, clenching his hands into fists. Oz turned around with a pinched look on his face.

"Why the fuck is Shantel in Del Mar?" he asked. I had one answer, but that wasn't my problem. That answer was between Shantel and that nigga Lawe because he would be the only reason Shantel would leave Union City.

CHAPTER TWO

CRESCENT 'CENT' WELLINGTON

I pulled at the metal handcuff on my right wrist while staring at this yellow-ass little dick nigga. I didn't know who the fuck he was when I first woke up, but since being here, I got to know enough about Roe a.k.a. Agent Rodney Gates. To me, I knew too fucking much, and that meant it wasn't looking good. The way he spoke rapidly into his phone told me my time was limited. The little information I did know about Henny wasn't shit in the grand scheme of things, but I could lie like it wasn't anybody's business. Whatever I knew about him or his U.C.K. business, I would never tell. I knew our work wife and husband thing floated around the hospital, but this shit was entirely too far. What the fuck was Pamela thinking? My first night in this shitty ass townhouse, I woke up to my hand throbbing and this bitch ranting and raving about my marriage to Hendrix. However, she clarified that I needed to tell her everything I knew about him if I ever wanted to leave this place.

I didn't correct the bitch when she stressed my relationship with Henny was the reason I was in this situation. While also stating, if I had only backed off, things wouldn't have gotten so far, but I did this to myself. She claimed I fucked niggas and moved on without a second thought leaving chaos behind me. What the fuck was she talking about? Who was she talking about because I didn't know this bitch until I got to Union? She was fucking crazy, and when I got out of this shit, she would find out how much chaos I would cause. What shocked me more was the pure hatred that couldn't all stem from my relationship with Henny. The fact this long titty, thin-lipped ass bitch thought she was running some shit had my blood boiling. The starvation and denial of water and care for my broken finger had her feeling like she won on some get-back shit. At first, I thought this bitch was a Roman plant, but I was way the fuck off. All she cared about was what Hendrix liked, when I met him, my reason for leaving Clapton, and how long I had been with Hendrix. The bitch was crazy as fuck. She wasn't asking for the information I thought she should have been asking about. It was like she didn't know the shit she stepped into, and Rodney didn't tell her who exactly Hendrix was. Either way, it all seemed…way too personal. Just to fuck with her this morning, I told her that I'd been fucking Hendrix since I started at Union, and I'm probably carrying his baby. I needed her on edge, enraged, and to do something to give me an out. The key to the handcuffs was always in her left pants pocket. I watched her enough to know she always stuck it back into the same pocket.

Pamela did exactly what I thought she would've done and launched herself at me. The slap across my face was quick, but the bitch forgot only one hand was cuffed. I couldn't give it as much force as I wanted, but I beat that bitches head in until she pulled away. I caught her with my legs and pinned her down as we twisted and turned on the bed. Pain radiated up my leg from the movement, but I pushed that to the side. I grabbed at her shirt and pinched the skin on her stomach, twisting it causing her to scream and flail around until I let go. I managed to get the key out of her pocket before she got away. I wasn't expecting the wild look in her eyes as she stared at me or the words that fell from her lips.

'Are you sure that baby is Hendrix's, or is it my brother's baby?'

My eyes widened at her words because who the fuck was her brother? My mind raced as she backed away, grabbing the keys from the beaten-up dresser. Was she related to Roman or some shit? It couldn't be Faxx. What the fuck? Pamela glared at me before looking down at my stomach with uncertainty.

'Bitch, we are going to find out if you are or not today.'

All that was twenty minutes ago when she stormed out of the house. I waited a few more minutes before trying to uncuff myself when I heard the door open downstairs. I heard his voice screaming for Pam as he walked up the stairs toward the room. Rodney didn't say a word about the wildness of my hair or the state of my clothes. He shook his head in disgust and disappointment. Rodney looked around the room before looking at a notepad Pam used. He threw it on the dresser, cursing under his breath as he pulled out his phone. He said the one name that stilled my body and had my blood running ice cold.

ROMAN.

How the fuck does he know Roman, and what the fuck was his plan with me?

I pushed the key under my thigh and stared at him while he spoke quickly and urgently into his phone.

"I don't give a fuck how you get this message to him, just tell him I have what he's been looking for. Tell him if he wants Crescent Johnson, then I need the location of Theodore Gregory Banks! You have one hour," Rodney gritted. My eyes were wide when he turned to face me.

"Wh—what do you want from me? I don't know what Pamela told you that I know, but I don't know shi—"

"This isn't personal for me. Apparently, this entire situation is only serving Pamela's insanity, and I've let it go on for far too long as it is. I need something that Roman has, and I have something he wants. This will be in the best interest of all parties," Rodney grunted. He turned away, and I listened as he left the house, leaving me in complete silence. Once Roman heard my name, he would come. I had to get the fuck out. I knew Faxx and the others were looking for me by the news I heard playing whenever the bitch watched TV. Unexplained fires and bombings were his signature, but how would he know that Roman or Alex didn't take me? How would they even know where to begin to find me? I had to get out, and now was the time. It had been a good ten minutes since Rodney left the house. I refused to wait any longer because I had no clue when that bitch was coming back.

I pulled out the key, fumbling slightly because of my fucked-up finger. I held back the tears from the pain in my finger and from losing my wedding ring. I could feel Fransisco's pain and Cece's torment like a stabbing sensation in my heart. I knew each morning when Cece woke up, and I wasn't there, would break her. Knowing how Faxx and Cece's minds work ripped me to shreds each minute I was away from them. I promised her I would never leave her, but this bitch took me from my baby. They took me from my family, but I would be damned if I wouldn't fight until I got back to them. Roman was coming back into play, and I wasn't protected. I heard a small snick, and the cuff opened. I sighed in relief as I scooted to the edge of the bed. My body throbbed everywhere as I moved, but once my foot touched the floor, I felt the sprain like it just fucking happened. I took a deep breath, closed my eyes, and pushed to my feet.

"Ah! Ah, fuck," I moaned. The pain had my eyes flying open. My adrenaline kicked in, pushing the weakness of my body, my mental fatigue, and everything else aside. I reached out, grabbing onto anything as I balanced myself. My head spun, but I blinked, trying to clear my vision so I could get the fuck out of there. If I could get to the street, I could get help. I didn't know where I was, but it was secluded enough that no one came when I sc reamed.

"Fuck it," I gritted. I hobbled my way to the door, wincing at the pain in my ankle and my hand. My stomach screamed for food, but I licked at my dry cracked lips, and kept moving. I didn't know where Pamela went, or if Rodney would come flying back through the door, so I pushed on. I made it to the top of the narrow staircase and looked down. The peeling yellow paint was dull, and the smell of something burning set me on high alert. Were they about to burn me alive? I grabbed onto the white railing and slowly descended the stairs. Once I hit the bottom, I quickly looked around for something to fuck someone up with if need be. The old tan and dark brown couches had seen better days, but I grabbed onto it as I pushed myself toward the front door. I heard the screen door creak, and my breath caught as I spun around on my heel.

"Fuck, fuck, fuck," I grumbled. I moved as fast as I could toward the hallway that led to the kitchen, I guessed. There had to be something in there I could use to defend myself, but the door flew open before I made it halfway down the narrow hall.

"What the fuck? Ahh naw bitch, where the fuck—"

I kept moving as the door slammed, and I took a chance to look over my shoulder as Pamela raised her gun.

"If you take one more fucking step, I will kill you. I don't care if you're possibly carrying my niece or nephew. It will break his heart, but fuck it," Pamela hissed. I slammed a hand against the wall as I turned to face her. Who the hell was she talking about?

"You are fucking delusional, Pam! Put the fucking gun down so you can catch these hands again. I will fuck you up with a broken hand and all bitch. I don't know you, your fucking brother, or what you want from me. I'm not even fucking Hendrix, you dumb stupid ass bitch!" I yelled. I rubbed my nose and blinked rapidly, searching for the burning smell, but I saw no smoke.

Pamela sucked in a breath, raising the gun just as something slammed into the door. Pamela jumped and turned around just as the door crashed in. I screamed, stumbling back, swearing that it was Roman and his niggas coming to take me. My ankle protested and gave out, causing me to fall to the floor.

"Fire department! We need to evacuate now! Now! The fire is spreading!" a man shouted.

"Wha—I didn't see any—" Pamela started as the man forced his way into the house, followed by—

Under the smell of smoke, I smelled an all too familiar scent. The only person with that smell was Henny. If Henny was here, so was Fransisco!

"Faxx—wait...Shantel?" I screamed in confusion and surprise. Smoke began to fill the house rapidly now that the door was open.

I saw Shantel take two quick steps toward Pamela, knocking the forgotten gun out of her hand before slamming her face into the wall.

"Ahh! Oh my—ahh," Pamela screamed as blood poured from her nose. Shantel didn't give her a second look.

"Kalvary, get Cent out of here," Shantel shouted.

"Shantel baby, let me do my job first. This all has to burn at the same rate," Kalvary smirked. Seeing his face with the helmet and firefighter gear on was hard.

"Who the fuck are you? Bitc—"

"You should fucking run, unless you want to be burned down in this prison you held my friend in, bitch," Shantel sneered. Pamela looked at Shantel standing in front of the door and toward me before she sprinted by me and into what I believed was the kitchen. I figured there was a back door, but why in the hell was Shantel letting her go?

"The door won't open! Oh my God! Oh my God!" Pamela screeched.

"Shantel! Don't let that crazy bitch—" I started, but she cut me off, looking at the man as he poured something on the floor. The smell of gas assaulted my nose, telling me what was about to happen.

"Kalvary, we need to move. I'm sure Faxx will not wait if we aren't there before he is," Shantel said, moving toward me.

"Don't let that crazy bitch go," I rushed out.

"Don't even worry about her, girl," she mumbled.

I pushed myself up from the floor just as the man came forward, leaning down and scooping me into his arms. I heard glass shattering in the kitchen as Pamela screamed. This bitch was going to get away!

"Cent, look at me. I got her, and I got you," Shantel said, touching my face. I saw the flat, dead look in her eyes as she clenched her jaw. Shantel moved by us with a look of murder in her eyes as she strolled toward the kitchen. I felt the heat of the fire across my skin as Kalvary gripped me tighter in his arms.

"Hmm, so you're the one Konceited was talking about. I didn't know you were this thick though," he smirked, carrying me down the hall and into the tiny, dingy kitchen.

"Konceited?" I sniffed. I glanced up, still hardly able to see his face, but the tattoo on his neck held the start of a K, and his toffee-colored eyes seemed to glitter when he looked back at the fire.

"Yeah, he said he saw you on a video call," he smiled. My eyes widened because he had to be talking about green eyes. That one fine ass nigga Faxx said I had to stay away from.

"Oh, shit. That seemed so long ago," I said, clearing my throat. I was so fucking thirsty because that bitch barely gave me enough to drink to fucking survive.

"Yes, too long. That nigga Faxx is wildin' in these streets, so we need to get you to him asap 'cause I don't need to be investigating any fires I didn't start myself," he said cryptically.

"Faxx? Where is he? Is he okay? Does he know whe—" I started to ask, but he smiled as we stepped through the door. All I wanted to do was see Fransisco and hold my baby girl. Anger filled me just thinking of how much harm Pamela had caused Cece. I was going to kill this bitch just as soon as I could move without feeling like I would pass out.

"It's all good. Your crazy ass nigga ain't completely lost it yet," Kalvary stated seriously. I looked up with a frown because I knew Faxx could get lost in that blackness of his mind. I opened my mouth, but he smiled. His straight white teeth flashed as he bit his lip, gripping me tighter.

"It won't be long," he stated. We stepped out of the house, and his eyes immediately narrowed as smoke-filled air hit me in the face. That shit never felt so fucking good, even if it was hot as hell. The flashing lights of the police and fire truck turned this morning into a scene straight out of a cop show. I turned my head away to see Pamela screaming at this sexy ass piece of chocolate. His tall, muscled frame was clearly noticeable because of how tightly his tan shirt clung to his body. He grimaced down at her with his bottom golds flashing as he smoothed a hand over the three sixty waves in his hair.

"Get out of the way! Can't you see that the building is on fire?" she screamed. Chocolate bit his lip as his fist clenched. God damn, that nigga was fine as fuck, and I was losing it because why was I staring this hard. The gold chains that hung from his neck flashed as she tried pushing by him, screaming for him to move as she looked back toward the house. Shantel was coming up behind her, and I saw the panic on Pamela's blood-smeared face. Before I knew it, Chocolate punched Pamela dead in the forehead with two quick jabs, dropping her where she stood.

"Karma! Why the fuck did you hit her like that?" Shantel shouted.

"She was getting on my fucking nerves, and she looked like she lies on loan applications," he deadpanned. The smooth bass of his voice and cocky-ass smile had my brows raising. Kalvary started to laugh as he made his way to the fire truck sitting there. Where the fuck was the fire crew?

"Nigga what? You know what, never mind. Where is Stasea?"

"Shantel, I'm serious. Her credit score is probably at three hundred and twelve," Karma argued.

"I'm right here. All I asked his ass to do was make sure she didn't move while I got the car," Stasea said, stepping up beside Karma. She wore plain clothes, but I could tell by the badge and stance she really was a cop.

"Pick her ass up, Karma," Shantel sighed as she looked over at me. I stared at her, and I could see the stress, anger, and fatigue in her gaze before she looked down at Pamela.

"Are we taking her to the *CLINIC* or the *RANG—*"

"Take her to the fucking *ASYLUM*," Shantel said, looking at Pamela. Karma's eyes widened, and he looked at Stasea, who moved closer to Shantel.

"Are you sure Sis? You haven't used—" Karma closed his mouth when Shantel's head snapped up. He raised his hands as Stasea held hers out in a placating gesture.

"Karma, little brother! I'm glad you're here but don't make me beat your ass this morning," Shantel stated flatly. She typed on her phone quickly before sticking it back into her pocket.

"Calm down, calm down, I got you. No need for the threats, big Sis, the *ASYLUM* it is," he said, bending to lift Pamela.

I jumped when I felt Kalvary's fingers on my face as he looked me over. He turned my head from side to side before lifting my hand to look at my finger.

"Shit," I hissed as he touched it. I didn't see Shantel walk over, but I felt her as soon as she was close.

"We need to set this and get you some fluids, Love," Kalvary stated. I blinked as the feeling of pure exhaustion came over me suddenly. I smiled at Shantel, so happy to see her, but her dark brown eyes looked me over from head to toe as they filled with unshed tears.

"The bitch hurt three people who are very important to me. She will pay for that Crescent, and when we get Rodney's ass, he will suffer. Bet on that shit. Let's get you fixed up and home where you belong," she smiled tightly. Her shaky fingers comb through my braids, lulling me to sleep. I saw the look of pure, unhinged hate in her eyes when Karma walked past with Pamela over his shoulder before my eyes slid shut on their own.

My eyes snapped open when the car hit a bump in the road, and I jerked slightly. I blinked twice and realized I was staring at the back of a seat. I took a deep breath, feeling a large arm across my chest that snaked up to hold the side of my face. When I moved, it tightened, and I felt a thumb caress my face instantly, making me slightly calmer than a second ago.

"It's all good, Cent. We're almost at the airstrip. I need you to stay still because I have fluids running into you," Kalvary insisted.

I didn't know how long I'd been knocked out, but I did a quick check of my body. I felt the I.V. in my hand. I could also feel a weight on my ring finger and left ankle while noticing that I didn't really feel any pain. I twisted slightly so I could look up at Kalvary to thank him, and I glimpsed a crisp white collared button-up shirt with a black tie and a badge that read State Fire Marshall. The shirt covered up the tattoo I had seen earlier, but I got it. I licked my lips and cleared my throat, praying my voice didn't crack.

"Thank you. How...how the hell did y'all find me?"

"That was all Shantel and her crazy fucking luck, but something is telling me that you would've gotten out of there yourself. No wonder that crazy ass nigga wifed you," he chuckled. I felt a warm hand on my arm and turned slightly to see Shantel. She was reaching back behind the seat, giving me side-eyed glances.

"Almost there, Crescent. I'm so sorry we took so long. This shit will never happen again," she promised.

"It wasn't anyone's fault, Shantel. That bitch is fucking crazy as hell and thought I was fucking Henny. I mean, that's my work man and shit, but she was trippin' trippin' for real. Then she kept screaming about how I did something to her brother or some shit. I don't know her or her damn brother. Henny better watch out because he got a fatal attraction bitch on his hands. I can't wait to tell—"

I trailed off as the vehicle began to slow. I didn't want to say shit about this to Tali, she was already beating herself down over the Jakobe situation.

"Shantel?" I whispered. Her hand left my arm as we pulled to a stop. I felt Kalvary's arm tighten as he helped me sit upright. My head spun slightly, but I was feeling a hell of a lot better than I had been earlier. I felt his arm steady me before he pulled away to take the hand with the I.V. and began to disconnect it. Shantel cut the engine and turned around to face me with a smile.

"Crescent, if I would have found out more about that bitch in the beginning, we wouldn't be sitting here. That's my bad, but trust, it will be handled. Now that I know who she really is, it will make things much easier to get what I need out of her," Shantel gritted.

"Listen, I didn't say anything to that bitch or Rodney. Did you see Rodney before y'all got me out? He was just there minutes before," I rushed out. I already knew how Shantel got down, and I wanted to be clear I hadn't said a fucking word. I also wanted to know if they caught that nigga Rodney as well. Shantel frowned and then smiled while Kalvary started to chuckle.

"Are you sure you want to fuck with that nigga Fransisco? I need some-body loyal like you," Kalvary smirked as Shantel shook her head. I looked into Kalvary's eyes, which looked like they flickered with flames. His uniform was at odds with the dangerous aura he exuded, which was also at odds with the tenderness he showed me. These men were—

"Cent, that was never a thought, and no, Rodney must have left before we arrived. But did she ask you anything about us? Trust me, we knew he was in on it and would be dealt with. We just can't figure out why he would've done it," she sucked her teeth. I swallowed before smirking at Kalvary as he placed a gauze on my hand and taped it down. His face sobered, though, as he waited for me to answer.

"She really wasn't asking me shit about U.C.K., almost like she didn't know Henny is a part of that. But I knew Rodney wanted her to ask about Henny. I just don't know what he wanted to know. All she was worried about was how long me and Henny had been fucking and why did I leave Clapton. Then went on and on about a brother that I don't fucking know," I sighed.

"She never gave her brother's name?" Kalvary asked.

"Naw, she didn't. I mean, how would she even know I came from Clapton because I never told anyone that shit. Not even Tali and Dea, so where would she get that?" I wondered aloud. Shantel bit her lip before checking her watch. She looked back up and turned to face me fully.

"Does the name Patricia Manning mean anything to you? Do you know her from Clapton or maybe someone Roman kno—"

I held up my hand, frowning deeply when I heard a helicopter in the distance. Shantel looked out of the Range Rover's front window.

"That's Faxx. When he says thirty minutes, that nigga means that shit," she sighed. Shantel turned in her seat and reached for the door. Kalvary began to do the same while he typed on his phone with a frown. He stepped out of the SUV and grabbed a dark blue blazer I had been using as a pillow.

"No! No, wait a minute," I shouted. Shantel turned her head back to look me over like she thought I was dying.

"What? What's wrong?" she asked frantically. She looked back at the helicopter before facing me again.

"Did you say Patricia Manning?" I asked slowly. Shantel frowned but nodded a yes as the helicopter came into view and began to descend.

"Yeah, do you know her?" she asked, pushing open her door. It wasn't her that I knew, but I did know who her brother was.

"No, I don't know that bitch, but I know her brother has to be Eric Manning. That's the only thing that makes sense by how she acts. That's the nigga Faxx damn near killed in the parking garage," I stressed. Shantel's back went straight as her brows crashed down, and the tick in her jaw had me leaning back.

"Was he ever at the house with you?" she questioned.

"No. I never saw him and don't think he would have been. Faxx fucked him up that night, and Milo basically told his ass to leave Union. Wait—Milo! Where is—is he—"

Shantel sucked in a breath as the helicopter touched down and I saw Faxx hit the ground. I didn't know how I climbed out of the SUV until I felt Kalvary grab my arm, pulling me to my feet. Everything in my head went completely blank, and I didn't see anyone else.

"Khaos, if I didn't know you had anything to do with saving her, I would shoot you in the face my nigga," Faxx seethed. His black eyes landed on me, and I couldn't fucking breathe.

"Nigga, I'm not entirely sure how you even got her to marry you. You probably forged that shit with your psycho ass," Kalvary chuckled. I felt Faxx's arms around me as he lifted me from the ground and turned me around.

"Shut the fuck up, Khaos. Where the hell is your twin? I thought Shantel told me you both would be here?" Faxx asked. I felt his hands running up and down my body, squeezing me before he threaded his fingers through my braids. I was so fucking tired, and the warmth of his body had me sinking into him.

"Naw, she wasn't close enough to be here in time, but her crazy ass is on the way back home. We're lucky because she probably would've burned down the entire street," Kalvary said.

"Bet. Once she's here, we all need to meet up. I'm still not sated, and niggas need to learn to stop fucking with us," Faxx condemned. I sucked in a breath, trying to inhale his scent, searching for the feeling of home.

"I hope you know, *Mi Amor*, that I'm going to chain you to our bed until I am one hundred percent that this will never fucking happen again. Now, breathe for me," he whispered against my skin. The air that left my lungs on a sob so deep I felt my body begin to shake as his hands gripped my waist, forcing my legs to wrap around him.

"Do you understand what I'm saying, *Mi Amor*? Tell me that you understand that I am not fucking around," he ordered. I swallowed hard as tears slid down my cheeks, and I tried breathing in his scent while shoving my hand up his shirt to feel his skin.

"*Mi Amor*, what do you say?" he warned. I took another breath and closed my eyes, ready to go home and deal with the rest later. I knew Faxx's threat wasn't just for talk. This nigga was serious. The crushing grip he had on me wasn't going anywhere anytime soon. I felt like he was suffocating me to the point I could barely take a breath, but it was exactly what I needed. I wouldn't deny his need to hold me tightly. Even if that meant being glued to his side. Fuck it.

"Yes, *Papi*."

I didn't know I had fallen asleep again until I woke up with a start. I felt a weight on me, causing me to jerk slightly. My eyes opened, and I sucked in a breath, moving my arms reflexively, thinking one of them would still be cuffed.

"You're home, *Mi Amor*," Faxx's voice helped ease the growing panic. I slowly opened my eyes to see our room in our house, not peeling yellow paint. I swallowed as Faxx traced circles over my thighs, and I brought my hand to his head. I smoothed my hand over his cornrows and let out a long sigh.

"Are you going to let me get up?" I smiled.

"Fuck no. Why? Where do you need to go?"

"Fransisco, you can't just keep me in bed. I need to get up, take a shower, see my baby, and—"

"I bathed you before I put you in bed. And let's just say you're lucky I didn't cuff you to the fucking bed. I saw the bruises on your wrists," he gritted. I traced his tattoos, causing him to flex as he raised his head. His usual dark brown eyes were still black as night and hard as fuck when he stared at me. I looked at my wrists and noticed that they had been bandaged. I could tell he had used the usual cream on them because it caused a slight numbing sensation. I was changed into my sleeping shorts and tank top. I licked my lips to tell him not to worry about the marks because they would heal, but his teeth sank into my thigh before he licked away the sting. My clit jumped at the contact even though my body was fucking exhausted.

"I'm not going to tell you that you don't know what it's been like without you beside me. I could tell by the way you wouldn't let me go, even in your sleep that you felt the same way. But *Mi Amor*, the anger I feel right now is still there even though I have you back. I don't think it's going to change until every nigga that's a direct threat to you is dead," he said in a monotoned voice.

"I fought every chance I got Fransisco. You know I did, and it wasn't like I meant for any of this to go down. Milo—and Dylan— where is Dylan? Did she—"

"Dylan is...she's in the hospital, but she is fighting. As for Milo, we didn't make it in time to do anything but gather his body. Now that you're home, we can lay him to rest."

I sucked in a breath, my heart breaking all over again as Milo being shot replayed in my head time and time again. If only I hadn't left the house. If I never picked up the phone for Gigi, he would still—

"Crescent! Stop! I know where your mind is going, but shit happens the way it happens. If you hadn't gone, more than likely Dylan would have died, and that would've eaten you up," Faxx stated.

"I should of—"

Faxx rose onto his forearms, pushing his body off of the bed to lean over me. My hands fell to the side of his face, and I hated that my ring wasn't there.

"The only thing you will do is never let this shit happen again. I feel like I really do need to write my name across your chest so mutha fuckas know the name of the last nigga they will see before they die."

"Faxx—"

"Naw, *Mi Amor*. I'm fucking serious. The tattoo is necessary because if some shit like this happens again, not one nigga, including my brothers, will be able to stop me from lighting a match to burn this bitch down. It's the fact that I'm not fucking finished, and I need everyone from Union, Clapton, P-Town, and Del Mar to understand who they're fucking with," Faxx thundered.

"Henny and—"

Faxx started to chuckle as his eyes grew heated the longer he stared at me. I could see the insane part of his personality showing as he grinned wider, like my words were funny.

"That nigga ain't wrapped too tight either, Cent," he smirked. Faxx leaned down until his face was inches from mine before he leaned in and kissed me. I felt like he was sucking the air from my lungs and refilling them at the same time. I didn't want him to stop, and I needed to be filled by him. I wanted to be filled in each and every way. My arm locked around his neck, but he pulled back looking at me as I moaned.

"You had a lot of people worried and mad as fuck, Crescent. Your work husband was one of them, he isn't as sweet as you think. You're going to have to take the punishment for all that worry you caused, *Mi Amor*," he whispered over my lips. My core tightened, and I felt the slick wetness between my folds at his threat. Faxx licked my lips as I tried to figure out exactly what the fuck that meant.

"But Papi, none of this was my fault. It was that crazy bitch Pam and Rodney's punk ass. Has...has Shantel said anything about Pamela?"

"You mean the fact Eric is her fucking brother?"

I clamped my mouth shut as his gaze narrowed at his name.

"Ahh, yeah, that and the whole infatuation she has with Henny," I said, trying to change his focus.

"Don't worry about Pamela. She's being taken care of, but as for your little boyfriend, that nigga is dead. As soon as he pops back up, I'll catch his ass, but right now, the focus is on Rodney," he lowered his body against mine. He moved his arm, so he could push my leg out that was bandaged, so it wasn't in his way.

"I never got the chance to tell Shantel what he said when he was there. Rodney was at the house before Shantel and the others showed up," I said, trying not to moan as his hands roamed my body.

"Tell me," he ordered.

"Before he left the house, he made a call. He realized that Pam wasn't getting the information he wanted. Why he didn't try himself, I don't know," I started.

"Either way we look at it, *Mi Amor*, he is still law enforcement. The less contact he had with you, the more he could deny wrongdoing. But what else?" he asked softly. My heart rate picked up as his tongue traced the tattoos across my chest, and I swore he was spelling his name.

I let out a slow breath, trying to concentrate on what the hell I was supposed to be saying.

"Ahh, hmmm, he ahh, he called someone so they could contact Roman. He wanted to trade me for information on Banks," I panted. Faxx stopped moving, and I could feel his entire demeanor change before he pulled away.

"Trade you? This nigga wanted to trade you like some kind of object?"

"That's all I could hear on my end. He said for Theodore Gregory Banks, and I don't understand why. I don't know what he would have to do with anything," I said quickly. Faxx gritted his teeth, but before he could say something off the fucking wall, the door opened. I turned my head, thinking it was Cece, but it was Tali. Her gray eyes were wide, red, and puffy as she stared at me.

"Cent!" Tali screamed before diving onto the bed. She landed on Faxx's back, and he grunted as she kissed my face.

"Tali, oh my God, I'm good," I laughed. Faxx's face was pushed between my breast, and his freak ass didn't even try to move.

"Cent, you can't be doing this shit. I hope Oz beats your ass again because...because—"

"I love you too, damn, I can't breathe," I laughed, trying to pull in air.

"Tali! Get off of Faxx like that before he suffocates," Henny chuckled. I couldn't see him because Tali's arms were wrapped around my head, but I felt the bed dip beside me.

"Tali's good where she is. I would die happy as fuck," Faxx said muffled. Tali moved back and slid off Faxx's back and to the side.

"I guess you would if you died between ass and titties. But I need to check Cent over," Henny's eyes gave away nothing. But the tightness in his jaw told me all I needed to know. This nigga was pissed the fuck off.

"Dr. Sexy!" I smiled as he raised my hand and began to feel my entire hand. His thumb traced over the bandage on my wrist before he smiled at me. His platinum grill flashed for a brief second. He looked over my face as Faxx turned his head, licking at my nipple. I tried to cover his mouth with my other hand, but he pinned it to the bed.

"So, I guess my work wife still hasn't learned her lesson. You had niggas over here worried burning down fucking blocks looking for your ass. I don't think Oz did a good job," he hummed. I cut my eyes over at Tali, but her punk ass was tracing the letters on Faxx's arm with her lips smashed together. *This bitch*! I looked at Faxx, and he raised a brow like I was supposed to have some kind of comeback.

"I...I...Dr. Sexy, I think we are all not focusing on the good things. I'm home, and you're here, Tali's here, and—"

"It's all good, Cent. I'm sure Faxx has already told you what will happen," he said, standing. I looked at Faxx while Henny unwrapped my foot and raised my brows.

"What? I can't help you, *Mi Amor*. You had everybody worried about you for over a week. You can take it, and you'll like it," he smirked. Tali choked, and I glared at her punk ass. She widened her eyes and then sat up.

"Okay, okay, leave Crescent alone. It's not like this was her fault even though it did give me a mild heart attack," Tali finished.

"Bissh!" I shouted as I tried to hit her. Tali rolled off the bed, not helping as Henny poked around my ankle.

"Ouch! Dr. Sexy, that shit hurts, and Tali, once I get up, I'm going to beat your ass," I threatened.

"My bad Cent. It's definitely a bad sprain. We need to do X-rays, but I'm pretty sure it will heal independently. I'll get you a boot to help stabilize your ankle so you can get around. After the X-rays, I have something that should help with the pain and speed up the healing process. You'll need it," Henny said, rewrapping my ankle. As soon as he was done, I heard a high-pitched scream that had me damn near falling out of the bed. Faxx was already climbing off, but I threw my legs to the side and tried getting up and almost busted my ass. I felt Henny's arm around my waist as he held me.

"Slow the fuck down, Cent. Let me help you," he said as Faxx and Tali ran out the door to get to Cece.

"Just…just pick me up! Something's wrong," I panicked as I hopped on one foot. I felt a sudden weightlessness as Henny lifted me and twisted me around so I could maneuver onto his back.

"You could rub some titties against me as payment for this ride," Henny chuckled. I felt his arms securely around my legs as he headed toward Cece's screaming.

"Shut up Hendrix. Just hurry up," I demanded while leaning on his shoulder. I bit down on his neck to make my point but the rumble I felt had my eyes widening.

"Cent. I don't want to hear shit when your screaming Platinum," he grunted and I was momentarily stunned.

"What did you—"

Then I heard my baby again and her cries were breaking my heart. I wasn't sure what the fuck was happening. If those fucking dolls were fucking with her, I was throwing all those bitches out of the window.

"Papi, Papi, they took her. They won't give her back! You'll leave, and then Uncle Link, Uncle Oz, Uncle Henny, an—" Cece cried. Faxx held her in his arms while Tali tried to calm her down.

"Baby girl. No one is leaving you."

I worried that this was my fault. Cece's head snapped up, and the curls all over her head smacked Faxx in the face as large dark eyes stared at me.

"Cent! Mommy," she cried as she pushed out of Faxx's arms. Henny helped me to the floor but held onto me when Cece crashed into me. I didn't give a shit about my hand or my foot as I lifted her into my arms.

"It's okay, Francesca. It's okay, I'm here," I whimpered.

"They said you wouldn't come back. They said you thought I was weird and didn't want me anymore."

I looked at Faxx, and his eyes darted to the closet. A table was pushed in front of it, with Travis sitting atop it.

"You know that's not true. I will always come back because I love you," I whispered.

"Travis said you would. He said no one that loves you would ever leave you forever," Cece mumbled.

"And Travis is right. I will never leave you forever," I whispered as I kissed her cheek. I hadn't noticed that Henny and Tali left until I felt Faxx guiding us over to Cece's Queen-sized bed. I climbed on, still holding Cece to my chest as I kissed her head, her eyes, and cheeks until she stopped crying. I felt Faxx behind me, and his arm wrapped around both of us.

"Travis also said that once you came home and we knew who took you from me, he would show me the best way to make them disappear forever. Can Travis play with me sometimes after school?"

My eyes popped open at her words, and I side-eyed Travis for a long minute. I turned slightly to see the frown on Faxx's lips, but I was also interested. Jesus Jerome Christ! He probably wanted to hear what Travis's ass had to say.

"Sure, baby. Then I can thank Travis for keeping you calm," I said, closing my eyes. I felt her little hand on my cheek before she kissed my nose.

"Papi, can you make it so Cent never disappears again?"

I opened my eyes slowly and found her staring at him like she was assessing the situation.

"That's the plan, Francesca. You will be able to see where she is at all times. Just like Papi," he answered. I felt the frown on my face because what in the fuck!? They were about to have my ass under lock and key. The sad part was that I didn't care as long as I was with them. I let out a long sigh, knowing I was being affected by their psychosis because I didn't see anything wrong with it.

CHAPTER THREE

Fransisco 'Faxx' Wellington

I slid out of bed slowly so I wouldn't wake up Cece or Crescent. I made my way downstairs, still seething about this bullshit. Even though I had my wife back, that shit didn't make up for the fact that niggas wanted to try us. I wanted to join Shantel in finding out what else Pamela might know about what this nigga Rodney's plans were, but I didn't want to leave the house. At least not until Crescent received her tattoo. I clenched my jaw because I hoped she realized that I wasn't playing about my name going across her chest one of these days. I pulled out my phone to check my messages, only to see a missed call from Stax. I blew out a sigh because he'd been on me hard about the way I was dealing with Cent's kidnapping. I already knew what to expect when I hit the call button.

"Fransisco, how is my little sister? Everything good?" Stax asked as I walked into my office. I figured Henny and Tali would've been gone because he said he'd need to deal with any fallout last week had brought to our doorstep. They had been staying here since Cent was taken. I knew they would be on their way here once Oz finished with Dea's OB appointment. At least we got news that Tali and Dea's mother was coming home in a few days.

"She's good. She and Cece are sleeping right now," I said. I sat behind my desk, opening up the coded laptop to see what Link had sent me. I knew he would have some information on how we could get close to Rodney to show him we ain't scared to hit his ass. He needed to know that his bitch ass could be touched no matter what agency he worked for.

"Good. I'll stop by later or in a few days. How are you?" Stax inquired.

I closed my eyes and let out a slow, measured breath because I knew this shit was coming. It was never a day this nigga could not be an older brother. Always monitoring, looking out, and giving advice when it wasn't asked for but—

"I'm good. I have a few things I need to take care of, and that's that. Why?"

Stax was quiet for a minute before he chuckled.

"Little brother, you really think I don't know you? I know for a fact that none of that anger has evaporated, even though Cent is back with you. Just like I know you're going to continue to hunt down everyone that directly or indirectly had something to do with her being taken," he confirmed. I sucked my teeth after typing in a few commands and waited until it connected securely before I opened anything.

"I have it handled, Santino. You worry too much. You already know Henny and the others ain't going to let me go too far off the deep end," I finished. That was a lie because those niggas had been right with me this time. This time shit was different, and we all had shit to lose. So, taking out everyone threatening what's ours was at the top of the list.

"Nigga, bullshit. Those niggas are on the same time you're on. All I want to hear is that you're going to end the lives of those niggas at the *RANGE*. They are serving no purpose being alive for you to torture now. Let them die and focus that rage on the niggas who deserve it," Stax urged. I leaned back in the dark brown leather chair and tapped my fingers across my desk. I let out a grunt before running a hand down my face.

"Fine. But I can't say the same when I get ahold of Roman, Alex, Rodney, and now that little bitch Eric. They all had something to do with this shit happening, not to mention Milo. I can't and won't let that shit go," I stated flatly. Stax was quiet for a long moment, causing me to check to see if we were still connected.

"Well, that's all I can ask right now. Call me if you need me, Fransisco. You already know whatever you need is a given," Stax emphasized. I already knew he would be beside me if I wanted to run into the DEA headquarters. It was never a question that my brother would have my back. He always would.

"Oh, and don't keep that girl locked in the fucking house," he rushed.

"She will be until that fucking tattoo is on her ass. This can't...it can't happen again. I think it caused Francesca's personality to split once again. I've made an appointment, so don't worry. It's handled," I said quickly.

"Get the tattoo and heal your family, Fransisco. It will all work out the way it needs to, but let me get back to work. I have surgery in an hour," Stax said before disconnecting the call.

I placed the phone on my desk and then opened everything Link had put together. The last call to Gigi's cellphone had been from Rico. That was good to know because Rico was sitting and waiting for our conversation. I looked through a few more things only to discover Alex thought it was a good idea to attack a few of my gun ranges. It was all good, though, because they meant nothing, but what surprised me was the picture of Marvin and

Tye. I sat back in my chair and chuckled because this bitch was on some real sneak-ass shit. A message icon popped up, and I read the quick message from Link stating Echo would be coming by to do Cent's tattoo. I leaned forward, typing in a message requesting every bit of information on Tye. I wanted her whereabouts, the properties she sold, and phone records. This bitch thought she was on some slick shit, and I wanted to see how far back it went. All this did was tell me I was definitely not the father of that baby. I scrolled through a few more pictures of Marvin with Tye. Then I saw one with Kaleb sitting in the car while Marvin held Tye's arm, leading her into a house that was for sale. I added the address of that property to the program and closed the file completely. While I let Link's program do its job, I finally reached out to *Neveena-Sonny Memorial* for a plot. The body was with Emerald Cremation & Funeral Services, already waiting for the go-ahead to get things started. Now, it was time to lay Milo to rest. During the time of the shooting and Cent's kidnapping, I found out that Milo had a younger brother that he was supporting. The kid was attending *Life Achievement Preparatory School* and getting ready to graduate. Apparently, he didn't know that Milo was part of U.C.K. or what he did to provide for him. It was apparent he wanted to keep his brother out of this life, and I would make sure I did everything to keep it that way. Mitchell wouldn't need to worry about shit even though the life insurance policy would make sure of it, but I would personally make sure his ass would never need to worry about a fucking thing. After that, I started looking into Roman and every business he was attached to. I wanted to know it all. After we bled that nigga dry in finances, took over his companies and destroyed them, then I would kill that nigga. I wanted him to wake up every fucking morning, watching his life crumble before his eyes.

I was deep into the finances of Dmar-Clap Productions and who exactly Theodore was when I heard a knock on my office door. I looked up to see Damari walking inside and dropping into the chair before me.

"When are you going to leave?" I asked.

"Now you know that shit ain't happening. Echo is here to do the tattoo, and Nia is here too," he laughed. I frowned as I exited out of everything and closed the computer.

"Is Nia good? Why is she here?"

"Well, she's not staying at Oz's house, that's for damn sure, and she's close to her due date. Sam is Oz's shadow, and we know how that shit would go with Dea. But she needs to be close to one of us, and here is the better choice," Damari shrugged. I wanted to ask how the fuck does their little situation work, but I really didn't give a shit.

"Dea, still not fucking with Nia?" I asked.

"They are cordial, but I'm not testing those limits. Especially while they are both pregnant, so this is the better way. Nia is all good in the guest house right now," Damari stated.

"Bet. It's whatever. But I didn't assign you or anyone else to me, so what the fuck are you doing here?" I questioned.

"Oz made the call, so here I am. Don't act like you didn't think one of them niggas was going to let you ride solo. You would've sent someone to them if shit was opposite my nigga," Damari insisted. I let out a slow breath because I knew I would've done the same shit without hesitation. I closed my eyes for a second, running through all the shit I had to do today. All I wanted right now was to get the tattoo on Crescent and head out to the *RANGE*. I leaned my neck side to side and released the building tension.

"I want you to put someone like Mitchell Norris at *LIFE ACHIEVE-MENT PREPARATORY SCHOOL*. They don't need to be seen, but I want him monitored to make sure nothing happens to the kid. Then I want you to call the *RANGE* and let them know to have my shit prepped. It's time for a little target practice," I ordered.

"Bet. Do you want to head to the *ASYLUM* first?" he asked. His brows rose, and I knew why. I stood up, rotating my arm as I thought about it. Shantel hadn't used that place in years, but I wasn't about to call her out on it. This situation must have really fucked with her hard, and I completely understood why.

"Yeah, let's check Shantel and then the *RANGE*," I confirmed.

"Bet," Damari said, pulling out his phone. I stood up so I could wake up Cent and get on with the day. I would let Cece have today, but I had to get her back to school tomorrow to get her back onto a normal schedule. I also made a mental note to hit up Sanchez about this Tye situation.

"Where is Echo setting up?"

"He said it would be best inside the spa area. So, he's setting up there," Damari stated while typing rapidly into his phone. Damari didn't look like he could fuck a nigga up whatsoever, but that's where people made their first mistake. After seeing him beat a nigga to death during an underground mixed martial art fight, I was impressed. I offered him a job, and then once I saw him laughing while taking out niggas for Oz that were going at Dea, I knew this nigga wasn't wrapped too tight. He fit in perfectly and wasn't afraid to speak his mind. None of us liked that *'yes man'* shit.

"Let him know we are on the way," I said, moving around my desk. I walked out of the door with Cent in my mind. She was about to get her first tattoo, signaling that she was U.C.K. and learning how to hit a target no matter how far away they were.

I walked inside Cece's room and saw that Crescent was already awake. She stared down at Cece who was lying on her chest and knocked the fuck out. I watched as she played in Cece's curls, content to stay where she was.

"I told you about standing there like a creeper, Fransisco," Cent whispered. I moved until I stood over them, staring down at them.

"I need to help you get dressed, *Mi Amor*. We have shit to get done today," I smirked. I leaned down, picked Cece up, and she laid her head on my shoulder. Cent frowned but began to scoot to the edge of the bed. I laid Cece back down and waited until she found a spot that she wanted to lay in. Her sleepy brown eyes lifted slightly as she rubbed them.

"Mommy, are you—"

Crescent leaned over Cece and kissed her head before brushing her hair out of her face.

"Shhh, go back to sleep. Papi and I have some things to do, but I won't go anywhere until you wake up," she whispered. Cece blinked a few times before she fell back to sleep. This was the longest Francesca has slept in a week. Cece would wake up screaming every night, even when she was with Dea or Tali. We waited silently until we heard small snores telling us she was out again. I leaned over, grabbed Cent around her waist, and helped her stand. I helped her into our room to get dressed.

"Papi, what are we doing today? I thought I needed to rest?" she asked. I grabbed the box for her boot that Henny must have left and began to open it.

"Well, you do, but I also need reassurance. I would love for us to stay in the house for weeks, but in this business, shit never stops. And until we put everyone that had something to do with you being taken from me in the ground, we don't get to rest, *Mi Amor*. Do you understand that?" I asked.

Crescent stared at me for a long moment as she played with the bandages on her wrist. I strapped her foot into the boot and pulled her to her feet. The sleeveless pink sweater jumper fell to the floor, covering her boot.

"I do get it, Papi, but if I'm being honest, I didn't think you would let me out of the house," she laughed. I smirked and pulled on a black and gray shirt with black sweats before I answered her. I didn't want to look at her yet because she would see it was exactly what I wanted to do. I wanted to use the cuffs on the bed to chain her to my side, but I refrained. That shit in itself was hard as fuck to do. I turned around, and she was right in my face, looking up at me like it was her first time seeing me. I reached for her face before kissing her then pulled back. Crescent managed to pull her braids into a French braid while I dressed. She reached up and pulled out my gold chain from under my shirt. I didn't miss the quick glance she gave her finger.

"You're only saying that because you know me. It's just that I can't do it yet and simultaneously can't have you out of my sight yet. So that means you stay with me. The first thing is getting your tattoo. And don't worry about the ring, *Mi Amor*. You will have something better soon enough," I said, taking her hand. Her heeled boot was slightly lower than the boot she had to wear for her sprain, giving her a little limp.

"Better? Do you mean bigger, so people don't miss it," she shook her head.

"Exactly," I stated. As long as she knew what was up, I was good.

"Tattoo though? I thought you would put a tracking device in my tooth or something crazy," she joked.

"Naw, *Mi Amor*. Shit like that could be knocked out. But a tattoo wouldn't even cross a person's mind," I smiled.

"Oh, my God! You really are about to fucking brand me," she gasped.

"*Mi Amor*, your entire body was branded the moment you let that Glock slide between your breasts," I chuckled.

"Seriously, Fransisco?"

"Am I lying?" I asked.

Crescent stared at me for a long moment, and I raised my brows at her.

"What if I want to brand you?"

"You can carve your name anywhere you want on my body, *Mi Amor*," I answered. I watched as her breathing picked up and her pupils dilated at the thought of it.

"If it's about to be some freak shit happening, stretch your arm out so it won't shake," Echo laughed. Crescent rolled her eyes at him, but I tipped my head, and he moved her arm further away.

"You need a ring," she squinted.

"And you need a collar. Something I can hold onto while you choke on my dick," I replied.

I smiled as she tried not to shift in her seat while she stared at me. Echo just laughed, shaking his head because he knew I was dead ass.

I stayed in the chair beside Crescent as Echo used ink with a blueish-purple look to it. I also could see the tiny amounts of silver in the ink. Link had created a technology that could track the person wearing it and react to the person's vital signs. Link was that quiet nigga that scared regular people with that shit he created.

"Do it," she said under her breath. I didn't think Echo even heard her speak she was so low. Crescent knew I wanted my name written on every available space on her skin, but I bit down on my tongue. I would wait until she begged me to do it. Today was actually the day she got her U.C.K. tattoo. Not only was she legally mine, but she also caught a body for us. Even though it was in defense of Tali, she still did it. I watched as each letter was placed inside of the crown with the Union City cityscape in the background. Crescent didn't move or make a sound, but the subtle way her eyes enlarged, and her pulse beat told me something was up.

"You need a break, Cent?" I asked with a raised brow. She looked at me and shook her head.

"No, I don't, but...this...this ink looks different from what I'm used to," she said. Echo glanced at me but kept on doing what he was doing. I watched his delicate strokes, finishing up the letter K before I answered Cent.

"Because your friend the Black Wolf developed a way to keep track of y'all asses that no one would detect," I said. Cent frowned slightly before looking back at me.

"So, Master Zaddy trying to lock my ass down too? Y'all niggas are possessive," she laughed. Echo choked, and I narrowed my eyes at Cent.

"When the fuck did you give this nigga a pet name? Don't get him killed 'cause you like playing games Cent," I threatened.

"Boy, bye! You know that's my side piece, Henny is my work husband, and Oz is Daddy Dom because he's.... just know, I'm not fucking with his crazy ass. He might beat me again for real," she shivered. I smirked because she had no fucking clue about her punishment for this shit.

"Did she just—"

"Don't fucking entertain her, Echo," I deadpanned.

"I'm done. You're good to go once I scan it into the program," Echo chuckled.

"It's starting to burn a little," Cent said, fanning her bicep.

"That is a side effect, but it shouldn't worsen. Let me spray it and scan it. By then, you would even feel it," Echo said as I stood. Cent stared at the tattoo with a look of shock, but she said nothing else as Echo finished. Once he was done, I grabbed her hand and helped her stand. As much as I wanted to stay in the house and lay between her thick thighs, we couldn't. Now that she was tatted, we had shit to do and enemies to handle.

"Let's go tell Cece we're leaving for a while. It's time to talk with Pamela," I sneered.

After we convinced Cece we would be back, I was glad when Santina and Santara showed up. Her cousins could always distract her from anything, but it wasn't until Cent promised that she would have Link upload the new software onto her tablet that Cece let her go. I texted Link to tell him what Francesca wanted as Damari drove us out of Union City and into Blackbay. We turned down a long, winding road that led up to the old Blackbay Sanitarium. It was shut down over twenty years ago, but we purchased this building not long after Shantel was rescued. Now, it was known as the *ASYLUM*. We stopped at a large gate that surrounded the entire property of the *ASYLUM*. Damari held his watch out of the window to a scanner. We waited for a few seconds, and then the gate opened.

I felt Cent stiffen beside me, and my hand resting on her thigh flexed. I knew she had caught sight of the large brick building sprawled across ten acres of land. But only a certain part of the building was in use.

"Jesus, she was serious," Cent whispered. I didn't think I was meant to hear her, but I did. I made sure she sat so close to me that nothing would be able to slide between us. I typed out a message before placing my phone in my pocket.

"Dead-ass serious. You don't have to—"

"Naw, fuck that, I'm going inside. I want to know why she went this far. I need to look into Pamela's face when she realizes how fucking wrong she was about me. I can't wait for her to realize she is about to suffer the consequences of her mistakes," Crescent blurted out. Damari caught my eyes in the rearview mirror before he stopped the Durango behind Shantel's Range Rover. I reached up, turned to Crescent's face, and stared into her brown eyes. How deep would she dive into this life for me?

"You're going to see some shit that you haven't seen before, Cent."

"It can't be worse than the *FARM*, Fransisco. I'm good, I can deal," she promised. Her hand came up, gripping my wrist as I stroked her face.

"Naw, *Mi Amor*, that was just child's play. You know us and the reputation that's both good and bad. More than likely, what you heard of the bad is probably true," I cautioned. I watched her eyes bounce between mine before she licked her lips.

"For better or worse, Papi. Either way, I have to see this. I need to see this," Crescent insisted.

"That just made me want to eat your pussy from the back, *Mi Amor*. Can you feel how hard those words made my dick?" I whispered against her lips. She tried looking away, but I tightened my grip as Damari exited the truck.

"Faxx," she moaned.

"I'm going to fuck you, collar you, and cum down your throat before the day is over Crescent. So, keep that pussy wet for Papi," I demanded before I pulled back. I opened the door and slid out.

"Hey! That...fuck, that is so wrong to say at this moment, Fransisco," she groaned as she took my hand. I stopped and looked down at her, her brown eyes staring up at me as I reached for her neck. I gripped it tightly, making her look up at me as I searched her eyes.

"Naw, *Mi Amor*, that isn't what you're supposed to say. What do you say to me, Crescent?"

She swallowed as she licked her lips, shivering slightly as I pushed closer to her. It wasn't like Crescent didn't understand my need to possess her and for her to feel that possession tightly around her neck like it was my hand.

"Yes, Papi," she panted. I leaned over licking her lips and pushing my tongue into her mouth fucking it like how I wanted my dick down her throat. Crescent moaned, and I released her and pulled away, smirking.

"Next time, you better act like you know what to say. Let's go, *Mi Amor*," I affirmed before turning and walking her inside the building.

"Jesus J. Christ, something is wrong with me," she whispered as Damari opened the large doors. As soon as he did, all you could hear was the echo of screams bouncing off the walls.

"No! No! No! Help me! Help—"

The scream was cut off as the lights began to flicker slightly.

"Oh, my God. What in the hell is she doing to that girl?" Cent asked. I lifted her and took the stairs to the next level as sadistic laughter grew louder and louder. I put Crescent on her feet and saw Damari sitting beside the door.

"You not coming up my nigga?" I asked. Damari didn't even look in my direction while he stared at his phone.

"Fuck no! If we're here, then Shantel is doing some wild ass shit. I'm good. I like to sleep at night," he declared. I started to chuckle and then laughed harder at the look on Crescent's face. I took her hand and led her to the room where Shantel obviously had Pamela.

"Fix your face, Cent. It's not that bad," I soothed. The look she gave me told me that she didn't believe a word coming out of my mouth. She rubbed at the spot where her tattoo was before breathing deeply.

"I'm pretty sure you're lying because what the fuck is that smell?" she frowned. I said nothing as I pushed open the doors to see Shantel standing over Pamela while holding her hand on a button. We stood there as Pamela's body lifted slightly off of the table. She wore a strait jacket, and her body was strapped down so she wouldn't fall off. When Shantel saw us, she let the button go and smiled.

"Ahh. Ahh, ple...pleasss...hel—"

Pamela's words were cut off when Shantel looked at her. Pamela began to cry softly, and I closed the doors.

"Cent! It would be best if you were home resting. Not here," Shantel said. She pulled off rubber gloves, stepped off the platform, and approached us.

"Mmmm, I had to be. Has she...what has Pamela told you?" Crescent asked. I let her hand go and made my way over to the table. Pamela's eyes were closed as she cried. She no longer had hair, and from the marks, I could tell Shantel wasn't gentle when she shaved her hand.

"We just got started. I had to wait for a little more information, but I have it now. Are you sure you should—"

I looked over at Shantel's sharp inhale as she looked at Crescent's arm.

"Got it today," Cent said.

"Oh shit! Oh my God! We need to have a get-together to celebrate. We'll talk later, but if you're sure, let's get started," Shantel gritted.

I stared down at Pamela until her eyes opened fully. I waited until she could focus on my face before I spoke.

"Take a good look at my face, Patricia. I want you to remember it because this will be the last face your brother will see before I blow his fucking head off," I forewarned.

"Wha...who...no! Please help me. Don't hurt.... he has nothing to do with—" Pamela sobbed. I saw her eyes grow wide in fear and hate as Crescent came up beside me.

"So, you've met my husband. Now that you see how much you've fucked up, let me repay you for the hurt you caused me," Crescent said, stepping back. I turned slightly, seeing Shantel hand her a hammer, and before I could ask what she was doing, I watched as the hammer came down twice on Pamela's ankle, splintering her bones.

"Ahhh! Ahhh! I'm sorry! Please stopppp, please.... I didn't know! He didn't say.... please," Pamela screamed as Crescent moved to the other foot. At least she didn't have a fucking cleaver.

I stepped back, watching as Shantel and Crescent moved around the table. I wasn't about to lie. I was hard as fuck. But I could see the hurt in Cent's eyes and the slight shake in her hands until Pamela spoke again.

"Fuck! Fuck you! Fuck You! None of this would've happened if you kept your legs closed! You—"

Shantel moved and hit a button that began to rotate the table in a standing position. Two arm tables came out on both sides. I moved closer as Shantel roughly began to take off the jacket and stood in front of Pamela. I pulled out my Glock from my holster and placed it directly in the middle of her forehead. I could feel Crescent watching me as I studied this bitch.

"If you only knew how badly I want to put a bullet through your head, you would keep your fucking mouth shut about my wife. The only things I want out of your mouth are the answers to the fucking questions my wife ask you. Blink if you fucking understand," I commanded. Her hiccupping and cries as I spoke only irritated me more until I felt a hand on my side.

"I...I.... I—"

"Do you fucking understand?" I shouted.

"Yes! Yes, just pleas—"

Shantel yanked her hand and pushed it flat on the table. Pamela snapped her mouth shut, but the tears ran freely down her face. I knew the pain in her ankles had to be intense.

"Only answer the questions, Pam!" Shantel shouted. She pulled over a small metal table that was covered by a blue towel. I pulled my Glock away as I watched Shantel placed an I.V. in Pamela's hand. Shantel hit the button on the table, and it moved once more.

"I'll tell you what...whatever...you...want to know," she slurred. Whatever medication Shantel pushed in had Pam feeling really good.

Crescent stepped closer to the table, clenching her teeth together. She sucked in a breath as Shantel sat above Pamela, placing a scalpel on her forehead. Shantel's crazy ass was about to give this chick a lobotomy. Who the fuck showed her how.... I closed my eyes because I was sure it was between Link and Henny.

"Go ahead, Cent. Let's get started while I prep her for a Trephination. Crescent, did you know I wanted to be a brain surgeon years ago? That was until...let's get started," Shantel smiled. She didn't look at either of us, but I could see Crescent assessing her. I saw in her eyes when she figured out something horrible had happened, but she just skipped over it, glancing at me quickly.

I watched as Pamela struggled against the leather straps that held her in place. I could tell Shantel hadn't thought twice about the straps digging into her skin. I glared at Crescent standing to the side of Pamela, trying to understand why she had done it, and she was desperate for answers.

"What did you want from me?" Crescent demanded. Her voice filled with anger. Shantel was neatly making an incision across her forehead like she did this shit every day.

Pamela's fear-filled eyes met mine, and I knew she could see the venom.

"You want to know why I kidnapped you?" she sneered. Whatever medication Shantel had running must've been the same shit Henny used. The shock of her crushed bones no longer bothered her, making her feel bold. "It's simple. I hate you."

"Hate me? What have I ever done to you? Bitch I don't even know you," Crescent asked. I looked up as the sound of a drill started, and I saw Crescent's eyes almost bulge out of her head.

Pamela let out a bitter laugh as her eyes rolled in her head.

"It's not what you've done. It's who you have. You took my brother away from me, leaving me to follow him here because you couldn't stay your ass in Clapton! I was supposed to be done with Rodney, but I needed his help to start over. I couldn't be mad when I met who he wanted me close to," she panted.

"Oh, this bitch is crazier than me," Shantel giggled.

"Then here you come again. I prayed the nigga you were with just fucking killed you, but no. You started over like it was nothing. Then, I finally saw my brother, and you fucked him too. I couldn't stand it because you weren't good enough. I saw you and *'Dr. Sexy'* as soon as my brother leaves for a few weeks, whore."

"Bitch, you are fucking insane, and me and Eric were nothing. Friends with benefits. I can't help how his mind interprets things even when shit was clear as fuck from the jump! But all this? Stalking and kidnapping me was for what?"

"I should have let Rodney call earlier, and then I would have Hendrix."

Shantel burst out laughing as she removed a piece of Pamela's skull.

"Crescent, do me a favor and check her sensations. Break her ring finger. That would seem poetic," Shantel smiled. I stayed quiet because I wanted to know more about Rodney and what else he had to do with all of this. Crescent moved around the table, grabbed something off Shantel's cart, and moved closer to Pamela.

I could see her pulse pounding in her throat as she watched Crescent with wide eyes. Crescent looked at me and then back at Pamela as her grip tightened on the handle of a bone saw. I looked at Shantel, and she seemed to be...enjoying herself.

"What else did Rodney have you doing for him? How many spies does he have at the hospital?"

Pamela's expression twisted as Crescent brought the saw to her finger.

"I can't wait to tell Henny about this," Shantel smiled.

"Wha.... what are you doing?"

"Answer the fucking question!" I snapped. Pamela's eyes met mine, and whatever she saw had her lips trembling.

"Nnn—no. I don't know what happened to ttth...the other girl. She disappeared, and I was moved.... even my handler chann—changed. But-tt—but that's because it was her fault! It's always her, fucking up a good thing!"

Crescent sucked her teeth and pressed down harder, and I heard the crack of bone.

"Ahhh! Oh shit! Wai—wait! Ahhh, ahhh," Pamela screamed.

"Well, we should hurry now. The meds are wearing off," Shantel said as she began drilling again.

"If you want the pain to stop, Pam, all you need to do is talk," I shrugged.

"Ahh, oh God help me please! I—I decided to take matters into my own hands. If I got rid of her, Eric would finally get over her, and I would finally have a chance with Hendrix. Rodney's petty bullshit didn't matter anymore! He doesn't understand that without planting evidence, there is nothing he could use to take down Hendrix."

That was always why we never truly worried about the hospital because nothing would hold up in court. The only thing that worried us now was that fucking video. Everything else was easy to handle.

"Does Eric know what you did? Does he approve of what you did to me? Stole a week of my life, scared my child, and hurt my husband. I am not fucking Hendrix, you dumb bitch," Crescent screamed before throwing

Pamela's severed finger in her face. Pamela screamed as another piece of her skull was laid out on the small table beside Shantel.

"You're all insane," she cried, her voice trembling with disbelief at what she was seeing.

"You kidnapped me just to get to Hendrix, and we're crazy? Bitch, you must not know exactly what insanity looks like, but let me show," Crescent gritted. I could see she wasn't mad about the kidnapping or treatment. It was because of what it did to Cece and me. That had me reevaluating everything because if the kidnapping didn't really bother her, what else had she been through where this was on the lower end of things? Both of my babies needed therapy. Fuck.

Shantel moved away, leaving Pamela's brain showing like some kind of fake Halloween costume.

"Did you see the expert incisions I made without damaging a thing? Let me send Henny a picture of it," Shantel said as Crescent moved the table to a standing position again.

"Don't you dare judge me, Crescent. I was willing to do whatever it took, even if it meant getting my hands dirty. Rodney already made the call, so now he will do whatever it takes to get you back. You will never have a moment of peace," she cried. The blood from her severed finger dripped to the tiled floor as she shook from head to toe from all of the trauma done to her body. Crescent stood before her, staring into glassy eyes, and shook her head.

"Did Eric know what you did to me?" Cent asked calmly.

Pamela's eyes were filled with a mix of fear and hate as she stared at Crescent.

"Who the fuck do you think told me where you lived," she slurred. Crescent's hand shook as she gripped the saw. I knew she was hurt even if she didn't have feelings for that nigga. Just another mutha fucka that fucked her over. I knew how Cent's mind worked, and I could say for sure I didn't like it. Shantel moved, grabbed Crescent's hand, and removed the saw as I got closer. Cent moved, and Pamela's glassy eyes stared into the mirror at herself.

"Ohhhh. Ahhhh wwwha—what have, oh fuck, please. Please, you stupid bitc—"

Crescent reached for her thigh holster as she pulled out Rose. No matter what she just did, killing someone who couldn't defend themselves would haunt her later. She had enough nightmares, and Shantel must have come to the same conclusion.

I held up my Glock, pointing to the side of Pamela's head as I stared at her in the mirror. Three shots rang out at the same time as Pamela's bullshit died with her. As the echo of the shots faded, everything became dead silent. I moved over to Crescent and pushed her arm down as she stared at Pamela's lifeless body. I pulled her to me, not sure if she was going to scream or cry at this moment.

"All this because this bitch was crazy. All she managed to do was paint another target on my back," Crescent whispered. She wasn't wrong because if Rodney promised Cent to Roman, he would want to collect.

"It's all good, *Mi Amor*. Because every single one of them niggas got a target on their heads. This time ain't shit going to hold me back," I promised.

"What's next? I think I should go to the hospital to see Dylan," she sighed. I could feel her body shaking from the adrenaline. I looked over Cent's head at Shantel, but she was staring at Pamela with her arms folded across her chest.

"Shantel, we need someone to get close to Rodney. He will be harder to touch once he finds out Crescent is gone. He's going to use whatever is at his disposal," I grumbled. Shantel slowly turned to face me, and I could tell she had an idea that gave her pleasure as she licked her lips.

"I think it's time Katrice paid her dues. I'm sure she is wondering what happened to her sister and that U.C.K. has something to do with it," she smirked.

"I have a better idea that I think Katrice would be good for," I suggested. Shantel raised a brow in anticipation of my idea.

"Tell me," she smiled.

"I need her to become real good friends with Tyenika. She's on some shit I don't like. Maybe Katrice needs to buy a house. All you need is to give her a few commands complaining about her cousins Tali and Dea, but she really has a special hatred for their friend Crescent. Then make sure she drops the nickname Cent in there as well. Give her enough to work with. You know what to do," I stated.

"Fransisco, I like how your mind works," Shantel nodded.

"Bet. What else did you learn about them," I gestured to Pamela's body. Shantel rolled her eyes as she typed on her phone before looking back at us.

"Patricia and Eric Manning, brother and sister from Clapton. Eric was in nursing school at Clapton Community College and seemed to have taken classes with you, Crescent," she said.

"I...I didn't know this nigga until I started working at Union," Crescent said, turning around. My hands slid down to her waist, and I rested my Glock against her hip. She shivered slightly, and this time I knew it wasn't from this bullshit.

"The classes were minor but very large to the point where you probably never noticed him," Shantel answered. She looked at me before facing Pamela's body again with a look of disappointment.

"Pamela was caught up on drug charges when she was caught selling hospital-regulated drugs. That's when she met Rodney. Then Eric graduated from Clapton a month after you left. I have no clue how he tracked you down, but I'm sure we can ask once we catch that nigga," Shantel stated. I let my Glock trace Cent's side up and down while I thought about our next move. Henny needed to be filled in on all this, so a hospital trip was a good idea.

"We're done here, *Mi Amor*. We will stop to see Dylan and see if there is any change, then head out to the *RANGE*. I have someone there who might tell us where Roman's bitch ass is hiding," I said, putting my Glock back into the holster. I turned Crescent around to face me and looked down to see her still holding Rose in a death grip.

"I'm bringing too much drama to your doorstep," she whispered. I raised a brow as I reached down, taking her gun from her grip.

"Naw, you're only giving it color, *Mi Amor*. You already knew everything was black before I saw you. Now, there is nothing I wouldn't do or no one I wouldn't kill to ensure you stay with me."

"You know I will do the same, right?" she asked.

I looked into her eyes, seeing the truth written in them, which told me I had corrupted her ass and I couldn't care less. Now it would be three of us saying, '*Be normal, act normal, and everyone will leave you the fuck alone*' before we left the house. Perfect.

"There was never a doubt in my mind about that Crescent. Let's finish our day so we can get home to our daughter," I acknowledged. I wouldn't ruin the surprise that she had also formally adopted Francesca when she signed those papers. I leaned down and placed my lips to her ear. I made sure to press her close to my body so she could feel what her words did to me.

"I think I might need to stick my dick in you before we get to the hospital. All you have to do is sit in my lap. Don't worry about Damari. He won't mind," he whispered. I felt her body shake as she pressed harder against me.

"Fuck," Crescent groaned.

CHAPTER FOUR

CRESCENT 'CENT' WELLINGTON

So many things were running through my mind that I didn't know where to begin. I knew what just happened, but it almost felt like a distant memory. Faxx seemed to have been anticipating some crazy shit to happen because when it was over, he helped me change clothes. That shit didn't even cross my mind, but why would it when I wasn't a psycho killer. It all made sense now why Fransisco always wore so much black because it hid the blood splatter.

What the fuck? Next thing I knew, I would be helping his ass hide bodies.

The thought of that fled my mind as Faxx's hands skimmed over my body as he pulled the long-sleeved crimson sweater dress over my head. I smoothed the material into place, then followed him out of Shantel's den of horror and into the SUV. I still found it funny. I wasn't even mad about the kidnapping bullshit because I'd been held prisoner before under worse circumstances. I pushed the memories away of being locked in a room until Roman felt like I learned my lesson. That nigga was crazy as fuck. I shifted through those memories, trying to see Eric before I met him in Union. Shantel was right. He could've been in a class, but I wouldn't have ever known by them being so large. But the question remained was how the fuck did he know I would go to Union City. No one knew where I was from, and I didn't talk to anyone at that college because I knew Tony or his brother, was watching me. I shook my head to stay in the present, still mad at Pamela.

I took a deep breath, waiting for the shock to kick in at what I had witnessed and what I had done to soothe the rage inside of me. Nothing happened. Nothing happened because, in my head, the bitch deserved the shit. After all, I knew what taking me would do to my family. I rubbed a finger over the tattoo on my bicep in disbelief. I was more shocked at the U.C.K. brand than being married. Now, because of that psycho-stalking bitch, I had to put the pieces back together.

"Crescent, I want you to know upfront that Dylan is being treated by the best, but it's still touch and go," Faxx insisted. His tatted hand gripped my chin so I would look at him. I watched as his dark eyes traveled all over my face. I guess he was looking for shock, regret, or denial.

"I know. I know y'all are doing everything you can to give her a fighting chance. What about Jacinda? Has she been here at all, or is she still trapped in the hotel," I smiled. It wouldn't be out of the realm of possibility that my mother would cut her losses and bounce if she got the chance.

"We had to bring Jacinda in because of Dylan's condition. She needed blood. Apparently, her blood type is rare, like yours. We were lucky when you got shot, but not so much this time. The hospital didn't have enough on hand," Faxx attested.

"That's one thing that Jacinda and I have in common. AB-negative blood type would be the only thing that connects us," I laughed bitterly.

"Yeah, well, let's just say she had some shit to say, and I almost let that fucking collar explode. But, more than likely, she will be there. She can't really go anywhere else unless it's back to the hotel, but I feel like she wants t o—"

"Make sure her investment stays alive. Trust me, I get it," I said, pulling out of his grasp to look out of the window. Union Memorial came into view, and I sucked in a breath.

"We'll check on Dylan and I'll call Henny while you visit her. He needs to know what little Pamela told us," Faxx said. She said little to nothing, but I knew Shantel and knew exactly what she could do. What else had she said before we got there?

"Did Shantel say that she said anything else?" I asked. Damari pulled up to the main entrance of the hospital. He turned around to face us, glancing at Faxx before looking at me.

"Let's just say the bitch was crazy as fuck. I did a little digging for Shantel on her. I can only say this wasn't the first unhealthy infatuation she's had. The last one ended up in prison because he didn't return her attraction. He went down for distribution of prescription drugs, sexual harassment, and embezzlement. Rodney was the lead on that, along with the man who was seen in those files," he said, looking at Faxx.

"Agent Thomas Higgins. So, please do me a favor and track him down. If anyone knows more about what Rodney is up to, it's him. I don't give a fuck about who he is or works for. All this tiptoeing is done. Make it happen," Faxx ordered. He opened the door and held out his hand for me to take. I looked at Damari, and he smiled at me before I reached out and took Faxx's hand. I let Faxx lead me into the hospital and toward the pediatric intensive care unit. My heart was slamming against my chest because I didn't want this. I fought to get to Dylan, and that bitch Pamela could cost Dylan her life.

"Are you good, *Mi Amor*? We don't need to do this now. We can always come back later," Faxx urged. We stopped at the elevators as he turned me to face him. He stood so close that I had to lean back slightly to look up at him. The dark brown of his eyes traced over my face before his thumb swept over my lips.

"I need to do this. I just...I need to see for myself," I whispered. The chime sounded for the elevators, and we stepped on. Faxx hit the button for the fourth floor, and I held my breath the entire time. All I could think of was what I could have done differently that night. Would things still have ended up this way? Would Pamela still have caught me if I hadn't decided to go? The doors opened, and I followed behind Faxx as we entered the room. Not one person said a word to us as we made our way to the room where Dylan was fighting for her life. As soon as Faxx pushed open the door, I rolled my eyes so hard those bitches should have been stuck.

"You actually have the nerve to show your face in here after what you've done?" Jacinda gritted. I took a step forward, ignoring Jacinda so I could see Dylan.

"Jacinda, I would advise you to tread carefully. It's only out of respect for this hospital that I don't set off that collar and blow your fucking head off your body. At least after that, we would have all the blood needed for the baby if it's called for," Faxx fumed. I glanced at Jacinda as she stepped back, visibly trembling with a hand to her neck. I looked away, but I felt the moment her hateful gaze landed on me.

"She's good, Papi. Let her talk because that's all she can do," I stated. I looked down at Dylan's fragile body and all the tubes connected to her fighting back tears. The tears weren't even from sadness, but anger.

"I'm not worried, *Mi Amor*, because her time gets more limited each time she speaks," Faxx gritted. I heard a buzzing sound, and I turned my head to see Faxx looking at his phone. He stared at me for a moment and then slid his cold eyes in Jacinda's direction before stepping out of the room. I turned to face Dylan and waited to see what she had to say. I already knew what she wouldn't ask. There would be no *'Are you okay?'* Or *'What happened to you?'* probably not even a *'Where have you been?'* There wouldn't be any concern coming from her, and I was good with that.

"So, you can't even speak for yourself anymore. You have him speaking for you?" she spat. I rubbed a finger over Dylan's leg before facing my mother.

"He is my husband," I shrugged. I waited as her eyes traveled up and down my body, landing on the boot, before she looked at my hand.

"So, all you came out with was a few bumps and bruises while your sister lays here dying, and you come a week later like it's all good. Do you have any idea how this...this...this is—"

I took two steps forward and got into her face. Jacinda tried stepping back, but her back hit the wall.

"All you give a fuck about is yourself. All you care about is ensuring she lives so you can get another payday. Let's not act like we both don't know why you are so fucking concerned," I seethed. I stepped back slightly as the rage-filled her eyes while she looked me up and down. Then, she slapped me. The sound of the slap was like a whip, and I smiled a little when I touched my face.

"You...you need to leave. Get out! Get the hell out of here, Crescent! It doesn't matter who you are fucking, I am still her mother and legal guardian, and I want you out," she said between clenched teeth. I leaned my head to the side as I looked her over. She believed she could still call shots like I was that same little girl seeking attention. The slap across her face was fast and hard, causing spit to fly out of her mouth. I leaned in close as I tried to control myself because I didn't want to kill my grandmother's child.

"The next time you touch me, don't be surprised when you find yourself bleeding the fuck out while I stare down at you, Jacinda," I smirked at her just as the door opened. "Let's see how long you will be called anyone's mother. Trust me when I say it won't last long," I said, stepping back.

"*Mi Amor?*"

Jacinda stared at me with hate, but I could see the fear beginning to replace that, making my smile wider.

Oh my God, I'm getting creepy, just like all of them! Be normal, act normal, and everyone—

I turned around quickly, not even about to finish that thought in my head.

"We can go, Papi. Are we meeting Henny?" I asked. I moved past him, out of the door, and he closed it behind us.

"Naw, we are going to have a meeting later today. We're heading to the bank and then *RANGE*," he said, taking my hand.

"Okay, but I need a favor," I sighed. I was done with Jacinda, and I wasn't about to let her do to another child what she did to me. At least I had my grandmother. Who would Dylan have?

"All you need to do is ask. You know that, *Mi Amor*," Faxx said, looking down at me. The brownness of his eyes was beginning to show, but I could still see the coldness in his gaze. I knew all I had to do was ask, but I rarely wanted anything from him except him. If I had made this same request to any one of them, they would have made it happen.

"I need custody of Dylan. Full legal custody," I stated. The doors opened to let us out of the unit as Faxx pulled out a matte black phone.

"Done."

"Oh, and why do we need to go to the bank?" I asked, confused.

I looked up at the towering brick building that resembled the banks from back in the day. It was massive, with huge archways and pillars lining the outside of it. Two armed security guards were standing at the entrance with the logo for Faxx's security company on their vests. This time, it seemed like we weren't going into KALM HORIZON NATIONAL CREDIT UNION through the front. Damari pulled the SUV down a side street and waited for the black iron gates to open.

"You never answered me, Fransisco. What do we need to do here, or what do you need to do?" I asked, turning to face him. Faxx had his phone pressed to his ear with his tatted hand rubbing along my inner thigh. He was keeping me in a state of hyperarousal while at the same time a little distant. I could tell that his trying to enforce some distance was hard as fuck for him because I was his. His touch owned every inch of my body and soul. Whatever was going on in his head wouldn't be enough to keep him from possessing me, my time, or my space. He moved the phone away from his ear with a slight smirk before looking at me. His dark brown eyes traced every inch of my face before they fell to my neckline.

"We need to add you to all my accounts, and I also need to get you entered in to get inside of the vaults when needed. And there is something here that I need to get," Faxx imparted.

"All your accounts and a vault? I don't think I need all that kind of access and shit. What if I'm trying to take you for all your money?" I asked.

"As long as you let me slide my dick between your breast while you lick the tip, you can have all the money I have, *Mi Amor*. It ain't shit to get that back," he grinned. His hand slid further up my thigh, brushing against my clit as I reached out and grabbed his beard.

"I do not need money for you to do that," I panted.

"Yeah, but her little ass needs some discipline," Damari insinuated.

"Shut up, Damari," I refuted. I did not need Faxx getting any Oz shit in his head. Damari looked in the rearview mirror and raised his brows as his stare almost swallowed me. I closed my mouth when Faxx chuckled and grabbed my chin. It still felt like his touch was still on my thigh, like it was branded or imprinted into my skin.

"Naw, Crescent. Damari might be right about that shit. You need that physical reminder not to fuck with Papi," Faxx pointed out. Faxx's hand slid down to my neck, running his nails along my skin.

"Yes, Papi."

I could feel my heart slamming against my chest while the sound of it filled my ears as his grip tightened. I hadn't noticed the SUV had stopped until Faxx's door was opened. He still didn't move as he leaned in close to my lips. I could hear someone shouting on his phone, but he ended the call and stuck it into his pocket.

"Have I ever hidden my OBSESSION that I have with you?"

"No. You've made it quite clear since day one, honestly," I answered.

"So, you understand when I mean I possess you, it means in every way. If you aren't in my dreams, I'll wake myself up because that means I must not be in yours, and I can't have that. I need you just as fucking obsessed as I am with you, so I always make sure I give you something to dream about. You will have everything you want and need, including the discipline you c rave, *Mi Amor*. There was no way to hide the pain and pleasure on your face when that thick ass was being spanked. Just like you want to feel that collar around your throat while I use it to force you to take this dick," he declared.

I had no idea what kind of shuddering breath left my body, but I swear I was cumming just from his words. I licked my lips, and my tongue swiped across his soft ones, making me moan. Everything he said was right. I did like it. I actually loved it, but now the thought of a collar wouldn't leave my mind. Now, I couldn't think of anything else.

"I understand, Papi," I whispered. His hard, dark gaze stared into mine for a moment longer before he smiled.

"There was never any doubt that you wouldn't. Let's get this done," he said, kissing me softly before pulling away. Faxx helped me out of the SUV on shaky as fuck legs in the back of the Bank. This must have been executive parking or something because only three cars besides ours was in the lot. Faxx held my hand as we walked toward a large brown metal door where Damari stood looking inside, shaking his head.

"Nigga, this dude is wild as fuck. These Union streets definitely ain't ready for his ass to be home," Damari laughed.

"I was trying to give him some time, but you know how he is about checks and balances," Faxx stated. As we approached, Damari widened the door so we could step inside, and my mouth fell open when I saw the tall, dark, chocolate nigga that was with Shantel when she saved me. A man stood to the side of him, wearing all black and holding a royal blue suit jacket over his arm, waiting patiently. Karma had his white dress shirt tucked into his royal blue tailored pants with striped suspenders over his shoulders. He had his sleeves rolled up, revealing a large gold watch. His thick arms had corded muscles as he rained down blow after blow on a man lying out on the floor while he lectured him.

"All payments are due on the first and last of the month, Jerry. I was even nice and let you have a grace period because I know and understand. I understand about hard times and all that bullshit, but you had the nerve to come in this bank thinking you could slide off with writing a bad check?" He shouted. Karma stood up, raised his leather-covered foot, and slammed it on the man's rib cage.

"I...won't...I—"

"Your banking and vault privileges are revoked, Jerry. You have until the end of the business day to settle your accounts with KALM HORIZON NATIONAL CREDIT UNION. We hope you've had a pleasant experience with us," Karma said, in a professional tone.

I stared at him as he used the white cloth the man in black handed him to clean his hands. I watched as he put himself back together, looking like an entirely different person. He slid his jacket over massive shoulders as he turned to face us. His wide smile revealed straight, even white teeth with dimples on each side of his face.

"Faxx, I didn't hear you come in. Is this a business call or a union call?" he asked, clasping his hands together. I stared at him with my mouth open, noticing his matching striped tie that went with his suspenders.

His demeanor reminded me of a younger version of Oz. Sexy as fuck and completely *insane*.

"It's business but not about my company. Personal business," Faxx disclosed.

"Oh well, shit. Navi, take Jerry to his car. Make sure he understands, when I say the end of the business day, I fucking mean five this evening. You know I have to eat dinner by six," Karma said as he dapped up Faxx.

"Yes, sir." The man's low rumble filled the space as he moved. Then Karma pushed Faxx out of the way and stared down at me.

"Nigga! What the fuck?"

"It's a pleasure to see you again, Crescent. I'm glad it's under better circumstances than before. I just have one question. Do you think that bitch would've lied on her loan application?"

I was staring into his chocolate brown eyes as he held my hands and slowly rubbed his thumbs across my knuckles. This nigga was dangerous.

"Well, she was lying about her name, so she for sure would have lied for a loan," I giggled when he smiled. Why the fuck was I giggling?

"Karma! Get the fuck away from my wife, my nigga. I don't want to break both of your hands, but I will," Faxx threatened, pushing him away from me. Karma chuckled, the professional demeanor rolling off of him like shedding skin.

"Fransisco, don't be a bitch, my nigga. You know I'm fucking with you. Tell me what you need, and I'll get it handled," he finished on a serious note. We didn't waste any time getting my prints, retinal scans, blood, soul, and whatever else made up my existence on file. I almost swallowed my tongue when I saw exactly how much was in my account now, but I died a little when I saw the joint accounts. I wasn't about to touch any of those cards, but I signed anyway while Faxx and Karma went to handle something. I looked over the last piece of paper. It displayed my name as the owner of an apartment building I knew all too well. From what it said, the building was currently under construction. When the fuck did this nigga do this?

"Aight, I need to get back to my office and handle some shit. Crescent, seriously, I'm glad to see you doing well. Try to stay out of trouble, so I don't need to pay out insurance premiums," Karma smiled as he hugged me.

"I will," I laughed as he pulled away. I held up the paper to Faxx, and he glanced over it and looked at me. I decided it was best to just leave that shit alone for today and worry about it another time.

"We need to go, *Mi Amor*," Faxx insisted. I grabbed my purse and sweater before reaching for his hand.

"What's next, baby?" I sighed.

"I need to clean up the *RANGE* after target practice before Stax does a surprise checkup or some shit," he chuckled. But I could tell his mood had instantly changed.

The ride to the *RANGE* seemed to be shorter this go around because I wasn't fearing for my damn life this time. I looked at the thick trees on each side of us as we drove up the dirt road that led to the property I knew of as the *RANGE*. Faxx's hand still stayed on my thigh the entire time, inching higher and higher to the point where I felt his fingers on the outside of my damp panties. I wanted to move, so I made him put some pressure on my clit, but at the same time, I remembered his words from earlier. If I pushed, I knew he would pull me on his lap and fuck me, not caring who the fuck was in the car.

I felt his lips at my ear and his breath along my skin, causing my breath to pick up.

"You do know my dick is still hard, *Mi Amor*. It will get worse when I watch you at target practice. Did you like how my Glock tasted the last time you were here?"

His voice was a rumble against my ear, causing me to shiver as the memories of the last time I stepped foot on this property and this nigga did some *Friday the 13th* shit.

"I'm not running through these woods, Faxx. I can barely walk," I panted.

"Naw, the only running you're going to do is from this dick," he chuckled. I closed my eyes as he applied pressure to my clit. I knew what he was doing and wasn't about to lie and say it wasn't working.

"I'm definitely not going to run, Papi," I murmured. I felt the truck come to a stop, and Faxx moved his head from my neck.

"Why in the hell is he here?" Faxx grunted. I opened my eyes and looked out of the front window. I screamed and fumbled for the door as Sanchez pushed off the driver-side door of a dark gray Aston Martin. His blind ass was driving now. He walked toward the truck with a furrowed brow.

"This nigga here early," Faxx huffed. I opened the door, and Sanchez came to my side as I scooted off the seat. His expression changed as his smile spread across his face.

"Cent! You know how hard it is to track you down since you married and shit," Sanchez chuckled.

"Shit Sanchez, you can see me now! I missed you," I said, hugging him. His arms wrapped around my waist as he lifted me briefly off my feet.

"Why are you like this? You know damn well I wouldn't not be able to see you," he chuckled.

"My nigga, put my wife down. We might share a baby momma, but we are not sharing a wife. And Crescent, did you forget what the fuck I told you about this nigga?" Faxx said, pushing us apart.

"Fransisco! This is my best friend! And you said I couldn't say I love you. I said I missed him," I said, smacking his hands. Sanchez kissed my forehead before he let me go, looking serious. Faxx leaned against the truck as Damari left and headed for the house. Everything was just like before, but it seemed a little too quiet. I felt Faxx's hands at my waist, causing me to step backward, pressing my ass against him.

"She loves me anyway, my nigga. I knew her first," Sanchez laughed, but it was strained. I frowned, beginning to get concerned.

"Why are you so early? I don't have all the details just yet on Tye," Faxx stated. I frowned harder because what fucking details? Sanchez ran a hand over his waves, causing his long-sleeved forest green sweater to pull tight across his arms. Now that I was looking at him, I saw the stress lines around his eyes and the frown on his lips. But it was the rage in his brown gaze that had my brows raising.

"Kaleb said a name that he shouldn't know shit about," Sanchez sucked his teeth. He began to pace as he clenched his hands like he was trying to reign in his anger.

"What the hell did he tell you, Sans?" I asked. Sanchez stopped and stared at Faxx for a second before he put his hands on his head.

"Kaleb said he didn't mind calling you dad, but would he have to call Jakobe his dad too? I need to know what the fuck is going on. If I didn't come here, I was going to her house to choke the fuck out of her. I don't know everything, but I know that nigga had something to do with that shooting," Sanchez shouted. I felt Faxx's hands tighten on my waist at the mention of Jakobe's name, but he was dead. All Faxx had to do was tell Sans that Ja wouldn't be a problem because Ja was dead. He could know that much, at least. Faxx stood straight and stepped to the side, leaving me to stand beside the truck. He got into Sanchez's field of vision until he stopped pacing.

"Listen to me. I need you to go home, pack all your shit and Kaleb's things and go stay at one of your other homes. One that Tye doesn't know about. Do not let her take Kaleb anywhere or pick him up for school. Did you get the emergency order?"

The seriousness in Faxx's tone was saying a lot, and I could tell Sanchez felt it as well. I was beginning to be afraid because what the fuck was going on?

"Yeah, for thirty days. But—"

"Bet. I will get someone to extend it until we take care of this shit. Just...just go and handle that. Get him enrolled at Cece's school and let the school know she cannot access Kaleb. I will update you once I have everything. I can't tell you anything else, and you know why," Faxx stressed.

"Naw, fuck that, Fransisco! Fuck that U.C.K. shit! This is my son! My fucking son nigga. What the fuck is going on?!" Sanchez demanded. I pushed off the truck with my eyes wide because I had never seen Sanchez like this, but I understood why.

"Because it's you, my nigga, I will say Jakobe don't need to be worried about. But Tye is fucking around with people more dangerous than that nigga could ever be. Do what the fuck I said, and once I know more, I will hit you up. But right now, pacing ain't doing shit but wasting time you could be using to make sure your son is protected," Faxx warned. They stared at each other for what felt like hours until Sanchez turned away.

"Don't fucking keep me in the dark on this Faxx," Sanchez pointed.

"Then maybe you need to make up your mind. It's not like it isn't something you're already thinking about," Faxx stated. I stood there as Sanchez slid into the driver's seat, slamming the door. He sat there for a minute, slamming his hands against the steering wheel before the smooth sound of the Aston Martin's engine came to life, and he peeled off.

"Faxx, what the hell is going on? If Ja is dead, why would—"

Faxx turned to face me as what sounded like a gang of ATVs came our way. Faxx's jaw flexed as he looked in the distance before looking down at me.

"I need you to get changed. I still have a few people hanging around that might give us some answers they don't know they have," he chuckled. I took his words literally because the last time this nigga had someone buried in the ground. We went into the house to change, I prayed there were pants this time because I was not trying to be in anybody's woods in shorts again. Fuck that!

I knew damn well I was squeezing the fuck out of Faxx's waist as he made his way deeper into this got damn forest. There was no way I could even figure out how I would make it back to the house. If I couldn't figure it out, then any person he had out here who escaped wouldn't figure it out either. They could be running for hours, even days, and still end up nowhere. The ATV slowed down once we got to a wooden fence. I looked around at the paper targets placed strategically and then saw it.

"Holy shit. You are fucking crazy," I whispered. Four men hung next to the paper targets that were the farthest away.

"Cent, this isn't anything new. You already know what's up, and the time to change your mind was over the moment you signed them fucking papers," he laughed.

"Nigga! I was under duress!"

"Dickmatized," he chuckled. He was absolutely correct, but I wasn't telling him that. I was trying to figure out why I wasn't hopping back on that fucking ATV and peeling the fuck out of here. I followed Faxx, and the closer I got, the more I bit down on my tongue.

"Plea...please...I don...I don't know where she is—"

"Fuck you! Fuck you!" another man screamed. Faxx said nothing as he picked up a case near a tree.

"Do you see that man right there?" he pointed. I looked up, and even though his face was swollen, I could tell exactly who he was by the large tattoo of clasped hands on the center of his chest. I sucked in a breath and shook slightly at remembering the small, deliberate cuts he used to give me when Roman wasn't happy with something I produced or if I was late delivering something. I jumped when Faxx's hand touched mine and blinked away the memory of that bullshit.

"Rico," I swallowed.

"Don't shoot him yet. I want you to aim for the head of the one behind him," Faxx said loudly.

"No! No...no...no...wa...wait.... I told you everything I knew! He didn't send us for your wife! We were only there for Gigi and the kid! Plea—"

"Please! Please! Shut the fuck up. At least I'm letting her use a gun and not the bomb strapped to your chest," Faxx laughed.

The large rifle felt heavier than before, but this time, I didn't feel any hesitation as Faxx helped me into position.

"Crescent! You don't need to do this! I can tell Roman you're gone. You don't need to listen to that crazy ass nigga! This ain't you baby—"

Before another word left Rico's lips, Faxx was on his feet, aiming his Glock. He pulled the trigger twice, hitting Rico in the shoulder and his left kneecap.

"Ahhh! Ahhh! You...son of.... Fuck, fuck, fuck—" Rico screamed as Faxx got back into position. The warmth of his body seemed to calm my racing pulse. It wasn't from fear, or nervousness, but anticipation.

"You've done this before, Crescent. You did it with Tony instinctively, so I know you can do it again. Just take slow, deep breaths while you feel the wind around you," Faxx whispered against my ear.

Yup! This nigga was trying to make me into some kind of assassin or some shit, but I did exactly what he said. There was so much I needed to talk to Tali about, but would she understand? Would she think I was losing it because I was tired of people thinking they could walk over me?

"Concentrate *Mi Amor*. Take a breath and—"

As I exhaled, I only thought about how I wanted it to stop. I was sick of running and looking behind my back, expecting someone to be there. I held the rifle, which was a little awkward because of my finger, but I was lucky to be right-handed. I was with Faxx on this one. Everyone had to go, so I breathed in again, and on the exhale, I pulled the trigger, hitting the man behind Rico in the throat.

"Oh shit," I gasped. I may have meant to hit his head, but hitting the neck damn near took his head clean off. The other man screamed and begged as he prayed.

"Oh my God! *Creo en Dios, Padre todopoderoso, creador del Cielo y de la Tierra*—"

"Not bad. Better than with Tony, and that's saying a lot," Faxx said, standing. He reached down to help me to my feet as Rico and the other dude screamed.

"I can't believe I just did that," I panted. My heart was racing as Faxx stared at me. I was staring a hole into Rico's head as my hands shook.

My eyes locked on Rico, the man who had held me hostage for Roman once upon a time. The memories of that experience were still fresh in my mind, but I pushed them aside, focusing on the task at hand.

"Rico, you know my wife, right?"

"I...I told you we didn't have—"

"Naw nigga, she will ask you a fucking question, and you answer the fucking question," Faxx boomed. I grabbed his hand as he helped me over the fence to get closer. Rico's pants were stained with blood, dirt, grass, piss, and whatever else he'd picked up outside. I had no idea how long Faxx had been holding him, but the hot glare he aimed at me just reinforced why all of this had to be done. If Roman told him to kill me, he would fucking kill me. I knew that for a fact, and I was done with all the bullshit. I was mentally checking myself, trying to figure out the reason why I was acting more and more like Faxx, but I knew the answer. It wasn't because of him but for him and Francesca. I needed to make sure the shit that was following me stayed fucking behind me, and being scared or hiding wasn't going to end it. I clenched my teeth together as I narrowed my eyes at him. I didn't know exactly how U.C.K. got him, but I knew the reasons he was st ill alive.

"Fuc—"

"Rico," I began, my voice steady and unwavering. "You know why you're here. I need to know everything you know about Roman and where he could be hiding," I demanded.

Rico tried to form his swollen lips into a sneer as his eyes filled with defiance. Faxx took a step forward, but I caught his arm. He tossed something black in the air, but I couldn't figure out what it was.

"You think I'm just going to tell you anything? Fuck you and that crazy ass nigga, Crescent. I'm going to die anyway," he hissed.

I felt a surge of anger rise, but I forced myself to remain calm even though I wanted to hop my ass back over that fence and shoot him in the fucking face.

"Rico, you held me captive, and you put me through hell. You remember that, right? Because I remember every fuckin' thing you and the others did to me. The sick little fucking games, the starvation, the threats, all of it. Trust me when I say I won't hesitate to use any means necessary to get the truth out of you. I mean, it seems like I have a lot of means nowadays to accomplish it," I laughed.

Rico's barely opened eyes darted all around, flickering with uncertainty.

"I don't know anything! I don't know where he is since, since, that crazy ass nigga blew up his house! I'm sure he's left wherever he was after that. He could...could be anywhere," he spat.

I exchanged a knowing glance with Faxx, understanding passing between us. I anticipated Rico's response, and it seemed Faxx did as well. The deranged smile on his face told me all I needed to know. Then I slowly began to wonder if this nigga really needed Rico.

Faxx stepped forward. His imposing presence caused Rico to flinch as much as he could as blood slowly leaked from his wounds.

"Rico, you know what I'm capable of," Faxx growled, his voice low and menacing. "Did you really believe that we needed you for this information? See, I was giving you a chance, a way to make your death a little less explosive. We have all of his files and the locations, I'm sure it won't be long before he uses one of them long enough to be caught. I kept you alive because your name sometimes slips out when my wife has nightmares," Faxx chuckled.

My eyes widened because I didn't know that, and he never told me about it. Which made his dream comment make more sense. What else could I have said in my sleep that he's heard? At this point, this nigga could have a list of fucking people somewhere for him to kill. I stared at him wide-eyed, and I wasn't the only one.

Rico's eyes widened, a hint of real fear creeping into his gaze.

"Okay, okay," he stammered. "I'll tell you what I know, just please, don't...don't—"

"Don't, don't, don't.... shut the fuck up my nigga. I watched some of those files on my way to get my wife, Rico," Faxx gritted. I swear to God, if my eyes could pop out my head, those bitches would be rolling across the ground because what the fuck! What had he seen? My heart pounded in my chest because this was what I wanted to talk about with Mena. I knew this would trigger him, and I didn't—

Faxx moved the ladder from the tree trunk and began to climb it. He leaned in closer, and his dark eyes bored into Rico's as he made a ticking sound.

"Talk, Rico. Time is running out," Faxx snapped.

Rico began to speak, revealing fragments of information about Roman's operations and potential hiding places that weren't in the files. His eyes never left what Faxx held in his hand. My gaze flicked toward the man praying in Spanish to see his eyes squeezed shut. But I could sense that whatever he thought would happen wasn't likely to happen. God was not coming to save him.

I could see Faxx's patience wearing thin, his frustration palpable as his jaw flexed. I didn't need to reveal where the cuts came from to him because he knew. If he knew, then that meant Link had to know as well. Without a word, Faxx grabbed Rico by the jaw, his grip firm and unyielding.

Rico crumbled, his fear overcoming everything, causing him to lose control of his own body.

I kept my emotions in check, focusing on the task at hand. I wanted to turn away as Faxx pried his mouth open and shoved the black object into his mouth. He turned it a certain way that it seemed to lodge itself in his mouth.

I swallowed as Faxx got down off of the ladder, staring at me, but it was like he was looking through me.

"Papi!" I snapped, and his eyes focused on me. I could tell he was grinding his teeth together and probably second-guessing all this shit we did together. All the sexual situations I allowed him to do to me and what he just declared to me. Would that change? Would we change?

"Mmmmmm. Mmmmmmmm. Mmmmmmm—" Rico screamed.

"Let's talk to this nigga and get the fuck out of here," he said, tilting his head to the side. He turned to look at the man still praying.

"Papi," I started.

"I can wait, but it won't stop me from tracking all these niggas down Crescent," he interrupted. He made his way over to the other man, who was only a few inches away. Faxx grabbed a rope that was tied to the tree and unraveled it. The man's body dropped low enough that when he opened his eyes, he stared directly into Faxx's cold, dead-ass stare. I watched him with my mouth clamped shut as he tilted his head to the side.

"I don't know...I don't know.... I don't know—"

I moved up closer to Faxx and placed my hand on his back as the man cried. I could tell the man had been shot already by the scar on his stomach.

Each time his body shook, the hole in his shirt moved, revealing a jagged scar stapled together. Faxx took in a deep breath before he looked down at me. I knew he could see the concern in my eyes or pleading for him to tell me what the fuck else he knew. He turned away, pulling out his Glock, and held it at his side.

"I don't give a fuck what you do or don't know. All I care about is the fact that you survived and Milo died. I wanted to let you die on the street, but it wouldn't have given me the satisfaction I've had these past few days. At least now I can watch as the light fades out of your eyes," Faxx said in a monotone. You would believe he had no emotions.

"It was a mistak—"

BANG. BANG. BANG. BANG. BANG.

I jumped backward and pulled Faxx with me despite his arm being still extended. His Glock was still aimed directly at the wound that was barely closed. The piercing scream faded as blood seemed to pour out of the man's body, and I couldn't find a fuck to give. Now I remembered his face, and he was the one who shot Milo that night. I refused to move until I saw for sure that he was dead. Faxx wasn't lying because he didn't move either until the light faded from his eyes. Then he stepped forward, pulling the tactical knife from behind his back, and stabbed it straight through the top of the man's head. I felt like I was paralyzed until he turned around and walked toward me.

"Let's go, *Mi Amor*," he said. I looked over at Rico, still screaming as he twisted and turned in his bindings.

"What about him?" I pointed as Faxx grabbed my wrist. We walked back toward the fence, and he helped me over it.

"Don't worry about him," he smirked. I climbed on the back of the ATV, wondering if the next detonator I received would blow Rico's head clean the fuck off.

I followed Faxx into the house as memories from being there the last time assaulted me. Now that I knew what he had seen, I know this had to be the reason why he was trying to distance himself. He was talking shit in the truck, but the fact he didn't do it or grab me in the usual way was telling. He walked into the bedroom and went directly into the attached bathroom. I stayed silent as he turned on the water and stripped off his clothes. He turned to look at me and started to remove my clothes. When I looked down, I noticed the blood for the first time and started to help him. I could see it in his demeanor that he was fighting within himself about something. I leaned on the counter as he helped me out of my boot and ace wrap. I finished undressing when he stood up and moved into the shower.

"Fransisco, what is the problem? You can't look at me now? Do you think I'm weak or something?" I asked. I stepped in behind him as he began to lather himself with soap—in quick, sufficient movements.

"Are you being fucking for real right now? Talk to me, Fransisco," I demanded. Faxx stopped washing his body and turned around so fast that I took a step backward.

"Cent, you asked me for time, and I'm giving you that. I can't help what I know and what I've seen. I just can't—"

Faxx caught his words, closed his eyes, and shook his head. I didn't know if I wanted to be hurt, agitated, or thankful he wasn't making me talk about it. The problem was that he clearly needed to because it was starting to affect him, which would affect us. I didn't know I was moving backward until I felt the cold tile on my skin. His dark eyes watched me like he was assessing me or trying to figure out a puzzle.

"Naw, say what you need to say. Since when have you bit your tongue on anything?" I noted.

"You're not going to let this shit go? You're just going to keep fucking pushing," he grunted. Faxx placed both hands beside my head, leaning down to look into my eyes. It wasn't like I was scared of him.

"You are damn right. I'm going to keep pushing. What has you so fucking distant all of a sudden?"

"It's all good, Crescent. I'm good. I just have a lot of shit on my mind and things I need to get done," he said, pushing off the wall. I pushed at his chest and almost slipped and busted my ass, but he caught my waist to steady me. Then he let me go and turned back around.

"Nigga tell me what the fuck is wrong. What did you see that's making you second guess us now? You weren't earlier, or were you?"

I possibly said the wrong thing because he had me pressed up against the wall when he turned back around. There was no room this time, and his body pressed against mine, and his hand wrapped under my chin as he held my jaw.

"You already know there is no fucking second guessing on us, Crescent. Don't ever fucking say that shit again. Yeah, I saw some shit, and yes, I do have a fucking list with Roman at the fucking top. But what I'm not understanding is how...why would you let me do the shit I did to you? You let me put a fucking blade to your skin, a gun in your mouth. I knew it was something with the tattoos covering scars, but I didn't think—"

"Faxx, it's not the sam—"

"What if me being who the fuck I am is the reason why you are triggered. Have you thought about that? Is that you're just used to that type of treatment, and you think that you—"

My hand shot up to grip his wrist as I shook my head because I could see where this was going. It was just like before when I compared him with Roman, and he believed he went too far.

"No, don't even fucking say it, Fransisco. You're letting what you saw get in your head like you are anything like those niggas. It's not the fucking same," I urged.

"I don't see the fucking difference Cent," he refuted.

"But I know the fucking difference! So, what, I can't like what the fuck you do to me? I have to be so weak that I'm looking for another abuser. I'm not going to let something that happened to me define me. I will not let it take away what I love about us, Fransisco. I never compared you to what they've done. This is the exact reason why I refused to really talk about it. You would take what happened to me and get it twisted in your head, ruining what we've built. I know what I want and what I like Faxx. Am I supposed to let them take away what makes me happy?"

"So all the nightmares and the flinches in your sleep don't mean shit? I can see the ghosts in your eyes when you open them after, Cent. When it happens again I now know exactly how they got there. They are triggers Crescent and I'm causing them," he debated.

That was where that dream statement from earlier came into play.

"Not with you! It was never a fucking trigger with you, Faxx. Please don't take this away from me. I already lost enough," I sobbed. It begin to make sense.

The collar.

Faxx had always known what to do and what I needed.

"Is that why you brought up the collar? Is that what you got out of the vault?" I asked.

"Faxx's hand dropped to my throat as he leaned down to kiss me. His tongue parted my lips, diving into my mouth as he sucked my tongue. His other arm dropped to my waist, and I pushed myself harder against him. I was still tired and sore, but he was what I needed. Fransisco was everything I craved, and nothing in my past or present was going to fuck this up. To be back in the confines of Fransisco's arms wrapped so tightly around me, had a moan escaping my lips. Our lips seared and melted—making tears prick at the corner of my eyes. His kiss was intoxicating to the point it was sucking the air from my lungs, making my toes curl.

I wanted to feel him closer. I *needed* to feel that he was real and to show him that everything he did to me was exactly what I wanted. He was and would be the only one I trust to handle my body this way.

A moan fumbled from my lips when he moved, pulling me with him. I felt him bend slightly, lifting me so I could wrap my legs around him. He let go of my neck and slid that hand over my body as he held onto me while maneuvering out of the shower. I felt the soft comforter on my wet body, and I let out a whimper when he pulled away. The deep brown of his eyes stared into mine, burning me as his gaze roamed my body.

"Faxx," I groaned, trying to pull him closer but settled for running my hands over his chest. I traced his tattoo to his neck when I caught his eyes again. When I saw his expression this time, I couldn't help but freeze.

My heart ached at seeing the troubled look on his face. His eyes seem deranged, almost in disbelief, with a hint of sadness tainting his features.

"I'm here, Faxx, and I'm okay. I want you and everything that comes with it," I whispered.

"I'm not going to be rough," he smirked.

"You're a fucking liar."

"This is the reason I brought up the collar. I wasn't sure at first, but the more I brought it up, the more I could see you needed it. You need to feel that I'm there even when you're dreaming," he confirmed.

His nose flared, and he took a deep breath as he leaned down to lick my neck. I stroked his beard before I pulled on it.

"I wasn't thinking of it in that way at first. It was more that I loved for there to be another way you claimed me. But I get it now, and you're right. I do need it. Is that what you got from the vault?"

"Yes. I had it made the day you were kidnapped. But anyway, I didn't understand the reason behind it. I just went with it," he said, leaning to the side. Faxx picked up a dark blue velvet box and placed it on my chest. He stared at me as I reached to open it, fumbling slightly because of my finger. Once I lifted it up, I stopped breathing. Nestled within the velvet-lined interior was a white gold choker covered with diamonds. I knew, in essence, what it meant because of Dea, but our situation was slightly different. I didn't think Faxx was fully into any of this kind of life style, but he could recognized what I needed that would help me cope.

"I'm not going to lie and tell you I don't want to see you wearing my collar. Just thinking about it eases something in me. If I can't keep you cuffed to this fucking bed, it was going to be some other way. This is something that we both need," Faxx explained. I stared at the collar, and he was right because it was designed to resemble small, intricately detailed handcuffs, each delicate link and shimmering diamonds. I reached in to pick it up, and it was heavier than I thought. The weight of the collar in my hands sent a rush of emotions through me. The symbolism of the restraints told me what I already knew. It wasn't like he hadn't just admitted it, and the feeling of it being right as I turned the collar over in my hands settled me.

"Put it on me," I said softly. I felt the box move, and his body slid along mine as he took it out of my hands. Faxx carefully fastened the collar around my neck. The feeling I got at the cool touch of the white gold against my skin, and the weight of the diamonds was unexplainable. It rested just as heavy as his hand against my collarbone.

"Do you know what this means, Fransisco?" I asked. His brows lowered as he stared down at me, probably trying to see if I was joking, but I wasn't.

"It means exactly what the fuck I told you when we stood in your apartment. I fucking possess you, Crescent. I'm the only one who would ever be able to take that off your neck. So, my question is, do you know what this means?" he asked. Faxx moved and curled his fingers around the collar, barely able to fit through the snug fit, and pulled. I sucked in a breath and licked my lips as he waited for my answer.

"That I belong to Papi," I smiled. The slow smile that spread across his face was that deranged one that would have a normal person side-eyeing him. "You're giving...giving serial killer right now."

"It means you sold your soul to a Horseman, Crescent."

Lawd, it's me again your humble servant. Send help because I believe exactly what this nigga just said, and I liked it.

"I could have lost you, Cent. But just because I got you back doesn't mean this shit is over. I'm going to burn Clapton to the mutha fuckin' ground until every single person that touched you is dead. Bet on that shit, do you understand me?" he seethed, his brows tightly knit together. The weight of his body and the pressure of his length against my pussy had me so wet I knew he could feel it. He moved, and the head of his dick bumped against my clit, making me spread my legs wider. It wasn't only his body, but his words made my core clench in need for him to fill me. He said it in barely a whisper, but I heard the steel in his tone. I reached up, bringing his face to mine, licking his lips before I bit down on his bottom one.

"I know," I acknowledged.

"*Mi Amor*, my entire world went *dark*, and then after seeing that shit, it's worse. Ain't none of these niggas making it out alive, Cent," he concurred. His jawline ticked, and he took a deep, shaky breath.

I believed every single word he spoke.

I could still see the hesitation in his eyes, so I wrapped my legs around his thick body, trying to haul him closer. He reached back, grabbed my sprained ankle, and rested that leg on the bed.

"Let's go *dark* together, Fransisco. For better or for worse, right? Just let me be drowned in you."

"*Mi Amor*, you shouldn't say shit like that to me. I'll pull you so far in, you will never get back out," he whispered. Goosebumps rose across my arms at the low rumble from his lips, especially how he looked down at me.

Faxx stared at me like I was a prize.

Like I was a pretty *fucktoy*, but also the love of his life.

I guess it was good that I wanted to be both of those things because I might have fought initially I didn't, but Faxx would prove it was always going to end this way.

Heat radiated from his broad, muscular chest as he towered over me, one arm on his side to not crush me. The other slid down my face, lips, neck, and over the collar. He dragged his hand back up and pushed his thick fingers into my mouth. Faxx rocked his hips while I sucked them. He pulled them away and placed his hand on my neck, above the collar pinning me in place. He squeezed tight before he shoved his tongue down into my mouth.

Oh my *God*.

It's funny how the world seemed to right itself whenever his lips were on mine—as if nothing else existed but the two of us. His other hand held my leg down, pinning it to the bed. I couldn't move or shift to get the friction my body demanded. I loved it and hated it at the same time.

It was so good, so right, and so fucking...*perfect*.

Faxx's demanding and rough kiss went on as he pressed me farther into the bed like he was begging for access to my very soul.

There was no way to deny Fransisco as my nipples beaded painfully like ice pickaxes while my core ached and pulsed with need. As soon as he licked into the roof of my mouth, a groan rose from my chest. We were pressed so tightly together that if I could move an inch, he would slip inside of me. It was what I wanted, and he knew that shit.

His rigid thickness pressed against my clit in the way I needed, but I couldn't move to get the motion I needed to cum.

"F-Faxx," I whined against his lips, wiggling under him. There's a burning inferno threatening to scorch me alive like I'm a burning match and he's the gasoline.

"D-don't...hold back Fransisco. I don't want or need that from you," I encouraged.

The look on his face now sent shivers down my spine, and butterflies erupted. His expression was so dark—like a predator playing with its prey before eating it. His eyes followed my every move while I licked my lips.

Before I could draw in my next breath, Faxx thrust down hard, making me gasp and my pussy *gush*.

"Oh fuck," I moaned. His thick long dick stretched me wide, causing my back to arch as it slid along nerve endings that had me shaking.

"Take that dick, Cent. You said you wanted it. You said you can handle it, so take that shit, *Mi Amor*," he rumbled. Faxx pressed his complete weight onto my body, and I gasped as he slid deeper. My nipples were painfully hard while my core spasmed around his girth.

"That's right, squeeze that shit. You're definitely going to be drowned in me, Cent. If you are not already pregnant, you will be."

Oh shit. I didn't think I could be, but this nigga was trying to make it happen by any means necessary. Stranger shit has happened.

"Papi," I choked. I raked my nails down his damp back as he pulled back and slammed back inside, pushing me further up the mattress.

"I want more."

"Naw, *Mi Amor*, you need more," he corrected. "Say yes, Papi. Tell Papi what you need, Crescent," he commanded.

"Mm, I need you, Papi. Please, I need you to make me cum," I gasped out as he eased off of my throat. A slow smile crossed his face as he slid out of me. I almost cried until he slid down and sucked my clit into his mouth as he got onto his knees.

The way his tongue slid into my entrance stole my breath away. He placed a thumb on my clit as he moved in circles while he slurped and sucked. My eyes rolled when his tongue came back up, sucking my clit into his warm mouth, and I felt two fingers slide into my core. My eyes snapped open as I moaned so loud. I was sure that nigga Rico heard it. I reached down and grabbed his head, pushing his face deeper. My eyes traveled over the tattoos that were intricately bestowed onto his body, making him a living piece of art as he moved. The way light and darkness bounced off those indents on his shoulders and arms every time he breathed and flexed had my hips rising to meet his mouth.

Faxx pulled away and looked up, licking his lips as he watched me. His two fingers moved in and out at a pace that I knew if he kept it up, I was going to cum.

"Naw, *Mi Amor*, that tight pussy not about to cum yet," he chuckled.

"Frans—"

Without hesitation, he moved over me, fingers still in my pussy as he pressed his mouth onto mine, making me taste myself. When he slid his tongue in between my parted lips, I couldn't help but open wider as he practically *fucked* my mouth with his tongue. My head spun as he sucked my tongue at the same pace his fingers moved inside of me.

My nails dug into his shoulders, and my core throbbed as I ground my body upward, pushing his fingers deep. He twisted them, hitting the bumpy ridges that had me screaming.

"Papi, please! Oh my...please Fransisco...I need—"

I could feel his lips ticking up with satisfaction before he pulled away and pushed my knees upward and out, creating a large enough space for his massive body.

He pressed down on my chest as he slid his dick into me in one thrust. His lower body started to move at a fast pace, slamming into me while holding onto my leg to pull me back down each time I was pushed upward.

"Ah fuck, Cent. Fuck," he groaned. The slapping sound with each thrust had my mind flying in different directions. Faxx leaned over me, pushing my leg up, causing the angle to change as his hand twirled around my braids.

"Do you like my dick stretching you out, *Mi Amor*? An entire fucking week I didn't have you. It makes me think your pussy has already forgotten the shape of my dick. Let me remind you," he insisted.

"Faxx," I whimpered. "Please, please...oh shit. Oh, shit, baby, I'm going to cum."

"Did I say you could cum Cent?"

I almost cried as my heart pounded so loudly that I was terrified it might just pop out of my damn chest. The faster he moved, the tighter his grip on my hair got, and there was no way I could stop if I came. The pricks of pain and the sensation of being completely filled had my walls tightening and my hips moving, wanting all of him.

Fransisco leaned forward, capturing my nipple in his mouth, and the sensation of it was almost too much.

"Fuck! Faxx," I screamed. He bit down lightly, teasing my nipple with his teeth, reminding me of the clamps. Especially the way he's perfectly playing with my body. Electricity zapped through every inch of my body, causing my hips to buck, trying to take in more of him.

"M-more, F-Faxx, Papi, ah—*ah*! More. More, *more*," I chanted broken-ly. The depraved, breathless pants and moans even startled me. My hands and body seemed to have a mind of their own as my fingers tugged at the end of his cornrows.

My back hollowed out almost demandingly as his tongue licked over my breast and up to the side of my neck. Faxx sucked my earlobe before pulling away and pushing his lips against my ear.

"I don't think you understand how I will burn the world down for you, Crescent. Then, shoot every nigga that was there in the street until I found you. Do you know how hard it was to see clearly or to sleep without you, *Mi Amor*?" he rumbled.

I shuddered violently when he pulled out to the tip, thrust past my wet folds, and back inside. His hips snapped against me as tears rolled down my cheek. I shook when I felt his tongue lick them away.

"F-Faxx," I moaned, my walls seeming to have no problem squeezing at the dangerous weapon.

My pussy had no problem drooling when he pulled back again and ran his head up my slit.

Maybe it's because it's him.

Maybe it's because I know that he wouldn't—couldn't—hurt me. Not in the way he was thinking because the pain he gave me turned into so much pleasure. I knew that shit was going to knock me the fuck out.

I whined, my head lolling side-to-side as he worked to go deep. His hands moved as he pushed my thighs down to the bed and slowly pulled back. Faxx began to push slowly in and out of me before his pace picked up. I could feel the stretch in my thighs as he held them in this position, giving me the pleasurable pain that made me addicted, especially knowing it was Fransisco. I felt one of his hands move off my leg, and he reached above me. He leaned down, licking my lips before moving his tongue in my mouth to the pace of his strokes. Memories of when he brought his knife to my skin or when he wrapped his hand around my throat played like a movie in my head. I needed it. I loved it, and I knew it was because it was him.

I wanted every single side of him, even that fucked-up depraved part of his soul, because he's mine.

"Do you want more, *Mi Amor*?"

Faxx pulled away from my lips and began to kiss his way to my collarbone.

"You wanna know what my Glock feels like, *Mi Amor*?"

"Oh my...oh fuck," I panted. Was he fucking serious? Just the thought had my walls clamping down on him so tight he groaned.

"Fuck Cent! If I were to push my Glock inside until the damn hilt hits that tight pussy, would you cum all over it?"

"Oh my God," I shivered.

"Oh, you like that shit," he whispered along my skin. I felt him grip the mattress as he pushed deeper inside of me. He was so deep I swear I felt him in my throat.

"Yes, yes, yes," I whispered. I don't know what the fuck made me say that. I was losing it, falling so deep I was scaring myself. I had to be fucking crazy at this point.

"I'll remember this conversation, Crescent. You're going to take that shit, cum on it, and fucking like it," he grunted. I don't know what kind of noise left my lips, but he smirked and then angled it up a certain way, and it hit a little bumpy spot that made stars explode at the back of my mind as I raised my hips to give more access.

I was just as fucking crazy and turned on by the shit he says because I knew he would do it. I could tell he could see, feel, and taste it by the way his black gaze stared at me. My pleasure was only making his obsession worse, and my craving for all things made him questioned the very little sanity I had left.

"*Mi Amor*, you look a little deranged, a little unhinged. Exactly the way I want you. I want to know that every time you open your mouth, the first word to leave your lips is yes, Papi. I want to consume your thoughts just as much as you own mine," he gritted against my cheek.

"Mm, Faxx. Papi! Lawd Jesus Jerome, what is he doing to me?" I cried while my body shook. "Pl-pl.... I...ahh...oh...hmm—" I mumbled as my eyes rolled to the back of my head.

"Use your words, *Mi Amor*. What do you want me to do?" he chuckled. I felt his hand slide up my thigh and over my body to rest against my neck. His thumb rubbed over my pulse before his grip became tighter.

I know full well he was teasing me, but I was too deep in the shallow water to do anything but give him what he wanted. The collar rested at the base of my throat, no longer feeling cold as my body heated it up.

Faxx wanted words, even with the little oxygen I had left, as he started to squeeze my neck.

"I want you. I need you to let me cum, Papi," I said with a shaky breath. Faxx slowly withdrew before rotating his hips and pushing deeper.

"You want this dick to make that pussy weep?"

I watched with heavy lids as he got onto his knees, pulling my legs around his waist as he grabbed something from the side of his bed.

The next thing I knew, my nipples felt as if they were on fire as he attached those nipple clamps connected by a thin chain that ended with a black device.

"Oh fuck. You're going to shock me again," I panted. The anticipation of that quick buzzing sensation had my pussy jumping.

Faxx's dark eyes looked over my body before he pulled on the chain, causing a gasp to escape my lips. With his arm under the leg with the sprain, he pulled the chain again while pulling onto his dick. He threw his head back with each thrust he pulled, and I cried out. I could hear the sloshing sound each time he moved, and I knew I grew wetter with each pull on the clamps. I found myself clawing blindly at his chest as he stretched my legs and pussy open to take every inch of him. Tears brimmed at the corners of my eyes because I couldn't hold back anymore.

"Shit. Shit, *Mi Amor*. Fuck," he said, grinding into me as I pushed down. I felt the sting of the clamps that made my toes curl just as a shock ripped through my body.

"Fuck!" I screamed.

Faxx's hand that held the chain grabbed mine as he held the box between us. I saw a light flash from his watch, but I was distracted when he moved my leg higher.

"You're so fucking tight, Cent," he groaned.

Faxx snapped his hips downward, pumping into me and pushing me closer and closer towards insanity. He was already on that cliff of insanity by the look in his eyes when I raised my hips off the bed. He dropped my leg, leaning over me, giving me all of his weight, and I gave him my complete submission. He pulled my other hand up and over my head to join the other and restrained my wrists with his hand. His thrusts became harder, deeper, and faster as he squeezed my wrist. His eyes widened, and I shook my head, trying to speak past the panting.

"I'm fine," I cried when he started to release me. His jaw flexed, but his other tatted hand ran over my face and under my chin, tilting my head up. He leaned down to kiss me, his hand squeezed around my throat possessively as I gasped.

The echoes of our skin felt like they were all around me as the *slap, slap, slap* grew louder and louder.

"Oh...I'm going to...fuck Papi—"

"You need me to fuck you harder?"

I didn't know if I was coming or going. I wasn't entirely sure if I even answered the question. In my head, all I could repeat was harder.

Harder.

Do it harder.

Fuck me.

Hurt me.

"Cent, Cent, baby, *Mi Amor*, open your mouth and tell Papi what you want," he rumbled, as he leaned down practically crushing me as his eyes pierced mine.

"Be a good girl and cum for me if you can't speak," he ordered.

Oh. My. God.

It's as if a spark rippled through my entire being, my back hallowed as a tidal wave crashed over us. My body tightened, and it was like I could hear the crackling of firecrackers as I bucked up uncontrollably, as a powerful orgasm washed over my entire being. I was squeezing the fuck out of his hand as he released my neck, rubbing circles on it as I came.

"Faxx!"

My thighs and body shook around him as an earthquake—unlike anything I'd experienced—rocked through my entire core. It continued to shock me that no matter how many times we've done it at this point, it's always like the first.

Ferociously.

Explosively.

LIFE-*ALTERING*.

Wait. Something was exploding.

One large hand was brought around my neck, tightening, causing my eyes to shift back to him.

"Naw, keep your eyes on me. So, I can watch you cum," he ordered.

My pussy clenched around his length, and his grip on my neck increased in response working with the weight of the collar.

"Fuck Crescent! Shit," he repeated like a broken record. I felt his last thrust slam into me as his cum filled me.

His cum spilled into me in long, hot spurts as he moved in and out.

Faxx filled me up to the brim as his dick pulsated between my wet folds, and I came again.

"Oh shit, shit, Papi," I gasped. My vision was blurry, and I felt his hand slide to my chest as I tried to catch my breath.

"That's it, *Mi Amor. Mi Corazón*. You're *mine*, Cent. Don't fucking leave again."

Fransisco kissed along my neck, almost like he was apologizing for being so demanding. I didn't need it, but I wouldn't stop him either.

I LOVE EVERYTHING WHEN IT COMES TO HIM.

With that, he tenderly pressed his lips back onto mine as he let go of my hand. As my heart slowed down and I was able to think, I opened my eyes as Faxx slid out of me and lay on my stomach.

"What the fuck was that noise?" I asked, frowning. Faxx started to chuckle before looking up at me, his brown eyes slightly darker than before.

"Rico had an EXPLOSIVE ending to his day."

I stared at him for a minute before I reached up and pushed his head back down on my stomach. I knew Rico deserved it, and I waited to feel remorse, but none came. Then I looked at that damn box and closed my eyes. How in the fuck would this conversation go with Tali and Dea?

This nigga was fucking crazy, but we're going to be okay.

CHAPTER FIVE

MALIKITA 'MALA' SAMUELS

I blew out a breath at the text I received from Shantel when I got up this morning. It only said 'FOUND AND RESCUED,' and that was enough. The hand wrapped around my heart finally eased at that moment, only to be replaced by a heavy feeling. If something like a kidnapping hadn't happened, Henny, Oz, Faxx, and Link would've pulled up. I didn't think even with Link and Faxx knowing what was at stake would've stopped them from coming after me and killing Charles. So, between that revelation about what happened with Crescent and Charles finding that tracker on his car, shit has been wild. I had no idea who put that tracker on his car, but I could tell it was federal. I also had no idea who the fuck this Teddy person was that Charles was grilling me about. I think whoever Teddy was and his disappearance were the only reasons Charles didn't look at me too closely that night. One thing was for sure. He was important and probably the man Charles went to see when he took his '*breaks*' out of the city.

I felt him behind me while I washed my face, and I knew he was staring a hole in the back of my head. I continued what I was doing and leaned over, splashing warm water over my skin to wash away the cleanser.

"Tell me how the fuck you did it?" he gritted in my ear. I sucked my teeth as I reached for the soft white towel to pat my face dry.

"I've told you not once, not twice, but multiple times that I did not put the fucking tracker on your car," I sighed. I put the towel down and stared at him in the mirror with my eyebrows raised. I saw the slight reddening of his ears that let me know he was good and mad.

"You know what the fuck I'm talking about, Kita," he seethed.

"If you're not talking about that, then I don't know what you're talking about. So can you excuse me so I can get to work on time," I stated. I began to apply my makeup when he slapped his hands on the vanity on both sides of me.

"What? What the hell are you going on about Charles? If you are referring to your little boyfriend, I don't know where or who he is, and I don't care. I told you I didn't put a tracker on your car! How about you ask Landon," I said sarcastically. I pressed my lips together, admired the matte red lipstick, and pushed his arms out of the way. Charles grabbed my wrist and pulled me hard toward him, spinning me around in place to look at him. My pastel rose pink silk camisole, and matching panties were the only things covering my body. He'd never physically harmed me, but I still felt vulnerable. I glared at his hand, his face, and then back to his hand that was still touching me.

"Any harder nigga, and you will bruise me, then nothing will stop your body from flying out of that fucking window," I hissed. His calculating brown eyes narrowed, and he looked at me in disgust.

"You act just like those no-good thug NIGGERS fucking up the city! I want to know how you managed to erase that video," he gritted.

"Careful, Charles, your unseasoned side is showing," I laughed. I snatched my arm out of his grip and rubbed it.

"And for your information, I have no fucking idea what you are talking about. Have you lost something else along with *YOUR* Teddy?" I smirked.

"You think because you were able to find the footage on my computer that you have the upper hand," he chuckled. I said nothing, staring at him and not giving away anything.

"Again, I don't know what the hell you are talking about. I can't be the one to help you with the career that you only have because of me, and find your little fucking video. But thank you for letting me know it's no longer there," I spat.

Charles stepped closer, his bare chest heaving as his jaw clenched in anger. My eyes dropped down to his hands as they flexed into fists at his side.

"Did you have Link come inside here and touch my shit, Kita?"

"You're fucking paranoid, Charles. It's not a good look! How the fuck would that be possible, and you not know! You're losing it," I smiled, shaking my head.

"Don't mistake me for those dumb bastards you call your family Maliki-ta. One wrong move from them and everyone in Union City, hell across the fucking world, will see them for exactly what they are. They are murderous thugs who gain power by blackmailing, bribing, cheating, and killing their way to the top. Play your fucking role Kita, if you intend to keep them all out of prison. Just don't make the mistake of thinking that's all I got on *those* people," he sneered.

"Fuck you, Charles," I fumed. I held his contemptuous gaze, refusing to let it go until he looked away with a small chuckle. I could still see that he was rattled. Just like I could tell, his usual cool demeanor was crumbling.

"Count your fucking days at that Casino, Kita. It's the amount of time you have left until you are officially Malikita Morgan," he smirked. I knew that he was stepping up the time on this bullshit engagement because he was feeling threatened.

"Is there gas in my car?" I deflected. His normal, irritating smile returned, taking pleasure in my words.

"Since Landon has appeared to have quit suddenly, I've had to hire other protection for you. Vincent has ensured you have enough to reach where you need to be today. Don't forget we are having dinner at the estate in two weeks. Just be sure to do something with...that hair. I can't have you come in looking like a hood rat from the streets. I'll need my grandparents' approval for my great-grandmother's wedding rings. You should be grateful to wear it, so be sure to fucking act like it," he ordered, before giving me his back. I bared my teeth at him, trying to reign in the urge to slam his head against that fucking mirror. This would be the first time I'd been to his grandparents' home in seven years, and even that time was unpleasant. I wasn't looking forward to going, but I knew nothing short of me finding that fucking original video would stop it. Link had taken care of the video on the computer fairly quickly, making me wish I had asked him earlier. But that idea was always scratched because we would end up in exactly the same place that night when Charles came to me. Henny, Oz, and Faxx would still be in jail, and Link would be dead, meaning U.C.K. would be nothing. Too many people depended on us, which was still the same today. I wasn't sure if Charles knew about the USB and that it was now in our hands, but none would matter unless we got the original. I was pretty sure he didn't know it was us, but he knew something was happening.

I turned away once the shower started and made quick work of getting dressed. I wanted to call Shantel or Henny for an update, but I knew I had to wait. I didn't want to fuck anything up with the rescue, so I would do what I did best. Take my ass to work and handle the shit Link couldn't at that moment. We had a shipment of machines being delivered today, and I had a meeting with the ignorant bitch Kami. I sighed as I pulled on my black straight-leg pants before pulling on the black tuxedo-style suit coat. The two silver buttons held a small crown with the U.C.K. letters inside. I normally wore the suit jacket alone but had to show professionalism. Shantel had a white suit identical to this one because she had them made for us. I slipped on the rose-pink heels and grabbed my purse so I could leave before Charles's bitch ass got out of the shower. As soon as I opened the door, I saw Vincent standing there dressed in all black, staring through me. I slammed the door and began to walk to the elevators thinking about all the ways I was going to fuck up Monica. It was like she was having a field day since Link had been tied up with the Crescent search. I would need to handle her after I dealt with the shit with the machines. Kami may be a bitch, but she didn't know anything about the compromised machinery, her daddy did.

"Ms. Samuels, I am going to need access to every part of the Casino you will be working in," Vincent stated. I didn't even look his way when the doors opened. I stepped inside, and he followed, hitting the button for the garage.

"Ms. Sam—"

"You can stop right there, Vinny," I sighed.

"It's Vincent and I need—"

"No, it's what the hell I say it is, and also, no, you do not. Let me explain something to you that Charles probably failed to mention. You will be staying in the fucking car for as long as I'm working. That is your job. Your job is not to fuck up mine," I stated.

"If I don't gain access, then neither will you. My job is to follow you step by step. If I can't do that, I will bring you back here," he said acidly. I sucked in a long breath as the doors opened. I stepped out but spun on my heel and slammed my hand against the doors so they would stay open. I had an extra few inches from my heels, but I wasn't even close to his six feet two inches. I looked up and smiled wide, showing every single one of my teeth. I already knew I probably looked a little crazy and deranged, but that's exactly what I was feeling. He stepped back, frowning down at me, his brown bald head shining in the elevator's lights.

"I take it that you know I'm working at Blackbay Casino and Resorts, correct?"

"That is where Mr. Morg—"

"Then you should know who fucking owns that Casino! If you know who owns it, then you would know ain't nobody that's not working directly for Mr. Moore walking around his fucking business. Save your life and sit in the damn car," I snapped. I let the doors go, and they began to close. I turned around and marched to my Benz, trying to calm down. I hit my key fob, hearing the chirp of the alarm.

"Beautiful, I love it when you are all fired up. That means we'll have an interesting day today," Konceited chuckled. I looked up and saw him leaning against a motorcycle the same color as his green eyes. He held his black helmet under his arm and smiled at me over my car. I heard the elevator doors open and knew Vinny dumbass would be coming.

"As a matter of fact, Green eyes, we are. We have a full day ahead of us," I smiled. Konceited always had a calming effect whenever he spoke. I still didn't understand why he was here and not at the Casino.

"Lead the way," he smirked. Konceited slipped on his helmet as Vincent slid inside his dark sedan, and I got into my vehicle. Now that I thought about it, I swear I saw this bike earlier this week. I hit the start button and pulled out, leaving whoever would follow behind me to catch up.

As I drove, I mentally counted the days in my head since I last saw Lakyn. It had been seven days since I saw or spoke to him, but I understood the reason entirely. If it weren't for Shantel and Henny keeping me somewhat updated on the situation with Crescent, I would've felt some way. I knew leaving with Charles that night probably fucked up his mind, but I knew, and he knew the reasons behind it. Until we figured this shit out, there was nothing I could've done differently at that moment but cut his damn throat. But then we still would have the same fucking problem, and ain't enough money in the world going to help us. The only thing I knew to do was to keep up this fake-ass façade and also run Link's business. I would hold shit down while he and the others ran through this city and others like the fucking plague. Charles had been acting erratic and even more unusual when I informed him that the tracker looked to be federal. I wasn't lying, but I wasn't sure he would initially believe me. But when I said it, the look of hate in his eyes confirmed Charles might know exactly who put it there. Whenever I questioned him about Teddy, he quickly clammed up or changed the subject. I didn't know exactly what the fuck was going to happen after they got Crescent back, but I knew we needed a fucking meeting. It had already been a few hours since the text, so Link could very well be at the Casino.

I pulled into the parking garage for employees and noticed Vincent going toward the front of the Casino like a good boy. He wasn't as stupid as he looked, and I was glad because my patience was thin as fuck. I pulled up to the valet and saw Ma standing beside the doors leading into the Casino with her tablet and phone. As I opened it, the new valet attendant rushed to the driver's side. I heard the loud noise of Konceited's bike as he pulled up and parked it in the non-parking area. I shook my head, handed the attendant my valet key, and went to Mallory.

"Hey, Boss. The shipment should arrive in two hours, but she's here already. She's throwing a fit that she is being asked to wait in the office on the main level," Ma said quickly. She opened the door as I walked, rolling my eyes at this chick. Kami really thought she would keep the same access as before. She was fucking trippin'.

"Okay, please watch the shipment closely and notify me as soon as it arrives. I don't care what I'm doing when it arrives. I want to be at that truck before anything comes off," I stated.

"Yes, Boss. I also did what you asked and...followed Monica again last night. I know for sure she met up with a man outside and handed him something last night when she left. But—"

Ma trailed off as I hit the button for the elevators. I heard the door open again as Konceited entered with a smile. His gaze slid over me easily, and then he looked at Ma.

"Mallory, every time I see you, I find something even sexier about you," he grinned. Ma took a deep breath before looking at Konceited with a small smile.

"And every time I see you, you're even more conceited than you were the day before," she blinked. The doors opened, and I stepped onto the elevator, laughing. Konceited bit his lip as Ma followed.

"Mallory, finish, please. What is the 'but' about? It's almost like you don't want to say it," I stated. Ma looked down at her tablet and hit a few things before she hit something else, expanding it. She turned it around to face me, and Konceited leaned over my shoulder to look as well. Monica's long arms were wrapped around a man, but his face was angled away. With the next swipe, she was kissing his turned cheek, and then the next swipe, he faced the camera.

"Oh shit," Konceited said. I took the tablet out of Ma's hand and began to go through each picture, studying it. I knew there was no way Monica was the person he'd been seeing this entire time. I knew about Charles. He knew how to play a person and was charming when he wanted to be. With each picture, I could see Monica's face, smile, and the light touches she placed on his arm. Monica's dumb ass was in love with a man that wasn't even checking for pussy. I looked up, seeing Mallory's sorrowful eyes.

"Oh! Oh, shit. Ma, there is no need to feel sorry for me at all. She is the least of my concerns regarding him," I smiled tightly. Even though she was my right-hand woman here, she still wasn't dialed in on everything related to U.C.K., but Konceited knew.

"Oh, okay. Thank God, because I didn't know how you would take it. I wanted to let you know last night, but—"

"It's all good. When Monica comes into work, I want her watched, and if she tries to leave, detain her ass. Tell Maurice to have one of his men keep track of her. If she manages to leave this fucking Casino, that person will be taken to the docks," I said flatly. I knew with the threat niggas would be on their P's and Q's. Because going to the docks only meant being transported to the *FARM,* and no one wanted that shit.

"I got it, Boss. It will be handled," Ma said quickly. I handed her the tablet back, but not before sending all the pictures and videos to my email. The doors opened to the offices' top floor, and I stepped off with Konceited on my heels.

"Ma, can you let Miss Kamille Indigo know I will be with her soon? Her appointment wasn't until noon, and she's early," I said. Mallory nodded and hit the button to take her to the main level. I turned away as Konceited followed me to the large doors at the end of the hall. I wasn't going to say a word about shit until we were behind those. I didn't know what kind of listening devices Monica's ass had in here. Since Link already knew she was on some shit, he made sure to sweep this area constantly, but I wasn't willing to take a chance. I held up my wrist, unlocked the door, and stepped inside. Konceited closed the doors behind me, and I immediately went over to my computer to change the codes for this office. Monica no longer needed access. It would automatically update on Link's watch when I finished. I smiled as I closed out of the computer, remembering the message I had received from Link that I had paperwork that needed my signatures. I shook my head because Link was wild with that one-page document. He probably thought I wouldn't read it in its entirety. Konceited cleared his throat, causing me to look in his direction.

"Yes."

"Do you think he's the one putting her up to stealing from Link?" Konceited asked. He dropped down in a chair as he removed his motorcycle jacket.

"No doubt about it, but for how long? How long has she known Charles? I guess we'll get all those answers today," I smiled. I hit the enter key as my phone chimed, pulling it out, I seen a text from Shantel.

> **Shantel: Everything is all good. She is home and safe, but I must wrap up a few things. I will fill you in later. The meeting is pushed back until later tonight.**

> **Mala: Understood. Link?**

> **Shantel: Unsure...**

I breathed, trying not to get in my feelings about him not hitting me up once Cent was safe. What the fuck was he doing? I mollified myself with the fact that he was still trusting me with his business and shook off my emotions.

"Beautiful. What are we going to do about the shipment?" Konceited asked. He ran his hand over his reddish-brown hair before leaning back into the chair. Even riding his bike, he still wore a fucking suit. He smoothed a hand over his black tie against a smokey gray button-up shirt with tailored gray pin-striped suit pants.

"Well, if Quinton was telling the truth, which I'm pretty sure he was, then the men delivering it are a part of the Cartel. We need to have a one-on-one with them," I smiled.

"I told you it was going to be an interesting day. I never expect anything less from you," he smiled.

Konceited followed me to the Casino floor to see exactly why Kamille was there. I felt calm when I hit the floor and the elevators opened. The flashing lights, the sound of slot machines, and the bustling energy of the casino seemed to calm me. I thought it was funny how quickly that happened. It felt like a home away from home. But now, I couldn't just enjoy my time on the floor because I had to deal with the bullshit that came with it. The first thing I had to do was see why Kami thought coming here now was a good idea or if it was because I was wrong, and she knew this shipment was going to be fucked up. Is she the distraction, or did she just have the wrong timing?

If it was just wrong timing, then what I learned today about her company would turn her world upside down. Because if it were what I thought, she would be in for a rude awakening. As the Gaming Manager and as a member of U.C.K., I took pride in ensuring the integrity and security of our establishments, while also ensuring no one fucked with our shit. There were too many snakes, and I could feel the shift happening. If niggas thought getting Crescent back would be the end, I knew for a fact they were wrong. It was about to get worse, so I knew taking care of this mess here would be one less thing to worry about. I saw Ma walking toward us and noticed her normally expressionless face was pulled into a deep frown. Her lips were pinched, and I tried not to laugh. I already knew what was going to come out of her mouth.

"Aww shit. It looks like someone pissed off little Ms. Mallory," Konceited chuckled. He was being light with it, but his eyes constantly scanned the area, waiting for someone to do something.

"Shut up, Konceited," Ma whispered as she got closer.

"What's up? Everything good?" I smirked.

"It's not funny, Boss. Somebody needs to knock that bitch the fuck out. If I weren't so restrained, I would've done it. She's lucky that she does business here," Ma grunted.

"What happened? Tell me everything so I can greet this hoe," I smiled.

"Kamille stormed into my office demanding to see Lakyn and asked how long she would be kept waiting. Screaming how she is one of this Casino's biggest business partners," Ma said, rolling her eyes.

"Is she still in your office or back in the conference room?" I asked. I began walking, trying to pull my mask of professionalism on before walking into a space with Link's ex-sub. I knew I had to stand my ground with her, and being dominant wasn't a hardship for me. I knew when and where to turn it on, and she would fucking fold, or I would fold her ass over that desk.

"My office," Ma hissed.

"We got this Mallory. Go and do you while I handle this bullshit. And let me know the moment that truck comes in. I don't care if I'm still in a meeting with Miss Bitch," I stated. Ma nodded and turned on her heel as I paused at her door.

"Got it, Boss," she said, hurrying away. I was sure she wanted to go far away from Kamille because I could tell she was on the verge of choking somebody.

"Let's not kill anyone on the main level," Konceited smiled. He stepped beside me and opened the door to the office. I waited, letting him step inside before he held out his arm for me to enter. My heels clicked on the office's cherry hardwood floor, causing Kamille to turn to face me with a scowl.

"Oh, you should smooth out your face, Kamille. We wouldn't want wrinkles too early," I smiled and sat behind Ma's large desk that matched the wood floors. I watched as her face went through many expressions before settling on indifference.

"Kamille, what brings you here today?" I inquired, maintaining a professional demeanor despite the tension in the air.

"You may call me Ms. Indigo, and you can cut the act, Ms. Samuels," she retorted, her eyes flashing with suspicion. "I know something is going on between you and Lakyn. If you think you can replace me and what I provided him, you're delusional," she laughed.

I straightened in the chair, placing a false smile across my face. No matter what problems Link and I were going through, he was mine and always would be. But that was none of her fucking business. I cut my eyes over to Konceited, and he was smirking while staring at what I assumed was Kamille's bodyguard.

"My personal relationships are none of your concern. We are here to discuss business, and that's exactly what we'll do," I informed her politely.

Kamille's expression darkened, and she launched into a tirade, accusing me of meddling in her affairs with Link. This crazy ass bitch had never once seen me before that day, and she thought that she fucking knew me. If this little meeting wasn't about business, then I didn't have the time, patience, or need to hear shit. I sighed, propped my arm on the arm of the leather chair, and leaned on my fist.

"Enough," I stated flatly, not hesitating to cut her off.

"Again, whatever relationship you had with Lakyn is over, and I'm who you will be dealing with from now on," I finished.

"Who the hell do you think—"

I sat up straight with a quickness she wasn't expecting and leaned onto the desk. I saw her bodyguard move out of the corner of my eye, but I wasn't worried.

"Nigga, if you want to keep your hand attached to your body, remove it from your hip," Konceited threatened.

"Who am I? I am the woman you will be dealing with if you continue doing business with Blackbay Casino and Resorts. Who I am is the bitch that will reach across this desk and slam your pretty face into it until I'm satisfied. You forget where you are, Kamille. You know, and I know who runs this fucking Casino along with this fucking city, so ask me who the fuck I am again," I demanded. I stared into her hazel green eyes, letting her see the seriousness in my brown gaze.

Kamille paused to catch her breath as fear spread over her face. I seized the opportunity to confront her about the corrupted machines. I leaned back in the chair, creating space to cross my legs as I stared at her open mouth.

"What do you know about the issues we've been experiencing with your gaming machines? I have evidence to prove something is amiss, and we won't tolerate it," I assured.

Kamille's eyes widened in disbelief, and she dropped back into the chair as if I'd slapped her across the face.

"I don't know what you're talking about. There is no way I would provide corrupted machines to this establishment or any establishment," she vehemently denied.

"I insist that you are mistaken," she said exasperated.

However, I was prepared with the evidence and was prepared to present it to her without hesitation. I pulled out my phone and typed a few commands to print it out. The laser printer in Ma's office began spitting out page after page of career-damaging evidence. It was all aimed back at her company, which, if she did have something to do with it, she would be the dumbest criminal in history. Konceited moved to grab the papers, all while keeping the large man in his sights with an easy smile. He placed them on the desk before Kamille and stepped back to lean against the door.

"Thank you," I smiled.

"Anything for you, Beautiful," Konceited smirked.

I watched as Kamille studied the proof I had laid out before her, and realization seemed to dawn on her face.

"It has to be my father. He has to be partnering with someone I don't know about because I have control over...everything else. This could ruin the company," she murmured, her voice tinged with resignation. "He must be pulling the strings behind the scenes. I have nothing to do with any of this. I haven't signed off on any of these changes," she stated quickly.

I listened as she explained her suspicions about her father's involvement in tampering with the gaming machines, and I could see the conflict and concern in her eyes. Despite our previous animosity, I couldn't help but feel a pang of empathy for her predicament, but those were the brakes. She took that company from her father ruthlessly. I could see Indigo partnering up with the Cartel to get back at his daughter, but he was unknowingly getting between two enemies. Indigo was being used and was too furious at his spawn to see it.

"Regardless of the source of the corruption, it is imperative that we resolve this issue swiftly and decisively," I stated firmly. "We cannot allow the integrity of our casino to be compromised any further. And we will not look weak in anyone's eyes, Kamille. Do you understand what the fuck I mean?" I asked.

"Ye...yes. But maybe I should speak to Lakyn about this, so he understands that I never—"

I stood up fast, leaning across the desk. I knew she didn't catch the motion until her face met the wood.

"Ahhh! Ahh, oh my God," she screamed. I could hear Konceited moving, and a loud thud hit the floor. I leaned down and pressed my lips close to her ear.

"I don't fucking like you, Kami, but this is the only time I'm going to give you a pass. It seems as though you think you have a right to speak to what the fuck belongs to me, and you do not. Pick up the fucking papers, grab your purse, and get the fuck out of my casino. Your father has fucked up, and it leaves you in the hot seat. He will die, Kamille, and nothing you do will save him," I hissed.

"No...no...he's old. He just doesn't want to give up contr—"

"Shut. The. Fuck. Up. Nothing you say will change what will happen. All you need to know is you, your company, and everything you own belongs to U.C.K., Kamille. You work for us now since doing business with your company has cost us significant money. You will pay it all back," I laughed. I pushed her face harder into the desk before I let her head go and stepped back. My phone beeped, and I looked down to see a message from Ma

.

> **Ma: The shipment arrives in less than five minutes.**

Kamille fell back into her chair with tears streaming down her face, mixing with the blood from her nose.

"Damn, you might need to see a doctor for that," Konceited said, nonchalantly.

"How much? How much do I need to pay you? I'll write a check right now—"

"Bitch, please. We don't need your fucking money but your services. Pick up your face, and you, along with your bitch ass bodyguard, can get the fuck out. You can try to call the police, hide, or refuse, but it will all end the same. Painfully," I said, straightening my suit jacket. I moved around the desk as Konceited opened the door. Maurice and two of his men were standing there.

"Need anything, Boss?" he asked, looking over my shoulder.

"Yes, escort them off the property and have someone sit on them after she is properly chipped," I ordered.

"Yes, ma'am," he said quickly. I nodded and began to head toward the back of the Casino, where we received all our shipments.

"Chipped?" Konceited asked, fixing his tie.

"Yeah, some new shit Link came up with. It enters the bloodstream, and we can track and hear what she is saying for a certain amount of time," I answered.

"Hmm, interesting. I'll need to see that," he murmured to himself. I rolled my eyes, knowing damn well this nigga was about to come up with something like it to fuck with Link.

I walked through the back corridors with Konceited beside me as he typed on his phone. I felt my other phone buzz, and I took it out. I was frowning until I saw Santina's number. I smiled and answered it immediately.

"Hey, niece, what's up?" I answered.

"Auntie Mala!"

I pulled the phone away at the shriek Cece made into the phone. I blinked a few times before putting it back to my ear with a smile.

"Hey, little bit. Is everything okay?" I asked, looking at my watch. I didn't think I was in the meeting with Kamille that long, but it had been over an hour.

"Papi and Cent said my friend Travis can come for a play date. You have to come with Uncle Link to pick me up tomorrow, but can you please tell him he has to be nice," she cried. I shook my head as we turned the corner leading to the shipping area as other people who normally unload the trucks began leaving the area. I knew Ma must have sent out an all-call for people to vacate. That made shit easier once the truck came through.

"Ahh, I will do my best, baby," I answered with a frown. Why in the hell would Link be mad over a doll? I shrugged because it was possible.

"Thank you! Santina said all the uncles are mean when we get boyfriends," she sighed. I burst out laughing, and Konceited looked at me in concern.

"Cece, I'm sure Uncle Link will not be mean to your boyfriend. If he is, I'll beat him up for you," I laughed.

"Yay! Thank you, Auntie Mala! I love you, bye," she screamed, and the call dropped. I shook my head as I put my phone away.

"So ain't nobody going to say anything about her doll being her boyfriend? Is it one of the ones that talk to her?" Konceited asked.

"I'm pretty sure it does, and Faxx is handling it," I defended.

"Well, I don't like it. How old is this Travis doll, and what is he saying to her? I don't trust that nigga," Konceited grunted.

"Nigga, it's a fucking doll," I laughed as we got to the doors leading to the loading area. Konceited pushed the doors open, and I followed behind him as the large tractor-trailer truck began to back in. We waited to the side as they pulled in, backing up to the large doors. The driver's door opened, and a man hopped out, closing the door. I heard another door close, telling me the other man had gotten out. We waited as they began to look around for the crew that was supposed to be unloading the new machines. We stayed close to the wall and moved closer as the two began speaking rapidly to each other in Spanish. We listened to the conversation between the two men, which was becoming heated. They talked in a hushed tone about the machines they were dropping off for the casino floor. I couldn't catch everything they said, but knowing we had the right people was enough.

"I'm telling you that something is off, Tomás," the man hissed. Tomás made a slashing motion across his throat, causing the other man to close his mouth.

"Enough, Raúl," he snapped, looking around to see if anyone heard them.

I looked at Konceited before I stepped away from the wall, but I didn't miss him picking up something from the ground. I knew I could count on him to have my back in any situation. Not only did Link trust him, but I held the same level of trust just by working with him over the last few weeks. We both knew the Cartel had been trying to get a foothold in this Casino and thought they would succeed. Those niggas were trippin'.

As we approached them, they looked up with surprise and suspicion in their eyes. I didn't waste any time getting to the point. They weren't the only snakes I needed to weed out of this garden on this good morning.

"Let's cut the bullshit. We know you're working for the Cartel, and we know what you've done to those machines. By the way, all the money y'all believe you stole should be about to—" I looked at my matte black watch. I tapped at the screen and looked back at the two men with a smile.

"It should be reversing right about now. I wonder who your bosses would blame for that fuck up," I grinned, slapping my hands together.

Tomás and Raúl exchanged uneasy glances, trying to maintain a façade of innocence, but I saw right through their charade. I leaned in closer, my gaze piercing through their defenses.

"Don't waste my damn time with the bullshit. You're deep in U.C.K. territory, and we are actually on a take-no-bullshit mandate. So, the only way you're getting out of this is by telling me everything," I directed.

Tomás scoffed, attempting to play it cool.

"We don't know what you're talking about. We're just here to do our job and collect our pay."

I felt the anger bubbling up inside of me, and I tried to keep my composure, but I was over the bullshit.

"Oh no, you should have just answered her questions, and maybe this wouldn't get so... bone-breaking," Konceited boomed.

"Listen, you think you know who we are, but let me assure you if you do anything to us—" Tomás started.

I reached around to my back for the holster that held my gun. I pulled out my Sig and aimed it at the men before they could blink.

What the fuc—"

I motioned for Konceited to step forward, and he moved in with an expression of anticipation that radiated an aura of instant death that couldn't be ignored.

"Don't fucking move, or this shit is going to hurt worse than you think. I tried to help you out, but y'all niggas don't listen," Konceited growled, his voice low and menacing.

"You've got one chance to start talking, or things are about to get painful for one of you."

"I told you this didn't feel right! I told you we needed—" Raúl began to speak, but Konceited moved to swing the lever that was used to jack up large trucks. The lever connected with his face, swinging Raúl's head to the left as blood and teeth hit the cement.

"Holy fucking shit! You son of a—" Tomás screamed while reaching into his waistband.

"Ahh! Ahh," Raúl screamed, dropping to his knees. Konceited was already moving, and he slammed the lever into Tomás side, causing him to slam against the side of the truck. I heard his ribs crack under the pressure of that hit.

"Fuck! Fuck, fuck, fuck you, fuck you," Tomás screamed while Konceited chuckled. Konceited rested the lever on his shoulder as I moved to squat down to stick my Sig under Raúl's chin.

"Ahh! Ahh—"

"Shhh. Shhh, calm the fuck down. Y'all have made a grave mistake by crossing us. You either start talking now or regret it for days. Because I will get every single piece of information out of one of you," I said softly. As Raúl cried silently, I tilted my head from side to side, waiting for the first one to give up the information.

I signaled to Konceited, and he moved swiftly, grabbing Tomás by the collar and pinning him against the side of the truck. He let out a yelp of pain as Konceited applied enough pressure to his injured ribs to clarify his point.

"Last chance. The first one to speak gets to deliver the message," I said, my voice steelier than ever.

"Where is the information from those machines going? What is the exact location?" I asked.

"It's...it goes—"

"Raúl, shut the fuck up!" Tomás shouted.

"I guess Raúl is the winner in this game," I said cheerfully. I stood up, gripping Raúl's collar and pulling him with me. I pushed him into the side of the truck and aimed my Sig at Tomás. Konceited took a step back, and I pulled the trigger.

BANG. BANG. BANG.

I put two in his chest and one through the center of his head.

"Oh God...what have you done...what have you done," Raúl slurred. Bloody drool rolled out of his mouth as he cried, looking at his dead friend.

"Shut the fuck up!" I snapped.

Konceited stepped forward, his imposing figure looming over Raúl as I holstered my Sig.

"Don't start with all this crying like a little bitch. You came to do a job, and I know this ain't the first time you've seen blood on the account of who you work for. So, give us the location," Konceited said in a monotone voice. Konceited's intimidating presence pushed down on Raúl, and I could see him cracking under it.

He began by saying the machines had been rigged to siphon off a percentage of the profits and send the money straight into a shell corporation. We managed to track that down already, but the origin of where it went initially was harder to trace.

Konceited grabbed Raúl's collar, lifting him off the ground to be at eye level.

"Where is the information being sent?" he barked.

Raúl stammered out the name of the location. It was in Puafton, and it sounded familiar to me. There had been a lot of shit about Clapton and Del Mar, so I figured it would have been in that area. I pulled out the untraceable phone and called Shantel.

"Yes?"

"What do we know about the location I just sent to you," I asked, frowning.

"Where did you get this? How? This—"

I wasn't sure what that tone was all about, but I wasn't feeling it.

"A friend of a friend fucking with our money. He said it all originates from that point, so whoever they are using for tech must also be located there. Why, what is it? Why are you sounding like that?" I asked.

"This address is...it's where...it's a place from the past," Shantel whispered.

What in the hell was going on? She didn't sound right, and I needed to know why.

"Shantel?"

"What's your plan?" she asked.

"I...I doubt anyone will mind when I send a little message," I beamed.

"We've got a lot of shit hitting the fan already, so I doubt one more thing would matter. Why, what do you have in mind?"

"Sending their machines back to them with an explosive surprise," I stated.

"I would say get it set up, and that will have to go through Henny. Just...just have it set up to move. I gotta go," she said quickly.

I looked at Konceited, and he waited to see what I would do. Shantel was right, and everyone needed to know this information before I leveled this shit.

"Knock his ass out and tie him up inside the cab of the trailer. Then I want to know how much like Link you are. Can you rig those machines up as explosives?" I smiled.

"Beautiful, it's like you fell from heaven and landed in my lap. Are you sure you're not the love of my life?" Konceited asked, before punching a whimpering Raúl in the temple twice, knocking his ass out.

"Green eyes, I'm more like the demon here to tempt you," I smirked, before turning away. I left Konceited to do what needed to be done so I could handle the rest of the shit for today.

As I strode purposefully through the back halls of the Casino, my heart pounded in my chest. I was still pumped up from the delivery situation. My watch vibrated, and when I looked down, I saw that Monica had tried to access the computer system by going through her terminal. I checked my phone and saw a text from Ma, saying that the elevators were on lock so that Monica couldn't leave the top floors. I hit the elevator button after putting the code in that would only worked for six people. The only people who could control these elevators would be Link, Faxx, Oz, Henny, Shantel, and me. The betrayal cut deep with Monica, especially since I had always considered her a close acquaintance. Link felt it was the right thing to do by bringing her on after her brother was killed. Being part of this family guaranteed her a modicum of protection, and she flourished because of it. She went to the best schools and was offered the best jobs. She never had to worry about a thing because her brother paid his dues and died because of it. Her smarts and knowledge of all things technical was a bonus, and it meant Link didn't have to explain what he needed or wanted in laymen's terms. Monica completely understood it, so what would make her betray the U.C.K. family like she had? But where the fuck did Charles come into play. My mind was racing with a mix of anger and disbelief that she thought any of this shit was a good idea.

I stepped onto the elevator and hit the button for the offices. I took in deep breaths trying to bring my anger under control. It wasn't enough that she crossed U.C.K., but she fucked with Link, and that's something I can't get with. I quickly texted Ma so she could have everything ready at the docks while Konceited took care of the shipment mess.

> **Mala: I need you to make sure the boat is ready to go at any moment.**

> **Ma: Will I need to accompany her to the *FARM*?**

> **Mala: Yes, but once she's secure, you can return to the casino.**

> **Ma: Got it, Boss. I sent more information I think you should review. It's damaging.**

The chime of the elevator sounded as I reviewed what Mallory had sent over to me. The information was other pictures and conversations Monica had about our operations. There was also a building Ma followed her to a few times this week that had my jaw firming and my anger beginning to spiral out of control. I slipped my phone into my pants pocket and looked down at my heels. I saw a spot of blood, so I leaned over and wiped it away as the doors opened to the offices. I stood up and saw Monica quickly getting into her chair, but she visibly relaxed when she looked up in my direction. I wrapped a tight rope around my anger so I wouldn't just shoot her in the fucking face. Her relaxation at seeing me was mistake number one. But who the fuck was I to tell her that? I stepped off the elevator, knowing it wouldn't move until I opened it again, unless one of the others showed up during the time Monica and I got some shit straight. After this is handled, everything with the casino would be on the right path, and Link would need to focus on one less thing. I pushed down my anxiety and sadness that I hadn't heard from him, but I got it. The shit still stung, and I knew I was going to have an attitude behind it, knowing damn well I shouldn't. I approached Monica's desk, and she looked up, grinning.

"Hey Mal—"

"Monica," I said firmly. "We need to talk."

Monica's brows furrowed, but I relished the shock of surprise that crossed her face at my tone. Her expression shifted from casual to uneasy as she noticed the seriousness in my eyes.

"What's wrong, Mala?" she asked, her voice strained.

"I'm just going to get straight to it because the disappointment I feel makes me...it makes me want to slam your head into that fucking computer screen," I said, cracking my neck.

"Wha—what is going on? I don't—"

"We know what you've been doing," I replied, my voice low and controlled.

"You've been stealing confidential information from Link's personal servers, thinking that you were so good that you wouldn't get caught," I smiled.

Monica's eyes widened in shock, and she stammered as I shook my head.

"I don't know what you're talking about, Mala. Link has to know that I would never—"

"Save the bullshit for someone who gives two shits what you think. Save it for someone like Charles," I interrupted, my patience wearing thin. Her eyes widened at that name, and she pushed back from her desk as I leaned on it.

"I have video, photo, and audio evidence of you accessing sensitive files and transferring them to an external drive. Don't bother denying it."

Monica's brown complexion seems to almost pale at my words. My jaw flexed, trying to keep it cool as she looked around nervously like there was someplace to go. But there was no escape, and I could see the fear of it written in her wide gaze.

"I... I can explain," she began, her voice trembling.

"Explain? What possible explanation could justify your betrayal to U.C .K.? You already know how we handle betrayal, so don't look scared now. You weren't afraid when you were handing off files or hugging Charles. Which is my fiancé," I laughed.

Monica slammed her hands on the desk, the first trace of anger taking over the fear. I smiled, knowing that statement would get to her.

"He doesn't love you! He's never fucking loved you, but you're necessary. Charles...he's, he's—"

"He is a fucking piece of shit, and he's also gay. So whatever love you think you have going on with him, you're dumb as fuck. He played you! Did you think you would walk away from this without...damage," I smiled, pushing away from the desk.

"No! You're lying! He said you would lie, cheat, and do whatever to make him look bad. That's why I had to keep an eye on you and Link! He didn't trust you two together because he knows that you are a whore. He chose me way before you came along! All through college and his internship with the mayor, but you came along with your demands for U.C.K., and you blackmailed him for powe—"

The way I almost fell on the floor laughing almost sent me. I knew damn well this bitch did not say I blackmailed him.

"Bitch you're trippin'. Why the fuck would we need him at that level? Why the fuck would I choose to be with someone I fucking despise? Tell me what the fuck you know about the man who is fucking every man that walks through his office doors," I snapped. Monica stared wide-eyed at me as the pieces clearly started to snap in place for her. I looked at the clock, seeing I still had a few more moments until the boat was ready.

"No, no, no.... he said...he said—"

"How many times has he brushed you off? How many rescheduled so-called dates have happened? Monica, you might be naive, but you're not fucking stupid. What the fuck did you think was going on, or what is going to happen because of your stupidity?" I asked.

Monica lowered her gaze, her shoulders slumped as realization forced her analytical mind to see what she didn't want to see.

"I...I was desperate, Mala. Charles, he's really good at getting what he wants and... he threatened me. He said association with you all would ruin my life, and it would be his job to see it happen. If I didn't help him get the information he wanted, he would have no choice but to take me down with you all. Even if he would hate to do it," she confessed, her voice barely above a whisper. She blinked, and I could tell she was replaying that conversation in her mind trying to figure out how she fell for the bullshit.

"What does he want with our data? What's his end game?" I questioned, my mind racing because I knew for sure this bitch had two masters.

"He said it isn't for him but for a rival that could help expose U.C.K. for the criminal organization that it is and the same organization that murdered my brother. He wanted insider information on our upcoming projects and developments of Link's inventions. I would be free, and you all would pay for letting my brother die. He said that he would definitely win the Mayoral bid with this. With the name Tilderman behind him, it was a guarantee," Monica explained, her eyes brimming with regret and anger.

"Are you truly this fucking stupid, Monica? We didn't kill Deon, and you know that. He died doing what kept food on your fucking table and had you going to the finest schools available," I gritted.

I should have felt a pang of sympathy for Monica because Charles was a bastard, and he knew what to use against someone to manipulate them. But with what I knew now fuck that! Loyalty was everything, and this bitch was another weed that needed pulling. Loyalty, above all else, is all we asked, and I couldn't see how that was so fucking hard to accomplish.

"You should have come to Link Monica. It's like you don't know how we handled situations you've found yourself in, and it's a shame. So intelligent yet so fucking dumb," I said, trying to keep my tone in check.

"I know, I know I fucked up, but...but I can fix this, Mala," Monica said, her voice choked with fear.

I sighed heavily, knowing no matter what this bitch said, it still wouldn't change her fate. One reason it wouldn't be fast is because this bitch still wasn't telling the truth about everything. I pulled out my phone and sent the pictures to Monica's computer. I knew each one was showing up on her screen, by the slack looks on her face. The last one was probably one she wasn't expecting. I pocketed my phone and pulled my Sig from my holster, letting my arm fall to my side.

"You knew about the machines and even helped with the coding. So, you are going to tell me everything you know about that location in Puafton," I gritted before slamming the butt of my Sig into her face. Blood gushed from her nose as I raised my foot and kicked her chair backward. The wheels moved across the floor and slammed her into the wall.

"No! Wait! You don't understand! You—"

I stood over her and began to reign down blow after blow to her face as I screamed.

"You set up that pharmacy shipment heist! You told the Cartel the best buildings to hide in Union City! You almost got Link killed on that fucking mission when our trucks were supposed to be hijacked, you stupid fucking bitch," I screamed. I grabbed her blouse and pulled her to me. Both eyes were swelling as she hissed through bloody lips.

"I...I.... I didn't hav—"

"It's time for your date at the fucking *FARM*," I condemned.

"No—" she started.

I reared back and punched her again, knocking her out. I stepped back, wobbling on my heels as I breathed heavily. I holstered my Sig before pulling out my phone to let Ma know she was ready. My hands shook as I texted the quick message. I looked down at my clothes, realizing that I was covered in Monica's blood. My head throbbed, and I figured if I went home and rested for a few hours, I could be ready to listen in on this meeting. After Ma, I sent out a mass encrypted email with all the information and explained everything that had happened. I pocketed my phone and pushed Monica's chair further away as I entered her computer. I typed in my code to release the elevators so they could take this bitch out of my fucking Casino.

I just needed a little rest, and I prayed that Charles's ass wouldn't be there, but with my luck, that nigga was still at the apartment. He was probably afraid of leaving because of those missing files, but it was whatever. I hoped my appearance would tell him to leave me the fuck alone.

CHAPTER
SIX

LAKYN 'LINK' MOORE

I sat in my office going over all of the CCTV footage of this past week. I knew it would take a minute to examine to ensure all of our bases were covered. Not only did I need to cover our tracks, but I had so much shit to catch up on with everything else going on. Henny was dealing with the Chief while Oz dealt with the information we were getting on the streets. Just because we got Crescent back, didn't mean shit was going to slow down. I knew Faxx like the back of my hand, and that nigga was about to be on a street-sweeping mission to take down the highest threats to Crescent's life. It didn't matter because it would be like killing two birds with one stone. Once Shantel provided the information that Damari gathered about

Pamela, I restarted the search to uncover what Rodney had missed when he was covering her tracks. Not everything could be completely cleared unless you were on the level of Lawe's capabilities. Damari managed to gain access to the computers of Clapton's community college. That made it easier for Pamela a.k.a. Patricia to completely disappear like she never fucking existed.

Now, I could focus on the connection between all of our enemies. I was aware that Mala was doing what she did best in handling the shit with the Casino, so I turned my focus to Rodney. Not only had this nigga participated in Crescent's kidnapping, but he'd been on some get-back shit for a minute now. He's always popping up everywhere he shouldn't. I reached for the phone next to me and dialed a number I rarely used, but it had to be done. I knew I was good, even among the greatest out here, on a computer tip, but I also knew the government had some good-ass security. But I knew one person who could help with that.

"Lakyn, I wasn't expecting to hear from you. What's up?"

"Lawe, I need a favor," I said, getting to the point. I knew that he'd studied us long enough to know I don't fucking do people. There were only a handful I could stand at one time.

"Hmm, and what might that be?"

"I need access to the Drug Enforcement Agency and all of the employees connected to Rodney Gates," I asked. We already had shit on him and his boss, but a little more information would go a long way. Also, I wanted to show his punk ass that niggas could fucking touch him. Getting inside of his agency will not only show him, but others as well who thought fucking with U.C.K. was a come-up.

"That's a tall order, Lakyn. Access would be one time and only six minutes exactly. So, can you do me a favor?"

"If it's possible," I answered. A window popped up on my laptop. The annoyance I felt was overshadowed by the amount of information being dumped into my hard drive. It wasn't like I didn't know this nigga could get into my shit. Once we merged businesses, his people could get into my systems and vice versa. It still didn't mean I liked that shit. I began to look through and download what I thought was needed, not wasting time because I only had six minutes. I could be traced if I took any longer than six minutes, and I didn't feel like having to destroy my hard drives or set fire to any places where I store my servers.

"Tell me what happened to Shantel?" he asked.

I paused in my typing and looked at the phone. The line was silent, but I knew that we were still connected.

"What would cause you to believe something happened to her, and why would you care?" I asked instead of answering.

"You know why I care? Because your implant follows her every fucking movement. And I'm sure it will be better once she gets tatted again. Also, anyone with enough training or who has been through a similar circumstance could see that something major happened in her life. So again, what happened?" he asked. I continued typing in my commands as my processor worked overtime to collect information.

"If you'd asked anything about business or even my personal life, I would gladly tell you what you want to know. As for Shantel, that is something I will not do. If Shantel wants you to know anything about her, she will tell you. That is a trust I will never break, no matter what's offered," I answered. The line stayed silent, and I worked faster just in case his ass decided to kick me out of his system.

"That's fair. I wouldn't have said anything either if I were in your position. Three minutes and the window will close," Ian said before disconnecting. The window that gave me access to the department's servers was now closed, and I finally looked up and acknowledged the captain, who had been standing there for the past six minutes.

"Yes."

"Mr. Moore, we will arrive at Blackbay Casino in ten minutes," he informed me.

"Thank you, Fredrick. I will call you if we will be moving anytime soon," I said, standing. Fredrick nodded and promptly left the salon as I put away my laptop. I felt my watch vibrate, letting me know information was being uploaded. The last time, it was Mala changing the access codes to m y office. So, by me getting this error information, it only told me Monica was trying to gain access. After that, we had a list of information about the machines and one person to speak to. I frowned at the coordinates where the information to the machines was going. I knew the place, but I had to be wrong, or this shit had to be wrong. As I continued looking at the information on my watch, I saw an attachment. I pulled out my phone and began walking.

"You know that you were way too engrossed in that phone to be aware of your surroundings?" Ace accused. I looked up and pocketed my phone as we stepped through the Casino doors. I fixed the diamond cuff links on each of my sleeves before smoothing down the gunmetal gray tie.

"I saw you when you exited the dark blue SUV across the street. Trust me, I've learned to always pay attention after y'all so-called crazy ass training," I stated.

"Just keeping you on your toes. I would've remained in the background, but Konceited is still here, and Mala just left for the day," he stated.

I already knew when Faxx found out that I asked Ace to keep an eye on Mala, and not me this week, he was going to be on some shit. I needed to fix this situation with Charles so she would be where the fuck she belonged.

"And Monica?"

"She's...Mala has her en route to the *FARM* along with one of the drivers for the shipment," Ace stated.

"At least she didn't kill Monica. That's a plus," I said. I turned in the opposite direction, heading for the parking garage.

"Oh, naw, she's alive, but I very much doubt that she wants to be after that fucking beat down," Ace chuckled.

"Do me a favor," I started.

"Hell naw. I did you a favor this week. Now that Crescent is back, I can tell you Fransisco will be on point, and you are not having his crazy ass coming at me," Ace shook his head.

"Fuck it. Call Sam and have him get someone to go through Monica's house. After they get all the electronics, burn it to the ground," I ordered. I took a breath because I knew there was a lot more shit I needed to go through, but before I could do any of that, I needed to see Mala. I didn't give a fuck what she thought about it.

"Done," Ace said. Ace faded into the crowd before I entered the hallway as he normally did. I stepped into the underground garage and headed for my new Denali. I was still mad as fuck about the other one, but I wasn't worried about getting that lick back. I already knew before the end of the week that every business Alex or his family owned was getting hit up. Konceited leaned against the driver's side door with his arms folded as I walked up.

"If you got time to be standing here, why the fuck you didn't follow her home?" I asked.

"Nigga, she's good. That bitch ass new security guard followed her home like he's supposed to," he shrugged.

"Why are you still here and in my way, Kodey?"

"Because Faxx is occupied, but I have what Kreed needs. He's going to need it sooner rather than later. Have y'all figured out who is going to help this nigga?"

"Yes, and apparently, she is already in Union City," I nodded. I hit the key fob unlocking the doors as Konceited pushed off the door.

"Stasea? Why in the hell would you have her doing this shit? She's..."

"She is perfect for the job, and I know she will get shit done. We can't fuck around on this, and Stasea will make sure it goes right," I said, opening the back door. Konceited sucked his teeth and moved over to a custom Kawasaki Ninja H2R. He grabbed the backpack sitting on the seat and walked back over to me.

"What is it?" I asked.

"Something your narrow mind wouldn't be able to dream up if you tried. Make sure he gets this shit," he smirked. I took the backpack, expecting it to be heavy, but it was light. I refused to dignify his bitch ass with a reply as I placed the backpack on the back seat.

"What are you about to do now?" I asked, opening my door.

"I have a therapy appointment. I'm already thirty minutes late, but...it is what it is," he laughed. I shook my head because Mena was going to fuck him up one of these days, for real. I swear this nigga forgot that she strangled all of her patients on her last client list because she felt they were too stupid to live.

"Keep fucking around with Mena and you will be the next cold case in Union City," I said, getting into my truck.

"I like it when her eye starts ticking and her teeth start grinding. That's how I know she wants me," Konceited said, getting on his bike.

"Nigga you can't...fuck it—" I said, slamming my door. I started the engine and pulled away from this delusional ass nigga. If he thought Mena wasn't thinking about ways to kill him, he's a fucking idiot.

It seemed like shit always happened the way things were meant to, even if it was fucked up. I already knew that once Landon went missing, Charles would switch companies, and he did just that. Not only was I now inside of all of Charles's networks but also any small security firms in Union City. I was sure to infiltrate as well while getting into Alex's companies.

GODDARD ARMED SECURITY SERVICES was hired the very next day when he couldn't contact his old security company because we blew it up after convincing Alex's brother-in-law to deliver a message to him. It was lucky for us that the Tilderman family owned the company. So we solved two problems at once. I parked in the shopping center across the street from their apartment building. I unbuttoned my dress shirt and reached in the back for my black hoodie. I got out of the truck and moved the backpack to the trunk. I grabbed my holster and pistol, then threw my hoodie on with the hood over my locs. I made my way to the garage across the street. Entering into the parking garage with my head down, I pulled out my phone and placed a call. I saw Charles car in his spot, making my lip curl in disgust. I should shoot this fucking nigga in the face.

"This is Vincent," he answered.

"Vincent, you are hereby relieved of your position at 3113 Coldstone Way, apartment 1216. We have been paid in full, and the confirmation for termination has been sent to your phone. Please confirm," I stated. The line was silent as I approached the door leading to the elevator. Since I didn't have a fob, I pressed the code into the box and waited for it to turn green. I stepped through the door, hit the button, and waited.

"Conformation is received. Please confirm the termination code," he grunted.

"4252421. Please report back to Goddard for reassignment," I said, disconnecting the call. The doors opened, and I stepped into the elevator. It didn't take long to get to Mala's floor. The doors opened, and a large man, bald about my height, with an off-the-rack suit, stepped inside as I stepped off. I chuckled as I walked to the door of Mala's apartment and pulled the small black box out of my hoodie. I opened the box, pulling out the copy of the key I made the night I saw her last. I looked out of the large floor-to-ceiling windows, seeing that it was now mid-afternoon. I stuck the key in the lock quickly and turned the knob, stepping inside as the door moved.

"So what! Do you really think I care right now if someone saw me leaving looking like this? At least I fucking took off the bloody jacket," Mala shouted.

"You cannot be walking around here looking like one of the home girls! You are going to be a fucking Morgan! Act like it!" Charles shouted.

I reached inside my hoodie, pulling my pistol from my holster as I walked forward.

"So you still got that little attitude because your man is missing? You still can't find Teddy and lost your poor little video. Nigga fuck you. And that's right, I said nigga because you still are," Mala snapped.

She was pissed, and it probably had more to do with what she'd been dealing with this past week. But still, she chose this fucking life. No one forced her, and none of us would have asked her to.

"Oh, please bitch do it. I want you to fucking do it. You can watch shit happen just like Kreed," Charles taunted.

I picked up the pace when I heard movement, and when I got to the doorway, I saw Mala across the bed, holding a lamp in her hand. Her brown eyes widened when she saw me, and I could see the slight tremble in her arms.

"Do it! Fucking do it, Kita. I want you to so that you can watch all of those nigge—"

Charles's mouth snapped shut when he heard the sound of the safety disengage and felt the weight of my heat at his fucking head.

"Please. Please say one more fucking word out of your mouth," I warned. Charles's mouth opened and then shut as he tried to turn around and face me.

"Nigga! Keep your ass still. Mala might give a fuck about the consequences, but I don't. So, make it easy and do something else," I demanded.

"Link! Link!" Mala shouted. I looked up at her as she sat the lamp down, holding out her hands as she held my gaze.

"What are you doing here?" she asked.

"I knew you were fucking hi—"

I used the butt of my pistol to hit the back of his head, causing him to stumble forward. He didn't move far because I grabbed the back of his shirt and pulled him backward. I put the barrel to his temple.

"Pack your fucking clothes, Mala," I said calmly.

"Lakyn—"

"Mala! I said pack your shit," I shouted. I saw the flex in her jaw, but she moved quickly around the room.

Charles began to chuckle as he held his hands up.

"If you do anything to me, Link, there won't be enough money or places you or those other thugs can run," Charles laughed. I tightened my forearm around his neck and pressed my pistol harder into his temple.

"Link! Lakyn, please let's go. I have what I need," Mala insisted. I felt her hand on my back, but I tightened up again as Charles began to struggle.

"Link! Baby, please. Not now, not yet," she whispered. I felt her head against my back and her fingers clutching my hoodie. I let out a slow, measured breath before I loosened my hold. Charles sucked in deep breaths as he began to cough.

"You might think you're winning now, Charles, but you just fucked with the wrong nigga," I said, pushing him away. Charles stumbled to his feet and hit the bed, catching himself before falling to the floor.

"You...you...you Kita, just...make sure you're here on the day of that dinner...or I will...I will bury all of you," he wheezed.

"Shut the fuck up," I gritted and aimed.

"Link!" Mala screamed. I pulled the trigger, sending four shots on each side of his body. Charles covered his head, screaming.

"Ahh! Fuck, fuck, fuck! Ahhh—"

With the fading echo of the shots, he slowly moved his arms, and I took quick steps forward, slamming my gun across his face. I leaned down to look into his eyes so he could see how fucking serious I was. FUCK IT.

"You've played this game with a stacked deck for eight years. Your time is done. Can you see how dark my eyes are?" I asked. I shoved my gun under his chin, pushing his bloody face up to look me in the eyes.

"Yeah, that's right, take a long fucking look. Do you see how dark they are? That's the darkness you're going to see when I choke the life from your fucking body," I seethed.

"Link," Mala whispered softly. I felt her hand on my shoulder, and I blinked. I removed my pistol and took the small duffle bag from her hands.

"Let's go," I gritted. Charles knew, and I knew that he still held a fucking bomb over my head. But I also now knew something that he wanted.

"Mala! You walk out that door with that...with him. You already know what's going to happen," he threatened. I turned back to look at him and tilted my head to the side.

"She'll be at that little dinner party. We wouldn't want appearances to get fucked up. I may even let Mr. Banks call you after," I smirked. I felt Mala staring at me, but I watched Charles's eyes almost pop out of his head.

"No! You're...you are lyin—"

"Am I? Can you take that chance because you already know I don't have a problem killing anyone? So again, say one more threatening word to her, and I will make you watch as I toss his weighted body over the side of his own yacht," I threatened. I saw the momentary fear and a crack in his defense as he swallowed. He used his hand to wipe blood from his face before his eyes shifted to Mala.

"Don't be fucking late, Kita," Charles gritted. I glared at him as I gripped my pistol tightly in my hand.

"I'm not afraid of you, Lakyn. No matter how you play it, I will marry Mala, and your secret will be kept safely tucked away," he grimaced. I looked him up and down, then began to chuckle because this nigga really believed he would win this shit.

"You should be afraid. At least for Teddy," I goaded. I saw his breathing pick up and his nose flare, but he said nothing.

I turned away, pushing Mala out of the door before the police could show up. I looked back and caught the burning hatred in his eyes as he watched us. Charles was rattled, and all that told me was I really did need to find that nigga Teddy.

"Fucking bitch ass nigga," I sniffed.

Mala tried to move quickly off the elevator as soon as the doors slid open, but I pulled her backward.

"Slow the fuck down. You don't need to be seen storming off this elevator like you were just in a confrontation," I said, letting her go.

"Where's your car?" she asked, hitting the button for the doors to open once again.

"We're taking your car."

Without another word, she headed for her Mercedes, hitting the fob to unlock it. Mala slid into the driver's seat, and I got inside after tossing her duffle bag in the back seat. The car was already moving before I managed to close the door.

"You got the nerve to have a fucking attitude when you're the one who walked away from me," I chuckled. Mala said nothing as she pulled out into traffic. Her hands were tightly wrapped around the steering wheel. I looked her over and saw the fatigue and irritation written across her face. Her jaw clenched as she tried to hold back her words.

"Say what you got to say, Mala. You don't need to hold back on my account. I ain't that nigga back there," I said.

"I need gas," she murmured. She was pulling into the closest gas station when two police cars flew by and turned the corner. I was sure someone called 911, but I didn't give a fuck. Let that nigga figure out how to spin that shit. They wouldn't get shit from the security cameras, so I wasn't worried. Mala pulled up to the pump and unbuckled her seat belt as she reached over my legs.

"Sit your ass in the car Mala," I grumbled before opening my door. I exited the car to fill up the tank, but I watched her through the window. She was wearing nothing but a camisole and a pair of dress pants. Mala's arms were folded with her eyes closed, talking to herself. Once the tank was full, I removed the pump and slid back inside the car.

"Where are we going?" she asked.

"The Casino," I said, staring at her. She started the car and pulled away, but I never took my gaze off her profile.

"What! Why do you keep staring at me?"

"Because I want to know what the fuck is your problem. If anyone should have the attitude, it should be me, Malikita," I countered. She slowed down and stopped at a red light before looking at me. Her narrowed gaze only had me lifting a brow at her, waiting for what she had to say.

"So, you don't think that running up in that fucking apartment was wrong? Do you understand what is at stake? Because I don't think you do, and you wonder why I never said a damn word," she hissed.

Mala slammed her foot on the gas when the light turned green.

"You're fucking kidding me right now," I laughed.

"No, the hell I'm not! Regardless of what you may or may not believe, I would do the same shit again. Look at you! How you responded back there. If I hadn't been there, you would've killed him," she pointed out.

"You're damn right. I would've taken his bitch ass out. What the fuck do you think this is?"

"And that's what I mean! You don't fucking think! You're too smart, Link! All of y'all niggas are so fucking smart, but at times like this you lack common sense," she shouted. "Especially back then."

"Yeah, let's do this, *Dove*, because we haven't really had the time to dig into that bullshit. If you believe I was going to let you stay with that nigga one more fucking night, you were trippin' for one. If shit wouldn't have blown the fuck up with Cent, I would have dragged your ass out of that nigga's car that night right after I put a fucking bullet in his head," I gritted.

Mala slammed her fist onto the steering wheel and screamed. She quickly brushed away the tear that rolled down her cheek. I reached out, pried one of her hands off the steering wheel, and held it.

"This is exactly what I'm talking about, Link. You already know what is at stake, but you were perfectly willing to kill his ass back there," she sighed.

"And I'm still thinking about doing that shit once I get you on the *LADY FRANCESCA*. Whatever he does, I will counter it. We will deal with it like everything else, but you...and this nigga holding you hostage is done," I said.

"Are you sure you didn't give birth to Cece?" she smiled.

"I'm her mother and father on a birth certificate," I shrugged.

Mala frowned, then opened her mouth and closed it. Then she shook her head and started to count to ten before blowing out a breath.

"Okay. I'm not even going to ask you to explain that, but have you ever considered the time frame when all of this shit happened? Shantel was barely fucking speaking at that time. All of y'all were still dealing with the fallout from two years previously when you got her back. Then! Then, not to mention Hendrix! Or did you forget? I watched as they cuffed Kreed and threw him in the back of that police van. I was right there watching, and none of us truly knew if he would get life or the death sentence. We didn't fucking know Link," she heaved.

"Mala, that is not the same as waiting eight years to—"

"Nigga! Kreed got fifteen years to fucking life for killing his bitch ass daddy! What do you think you would have gotten? What sentence would Oz, Henny, and Faxx have gotten for...for taking out the Mayor? Kreed only got that retrial because of who y'all became after that! If y'all went down, then where would he be? Where would all of us be right now? Fucking think Lakyn!" she shouted. She used her other hand to wipe the tears from her face, but I could still see the anger and rage in her eyes.

"But to give in to what this nigga demanded was insane," I stated.

"Do you think I didn't fight? Do you think in that first fucking year I didn't try to take his ass out, because I did. And you know what he said to me? He told me to do it just like earlier. Charles likes pain and control, so he loved what he was doing. Charles simply told me to kill him and watch you, Henny, Oz, and Faxx go down just like Kreed. He knows I can kill him, and he is prepared for that. While I held that butcher's knife to his throat, he convinced me to wait. Not long after that, a window popped up on his computer with a mass email chain of the footage showing your faces committing a crime that would give you the death penalty," she sighed.

I stared at her for a long moment, studying her and reading every movement she made. My brows furrowed as I went over all the details that she said and what she didn't say.

"Mala. I can understand that shit, but eight fucking years and you didn't say a word. How long would you keep it up? What if you never found it? I could've gotten rid of the files long ago," I stated. I thought back to that time when we were all young, but making a name for ourselves. Union City Kings were on the rise, but a lot of shit had happened in those two years. Yet we still would've handled it. She shouldn't have ever had to deal with this, and she wouldn't have unless there was something else she wasn't mentioning.

"I would have kept that shit up as long as it took for me to destroy the information. No matter what you think, Charles isn't an idiot, and he shares the same DNA as Ian and Lennox. But, he also has a name that carries weight. Charles comes from old money, and they had or have resources we don't know about," she said tightly.

We turned into the Casino's parking lot, and I pointed toward the docks. She turned toward where I pointed before pulling into a parking space. I looked away at the large, sleek, customized black, gold, and white super yacht waiting for us to board.

I let her hand go and got out of the car. I grabbed her bag from the back seat and closed the door while analyzing her words. It wasn't like I forgot that Charles was technically Oz and Ian's younger brother because it didn't fucking matter. I knew Oz didn't claim that nigga, and even if he did, the shit he was doing would call for his head on the chopping block. But it didn't mean he wasn't ruthless, just like them. I rounded the car and opened Mala's door, reaching for her hand as every scenario ran through my mind. What else could have happened to cause Mala to stay? To put up with such treatment that she was willing to suffer for us.

"Link, baby, you're thinking too hard. It's loyalty. I would do whatever I could to ensure every one of us is safe," she emphasized.

I gripped her hand tighter as we walked closer to the yacht. Captain Fredrick stood next to the boarding ramp, and I watched as he signaled the crew.

"Nice to have you back, Sir. Malikita, it is always lovely to see you again," he smiled.

"Thank you, Fredrick. How is Vivian?"

"She is well. Thank you for asking. Will you want dinner this evening, Sir?" Frederick asked. We boarded the yacht as every possibility ran through my mind.

"No, we'll make do, Fredrick. Just take us out," I stated, leading Mala to the salon. Suddenly, I stopped, causing Mala to run into my back.

"Link, what the hel—"

I turned around and stared down at her, trying to read her eyes, and then I saw it. Fear. But fear of what or who?

"Tell me," I grunted. Her brown eyes bounced between mine as she seemed to weigh her options, and I knew she saw there was none in my gaze.

"Now, Malikita," I demanded.

"The first and only time I visited Charles's grandparents' estate, I was told by his grandfather to play along with his only grandson's little game as long as he wanted me to. Charles said the only way for his game ever to end was when he was dead. I wanted to take the golden cutlery and slit his fucking throat right there, but I knew what would happen."

"We would go down," I nodded.

"Yes, but when Charles left the table to get something his grandfather asked for, he...this old bastard leaned across the table and told me that as long as I played along, the things that happened to Oz's mother wouldn't happen to mine, Stephanie, or...Mrs. Laverne. His grandson stated the terms of his game, which I have to play by. Not you, Henny, Oz, Faxx, or Ian knows who killed their mothers. But every other week on a Tuesday, no matter where the fuck I am, I find pictures of all of them, and it doesn't matter where they are. Now, after knowing this entire time that Ian, with all his resources, still hasn't figured out who this person is, I'm glad I kept everyone safe for eight years," she lamented.

Fuck.

I swallowed and turned away to pull her inside of the salon as we began to cast off.

What I wasn't expecting was the shit about Charles's grandparents. It wasn't like Ian hadn't confirmed that Kenneth had some kind of backing that kept his shit clean by killing what was causing the problem. That was another reason why we had to use him wisely and safely for Seyra's sake. Now, not only her but my mother, Vanessa, and Stephanie were at risk. How? How was this person able to evade Ian or myself? How did this person move like a ghost in Union City and wherever Mala went? The only way I see ending that particular problem was to find the original file and kill Charles. Even though his grandfather seemed to like to stick to the terms, people did shit out of emotions, and he could very well order this ghost to kill. So, that meant we needed to handle this Charles situation first, then kill him and his entire fucking bloodline.

And the best way to accomplish that was to find his weakness. We needed to find Theodore Banks and we needed to find the original footage of the murder.

"Then, when I spoke to Shantel, she got all cagey when I told her the location. I wasn't thinking too hard on it before, but is that—"

"Yes. That's where we found her, but this structure is new. Faxx made sure that place was leveled before we left," I said, closing my laptop. I leaned back, watching Mala as she bit down on her lip and clenched her hands into fists.

"We need to finish questioning Monica about this shit. Are we going to the *FARM* now?

"No," I answered.

Mala stopped in her tracks and turned to face me with both brows raised in question.

"Why not?" she questioned.

"Because you've put a stop to all the bullshit at the Casino for now. And as for Monica, it ain't nothing she's going to be able to do anymore. Our focus now is on Roman, Alex, Rodney, and this fake ass nigga Charles," I noted.

"Okay, so why do all this? Why run up into the apartment the way you did then? As you said, everything for the Casino was taken care of. You've received all the information, and there isn't shit we can do right now, so why risk it? You knew why I had to leave with him, just like you know I will have to return to him. You understand why that is so important now, right?" she assumed.

I stood up, holding eye contact with Mala, infuriated by her stubbornness and lack of understanding, she'd fucked up when she went looking for the Black Wolf.

That night was like she put my world in order, only to drive me insane and walk away three times now. I told her that shit wasn't happening again, and I meant all of it. Mala was like a drug, and I was addicted to her in every way. That was her fault for coming back into my life and thinking she could just walk out. I could see her angle and what she had been thinking, but it would never sit right with me that she had to do that. The sloppiness of that night will continue to haunt me, reminding me of how I lost eight years with Mala.

So, if she thought I wasn't going to do exactly what I did once shit was settled, then that was on her. I was ready for my next high, even if it meant I might end up killing Charles earlier than expected. With this new information, I had to step back and look at all angles regarding my parents or any of my family. I sent out a text about this problem, knowing damn well Faxx was going to have more people sitting on my parents, Vanessa, and Stephanie. But right now, I needed one thing. I needed one person to understand that it would be over my grave before I ever let another person think she was theirs. Every time Charles bitch ass would look in the mirror, he would remember how close to death he was, and if he didn't, the next time I would strangle that nigga—Mala was mine in this life and the next.

"Oh naw, why are you stalking me like that? It's not the time, Lakyn," she said, backing through the open doors.

My jawline ticked as I watched her turn and exit the yacht's salon before we finished our conversation. There's nothing much to it to begin with because there's no way I'd allow anyone to think she belonged to anyone else if it wasn't with me.

Mine.

No one else.

She took my damn heart, and honestly, I didn't want it back.

In turn, I just wanted her—body, mind, soul, and everything else.

I kept moving, following her toward the sundeck.

If I wasn't so angry about everything that went down, I might have enjoyed the view of her luscious curves every time she walked and swayed her hips.

"Link, stop fucking stalking me. I'm not in the mood right now. I really need to figure out how to keep this nigga from doing some tit-for-tat shit," she sighed.

As I stepped onto the yacht's sundeck, I was immediately struck by the breathtaking view of Blackbay stretching out into the horizon. The breeze had her folding her arms, trying to stay warm from the chilly air, and her eyes were fixed on the distant shoreline. Despite the tension and all the bullshit that needed to be done, I had to make her understand she wasn't doing this shit alone any longer.

"Stop following me, Link. I need a minute. I have never said any of this shit out loud for fucking eight years," she growled as she turned towards me. The twists in her hair flew behind her like a whip I was about to wrap around my fist. It was taking everything in me not to pull her toward the lounge chair, lay her flat with her ass up in the air, spank, and then fuck the shit out of her until she understood how serious I was. Or maybe that's exactly what she wanted.

I strode toward her, closing the distance even though she looked ready to knock my ass out with her perfectly manicured hands and then throw me overboard. She didn't move as I stepped into her personal space and grabbed the back of her neck possessively. I crushed her sinful body toward my chest so her body could press against mine. I wanted her to feel what she did to me, but the way she moved, spoke, and whenever she thought she was threatening me.

A gasp followed with her eyes widening when she felt my need for her, causing her to moan. I could feel her pushing closer when she dropped her arms to wrap around my waist.

Good.

"Now I prefer you tied and stuffed full of this dick until you and I both know who's in charge," I chuckled. I let my fingers find their way into her twists and pulled downward, so she'd look into my eyes.

"Until you understand who you belong to."

Rather than submitting, she had the audacity to roll her eyes.

"Link, your crazy is showing again if you think you can boss me around. It's like you forgot I know what you like as well," she grinned.

Oh, she was talking big shit.

"Do you need a reminder?"

"Do you need a reminder?" she snapped back with narrowed eyes. One arm around my waist moved and crept up my back to pull my locs. The slight pain from the tug made me smirk and tighten my grip. That fierceness slipped slightly when my other free hand squeezed her ass, and her teeth flew down to clamp at the bottom of her lip to subdue the moan as I leaned in closer.

"You're going to be the fucking death of a lot of people who thought it was a good idea to keep you away from me, *Dove.*"

I could practically smell her arousal as goosebumps broke around her skin. Mala's eyes widened slightly at my words, and her hips moved, so I knew she liked it.

"What are you going to do?" she whispered, voice low and husky. I could feel her nipples protruding through the thin material of her camisole as she got onto her tiptoes and leaned in even closer to get even.

"Tie me up to keep me from leaving?"

My entire body was so tightly twined together, ready to combust at a moment's notice at her suggestion. That seemed like a plan to me, and I was willing to bet everything I owned that she wanted that too. She wanted me to punish and choke the shit out of her. I could see it in her eyes as her breath picked up speed, and she trembled against me. She wanted me to dominate and remind her who she belonged to. I could read the thoughts running through her mind and tell she needed me to mark her in a way she'd know, and everyone else knew she was mine in every way.

"Maybe I should do that," I declared sinisterly. I watched as Mala's mouth parted questionably. I released her twist and stepped back. I turned her around, grabbed the back of her nape, pushing her down so that her face was on the arms of the sofa with her ass high in the air.

"Link—"

Her legs automatically adjusted to balance herself, and I stepped between them. I pushed my dick against her, my eyes zoned in on the item lying on the table just next to us.

Bet.

I grabbed the thin rope often used to tie down the chairs loosely when the yacht was docked. I worked quickly and sufficiently with speed before she knew what was going down. By the time Mala's mind played catch up, I had already managed to tie her hands.

She wiggled out of my hold, whirling to glare at me.

"Nigga, we don't have time to play your games," she huffed.

"We got time. You did some shit you need to pay for Mala. It ain't nothing we can do until we get to where we're going, and we have hours before that fucking meeting," I chuckled.

"I swear I should kill you," she hissed.

"See, that's the shit I like. You always talk that good shit when you're mad," I taunted. She knew I liked that shit.

"You know damn well I would love you to try that. I'm already fucked up in the head enough that just a threat like that coming out of your mouth is making my dick throb."

"Oh my freaking God, Lakyn. You're *insane*," she laughed slightly.

"If you leave me again because of your fiancé, I really will fucking go insane," I growled, stepping closer to her. I knew now that she was tied up. There wasn't much she could do, and nowhere she could go. I had already told the captain we needed the bare minimum crew, and none were needed for the rest of the day.

"Lakyn, listen, it wasn't because I wanted–"

"If you do, I won't be responsible for what I would do," I warned.

"Fake fiancé, Link. None of it is real, and you know that. Stop acting like I haven't always belonged to you," she said, struggling against the ropes.

"I don't give a fuck. Fake fiancé is still a damn fiancé," I seethed.

"You're insane! I'm not going back and forth with you. You already know why we need to do this shit, and I'm not going to stop until we have what we need," she shook her head.

"Okay, and I told you that you're mine. End of story, case fucking closed. You're not doing this on your own anymore, Mala. I see what you did, and I can see why you did it the way that you did, but I don't give a fuck. They're applying pressure, but them niggas won't know pressure until my arm is wrapped around their throats."

Mala glared at me with exasperation written clearly over her face, enough to make me chuckle. If only she knew half of just how insane I could be, but I was sure she did.

"You always knew how to hide the psycho side of you, but it's showing more than usual, Kyte," she theorized. My dick got harder.

"Only when it comes to you, *Dove*," I chuckled, turning to grab a throw cushion and throwing it in front of me. She stared at the pillow in confusion, her brows knitting together as her eyes found mine.

"*Kneel*."

Mala's eyes narrowed. "Do you think—"

"*Kneel*."

I needed this control right now, and when her eyes locked onto mine, I knew she could see how on edge I was. She slowly dropped onto her knees, gazing up at me.

"There," she grumbled, the anger still dancing in her eyes alongside something else—

Need.

Her twists fell back behind her shoulders. I leaned down, dropping my mouth to hers, and kissed her so intensely that I knew she could feel how much I needed this—how much I needed this control, or I might just set this entire yacht on fire to have her to myself.

I grabbed her by the chin, squeezing gently as our eyes connected. All that fire inside seemed to molt and dissolve ever so slightly. My other hand shoved my pants and boxer briefs down enough to just free my length.

Soon as I released her mouth, her gaze darted straight to my dick as pre-cum beaded at the tip.

"Now be a good girl and lick daddy's dick for me. We're not leaving this yacht until you understand just how fucking serious I am."

"Link," she whimpered and swallowed, brown eyes looking up at me.

The sight of my dick casting a shadow over her face was enough to make my balls ache, painfully. I towered over her frame, nose flaring as I watched while she licked her lips before leaning forward to use her tongue over the head of my dick, kissing lightly.

"What did you say, Mala? I didn't hear what you called me," I groaned. I gathered her twist into a loose ponytail at the base of her head. I held her away from my dick, but her eyes kept dropping to look while her breaths became shallow. She tried to move and lean forward. I wanted her to, but she needed to answer, or neither of us was getting shit.

"Lakyn! I said Lakyn! What else do you want me to say?" she groaned.

"That's all you needed to say, *Dove*. Now, all I need for you to do is choke on my dick since you wanted to try and leave a nigga again."

I tugged her face forward until her plump lips were pressed onto my head, causing them to spread and stretch. She opened her mouth wider, but slowly closed around it, sucking hard. She pulled back, making a popping sound before licking her lips. Mala leaned over, slathering the tip across her lips like she was putting on Chapstick. Then, she glided her tongue over it—swiping that thick precum gathering at the tip again—swirling her tongue across with the kind of skill that was easy to remember. She knew me and knew my body because we taught each other together. For years thoughts of her doing this shit for another nigga tore me the fuck up to where I stopped feeling shit unless it came to my family.

A dark cloud rolled over me, and I wanted to make sure that no one would ever be able to satisfy her in any way. I wanted her to feel like I did when I didn't feel like I could take a full breath unless she were near. I wanted her to feel that way when I'm not around, so the next time she knows that she couldn't breathe without me.

I could tell she was already struggling to open wide enough to accommodate the entirety of my thickness. Yet, I enjoyed the idea of choking Mala with my dick, being the person to decide if she had to breathe through it or gag.

If it was possible, I wanted to own every damn part of her—to make her reliant on me only, but she would fight it and try to reverse it. I wanted her muscles, body, bones, and blood to be made from what I gave her.

She moaned around my length, and it filled my ears, urging me to continue to push forward. I pulled back slowly, then slowly thrust back, giving her time to adjust accordingly as I dragged my length over her tongue. When I managed to get the head of my dick down her throat, I saw the way her face twisted with the urge to gag.

I didn't pull back. Instead, I pushed forward, working past Mala's instinct until she swallowed all around me. All the while making sure she kept her eyes on me.

"Good girl. Such a...fuck.... you like to be choked like this. You know just how to breathe through that shit Mala. Does it feel good, *Dove*? Do you need more of my dick down your throat, or you can't handle it?"

And because she was made for me, her submissive nature slipped into place, making her nod as she twirled her tongue.

"*Mm.*"

The feeling of how she sounded made me almost cum, especially with her lips tightening like a vice around me. The vibrations from her agreement made my balls clench up toward my body, my dick throbbed painfully and thickened further. Judging from the way her eyes widened, she could feel it. I pulled on her twist as she slid her tongue along my length, circling around the head before she pushed back down, hollowing out her cheeks.

"Fuck, *fuck*, I'm not going to nut down your throat if you keep choking on my dick like that," I groaned. The slide going in and out of her had my hips moving faster. I knew if Mala's hands weren't tied, I knew she'd be clawing at my thighs. I was feeding into her need to please me while denying her need to mark me. I pulled my dick out of her mouth at the same time I pulled her hair.

"Breathe. Breathe, Mala," I demanded. Her eyes were wide as her chest heaved, but her gaze pleaded as I held her in place. Looking at her had me remembering just how much she liked to suck dick. She gasped a handful of air before I eased my grip and slid back between her lips, giving her part of what she could take inside of her mouth. I wanted to be buried in the back of her throat when I made her drink my fucking cum and to have that part of me in her.

"Do you want to breathe, *Dove?*" I questioned, making short, shallow thrusts in her tight throat. I was so deep that I knew she would be sore tomorrow, but she would be thinking of me with each swallow or movement.

"Or do you want this dick?"

"Mmm...ye...yess," she muffled as drool slid down her chin.

"Whose dick?" I gritted out with the patience and strength of a God to not cum yet.

"Ywors," she said muffled. Her body wiggled, hoping to get more, but the ropes were tight, and I knew she couldn't get out.

"Yeah, that's what I thought," I murmured. My toes curled as I felt the boat bobbing as I slowly withdrew and thrust deeper.

"Mm," Mala moaned, bobbing her head as much as my grip would allow. Her sounds were vibrating even more intensely as I stared down at her.

She fed into this part of me I knew no one else would ever be able to fill.

Just her, and she knew that. I pulled back, and she gritted her teeth, looking up at me.

"I thought you were going to choke me on your cum?"

I raised my brows at her as I forced my growing orgasm down just because I knew she wanted me to.

"The Wolf would have made me," she panted. I tilted my head to the side and looked at her like she was fucking crazy.

"Then fucking take it, and you better breath through all that shit Mala," I taunted. She opened her mouth again, and I knew she was going to say some more shit, but I smirked. I guided her head back to my dick, twisting my hand around her hair to hold it better as I fed her what she craved. I nudged her throat as she took me deep, fucking her without holding back or any remorse since she wanted it.

Because she was *mine*.

"*Mmm*," she groaned.

It didn't take long until I was fucking her throat in fast and hard movements that made her gag as she moaned around me.

"Look at me, Malikita," I command.

She pried her eyes open as she swallowed around the head of my dick and hummed. I felt my orgasm deep from the depth of my existence. I could tell she was barely able to breathe sufficiently, and I was caught between ignoring it or craving more and letting her breathe. I loosened my grip, beginning to pull her off me, but she swallowed again. I felt her tongue on the underside of my length as she twirled around it.

"Fuck! You call me insane, but you need this because you need me as I need you," I grunted. My drive was manic, aggressive, frantic, and I could feel my muscles flexing and pulling tightly. With her continuous moaning and slurping sounds, I would give her what she was working for. I pumped past her gag reflex, watching like a crazed man as her eyes watered. It only made my erection stiffen and harden in the way my balls dragged and slapped down her smooth chin.

"Mmf. Wolf...Cu—"

"I know," I groaned, pulling free from her mouth as a thick string of saliva connected us. She gasped, taking a deep breath before I grabbed her face. Squeezing her cheek, she instantly opened her mouth as I stroked, edging myself towards the inevitable.

"Open your mouth and stick out your tongue."

Obediently, she did as she was told and gave her what she demanded. I slid my dick to the back of her throat, and I felt her muscles constrict around me. She moaned before her lips wrapped around my dick, and she swallowed every fucking drop.

"Fuck, Mala," I grunted.

"*Mm*"

I opened my eyes, staring up at the sky, judging the time and where it would be easier to tie her ass up. I warned her before, and she probably thought I was playing, but that shit would happen. I looked down, my eyes low, as I watched her draw her tongue back over my length as she swallowed.

I pulled back, releasing her twist, and watched as she caught her breath before I helped lift her quickly to her feet. I reached out, grabbed her neck, and pulled her to me. I shoved my tongue in her mouth, and she moaned before I felt her tongue wrapped around mine, sucking on it. I knew her mouth was bruised, but she didn't seem to care. Mala opened her mouth, greedy for more. A groan fell from my lips.

I wasted no time taking over her mouth, sucking her tongue, and taking her breath before I pulled away to lick her lips. Slowly caressing the column of her neck as one hand went to her pants and pulled them over her hips along with her soaked panties, then plunged two fingers right into her warm pussy.

"Oh," Mala choked out when I used the thumb to rub at her swollen clit as I worked two fingers inside her tight walls. My other hand went to hold onto her hips so I could control her movements. She whimpered and bucked her hips, wiggling against my body, trying to get the friction she needed.

"Fuck, your pussy is soaked, *Dove*," I rumbled while she let out a whine, my dick hardening again. Despite just cumming, my dick was still throbbing hard and ready to fuck the shit out of her.

"I need you, Lakyn," she whispered.

"I know," I gritted out.

"I needed you just as much when you walked out, but let me make that shit impossible. I need to be inside this tight pussy where my children will be born and where my perfect obsession will finally get her release. Who do you belong to?"

"Oh, fuck, you. I belong to Lakyn," she moaned, completely relaxing while her head lulled to the side, showing me her neck.

"Don't run to another nigga Mala. It's all good though, *Dove*, I got you," I promised.

"There...there isn't anyone...else, Link. You know that," she gasped. I licked the side of her neck as I pulled my fingers out of her pussy. I leaned away and stuck them in my mouth as she watched me. I sucked up her nectar just like that peach while staring into her aroused, lust-filled eyes. I knew Mala meant every word, but it didn't mean she still wouldn't try to leave me thinking she was doing the right thing. That was something that wasn't happening. I pulled my fingers from my mouth, grabbing my pants to pull them up enough on my hips that they wouldn't fall. I used the hand on her hip to reach around and tugged the rope. She stumbled back slightly, trying to catch her balance as the yacht moved.

"Being funny, Kyte?"

I smirked, stepping around her and leading her to the other side of the yacht toward the jacuzzi. That way, we would be overlooking the lake close to the *FARM*. As I released the rope, I looked toward where the docks would be in about an hour or so.

"I swear I forget how huge this thing is. Are you letting me relax or something—"

"Fuck no. Ain't no relaxing Malikita," I said, reaching to the hem of her shirt. She assisted me in taking it off, revealing her lacey bra. I ran my hands over the front clasp and popped it.

"Take your pants off, *Dove*," I demanded while rubbing a thumb over her nipple. I never stopped touching her as she did what I asked. I pulled back, taking off my t-shirt, and dropping my pants and boxer briefs simultaneously. I stepped into the hot tub and held out my hand to help her inside. Once I found the spot I wanted, I reached out and sat her on top of my thighs with her parted legs resting on the side of my hips. Her hands came down on the side of my head as she gripped the edge of the jacuzzi. She was essentially caging me in. Mala was the only one that I would ever allow any kind of dominant position over me like this. She knew it, and I needed her in my world of craziness to make it all make sense.

Capturing her lips, I cupped the back of her neck and the other around her soft waist, pulling her closer.

"Shit, baby," she murmured against my lips as the head of my dick bumped her clit. I tilted my head to the side, simultaneously opening my mouth as our tongues collided. Ever so slowly, my hands smoothed over her skin up to her shoulders, where I held her in place as I thrust against her clit.

"Lakyn, shit, please," she moaned. I pulled away, licking down her neck and over the top of her breast. I felt her fingers dig into my shoulders. She clutched my shoulders tighter as the water splashed. I kept following a path across her skin with my tongue, causing her to grind her hips, seeking my dick. The noises she was making were probably audible across the yacht and lake. I didn't give a fuck. I wanted to hear her louder, just like she was in *MYTH*.

My hands never stopped their movements, and my palms slipped downward to the swell of her ass. I slapped it, making her jerk up enough that my dick sat at her entrance. I held her hips still, so she could ease her wet pussy on me, making her hiss in agitation.

I pulled my mouth away, kissing up her jawline, gently sucking her lips and tongue. I gripped her tightly, lifting her enough so her breasts were at the level I wanted. I began to tease her nipples with my tongue, circling it around her areolas.

"*Dove*," I groaned.

"Lakyn," she moaned, grasping my locs and pulling me forcefully into her breast.

"*Mine*," she gritted, tightening her grip as she tried to move, but I found myself grinding harder with that word. I let her go, and she slid farther down, making us both groan.

"Fuck Mala," I moaned. I grasped her ass with both hands, bucking her back and forth on my length, sliding further and further inside of her.

"Link, please, baby," she panted. I could feel Mala's pussy trying to grip my dick as her pussy clenched and begged like she knew what was already coming next.

"How long can you hold your breath, Mala? I feel like we should find out," I said against her skin.

"Oh, fuck. Fuck, Link," she cried while quivering from head to toe before drawing me in for another kiss. She lifted herself upward and put her hand on my shoulder for balance.

I shuddered at the loss of her wetness that was trying to slob down my length. Mala removed one hand from my shoulders as she held eye contact. I felt her fingers wrap tightly around my dick as she stroked. She squeezed the head before she guided my dick right to her weeping entrance.

"Are you sure we will not find out how long you can hold your breath?" she asked. Mala stared into my eyes as she rocked her hips slowly over every inch and vein. She bore down on me, causing my head to fall back.

"Shit! Shit," I repeated as her tight walls gripped my dick. I could feel her pussy pulsating and squeezing. The way her wetness was coating me entirely until she was settled at the base of my dick with my balls resting snugly on her ass.

"Fuck, *Dove*, you're gripping me so *damn* hard. Fuck me, Mala."

"Mm, yes," she moaned.

Using the slow lulling motion of the water as her rhythm, she steadily rode my length. Each time the yacht bobbed up, she would push herself up before taking me to the brim when she came down. She slammed my length deep into her wetness. Her thick thighs were restless on either side of my hips, trying to squeeze me as she rode my dick like she was in a rodeo.

"That's it, *Dove*, ride this dick," I groaned, spanking her ass and starting to help her bounce faster on my dick. All I could hear was her panting and our skin slapping along with the water.

"That's right, Mala. Fuck me. We aren't going to stop until you're *limp*."

I used my hands to slam her down, pushing deeper and faster into her walls.

"Get it through your head, *Dove*, it ain't no going back. There is no handling this shit. You came to me willingly, and I ain't fucking letting you leave. Do you understand me? Because I'll fucking kill anyone who even thinks about touching or taking you from me." I promised.

"Yes, yes...ah, you're...so...*deep*, Lakyn, please," she whimpered.

"Deep? Show me how you want it."

Mala's hands gripped the back of my neck as she grinded over my length, slipping further inside as she rotated.

"H-here. I want it right here," Mala stammered out. She pulled away and trailed her finger toward her pelvic region. That was so fucking sexy for some damn reason.

My dick throbbed, and jerked inside of her making her eyes roll to the back of her head. I started to thrust faster and deeper like a man possessed.

I could feel her fingertips on my dick each time she rose and fell hard on my length.

"Take that shit, Mala. Bounce on that dick and take all of it," I chuckled.

"Oh God! Shit, fuck," she screamed.

"All the way up there. Let me feel that pussy cream all over this dick baby. I'm going to stir up your deepest depth. I'll make sure no one will ever be able to make you cum the way I can."

"Lakyn...please," she babbled.

Grinding her hips and curving her back as an offering of her breasts, but I had other ideas. I pushed off the ledge and leaned over, licking a nipple while lowering in the water. I captured a beaded nipple into my mouth as she continued riding me harder, letting her pussy squeeze the shit out of my thickness. I let one of my hands roam the length of her body until it got to her neck. Her face was above the water as her core worked to suck my dick deeper into her womb, trying to fill herself with me as I hit that spot she liked repeatedly.

"Oh fuck! Oh my God! Oh God! Ahh, Link. Shit, Lakyn. Lakyn," she repeated as she circled her hips. The sounds she was making echoed all around me as I squeezed her neck, pulling her harder on my length.

"That shit sexy. Take it, Mala, and scream for more of it," I gritted. Her screams of my name only fueled my insanity. I didn't even know what kind of face I was making as her pleasure slid down my length. Mala trembled and continued riding me as I lowered her more and more into the warm water.

From the angle alone, I began slamming right into the spot between her cervix and walls.

"Shit! Please, Oh God. I'm going to cum. Lakyn! Oh, shit right there. Right there, please," she gasped.

"Fuck, how are you this tight still?"

"B-because...it's made for you."

Ah, she really knew what a nigga needed to know, but I was just glad she understood.

I sped up and egged her on by pulling her lower in the water with only her nose and mouth visible. I knew if we weren't in the water, her juices would be running out of her pussy and drooling all over my balls.

"*Dove*," I grunted. I gripped her neck harder as my other hand used her hip to slam harder. I was getting lightheaded and panting as sweat rolled down my body rapidly as our bodies met deafeningly loud. I used my grip and pulled her out of the water by her throat. I pulled her toward me and licked into her mouth, sucking her tongue as she panted. I licked the roof of her mouth, and she squeezed her walls around my length. Fuck.

"Shit, *shit*, baby, I'm about to—"

"Me too," she cried.

"Fuck!"

I pushed her back down, and this time under the water as I thrust harder, deeper, faster, angling up to hit that spot she liked. Mala's hips bucked as she fought to come up, but I was close. I grinded into her wet pussy, feeling her wall spasming around me, telling me she was about to lose it. I pulled her up, and she sucked in a deep breath as the water slid over her skin like diamonds. Mala pried her eyes open before throwing her head back.

"Come inside of me, Lakyn. I don't want anything between us because that's what it means to be yours, right? I want to feel you inside of me. please...I want... you and everything that comes with it. Fuck it, f-fill me up," she moaned.

While her voice and tone came out innocent and naïve, her hands going to wrap around my neck was an entirely different story. It was like she was telling me she was still the one in charge, using what she knew to dominate me. That was all I needed to push me over the edge when her nails dug into the flesh of my neck.

"Cum for me, Lakyn," she ordered.

I dug my fingers into her quivering hip, hauling her to take my entire length as I erupted inside of her. I could feel my world-shattering as hard spurts of my thick cum filled her up, and I kept pumping until she had it all.

"Take it. Take it all, *Dove*," I grunted, even though I couldn't breathe properly from how hard she was strangling me. The black spots on the edges of my vision appeared, as my hips ground into her, using my body to bump her clit as I pushed down harder. I didn't seem to care in the slightest, even though the black spots were now growing. Mala eased off, and I sucked in a breath as I held her on my dick as it jerked inside of her.

"Who do you belong to? Shout it for the whole world to hear."

"Lakyn!" She screamed as her body jerked and shivered. I felt her walls collapsing around my rigid length. Every inch of my dick was being imprinted inside of her as the rippling waves crashed into her from all sides. I felt my thick semen flooding her as her walls contracted, pulling me deep into her body.

"Fuck!" I screamed.

Mala's hand still was wrapped around my neck, and she tightened it, making my dick jerk while she strangled the remaining air out of me.

Her inner walls sucked the last rope of my cum right out of me. I let go of her hip, reaching back for the rim of the hot tub and sat on the ledge. Mala removed her hand, and I pulled her in for a kiss. We gently rocked to the lull of the yacht. I could feel her shiver as she straddled me, but she wrapped her arms around my neck.

"I won't go anywhere, Lakyn. I see it in your eyes, but I won't, I can't," she whispered against my neck.

I still saw her leaving me every time I closed my eyes, and I hated it.

I needed to ensure she understood her place would always be next to me.

Forever.

MALIKITA 'MALA' SAMUELS

I was lying across the bed in the yacht cabin while Link sat at the desk with the laptop open. I listened as they discussed the niggas from the delivery, Monica, and Landon. I could hear the rage in all of their voices when they found out where the signal was going. Shantel didn't say a word, and they quickly breezed past that subject. I knew the four of them would deal with that shit later.

Everything was running through my mind. How and where was the footage? I rolled to the side of the bed and stood when I heard Henny asking about Charles. I knew it had come time for me to say what I had dreaded for years. I was sure they all knew the bare minimum the night I had to leave when Charles showed up, but with everything else going on, it got pushed to the side.

"So not only was this nigga Charles playing us on this hostage bullshit, but he's fucking Rodney? Both of them niggas ain't doing shit but adding more nails to their fucking coffins," Henny grumbled.

"When I went to place a tracker on Charles car, I noticed that two were already there. One of them had to be from Rodney because the other was ours," Link stated. He cut his eyes at me to tell me to get over here. But I was stuck because that's who was in his office that day when I ran into Link.

"I think Rodney has an idea about what Charles has, but Charles likes to play games and shit. He's probably stringing Rodney along, but all that is going to stop soon, apparently he's reopening the case he had on Theodore Banks. From the information I got on Rodney's files, it got shut down quickly a few years ago, and I think it was because Charles made it happen. It fits," Link said.

"So, the Banks nigga is fucking with Charles too? Shit, is he fucking Monica?" Oz asked.

"No, I can tell you that upfront. He's not fucking any women whatso-ever. But he is very good at what he does, and that's manipulation, telling a person exactly what they need to hear to comply," I sighed as I stepped into view of the screen dressed much like Shantel. For the most part, she always had on somebody's clothes. Today, I could tell it was Oz's. The large black and gold hoodie that said Wiz on the hood and the way too large shirt said it all. I saw Crescent looking slightly tired, and I could tell she seemed less like herself when she smiled at me. She moved closer to Faxx, who adjusted himself so she could lay on his chest. The tattoo on her arm made me smile, and she smirked. I mouthed 'celebration' at her, and she shook her head, looking at Shantel. I cut my eyes over to her, knowing damn well she had to be already planning something. She nodded before looking in her lap, which told me she was on her phone. Link reached out and pulled me down in the chair next to him, forcibly moving it closer. He pulled my hand into his lap and held it as usual. He wasn't a touchy-feely person, but it was entirely the opposite with me. Henny looked over me, and I caught the slight tightening in his expression. I was wearing a pair of jeans and a black tee shirt with Link's hoodie zipped to my chin, and Henny's quick glance had me nervously messing with the zipper. Fuck, fuck, fuck! I was going to hear it. I know someway somehow this nigga was going to show up out of the fucking blue and corner me. I knew it wasn't because of Link's situation and me, but because of Charles. His light honey-brown eyes shifted and narrowed in Cent's direction. She closed her eyes like if she did that nobody could see her ass. Then, they moved to Link, and he r aised a brow.

"And we still don't know where Banks is?" Henny stated. The tightness I saw in his jawline was a little more of a statement. I knew them all, but I knew my cousin very well, and this nigga was pissed. I just didn't know if it was me, Cent, or this entire fucking hot ass mess we found ourselves in. Oz, Henny, and Shantel were the only ones at the CLINIC. Link, me, Cent, and Faxx were on video. Another screen popped up, and that fine-ass nigga Ian came on. He sat back in his chair, arm extended across his desk as he nodded a greeting. I didn't miss the quick glance he threw at Shantel. And I definitely didn't miss her shift positions. Gone was the lounging over the table, picking at Henny's sleeve to annoy him. She picked with him so he would ignore her and wouldn't pay attention to what she was doing, but I guess there was no longer a need for it when she sat her phone on the conference table.

"No, I don't think anyone knows where he is. If Roman or Alex had Banks, then Roman wouldn't be coming so hard at us. Yes, he wants Cent, but he would have already come at us if they had the USB. Meaning if he had Banks, they would've already been on Charles's ass for another one," Link surmised. Henny looked at me and pressed his lips together before breathing.

"Do you know anything about Charles and Banks?" Henny questioned.

"No, not until last week, at least. I knew there was someone, but not who. He would go away occasionally, and I finally tagged his car when they all became lax. Since I was looked at as complying, they didn't see what I was doing," I said, looking at each of them. No one said a word, and when I glanced at Oz he was staring at me, drumming his fingers across the table. Fuck! I wasn't worried about Faxx because he already knew what was up. It was those two I was worried about. Oz leaned forward and stared into the screen until my eyes focused on his cognac-colored ones.

"Malikita, I want you to finish. I want you to say it all, so we know who and what we are dealing with. Then after this is all said and done, I'm going to beat your ass," Oz warned. I squeezed the fuck out of Link's hand. I looked at him, and he was busy looking at his damn watch. I looked at Crescent her eyes were wide. She pointed to herself like, '*Remember me bitch, he'll do it.*' I knew that. Damn it.

"Ahh, see this...ahh—"

"*Dove*, start at the grandparents' house," Link said, facing me. I closed my eyes and opened them to see everyone staring at me. Ian's head tilted to the side, and Oz leaned closer. I drew in a deep breath and released it slowly.

"Okay. So, after I left at eighteen the first night, I tried to kill this nigga. And I would have, if he proved to me how things were set up. If he were to disappear or die, all of you would've gone down. Once I saw that, I knew I had to change my entire strategy, but he told me we needed to see his grandparents for approval. I can count on one hand how many times I met his mother and father over the years. As for his grandparents, mainly his grandfather, I've only seen those people once," I grinned.

"Mr. Cornelius Phineas Astor," Ian smiled as he watched me. His smile was sexy as shit, but I could see beyond it. Ian's eyes reminded me of Cornelius in a way. They were cold, calculating, and dissecting.

"I am sure you know my dislike for the man," I said, nodding.

"We know who they are, but they never tried us like Alex has," Henny said, leaning an elbow on the table. He rested his chin on his fist and frowned. He squinted at me and then sat up straight.

"How did he threaten you? That family has long, old money, and that's what they do," Henny stated.

"When he asked Charles to get him something, he told me how Charles loved his little games. Cornelius said that this game he's running this time may be more lucrative and that he will do whatever to keep playing until he's ready to stop. But, since Charles acknowledged he would never stop until he was dead, his grandaddy added his two cents," I laughed bitterly. I looked at Henny before gliding at Oz and then at Ian.

"He threw old pictures on the table and pointed at each of them as he told me, and these were his exact words, *'You will keep playing. If you do not, what happened to Ian's mother,'* who I didn't know at the time, *'and the whore who is mother to your little friend along with yours will get the same treatment,'* and he smiled. I swallowed as my throat went dry. Link leaned into the screen, his near-black eyes burning with hate.

"And he said that my mother, Stephanie, and Vanessa would all die the same way," he grunted.

"Is that why you put in the order for extra measures?" Faxx questioned. Link shook his head as he leaned back. Ian sat forward with his hand clenched in a fist while Oz bit down on his lip as he stroked his beard.

"Yes, it's needed because we don't know who it is that they used to accomplish that shit," Link complained. Ian cracked his neck, and Shantel seemed to stiffen in her seat. Henny looked over at his screen, and I could see the aggravation and fire in his eyes. My mother was the only parent figure he now had, so I knew he was feeling it. Just like I knew he was going to pull me up.

"Lawe, tell me you got something," Henny demanded. Ian looked at me before taking a breath and blowing it out. His clenched fist was the only thing that told how mad he truly was.

"Fuck no. This person is a ghost or protected more than I am. I've always known that family had a hand in the murder of our mothers, but nothing I could find told me who the fuck it was. We know who put the hit out, but even Cornelius would never say the name," he fumed. "They come from older, harder stock, and have enough money and power not to be afraid of people that come after them," Ian seethed. Everyone was quiet for a long moment until Oz stood up and stepped around the black leather chair. He placed both palms on the top of the desk and leaned into the screen.

"They aren't afraid because they haven't met the right fucking niggas," he gritted. His eyes seemed to darken when he turned to look at me.

"I completely understand your reasoning, Mala, but we all know you are still catching it just like another person. Crescent don't think I can't see your thick ass because your eyes are closed," Oz grunted. Faxx smirked and tightened his grip on her. I could tell the last week was replaying in his head on a loop, and the only thing that would stop it was when everyone who was an immediate threat was dead.

"I have been properly punished, Oz. Come on," Crescent said, sitting up. Henny looked at her before he started to chuckle.

"Work wife, the fact that you think you have, is comical," he said, tapping his lip. Henny looked at Ian, then at Faxx, Oz, Shantel, Link, and me.

"First thing is first. We need to find that nigga Teddy because I am one hundred percent sure Charles told him where the original is. Then kill Charles and his entire fucking family. Well, the Astor part, not y'all niggas. All the while taking out these fucking people who keep testing us. We got hostages, use them, find more fucking answers. But, until we know everything, the streets run red. When I say streets, I don't just mean Union. If we're taking Clapton, Puafton and Del Mar, bloody them bitches too," he said, slamming his palm to the table. Oz pushed off the desk and slapped Henny's shoulder but stopped with his finger up.

"You know what? Shandea would've killed me if I had forgotten this. We're throwing Cent a little welcome party at *MYTH* this weekend. Since she wants to see the lower levels, I guess I can get her in," Oz smirked.

"Daddy Dom Oz, see, this is why I fucks with you," Crescent danced. She looked over at our screen and grinned. "Is the Black Wolf going—"

Faxx's screen cut out, and Link laughed before closing the laptop.

"That girl is dumb as hell," he chuckled, pulling out his phone. He put it on speaker.

"What nigga?" Faxx barked.

"Master Zaddy, help me! He's crazy, and he got me tied to this bed and—"

"What are you doing to that girl?" I asked.

"She aight, now what do you want, Link," Faxx snapped. Link's dumb ass was damn near on the floor laughing.

"Yo, yo wait, tell my Phatty Cake I'm going to try and be— did this nigga hang up?" he screamed. The phone started to ring again, and I hit the accept button.

"Hello," I said, giggling.

"Mala put this nigga on the phone," Faxx grumbled.

"It's on speaker he can hear you," I answered.

"Nigga, make sure you pick up my baby tomorrow, and don't be late! Her '*friennnd*' Travis is coming for a play date," he said.

"The Chucky doll?! I guess...whatever makes her happy," Link agreed.

"And when you find those flat ass tires on your car, don't fucking call me for no ride or to pay for shit because fuck you, my nigga," Faxx threatened.

"Hold up, hold up for real, don't hang up. I just wanted to ask Crescent a serious question," Link said, clearing his throat.

"Anything you need to ask my wife, you ask me first," Faxx said, sucking his teeth.

"All I really need to know is if she's going to let me lay on them soft ass pillows she calls titties and—"

The phone disconnected, and I slapped Link's shoulder as hard as possible.

"Why do you keep fucking with that crazy ass nigga?"

"Because it helps him to refocus. Did you see it," he said sobering. I blinked, knowing Link was right because the black of Faxx's eyes hadn't changed. If anything, they looked...COLDER.

"I do. But I absolutely feel you on that shit 'cause those titties do look soft as fuck," I laughed.

"See! This is what I mean," he chuckled. I stared at him, and I loved it when he laughed because he was always so fucking serious. He only became Lakyn around his family.

"*Dove*, you keep watching me like that, and I'm going to bend you over that railing and fuck the shit out of you."

I stood up with a smile because it was what I wanted, but I also knew we had shit to do.

"Too bad we need to see a man about a late delivery," I said, pulling on his locs.

I followed Link as we made our way from the docks and up the hill to the *FARM*. The large white house sat further back than the other smaller buildings on the land. I looked around, trying to take it in because this was a working farm.

"You really went and did it, Link. I can't believe you have this place really running like a full-on farm," I exclaimed. Link looked over his shoulder because my ass was walking all extra slow with my mouth open. He legit had farm animals on this bitch like it wasn't used to make bodies disappear.

"We said that we wanted a place away from the city. You said that you wanted a farm because you wanted horses and shit. But it's a good investment and a huge tax write-off," he answered. Link stopped before a medium-sized building and held his hand out for me to catch up. Everything he said was true because I couldn't take my eyes off the horses grazing in the field. I felt his hand wrap around my wrist as he pulled me into the building that smelled like chemicals. I turned to face him as the door shut behind us. The building opened up in a large open area where men and women moved between large steel containers.

"You say tax write-off, and I say it's a great way to hide a counterfeit operation," I laughed.

"Potato tomato," he shrugged as he waved over an older man.

"What?" I laughed as the dark-skinned man's brows raised for a quick second before he noticed who was waving him over.

"What? Why are you acting like you can't hear me?" he frowned.

I watched as the man handed the woman next to him his clipboard and walked toward us.

"You do understand that is not how you say it, right? Or are you fucking with me," I questioned.

"If you say so."

"Nigga, I know so," I laughed. He squeezed my hand as the man stopped in front of us.

"Mr. Tom, how is everything looking? Will the next batch be sent out on time?" Link asked, pulling me forward. Tom looked at me and back to his boss, kinda nervous.

"Ahh, yes, yes, it's just that—"

"Mr. Tom, my name is Mala. It's a pleasure to meet you," I said, holding my right hand. Tom rubbed his left hand on his jeans before taking my hand firmly.

"It is a pleasure to meet you as well."

"Great. So, tell me what seems to be the problem. By the look of things, it's like you're running a tight ship," I smiled. Tom relaxed slightly and smiled down at me as he pushed his gold-wired framed glasses up on his nose. He had to be in his late fifties, but he still looked good, just scared. This man was an entire nerd in these streets.

"Yes, yes, I do. There isn't a problem on my end, but there has been a problem with receiving the needed ink," he huffed.

"Really? Let me know your problem, and we will see how to address it. Whatever problems you have in the future regarding this, please get in touch with me," I said, pulling my hand from Link's. I reached into his hoodie pocket and pulled out my phone.

"Yes, sure, that is not a problem at all," he said with relief in his eyes. I glanced at Link and shook my head. This man was too scared to fucking talk to this nigga.

"Great. Let me see your watch," I pointed. I held my phone over it, and my information transferred to it and his to my phone.

"Now, tell me about this problem, and it will be handled," I smiled again. I stuck the phone back into my pocket, and Link reclaimed my hand again.

I stood there as Tom explained the hold-up at the airport because the routine had changed. Tom talked to me the whole time without looking in Link's direction. That's what I wanted because I could tell this man was scared as fuck. I held up my hand to stop Tom in his sentence.

"Got it. Use what you have available, and we will take care of the rest," I nodded. I watched the tightness in Tom's shoulders ease as he nodded, thanking me before walking away. I waited for a minute before looking at Link.

"What?"

"Why the hell do you have that man so scared he could barely get his words out?" I asked.

"That's why I brought you here first, or it would've taken all fucking day," he answered. I stared at him, but he tugged me toward a set of metal stairs that led to an upstairs office.

"That wasn't my question, Kyte. Why do you have that man stuttering?"

Link ran a hand through his locs, chuckling, as we descended the stairs.

"Probably because the last time there was a problem, I pushed his partner into that," he pointed. I looked over the railing and into what looked like water, but the smell told me it wasn't. I knew it was the chemical used to wash the money and create the new bills.

"So, you over here playing Batman and trying to create a Joker," I said, leaning back. Link opened the door and held it until I entered. There were only three chairs, a massive metal desk, and a couch. I heard him chuckling as he closed the door and locked it.

"Naw, but it ensured there wasn't another mistake," he said. I looked at him as he walked past me and over to a door I wouldn't have noticed until he pointed it out. He typed in a code, and it opened. I followed behind me, and the door shut on its own.

"And the mistake was…"

"He hired a family member to deliver the bills where they needed to go. The nigga stole one of the boxes, so—"

"So, they both had to pay for it. I got it," I said, following him down a set of stairs. Where the other building was warmer than usual, it was cold as fuck here. We hit the bottom, and he pushed open another door, and the smell of animals, hay, and whatever else you could think of on a farm assaulted my nose.

"Yeah, and ever since this nigga be stuttering, but I knew you could handle it," he said. I rolled my eyes, then pressed my lips together, trying not to say a word. He'd done exactly what we talked about on his own and never said anything about it.

"So, you really used my idea?"

Link stopped walking and turned around, seeing me still at the door. My heart began to beat rapidly as he stalked back in my direction. His hand slid up my neck and I was mesmerized by the small wolf tattoo he had on his hand. Link tipped my head back and looked down at me. His dark brown eyes felt like they were staring into my soul, but this time, he wasn't about to let go.

"Yes, I used our dream Malikita. That was the only thing I had left when you walked away," he said, staring down into my eyes.

"You...you know why I had—"

My air was cut off as his hand grew tighter around my neck, and he leaned closer, his lips ghosting over mine.

"And it won't fucking happen again, *Dove*. Now help me make sure niggas understand what it's like fucking with U.C.K.," he whispered. I flicked my tongue out, and he grabbed it with his teeth before he parted my lips. If I didn't know any better I would've thought this nigga was trying to take the rest of the air from my lungs. His hand eased, and he pulled away, leaving me slightly dizzy. I reached out and gripped his bicep to steady myself as I sucked in the air.

"Oh.... okay," I panted. "Let's get it done," I said, licking my bottom lips as he stared at me. His long locs were loose around his shoulders. He ran another hand through it before looking over his shoulder.

"Mmmmmm, mmmmmm,mmmmm," Ràul tried to scream.

The interior of a dimly lit barn was similar to what I saw before with Shantel and the girls. I looked around and noticed that it was the same barn we had just entered from a different direction. I followed Link to one of the stalls where a red-faced screaming Ràul sat tied down to a chair next to a metal table with a drain. As I stood facing him, his head was covered with a black cloth bag. Link tore the bag off his head, and his shifty-looking eyes darted around the room. His brown gaze landed on me, and they widened until Link leaned down in his line of vision.

"Welcome to my *FARM* Ràul. I heard you had some information I needed. Tell us what we need to know, and you will be able to drive your ass right out of here alive," Link smirked. Link stood up and moved back over toward me. He leaned against the wooden wall with his arms crossed, a steely look in his dark eyes that stayed trained on Ràul. I took a deep breath, regaining Ràul's attention, and he shifted nervously in his chair, trying to avoid my gaze. I walked closer to his, reaching down to rip the black tap from his mouth.

"Ahh. Ahh, shit. Come on, I don't know anything more than what I gave you," he cried.

I leaned in close to Ràul and smiled.

"You know why you're here, Ràul? Just like you know what came out of your mouth is a lie. We have evidence about the signal, and you already gave up the location for it, but we both know that's not all you know," I said, tapping his nose.

Ràul already stunk of sweat, but beads of perspiration began to appear on his temple even though it was cold as fuck. He closed his mouth, trying to remain defiant as I walked around him.

"I...I don't know what you're talking about. I ain't done nothin' else but what I was told. We picked up the truck at the spot and took it to the Casino. That's it. The older dude and the big one was always there like shit was all good," he rushed out.

"Cut the shit, Ràul. We know you're involved. We just need to know where your people are located in Union City. Because I'm sure they all know that Union belongs to U.C.K., and ain't shit happening without our say-so," I screamed.

Ràul began to shake his head. I reached out and grabbed a handful of his brown hair and yanked his head back. I held out my hand and felt the rubber grip of my Sickle Machete. I stepped around the back of his chair and brought the machete to his throat. It cupped the place under his chin perfectly, and I could tell the cool metal of it seemed to burn his hot skin.

"I don't know! I don't know. I don't know what you're talking about! I'm just a middleman! I'm nothing to the Cartel but a runner. Now...wait...wait—"

He screamed as I pulled the blade tighter, causing a trickle of blood to run down his neck.

"Oh my God," he screamed again as he started to pray in Spanish.

I looked at Link, and he stepped forward, his expression cold and intimidating. He squatted down in front of Ràul and rubbed his hands together.

"You don't want to play it this way, Ràul. Trust me. I could have some-one else deliver the same fucking message, but we're choosing you. But if you don't answer her fucking questions, I'll be forced to take you over there," he nodded to the corner. There was a large trough filled with a dark fluid. Link moved and grabbed Ràul by the collar while using his other hand to unlock the bolted chair to the ground. I pulled back just as Link pulled him and the chair toward the trough as Ràul screamed.

"No, no, wait, you don't understand. The one you killed was the nephew of....wait, no, no—"

"You're either going to tell us everything we want to know," Link urged. He pushed Ràul's head down, causing the chair to flip up and his chest to hit the burned metal container. Link looked up at me as he held Ràul's head under dirty ass water.

"You might want to break that one in on Monica instead of this piece of shit," Link said in conversation. I looked at the silver and black sickle machete and smiled at the thought.

"You might be right, but it did make him piss himself, though," I said, nodding at Ràul. Link pulled back while I used my foot to push the leg bar of the chair. Link used the back of Ràul's neck to haul him out of the water just as I pushed, causing the chair to slam back to the ground. The shit was weird and natural with us. It was like time was never missed, but I knew that wasn't the case.

"Might as well make it easy on yourself," I said. Ràul took in raged breaths as rivulets of water ran from his hair and down his reddened face.

"Please! Please! I don't—"

I slammed my fist across his face. I pulled back and did it four more times, causing blood to run from his mouth.

"This nigga is beginning to look like Rocky after the Russian whipped his ass," Link chuckled. I looked up at him, and I knew his ass was enjoying this shit. I shook my head as Ràul wheezed and spluttered.

"Please, I'll die if I—"

Link moved so fast I barely saw him. He grabbed Ràul by his face and pushed his head back, making him look him in the eyes.

"Nigga do you really believe I won't fucking kill you right here? At least they will just probably take your head. Naw, naw, not me. I'm going to make it last and make sure it hurts while I do it. Place your bet and see which mutha fucka will do worse because I guarantee them bitches ain't got shit on me. Speak my nigga," Link ordered.

He pushed Ràul's head backward before punching him in his stomach over and over until Ràul began to cough up the water he'd ingested. Link back away as I kicked the chair to its side just as the water spilled from his lips. I watched as Link squatted down to watch as Ràul choked and coughed up blood and water.

"Okay, okay, okay, just plee...please don't send me back—"

I folded my arms across my chest as I tapped the machete against my arm, narrowing my eyes at Ràul before flicking to Link. He nodded and stood back up to his six foot three height.

"Then start talking, Ràul. We don't have all day," I ordered

Ràul coughed again as he shook in his restraints as the coldness of the stall started to creep in.

"It's...It's—"

Link leaned down, lifting the chair and Ràul up so he could talk. I stepped into his line of sight, looking into his red-rimmed brown eyes. His body was shaking, and his lips trembled as tears rolled from his eyes.

"It...it all happened because of Monica. She's the one behind Redd and Quinton's involvement even though they didn't know."

"So, you're telling me that she's working for the Cartel? And I'm supposed to believe that bullshit?" I asked. Honestly, I wouldn't put it past her ass to be working for them or unknowingly working for them. I glanced over my shoulder as Link stepped closer to my back. His strong hands gripped my waist as he massaged circles against my skin.

"She's the one that took the money and chose the location because she said no one would ever look there. And she was right because no one came to that place even after it was rebuilt. Monica didn't know about our involvement until it had already started. She screamed about a man named Charles but...but...from...from what I know, we gained her assistance through a mutual contact. Alex Tilderman. All I did was follow orders. I have kids, man...I have little ones, you understand," he cried.

"So, where is she?" I asked, trying to control my excitement. I had felt my phone buzzing in my pants, but I knew who it was. It was no one but Charles sending threats and still believing he had the upper hand.

"I was going to say we can set shit off tomorrow because I believe a lot will be going down at the same time. From what I can see, Faxx is on a mission to shut down every fucking business Roman and Alex owned. So, this right here will just add more insult to injury while taking down that fucking building. There should have never been anything on those grounds, and it won't be after tomorrow," Link promised.

"I need to call Shantel. I know this brought up a lot of shit with her," I said absently. Link stopped and grabbed my wrist, pulling me to his side. His arm slid around my waist as he led me across the gravel road and to the large tractor-trailer truck where Konceited probably rigged some psycho shit up. Link squeezed my hip, showing me that he already knew how I felt about this shit with Shantel and how if I had just caught the bus with her that day, she would've never been taken. It was exactly what had been running through my mind since the meeting.

"You had to make up a test that day, Mala. Even if you were there, they would have only taken you both. How about we go find out what your muscle has done to these machines," he said. I knew he was trying to ease a guilt that would never disappear. But I loved him for trying. At least he understood how that emotion worked.

"How about we do that first, and after you help me figure out how to duck Oz and Henny," I suggested.

"Naw, *Dove*, sometimes you must take the punishment you deserve. As for Hendrix, he's going to catch your ass either way. Toughen up and take it like a big girl," he said, slapping my ass.

"Fuck you, Kyte. Fuck you."

I barely wanted to open my eyes, but I could no longer ignore the warm body between my thighs. I rethought my request after we looked over the truck and the machines. Konceited had each machine connected to some kind of water-cooling system so that once the truck reached its destination, it would automatically kick on, and each would begin playing a game. Any combination of three in a row would cause it to explode. I just shook my head while Link mumbled about him stealing an idea he had in camp. These niggas were crazy as shit, but it was what it was. Henny called me twice last night, and I didn't hit ignore, but I ignored it. I knew it was only making shit worse, but I just wasn't ready for the third, fourth, and fifth degree of bullshit. Then I sat and watched Link rigged up something in the truck so it would drive to where Shantel was held all those years ago. When Ràul said the coordinates of the place, I didn't catch on. It wasn't until I received all the rest of the information before confronting Monica that I knew what it was. I was ready to dead that bitch as well, but it was all in due time.

"Mmmm, baby fuck," I moaned. My hands roamed down my body to the top of Link's head. I fisted his locs in my hand and pressed him harder onto my clit. The circular motion of his tongue had my hips moving and my core seeking something to latch onto.

I pulled at his locs, causing him to raise his head slightly. Dark brown eyes stared at me as he flicked his tongue and slurped my clit between his lips.

"Oh fuck," I groaned. Link closed his eyes and inhaled deeply, savoring my taste like breakfast. He pulled away, my juices covering his beard as he licked his lips.

"*Dove*, lay back and let me finish my food. I need a balanced breakfast to get through the day," he rasped.

I held my breath as his hand skimmed my thighs, and his finger slid down my slit. I watched as he twisted his index finger into my velvety walls.

"Oh, shit, fuck Lakyn," I cried out. The warmness of his tongue greeted the bundle of nerves that he knew would send shivers of delight down my spine. With small, delicious swipes of his tongue, my hips began to rock, but he used his other hand to hold me down. He pulled his mouth away and opened his eyes as he pulled his finger out. My juices clung to his finger, and he brought it to his lips while he stroked my thigh softly.

"You taste so good, Mala. I need you to spread wider for me, *Dove*," he demanded.

With slow, deliberate motions, he traced the outline of my mouth with his finger as I did what he asked. I parted my lips and began sucking his finger the way I wanted to suck his dick. I savored the sensation of his finger moving gently in and out of my mouth. A soft sigh escaped my lips when he moved his other hand and slapped my pussy, making my clit throb. I savored the anticipation of the impending orgasm I knew was going to come when he pulled out his finger.

Then, with a glint in his eyes, he slowly slid his two fingers back into my entrance, twisting them before rubbing against the ridges and hitting my g-spot.

"Oh God! Shit, Lakyn, please, I'm going to cu—"

"I want you to cum. I want to taste that delicious cream. I want you to cum down my throat," Link smirked. Link leaned back between my legs, licking and sucking at my clit while moving his fingers in and out. He pulled them out and stuck his tongue between my fold and sucked. Oh my God, he was sucking me like that fucking peach, and I was going to pass the fuck out. He pulled back and stuffed three fingers in this time as my cream coated his lips, beard, and tongue. He closed his eyes and let out a content hum, reveling in the decadent pleasure.

"Link! Fuck Lakyn, I'm going to cum," I panted. Link leaned down, his movements never slowing as his mouth covered my pussy. Each touch of his tongue against my skin, my clit, or inside my walls sent ripples of pleasure through me, causing my hips to buck and my mind to break into pieces. The way he used his tongue, lips, and teeth had me feeling as if the sheer decadence of the experience was carrying me away. I felt like my head was in the clouds as wave after wave of pleasure assaulted me. I felt the dam break, and I screamed.

"Fuck! Oh, shit, baby, I'm cumming," I moaned. I felt his strong hand on my hip holding me down, but my other leg wrapped around his head while I pulled at his locs, not knowing if I wanted him closer or to push him away.

"Ahh, please, please, baby, ple—"

I knew I was rambling, but with each flick of his tongue and twist of his finger, my body jerked, and I knew his face would be covered in my essence. I was so sensitive now that even the slight brush of his beard shook my body.

"Mmm, thank you, *Dove*. Now, I can get through the rest of the day. Just think about how you could've woken up each day," he smiled. This nigga was petty as fuck, but words made no sense when I opened my mouth.

"I...I...oh shii—"

With a satisfied sigh, he leaned back, pulling his fingers free, looking utterly content and rejuvenated by the intimate and indulgent experience.

I blinked as my body and brain began to turn back on when the golden light sunbathed the room in a warm, comforting glow.

"Get up, *Dove*. We need to kill a few niggas before picking up Cece. We also need to find a present for Shandea. You are good with that baby shit," he chuckled, looking down at me. I swallowed as his words hit me while his warm body moved away.

"Wait, what? Who's planning the baby shower?" I asked, pushing myself up on my elbows. I watched Link pull his hair into a ponytail before entering the connected bathroom. If I were being honest, sleeping in the farmhouse was the best rest I have ever had in eight years. It just felt like home.

"Henny said he's been trying to call you to talk about it," he said over the running water. I pressed my lips together before swinging my legs over the side of the massive bed. I stood on wobbly legs, knowing damn well that Dr. Pharma was being fucking slick, but now I had to call him.

After we showered, I still did not call Henny's ass back. It would be better to do this in person. Maybe he could see my sad eyes and get over it. I knew what he was feeling, and he had every right to be pissed the fuck off. Vanessa was also practically his mother. The threat to her life, that he knew nothing about, probably wasn't sitting right with him at all. I followed the path with Link slightly ahead of me to where Monica was being held. I wanted to take her ass out to the fucking lake and drown her, but this way would make a bigger statement. We needed to make everyone understand that we were onto them, including the Cartel. I wasn't sure how Link would make that happen, but I fully trusted his abilities.

"*Dove*, try not to kill her yet. She has a role to play," Link said, stopping in front of a smaller building. It looked like a place where you would keep tools, but I knew what it was because Katrice had the misfortune of staying here.

"Baby, it's you that we need to worry about. I managed to control my anger, and I beat her ass yesterday," I seethed. I felt the wave of anger wash over me again as I gripped the handle of the sickle machete. I was in love with this thing. It gave such fond memories of me taking out that doctor who refused to help my father. I bet if he could've made that decision over again, he would have. Pieces of his body were probably still in a duffle bag chained to a cement brick at the bottom of Blackbay.

"I always keep my cool, *Dove*. It's not like I haven't suspected her already. Now it's just having to remove the tattoo from her body," he said, pushing open the door.

I walked alongside Link, my heart pounding in my chest as we entered the small, nondescript building. The air was thick with tension and the weight of the task ahead, but there was no sympathy. Monica was once a member of U.C.K., but her betrayal landed her in this position. It was like she forgot who and what we were. Sometimes, I forget how we appear to people looking from the outside. We'd fooled many people over the years, but she should've known better. She aligned herself with Charles, and that nigga played her like a fiddle. She was selling out her services and tech knowledge for his own agenda. Even if he hadn't known that Alex was fucking with the Cartel, he was still fucked up for what he was doing. All these people threatened our territory, and we couldn't let anyone escape it. Not only will Monica lose her tattoo, but also her fucking life. It was a waste of manpower and talent. It was also a slap in the face of her brother's memory. All he'd done for her to live a good life, and she tossed that shit out the window.

The small, dimly lit hallway stretched before us, our footsteps echoing off the walls. The place felt like a sterile clinic, and that's exactly what it was. I saw a black duffle bag sitting next to the door and frowned. Link swung it open without a word, revealing a small room and Monica. She lay on a hospital bed in the corner, her eyes wide with fear as she looked up at us. I could see the guilt and desperation in her eyes, but it was too late for a second chance. She could have gotten out of it and had plenty of time to come clean. Monica had made her choice, and now she had to face the consequences.

"Monica, you know why we're here. You betrayed us, and now you're going to tell us everything else you know about the Cartel's operations," I said, my voice cold and steady.

Monica's eyes darted between Link and me, and I could see the fear in her expression. She held Link's black gaze but looked away quickly. I knew what she saw, and there was no longer life in them, only the cold grip of death when he looked at her now. I shivered slightly because I never wanted them to be aimed at me. His silence said it all, and Monica knew it. She gave me a lot of information, but it wasn't everything. She was holding cards close because she figured if she told Link, he would show mercy. There wouldn't be any mercy this time, though. It was called before but reiterated in the meeting. Henny wanted scorched earth, and that's what he would ge t.

Monica began to stammer, trying to devise excuses, but we wouldn't let her talk her way out of this. Link walked over to the bed and grabbed her by the arm.

"Link, please. I wasn't thinking straight. I—"

"Monica, I would stop fucking talking unless it's to show me and Mala how you're going to redeem yourself. Anything other than that is just a bunch of bullshit running out of your mouth," Link gritted. He pulled her out of the bed and to her feet, his expression hard and unforgiving.

"Ahh! Wai—" she started before he threw her into a chair in the corner. The chair was tall, and it had an arm that you could move around to make it easier to draw blood. Link pulled at the same arm, turning it around until the inside faced up. The small U.C.K. and crown tattoo showed back at us like a taunt.

"Listen, Monica, we know everything that you've done. The worst thing you could have done wasn't to steal my projects, but it was choosing that location. That fucking location you knew should've remained dead!

You've been given every chance to tell us, hell, tell me about what was happening, but you chose the wrong. Now, you're going to die where you thought it was safe. You, of all people, should know the price of disloyalty. You disgust me, and I know for sure you would've disgusted Deon," Link s aid.

"You! How dare you say his name! If it weren't for you, he would still be here. If it weren't for you, he wouldn't have been in this sick fucking life," she screamed. Monica struggled against Link's grip, but she was not strong enough to break free. I could see the internal conflict in her eyes, the anger warring with her desperation to save herself from death. I knew we had to push her to the breaking point if we were going to get the information we needed. I stepped closer, raising the machete and placing the blade on her arm right above her tattoo.

"Deon died protecting family! He died on the same ground you've been betraying us on! He died by the hand of the people who would have taken your body and sold it at an auction. You wanted to please your little boyfriend and dishonored your brother while doing it. At least die with some fucking dignity and tell us everything. Maybe keep your tattoo, knowing you did what you should have done long ago," I commanded. I knew my voice was biting. The tension in the room was thick as fuck as Monica stared between us with hate, but the pressure of the blade had her fear winning out.

"Every detail about their operations, who their leaders are, and their plans. We need to know it all, Monica, or the tattoo won't be the only piece of skin I remove today," I hissed.

For a moment, she hesitated as she blinked rapidly, trying to hold back the tears that ran down her swollen face.

"Fuck it, take it, Mala," Link commanded. With a flick of my wrist, the machete moved, cutting through her flesh like butter. With one quick motion, her U.C.K. tattoo was on the floor below our feet.

"Ahhh, ahhh, ahhh, oh my God, please! I don't know. I don't know anymore," she screamed. Link let her arm go and moved behind her, grabbing something from the small table. Before I knew it, he had a clear plastic bag over her head, pulling tightly over her face as she screamed.

"Did you want to take Cece to the mall? I'm thinking about a newer tablet for her since she's getting older," Link asked casually.

"That's fine, but you can't be mean to her boyfriend," I laughed. I held down Monica's hands as she jerked and kicked her long legs in the chair.

"Boyfriend? What boyfriend? She doesn't have my permission for a boyfriend," Link said seriously. Link released the bag and pulled it over her head as Monica drew in a deep breath.

"Oh my God, Link. You and Konceited are ridiculous about this shit. It's Travis. The damn doll," I laughed. Monica heaved and coughed as Link screwed up his face.

"Ppp—please—" Monica wheezed before coughing again. She took another breath, but Link placed the bag back over her face before she managed another one.

"I really wish I installed the chairs and tub like at the cabin," he said, looking down as Monica clawed at his arms.

"You should have it done if there is room. It probably would only be one, though," I shrugged. I fought Monica and grabbed her arms, pinning them down.

"Now, about this damn doll. I need to talk to Faxx about this boyfriend shit. I mean, I guess it could be worse. At least she's not old enough to think she can have one. It's probably those triplets! Well, at least two of them. I know it's Santina, and Santara is filling her head up about it. I'm going to pull up on their asses when shit dies down," Link warned. I rolled my eyes, making a mental note to warn them about the incoming bullshit coming their way. Link released Monica again, and I let her go. Her arms flew to her neck as she coughed and sucked in air, trying to fill her lungs in case she

got the bag again. I leaned down and pulled at the short strands of her hair
.

"Are your lungs burning yet? It's only going to get worse," I taunted. I dropped her head and stepped back as she coughed, holding a shaky hand.

"Please...pl...please. I'll tell you all...all that I know," she gasped. Then the floodgates opened. She started to speak, her words tumbling out in a rush as she revealed everything she had learned since turning her back on us. The Cartel's smuggling routes, distribution networks, and contacts within the city government. The fact that since removing the old mayor, U.C.K. effectively removed the person that was making shit easy for them. Link glanced at me, and I breathed, figuring this was probably why they'd been at us. Apparently, trying to get us to join them was their first attempt, but that failed. Jakobe and his plan failed, so it left a war.

It was all laid bare before us, and I felt a surge of grim satisfaction as the puzzle pieces fell into place. They were trying to surround us and use the people who wanted us out of the way to do the work for them. I saw it in Link's eyes that he felt the same. He typed something on his watch, and I was sure this little scene was recorded and sent out to everyone, so they knew how to proceed.

Monica had fucked up and found out, and now she was feeling it. Knowing who her brother was to us brought a tiny bit of pity to the forefront because this would have gutted him. But loyalty to U.C.K. and our determination to protect our territory overrode any sense of pity.

After what felt like an eternity, Monica finally fell silent, her eyes downcast as she realized the magnitude of her betrayal. Blood rolled down her arm as Link moved around the chair to leave the room, but only long enough to grab the bag. I raised my brows as he threw it to the bed and pulled out a vest.

"Oh, are we pulling a Faxx today?" I laughed.

"You know, sometimes his methods of creating a sandstorm are valid. I want that place to be dust, and Monica will do it. Isn't that right, Monica?"

Link said, turning to face us. I reached out and took the vest from his grasp as he squatted down in front of her. I bit down on my tongue as he reached up to cup her face, making her look at him. Her glassy eyes stared into his as he snapped his fingers once, twice, and then a third time. After the third one, he tapped her shoulder and quickly repeated the same sequence of events.

"Thank you, Monica," Link's his voice was softer now but no less resolute.

"You've given us what we needed. Maybe now you can start to make up for your disloyalty by wearing this vest."

"Yes. I can compensate for my disloyalty by wearing this vest," Monica repeated.

"You will also drive the location where your servers are housed and stand in the middle of them. You will only get out of the truck when you hear the sound of a jackpot win. You will drive and stop for no one," he instructed.

She repeated. Link glanced at me and nodded for the vest. I began to help Monica put it on as she got to her feet.

"Once you get close to your servers, you will enter your password into the computer, at which point you will be in full control," Link said. I watched as he adjusted the vest and typed in commands on the small screen. He hit a button and held up his watch before looking into Monica's eyes.

"Yes, I will be in full control," she repeated.

"You are fully aware of what is happening but will obey," Link stated.

"I will obey," Monica said as her eyes filled with a mix of relief, but soon they were consumed with fear. She knew there would be no coming back after this.

"When I snap my fingers three times, you will awaken and be alert. But follow all instructions," Link said.

"Follow all instructions," she cried. But maybe, just maybe, she could find a way to redeem herself in some small measure.

"Oh my God, no...Link, please don't do this," Monica cried.

Link put a hand on my shoulder, his expression grim but determined as he looked at Monica, who pulled at the vest, but there was no way to get it off. I heard footsteps and looked behind us as Ace filled the doorway.

"We did what we had to do here, *Dove*. She made her choice, and now we need to go pick up my baby before she says I was late," he said, turning away.

"Ace, take Monica and then strap Ràul to the passenger seat and send them on their way," Link said. Grabbing my waist, I transferred the Machete to my other hand and laced our fingers together.

"I got you," Ace nodded as he moved into the room.

"Link! Link! You can't do this! You can't just do this—"

The door to the room closed as Monica screamed, I wanted to do more to her, but we had a long fucking list of people to handle.

"Let's take Cece to the mall, and while you get the tablet, we can shop," I smiled.

The dangers lurking in the shadows would always be there, but as long as we stood together and remained loyal to each other, we would find a way to weather the storm. This was the entire reason why I refused to let anything stop the *Union City Kings* from rising.

Even though I loved the yacht and the farm, it felt good to be sitting in my car. I was never the boating kind of girl, but I knew how much Link was fascinated with water. My right hand rested on his thigh as we waited outside of Cece's school in the pick-up line. I was worried about having a booster seat, but apparently, Link kept a few on the yacht just in case. This nigga really did think Francesca was his child, and I shook my head because his crazy ass might really have a damn birth certificate. I couldn't say anything, really, because we all were attached to that little girl and would kill whoever got close to her.

"Is that her right there," I asked. I was moving my head, trying to see through the children who were running to cars in the line.

"Naw, that's not her, she's...there she is," Link said, opening the door. He got out of the car as Cece ran toward him.

"Uncle Link! Uncle Link, you're on time," she screamed. I closed my eyes, trying not to laugh as he scooped her and that damn red-headed doll up into his arms.

"I was late once, and you didn't even know it yet," he said, kissing her cheek before opening the back door. I remember when Link made the mistake of saying he was late to the day of her birth, and she hasn't let him forget it since. Cece was like four at the time, and I was trying to figure out how the hell she remembered this shit.

"Auntie Mala! I missed you," Cece said, leaning between the seats. Link got back into the car and pulled on his seatbelt.

"I missed you too little bit. Now, get in your seat and buckle up. Make sure Travis is buckled in, too," I said, watching her. As she fiddled with getting the seatbelt into the hole, she talked about school and how she didn't have to see some kid named Jonny anymore because his daddy lost his job. When I heard the click, I looked in my mirror and pulled out int o traffic.

"Oh, well, that's too bad for Johnny's daddy. *Little bitch*," I looked at Link as he said the last part under his breath, and he blinked at me. I shook my head because I was not about to ask what the hell they did.

"Uncle Link, can you take me to the Rec. Travis is playing basketball, and I said I would watch," Cece asked. I looked at the doll sitting next to her and then at Link. He was doing the same.

"You mean Travis wants to play basketball?" he asked.

"No, he's playing, and I wanna watch it. Please, please, please. Papi said he could do a play date but we couldn't because he wants to play basketball," she sighed. She blinked her large brown eyes up at us while she pulled at the end of one of her French braids.

Link shrugged at me and pulled out his phone.

"I don't see why we can't," he sighed. I turned on my blinker to make a U-turn and head in that direction instead of the mall.

"Yeah, watching a game will be fun," I smiled at Cece.

"Yes! Yes! Yes! Auntie Mala and Uncle Link are the best! Yesssss," she cheered. I looked at Link, but he was frowning at his phone. This was different for Cece, but as long as she was smiling and not asking to blow shit up, I was good.

We pulled into the parking lot, and Cece unbuckled and pulled at the handle.

"Francesca Wellington! You know better," Link scolded.

"Sorry, Uncle Link. I'm just excited," she grinned.

"You're so excited you're about to leave Travis," I pointed as I opened my door.

"Oh no! I can't leave him," she said, grabbing the doll. Link exited the car and opened Cece's door, taking her hand in his.

As soon as we entered the Recreational Center, a game was happening. Cece let go of Link's hand and ran to stand at the court line, holding Travis in her arms. We followed as she and others screamed as one kid with braided brown-tipped locs shot a three-pointer. The little boy was so cute, with the most beautiful brownish-gold eyes framed with long lashes. I stepped forward and squinted because he looked like a smaller version of Link.

"Yes! Go, Papi, go. Go, Papi!" Cece screamed. I already knew my mouth was open because what the fuck. Link already had his phone out but looked up as Cece screamed.

"We have a ball of fire running down the court, and nothing can touch him because he is too hot. Can no one stop the madness?!"

"No, Bob, they can't, as Cortez gives us another amazing three-point shot putting the UNION CITY FLAMES in the lead!"

I began to clap with everyone as Cece screamed again. I shook my head as he ran that ball like he was playing professionally.

"Go, Travis! Go, Travis," she shouted. The little boy named Cortez on the back turned around to look at Cece. I slapped my hand over my mouth, trying not to laugh because my little bit found a little boy that looked like her damn Uncle. *Lawd*. All I could say was that my baby had good taste, and her uncles were about to lose their minds.

"No. No. No, this isn't happening," Link gritted. Travis smiled and ran over to her, kissing her on the cheek before running back onto the court.

"I'll talk to you after I win, Francesca," he smiled over his shoulder.

"Oh, it looks like Cortez has his own little cheer squad! Young love, right Bob?"

"What the fuck! Francesca! Ahh, hell naw! I...I'm calling Faxx! This little nigga is a GROWN-ASS man," Link said, damn near hyperventilating. I knew my eyes were wide because I didn't believe Cece was ever talking about the fucking doll since the beginning.

"Link? Are you serious," I burst out laughing.

CHAPTER EIGHT

LAKYN 'LINK' MOORE

I looked at everybody inside of the Rec like they were fucking crazy cheering for this little nigga Cortez. What in the hell was going on, and why was my baby jumping up and down waving that damn doll in the air. I looked back down at my phone as Faxx texted me back.

Faxx: A grown-ass man? And he's still alive?

Link: This nigga named Travis! You need to get here now!

Faxx: I'm already on the way.

Henny: What the fuck do you mean somebody kissed Cece?

Oz: Is this the Union Recreational Center we just helped with the building fund? Close to the hospital?

Link: It's the same one, and it's someone on their basketball team!

Henny: The only teams they have are for kids??

Link: Nigga! Ain't no way this is a child! I'm looking at him now!

Oz: OMW

Faxx: 2 mins

Henny: Say less.

I moved closer to Mala and noticed her laughing while shaking her head.

"What in the hell is so damn funny? I don't see shit funny about this grown man playing with these kids. Look at him," I pointed.

"Lakyn, you can't be serious right now. That little boy is eight years old at the max," Mala bit her lip.

"Little boy! Do you or do you not see that big ass nigga running game on that court. He got to be like college-age to play like that," I sucked my teeth.

"Link! Stop, that is a child. Stop calling him a nigga," Mala admonished. I rolled my eyes and pushed her back so I could get to Cece and find out how long this shit had been going down.

"Nigga don't push me out the way," Mala laughed. I wasn't even about to look at her right now as I squatted down in front of Cece.

"Baby girl, who was that that just came over here?" I asked. Francesca tried looking around me to see the court, but I reached out and brought her face around to look at me. She squeezed the doll tighter when her eyes met mine and smiled.

"That's Travis, Uncle Link. He's my...he's my friend," she smiled. I narrowed my eyes, but she glanced at Mala. Ahh, hell naw, this little secret will stop right here.

"Oh, okay, well, how did you meet this man...I mean, boy," I said. Cece squinted at me before she started rocking from foot to foot. That was her nervous habit when she didn't want to have a conversation.

"Francesca, I asked you a question," I said, raising a brow.

"Aww, Uncle Link, not you! Santina said all of you act weird when we get boyfriends," Cece huffed. I was going to kill Santina and Santara when I got to them.

"No, no, I just like to know all of your friends. That's all, Cece," I smiled.

"We go to the same school. Travis is new, but he's so smart, Uncle Link...and he doesn't—"

She leaned closer to my ear, "And he doesn't think I'm crazy," she whispered. I had to work to control my fucking face because each time she said that, I wanted to take Tye and tie her up to the fucking train tracks.

I forced a smile at her as she watched me.

"Good, he's right. But he's a little old for you to play with, right?" I asked, holding my breath. I saw Mala step into view and place a hand on Cece's shoulder, causing her to release an irritated sigh. She was irritated with me! Me! Naw, who the fuck was this little nigga because I wasn't feeling these changes.

"He's only eight, and we're in the same class. We're both in the gifted program," she smiled.

"Another shot by Cortez from the three-point line! It looks like the Flames will be going home today with the win!" The announcer shouted.

"See, Lakyn, nothing crazy. They know each other because of school. Come on, Cece, so that we can watch the game," Mala said, pulling her around me. I knew for sure that nigga was about eighteen at least.

"Yayy! Papi! Go, Travis, go!" Cece screamed. I closed my eyes as I stood and turned around, seeing Faxx and Crescent coming into the Rec and looking around. I held up my arm, waving them over as Faxx scanned the area, looking for the Cece.

"Where the fuck is this nigga?" Faxx asked. His black eyes lightened slightly when he saw Cece jumping up and down next to Mala.

"Link, are you sure that you saw what you said you saw?" Crescent asked, looking around, confused. There was a crowd of people here cheering for the teams playing.

"Hell yeah, he's right there playing ball like he's in the fucking NBA!" I pointed to the court. They both looked as this nigga made another damn three-point shot.

"Link, that is a whole fucking kid. He is not and does not look like a grown-ass man. You wild for this," Crescent laughed.

"Yo! Where this nigga at," Oz stated. He held a hand to Shandea's back as she passed on a tired smile. I reached out and pulled Cent to me as I stared at Faxx.

"She called him Papi, my nigga," I said.

"She said what?" Faxx asked with a frown.

"Go, Papi," Cece shouted. She swung the Chucky doll around as she danced next to Mala.

I squeezed Cent while she tried to push me off and raised a brow at Faxx.

"Wait, I thought you said it was a grown man. It's a kid," Oz said, frowning. The doors opened again, revealing Henny and Konceited. Henny came in wearing scrubs as he scanned the court looking for this nigga Travis.

"Where is he?" he asked, standing next to Dea. He looked her over real quick before kissing her forehead.

"U.C.K. is in the building! Let's warmly welcome the people responsible for our brand-new state-of-the-art facility!" The announcer screamed. The crowd began to clap, and some chanted U.C.K. as I closed my eyes. Fuck.

"Give me my wife, Link," Faxx grumbled as he held up a hand. I let Cent go as Oz held up a fist and motioned for things to continue as Henny stepped closer, watching Cece. Crescent punched my arm before I could grab her again.

"Look at this shit, ain't no kid able to play like that. He's a grown man," I said, pointing. That's when he made the last shot, and the game was called.

"The UNION CITY FLAMES wins and will be moving on to the next tournament against—"

"Yay, Papi, you won. Travis, you won," Cece said, letting Mala's hand go to run over to this Travis nigga. Faxx's mouth was open as Dea and Oz moved closer, looking at the two hugging.

"Y'all see this shit, right?" I asked.

"Who the fuck is he? Who's his people?" Oz asked, squinting.

"I told you Beautiful! It wasn't any damn doll. I knew I didn't trust this nigga, Travis," Konceited shook his head. For the first time, we agreed.

"Hey Konceited," Crescent smirked, and he winked at her.

Mala waved him off while smiling down at Cece. This was out of control.

"See, even his ass sees the problem," I said, waving at Konceited.

"All of y'all need to chill out. Seriously, look at her," Dea said. I felt a warm hand slip into mine, and I looked down at Mala, trying to hide the smile on her face.

"Shandea, this is my child," I said, grabbing my chest. I was about to pass out, and the only person taking this seriously was Konceited! Dea tried and failed not to laugh as Cent put her head down.

"Faxx, are you going to do something? What kind of parenting is this? Let me get my child 'cause y'all niggas actin' real slow," I said, turning.

"Really, y'all, she has a friend. A real friend. Do any of you want to take that from her? Her first real LIVE friend that doesn't think she's weird for being different," Dea asked calmly. I looked at Cece, and she pulled Travis with her as she approached us.

"Hold up, his last name is Cortez," Konceited frowned, and then his face smoothed out.

"I still need to know who his peoples are. Fuck that," Oz grunted.

Faxx stared at Cece with an expression I couldn't place, but the flicker of hope in his eyes grew as they came closer.

"Papi and mommy, this is Travis. I named my doll after him," she grinned, looking at Faxx.

"Hi Travis, it's very nice to meet you finally," Crescent said.

"You too, Mrs. Wellington. Francesca has told me so much about you," he smiled. I saw his gaze slide to me, and he rolled his eyes. Aww, hell naw.

"Oh, you're so polite. Cece, you did good, girl," Crescent said, rubbing Cece's cheek. Faxx's eyes slid to Dea as Henny tilted his head to the side, releasing a breath.

"Dea is right, Faxx. This...this is a good thing," Henny said begrudgingly.

"This is wild," I said, tossing up my hands in the air. "Nobody saw that," I said, pointing.

Faxx looked at Cece and smiled before getting to their level.

"Oh, so this is Travis. What's up, Travis? You were doing your thing out on the court," Faxx said.

"Thank you. I got a little worried that Francesca would run out on the court, so I just wanted to win fast so she wouldn't get hurt," he said, looking at her and then at Faxx.

"Awww, he's so sweet."

I looked at Dea, Crescent, and Mala like they had lost their minds.

"And he looks like a little Link," Dea said, covering her mouth. Oz, Henny, and Faxx frowned as they reassessed the kid.

"Is that why you're so mad? Because he looks like a baby wolf," Crescent smirked. I had something for her ass later.

"Naw, no, he doesn't. That nigga doesn't look anything like me," I said flatly. Mala punched my shoulder, but I was serious.

"Naw, Link," Konceited started to chuckle, "are you sure you don't have no loose ends running around out here," he laughed.

"Fuck no," I snapped.

"He's not my dad. No way he could be," Travis said, looking at me. I was about to take a step when Mala yanked on my arm. Cece turned around and looked up at me.

"Uncle Link, he's so smart. He's really good at computers, and he helped me fix my tablet in class," she smiled.

"Shiddd, he might be his," Crescent said under her breath. I shook my head at her, and she widened her eyes. I looked at Henny, but he was watching Cece.

"Papi, Travis couldn't come over today 'cause he had a game, but can he come over this weekend?"

"Whose kid is this?" Oz said looking around. Konceited came closer, and though he was laughing, he looked skeptical.

"What's your father's name, Travis?" Konceited asked.

"His father is named none of your damn business Kodey," a man said, pushing through the crowd of people.

"Dad! You missed the game, but we won," Travis said, moving to the man. We all looked at the man as Travis approached him, still holding Cece's hand, and hugged him. Konceited spun around, and he smiled as he walked over.

"I'm sorry, son. I tried to make it, but I won't miss the next one," his father said.

"Wow, what the fuck are you doing here, Cortez? I saw the name on the jersey, but then the eyes had me questioning, but I wasn't sure," Konceited said, dapping this man up.

"Yeah, that's me," Cortez said.

"Dad, this is Mr. Wellington Cece's dad," Travis pointed. Cortez held out his hand, and Faxx took it.

"Nice to meet you, Fransisco, and the rest of the crew. Oz, Link, and not sure of your name," he nodded to Henny.

"Why would you know it, detective—"

"INTERIM Chief Cortez. I assumed you were a part of this...crew," Cortez said, dropping his hand.

"You know what they say about assumptions, Chief," Oz said, stepping slightly before Henny.

"Mr. Anderson, I hope things are going well with your club after the trouble recently. My condolences on the death of your brother," Cortez nodded. Oz's jaw clenched, and I stepped closer because what the fuck?

"My brother is doing well, actually. He's finally been able to take that vacation he's been meaning to take," Oz intoned.

"Oh, I do apologize. I was speaking of Jakobe Howard. Y'all were close, right?" he said, looking around. None of us said a word as he met our eyes, and then his gaze landed back on Konceited, before he nodded again.

"Well, it was good to see you, Kodey, and lovely to see you again, Miss Francesca. Travis, we need to head out. We have that draining of the bay in three days or less. I need to supervise the planning of all that. Takes a lot of man hours," he stated. My eyes were locked on Cortez, but I still noticed this nigga Travis kiss Cece's cheek before he walked off with his father. Oz turned to Konceited, but we all stayed silent until the last person left the gym.

"Okay, so are we going to deal with this problem," I said quickly.

"Exactly, Link. Who the fuck was that nigga?" Oz demanded. Konceited stared hard at the now-closed doors before shaking his head. He drew in a breath and released it like he was in shock.

"He's from P-Town. We grew up together and went through a lot of shit together at one point. So, it's not like he doesn't know the streets or the talk on these streets. I never really knew why he disappeared and went on the straight and narrow, but I guess I do now," Konceited said, rubbing his chin.

"Uncle Kode! You didn't tell me you were here," Cece said, hitting Konceited's leg.

"Oh, dang, don't put me in the hospital, pretty girl. Uncle Kode is getting old," Konceited laughed picking her up and kissed her. Faxx was still looking at Cece, and Crescent looked from him to her before she moved.

"Cece, let's go and talk girl stuff with Auntie Dea and Mala," Crescent said, holding her hand. Yeah, that was best because I needed to know what the fuck we were going to do. I waited until the door closed before getting straight to the point.

"So, what are we going to do? How do we need to handle this new threat," I asked. Konceited shook his head, waving his hand back and forth.

"Naw, naw, I don't think it was a threat at all," Konceited analyzed. Oz folded his massive arms and pulled at his beard, looking at Konceited.

"Why not? This nigga knew exactly who we were except Henny, but that is by design. Not only that, but he also made it a point to let us know he's been clocking us," Oz pointed. Henny ran a hand over his waves and looked toward the door, frowning because he should have known this guy was coming in. Not only that, he seemed to have been in Union for a little minute now, but that wasn't the issue.

"If he was threatening us, I don't think he would've said out loud about the bay shit. The question we should be asking is how we didn't know about this and how fast can we take care of the situation or get it delayed," Henny stated.

"Henny is right. I can say that Cortez doesn't slip up on no shit like that. It wasn't a threat but a warning," Konceited concluded.

"Nigga you basically a fucking cop yourself. Why the fuck should we trust you," Faxx said, snapping out of it.

"Whatever, you just mad 'cause your wife was over there rethinking her choices," Konceited smirked. Faxx stepped forward, but Henny cut in before them nigga started a whole who's lighter and brighter war.

"Konceited, what makes you think that? I feel like I can agree with you on it. It was his vibe, but I need more information. I don't like being last to know shit in our city," Henny noted.

Konceited cracked his neck and shrugged.

"That nigga is just as much street as the rest of us. From what I know, he understands how shit runs. He understands the necessity of how shit is ran. He knows power, and if he can work with it to keep the streets quiet and on the low, he will do it. I just didn't know he was coming here. That's the problem. That was some hush shit because I should have been flagged to let you know, so this is some off-the-books movement," Konceited reasoned.

"I need to make some calls," Henny said, pulling out his phone.

"Okay, all this is good, but can we get to the problem?" I shouted. Henny looked up and frowned, moving over to me to look into my eyes, doing that examination shit.

"What nigga?" I said leaning away.

"My nigga you good? I mean, seriously, are you okay because this is an emotion I haven't seen you show since I've known you," he observed.

"He's good, Henny. Link is just worried that someone is stealing Cece from him. You know this nigga got abandonment issues," Faxx surmised. I was about to shoot everybody in this bitch for laughing, but Faxx stared at me seriously.

"You don't see a problem?" I asked him.

"Think about it Link. This is a major step for her and could help her, like Dea said. She has an appointment in a few days. Take her and ask Mena about it," he suggested. I narrowed my eyes and screwed my face up before walking past them.

"I'm taking full custody. Y'all taking this shit too lightly for me," I said, pushing the door open.

"Lakyn? The bay?" Henny called out.

"I got it handled. Just get that shit set up for Rodney bitch ass," I said.

"Why is this nigga trippin' over his look-a-like? At least she picked someone that looked like him. I mean, I wanted to trip his little ass for that handholding, but he's a kid. Puppy love and shit," Oz questioned.

"Fuck y'all niggas," I shouted.

I stepped outside with too many issues on my mind. The bay shit was fucking with me, and I knew I needed to move on it soon because there were a lot of bodies there. I looked at my watch and sent Ace a message to see if Echo could do a deep dive and figure out how we could move my killing field.

Crescent was the first one to see me walking over toward them. Cece turned around and looked up at me, smiling. She ran over to me, and I lifted her up, hating the fact that nigga Faxx might be right. Fuck. I thought I had that shit dealt with, but...

"Uncle Link, are you picking me up tomorrow, too?" she asked. I could feel her hands playing in my locs and tell she was uneasy. Shit.

"No, not tomorrow, but I'm going to pick you up on the day of your appointment so we can go together," I said, putting her down.

"Oh yes! Mommy said I can't go to hers this time, but we can have a family one next month," she said, turning around. I looked at Mala, and I could see that she was staring directly into my fucking soul.

"Are you ready, baby?" Mala asked, looking at the doors. I knew her ass wanted to leave before Henny came strolling out, but I was ready. I needed to see my mother.

"Yeah, I need to check up on Mother and Father really quick. I need advice on this shit," I said, walking toward her car. Cent pushed herself off the hood and approached me, wrapping her arms around my waist.

"I'm sorry for laughing, Master Zaddy. I promise to get more information on this Travis situation," she said, letting me go.

"Yeah, you know what's up, but that little hug ain't saving you. And Shandea! Get in the damn truck. You should not be standing for this long," I shouted as I opened the door. Mala slid inside, and I rounded the car to the passenger side.

"Oh my God, Link, I'm fine! You act just like Henny and Oz," she sucked her teeth but opened the Navigator's passenger door.

"I thought so," I said, sliding inside. Crescent walked Cece over to the Wagoneer, and Damari opened the back door.

"How long do we have before Monica gets to the location," Mala asked. I looked at my watch before pulling out my phone as she pulled into traffic. I could feel her eyes on me as I looked over at the truck's location and how long it would take before the fireworks began.

"Malikita, say what you want to say. Staring a hole in my face won't answer your question," I said, not looking up.

"This is because of me, isn't it? When did this start?" she asked.

I breathed in because I wasn't the one for all this fucking therapy bullshit. Henny hadn't pushed it, and I didn't need to tell him to go fuck himself. I was good. I was handling it until now. Fuck.

"You should see Mena," she sighed.

"For what? To tell me what I already know about myself. Naw, I'm good. And yes, it is a partial thing. When you left, I was fucked up, and understandably so, but I handled it," I said, hoping the conversation was over. I knew, and Mala knew that I would always answer her no matter how uncomfortable it made me or her.

"Why are we discussing this?" I asked. I looked at my watch, which showed Monica had about an hour to go.

"Because you just had a fucking meltdown at a kid's basketball game. They are children Link. I doubt they even understand the boyfriend and girlfriend thing," she laughed.

"Did you or did you not see that grown-ass man-child in there? He was damn near my height," I yelled.

"Nigga he was shorter than me, and I'm five feet seven inches. Ain't no way he was almost your height. Maybe he's a little taller for his age, but not overly so. You're trippin', and you think Cece is trading you in," she shrugged.

"We'll see once I talk to my Mother. She'll guide me on how to go about this custody process because y'all not up on game," I said, pocketing my phone after calling my mother's line and getting no answer.

"Oh my God! You're...you.... baby, I love you, but your crazy is definitely showing. Like for real, real showing," she shook her head. We got off Highway 282, taking the exit to my parents' middle-class neighborhood. Why they wouldn't let me move them, I didn't know. Why they couldn't just move themselves, I had no idea. They didn't need to stay here, but I understood more each time I returned to the house. It centered me, and I think that was the entire reason they hadn't moved. I believed it did the same for us all, so I had to stop asking about it.

"The last time it happened was when Lakina went to that fucking boarding school. But I handled it just like I'm going to handle this," I stated. I felt Mala flick her gaze, so I looked at her. Her lips pressed together, and I could tell she was trying to hold something back.

"What? You don't think I can handle it like I did with Kina?"

"Baby, if you call sitting outside of her dorm every night until you manage to replace all the security cameras in the damn school handling it, okay," she huffed. The only person that ran their mouth about that shit had to be Shantel. I knew it was her, and I was going to fuck her up. I told her to keep that between us, not go off and tell Mala about the shit.

"And no nigga, Shantel did not tell me shit. It was Kina. And yes, I know you told Shantel because you tell her everything," she rolled her eyes.

I pulled out my phone, retrying my mother, but still no answer. When I looked at her location, it said she was at the house. I checked my father's, and it said the same. I was worried and not at the same time because I knew my parents could handle themselves, but with this Charles shit, I needed to lay eyes on them.

"You're jealous."

"Nigga, please. Shantel will never be a person I worry about, and you're deflecting, but it's cool. Let's get Mama Laverne to sort your shit out," she laughed. I got out before she could cut the engine, walked around to her side, and opened the door.

"My Mother will understand where I'm coming from. This has nothing to do with what you think it does. This is about proper parenting for my baby," I said, walking toward the door. I saw both of their cars in the yard, so I knew they were there.

"Kyte, that is Faxx's daughter, and he's handling it correctly. Just give it a minute and see," she urged. I said nothing as I entered the code for the door to open. I stepped inside, hearing low music, knowing they were there. The dining room was empty, but the music came from the living room area.

"Mother! I really need your advice on—"

"Oh shit! Oh my God, oh my God," Mala said, turning around. I think all these niggas were trying to take me the fuck out. All I could see was the large tiger tattoo on the back of the man who had my mother pressed against the wall with her legs around his waist. I looked at the couch and saw my father with another woman lying on his knees with his hand on her ass.

"Lakyn! Wh—what are—"

The man turned slightly, and my eyes got bigger because what the fuck was happening.

"Meridian!? Mrs. Noelani? I can't unsee this shit. Fuck! What the fuck!"

"Lakyn Moore, this is none of your business, and you will check your tone," my father ordered. I kept my eyes closed because I know fucking well I didn't just walk in on some swinging-type bullshit with my parents and their friends. It felt like everybody was out to fuck my shit up today.

"Naw, fuck that. Y'all nasty, I can't—"

"Link, stop. Now you know you can't throw any shade at them. It must be where you got it from," Mala whispered.

I heard the door open, and my heart rate picked up, thinking it was Kina. She would fucking lose it.

"Yo! Where is everyone? Ma! I've been trying to reach you, and now I have to track you down here. Are we having dinner—"

I looked behind me and saw a shocked Karma staring at the scene in front of me.

"Dad, you always had that walk about you that indicated you were on this freaky shit, but mom!" Karma shook his head.

"Oh my God. Horizon, why are you tracking me? This...okay, will y'all get out so we can get dressed? It isn't like y'all haven't seen or done anything like this. Jesus," Noelani gasped.

"You know what? I'm good. I can deal with all this shit on my own. I can't—"

"Lakyn, baby, what is it? What happened? Give me a second and."

"You're good. You're good, Mother. I just...I need to kill somebody," I said, turning and walking toward the door. Karma stood there for a second longer, shaking his head like a disappointed parent.

"Lakyn, son, just hold on," my father chuckled. I walked faster toward the car. With all the shit that was going on, life still had time for this bullshit?

"Link! Link hold up. Just hold up. Get in the car. It's all good," Mala chuckled.

"Mala, they old as fuck. They like eighty," I stated.

"And they still getting it in. But I don't know why your numbers are so off today because they are not even out of their fifties yet. Just get in," she demanded. Is this what normal people have to deal with? Fuck. Maybe Mala should've stayed the fuck away if my head was going to be fucked up like this. Naw, naw, that wouldn't work. What the hell? I blinked and looked up, noticing we were pulling into a car wash.

"Why are we here? I need a fucking drink and to go to the *Clinic*," I said.

"No, you need something else first. I think I know the problem, and the *Clinic* will elevate the rest," she stated.

"Mala, I don't know what the hell you think a deluxe carwash will fix, but I guarantee you it won't work," I grunted. She said nothing, reaching across me and opening her glove department. She pulled out a small wallet and took out a card. Mala leaned out the window and stuck the card inside the machine.

"Mala?"

"Kyte, I need you to trust me for a minute. Can you handle that?" She asked. I closed my mouth as she leaned back into the car and rolled the windows up. The light in front of us turned green, and she moved forward. I stared at her as she put the car in park, and the rush of water began. Mala unbuckled her seatbelt and reached to do mine.

"Put your seat back, Lakyn," she said softly. I tilted my head to the side, momentarily forgetting everything that just went down as she slid her jeans down.

"*Dove*, this ain't going to be enough time," I gritted. I was saying that but doing what she told me while unbuttoning my jeans enough to free my dick. Watching her already had me half-mast, but when she moved to hover over me, my hard as fuck dick bumped her clit. I licked my lips as I watched her lower herself inch by inch onto my length. Her warm walls gripped and sucked me into her pussy, but I needed more. My hand came to her hip, and I slammed her down hard, making her gasp.

"Fuck! Fuck, Mala," I groaned.

"Ride my dick, Mala," I whispered against my lips. I moved my hips and hers, making her rock faster against me. I spread my legs as far as I could and pushed my length deeper into her.

"Yes, Lakyn, fuck," she cried. Mala placed her hands on my chest as she rose up and slowly sank back down on my throbbing dick. I moaned, throwing my head back against the seat as her warm pussy massaged my length, sending pleasure coursing throughout my body. Her pussy was tight as fuck, but the slight pain crossing her face turned to pleasure with each movement. Mala circled her hip, and nothing could compare to her body, her taste, or the knowledge that she knew me. I sucked on her tongue as her hands slid up my shirt, as she dragged her nails across my chest. I felt one hand moving further as her fingers wrapped lightly around my throat. The tingling feeling running through me at that movement had me tighten her grip on her hip and twists.

"What are you doing, *Dove*?" I asked. The sound of the water slamming against the car gave me a feeling of being underwater as she stared into my eyes. I rocked into her deeper, dropping her hair to brush my fingers along her hard nipples.

"Lakyn," she moaned. The hand wrapped around my neck tightened, and she pulled me forward as I pushed upward. I felt her tongue against my lips as she squeezed my throat.

"Fuck. Slam that pussy on this dick, Mala," I groaned against her lips. Mala moaned circling her hips. Mala's pussy tightened around my dick like a vice grip at the same time as her hand squeezed. I held her hip and slammed into her harder, making sure she took all this dick. I felt my head hitting that spot as she screamed.

"Oh my God! Oh...fuck," she cried, moving faster. The sounds of her ass slapping against my thighs made my dick harder. Mala squeezed my neck tight as she moved. My eyes slammed shut as the lightheadedness began to settle in.

"I'm not leaving Lakyn. I swear to you I will never leave again. Even if it kills me, I will never...never fucking leave you," she whispered. I could feel her chest pressed against mine as she slowly released my throat.

"Fuck! Fuck this dick Mala and cum all over it. You are saying all this like I don't know. You can't escape me. If I have to tie your ass to the fucking bed every night, I will," I threatened. I grinded upward as she pushed down on me. My eyes closed as she licked over my lips and pulled on my beard. Mala pulled away as my grip on her hip got tighter, and my other hand traveled over her stomach to her clit. I pressed on it and started to rub. I watched as her eyes rolled back from the sensation. I held her hips down and jacked up into her.

"Oh, shit. Yes, Lakyn! Lakyn, baby, right there. Lakyn, I-I love-love," she c ried.

I felt both her hands slide over my neck, and she used that pressure to press me into the headrest as she bounced. I could barely breathe, and the spray of the water splashed against the windows as her pussy made sloshing noises with each movement. Her grip grew tighter, and my head spun, and I was sure I stopped breathing as a powerful orgasm came rushing from the base of my spine.

"Oh, you think that shit isn't mutual. You will never be able to walk away from me, Lakyn. You want my breath, my mind, my body. You want everything while you forget without me, you can't fucking breathe. I control every breath you take," she panted. The sound of the carwash was fading, but I heard the water stop when the car began to move. Mala rocked faster as we both chased the orgasm we could feel coming.

"Oh, fuck," gasped. The black dots began to pop into my field of vision. Mala leaned over into my ear as I slammed into my channel harder and deeper. Both my hands landed on her ass, and I pressed down harder, knowing I was going to leave a mark. The skin-to-skin contact filled the space in the car. I spread her cheeks apart and used them to slam me down my dick loving the sound her ass made with each stroke. I was deep and stretching her out so much that I knew she would be walking funny. This pussy was my home, and it would only know his dick.

"Lakyn! Oh God, I can't...I can't, please. I'm going to cum" she moaned as she released my throat, but I didn't stop. I knew the carwash was about over, but I was balls deep inside her. Mala's mouth fell open. She tried to pull back when she noticed the car moving forward, but I held onto her.

"Naw, don't run, Mala! You did this. Wasn't this your idea? Take this dick, *Dove*. Cum on it. Let me feel it," I demanded.

"Shit, Link. The...the dude...the det...detail—"

If that nigga holding that fucking rag knew what was good for him, he would make sure not a word left his lips because I wasn't stopping. I pushed as deep as I could go. Her walls spasmed around me, and her nails clawed at my chest. I leaned closer and grazed my teeth over her ear lobe.

"Fuck that nigga. Let's not act like people watching me fuck you like this don't get you off. Let them watch because ain't no nigga ever touching you, Mala," he grunted. Her eyes rolled back again, this time at my words. I knew what she needed and what she wanted because her pussy never lied. By the way, it clasped around me. I knew she was about to cum.

"Mmmm, yes, *Dove*. You like that shit."

"Lakyn! Yes, yes, Lakyn," she cried.

"Fuck, Mala," I panted.

"Damn, Mala. Let Daddy inside, *Dove*. I want you to nut on it, cum all over this dick," I hissed. I pulled out to the tip, then slammed deeper into pussy.

"Oh God, Lakyn! Right there, Daddy. Lakyn," she screamed.

"Scream for me, Mala. Cum," I demanded.

"Lakyn," she moaned as her body shook. I could feel her pussy tightening around me, and I pushed in deeply. I felt my dick harden and throb as I exploded with one last thrust.

"I love this pussy, Mala. No escape. You agreed," I gritted.

"Lakyn," she moaned repeatedly, voice going hoarse.

I groaned her name until the last bit of nut left me. I was dizzy as fuck when I pulled back and looked out of the window. Mala's face looked drugged as she blinked at me. The middle-aged man stood there with a towel in his hand and mouth open.

"Pull your shirt down, *Dove*, or you're going to give this man a heart attack," I said. Before I fixed my pants, I helped her slide off my lap and into the driver's seat. I hit the button, letting the passenger window down.

"Ahh...ahhh, did you need—"

"Naw, we good. I got what I needed," I said. I pulled two-hundred-dollar bills from my wallet and dropped them in his box. Mala managed to pull it together and put the car in drive. She pulled out, and then she burst out laughing.

"Now you can't say shit about your parents because you're just as out of control as them. If not worse," she laughed. My watch buzzed, letting me know Monica would arrive at her final destination in less than forty minutes.

"Shut up, Mala. Get us to the *CLINIC*. I want to watch this on the big screen," I chuckled, feeling something settle and snap into place when her hand slid over my thigh. She uncurled my fingers and laced them together with hers without saying another word.

Walking into the *CLINIC*, I noticed Henny's Bentayga and Shantel's Rover. Mala pulled next to Shantel's SUV, blowing out a breath as the doors to the large warehouse closed behind us.

"You weren't going to be able to duck your cousin forever. You knew eventually he would catch up to you," I said, opening my door. Mala screwed up her face as she unbuckled her seatbelt. She quickly buckled her jeans and opened her door. I stood up, nodding to Ace as he exited his black-on-black BMW XM Sport.

"Yeah, but I didn't want to have this conversation smelling like your cum while I tell him all the reasons why I had a fake fiancé," she sighed. I checked my watch and saw we had three minutes before the show. I looked her over as we approached the stair and didn't see a fucking thing wrong.

"I will get him to help me with a little something while you shower," I said. We climbed the stairs just as Shantel exited a room from the side hall, looking down at her phone and shaking her head. She looked up and smiled, walking over to us.

"Bissh, I watched that video of you whipping Monica's ass a few minutes ago and about died," Shantel laughed. It was rare to see her with a huge smile or shedding the hard demeanor of the take-no-shit businesswoman who ruled the businesses with an iron fist. I didn't know if it was because Mala was home or someone else. I would ask her later about that shit because I didn't miss her action at the meeting when Lawe came online.

"Girl, I had to hold back. I wanted to kill that bitch. One more hit and I was sure she would've been in a fucking coma," Mala laughed. I reached out, grabbed Shantel, and tried to remove my fucking dress shirt and the black wolf cuff links she was wearing like a damn outfit.

"Nigga! Stop, you said I could wear it," she said, smacking my hands.

"When? I know damn well I never said that shit. Especially not my cuffs," I stated.

"Stop Link! After all, I did get that dude Landon ready for you. Not to mention hooked up the screen so we can see this bitch blow up live," she smiled. I narrowed my eyes, moving passed her knowing full well her ass was up in my penthouse in the Casino. I heard her and Mala talking as I pushed through the doors, seeing Henny sitting in the chair. He was looking down at his phone like he was going to murder it, so I wasn't saying shit. I took the chair beside him to use the keyboard to tap into the network and pull up the drone that had been following Monica.

"You good my nigga?" he asked. He changed out of his scrubs, but he was still in all black, like he was about to get into some shit.

"Yes and no."

I said nothing else as I took control of the drone to see into the truck's window. I tapped a few keys to listen to whatever conversation they were having.

"Francesca will be fine, but you know how important it is for a child so young to have friends. You know how important it is to understand other people's feelings. It's how she will learn to navigate the world when she's older," he stated.

I was less annoyed by this temporary situation with Travis, but I also knew Henny was, unfortunately, correct. Without those connections early on, she could become the younger version of me—no understanding of the feelings or emotions of other than my parents. I didn't understand the meaning of friendship or allyship at that time. I sometimes think how much colder I would've become if I hadn't met Henny. If he hadn't been there to help me understand that just because I was a genius didn't mean I wouldn't get caught or outsmarted by someone with more intelligence. When I found him sitting on the boat that I used to take people to the bay with the body of one of the niggas from the underground gambling house, I was intrigued. I intended to take him out because he robbed me, but he was larger and older than I was. I had no one on my side, friends, or people I could trust. So, when I saw him, I had to know what this kid knew even though he was only a few years older than me. What did he know that I didn't, and how had he accomplished it alone? That's when I met Jakobe and Malcolm. What it all boiled down to was he knew how to fit in enough to move through life, making people think we were normal.

He also knew how to form connections with others, and the easiest way was finding others who thought and moved just like you.

"So, you agree with Faxx, and I have abandonment issues or some shit?" I asked.

"Yes, you were mad as fuck at me when I had to go to medical school, and you were pissed the fuck off about Faxx when he had to deploy. We know where it was from, and it has been managed so far. This shit with Mala just shook you up," he said, blanking out his phone's screen.

"What, are you a therapist to my nigga? Don't psychoanalyze me," I said, hitting the speaker. The door opened again, revealing Mala and Shantel. Henny smirked at me but glanced at Mala when she sat on the opposite side of him.

"Hi, cousin," she said, leaning on his shoulder.

"I've decided not to even lecture you on this. I'm sure you got enough of it from Link," Henny said straight-faced. Mala sat up and opened her mouth when the voices began to play through the speakers.

"What are you doing? Stop! Just fucking stop the truck. You're not tied down! You can stop the truck," Ràul screamed.

"I can't! I can't! Don't you think I want to, but I can't," Monica cried.

The truck turned left onto a dirt road lined with trees. I felt Shantel next to me and her gripping my bicep tightly. I reached over to the arm of her chair and pulled her closer to me. She probably would have been in my lap if the leather arms weren't in the way. I hated feeling her body go motionless and hearing her breathing stop.

"Bitch! Just fucking stop! Do you understand what will happen to me when they find out—"

"I can't!" Monica screamed as she slammed on breaks.

"Dios ayúdame, God help me, God help me," Ràul cried.

Tears ran down their faces as Monica stopped inches from a medium-sized building that housed her servers. I felt Shantel's nails into my skin, but I didn't move or say a word as she watched. Even though it wasn't the same building, the area never changed.

Monica sat in the truck, her hands on the steering wheel, tears streaming down her cheeks.

"This bitch got the nerve to cry after the shit she did. What did she believe was going to happen?" Mala scoffed. I looked over at her as she stared hatefully at the screen.

"That she wouldn't get caught," I answered. "Monica got it in her head that she was the smartest in the room because she felt as though she was getting away with shit. She forgot that it's always someone or someone who is smarter," I concluded. Henny looked at me, and I caught the flash of his grill before he turned his attention back on the screen.

Monica suddenly moved and began to unbuckle as the winning sounds of jackpots reverberated through the truck.

"Hey, hey, hey, what does that mean? Where are you going? Hey! Hey! Monica, where the fuck are you going!" Ràul shouted as he shook from side to side, trying to get out of the restraints.

"No, no, no, I can't believe this is happening. You son of a bitch! Fuck you Link, fuck all of you! How am I going to get out of this? It has to be a way. Type in the password, and then I have a second to bypass whatever he did to this vest. Oh my God, you bastard! Please, please," Monica ranted.

Rows and rows of servers were lined up in rows, filling the entire building. Monica moved through the space toward a small workstation in the back. As she approached the computer, I was moderately impressed with it. The Edge XT2ATR Workstation lit up as Monica got closer. Her hands automatically came up when she was within reach of the wireless keyboard.

"Are you sure you want to destroy it before seeing what she has," Shantel questioned. My fingers were already typing in the commands for the vest to do what I had invented to do. It worked much like watches, and as soon as she entered her password and hit enter, I would have every file sent to every server in that building.

"Oh, we definitely will have everything she has ever worked on," I stated. Henny leaned closer, his two thumbs resting under his chin. Monica began to type in her password, and I could see her hands shaking just as she hit enter. I did it at the same time as she did, and as soon as it was done, her body went limp. Monica shook her head as she realized she now had full control of herself.

"Oh fuck, oh fuck," she screamed.

I leaned back in my chair, peeling Shantel's hand from my arm, and held it. Monica began to search for a way to remove the vest but focused on the device connected to it when she saw it was impossible.

"All I need to do is get—"

She never finished her words as everything on the screen turned bright white.

Boom. Boom. Boom. Boom. Boom. Boom.

The drone following Monica was destroyed, but as soon as it cut out, the one hovering over the truck caught the tractor-trailer, exploding along with the building before we lost connection.

"Shit! What in the hell did Konceited put in the fucking machines," Mala wondered aloud.

"That nigga won't tell me. He's an asshole, and that's why I don't fuck with him," I stated.

"Nigga, I still don't understand what Eli was thinking about sending you to that camp, but at least you met another crazy nigga just like you," Henny smirked.

Mala turned in her seat while I had another drone flying over the property to ensure that seat was dust, but that bitch was still burning.

"Henny, what the hell do you mean that you aren't going to say anything? I don't trust you," Mala hissed. I knew she was sure Henny would back her ass up. Henny smirked as he looked down at his phone and back at Mala with a smile.

"Naw, I'm going to let Oz handle it. Plus, Aunt Vanessa has a lot she wants to say to you. I'm good," he shrugged.

"You snitched!?" she shrieked.

"You're fucking right I did, and she is mad as fuck," he chuckled.

"You on that sucka' ass get back! You're wrong for this shit. Damn it," Mala said, standing.

"You were wrong to keep that bullshit from me, but it's all good. Payback is a bitch, and you know how ya' mama is," Henny laughed harder.

"Come on Shantel. We need to hit up Cent about the arrangements for Milo. She just texted me," Mala said, pushing Henny in the back of the head. Shantel let my hand go and stood, not saying a word, but I knew Mala would bring her back. I felt her fingers run through my locs before she grabbed Shantel's arm and pulled her out the door, still cussing Henny out.

"You know that was fucked up," I said, moving the files from Monica to a different server. I set the program to unzip and store everything on the categories I set up before looking at Henny.

"It was best. I would have said some shit that hurt her, and she's—"

"Sacrificed enough. Yeah, but it's still some fuck shit," I gritted.

"Not saying it isn't," he said as his phone rang. Henny hit the speaker button and answered.

"Briggs, what the fuck is going on? I don't like not knowing that we have an interim Chief out of the blue. Just like I don't fucking like not knowing they will be draining the bay. Why am I hearing this shit on the street Briggs and not from you?" Henny bit out.

"Listen, listen, I was just as in the dark as you were. When I got the message, I started digging and inquiring quietly. From what I know, someone is pulling strings and purposely keeping me out of the loop. Once I got confirmation, I stormed the meeting they were having today. It wasn't being held anywhere near my offices, but you know I have people loyal to me. I met this...this Cortez and the agent that apparently was spearheading this investigation. They have enough evidence that says there are bodies down there and that I knew about it. I don't know where they got it or exactly what it is, but they got a judge to sign off and fucking I.A. breathing down my neck saying I'm on the take," he panted.

Henny's jaw firmed as he sat back in his chair. He ran a hand over his face before slamming his fist to the table.

"All I need you to do, Briggs, if you want to live a happy retirement, stress-free and wealthy, is to keep your fucking mouth shut. Let me handle this shit. Send me the meeting address, and I'll take it from there," Henny said, hitting the end button. He looked at me, and his flat stare was enough said. His phone beeped once, and he turned it in my direction. I typed in the address and then infiltrated the building's security systems. It was easy because we had already taken this the other day.

I sped through the footage starting two hours ago. Within a matter of minutes, a few cars pulled into the parking lot. I recognized Cortez as he stepped out of an unmarked car and was met by none other than Rodney.

"I knew it would be this nigga. I'm sick of him and his petty ass vendetta he has. I'm calling in his shit. I'm sure Oz is finished with whatever he's setting up. It's time for this nigga to realize who he's fucking with. I'm over this nigga. I want him down so bad that he can only go to a cheap motel. Send out the alert. It's time to play his game and end his shit," Henny said, standing.

"Bet it's done. I feel like seeing what the fuck Landon knows. I want to know where Charles has been going for all these years," I said, exiting out of the system.

"I want to get this shit out of my system before the funeral. It seems as if it will be the same day as the great draining of the bay. Have you heard from Echo?" Henny asked. I looked at my watch and stood up, leaning my neck from side to side. I pulled my locs back and used one of them to hold them together.

"He has two hours before he reports in," I said, moving toward the doors.

"How many bodies do you think we will have to relocate?" he asked, following me out of the doors.

"Including the ones from college and before. Around one hundred and forty-four," I said. I knew it was the exact amount. I just didn't want to look too crazy. Henny was quiet as we approached the door where Shantel had Landon strapped down. I had no idea how she set it up, but I was sure it would be perfect because she knew me.

"Why are you so quiet? Do you think you failed in helping me curve my urges?" I chuckled, stepping into the room.

"Actually, it's less than I thought, so it's a win-win, in my opinion. The compulsive need you felt that you had to do in that way was curved by the FARM. So, in essence, I managed to psychoanalyze your ass while pointing you in another direction to express those urges," he laughed.

We stopped in front of Landon, who hung upside down from a chain as a jet blast of cold water sprayed him with the power of a fire hose.

"Ahhh! Ahhh! Ple...pleas... make it st...st... stooopp."

I ignored Landon and faced Henny, who stared at me with a smirk on his face. His platinum grill flashed in the low lighting.

"You are a fucking asshole. You...you fucking bitch," I pointed. He shrugged, and I shook my head.

"So, because I decided I didn't need to see Mena, you would become my therapist?"

Henny laughed as he moved around the room, hitting the button to stop the water.

"Fuck naw my nigga. I double majored and minored because your ass needed a fucking psychiatrist. You are fucking crazy, Lakyn, and I knew you would refuse to look closer at your shit. Where do you think I met Mena?" he smiled.

"This is exactly why I don't fucking talk. You got crazy analyzing crazy. Please tell her how that shit works," I questioned.

"Because who is better to know the mind of a psychopath than another psychopath? You know this. Deep down, you knew what I was doing. You just accepted it from me," he answered.

"But you let your cousin, blood family, be with someone like me. You sound like the true crazy nigga," I chuckled.

"Nigga, please. Mala's ass is fucking nuts, but y'all balance each other and always have. That's why I couldn't understand when—"

"Please, please, I don't know anything else. I shouldn't be here. I just do security," Landon shuddered.

I turned to look at Landon. His partially naked body shook from the extreme coldness of the water. My gaze dropped down to the medium-sized barrel filled with the same cold water. I guess Shantel was thinking about me.

"See, Landon, that's where I think you're lying. I bet you've been waiting for your rescue and shit from your little security group because of that tracking device you had," I stated. His eyes went from fear to uncertainty. I tilted my head to the side and leaned over to look in his face.

"So, the lies and bullshit you're prepared to say you really should reevaluate," I demanded. I stood up and looked at Henny. He pulled on a pair of sterile surgical gloves and began pressing against Landon's upper body.

"Wh—what is he doing?" Landon asked, teeth chattering.

"He's a doctor. Don't worry about him," I said. I glanced at my watch when it beeped, telling me that all the files from Rodney had been downloaded, and three of them had been flagged.

Landon glared at me with defiant eyes as he tried moving his arms bound behind his back. I walked around him as Henny examined his body. I knew my expression was blank and cold as I watched him. I could tell he was trying to think of what he could get away with saying and what he could hold to keep him alive long enough for someone to show up. The problem with that was no one was coming.

"Where does Charles go every couple of weeks, Landon? I know you have the information I need," I demanded, my voice steady and unwavering.

Landon scoffed, and his eyes filled with disdain as he shook his head. I smiled when I stopped in front of him. I could tell all the blood was rushing to his head as his ears, face, and neck turned crimson.

"I don't know what you're talking about. I don't know what tracker you are talking about or anything about Charles. I was hired to follow the woman. Ahh, what the hell are you doing?" he spat.

"It was just an injection, my nigga, calm the fuck down," Henny said, stepping backward. Henny turned to walk back over toward the wall to lean against it.

"Wh—what the hell did you give me?" Landon demanded as she twisted in his bonds. I leaned in closer, my gaze fixed on his face.

"Nigga, you are worried about the wrong shit. You should worry about answering my question instead of what he just gave you. Maybe this will get your attention," I said, looking over my shoulder. Henny hit the button as

I stepped back. The chain holding Landon's body released, dropping him into the barrel.

"I have three flags from Rodney's files. One has to do with Teddy bitch ass, and the other two are personal. Rodney never planned on returning to Union. Someone sent him here, knowing full well he knew us. From what I got, Rodney was sent here to take us down at any cost. I should get the full one hundred when I get to my laptop," I grunted. I waved my hand, and Henny hit the button, raising Landon out of the water.

Landon sucked in a breath as his body shook uncontrollably. I leaned down and stared into his face while I waited for his reddened eyes to open. I saw what I wanted to see—Fear.

"Send the first one over to Faxx," Henny imparted.

"Bet," I said, staring at Landon.

"We can make things much easier for you if you cooperate," Henny lied. Landon's eyes darted in his direction before focusing back on me. I noticed his respiration increase and rapid pulse beating like a drum on the side of his neck. I watched as his blue lips trembled, and he looked at Henny again. I turned around, and Henny stood against the wall, his arms crossed, his expression cold and unyielding. He tapped another syringe as he stared at Landon. He knew as well as I did that people always thought someone would come if they could just hold out.

"You heard him, Landon. Don't make this harder than it needs to be," I added, my voice low and threatening.

Landon remained silent, his jaw trembling in defiance, fear, and hope. I sighed and stood up, motioning for Henny to drop his ass again.

"No, no, nooooo!" he screamed.

"How would Rodney know about the bay? I've been thinking about this since we saw him in that parking lot," Henny said, hitting the button to raise Landon.

"I'll find out soon enough," I said as Henny cracked his neck and advanced toward us. The glint in his eyes as he pulled the cap off the syringe to look at the clear fluid told me he was experimenting.

Landon gasped as Henny came closer, grabbed his jaw, and turned his head to the side forcibly. He jammed the syringe into the side of his neck. Landon struggled against Henny's grip, but it was no use. I watched as Henny applied just enough pressure to make Landon wince in pain.

"Tell us what we want to know, and this can all be over," I urged, my voice laced with urgency.

Landon's teeth began to crack under the pressure. He winced and grimaced in pain as he screamed.

"Stop! Jus—okay, okay!" he gritted, his voice strained. Henny to release him, and Landon pulled in a breath before beginning to breathe heavily.

"What the fuck—wh...what the hell is wrong with me?"

"Where does Charles go, Landon?" I pressed. My eyes locked onto his, holding them without blinking.

Landon's breathing became labored as he finally started speaking, his voice low, defeated, and raspy.

"We've only managed to track him to a rest stop outside Del Mar. He goes there every couple of weeks to meet with a business partner name... named Banks, and they spent two to three—three days...days...days there before returning...returning to...to his car," he gasped, his eyes beginning to bulge.

"So, Banks was picking him up outside of Del Mar? Is that on the Union side or P-Town?" I asked.

I nodded as his breathing picked up significantly. He leaned in, studying his eyes, looking him over like he was checking his symptoms.

"Words, Landon," I snapped.

"Pppp...P-Town," he coughed. Small amounts of water bubbled up and poured out of his mouth as he choked.

"Good. Now let me help you," I said, turning away.

"Ple—pleas—please, I...I can't...my ches—"

"I bet Mala felt suffocated with you down her throat all the fucking time. Let me show you what it feels like not being able to breathe.

I walked over toward the wall, slamming my hand on the button and releasing the chain, dropping his body into the water.

"What the fuck did you give him, Doc?"

"Something I wanted to test out before using," he answered.

I looked down at my phone, seeing Faxx's reply.

> Faxx: Do me a favor and notify D-Mar Clap Productions they will be audited.

"What's the plan for this Charles?"

I looked up before typing my reply, feeling the rage running through my veins. Not only had this nigga stolen eight years, but he thought he could play U.C.K., and that wasn't happening.

"Bring him back to the *FARM* so I can watch Mala peel his flesh from his body for eight days," I intoned.

"I guess you will need my assistance keeping him alive to enjoy it," he nodded. I hit the reply button with only one response.

> **Link: Done.**

Right after I sent that message, I received another one, but this time it was from Echo, and I quickly opened it. The images were slightly grainy, but I could make it out. I read the message twice, my blood filling with rage that someone dared to fuck with my shit. Anxiety clawed its way into my chest at what this shit could mean. Except one thing was tapping at the back of my mind—something I had seen recently and a few weeks ago. I looked at the message again before raising my head to look at Henny. When he walked over, the frown on his face told me he could feel my unease. I turned the phone to face him so he could read what Echo reported.

Echo: There are no bodies. There is nothing in Blackbay.

CHAPTER NINE

CRESCENT 'CENT' WELLINGTON

I stood in the mirror while fixing my scrub top with Tali on speaker-phone.

I missed you so much. I told Henny we should stay at y'all house, so I was sure you weren't a hallucination," Tali giggled.

"You know what? You are a whole damn fool. But let me tell you about Travis, and not I'm not talking about the doll," I laughed.

"Bitch! Hendrix came home last night on one about how he was dying on the inside because his baby got a boyfriend. Bissh, when I tell you I had to let him lay in my lap and promise that whenever we had a baby if it's a girl, she couldn't get a boyfriend until she was twenty," she huffed.

"Why the hell are you lying to that man like that? You wild as hell, I can't, I just can't," I laughed while leaning over the sink, trying not to fall the fuck out.

"Girl, no! I am dead serious," she chortled.

"He was so calm and helpful at the game, though, and Travis is so cute! He looks like a little Link," I whispered.

"He did tell me that. Our Cece likes them chocolate, girl."

"She does because I taught her well, baby," I laughed.

"Okay, you might be right, but you're still coming into work anyway, right? I have interviews all day with people for the new charge nurse position. Also, Cressida has been asking for you. I don't think I can stall any longer," she sobered.

"It's all good. I'll be in today so I can talk to her. I need to be doing something, and now that I have this tattoo, I don't have to be on lockdown and glued to this niggas side."

"Girl, bye, you like that shit," she rebutted.

"And do. So, what," I said, walking out of the bathroom.

"Nothing because I got mine as well, so I feel you, but are you ready for *MYTH*? Like the real shit?" Tali asked.

"Girl, yes. I'm just trying to see what happens down there. You know them niggas not going to let us participate."

"Chile, I know, but they do need some kind of distraction for at least a night. So, it should be fun," she sighed.

"Okay! Let me know once you get in," Tali said before ending the call.

I felt light while taking my time going down the stairs, listening to Cece talk Faxx's ears off. I still thought Milo would pop his head around the corner whenever I came down, but I knew it wasn't happening anymore. I blew out my breath and made my way into the kitchen, running down the list of shit I needed to handle. I didn't want to say anything about Pam over the phone so that I would get that shit off my chest later today.

"Mommy, Papi said that you are going to work," Cece said, chewing. She stopped chewing, her eyes going huge as she stared at me. She started with the whole mommy thing and hasn't returned to Cent, but I was thrilled about it. Faxx stood at the counter holding a bowl of fruit. He smirked at me as he bit into the strawberry. I sucked in a breath and made myself look back at Cece as she stuffed a piece of turkey bacon into her mouth.

"I am. You don't like my new scrubs?" I said, holding out my arms. Her brown eyes looked me up and down, nodding at the light blue scrub set that was the uniform for the clinic.

"Yeah, I like them, but I love your necklace," she grinned. "But Auntie Tali let me help pick it out when—"

Her voice faded, and I moved closer and slid onto the stool beside her. I kissed her cheek and took a slice of toast from her plate.

"Thank you!"

"Hey! That was for Travis," she said, looking at the doll.

"He said that I can have it," I shrugged. Cece looked at Travis, having some kind of mental communication as I looked over at Faxx. He stared at Cece briefly before sitting his bowl down and approaching me. I put the piece of toast on Cece's plate when he pulled my braids to tilt my head up. He leaned down, pressing his lips to mine. I could taste the burst of flavor from the mixture of fruit he was eating. Faxx pulled away and sat down across from us.

"So, Crescent is going to work and staying at work. Francesca is going to school, and Aunt Vanessa is picking her up today," Faxx said. He lifted a black sports bottle to his lips as he stared at us. Cece turned around and frowned at him.

"Papi, that's...wait a minute. Uncle Oz and Auntie Dea are posed to pick me up," she frowned.

"It's supposed Cece, and something came up. You know that happens sometimes but not always," Faxx stated. Cece sighed but then perked up when she looked at me. I heard the side door open, revealing a belly bigger than Dea's as she walked inside.

"Nene!" Cece screamed as she slid off the stool. Nia was on the phone but pulled it away from her ear.

"Niece! I can't bend down," she said as Cece climbed onto the chair and hugged and kissed her.

"Is the baby coming yet?"

"I hope so. I can't wait for you to meet him. As soon as I finish this call, we will have a girls' chat about this boyfriend," Nia smiled. Cece smiled as her body shook in place.

"You got to say it really quiet. Papi said I'm too young to have a boyfriend, but I don't know what to call him. He's a boy, and he's my friend. Boyfriend," she shrugged.

"Exactly, baby. We can talk about it before you leave. Hey y'all," Nia waved before wobbling to the dining room.

"Ha! That's exactly what it is, Francesca," Faxx said.

"Nia, I really need you to sit your ass down somewhere 'cause I'm not delivering no baby," I said, pointing.

"She's right, Nia. Don't make me get Damari in here for that ass," Faxx threatened. Nia moved slightly faster at the threat but waved us off as she stepped into the other room, getting back to business. I turned around and saw Faxx staring at me hard. His dark eyes roamed over my face and to my wrists.

"Fransisco, really?" I asked as Cece grabbed her plate.

"Oh, Mommy, can Auntie Vanessa take me to Travis's game?"

I looked at Faxx and watched his jaw flex as she smiled. He looked manic.

"Ahh, baby, that is up to Auntie Vanessa. You're going to need to ask her if that's okay when she picks you up," I answered.

"Okay," she danced. I watched as she placed the plate in the sink, and grabbed Travis before leaving the kitchen. I looked back at Faxx with his head in his hands.

"It's not that serious. It's child's play, baby," I laughed.

"I'm good, *Mi Amor*. It's just that I know how it starts. I went through it twice already with my nieces," he sighed.

"So, tell me why you were staring at me like a serial killer who was searching for his next victim," I queried. Faxx stepped around the table. I pushed away from the table and looked up at him with a raised brow. His tatted hand slid around my neck, as he used his thumb to push my head up.

"*Mi Amor*, I already found our next victim. But I need to finish getting your wedding gift together," he chuckled. He leaned down, pushing his tongue into my mouth. Faxx sucked my tongue before pulling back, fogging my thoughts. What the hell did he just say?

"Hey, hey, what the hell does that even mean? And what gift? Hold up, Fransisco," I laughed.

"I'm not riding with you today, but I will be there for lunch. I should have something about Dylan by then," he said.

"Fransisco—"

"Oh, my bad, *Mi Amor*. I forgot to tell you that we have to bake the cheesecake for Dea's party thing," he said, backing away. I opened my mouth and then closed it because I know damn well I never said I was baking a damn thing.

"That was all you, my nigga. I ain't never said that I—"

"Cent, we're married. When I say me, it means us. So, if I say I will bake the cheesecake, it means we will do it. We're one," he pointed between us, smiling. I narrowed my eyes but said nothing about it. He wasn't fully one hundred, but he was coming back more and more.

"I love you, Fransisco," I said instead.

"Te amo, Crescent. Oh, your food is in the warmer, and you have mail. Cece is with me," he tipped his chin. I watched as he walked away before looking at the pile of letters at the end of the counter. I stood up, grabbed my plate from the warmer, and picked up the mail before entering the dining room. I sat down across from Nia as she talked some large ass numbers with someone while I picked through the mail. I cut into the omelet and frowned at the official-looking letter with my name on it. My new name that I hadn't even gone to get my I.D. for yet. I chewed as I tore it open and read the first few lines. My hand began to shake as I read words I wasn't expecting.

Certificate of Adoption. This was to clarify that stepmother Crescent Wellington has formally adopted FRANCESCA LAYKEN WELLINGTON—

"Oh my God," I gasped as Nia ended her call. "How the fuck did this crazy demented ass nigga get this shit done? I wasn't even here," I whispered.

"Cent!" Nia shouted. I looked up, blinking fast as tears hit the table.

"Yes," I choked.

"Crescent, baby, what is it? Who did it? Did that nigga Roman find you here? Did he send some shit because pregnant or not, I will fucking shoot his balls off before I—"

"I'm Francesca's mother," I said, still looking at the paper.

"Oh. Oh well, I thought this was established. You and Faxx got married, and her biological mother is a bitch who really has no claim to her," Nia said, watching me worriedly.

"No, Nia, like for real. Legally! She's mine. She's all mine," I said, turning over the certificate.

"Oh! Shit congratulations on that and the collar! I mean, you had to see both coming. He's...calculated," she winced.

"No need to take up for him, Nia. I know just how persuasive he can be," I said, staring at the table. I probably signed my damn life over that night.

"As long as you know," she sang. Nia's mass of curls was pulled into a long braid that lay on her shoulder. She touched her belly and sighed as she tried to get comfortable.

"Nia, girl, you are ready to pop. Are you sure you're good?" I asked while sticking my certificate back into the envelope. I frowned because I noticed there was no postage stamp or anything that would say it had been mailed. How long had this nigga had this shit?

"Ugg Cent, I know. Look at me. But I got some work done before I'm out of commission. I'm trying to help out behind the scenes as much as possible to make sure shit stays stable until I come back. I did just hire a replacement for that Fed bitch," she sneered. Then her face twisted up before it smoothed out.

"Nia? Do you want me to call Damari or Sam? Both? I don't know how this works," I said, standing. She waved me down as she blew out her breath while holding her belly.

"Girl, I'm good. So anyway, I got this new Dominatrix that I'm excited about because she is good with her shit. She's going to take over Shantel's place while she's handling all this shit," she waved in the air.

"Wait! Hold up, Shantel is a Dominatrix! I mean, she does know how to command attention," I moved around the table. I pulled out my phone as I moved.

"I would've said Seyra because you know she's always on everyone's ass," I laughed. I dialed Damari, knowing he was probably waiting for me to call somewhere on the property.

"Girl, hell naw! Seyra has way too much on her hands for this. Her name is Emmilee. But check this out. They call her *Professor E*. She comes in all buttoned up, but under, she is fully leathered up with chains and hooks hanging. It's about to be a time up in *MYTH*," she panted.

"Damari, I need you to bring your ass in here. Nia is in labor," I rushed out. I hung up on him and rushed to Nia's side.

"Bissh, I am not ready for this," she gritted. I raised my brows because it was too late for all that shit. And by the looks of things, she would have to pop out another to keep the status quo.

I stepped into the Women's Center, rocking on my boot. My ankle was slightly throbbing, but I knew I would be good as soon as I sat down. I breathed out a breath as I turned the corner and saw Tali rushing out of her office.

"Tali," I called out. She looked my way and then kept moving. I frowned and picked up the pace toward the front desk. The department was now fully open, and the doors opened in thirty minutes, but with Tali's acting, something felt off. I unzipped my jacket as I turned the corner.

"Do you really think this is in your best interest, Ignacio?" Tali hissed. I slowed down but never stopped moving in her direction. I came up behind Tali as Dr. Tremont took a step closer.

"I don't know who you people think you are, but I'm sure your little nigga doesn't have everyone under his thumb. If everything is up to code, it will all work out, won't it? I'm going to help you, Tali. To teach you a lesson that you won't need to learn later in life," he scoffed.

"You are a fucking idiot. Whatever fucking happens isn't on me, Tre," Tali seethed. She spun on her heel. Tre reached out and gripped her upper arm.

"Get the fuck off of me!"

"You need to listen for your own good or at least your license," he hissed.

"Nigga you aren't my damn daddy! I don't need to listen to anything you've got to say. You need to leave," Tali demanded.

"Stop acting as if you need a daddy. That's your problem, right? Daddy issues," he sneered. Tali looked like she was about to stab this nigga with a ballpoint pen.

"Dr. Deadman walking, I would advise you not to do that," I snapped. I put my jacket, purse, and phone on the desk. I held his eyes as he screwed up his face. Tali flexed her arm and yanked it out of his grasp.

"Excuse me? This is below your fucking pay grade. Who do you even think—"

"Nigga who—"

I snapped my mouth shut, and my eyes widened. Tali's breath caught as she looked around, ensuring no one else was in the vicinity, but I didn't think it mattered. Dr. Dumbass just fucked up.

Shit, shit, shit.

How much had he seen or heard? Damn, I was having an almost normal kind of day.

"See Tremont, it's niggas like you that don't fucking learn their lesson. I come in here seeing you touching shit that doesn't fucking belong to you," Henny gritted. He stepped closer to Tre with every word, causing the man to back up and hit the wall. Sometimes, it was hard to see when his personality switched. You had Dr. Pharma, Hendrix, and then there was Henny. This was Henny and not the one that should even be in the fucking hospital.

"Dr. Sex—"

"Quiet Crescent. I'm trying to hear this bitch speak since he had all that fucking mouth a few seconds ago," Henny gritted.

"You can't—" Tremont began, but Henny bunched up his white coat and slammed his back against the wall hard enough for a few pictures to fall.

"You're—you're fucking crazy," Tremont grunted, but Henny's forearm came across his throat, stopping any other words from leaving his lips.

"Hendrix, baby, hol—"

"Naw, he wanted the nigga. Well, here I am. I don't like people thinking they can touch what the fuck I possess, and then you disrespect my work wife," he chuckled.

"Ahh shit. Tali, we, I—" I had no idea what to say or do. I swallowed as Tali's wide gray eyes glanced at me. She smoothed down her skirt and stepped closer, touching Henny's shoulder.

"Baby, I think he's got it. You got it, don't you, Tr—"

The glance Henny gave Tali had me shrinking to the floor while at the same time making my nipples hard. Tali sucked in a breath, and I saw her press her legs closer together, and it almost made me laugh.

"You got the message right, Dr. Tremont," Tali said, clearing her throat.

"Yes," Tremont hissed. Henny pressed harder into his throat as Tremont's hands came up to try and move Henny.

"Get the fuck out of my hospital, my nigga," Henny ordered. I looked around the small area, hoping no one would round that fucking corner just yet. Tremont wasn't a small man, but I could see the strain he was using trying to remove Henny's arm. Henny pulled away, and Tremont damn near fell but caught himself. He slid to the floor, coughing and gagging as he dragged in breath after breath as he held onto the wall.

"You're.... you are finished Pharma. The cameras... there are cameras everywhere," he said, voice cracking.

"You got two fucking seconds before I chop off your fucking hands," Henny said, leaning his head to the side. Tremont started to open his mouth, but the glance at Tali told him to run. Tremont used the wall to make his way toward the doors leading to the parking garage.

"Tali, I need you to look over the list of people who require lungs, kidneys, and a heart," Henny said casually.

"Hendrix, he called Joint Commission, and they are here. In the hospital," she said urgently. That nigga was a Deadman walking for real. I wasn't entirely sure he would make it off hospital grounds.

"Hendrix? Baby, did you hear me?" Tali said, stepping in front of him. I moved around the desk and came up to his other side. He was still staring in the direction Tremont had run.

"Dr. Sexy, I can't even get a hug or kiss this morning. It's my first day back, and my work hubby is not even paying me any mind," I said. He blinked and looked at Tali before releasing his breath.

"Don't worry about Joint Commission. Just perform as usual, and it will be fine," he said. Then he looked down at me with a raised brow as he held out an arm. I wrapped my arms around his waist and breathed. Why this nigga always smelled so fucking good. Damn. I still could feel the tension in Henny's body, but his lips pressed against my forehead.

"Aight, get off me. I don't feel like fighting with your husband about the rules this early, especially now," he chuckled, looking at my neck.

"Hilarious. And rules? Fuck the rules. We were married first," I laughed, pulling back. "You know Nia is in labor, right? That's what I was coming to tell you, Tali," I said, looking between them. Henny caressed my back before he pulled away and removed his black-framed glasses from his inner pocket.

"Yes, I was coming to tell you Seyra will be tied up, and you will need to handle Joint Commission. Trust me, it will be all good, *Thickness*," he said, stepping closer to Tali. I could tell his ass didn't give a fuck about anything at this moment when he damn near sucked her soul out through her mouth. I was trying to tell myself to move or turn around, but I was stuck, like stuck, stuck watching them. It had me wondering just how he would eat a Mango because.... shit. Henny pulled back, looked Tali over, and then turned away.

"*Thickness*, you got this. I need to handle a few things, but I'll be back to eat you for lunch," Henny said, walking in the same direction as Tremont.

"Wait, run that shit back. Did he say for lunch or eat you for lunch?"

"You heard what the hell this fool said. Fuck, my nipples hurt. But bump all that you handcuffed for real. If it was one nigga that could figure out how to do it, it would be Faxx," she whimpered, rubbing her chest. "But seriously, it's beautiful," Tali said, drawing in a breath as she looked at her watch before closing her eyes and shaking her head.

"Thank you, and we can handle this mess, Tali," I said, touching her arm.

"I know, I know, it's just I've got so much shit to do. We have this mess, and I had interviews," she sighed. I watched as she pulled herself together and held her head higher. Tali shook out her hands and then looked at me.

"Okay, so Nia is having her baby now. That means Seyra can't help until she's done. We no longer have a charge nurse, which is fine since we aren't taking in procedures until next week. So, this should be fairly easy for us," Tali said. I smiled as her professional demeanor settled into place as she fixed her light blue blouse and high-waisted black pants.

"That's right, we got this. All we need to do is make it through today with this bullshit and tomorrow," I said, looking away. I felt Tali's arms around me and buried my face in her shoulder.

"I don't know if I can do it. It's my fault, Tali. He shouldn't have even been over that way. If I—"

"Crescent, listen to me. Milo knew the life. He also had a job, and he did it, so let's not ruin his memory like this. He would be cussing you out right now if he heard you. Whoever pulled the trigger will get theirs," she whispered. I squeezed her tighter and let her go so she could look into my eyes. Her marble gray eyes stared at me intently as I licked my lips, nervous at her reply.

"He got exactly what he deserved. I am completely sure of it," I stated. My tone was hard and flat as her eyes bounced between mine as she breathed.

"Good. He deserved everything he got then," Tali rasped.

"So did Pam," I said quietly. I licked my lips again, and my mouth suddenly felt dry as I confessed to murder without saying the words. Tali pulled back with a frown, but it smoothed out the longer she looked at me.

"That is a conversation over drinks bitch. Let's—"

Tali's words were cut off as an announcement occurred over the loud-speakers throughout the hospital and connecting buildings.

"Good morning, Union Memorial guests and staff. Let's all warmly welcome our special visitors who are here to ensure we are giving our patients the best care possible."

"Let me reschedule these interviews, chile," she huffed before walking away.

Everyone and their mama who worked in this hospital knew what this was all about. I looked back at Tali, but all worry faded as her business persona showed on her face.

"Hendrix said it's nothing to worry about, so then it's nothing to worry about. Let's get the doors open and get to work," she said, spinning. I took a deep breath, completely agreeing with her. I made my way over toward the main doors and pushed the Joint Commission and Tremont's dumb ass out of my head.

As I walked into the staff break room, my heart raced with anticipation. Joint Commission was on the way toward the Women's Center. I glanced at Tali and tried to read her expression. We had worked tirelessly to ensure that every aspect of the new department was in order, but the thought of being confronted by the Commission's members still made me anxious. What in the fuck had Tremont said to them, and what could they be looking for here? We just fucking opened.

Tali and I would represent our department in front of the Commission. We sat down at the table, our eyes meeting briefly, sharing a silent understanding of the task that lay ahead. A few other nurses and techs were in the room, hoping they wouldn't be asked to do anything. I wasn't sure if they would ask to follow a patient's chart or if they would walk around looking for things that weren't up to standard. Honestly, I wasn't too worried about that because Henny never cut corners on any of his shit. He definitely wouldn't, since he built this specifically for Tali.

"Only answer the questions that they asked. And we only show them what they want to see. We aren't doing procedures, so there is no need to go in the back unless they want to check dates on supplies," Tali whispered.

"Bet, it's all good. Not my first rodeo," I danced, making her laugh. Everyone else already knew the deal, and each of the staff members I knew from experience was praying they didn't get asked any questions.

The door opened, and a group of five individuals entered the room. The tall, dark, brown-skinned woman with locs was the first to enter the room. She wore a black business pantsuit and heels, making her look six feet tall. Her dark brown eyes landed on us, and her matte red lips curved into a polite smile. The next three almost had me choking on my own spit when Konceited, Kalvary, and that dude Karma walked in behind her. But a stunning dark chocolate-skinned woman followed behind them, closing the door behind her to steal the show. She had to be about five feet nine inches without heels if not even six feet. What caught me was the wild curls of her hair tipped in a light honey blond, but she had the same shade of toffee-colored eyes as Kalvary.

I knew damn well my mouth was open because, one, I had to be out of it when he carried me out of that house because that nigga Kalvary was fine as fuck! He was a shade lighter than the woman standing beside him, but I blinked when he smiled at me. Yeah, that was the same man. He just wasn't wearing that Marshall uniform. I looked at Konceited, but his entire persona seemed different. I was used to the suits, but they were worn with a more authoritative feeling this time. What in the hell was going on? Everyone in the staff room was quiet as fuck after they entered, but I understood why. The feeling in the air pressure seemed to condense and press in on the senses like they were stealing all the air out of the damn room. I glanced at Karma, but I caught Tali's slack jaw as she stared at that sexy chocolate nigga. I bumped into her arm on purpose, accidentally, and she blinked and stood up.

"Hello, my name is Tali Saunders. It's nice to meet all of you. What can we do to help you do what you all came to do?" she smiled, holding out her hand.

"Hello, Tali, it's wonderful to meet you. I'm Noelani Kalm, but you may call me Noelani," The older woman smiled as she stepped forward to take Tali's hand. Konceited stepped forward to shake our hands, introducing himself as Kodey Kreu. Karma, or should I say Horizon, was next, then Kalvary, and finally Kalamity. After introducing themselves as members of the Joint Commission, they took their seats at the head of the table. I could feel the weight of their authority as they began to address us.

The leader of the Commission, Noelani, held a stern expression with sharp eyes, wasting no time diving into the purpose of their visit. She explained that they had received an anonymous complaint regarding the practices and conditions within the Union Memorial, including the newly opened Women's Center. Tali and I exchanged glances because what the fuck. How the hell was Henny pulling this shit off? How in the hell had U.C.K. infiltrated all aspects of the healthcare field? What kind of black magic shit they had going on. But we maintained our composure as the members of the Commission began to ask us questions about our department. I could tell it was all for a show as they asked each person sitting at the table questions and dismissed them once they were finished. The entire time, Konceited and Karma were on their tablets. I wasn't sure exactly what they were doing, but I wasn't about to ask. Noelani took charge, and the rest sat quietly as she asked the needed questions.

Noelani finally returned to us with a warm smile but directed her next questions at Tali. She inquired about our patient care protocols, the qualifications of our staff, and the measures we had in place to ensure patient safety. Tali answered confidently, outlining the rigorous training our staff had undergone and the comprehensive safety protocols we had implemented. She spoke eloquently, her passion for nursing shining through as she addressed each query with poise and professionalism.

As Tali finished speaking, Noelani turned to me with a tablet. She delved into the specifics of our daily routines, asking about our patient care technician duties and our level of involvement in the Women's Center. I took a deep breath and began to explain the vital role we played in supporting the nursing staff, ensuring the comfort and well-being of our patients, and maintaining the cleanliness and organization of the facility. I emphasized the importance of our work in creating a positive experience for the women under our care. She nodded at my explanation and then finished her questions with the last two staff members who were left in the room. After she finished, she dismissed them, and once the door closed, she breathed a sigh of relief.

"Well, Kalamity, did you get all of that? I want everything recorded and uploaded showing we followed through with the complaint and closed it. Kodey, tell me what you found," Noelani demanded. Konceited sat back, his usual easy smirk crossing his face as he winked at me. Fucking Green E yes.

"Well, I went through everything Link sent over. I added a few more discrepancies to Tremont's trail in the system. He actually was doing everything by the book, but after I finish, his documentation will be a fucking mess and look like he's negligent in his specialty projects.

"Good. I really respected Tremont's work as a fellow medical professional, but what can we do?" Noelani sighed.

"Konceited, what the hell are you doing here?" I laughed. Konceited looked up from his tablet and smirked.

"I do have other skills instead of being fine as fuck, Cent," Konceited smirked.

"Conceited ass nigga," Karma mumbled.

Konceited cut his glance to Karma, but looked back at Tali and me, smirking.

"But naw, seriously, I specialize in computer forensics," he said, looking back down. My mouth fell open but closed when Kalamity laughed while raising her hand before looking up.

"Everything is documented and sent over to the main headquarters for review. That nigga thought he was about to do something," she rolled her eyes.

"Great, Kalvary?"

"Of course, everything is up to code. I've already sent my report on it, so the Marshall for this city shouldn't do a pop-up visit. Even if he did, there would be nothing for him to find. So, if we are done, I will take my sister out to eat before seeing Kreed," Kalvary stood.

"Wait, wait, hold up! How? I mean, you know what? I don't even want to know how this shit is possible. Got me all worried for nothing," I said, leaning back in my chair. Kalvary smiled at me while Horizon, a.k.a. Karma, and Konceited finished their work. This insane fine chocolate nigga owned a bank! It was hard to reconcile Karma being named *Horizon*, which was the bank's name. Going by their last name, his family owned the credit union.

"Karma, I didn't get to really thank you for helping me, too," I said. When he met my gaze, he looked up with a frown that smoothed out into a smile as he looked at my neck.

"We're good, and there is no need for all that. We're family at the end of the day. But mom, I'm going to head back to the bank. This niggas finances ain't going to hold up if he's ever taken into custody," Karma said, closing his tablet.

"I'm going to head down to the emergency room and see if Stax is there. He said he would be helping out because they are short staffed," Kalamity said standing.

"Perfect. Thank you all for coming on such short notice," Noelani smiled.

At this point, Tremont was about to go down as one of the most corrupt doctors in the country and then disappear like he never existed.

Noelani laughed, and I could see the resemblance between her and Karma as she fixed his collar before he stood. Noelani looked back in our direction, a wide smile covering her face as she focused on me.

"Now, Crescent, tell me all about how my sweet Fransisco proposed to you," she smiled.

"Ahh shit," Tali mumbled under her breath.

"Sweet! That nigga?" Konceited shouted.

I felt Tali's eyes on me as I sat there dumbfounded at how to tell this lady her sweet Fransisco fucked the shit out of me across the dining table while I signed away my life.

I sucked in a breath and opened my eyes as a warm hand caressed my stomach. I tried moving, but Faxx's body pressed me firmly into the mattress. I blinked slowly as he ran a finger over my nipple, causing it to harden. I glanced at the clock. It was only five in the morning. I knew today was going to be hard as fuck, but I knew it was past time to lay Milo to rest. I sighed as I used my left hand to rub over Faxx's back as he placed kisses along the tattoo's that covered the scars on my body. Roman had made my life a living fucking hell and made me feel like shit every chance he got. I never experienced that with Fransisco, and I knew I never would.

"Fransisco, why do you insist on chaining me to this damn bed like I'm going to go somewhere," I moaned. His tongue traced a path over my navel and lower until he flicked my clit.

"Fuck," I moaned. Faxx took another long lick before sucking the sensitive bundle of nerves into his mouth. My heart rate began to speed up, and my legs moved independently. I widened for him instinctively as one long finger entered my core.

"Shit, baby," I panted as he slid another finger inside. Faxx pulled away and looked up into my eyes. His finger never stopped the slow in-and-out motion that caused my hips to move.

"Because it's a reminder," he reasoned.

"A reminder for...for what," I moaned. I closed my eyes, but his finger tugging at my nipples turned into pinching.

"Look at me, Crescent," he demanded. I opened my eyes and bit down on my lip. My foot was resting on top of the pillow, and I tried not to move it.

"Faxx, please, faster," I begged.

"Naw, I like this slow pace. When it's slow, you beg more for Papi," he smirked.

"Shit, Papi, please," I begged.

"But to answer your question, the cuff reminds you that you belong here. You belong to me, and you can't escape that. Not now. It's too late," Faxx said, pushing deeper. Faxx curled his fingers before spreading them apart as he moved a little faster.

"Papi, the chokehold you got me in, I can't even escape you in my sleep, so why would I try in reality," I stressed.

My hand dropped to my side, hitting something, causing me to turn my head. I moved my hand to try and cover my nipples, and he chuckled.

"What's that for?" I asked. His fingers increased speed, and I shuddered violently. He reached for the black case with one hand and flipped it open.

I tried leaning forward to see what exactly he was doing when his thumb pressed against my clit.

"It's a gun case," he said nonchalantly. I couldn't help the way my walls contracted and clamped down on his fingers at the word. I swallowed and tried to force some kind of sentence out of my mouth. I closed my eyes as he massaged my clit but opened them when I felt something cold, hard but smooth brush along my skin. I pushed up, but he settled his body over me, pulling out his fingers and bringing them to his mouth. My gaze was fixated on that action when I felt the same hard and cool sensation on my clit. Before I realized what exactly he had, he was slowly thrusting it past my wet folds.

"F-Faxx," I cried, my eyes wide, and my pussy seemed to have no problem squeezing at the dangerous weapon. Oh my God! What in the hell was I thinking? I slowly fell into a sexual world I wasn't sure I was ready for, but at the same time, I craved it. My pussy was wet as fuck from his fingers, but now it was drooling when he pulled out his gun and ran it up my slit.

Maybe it's because it's him that I couldn't find a fuck to give.

Maybe it's because of what he said that I felt comfortable showing the crazy shit I liked in my head because he wasn't going anywhere, and I—and I couldn't escape.

Or maybe it's because of the thrill that rushed through my body as he slowly worked the barrel into my tightness. I blinked as my hips moved and realized he was watching me, waiting for me to meet his dark gaze. As soon as I did, he thrusted in again, and my mouth opened. I felt the warmth of his lips on my neck as he licked a trail up my neck and sucked my tongue into his mouth.

"Mmmm," I moaned as he pushed deeper. He was fucking me with his Glock while fucking my mouth with his tongue at the same time.

He worked his Glock into my wet pussy like it was a dildo, or his fingers, rather than a dangerous weapon that could potentially kill me— the same gun that he used to deep-throat me. I was fucking losing it. I could hear myself whining as my head lolled to the side while he worked the Glock into my tightness. It's that pleasurable pain that made me addicted to him, just like when he brought his knife to my skin or when he choked me while watching me take every inch.

I wanted it, and he knew what I wanted. He knew what I needed and craved.

I kept my eyes open, and so did he as he licked the roof of my mouth. I pulled at my cuffed wrist, wanting to touch him because my other hand just wasn't enough. I wanted to touch every inch of his body just like I wanted every side of him.

"Oh, Papi," I moaned as he pulled away. I pulled again at the cuff and raised my hips, but he pushed his body down, sliding in deeper.

"Do you want more, *Mi Amor*? Tell me what you want, Crescent," he hummed against my skin. Faxx kissed his way up to my collarbone before licking my neck and sucking my earlobe. He pressed his lips against my ear and groaned.

"Do you remember when I asked if you would cum all over it if I pushed it to the damn hilt?"

"Oh, fuck me. Shit Papi, Papi, wait, oh God."

"You look fucking *drunk*, baby, because you like that nasty shit. Do you trust me? Do you trust me to give you everything you need?"

"Yes! Fuck yes! I do, I do," I screamed. I could feel my body shaking, but it was almost like I was floating. My cries and screams felt less embarrassing, showing me just how far our brand of insanity went.

"Good to know," he grumbled close to my ear. Faxx sat up, slid the Glock from my core, and trailed it up my body. I felt my wetness as it slid over my titties. I looked down and opened my mouth to ask where he got that thing, but he slid it between my lips.

"Now, do you understand why I can't get enough of that pussy? Do you see why I need to wake up every morning with your taste on my tongue?"

I couldn't answer him with this Glock-sized dildo sliding further down my throat. I felt him position his dick at my entrance as he pushed inside. He pulled the dildo gun out of my mouth and threw it to the side. I felt his large hand travel back up to my side and then to the cuff, releasing my arm. My hands fell to his shoulders as he angled up a certain way, hitting the little bumpy spot that made stars explode at the back of my mind.

"Mm, Papi. Yes Papi."

With every hard thrust, his pelvis tapped onto my swollen clit. In seconds, he had me falling apart and repeating his name like an anthem.

"Fuck, *Mi Amor*, you know I can't live without you, right? You know I'm going to kill every nigga that put a mark on you," he gritted.

His other hand slid under the back of my knee, and he raised my leg, changing the angle as his pace picked up.

"Yes, Papi, I know," I whimpered.

I felt his nails dig into my thigh, and he slammed into me, sinking further as my walls gripped his length. Faxx leaned down, circling my nipple with his tongue as he used the grip on my thigh to slam me back on his dick. The rotating of his hips as he slid in and out, along with his teeth over my nipples, had me losing it. I clawed at his back one minute and held his hips down as he deep stroked my pussy. The way his thick long dick filled and stretched me had tears brimming at the corners.

"Shit. Shit, *Mi Amor*, you feel so fucking tight. That's right, Cent, tighten around this dick like you don't want me ever to pull out. Let me slide in so deep you will feel me with each step you take," he grunted. His hand on my neck began to tighten as his thrust became faster and harder.

"God, yes! Please, Papi," I moaned. My fingers smoothed up his beck to grip his hair. I pulled, lifting his head away from my nipples. He leaned down, licking over my lips as he pulled out to the tip and slammed back inside. I felt the headboard behind me telling me that he was fucking me to the top.

"Mmmm, I wanna see that ass bounce, Cent," he chuckled. I opened my mouth, but he was already slipping out and flipping me over. I tried pushing my body up on shaky arms, and his hand around my waist helped. Once I was in place, I felt a hand in my braids as he gathered them into his fist. Faxx pulled my head back at the same moment he ruthlessly pushed inside.

"Oh fuck! Fuck," I cried as he snapped his hips downward, thrusting into me like a savage, and I was loving every part of his insanity. He angled my head enough that I could look back and see just how fucking crazy he was. The normally flat or dead black seemed to burn my skin as his eyes roamed over me.

His other hand glided over my breast as he wrapped his other around my neck and squeezed. He held me up as he pounded into me possessively as I gasped.

The echoes of his punishing thrust and the sound of his skin hitting mine made the nastiest of sounds I had ever heard. I could feel my channel flood with my juices, giving it that wet skin sound as he moved.

SLAP, SLAP, *SLAP*.

"*Mi Amor?*"

My nails dug into his wrist as he eased his grip slightly. I sucked in a breath as my pussy began to squeeze with a built-up hunger. He made me feel like I was starved, and I needed to feel his cum inside me. I just wanted more of what he had to offer and what he was still holding back.

"Fuck me harder," I cried.

"Cent, Cent, baby, just remember I give you what you want, what you need, and what you can take as long as you can trust me," he affirmed.

"I do, I swear I do, Papi," I moaned.

"Then cum for me and make sure you stay on your fucking toes," he warned.

A spark ignited and rippled through my entire being. His grip on my throat tightened again as his strokes became fast, harder, and deep as he fucked me down to the mattress. His hand turned my head to the side, loosening his hold as my body tightened. Sparks of light flashed in my vision as an uncontrollable orgasm washed over my world.

"Fransisco!"

My pussy clenched around him when he rotated and pulled back. He slammed in again, and I felt his hot thick cum pour into me.

"Fuck! You like that slutted out shit. I want you to remember all this Crescent. When it's over, all I want to hear is you saying thank you, Papi. Now, what do you say?" he asked. I swallowed as my heart pounded in my chest.

"Yes, Papi," I said breathlessly.

When my eyes opened again, the clock said it was close to eight-thirty. I groaned and rolled over to my back, realizing I was wearing one of Faxx's tee shirts. I pushed myself up to care for my personal needs and get dressed. When I sat up, I frowned at Shantel in the closet.

"Shantel?" I asked, rubbing my eyes. I swung my legs off the bed, testing my ankle to see if I could stand.

"Hey girl, I got Cece up and dressed. I did her hair and made breakfast. Do you have anything red?" she rushed out. I yawned and stood, giving my other foot most of my weight.

"Yeah, yeah, but I don't think you could fit my clothes, boo," I said, hopping to the bathroom with a sore pussy. Shantel stepped out of the closet, showcasing her ivory-tailored peak-lapel jacket paired with slim, narrow bootcut trousers that cost more than my Audi. Her large, red-brimmed hat damn near covered most of her face. Shantel raised the pants' legs, showing off her red logo-heel leather pointed boots. When I looked closer, I saw the letters on the heel that said U.C.K. I was jealous.

"You like that?" she smirked.

"I want a pair," I yawned again.

"I'll think about getting you some made while you put a warm cloth on that beat-up cat so you're not limping into the Lord's house this fine morning," she replied. I almost choked on her words as I started laughing.

"Shut up, I don't even have a comeback," I said.

"Ooouu, yass, I like this. I'm sitting out your dress. Since Milo's favorite color is red, I figured we could wear it for him," she said as I turned on the water.

"Got it! Wearing red," I shouted. I took a deep breath as I prepared myself for the rest of the day.

As I stepped out of the white Maserati Limo, the weight of the day pressed down on me like a physical force. The red asymmetric cape midi dress and exotic limo had me feeling like a stuck-up rich bitch. I said as much to Shantel, who replied that the high neckline is balanced with a below-the-knee hemline, while the cape sleeves deliver a high-impact yet sophisticated look. I nodded and said rich bitch. She smirked at me, telling me that I was now, and to act like it. When I asked Faxx about the limo, he said it was because that's how we did things. We do it big for the people we lose and celebrate their life. I cried like an idiot, and he held me until I pulled it together. No matter what anyone said, this shit was my fault. I exhaled as Tali made her way to my side, wrapping her arm around mine.

"All this is a see you later. Not a goodbye," she whispered.

The air was heavy with grief, and the sad notes of a distant piano drifted through the church, setting the mood for the event that would change the way I moved forever. I took a deep breath, trying to steady my nerves, and reached for Faxx hand. He squeezed it reassuringly, and together we made our way inside. It was packed, but we moved down the aisle as one. The entire crew followed behind us as we made our way closer to view the body.

Cece wiggled out of Mrs. Laverne's grasp and ran over to us, taking my other hand as she walked silently beside us. Her eyes were downcast, and her expression was a mirror of the sadness I felt. She clutched Travis against her chest as she spoke softly to him. Everything was decked out in shades of red and white, Milo's favorite color. He had been more than just a bodyguard to me. He had been a friend, a sounding board, and a brother to us both. His loss was a wound that cut deep into my heart, and I knew Faxx felt the same.

As we approached the open casket, I spotted Milo's brother Mitchell standing there, his face etched with grief. I felt a lump form in my throat as I watched him, knowing that he had lost the only relative he had left. I couldn't imagine his pain, and it only added to the burden I already carried. He looked up and smiled as we approached. I hugged him and made sure he sat next to all of us. Faxx spoke softly to him. I wasn't sure about what, but I knew he wanted to ensure that Mitchell knew he wasn't alone.

The service began, and the pastor stepped forward, his voice filled with compassion as he spoke of Milo's bravery and selflessness. He recounted the events of the shootings and how they took away so many of us too soon. Tears welled up in my eyes as I listened, the guilt and sorrow threatening to overwhelm me.

If only I had been able to protect him as he had protected me.

I could see Faxx out of the corner of my eye, his head moving and his face sitting in lines of fury. I looked at Link holding Cece against his chest as she played with his locs. His face was tight right along with Henny and Oz. What the hell was going on?

The pastor shouted for an Amen, returning my attention to him as he preached. His words were a balm to my wounded soul, and I found a measure of comfort in his sermon. The pastor spoke of love and sacrifice, the bonds that held us together even in the face of tragedy. His words stirred something deep within me, and I felt a renewed sense of purpose, a determination to honor Milo's memory in any way I could. I also felt a deep need for revenge on the real people behind it. Because Milo wasn't the only one hurt. Even though Gigi was a bitch at the best of times, she was dead. My sister lay in PICU because of them. Even though I still felt the blame, others still alive were responsible. And I wanted their heads on the fucking table.

"Cent, I'm going to need to use this hand later," Tali whispered in my ear. I jumped slightly, and Faxx hand landed on my thigh.

"Sorry, sorry, I was thinking," I said softly.

"About?"

"Roman and my father's head on a fucking table," I seethed. Tali turned to face me, her brow rising slightly.

"Did you know that Oz actually has a butcher's table?" She asked just as softly. My brows came down as her words drifted through my thoughts. Then I replayed her words in my mind, coming to a realization. First, that Tali didn't flinch at my casual statement of murder, and two, that Oz was the fucking Butcher. How the fuck hadn't I put that together?

"Are you telling me that Daddy Dom is the... Butcher?" I said through my teeth.

Tali nodded her head as the pastor raised his arms in the air. We all stood, and I looked around the packed church, seeing some people I'd met but many unknown faces. That was until I spotted that nigga Rodney. He was turning to leave the church as they began to close the casket.

"Fransisco—"

"I know *Mi Amor*, don't worry about that. Let's get Milo buried," he gritted.

I followed behind him as they pushed the casket out of the church.

Faxx held out his hand to help me out of the limo, and the weight of the knowledge that this was it pressed down on me like a ton of bricks. But we made our way through the crowd, but I couldn't shake the feeling of impending trouble. I knew I was probably picking up on whatever Faxx felt, but we pressed on. As we approached his final resting place, I felt a deep ache in my chest, a pain that threatened to consume me whole. I was glad that Mrs. Laverne and Mr. Elijah agreed that taking Cece home after the funeral was best. I didn't want her to see this, but a feeling pricked at my skin that something was up.

Faxx walked beside me, his usually flat-ass expression etched with sorrow. Milo's death had hit him hard, but I didn't expect to see him like this. Tali was on his opposite side, with Henny next to her. His usual expressionless face looked at Faxx in concern. I knew Milo was more than a bodyguard to Faxx – he was a friend and brother. He was U.C.K. family. I watched as the red casket etched in gold trimming with a large crown on the top moved slowly down the walkway to the open plot. I looked in the direction of my grandmother's grave reminding myself that I needed to visit her grave as well. Neveena-Sonny Memorial maintained the cemetery beautifully.

We reached the gravesite, and the air was chilled. I felt the weight of the stares from the mourners, their silent condolences hanging heavy in the air. Henny, Oz, and Link flanked us. Their expressions each reflected the turmoil within all of us.

As the funeral director began to speak, Faxx cracked. I was startled, concerned, and confused. He turned away, his shoulders shaking with silent sobs.

"Take me! They took him too soon! It should have been me," he screamed. I reached out to him, but he threw himself at Tali before I could say anything.

"He was a child! He didn't deserve to go out like this," he cried on Tali's shoulder. Henny, Link, and Oz looked at me like I was supposed to do something.

What the fuck was happening right now?

I didn't know what the hell was wrong with him because I'd never seen him act this way or show such emotion. I was stunned. Tali wrapped her arms around him while his simple ass cried on her shoulder. My heart broke because he was showing so much emotion, and none of us knew what the fuck to do. He wrapped his arms around her, turning her toward the grave as he rubbed her butt.

This nigga.

"I know damn well this nigga ain't feeling up my shit at a funeral," Henny grunted.

I opened my mouth to try and defend him from it when he cried out again.

"Milo! You were my nigga!" Faxx shouted, raising his head and shaking it from side to side.

"Move Oz, Y'all can't see he's hurting. Oh, come here, baby," Shandea said, pushing from under Oz's arm. She went to Faxx as I stared at his ass like he was crazy. I didn't know what was happening but stepped closer, rubbing his back as Dea approached him. Faxx leaned over, laying his head on Dea's breast, and I choked. Oz's expression was priceless, but I knew this wasn't the time to laugh.

"I know you fuckin' lyin'. This what that nigga be doing when he gets his hair braided? Henny, you need to get this nigga under control. What in the hell is wrong with him?" Oz grunted.

Mala and Shantel pushed through them as Link stared incredulously as we all tried to calm Faxx down.

"This nigga has finally lost that last screw. I... I don't know how to take this. Henny, you're a doctor," Link stated. I turned to look at them as Faxx moved us around like, *'help me help us,'* but these fools looked dumbfounded.

"This is out of my expertise. Where the fuck is Mena?" Henny said, then his face changed when Faxx raised his head. People were murmuring in confusion, and the looks on other people's faces were of stunned expressions.

"Why him, God! Why him," Faxx shouted, but on that last 'him,' it came out just as flat and dead as his eyes could be. His gaze stared off into the distance. Before I knew what was happening, Faxx managed to move us next to a large stone statue of an angel holding a sword pointing toward the ground. Then chaos erupted as I heard the sound of gunfire. My heart sank as I recognized the faces of people that I knew. Roman people chose this day, of all days, to make their move. My blood ran cold as I realized what was about to happen. I threw my body over Shandea as Mala and Shantel turned around, facing in the outer direction with guns raised. Screams and shouts filled my ears as I covered Dea as best as possible. Tali was right next to me, covering her other side. I turned my head to see Faxx signaling to Henny, Oz, and Link. I watched them and could tell they had trained for such moments, prepared for the worst. As the shots rang out, they sprang into action, taking cover behind headstones and mausoleums. Faxx moved us furthest away with a line of trees to our backs and the statue protecting our fronts.

"Y'all, stay there and stay the fuck down!" Oz shouted. His voice was barely audible over the din of gunfire. He pushed Mitchell in our direction, and Shantel grabbed the boy, pushing him behind her and close to us. I could see the rage and grief in his eyes, but I knew the rage would win out. Shandea was pregnant, and not only that, but they also chose to desecrate Milo's memory. Faxx nodded at Link, his jaw set with determination. My heart pounded as bullets whizzed past them as they returned fire. People ran in all directions, and I couldn't tell if the people on the ground were hit or just ducking for cover. Each shot was a grim testament to the violence that had shattered this solemn occasion and pissed me the fuck off. I wanted to move and react, but what would I be able to do because I didn't have Rose

.

"Cent! What's happening? Who is it?" Tali shouted.

"Oh my God, oh God," Dea said repeatedly.

"Just stay down! Don't move and stay down. Mitchell, make sure they're covered," Shantel ordered.

"I got them. I got them," Mitchell said, panic written over his face.

"Shantel!" I screamed as a man came out of the woods, aiming in her direction. Shantel spun on her red heels, knelt in the mud, and pulled the trigger. Before the man could let off a shot, he fell backward just as another stepped out. Mala swung her arm to the side, pulling the trigger and hitting the man once in the neck and twice in the chest. Then I heard a loud crash. I whipped my head around, panicked that one of them had gotten hurt, but I realized that a bullet hit the machine that lowered the casket to the ground. The loud crash was Milo's casket hitting the dirt bottom as more people screamed. I saw even more people coming out of the tree line, but they moved differently. They carried themselves like they were one body. I could tell that those Clapton niggas were now thinking twice about what they stepped into. That was their problem. They had no intellect and followed Roman mindlessly.

"Go, go, go, go! They're locking the gates!" Someone shouted.

The air was so thick it was suffocating, and the sound of screaming and shouting seemed like it wouldn't end. I saw Henny and Oz alongside each other, their resolve unwavering as they kept pressing forward. Faxx and Link stood and ran together, aiming and shooting, hitting some in the head and others in the gut. Every shot we fired from our side was driving back the Clapton niggas. I couldn't believe they thought it was a good idea to come to Union City.

"Hold that nigga!" Faxx shouted. Link held someone down with his foot on his neck.

"Nigga move one more time," Link threatened. I was guessing the man moved because I saw Link aim and shoot the man in the knee.

"Ahhh! Ahhh!"

His screams blended in with other whimpers and cries as the dust settled and the gunfire began to fade. The people who dressed entirely in black pressed forward, taking headshots of people who were down on the ground. I allowed myself a moment to catch my breath. I slowly pulled away from Dea, letting her move enough to lift her head, seeing that the only people standing had some form of red on except the team of people that came from the woods. I looked around, shaking slightly as the adrenaline left my body.

"Y'all good?" Mala panted. She looked us over while I looked at the cemetery as it lay in shambles, a stark reminder of the violence that had erupted on this hallowed ground. These niggas had no shame, no code, and no respect for shit. I frantically looked around until I saw Faxx dragging a screaming man by the ankle across the grass. I let out a breath seeing that he was safe, but I knew it was going to be a completely different story for any nigga that survived.

"Crescent! Look at me. Are you okay," Tali asked, holding my face. I blinked once, then twice, before sucking in a breath.

"I...I WILL BE, WHEN FUCKING ROMAN AND ALL HIS NIGGAS ARE DEAD."

CHAPTER TEN

Fransisco 'Faxx' Wellington

These niggas ain't got no fucking idea the shit they just brought on themselves. I stood next to Link as he typed on his laptop and watched Oz as he dragged the nigga I shot in the knee onto his Butcher block. I had no idea why Rodney was at the funeral unless he was salty about the bodies not being in the bay.

"Ahh! Fuck y'all niggas! I ain't telling you shit! Fuck Union," the man shouted. I knew something was up when I saw a few people enter and leave the funeral. Their movements and mannerisms were off, but the appearance of Rodney threw me off. It very well could have been his attempt at trying to get someone in on the inside to find out exactly what happened with Milo. No one knew he was there that night of the mass shooting or any real idea how he'd died. Roman came to the funeral searching for answers or evidence because everything he was trying to do was failing. But I really figured shit was up when I noticed another small gathering at a few graves around the cemetery. The spacing and position the parties were in had us almost surrounded. Before we made it to the grave, I had that boxed-in feeling I knew all too well.

"Fuck Union, my nigga? What the fuck makes you think I need you to tell me shit! Henny, did you hear me ask this nigga a question?" Oz boomed.

"Naw, I didn't hear shit," Henny answered. I looked at my watch and set a time that I would need to make my way to Henny's spot. Crescent wasn't too happy about me leaving after that bullshit, but she got it. There was no way things could go unanswered after this disrespectful ass shit.

"Wait! Wait a minute. What the fuck are you—no! No!" The man screamed again. I looked up to see Oz raise his cleaver in the air, and it came down, cutting through the man's arm in one smooth motion.

"Did you fucking wait before you started shooting? Shooting at a place where my pregnant wife was at? Naw, my nigga, I need no words from none of y'all niggas. I need blood for that," he said, turning to look at the others.

The high-pitched scream of pure pain filled the room. The blood from the lost arm sprayed Oz's crisp white dress shirt but blended in nicely with his tie. Henny reached over with his sleeves rolled up with his black latex gloves covering his hands. He tied a tourniquet above the wound before reaching for the blow torch.

"Fuuuucccckkk! Ahh! Ahh! Wh-wh—ahhhh."

"Why the fuck are you screaming? It's only right that we take that arm since it's the one you used to shoot with," Henny confirmed. "I mean, you are the one whose shots were so fucked up that you hit the fucking casket. You desecrated the body of someone from U.C.K.," Henny exploded.

"Ple...I...I'll.... I will tell you anything," the man cried.

"Oz, he said he would tell us anything," Henny stated calmly.

"How? I want to know how when this mutha fucka ain't got no tongue," Oz raged. I watched for a second as Oz grabbed the man's face and squeezed his jaw so tightly that his nails drew blood. He forced his mouth open with a small knife and pulled out his tongue. Henny backed away from the table as the man began to scream and pulled his gun from his holster. Even though we were at the BUTCHER SHOP, Henny still had medical supplies here to do what he liked to do. I didn't think Henny was feeling that shit this time. My gaze followed him as he walked toward the other bound men. It wasn't like these niggas really knew anything. Roman knew exactly what kind of assholes to send that didn't know any better.

I turned to look at Link and caught the wide eyes of the other four people who were caught up at the gates trying to escape. Their duct-taped mouths kept them quiet, but the screams in their eyes told me all I needed to know. The horror and fear on their faces brought a slight smile to my lips as Henny raised his gun to the first one's forehead.

"You stepped in fucking Union City and endangered my fucking family? And you thought y'all would just walk out of here? That bitch nigga Roman sent all of y'all to your deaths stepping foot in my city. Fuck you," Henny said, and pulled the trigger.

He moved to the next man, who tried to get out of his restraints as Henny aimed at his head.

"Fuck you," he said, moving down the line and repeating the same thing as he moved down from person to person. When everything went down, I already knew Ian would contain it. Being the owner came in handy in multiple ways when shit started to pop off. Ian had already initiated a lockdown of the cemetery before anyone managed to escape. Those who were there for the funeral made it out safely with a more sizable retirement than they had that morning. We had to keep this quiet, but I was sure something would get out, but it wouldn't fall back on us. We didn't need this new Chief nigga showing up again talking shit. I checked my watch again as the rage I felt for Roman had me seeing red. What if my daughter was there? What if Crescent, Dea, or Tali had gotten hit? A few people were injured, but it was nothing serious. Roman came at us like all bets were off for him. Even his obsession with Crescent seemed to have run its course and is now taking a backseat. That was fine because I was with the shit. I had a few hours to send the message that needed to be sent before I needed to get back home.

"Link, what the fuck happened with the bodies?" Henny questioned. He turned to face us, his jaw ticking and fist clenching. I took note of his cues which normally didn't show, and it told me he was getting ready to be on some shit. I could tell he was on the edge, and it took a lot to get him there, but I was with it.

"I knew I saw this in the files before, but Lawe confirmed it. This nigga moved the bodies the night of the charity event. There was a file that I hadn't gotten to when we merged systems, but I remembered it because it said KLM," he grimaced. I already knew he was feeling some type of way about that shit, but at least that was one thing we didn't need to worry about.

"So, we'll deal with that later. I'll also have the places Alex will be by tomorrow. Certain parties happen that he likes to attend. But more importantly, what about the body of the mayor? Did he move that too?" Oz said, turning around.

"Send me everything you get on Alex as soon as you get it," I noted.

"I got you. So, what about the body," he repeated.

"When I spoke to him, apparently, he had no idea about that. He also said that from his end, he doesn't see anything on the back channels about what's on the USB. When I checked, I came up with nothing as well. So, it tells me that it isn't on a computer, and if it is, it's not connected to any form of internet. We just need the location, and I feel like that nigga Teddy is my best bet," Link gritted.

"Without the evidence of the file, that body means nothing. We just need to make sure Rodney looks like he is on a witch hunt to make a name for himself," Oz stated.

"Then the plan remains the same. Find that nigga Teddy and take out Charles," Henny nodded. That was my cue to stand because all this shit ran together, and we could handle a few different things at one time. I stood up, looking over the bloody scene and chopped-up body Oz had created before looking back at the rest of them.

"Faxx, you know these are Clapton niggas. How do you want to handle this shit because I say blood," Henny queried. I looked down at my watch again and read the text Whisper sent. She had confirmed that the two people I most wanted had showed up today and were in the building. Whisper also confirmed her pick-up, which might help with Henny and Oz's frustration before tomorrow's party. I had agreed with Crescent last night about not rescheduling the party, but with all this shit happening, maybe we should have.

"I say make these Clapton niggas think fucking twice. I don't want no shit happening tomorrow. Dea can't handle another stressor like that. Make sure they can't come back from this," Oz fumed.

"Bet, it's about time for Dmar-Clap Productions to be audited anyway. They won't even give it a thought when bodies start falling from buildings. While Link and I handle the response to Clapton, y'all will have an appointment at the *CLINIC*," I finished. I reached for my holster and pulled it on before reaching out for my black riding jacket.

"Who?" Henny asked. The door opened, and Sam walked inside with a garment bag and a medium-sized box.

"I figured you would look like this. Shandea sent you clothes and this," Sam notified Oz.

Oz moved around the table toward Sam with a frown at the box.

"What's in the box?" he asked, taking the bag.

Sam let out a short, biting laugh before shaking his head while staring at Oz.

"It's.... it's so fucked up. It's only really fucked up because it came out of Dea's mouth. I just can't believe it," he huffed.

"Nigga what the fuck did she say it was for," Oz demanded. He turned away and started for the door in the back that led to a small bathroom.

"She said she wants the head of the nigga that made Milo's casket fall," Sam said straight-faced. I looked at Sam, and I could feel Link and Henny staring at him as well. Oz turned around slowly and frowned before looking at Henny.

"Nigga does pregnancy make a woman homicidal or some shit because she's been on one lately. Extra.... extra crazy," Oz questioned. Sam started to laugh and shook his head, setting the box down.

"Wiz, I'm ninety-nine percent sure that she got that shit from you. I mean, exchanging DNA can change a person," Sam smirked. Oz glared at Sam, who just let his smile get bigger.

"Shut the fuck up nigga. Whatever, put that nigga head in the box. Now who the fuck is this new patient?" Oz asked. He hung the bag on the door and then began removing the blood-soaked dress shirt. Henny opened and then closed his mouth before turning to face me. He raised a brow, choosing to ignore Oz's question.

"Agent Thomas Higgins. It seems he's been poking around about Pamela's whereabouts for her worried brother," I chuckled. That nigga should be worried about his fucking self.

"Bet," Henny nodded. Sam stepped in my path, looking into my eyes, and I waited for a minute to see what the fuck he wanted.

"I can't see it, but I would've killed to see those fake ass tears," he laughed.

"Fuck you, my nigga. Take your ass back to the hospital with your son," I said, pushing by him.

"Faxx, it's hot as fuck in all surrounding cities. It's all over the news about the businesses, homes, and missing people being taken out," Sam said, raising his brows.

"We're all good. This will be quietly loud as shit," I said, pushing the door open.

"This nigga is entirely too calm. Call Ace and Ech—"

Oz's words were cut off, and I walked up the stairs, opened the other door, and stepped into the small storage room. I hit the screen to look outside before pushing the door open and walking over to my metallic matte black and pearl white Hayabusa. I stuck my hand in my pocket, pulled out my gloves, and began sliding them on when the door opened again. Link stepped out, zipping up his red and black riding jacket while walking over to his matte red and black GSX-S1000GT that was pushed to the max with a power commander. He pulled on his black gloves before picking up his matching black helmet.

"Are we keeping it standing, or is it coming down?" Link asked.

I grabbed my helmet and looked up at the sky. The sun was high, and I knew the streets would be busy as fuck.

"It's already laced up just like I like it. All that shit is coming down just as soon as we get what the fuck we need. I want that nigga Roman to keep thinking hiding is going to save his ass. He'll be in my container on the RANGE very soon," I grunted.

"Bet. I want to be there for that shit," Link noted.

"Let's get this shit done so I can get home and make this fucking cheese-cake for tomorrow," I chuckled.

"Don't forget about Shantel's cheese—"

"Nigga ain't nobody forgetting about her spoiled ass. Who are you, her fucking spokesperson?" I speculated.

"Fuck you," Link chuckled as I shoved the helmet over my head and made sure my hair was under my collar. I swung my leg over my bike, starting the engine. Once I released the brake, I hit the throttle and pulled out from behind the shopping center. Once we hit the highway, I let this bitch open up.

We walked up to the towering glass building where Dmar-Clap Productions was located in Clapton. It would have been better if we were on foot, so we parked up the block on a side street between a consignment shop and an old carpet cleaning business. One was still closed, while the other had no customers at all. Both of their security systems were non-existent. They were for looks only because they weren't recording a fucking thing. I could feel the tension in the air as Link, and I pushed through the glass doors and entered the lobby. I didn't give a shit about the security cameras surrounding us because they were already scrambled. As for this building, I wanted this nigga to see us here. I already knew the two employees were here, probably trying to figure out why they were being audited or trying to locate their boss to deal with it. None of the people who worked for Dmar-Clap Production was on the up and up. All of them niggas were on some shady shit.

"So, are we not going to talk about the Cece situation and what you're planning on doing," Link asked. I hit the button for the elevators and glanced toward the large, wooden, empty desk where the security should've been sitting.

"I have been meaning to ask what you think we should do about Cortez. He seems to know a lot about us. Have you been able to find anything out on him yet?" I asked. I could honestly say I wasn't feeling that this new chief knew shit about us. He knew enough that he knew how to point each of us out with our names.

"We know what Konceited knows about him, but I want to know the real reason why he told us about the bay. What is his end goal and will he become a problem," I said as the doors slid open. Four people got off of the elevators that I could tell worked on a different level than the production company. Dmar-Clap was located on the top floor of the tower.

"Man fuck that nigga. I got the information Konceited sent, and I've also got something running on him to find out what we don't know. I'm talking about that little nigga Travis," Link stated. I hit the button for the top floor and waited until the doors closed to look this nigga in the eyes.

"Lakyn, you know, and I know that they are children. I'm going to be straight up with you because I feel the same way as you and so do Henny and Oz, but what you aren't thinking about is what if we take this friend away from her? She is attached right now, but that shit could fade in a month, a year, shit two weeks. You saw what happened to her when Crescent was gone for just a week. What the fuck do you think will happen if we remove her first friend?"

Link was looking at me like I had two fucking heads growing out of my body. I knew how he felt because I felt the same fucking way, but there was one difference. I knew what the voices in her head could turn into, and it could be something she never came back from, just like my mother. Also, a phone session with Mena and Crescent talking over the situation cleared my vision enough to do what I think was best for Cece. I was actually using what Cent said last night word for word and just switched the names.

"This sounds like that shit Cent be talking about. I told you fucking with her classwork would fuck with your head. I can see I'll be raising her alone," he gritted.

"Nigga! You're wildin', I need you to snap out of it. Francesca isn't going anywhere my nigga. She just asked to stay with you for the weekend," I shrugged. I was lying like shit.

"Oh, oh, aight, aight. That's cool, I just need to rearrange some shit but it's all good," he nodded as the doors slid open. I chuckled stepping off the elevators and reminding myself to tell Cent this shit. Henny was right about me being too calm because I was, and that's normally when shit was worse. I felt the blackness slipping in and following through my blood like ice water. All I could see was my target and the information we needed. I pulled my Glock from my holster and walked toward the voices. Link followed suit pulling out his pistol and tapping it against his leg. I raised my arm looking at my watch as I tapped the screen. I sent the alert that would make all the floors have a fire alarm in the next twenty minutes. The desk was empty just like I expected it to be. I looked at the words written in the wood behind it and sneered. The lobby was sleek and modern, with the Dmar-Clap logo emblazoned on the wall in bold letters. This was the reason Cent had been practically held like a slave just to make a nigga some money. It worked for a while to is what's crazy and the reason why he was able to move so freely was because he didn't have to touch his money. If anything were to ever happen all that shit would've landed on Crescent.

I tilted my head from side to side shaking out my arms as the cold spread through my body as we moved toward the large open door. I stepped up just as the man in a pin-striped business suit stood up and moved closer to the desk where the young woman sat.

"Tarryn, I don't think you fucking understand what the hell is happening. We don't know when these leeches will show up, nor do we have access to grant them into the systems. Where the fuck is Banks?" he seethed.

"And again, Jim, I said I don't know! What the hell do you think I've spent the last twenty-four hours trying to figure out? I can't get into his files! How about you do something! Call...call Roman!"

"Who the fuck do you think ordered us, meaning you, to find Theodore. Have you seen the fucking news lately or what? People are dying left and right! People we fucking know Tarryn. Our biggest artist is locked up and no one can contact him. Not even the lawyers we send down there daily. Theodore is like a fucking ghost and Roman.... if we don't get him something to go on, we will be the next names on the damn list," he seethed. Jim slammed his fists on the desk making the laptop Tarryn was working on bounce. Tarryn looked up her brown eyes assessing Jim and she pushed her round-framed glasses higher up on her nose. So, we found the accountant who was also Theodore's personal assistant. She was a young brown skin woman with a harried look, that quickly turned to rage. Jim

Bradley the talent manager and also the one who set up the meeting on Soundisland for Crescent to come here.

"I'm going to need you to back the fuck up, Jim. I'm not these young dumb girls that come in here afraid of their own fucking shadow," Tarryn retorted.

The atmosphere was thick with tension as we moved further into the room. It was clear these two knew the backends of this piece of shit company. And it also sounded like Jimmy Boy had contact with Roman.

Jim loomed over the desk, leaning in close to Tarryn's face. His voice was low and threatening as he demanded through clenched teeth.

"Find the fucking location of Theodore before we are both found with our necks broken," he gritted. That seemed to catch Tarryn's attention because she was visibly distressed and began insisting that she was trying to find Theodore but didn't know where he was.

"Well, you better, because if not Roman will make sure we are the next people that can't be fucking found Tarryn," Jim said. His tone turned darker as he issued the chilling threat.

I stepped forward, and interrupted their stare down, with a chuckle as I started the timer on my watch. Tarryn's head snapped up and Jim turned around with his face revealing shock, then fear. That right there told me he knew who the fuck we were. So, I would start with this bitch ass looking nigga. Link raised his pistol as he casually walked closer to the two, but his focus was on the laptop.

"It doesn't look like I need to tell you who the fuck we are so let's get to it, Jimothy Bradley. We know how tight you are with Roman so let's not act as if you don't fucking know where that bitch is hiding. College roommates and longtime friends. So, lets cut the bullshit," I smirked.

"Y'all niggas real quiet all of a sudden. One of you better start talkin'. It will make things so much easier," Link stated. He used his pistol to point at Tarryn to stand up from the desk.

"I know exactly who you are, but this isn't Union City. Y'all U.C.K. thugs got the wrong idea about us because we don't know anything about where anyone is," Jim shrugged. I smiled before lowering my Glock slightly and shooting.

"Ahhhh! Ahhhh! You.... fuck! Fucking bullshit," Jim screamed as he fell to the ground. Tarryn screamed but closed her mouth when Link put the pistol to her forehead.

"Now, that we all are clear how this shit is going to go let me try this shit again. Where. Are. They? Tell me where the fuck is Roman Sharpe and Theodore Banks," I gritted. Link had Tarryn moving closer to a screaming Jim as he sat down behind the desk.

"I.... I already told you! We... we don't know.... we don't know where either of them are," Jim gritted. He held pressure to his thigh in the exact spot that nigga took a knife and cut Cent for Roman's entertainment.

I stepped closer, stepping on Jim's thigh and hand, smashing my foot down as he screamed.

"Ahh...ahh...fuck, fuck, fuc—"

"Listen, all I do is handle the money and meetings. I just work for them, that's all. I don't know where they are. So...please—"

"Shut the fuck up. You're not as naive as you're making yourself look Tarryn. You know what the fuck has been going on and the one that deals with the money knows where the bodies are hiding," Link said closing the laptop.

"I...I account fff...for the money but I don't—"

I snapped my head in her direction as I pressed harder onto Jim's leg and Tarryn clamped her mouth shut.

"Bullshit! Don't fucking lie to me Tarryn Maynard," I smirked. Her brown eyes widened as her glasses slid down her nose.

"Yeah, that's right. I know who the fuck you are, and I know exactly what you do. Yes, you fuck with the money, but you also take care of that nigga Banks personal shit. You even deal with his properties," I smiled.

I stared at her while I aimed my Glock at Jim's head. I could see Link standing and picking up the laptop. Tarryn exchanged uneasy glances, her facades of lies about not knowing something was beginning to crack under the pressure.

"She doesn't know shit! If she knew, we wouldn't fucking be here you son of a—"

I turned my Glock to the side and smashed it across his face once, twice, and a third time.

"Stop! Stop! Please... if we knew somethin', I would tell y'all ...but y'all don't get it. It's Clapton and Roman...he...runs Clapton," Tarryn screamed. I saw her looking toward the doors, probably expecting security to come walking in any moment because of the shouting.

"Fuck it Faxx, maybe a little pain will help her memory. We have less than ten minutes. It's funny that she's worried about that nigga Roman. I think we should show her who the fuck she should be afraid of. I've broken the code to Teddy's little files," Link said glancing at his watch.

"Wa—wait a minute. I don't know what you think I can do," Tarryn cried.

"Tarryn just keep your mouth closed," Jim gritted. I leaned down and grabbed him by his jaw. I squeezed harder, forcing him to look into my eyes so he could see the rage.

"Your loyalty to that nigga is what put you in this position now. I don't give a fuck about how long you and he went back. The moment you saw that nigga lay a hand on Crescent is the moment your life was forfeited my nigga. I ain't here for you anyway but I knew you would be here to oversee his bullshit. You made my wife bleed," I hissed. I pressed harder on his leg, and he grimaced in pain before screaming. I leaned back watching the pain cross his face.

"Ahhh! Bitch! Th...that bitch....is what caused all this shit!" He screamed.

I looked at my watch before reaching down and pulling this bitch ass nigga to his feet. The scream that tore out of his body wasn't going to be anything compared to the one that was coming soon. I pulled him close to my face as that of his hands reached for his leg while the other gripped onto my wrist as he ground his teeth together.

"The only bitch I see is you, my nigga. Another bitch on my list that needs to take a fucking flight," I intoned. I raised my arm and aimed at the large floor-to-ceiling windows that looked out over Clapton. I stared at its twin across the street before pulling the trigger six times. The large glass began to crack on the fourth shot. The last two made the glass so fragile a touch would have glass falling to the sidewalk.

"Please, stop! Please!" Tarryn screamed. Link grabbed her by the bicep and yanked her onto her toes.

"You got a choice to make, Tarryn. You wanna keep playin' dumb, or you want to do what's needed to save your fucking life?" Link snarled. "Time's running out, Faxx," he said tapping his watch.

"Jesus fucking Christ! Alright, alright. Look, I'm not entirely sure but if I'm right it's on the outskirts of Clapton! Not one of his locations but the distribution warehouse for *Silk*! He's where we keep the fucking *Silk*," Jim rushed out.

"Location?"

"I don't...I don't know for sure because I've never been there. That's...that's that Cartel shit! That's all we know, I swear! I fucking swear," he pleaded.

"What about Theodore? Where's he at?" I asked.

"I... I don't know, for real. He's been moving low-key for weeks now. I haven't seen him," he babbled.

"Bet," I said putting my Glock away. I used that hand to raise this nigga to his toes letting him see his death before it happened.

"You're going to let us go, right? I told you...what...I know. My leg needs—"

"Hell yeah, I'm going to let you go. You'll be the first one to get to the ground floor," I chuckled. I held onto his lapels with one hand as I punched him repeatedly in the face, causing his nose to break and his teeth to crack. And then I threw his bitch ass at the cracked window causing it to break completely as he crashed through it.

"No! No! Ahhhhhh—"

"Oh, my fucking...oh shit, shit, shit," Tarryn cried. I turned away not needing to see what happened. I already knew what a body looked like when it hit the ground from this height. It was time for us to go. Whoever was still in the building at this point was no longer my concern.

"Let's move. Ace is in position," Link said, pushing Tarryn forward. I moved faster hitting the button for the elevators that opened instantly. I stepped inside and hit for the lower level so we could leave through the underground parking lot.

"Oh my God. Thank you, thank you, thank you," Tarryn whispered as the door shut. The drop was fast to the bottom leading me to think no one else was left in the building because it didn't stop.

"Don't thank us yet. Thank us when you do what the fuck we need you to do. Because if you can't, there is always another building with another fucking window," Link grunted.

"God," she whispered closing her eyes. I glanced at Link before looking at my watch again. The door opened and I stepped off and began to jog toward the opening. I heard the click of heels as Tarryn ran behind me with Link following. I already had some idea's how to figure out where the fuck Roman was, and I would put Konceited on that shit asap. I already knew Link would be tied up and he needed to focus on that Teddy situation.

We exited the garage on the opposite side of the tower with one minute and forty-five seconds to spare. I reached back, grabbed Tarryn's arm, and began to pick up speed. I could hear the sounds of sirens and I knew the streets would be cleared so the firetrucks could get through. They were close and would make it just in time to see the building fall to the ground.

"Time," Link shouted just as a loud explosion sounded. Then all you heard was an explosion after explosion rocking the street. We kept moving as Tarryn screamed as we put distance between us and the crashing tower.

"Oh shit, shit," Tarryn screamed, tripping over her feet as a cloud of dust covered the area as each level to that fucking building came down. I reached down pulling Tarryn to her feet as we moved, not caring that she lost a heel. I pulled up the scarf that was around my neck and put it over my mouth. The entire street looked like it was covered in a sandstorm of concrete and glass.

"Van! Van!" Link shouted passing by us. He reached the blacked-out van and threw open the sliding back door. I lifted a screaming and crying Tarryn and threw her into the van.

"Wait! No! Where are they taking—"

"Close your fucking mouth. Do what you do best and use this to find your fucking boss. You want to live make that shit happen," Link ordered as he tossed the laptop inside. As soon as he slammed the door shut, and banged on the side, it took off.

As soon as the van pulled off, we ran toward the bikes. At least that bitch Monica would be good for something because she not only was dealing with the Cartel, but she chose their locations. I climbed on my bike and felt the vibration on my waist seeing there was a message from Oz.

> Oz: Earlier than I thought 8798 Canterbury Lane is where the next party is held. Meet me.

Before starting up my bike I sent Damari a quick text to take Crescent home. I didn't want to miss the opportunity that I could get to Alex if I had it. I just wanted to finish so I could go home, bake this fucking cheesecake, and lick my wife's pussy.

"One more stop. Keep up," I smirked. I pulled on my helmet and started the engine just as Link pulled beside me. He raised his visor and stared at me.

"Canterbury?" he asked. I just nodded and hit the throttle. "Bet, let's see who makes it first," he said, slamming his visor down as police, fire engines, and ambulances zoomed by. As soon as it was clear I released the brake and peeled out on that nigga.

As we approached the sprawling mansion right on the line between Union City and the surrounding county, I could feel the adrenaline coursing through my veins. The power of my Hayabusa always gave me a thrill but when I hit its top speed, I get hit with that rush that I knew diving deep into some pussy would be the only thing to bring it down. The day was getting later sliding into mid-afternoon, but it was alive with possibilities, and the air crackled with the promise of dangerous explosions. I lived for moments like these—moments when the line between chaos and control blurs, and the world becomes a playground for a U.C.K. nigga.

Oz had been tracking Alex's movements for weeks. The rumors of these parties had been floating around, but it wasn't our shit. It never interfered with our business in U.C.K., until one of its members started trying to put his foot in our fucking city. If that wasn't enough, he was the true reason Crescent was put in the position she was in. If it hadn't been for him putting her on Roman's radar none of that shit that happened to her would have happened. The information Oz ended up getting from the Country Club had led us to this opulent mansion, where a party was rumored to be. We all knew it would be filled with Union City's elite which might help also get us information on Charles' people. Oz was waiting at the entrance, already managing to take out the security at the gate, so that we could get in. I knew if some rich-ass old niggas would be here his ass would be as well. He was always searching for more clientele and more information. Oz pushed off his Navigator and stood to his full height. I was surprised he wasn't wearing a suit but was decked out in all black down to his feet. The only thing of color was the red tree on the side of his boots. He reached inside of his SUV as we came to a stop, pulling out the specially made fitted vest.

"None of us can get fucked up. Shandea will lose her shit if we all ain't at this fucking party tomorrow," Oz said, handing us our vest. He reached back inside, grabbed a large black duffle and pulled it out. I smiled knowing it was Whisper who probably sent this shit with him. But I felt him on that Shandea shit. I knew he would do whatever it took to keep her ass happy. It was all good with me because I didn't want shit standing in the way of tomorrow night. If I could get to Alex or Roman by then, then it would make that shit even better.

"Bet, so how do you want to handle this?" Link said pulling on the vest and making sure everything was covered. I did the same and blew out my breath because it ain't any more subtlety about this shit. Alex was quiet while he made backhanded deals or stole my shipments. Why the fuck should we?

"Kick that bitch in and whoever pulls out on us they can be the first to go. Get what the fuck we need then flatten this bitch," I demanded.

"I'm with it. Let's go," Oz said, moving towards the house.

"All this nigga wants to do is to see who the fuck is here and use that information later," Link snorted. I smirked because that nigga was right. Lennox Anderson would always show up when it could grow his business legally and illegally.

"I can't see the lie in that my nigga," I chuckled.

We approached the ornate front door. It was large and looked wooden. I could tell that it was reinforced. I gave Link a nod, and without a word, he raised his wrist and began to hack into whatever security this place had. I was sure they had something expensive, but I wasn't worried over that shit. I reached into my pocket pulling out a grayish-black container that held a gray almost Play-Doh-like substance. I pressed it against the hinges of the door holding each of them for one minute.

"We good to go," Link stated as I backed away. I counted to fifty in my head when the door exploded. The blast had the thick door splintering and crashing to the floor leaving a trail of smoke. The music and laughter from inside came to an abrupt halt as we stormed into the opulent foyer, drawing the attention of the well-dressed guests wearing less than nothing. High-profile people from Union City, Del Mar, Puafton and Clapton mingled in the decadent surroundings, oblivious to the intrusion about to shatter their evening. The music was loud and the laughter even louder until two more people looked toward the blown-out door.

"This is exactly what it felt like walking in on my parents the other day," Link murmured. I frowned but I was going to have to ask about that statement later.

"What the fuck my nigga," Oz asked incredulously.

"Move, move," I said instead as we moved quickly inside scanning the room. Two men came out of a room to the side of us. Oz never hesitated. He turned punching one of the men so hard in the chest it visibly caved in as he hit the wall. The other man stopped in his tracks as Link pointed his pistol at him and raised a brow.

"Who—"

The guard's mouth hung open and his eyes were wide as Oz's cleaver came down on the top of his head. Oz pulled back with a forceful yank and the man fell to his knees before falling face-first onto the floor.

"Trying to keep things quiet for a moment," Oz boomed. His eyes began to turn the same shade as mine. I saw a man stand and head in our direction wearing all white from his hair down to his shoes. I looked away and my eyes locked onto a familiar face. Alex's father, who was standing near the grand staircase, had a look of shock on his face. But as our eyes met, I could see a flicker of awareness, recognition, and confusion in his expression. When I tilted my head and smiled, I saw the flicker of fear enter his blue eyes.

"Gentlemen, how may I help you? This is a private invitation-only party," the man smiled looking us over. He didn't look afraid or bothered by the violence and I found that shit odd. Oz stepped forward, smile wide on his face showing the bottom row of his golds.

"Milford Winthrop, I never expected you would be running this...this scene," Oz smirked.

"Mr. Anderson, I didn't notice it was you. I'm sure you understand the need for these parties. We used to hold them at *MYTH*," he grimaced.

"Oh, still salty the old man left his business to the help, and not his son. So sad for you," Oz said looking around. When Oz said that Alex had certain proclivities, I wasn't thinking that shit would run in the family, but it would make sense. *MYTH* had some wild shit about it including sexual experiences that people wouldn't think others would enjoy but this shit, this shit looked like a borderline slave auction. The women and men on the platform had their heads bowed as they stood there while the other people in the room held up numbers. Some people began to duck their heads and stuff the numbers they held under their seats.

"This is not the place for you, Oz. You don't belong here just like you didn't deserve my fucking birthright. Because of you, I had to start from scratch, you stole my list," Milford gritted stepping closer.

"Ford shut the fuck up and stop crying like a little bitch. Cry after you lose these people because I couldn't ask for anything more with this shit," Oz chuckled.

"You nigge—"

"Watch that shit Ford. I don't want to kill your smart ass out of respect for Sinclair," he retorted. "We ain't here for you or whatever you got going on," Oz stated aiming his desert eagle at his chest. Oz was saying that shit, but the watches and vest were recording every fucking thing. I turned my attention back to Alex's father as he moved quickly up the stairs.

As the initial shock subsided, the guests began to murmur and cast wary glances in our direction.

"Get. The. Fuck. Out," Milford growled. Oz smiled and tipped his head at us to grab up Elton Tilderman's bitch ass. I could feel Milford's rage and confusion because where the fuck was his security team? Little did he know they were locked in the security room after Link took control.

"Naw, once we get what we need then we will leave you to your shit. Let's go sit with your friends," Oz said stepping forward. The gun was at Milford's chest, and I saw the realization in his eyes when he figured out no one was coming to protect them.

I moved, leaving Oz to deal with those people as Link followed me up the stairs. Elton had a head start but that nigga was old as fuck and out of shape. We reached the top and I saw him push the woman he held on a leash into a room and slammed the door. We made our way down the hall, and I intentionally placed the grayish-black puddy at different points on the walls.

"Was that nasty nigga wearing a dick cage?" Link asked. I flicked my eyes over at him before facing the door. I raised my booted foot and slammed it against the hinges.

"You know exactly what you saw," I laughed as I kicked down the door. Link followed closely behind me as we burst into the room, our eyes scanning the room for any sign of Elton or Alex Tilderman. A few people were sitting on couches talking, but now sat in stunned silence as we looked around.

The air was heavy with the scent of expensive perfume. We made our way through the lavish room that opened up into another section of the mansion. I caught sight of Elton, but I didn't see Alex. It wouldn't matter because his father would do. Elton was rushing down the hallway dragging a woman along as he checked doors. Link had moved inside further to the people who were engaged in a hushed conversation. I recognized a few of them, but they weren't who I was here for.

"Get the fuck up," Link ordered. He pulled open a door and looked inside before stepping back.

"Who.... What is the meaning of this?"

"Nigga get the fuck up. Old Colonel Sanders lookin' ass nigga," Link said sucking his teeth. He got the people out of their seats and pushed them through the door he'd opened. I turned back to the hall and watched this old sagging ass man wobble down the hallway. I moved and started down the hall while Link secured the door so no one could come up behind us.. He dropped the leash and started ramming in the door. The woman seemed to scurry to the wall and cover her head instead of running. What the fuck did these niggas have going on?

I pounced on Elton kicking him in the back of the leg causing his knee to buckle under the pressure.

"Ahh! Ahhh shit! What do you want money? Who...who—"

His words turned to screaming as I dragged his ass away from the door by his gray hair. I kicked the door making it swing open before tossing his dick-caged ass into a secluded room.

"Ahhh! My Cock! My fucking cock you.... Fuck," he rolled. I stepped into the room shoving my Glock into the back of his head.

"Shut the fuck up. Get on your fucking knees," I grunted. Elton turned his head slightly as he pushed from the floor and climbed to his knees. Panic flickered across his face as he realized the gravity of their situation. I didn't give a fuck who he was or who the fuck party this was. I was here for one fucking reason.

"Where is Alex?" I demanded, my voice low and menacing. "I'm sure he's been in contact with you. Don't fuck with me Elton," I warned.

Elton Tilderman tried to maintain his composure, but his eyes betrayed his unease. I figured it was hard to play some tuff shit when your dick is out and in a cage. Any more movement in the sharp ends that were inside would begin to poke him.

"I don't know where Alex is," he insisted, his voice strained.

"You expect us to believe that shit? Do you really believe I think you don't know your son's every movement," I scoffed.

Without warning, Link gripped Elton's hair pulling so hard he had no choice but to get to his feet.

"Fuck! Shit, shit God damn it," Elton screamed before Link slammed him against the wall, his grip unyielding.

"Tell us where Alex is, or that cage will turn into a body-sized one for you, your wife, and the rest of your fucking ignorant ass children," Link hissed.

Elton winced in pain, his resolve weakening as Link pressed his pistol into his temple.

"I swear, I don't know where he is!" Elton shirked.

Link was leaning as far away as he could from the naked man, but I stepped up close to his side.

"You're all implicated in Alex's activities, whether you're directly involved or not. You better come up with something better or I will walk your naked caged dick ass down the middle of the streets in Union City. Fuck with me," I promised.

The weight of our presence bore down on him, and I could see the fear in his eyes at my threat.

"I'll... I'll te—tell you what I know," he stuttered, his voice resigned. "But you need to make sure to leave the rest of my family out of this. I've wanted nothing to do with his bullshit," Elton mumbled.

"We'll consider it, so start talking," I gritted.

It became clear that Alex had been behind the scenes for years slowly moving in position to take Union City until U.C.K. happened.

"He's been quiet and distant after my son-in-law showed up barely alive," he sneered.

"You've said a lot of shit my nigga but where he is," I said raising my Glock. Link pressed harder against his temple.

"Fuck! Yes, yes I know! I don't know where he is now is what I'm trying to say. I know where he will be," Elton huffed. I pulled back and waited for Elton to look in my direction.

"Location," I said.

"He— there is another party being held and he will be there," Elton heaved.

"What the fuck makes you so sure about that?"

"He has to attend because after the bride will have to be initiated into this life.," Elton panted. Link shifted and pulled his pistol away from his head.

"Where and when?"

"Trust me, you will know when and where because it will be everywhere once an Astor heir gets married." I barely saw Link move, but I felt the breeze of his swing as hit after hit landed on Elton beating him down to the floor. I stepped back realizing what the fuck this meant. Charles and Mala's wedding is where Alex would be. I waited a few more seconds before I moved and caught Link in the crook of his arm pulling him away before he killed him.

"Do you understand what the fuck this bitch just said?" He raged.

"I did and we know fucking well that shit ain't happening Link. We'll handle it," I said, shaking him. I never felt so much blind anger in my life. Link twisted and I let him go and he moved back over toward Elton. I wouldn't stop him this time. Whatever happens, happens this point. Link dug into the vest pocket and pulled out something that looked like a syringe. He jammed it into Elton's neck and pulled away only after he kicked the cage.

"Ahhh," Elton moaned.

"We got what we need. Elton, I advise you to get the fuck up," Link grunted.

We stepped into the hall and the girl still sat with her back to the wall with her arms and legs zip-tied together. I pulled out my knife moving to cut the ties off of her and pulling her to her feet. Link was already moving down the hallway and into the room we came through.

"Hey! Is anyone else like you here?"

Her bruised body shook but she mumbled out a no sir. My jaw flexed and I pulled her down the hall just as Link threw the last guy out of the closet and toward the door.

"Move! Downstairs, now!" he shouted. His pistol was aimed, and the two men and one woman began to move swiftly down the hall and toward the stairs where I could hear Oz laughing. As we hit the landing, I pushed the girl toward the others who were dressed similarly to how she was. The woman had on a tan bra and panties set and nothing else. The men just a tan pair of briefs and nothing else.

"You know Milford, it's been all good fucking with you, but it's time to go. Thank you all for the contact information. I'll be taking your product off your hands once again," Oz said, standing.

"You'll regret this, Anderson. I'm not the same boy you knew back then," Milford gritted.

"Go back to Puafton with your bullshit Milford, and stay the fuck out of Union City. This is the one and only pass you will get from me. Father or no father I will cut you limb from limb. Tell me you got me, Ford," Oz ordered. I looked out of the windows seeing two black vans pulling up, and Sam stepped out of one, Echo the other.

"Yess," Milford hissed.

"Good, I'm glad we had this talk. Y'all really should leave as soon as we do," Oz nodded. We backed away toward the opening, pushing the people that would have been auctioned out of the opening.

"Milford if you don't want to go down for murder, I advise you to find Elton Tilderman upstairs. His cage got him by the balls," I said, stepping outside. I heard Oz telling Sam what needed to be done as Link stalked his way to his bike. I set the timer on my watch for the explosion. Because, in less than twenty minutes this would be all over the news. What made me sick to my stomach was the fact that...this is exactly how we found Shantel years ago.

CHAPTER ELEVEN

CRESCENT 'CENT' WELLINGTON

I sat in my dimly lit living room, waiting on Faxx as the eerie glow of the television screen cast shadows across the walls. Damari told me we needed to get home because Faxx was going to be later than he first thought. I wasn't sure what happened, but if he wanted me home, that's where I would be. I was already feeling a certain way about what happened this morning and really wanted to be by myself. Roman probably wouldn't have ever been a factor in their lives if it weren't for me. I tightened my hand into a fist wishing I could put that shit through his face. If Dea had gone into labor or gotten hit I would've lost it. If something were to happen to Tali or any of them, I don't think I would be able to handle it. I needed my husband and each time I thought of that sentence my heart squeezed. I was trying to figure out why I was fighting him so hard in the beginning, when I knew exactly what I felt for him. I knew the upcoming appointment with Mena would address that as well. I still didn't fully trust myself, or my decisions.

I sat watching the news as it reported what was happening around the city. I was watching about the recent string of explosions that had rocked Union City and its surrounding areas. My stomach churned with a sickening mix of dread and apprehension as I listened to the details of the devastation that had been happening since the night I was taken. I couldn't tear my eyes away from the screen, even though every fiber of my being wanted to look away.

"Lawd, who does this shit? My man that's who," I whispered.

The fact that they showed Pamela's house and spoke about her disappearance had me bringing my hand to my throat. The only house that exploded was hers and none of the surrounding homes had been touched.

The news anchor's voice filled the room, solemn and grave.

Union City's Channel 7 News

"*Good evening, this is John Goldwin along with our beloved Natalie Bass and you're watching Union City's own Channel 7 News. We interrupt your regularly scheduled programming to bring you breaking news. A series of explosions has rocked Union City and the surrounding areas, leaving a trail of destruction in their wake. The authorities are still struggling to ascertain the cause of these attacks, and the public is urged to remain vigilant and report any suspicious activities to law enforcement.*"

"*Exactly, John. It has been a truly terrifying few weeks here in Union City the destruction seems to be spreading,*" *Natalie said solemnly.*

My heart pounded in my chest as I watched the images of billowing smoke and crumbling buildings flash across the screen. The cloud of dust looked like it could have been a sandstorm, and now I understood his call sign. Faxx was a man of action and didn't fuck around about his get-backs, but I never imagined he would be this extreme.

"John our viewers need our continued coverage of the series of bombings that have rocked Union City and its surrounding areas. The situation remains dire as authorities struggle to identify the perpetrators behind these heinous acts of violence."

"That's right, Natalie, and we will do a deep dive into this story. The latest reports indicate that the explosions have left a trail of devastation, leaving the citizens of Union City on edge. The big question on everyone's mind is, who could be behind these coordinated attacks? Is this a calculated movement or is this being done by the mind of a crazed individual?"

"Absolutely, John. The police have yet to identify any suspects, and the public is understandably anxious for answers. There's been a lot of speculation swirling around, with some pointing fingers at radical groups, while others suggest the possibility of a lone individual with a personal vendetta against the city."

"Indeed, Natalie. The lack of a clear motive or a discernible pattern has only added to the confusion. Joining us now is our esteemed commentator, Dr. Mena Malone, to provide some insight into the possible motivations behind these attacks. Dr. Malone, what are your thoughts on the current situation?"

I know you're fucking lying! Wasn't no way, it just wasn't no way. I reached for my phone on the table sending Tali a quick message to look at the news because what the fuck! Mena!! Fucking Mena!

"Thank you for having me. It's a pleasure to be here, albeit under such troubling circumstances. In my opinion, we must consider the possibility that these bombings are the result of a long-standing *feud between rival factions within Union City. There are whispers in certain circles about a clandestine war between the Union City Kings and their adversaries, and these recent events may very well be a manifestation of that conflict."*

"A clandestine war, you say. That's certainly a compelling theory. Can you elaborate on what might be driving this alleged conflict between the Union City Kings and their enemies?"

"Certainly. The Union City Kings have long been a dominant force in the city's underworld, with a stranglehold on various illicit enterprises. However, recent rumblings suggest that rival factions vie for control of the city's lucrative criminal underworld. These bombings could be seen as a brazen display by others from Del Mar or Clapton."

"Fascinating. So, you believe that these attacks could be a form of retribution or a show of strength in this alleged power struggle?"

"Precisely. It's important for the public to understand the underlying dynamics at play here. While the authorities continue their investigation, it would be prudent for citizens to remain vigilant and consider the possibility that this may indeed be a war for Union City's streets. To be honest the Union City Kings may be the only people to stop it. Why have the authorities not been able to stop these attacks, but they have now slowed down here in our city as if the other factions have pulled back."

This bitch is seriously on the news getting people on U.C.K.'s side. I'm fucking dead.

"Thank you, Dr. Malone, for your valuable insights. As we navigate through these turbulent times, it's crucial to remain diligent and consider all possible angles in the quest for answers. We urge our viewers to exercise caution and report any suspicious activities to law enforcement as we await further developments in this ongoing crisis. I don't know Natalie, is Dr. Malone correct and the Union City Kings may be the answer to this ongoing situation?"

"I can't answer that John, but I know that we all would love for this war to end," Natalie said looking into the camera.

"In other news, a mansion owned by the Sinclair family has just exploded. But Channel 7 News just received video information on a human trafficking ring being run by this influential family. Natalie let's take a look. Viewer discretion is advised for those under the age of eighteen—"

As the news report continued, I heard snippets of interviews with witnesses and survivors, each account painting a picture of fear and confusion. It was a surreal experience, sitting in the safety of my own home while the city was teetered on the brink of chaos. A few witnesses said how lucky they were to get some kind of notice, or nothing touched their homes at all. People whose homes were impacted by this praised their homeowner's insurance for swift action and reimbursement to get back on their feet. As soon as they went on a commercial break an insurance company commercial for NEW HORIZON'S INSURANCE COMPANY began to play. This nigga really did have to pay out Premiums.

I reached out grabbing the remote to mute the TV before picking up my phone again to call Tali. I couldn't believe this shit. I was damn near too stunned to speak as I scrolled for her number. Before I could hit send, I heard the roar of Faxx's bike. I dropped the phone on the couch, and pushed myself to my feet. I was getting so sick of the boot, but whatever injection Dr. Sexy had been giving me seemed to be helping accelerate the healing process. I was heading for the stairs to the basement because I knew he would come up this way. I heard the door open and close as I got to the top.

"Mi Amor, don't you bring your limping ass down these stairs. I need to make a few calls then I'll be up in a few minutes after I shower," he said looking at me from the bottom.

"Fransisco, you smell like you were in a fire or something. Are you okay? Did you get hurt? Is everyone—"

"It's all good Cent. Give me ten minutes and I'll be up there. I need a minute, then I need you to help bake these cheesecakes," he smirked. I smiled at him, but I could see the literal shadows in his eyes before he turned away and went down the hall. I started to take a step and go down anyway, but I stopped. Whatever it was I knew he needed to get himself together before coming to me. I took a step backward from the stairs and went upstairs to shower. Whatever he had to say, I knew it was going to be some heavy-ass shit. I just prayed tomorrow would be as normal as shit could be when with all of them.

I stood behind Faxx as he faced the counter, the tantalizing aroma of vanilla and cream filled the air. It was getting later into the evening and Mrs. Laverne said she was keeping Cece for the night. At least I could talk to him about what I saw on the news and what Cece told me over the phone just now. My eyes were fixed on him, his strong hands expertly maneuvering through the ingredients. Had I been upstairs that long that he already had one in the oven?

Who even taught this nigga how to bake?

I shouldn't really be shocked that he knew how to bake because he seemed to master every damn thing. I wasn't by far an idiot or slow on the uptake but low-key this nigga was passing my classes on some genius-level type shit. Tali said he'd read through the textbook once and that was it. Every movement he made was filled with grace and precision, and I couldn't help but feel my heart skip a beat as I watched him. I was starting to feel like him and Cece with this stalking shit, but I guess it ran in the family. While studying him I could see the calming effect going through these motions had on him, and it made me smile. His crazy was receding. Somewhat.

"So, my baby just called and said she's glad she doesn't need to blow up any more houses," I cringed. Why in the hell Faxx and the others thought that shit was a good idea I didn't know but we couldn't have her running around here thinking that was the way to fix things.

"It was all good *Mi Amor*, I made sure no one was inside of the house," he said turning to look at me. My eyes followed his tattooed skin as he leaned against the counter with a smirk. The deep brown eyes were less dark than they were earlier, but I saw the hint of a ticking time bomb hiding in the background.

"Mmm, really? Even in Roman's house. You know that big white house with the gate and circle driveway," I raised my brows. I stepped closer deciding to leave my boot off to test out my balance. There was still a little pain, but I felt surprisingly stable. Faxx tilted his head to the side as his gaze roamed over me. I watched him watch me and his eyes got stuck on my chest before meeting my gaze.

"I absolutely made sure everyone inside of that house was dead before it…it exploded," he smiled. His slow sexy as fuck grin had me pressing my thighs together as he kept watching me. I heard the sound of the alarm beeping as the door opened. I knew Damari had left for the hospital once Faxx got here, and everyone else never came into the house. I turned around but warm arms came around my waist his Faxx's lips pressed against my face. His tongue traced a path up the side of my neck before he spoke.

"It's only Echo. He's getting my bike, having it cleaned, and changing the paint. Now come here and help me," he whispered. I squeezed my thighs together as I turned around and followed him to the counter. I washed my hands as I watched him mix the ingredients together making a smooth creamy mixture.

"That looks so good," I said drying my hands.

Faxx's voice was smooth and velvety as he spoke, his words laced with innuendo that only we understood.

"It's as smooth as your walls when I slide inside," he smirked.

The not-so-hidden meaning in that statement told me what time it was. He was going to fuck with me the entire time, but I couldn't deny how this seemed to calm him. The air crackled with anticipation at his next seductive verbal comment.

I leaned against the kitchen counter, my eyes never leaving Faxx's form. His fingers moved with such finesse, skillfully measuring out the perfect amounts of sugar and butter. The way he dropped chunks of the fruit into the bowl, then slowly mixed it making small swirling designs, sent shivers down my spine. Everything this nigga did was sexy, or I was just extremely horny. I could just be a hoe for my husband, and that's okay.

"Why are you standing there and not helping me? You licking those thick lips is about to have me sliding my dick between them," he taunted.

"I don't even know why you insisted I be here. You got all this handled Fransisco," I smiled. Faxx turned to me with a mischievous glint in his eyes. He dipped his finger into the creamy concoction, a portion of it clinging to his finger. Slowly, he brought his finger to my lips, his touch sending an electric jolt through my body. I parted my lips, welcoming the sweet taste, savoring the forbidden pleasure and taste of mango. Faxx slid his finger in and out of my mouth watching intently as I licked it clean.

Our eyes locked, and in that moment, time stood still. The room seemed to fade away, leaving only the two of us, connected by this shared intimacy. He pulled his finger back and smirked at me.

"Ain't no way you can serve this fucking cheesecake at the party," I said licking the remnants off my lips.

"They are already in the oven, *Mi Amor*. I made the mixture up last night when I couldn't sleep. This one is yours. I thought you liked mango."

"I do," I said quickly. Faxx stared at me for a long minute before leaning over and licking my lips. He pulled back and I leaned forward trying to get closer to his ass.

"How does it taste?"

"It's sweet," I answered.

"The cheesecake will be even sweeter when it's baked," he said, his gaze never wavering from mine. I could feel the heat rising between my legs, my breath hitching in my throat as his words ignited a fire. I knew his ass wasn't talking about no God damn cheesecake, but he was going to fuck with me.

I watched him pour the batter into the gram cracker crust, his movements were purposeful and deliberate. Regardless of what he was doing or how at peace he was right now, I knew some shit went down. But I could also tell whatever happened he wasn't really ready to talk about this shit. I stepped closer leaning against the counter and watching him closely. I couldn't tear my eyes away from him, his every action a seductive invitation.

"So, baking calms you?" I asked.

Faxx put the cheesecake in the oven and turned back to look at me. The large kitchen rivaled a restaurant's and I wondered if this was what he did all the time.

"It was something my mother did with me and my brother when...when she was more herself," he stated. I swallowed knowing a little about his mother and past. He didn't like to talk about it, and from what I knew his brother basically raised him.

"You seem to enjoy it though, like you do cooking. Why in the hell did you need me here anyway? You had all this shit prepped last night by both of the ovens going," I smiled. I saw the slight tensing in his jawline the longer we stayed on the subject of his mother or liking for baking and cooking. So, I switched tactics and he chuckled.

"*Mi Amor*, I think you forgot I've been in your books, keeping your shit current. I know all the little tricks you got," he said stepping closer. Both his arms came down on the counter caging me in as he looked into my eyes.

"Okay, and so what? I'm asking because I want to know everything about you. The good, the bad, and the crazy. You don't need to be normal or act normal because I will never leave you the fuck alone Fransisco," I panted. His chest pressed me against the counter as he looked at me with a grin I couldn't figure out. A little crazed, unhinged, or was it predatory?

"That sounds a little obsessive Crescent. Are you obsessed with me? Did I accidentally on purpose make you insane just like me?" he chuckled. He leaned down, his nose running over my collarbone as his warm breath tickled my skin.

"Yes. And I think it was a calculated move of yours," I moaned.

"Everything I do to you, for you, around you are a calculated move. Bending you over that table so you could sign yourself over to me was one of them. Seeing how you came for me on top of the table in the conference room when your friends were watching was another one. It's all calculated so I know what you can and can't handle. So, I know what I need to do to make sure you're happy because it ain't no escape. So, I do shit to make sure if you thought about it, you would chain yourself to our bed," he whispered.

"Oh my God," I moaned.

The timer chimed on one of the ovens, signaling the completion, and Faxx looked up as his hand came to my face. He smoothed his thumb over my lips before wrapping his hand around my throat.

"You know I will do whatever it takes to make sure you're happy, safe, and satisfied. So when you hear about the body of Jimothy Bradley was found just know I mean what I say," he gritted. He kissed me so hard it stole the rest of my air sucking the taste of the mango right off my tongue before he let go. Faxx pushed from the counter and moved toward the ovens while I tried to catch up to what he just fucking said. I swallowed catching myself on the countertop so I couldn't slide down that bitch because my pussy was so wet.

"You should help me taste this one," he said, his voice laced with promise as the delicious scent of the cheesecake and his voice sent shivers down my spine.

"Fransisco, it needs to cool," I said as the bits and pieces of his words began to make sense. Wait. Hold the fuck up, because how did he even know what name? This nigga had a list and some fucking footage he'd seen. I did a slow pan in his direction as he placed the two cheesecakes on the counter before going to the refrigerator. He pulled out a covered dish and placed it on the table.

"I made this one first. I like to make sure it comes out how it's supposed to. Come and sit on Papi's lap Cent," he said sitting at the table. I turned toward the counter and grabbed a fork and knife before reaching for a small plate. I turned back, walking over to him as he uncovered the cheesecake. I slid onto his lap and he positioned me right over his dick and pressed down. Please give me strength, dear lawd. Please, because WWJJD! What would Jesus Jerome do?!

"So, I said that name to? I don't even remember," I whispered.

"Yes, but trust me, that nigga will never be a factor again. I made sure he took the fastest way to hell. But fuck that nigga and all the rest. Open your mouth for me, *Mi Amor*," he demanded.

He took the knife and cut a slice before using the fork slowly bringing a piece to my lips. My eyes locked with his as my mouth covered the fork and the creamy, decadent cheesecake melted on my tongue the burst of flavor of the mango had me going back to that day. I couldn't help but feel that this moment was just the beginning of another live fantasy my ass should've been having. I felt his other hand on my bare thigh traveling up my shorts and brushing over my lower lips. He pulled the fork away and sliced off another piece as his finger slid down my slit causing me to rock my hips as I licked my lips savoring the flavors in my mouth.

I watched as the fork pierced through the layers of the cheesecake. I felt a shiver of delight run down my spine at another taste as his finger brushed over my clit.

"Fuck, Fransisco," I moaned.

The crust crumbled delicately under the gentle pressure of the utensil, revealing the smooth, velvety texture of the cheesecake beneath. He brought the morsel to his lips, and he closed his eyes.

I watched as he savored the moment as the sweet aroma of ripe mango and rich cream filled his senses.

"Mmmm, didn't I say it would be sweet? Just not as sweet as the taste of your pussy," he grunted.

Faxx put the fork down used his finger for the next piece and slid his finger between my lips. The taste touched my tongue, I couldn't help but let out a soft moan of pleasure. His other finger rubbed circles over my clit at the same pace he moved his finger in my mouth. The sweetness of the mango danced with the tanginess of the cream cheese, creating an exquisite symphony of flavors in my mouth.

"Mmmm," I moaned trying to rock my hips to make him move faster. I relished the sensation, allowing myself to be completely enveloped by the indulgent pleasure of each mouthful.

The creamy filling melted against my palate, leaving a lingering, decadent sensation that sent waves of delight through my entire being. Faxx pulled his finger from my mouth dipped it into the cheesecake and slid it back inside.

"Do you see what I mean Crescent? Do you taste how smooth, creamy, and sweet that is? That's what's it like to eat that pussy," he said with his lips pressed against my ear. "Take your time and savor every bit just like I do every morning. You understand why I can't get you out of my head especially the way you are sucking my finger," he grunted.

Tasting the luscious dessert caressed my taste buds with each delicate movement of his finger and his words had a wave of heat rolling over my body. I heard a beeping noise, but all that shit went out the window when his finger slid down and pushed into my core.

"Oh, oh shit," I moaned.

"Oh my God. Fucking food porn," a distant voice said. Faxx pulled his finger out of my mouth again and swiped at the cheesecake again, but this time sucked his finger into his mouth as I watched. I felt the twist and curl of his finger and I groaned moving my hips to get more feeling.

"See, this the shit Oz was talking about. It's this nigga that's the problem."

I knew the voice was Henny and I wanted to look his way, but I was so wrapped up in the way Faxx's tongue licked the white filling from his finger. I felt a growing sense of euphoria, lost in the movement of his finger deep in my core and his thumb pressing against my clit. While still tasting a combination of flavors, textures, and the pure indulgence of cheesecake.

"Did y'all have tongue implants or something? Why are they so...so fucking long?" Tali groaned.

"Why? Do you want to know who's the longest *Thickness*?"

"Huh?"

I tuned out the voices when Faxx removed his finger grabbed my face and shoved his tongue down my throat. He added another finger in my pussy my muscles clenched hard around them as he massaged my walls sending me into a state of blissful reverie, making me forget about the world outside, the voice in my kitchen, and about the problems that never seemed to end.

"Fuck, fuck, Fransisco," I moaned.

"That's right, *Mi Amor* cum for Papi," he growled against my lips. His teeth came down on my bottom lip as my eyes rolled to the back of my head.

"If cheesecake going to make me cum like that, I want one every fucking day. I'm just saying, and it's mango!"

Faxx pulled away from my mouth and pulled his hand out of my pussy, grazing my thigh before lifting them to his mouth. My head fell on his shoulder while I thanked the good lord that it wasn't a fucking bodyguard or some shit.

"That is the sexiest shit I've seen lately. This...this shit, all this shit should be illegal," Tali murmured.

I cracked an eye open as Faxx chest moved because he was laughing. Henny stood against the counter, holding Tali to his chest with an arm across her chest and his brows raised.

"What? Why are you staring at me, Dr. Sexy?" I rasped.

"What do you mean? I'm not allowed to watch my work wife cum. She watched me, right?" he smirked. His voice lowered on the last part as he kept eye contact. I squeezed mine shut, and that shit didn't help because the night of the VIP came back clear as fucking day.

"We can still see you, Crescent," Tali laughed. "I like this voyeur stuff, it's...mind-blowing. Right Cent, it was mind-blowing," she smiled.

"Fuck you, Tali," I whispered. Faxx chuckled and repositioned me, so my legs were on either side of him as I rested my head on his shoulder.

"What the fuck are y'all doing here," Faxx asked.

"We came here so I could give Cent this last shot, and to see if I could get some cheesecake but I'm not sure if any of this is edible. I take that back, are you edible Crescent?" Henny asked.

"Oh my God, why? Why? Don't y'all need to blow some shit up or surgically attach a head on another body," I groaned.

"That's...interesting, but I was asking a serious question," he said.

"Yes! Yes Hendrix, it's edible! Why do you want to taste it?" I snapped. I looked over my shoulder and glared at him because he knew he was messing with me, and I was tired damn it. He chuckled letting Tali go as he stood. My eyes got wide, and Tali pressed her lips together. This bissh was never any help.

"Hold up Dr. Sexy—"

"Naw, Crescent, keep that same energy. Call me Hendrix because I want to know if you're offering," he said, stepping closer.

"Oh my God, Fransisco make him stop," I whined as my traitor ass pussy throbbed.

"Henny, leave my wife alone, she had a hard day," Faxx chuckled.

"Bet, for now," Henny said. And I wanted to know what in the fuck did that even mean! None, absolutely none of this shit was normal, and I was beginning to question if I was just pretending to be normal my entire life. Just like Fransisco.

When we pulled in front of Tali's mother's house, I couldn't help but feel a sense of excitement.

Act normal, be normal, and everybody will leave you the fuck alone.

As that thought ran through my head, I let out a breath just ready for a normal fucking day. Just one. While lying in bed Faxx told me about the women that was found about what was planned and that was probably the true reason why everyone wanted those ports. Either way we looked at it Faxx and Roman would've eventually crossed paths so meeting me first was a bonus, so he said. I was also horrified and satisfied at the knowledge that Jimmy's bitch ass took a nosedive out of the fucking top floor window at the tower. I also felt a sense of excitement at the knowledge they may finally get a location on Roman and when they did this shit would be over.

"*Mi Amor*, I'm going to go around the side to the backyard. Those niggas act like they can't get the fucking tent up," Faxx said pointing.

"Just make sure they got the heaters running, so it's warm before Mrs. Naomi shows up," I said. Faxx leaned down kissing before turning away. The white tee shirt with the same crown on the back of it as the ones tatted across his body claiming him as a U.C.K., nigga for life.

"I got it handled. Get inside of the house Crescent," he ordered looking over his shoulder. I waved him off, but started towards the house walking up the freshly laid driveway. Tali had been talking about the renovations she and Shandea had done for their mother for weeks before I was kidnapped, and today, I was finally going to see the results for myself. From the pictures Mrs. Naomi had shown me of the girls, her husband, and the house it had always been beautiful, with its classic architecture and small garden. But Tali and Dea had promised that the renovations had taken it to a whole new level while also making it a lot easier and safer for their mother to get around.

I walked up the front path, just as Tali swung open the door, her face beaming. I could tell she was thinking the same shit as I was. Stress-free fucking day with family and the church people.

"Crescent, it's about time y'all got here! Where's my side piece?" She asked, frowning.

"He went around the back. Something about helping with a tent or whatever," I said stepping up onto the steps.

"Keep playing around. Let Henny hear that bullshit, he's going to beat your ass," I smirked.

"First off, that nigga got a whole fucking work wife. I can at least have eye candy. Now hurry up before Dea and Oz get here with Mama. I've been dying to show you around," she exclaimed. giving me a quick hug before leading me inside. The moment I stepped through the door, I was greeted by a flood of natural light streaming in through the newly installed skylights. A picture hung from the ceiling revealing what it looked like before it was redone. The once-dim foyer now looked and felt open and inviting. I couldn't wait to see the rest of the house.

"The pictures are a nice touch girl. Yass, the interior design is on point," I smiled.

"All thanks to…Nia, but that's neither here nor there," she waved.

"What? Nia? How have I never heard of this before? How did that conversation even go down?" I asked, folding my arms because I had to know. Tali rolled her gray eyes and shrugged.

"Girl, I don't know. She came to speak with Dea and shit was…cordial, but I think she wanted to extend an olive branch. I didn't ask for more details. As long as Dea was good I was good," she sighed.

"Nia really is cool peoples though. I get Dea's hesitation on it, but it honestly wasn't on her," I said. I knew full well I probably would have quite possibly acted the same way, but only in the way it happened. I couldn't fault a nigga for shit he did before me.

"Yeah, yeah, I know and so does she. I think she holds Oz at fault more, but she's basically over it," Tali said.

"Okay, okay show me this million-dollar redo," I said, clapping my hands.

Tali led me through the living room, which had been transformed with fresh paint, new furniture, and elegant décor. The space felt cozy yet sophisticated, and I found myself admiring the attention to detail in every corner. From the before picture, I could tell that Mrs. Naomi had a knack for blending modern touches with the home's traditional charm, and it showed in every room we passed through. Next, we ventured into the kitchen, which had undergone a complete overhaul. Gleaming countertops, state-of-the-art appliances, and a spacious island took center stage, and I could tell that it had been designed for wheelchair use or the perfect height when standing. I knew how much Mrs. Naomi loved to cook and this would be the perfect culinary space. I couldn't help but imagine the delicious meals that would be prepared there and the laughter that would fill the room during family gatherings. Ones that I wanted and only had when my grandmother was alive. Tali pulled a covered dish out of the refrigerator and sat it on the island while she took out another.

I looked at the picture on the island that showed just how much work was put into it. I knew Tali and Dea had a hell of a time trying to explain why remodeling the house was a better option than just moving their mom to a bigger and better place. I got it, it's what she knew, and the home she made with her husband and kids. It was the reason why I would never get rid of the home my grandmother left for me. Once it was fully in my name, I planned on doing a complete remodel and using the space to help teens who had no place to go. The plates were gone, and I turned to follow Tali into the dining room where the rest of the dessert was sitting on the table. She placed the two plates down as she removed the cover, raising her brows.

"Don't be eyeing that cheesecake all suspicious and shit," I laughed.

"Girl, I don't know. From what I saw last night, every food item that comes out of your house needs a close inspection," she grinned.

"Bissh," I tried hitting her arm, but she moved out of the way laughing. Before coming over here, we went by Mrs. Laverne's house to see Cece, and apparently she wanted to stay there because the triplets and Kina were going to be there tonight. Faxx rolled his eyes because she was supposed to be with Link, but whatever Cece wanted Cece got, to a certain extent. I could hear Mala and Shantel's voices as footsteps came down the stairs.

"Tali, Nia really put her foot into this. It was a good idea to keep the house for sure. Property in this area is going for close to eight hundred thousand, easy. Never give up property," Shantel lectured as she came to stand next to me. She placed her arm over my shoulder and leaned against my head.

"Shantel is right Tali. You and Dea did the right thing. The boys are always trying to move too fast without thinking first. This is a great investment and now that it's paid off it's even better," Mala stated as she walked through the kitchen.

"We both knew that this was where Mama would be happy, and she knows everyone on this street. After all she's been through, I wouldn't want to take anything else from her," Tali attested.

"I agree with you. She loves this house and this street. She would have cursed y'all out if you moved her," I said. Shantel and Mala moved toward the back saying they wanted to make sure Henny, Faxx, and Link knew what they were doing.

So, I followed Tali upstairs, and I marveled at the transformation of the once cramped and outdated staircase. The before picture hung on the wall and it was totally transformed. It also had lift access if she needed it in the future. Tali and Dea had expanded the landing and installed a stunning chandelier that added a touch of glamour to the space. The upper floor revealed even more surprises, with each bedroom boasting its own unique style and character. From the serene master suite to the vibrant guest room, it was clear that Tali and Dea had spared no expense in making every space feel special. They were finally living in wealth they now possessed but I knew neither was used to it. Dea adapted more easily to the lifestyle but Tali still struggled slightly Dr. Sexy was working on her ass. Literally.

Finally, we stepped out onto the newly renovated balcony, where a breathtaking view of the landscaped backyard awaited us. The outdoor space was transformed into a tranquil oasis, a complete fountain, and comfortable seating areas with a fire pit. It was the perfect place to relax and take in the beauty of the surroundings, almost feeling like we weren't still inside Union City.

"Let me guess, Link put some kind of security system in place already," I laughed.

"You know it. That was one of the most expensive things in this house I didn't fight when he told me what he was going to do. None of us are stupid here, Cent. We all know that shit can happen, and I want my Mama protected as much as possible," Tali maintained.

"I feel you," I hummed.

We made our way back downstairs, I couldn't contain my excitement when I heard the door close outside. I had missed Mrs. Naomi and our talks at the hospital. She reminded me so much of my grandmother, and I felt like she was the mother I should've had. She told me as much when I talked a little about Jacinda. The doors opened, and the first thing I saw was a belly, before Dea stepped inside.

"Hey, y'all. People are already arriving," she said, hugging us. Oz held Mrs. Naomi's arm as he helped her inside the house. Her light brown eyes widened as she stepped inside. Her hand went to her mouth as her breath caught.

"Oh my God this...this...this is more than I thought it would be. I was looking for some new paint and furniture. Not a room that could be featured in *Homes of Union*," Mrs. Naomi gasped.

"I'm so glad you like it Mama, but you haven't seen it all," Tali smiled. Mrs. Naomi's eyes finally looked in our direction and she lit up.

"Oh my baby. Oh, that is a beautiful necklace," she said, moving out of Oz's hold. Tali opened her arms wide, but Mrs. Naomi wrapped her arms around me. Dea raised her brow as Oz chuckled. Funny ass niggas.

"Ain't this some bullshi—"

"Tali Saunders! Not in my house," she corrected. I hugged her back as Tali rolled her eyes.

"Crescent, baby. I missed you so much. I haven't talked to you in over a week," she said, pulling back.

"Mama, can I get a hug too, dang. I am your last born," she pouted. Oz stepped forward, reaching out for Dea, and helping her sit down.

"I'm going to see if they have everything together before more people arrive," Oz stated.

"Oh, thank you, Lennox. You're such a sweet young man," she smiled as he kissed her on the cheek.

"That is a whole li—"

I cut off my words when Oz pulled away and looked me over. He reached out, hugging me tightly before whispering in my ear.

"You keep digging that hole deeper and deeper, Cent. I'll use that collar to choke you until you cum," he said as I pulled away. I looked over at Dea, and her punk ass was cleaning her nails. I knew damn well she heard his ass. Oz stepped out of the room, and I turned back to Mrs. Naomi and Tali as she finished fixing Tali's hair and then her low-cut top that was half-off the shoulder. A knock sounded at the door, and it was the sign that the party was about to get started.

The sun dipped below the horizon, casting a warm golden glow over the backyard.

The tables were adorned with vibrant flowers, and the air was filled with the delicious aroma of sizzling barbecue, desserts, light smell of alcohol. Church people or not that didn't mean they couldn't drink. Laughter and chatter filled the air as friends and family gathered to celebrate Naomi's homecoming. My shoulders eased and I felt myself relax against Faxx as he and Link debated over who won their race the other day. I felt Faxx's warm hand on my thigh as he squeezed causing me to close them. That only made his ass push higher up.

"Dea, I had Faxx make you a peanut butter-topped cheesecake. It's actually good as shit," Oz said, setting down the plate. Dea's face scrunched up before she pushed it away.

"Eww Oz. I can't eat that. Cold peanut butter, no thank you," she shook her head. Oz stared at her like she had four heads and one of them fell off. Shantel covered her face as she stuffed her third piece of chocolate cheesecake in her mouth.

"Are you serious? No, no never mind," Oz said pushing it toward his side.

"Baby, can you get me what Cent has? It looks good," she licked her lips. Oz frowned, looked at my plate and then narrowed his eyes on Dea.

"So, you mean to tell me, you want a mango cheesecake?" He asked.

"Oh my God, that sounds so good. Thank you, baby," she said, pushing him. I covered my face, but I didn't miss the pointing he was doing at Dea to Henny behind her back. One of the older men at another table just patted his arm.

"Shandea, why the hell are you messing with that man?" Mala snorted. Dea tilted her head to the side smiling slightly.

"He needs to be on his toes every once in a while. It's not good for him to think he can always control something," she said softly. Henny looked at Faxx and Link who raised a brow.

"That nigga Sam might have been onto something," Link mumbled.

As the evening progressed, the mood was joyous, and the atmosphere was filled with love and warmth and I was fucking content. Is this what it felt like to be with a large family? Is this what it felt like to do something so mundane that it was one of the best days of my life?

I was feeling good as hell until I heard a familiar voice that I hated. I shouldn't even have heard it since the bitch was dead. The tranquility was shattered when two women stepped around the side of the house. They both walked with an entitlement that neither should even fucking possess. I saw Tali's eyes flare hot and Dea's fists clench together. Mrs. Naomi's sister, Danita, had arrived, and trailing behind her was her daughter, Katrice.

"I know you're fucking lyin'. How the hell do they know about this?" Dea hissed. From what I knew about the family dynamics, Danita had always been a troublemaker, and her arrival cast a shadow over the near-perfect day.

Bitch.

I noticed Mrs. Naomi's smile falter as she exchanged strained pleasantries with her sister. Tali and Shandea tried to maintain their composure, but I could see the tension building in their expressions.

"Calm down *Sweetness*. You know better, Shandea," Oz scolded. Shantel was staring at Katrice like she was a bug on her windshield, but I could tell she was cooking up something. That was when I picked up on what Danita was saying. Katrice hadn't even looked in our direction as she looked over the yard and the back of the house. She started forward like she was about to enter when Link spoke up.

"Naw, that ain't your house to be entering. Did you get permission," he asked. Katrice looked at him and kept her mouth closed. Her hateful gaze traveled over us, but seemed to slide over Shantel like she wasn't even there. Katrice turned around, mumbling under her breath as she stomped over to her mother. I felt the warmth of Faxx's hand leave my thigh, causing me to look down. His hand was reaching under his shirt gripping his Glock as he stared.

"Dea, do you want me to shoot that bitch?" Faxx asked.

"Yes," Dea said without hesitation.

"No!" We all screamed at once. Faxx's dark brown gaze turned a shade darker as he leaned back in his chair. He pulled out the Glock anyway, but rested it on my leg.

"Dea, don't tell his crazy ass no shit like that unless you want a target on her head," Oz said, keeping his voice low.

"I do. I want a huge red target on her fucking forehead. That bitch," Dea snapped. She stabbed the fork into her second piece of cheesecake and moaned.

"Faxx, don't you move," Henny chuckled.

Danita's behavior became increasingly disruptive. She began to make snide remarks about Tali and Shandea, insinuating that they had something to do with the disappearance of her other daughter, Yasmin. The accusation hung in the air like a dark cloud, poisoning the festive atmosphere. People began whispering as confusion and frowns began to appear around the group. I saw the flash of hate and fed the fuck up in Tali's gray eyes. They became hard as marble as she shoved her chair back. Henny gripped her wrist stopping her from moving further.

"How dare you accuse us of something so heinous? We have nothing to do with Yasmin's disappearance, and you know it!" Tali's voice rose in defense, her eyes flashing with anger. The funny part was I almost, almost believed that shit.

"You always were the troublemaker, Tali. I wouldn't put it past you to have something to do with Yasmin vanishing. Neither one of you seemed to be even doing anything about it," Danita sneered. "Let it play out. Just let it play out," Shantel said under her breath. Henny frowned slightly, but released Tali's wrist. He tilted his head to the side staring a fucking hole into the middle of Katrice's chest. Whatever was happening fucking psycho ass hypnotizing Shantel had something up her sleeve.

"Then why was it me and Dea that reported her missing? Neither of you has, so maybe y'all trifling asses did something to her! What, did she try to kill you too, like she tried to kill my Mama you old dusty pussy bitch," Tali shouted.

"Now Danita and Tali, this is not the time. This is a celebration for Naomi," an older woman said, standing.

"Oh, shut the hell up, Mary! I thought Dea was supposed to be marrying your grandson, but she is sitting up here pregnant by another man just like her Mama, a slut" Danita smirked.

"Excuse me bitch," Dea said, turning to face Danita. Aww shit.

"Danita, that is none of our business, they will work that out on their own time—"

"The fuck they will," Oz gritted.

"Mrs. Mary please sit down. Mama don't even get yourself worked up. That's all she wants to do, isn't that right Danita? No real life of your own so you want to ride someone else's coattails," Tali laughed.

Danita started to laugh as she spun on her heel pushing Katrice behind her as she stared at Tali. Then she slowly looked over at the table. Dea's hand rested on her stomach and the other laced with Oz's. I could see the death grip she had on him as she ground her teeth together. I scooted my chair back slightly, just in case that bitch needed a chair across her fucking head.

"That is classic Tali. You are talking all that big mess, but bringing thugs and killers into your mother's home. A home that honestly should have belonged to me in the first place," Danita spat.

Faxx leaned back in the chair throwing his arm over the back of my chair his Glock in full fucking view.

"Oh, you mean the house my father brought for my mother? Bitch you need to move the fuck on like Yasmin probably did. More than likely, she was sick of both of y'all shit. She probably faked her own disappearance just so she wouldn't have to look at a stank old ran-through bitch like you," Tali sneered.

"Oh! Boom! Shots fired," Mala called out.

Before anyone could intervene, Katrice leaped to her mother's defense, her face contorted with rage.

"You're a liar, Tali! I know you did something to Yasmin, and you're going to pay for it!" Katrice shrieked.

"Ahh bitch I have been ready to beat that ass again," Tali said stepping away from the table.

"Tali stop! Danita, you need to leave. Get off my property and don't come back. We have nothing to talk about. I pray you find Yasmin, but that's all I have for you," Mrs. Naomi sighed.

"Fuck you, Naomi," Danita said looking behind her.

"I know this bitch didn't yell at my mother," Dea said, hitting the table.

The situation escalated quickly, and I knew I had to step in because Dea's ass couldn't fight. Mala was sitting back with a slight smile, but I knew if her ass got involved somebody would die. I moved to stand beside Tali.

"Enough! Y'all need to get the fuck on, or thoughts and chairs is all you're going to get," I exclaimed, my voice cutting through, yelling.

"This is my kind of party," Mala whispered.

I knew her ass was fucking crazy. I was hoping my ankle wouldn't punk out on me, but I felt good as the adrenaline rushed through my veins.

"There's no evidence to support that claim, Danita. Accusing Tali and Shandea without proof is a bunch of bullshit," I shouted.

"And who the fuck are you?"

"Crescent."

Danita scoffed, her eyes flashing with malice.

"Stay out of this, Crescent. This is none of your business, you ain't in no way family," she dismissed me.

"Mala, this is how I first saw her in *MYTH*. All crazy with no hesitation," Faxx chuckled.

Before I knew it Katrice lunged at Tali, her fists flying in a blind rage. Tali defended herself, but Katrice grabbed her locs and pulled. I moved to pull her off when I felt Danita grab my arm as people shouted.

With a surge of adrenaline, Tali twisted and punched Katrice in her stomach before grabbing a plate and slamming across her head.

"Ohhh shit! Look at my sis, move over here Dea," I chuckled. I grabbed Danita's wrist twisted and then elbowed her in the face. I didn't want to use my hand because of my finger, but fuck it if it breaks again.

"Ahhh bi-bitch," Danita screamed. Tali threw Katrice to the ground just as she tried clawing at Tali. I grabbed the chair Oz was sitting in and slammed it on Danita's back making her fall to the ground. The scuffle was chaotic, with limbs flailing and shouts filling the air. I raised my foot and was getting ready to slam it on her head when someone grabbed me up.

"Chill, chill *Mi Amor*. Don't kill her," Faxx chuckled. I twisted but Faxx's grip tightened as my eyes fell on Tali.

"Let me get my baby before she tries and kill this girl," he sighed like he was disappointed.

"Stomp her ass, Tali! Hit her for the baby!" Dea screamed.

"Shandea! You need to go to your mother," Oz snapped.

Despite Katrice's ferocity, Tali overpowered her on the ground slamming her face in the dirt. Tali stood up and started stomping her out before Henny grabbed her up. Panting and disheveled, Tali was fighting to get out of Henny's grip. I didn't know what he was saying in her ear, but she started to calm down slightly. I went still hoping Faxx would put me down so I could run over there and kick that old bitch in the face for coming at Mrs. Naomi like that.

"You're not slick Cent, keep that thick ass still," Faxx said, setting me on my feet. His hand wrapped around my waist, pressing me against him, so I couldn't move. I could feel the weight of the other people's stares on us, but I remained focused on making sure that bitch didn't run her mouth again. A lot of people were still here, but some left scared things would get out of hand even further. Henny walked Tali over toward us as Mala and Shantel ran to Katrice, rolling her over. Shantel was snapping her fingers in her face while Mala held her jaw so she would face her. I blinked twice and saw Mrs. Naomi rushing to our side, her eyes filled with concern and frustration. Danita pushed herself to her feet and swayed slightly.

"I swear I will press charges against both of y'all bitches. This is assault," Danita said.

"Danita, that is enough! You've caused nothing but trouble since you arrived. Leave my daughters and their friends alone. Get off of my property before I call the police and press charges. You ever come here again, and I will call the law," Mrs. Naomi shouted.

Danita's gaze flickered with defiance, but she turned away looking for Katrice. Shantel had her sitting up as she spoke quickly to her as Danita approached. She reached down grabbing Mala's shoulder. Mala reached over and twisted her wrist as she stood to her feet.

"Naw bitch, I ain't as delicate," she sucked her teeth pushing Danita away.

"Ahh! Fuck all of you! I know who you are, and I will press charges. They will believe me, and I got witnesses," Danita shouted as Shantel stood. She stepped back as Danita rushed forward when no one spoke up to help her. She leaned over and pulled Katrice up to her feet. Katrice teetered for a second but caught her balance looking out of it. As they retreated, Danita shot one last venomous glare in our direction before disappearing around the house.

The tension slowly dissipated, and the onlookers began to disperse, leaving only Mrs. Naomi, Tali, Shandea, Oz, Link, Faxx, Mala, Shantel and me standing in the aftermath of the confrontation. I looked at Link and he was holding his phone up smirking before putting it in his pocket. Emotions ran high as we tried to make sense of what had just transpired.

"What was that all about? What is she talking about Yasmin is missing?" Mrs. Naomi asked. Oz finally let Shandea move, and she walked slowly closer to her mother.

"Mama, we don't know where she is. After we found out what she had done she just...she vanished," Dea shrugged. Her quick glances at us told us how uncomfortable she was with lying to her mother, but it was for the best. She couldn't know Yasmin was living on inside someone else.

Mrs. Naomi shook her head before she embraced her daughters, her eyes brimming with tears.

"I'm so sorry you had to endure that. I never wanted things to escalate like this. I thought she was past all this stuff. All this happened so long ago," she sniffed.

Tali hugged her mother tightly, her voice trembling with emotion.

"It's not your fault, Mama. We're just glad you're home safe. I'm sorry this ruined your party," Tali sighed.

Shandea nodded her expression, a mix of relief and lingering anger.

"We'll figure out a way to deal with Danita. We don't need her coming around interfering with your recovery," Dea said.

I placed a reassuring hand on Mrs. Naomi's shoulder, offering her a small smile.

"We're here for you, Mama. Things will all get figured out in time," I reassured. Tali stared at me as Mrs. Naomi kissed my cheek. She was going to try and take Katrice out the next time she saw her. It was going to be onsite, and I would help her. I knew that our bond was tight enough that she caught the agreement in my eyes. I saw Henny speaking to Shantel and the smirk that crossed his face told me all I needed to know. This bitch would get what was coming, and I would hate to end up on his table under those circumstances.

CHAPTER TWELVE

MARVIN HOWARD

I leaned back in the dimly lit room, the smoke from my cigar swirling lazily in the air. I may have been a bastard of a father, but that didn't mean I didn't love my son. Those bitch ass niggas took my legacy from me along with the knowledge of where the fuck he hid the banking information for the money we stole over the years from the Cartel. I had my suspicions that Jakobe was going to try and run, but I always knew what my son was thinking. I made sure it was that way since birth. The phone on the table buzzed, and I snatched it up, recognizing Tyenika's number. She was the key to helping take down U.C.K., and I needed her more than ever now that the plan was in motion.

Not to mention she was carrying my second chance. Jakobe's seed would be my second chance at making sure my legacy survived, and for me to mold him better than I did my own son.

"Yeah?" I answered, my voice low and commanding.

"Listen Marvin, I have a lot of shit going on right now. Since y'all wanted to be stupid and hit them openly they are on high ass alert. I can't see my daughter, which means I have no reason to even contact Fransisco. It's beginning to get too risky for me and my baby. I've done what I can with locations and shit. I refuse to do anything else," Tye rushed out.

"Excuse me? Did you forget who the fuck you are speaking to little girl?"

"I did not for—"

"No! You fucking forgot or you wouldn't have thought to open your mouth with that bullshit. Number one, that baby is coming with me when he's born, like that shit or not. Number two, you better figure it the fuck out Tye because you know damn well that I have no problem doing what's necessary to make sure you comply," I interjected. My fist slammed hard on the desk, causing the lamp and other accessories to rattle. Things were quiet on the other end but I could still hear the bitch breathing. I raised my hand in the air waving over a guard just in case I needed to give the order to kidnap this bitch and her fucking son.

"Marvin, you gotta do something for me first," Tyenika's voice crackled through the line.

I clenched my jaw, already knowing where this was headed. She always had a way of making things complicated but if money could solve this issue faster it was what it was.

"What do you need, Tyenika?"

"You gotta take out Sanchez, and then you gotta bring me my son. He's taken him and had some fucking emergency order placed on me, which stops my funds. I don't like that shit, and I don't like that he believes he can play me while fucking all these bitches like shit is sweet," she demanded, her tone unwavering.

I knew who Sanchez was to her, and I also knew that he was an associate of Henny, Oz, Link, and Faxx, the niggas that murdered my son and didn't have the decency to leave his body to where he had an open casket. Fuck ass niggas. My question was, what exactly did Sanchez know about his business associates, and could I use this opportunity to send a fucking message?

"You know that ain't an easy task, Tyenika. I can't just waltz into Union City and take an associate out without some kind of retaliation, it's already hot," I disputed.

I didn't give a shit about any of that, but I knew how those niggas got down. If this Sanchez was in any way close to U.C.K., then he had some value to me. I just didn't need this bitch thinking she could order me around like I was her fucking tool.

"I don't care. You want my help, you do what I say," she shot back, her words slicing through the air.

I gritted my teeth, my mind churning with the weight of her words. The Kings had taken something from me, too. They had gunned Jakobe down over some bitch, and I wanted revenge just as much as she did, but this was pushing it.

"Tye, you've finally lost your fucking mind speaking to me the way you are. You're alive for one reason and one reason only and that's because of my grandchild you're carrying. But that doesn't mean you can't do that shit locked in a room and chained to the mutha fuckin' bed! Do you see where I'm coming from?" I seethed. I covered the mouthpiece ready to send out the order to bring this bitch to me when she laughed.

"See, that may be the one thing Marvin, but it's not the only thing. Here is the thing, your son liked to run his mouth a lot when I sucked his balls out through his dick. Not only am I carrying his child, but I know exactly where to find that hard-drive containing the banking information to the Cartel's money you stole. So, let's start back at the beginning," she rebutted.

I leaned back into the leather chair and sat the cigar down. I waved away the guard as I ground my teeth together at the stupidity of niggas with bitches like Tyenika.

"Get out!" I shouted. The guard moved faster toward the door pulling it open and exiting shutting it quietly behind him. I trusted my people as far as I could throw them niggas. I knew Alejandro and Carmelo had plants embedded throughout my guards and I refused to take a chance. Even though Larson had been with me from the start.

"You know what we did, Tyenika. I assume that you know the money Jakobe and I took from the Cartel could come with a heavy price if you even think about trying to use it yourself," I reminded her. The memory of that chaotic day flashed through my mind when I found out about Jakobe. That knowledge that he had hidden the information somewhere without telling me had such a rage burning inside me that I ended up burying that nigga in a casket full of concrete.

"You think you can just use that against me?" I hissed into the phone.

I would kill this bitch but not before I got my grandchild. I would rip that baby from her womb and watch her ass bleed out and die.

"I know exactly what I'm doing, Marvin. And if you are even thinking I want something to do with that dirty ass money you're wrong. I wouldn't touch that shit with a ten-foot pole. That's what a child and life insurance is for old man. But what I will do is toss that fucking hard drive in the nearest landfill. You need me as much as I need you," she retorted, her confidence unshakable.

I blew out a huff of air as I chuckled because, secretly, I liked her cunningness. I picked up my cigar and took a long pull as I stared up at the ornate ceiling. I tossed the cigar into the ashtray, my mind racing. I needed her a little longer, and she knew it. The Cartel was closing in on Union City, and we needed to take out the Kings to secure our hold. Tyenika was my link and I couldn't afford to lose her. Not yet.

"You like playing a dangerous game with dangerous men Tye, but fine. I'll do it," I grumbled, as the weight of my decision settled heavily on my shoulders.

"Good," she retorted but I could hear the relief in her tone.

"But, where the fuck is he? Does he have men watching him? Because, from my knowledge, he hasn't been seen lately," I said.

"That's because he left his fucking house and took my son with him. He even went as far as banning me from his school to where I can't go near it! But, you can't erase the love a son has for his mother. Kaleb called me and, in that conversation, he said they were staying in a new house but he doesn't know where. What he did know was that his daddy was going out tonight. He was going to his 'Uncle Oz,' and we both know what that means," she theorized.

"So, Sanchez will be at *MYTH* tonight is what you're saying. And all I would need to do is follow him to where he's staying," I finished.

"Exactly. So, when it's done, then we'll talk," she said, and the line went dead.

I rubbed my temples, frustration and determination warring within me. I had to focus. The plan was in motion, and I couldn't afford any distractions. I couldn't afford for Tye to do something stupid while at the same time, she just gave me more leverage. If she thought Kaleb would be coming back to her after I killed his father, she was crazy. Once I had what I needed from that bitch, I might fuck her then seal her away until it was time for her to deliver my grandchild. When she gave me that fucking hard-drive, all she had to do was get Fransisco alone, which would be easy if he believes there was a problem with the baby. But after that, that bitch is done for thinking she could blackmail me.

I reached for the phone again, making the necessary calls to set everything in motion. Sanchez would tell me everything he knew about those niggas before I killed him. That would send the message I needed when they found his body. Then Tyenika's son, my grandson, would soon be in my hands.

"Larson!" I shouted.

I waited for a few seconds when the door opened and he poked his shaved brown head in side with a raised brow.

"What's up Boss?" he replied.

I smashed my cigar in the ashtray and leaned back my hands lacing together over my stomach. I blew out the smoke and leveled my gaze on his hard brown eyes.

"Get everyone together. We're going to *MYTH*," I declared.

It was time to show these Union City Kings what it looked like to fuck around and find out.

I gathered my men, steeling myself for what was to come. Tyenika's son was one ticket into the heart of the Kings' operation, and Sanchez's demise and the kidnapping would shake their foundation. If we moved with precision, and our every step calculated and deliberate those niggas would see any of this coming. This was it, the moment I had been waiting for. Stripping the power U.C.K. had over Union City will be satisfying but watching them suffer as they lose it all and then their lives will be priceless.

BEHIND THE CURTAIN

I, _____ (Print Name), hereby acknowledge that I am over the age of 18 and voluntarily agree to participate in all activities at *MYTH'S* Owners suite/ *'BEHIND THE CURTAIN'* will hereby be called *BTC*. I understand that the activities at the club may involve physical, emotional, and psychological elements intended to be consensual, and safe.

I understand that these *BDSM* activities may include, but are not limited to, bondage, discipline, dominance, swinging, submission, sadism, masochism, group sex, voyeurism, exhibitionism, and other related activities. I am aware that these activities may involve physical contact, restraints, impact play, and psychological role-playing scenarios whenever entering *BTC*.

I agree to the following terms and conditions:

1. I am participating only in *BTC* activities at the Club *Myth* of my own free will and consent.

2. I acknowledge that I have the right to withdraw my consent at any time during the activities.

3. I understand the importance of clear communication, safe words, and aftercare in all BDSM interactions.

4. I am aware of the risks associated with BDSM activities and will not hold Club *Myth* or its affiliates responsible for any injuries or emotional distress that may occur during or after my participation. However, if *Club Myth causes distress or injury,* we will provide all health and mental care for a period of one year.

5. I agree to respect the boundaries and limits of others and will not engage in any activities without obtaining clear and enthusiastic consent or without your partner being present.

6. I understand that alcohol and drugs can impair my judgment and ability to provide informed consent, and I agree not to participate in *BDSM* activities under the influence of alcohol or drugs.

7. I acknowledge that Club *Myth* has safety protocols in place, and I agree to abide by these rules and guidelines for the well-being of all participants.

8. I understand that any violation of the club's rules, including consent violations, could result in immediate expulsion from the club and legal action if necessary but more than likely death.

I have read and understood the above statements, and I agree to adhere to the rules and guidelines outlined in this consent form. I acknowledge that I have the right to seek clarification or ask questions regarding any aspect of this form before participating in any *BTC* activities at CLUB *MYTH*.

Signature: _____   Date: _____

Please provide emergency contact information:

Name: _____

Phone number: _____

Please retain a copy of this form for your records. All forms are kept on file on the club's privately owned servers.

CHAPTER THIRTEEN

CRESCENT 'CENT' WELLINGTON

I was still vibrating on ten as Faxx drove through the city. I was mad as fuck because I didn't get to stomp that bitch out like I wanted. Tali was just as mad as I was, and I knew she was plotting on catching that bitch. The fact these niggas had us on lock right now made what we wanted to do harder to get away with. I knew they didn't give a shit about what happened to Katrice, but all we heard was '*Not yet.*' There wasn't any reason why that bitch couldn't go lay in the grass with her fucking sister. I sucked in a deep breath trying to calm down because I was becoming just as bloodthirsty as Dea.

I looked down sharply pressing on my stomach trying to feel if something was in there like an idiot.

"What are you doing Crescent? Imaging my baby in there," Faxx smirked. I cut my eyes at him as he turned on Concord Ave.

"Are you intentionally trying to get me pregnant? What if I don't want a baby right now? Would it matter?" I asked. Faxx shifted in his seat, tilting his head from side to side and cracking his neck. He swallowed as he slowed the SUV to a stop at a red light. Faxx turned to look at me taking his hand from the wheel and ran a finger along my jawline.

"Of course, it matters. If you don't want to get pregnant it's a fine time to say you don't. I damn sure know as deep, and as hard as I fuck you, you're for sure going to be carrying my baby. If you're not already," he smirked. I stared at him until he turned away and hit the gas. His hand fell to my lap, and I turned his tatted hand over and traced the crown that covered it.

"You're definitely trying to keep my ass from escaping," I sighed.

"At least now we are on the same page, *Mi Amor.*"

"Yeah, yeah, I know. I wanted to be trapped anyway," I answered leaning against the headrest.

"Now, all I have to do is put you in my web," he said, slowing before he turned. I caught sight of a burgundy truck turning with us and I swore that was Tali's car.

"Papi, where are we going? I thought we were going home," I said, sitting up. He made another turn and so did the car behind us.

"I need to make a stop first," he acknowledged.

"Are we being followed?" I asked, getting nervous. I was ready to reach down and grab my purse to pull out Rose. After the entire funeral debacle, I refused to go anywhere without it. Faxx glanced into the rearview mirror quickly before making another turn.

"Yes, we are. I got you Cent," he said looking in his mirrors. I looked around at the alley, it seemed tight, but at the end it opened up. All the buildings were nondescript as Faxx pulled to a stop behind one of them with a huge steel door.

"This is it! This is where I get taken out," I spluttered. Faxx's hand tightened before letting mine go. I rolled my head to look at him and he stared at me shaking his head. He leaned over the console as his hand gripped my neck pulling me closer as his tongue traced the seam of my lips. They parted automatically because there was no thought behind the action. His tongue slipped in slowly and steady as he tightened his grip on my throat before he started to suck on my tongue.

"Mmm," I moaned.

KNOCK. KNOCK. KNOCK.

I jumped slightly and tried pulling back but Faxx held on tighter continuing to take his time as he stole the air from me. The problem with that, that I had, was I wanted to give it to him. He pulled back staring me in the eyes and the dark brown of his darkened. But it was different from the homicidal manic I called my husband. This was.... suck on my Glock Faxx. The run in the woods Faxx was staring at me. He licked his lips before letting my neck go but his eyes never looked away as he unlocked the door.

"Get out of the car, *Mi Amor*," he said dangerously. My eyes widened as my door opened revealing Shantel.

"It's about time nigga, damn. I have places and things I need to do tonight after this," she ranted.

"Where are we, Shantel?" I asked. Shantel reached across me unbuckling my seatbelt.

"Girl come on. I am about to make your wish come true, chile," she said, as I slid out of the SUV. It was Tali's SUV that was behind us, but she wasn't in the car or standing out there. I couldn't even tell where here was at this point.

"My wish is to go home and twirl on my man's dick before I go to sleep. I think I fucked up my finger again," I said switching subjects. My ass was tired as hell and beating bitches assess had me ready for a shower and bed. But Shantel pulled me by my hand toward the doors where I hadn't noticed two big ass niggas standing before. They were dressed all in black with a black scarf covering the lower portion of their faces, the symbol of an 'M' over the mouths. As we approached one of them opened the door just as we got close. The inside was dark as fuck, but a low, red light lit the hallway almost beckoning me in further.

"Welcome to MYTH UNDERGROUND. Enjoy your stay and cum for us again," he stated in a low baritone voice.

"Wait, what?" I said as the doors closed leaving us in semi-darkness.

"Bissh, what the hell are we doing here? I thought it was going to be tomorrow or something," I said, following her deeper into the building.

"I think we all need some downtime after that little get-together. I mean, I won't be able to stay because I have to help Link and Mala really quick with some shit," she waved off.

"Leaving? Come on Shantel, seriously? We never get to do anything together."

"Girl bye, I have planned out an entire party once Dea drops that damn baby! They finally have women that can manage their crazy asses and now I can chill," she smirked over her shoulder.

I shook my head as we walked through the dimly lit hallway, the crimson glow of the red lights casting eerie shadows on the walls, creating an atmosphere of mystery and anticipation. Shantel navigated us through the underground part of MYTH that I didn't even know had an entrance. The sound of muffled music grew louder as we ventured deeper into the heart of the establishment. The hall was lined with doors all the same color but with different numbers attached to each. The air was heavy with the scent of incense and excitement, and I couldn't help but feel a flutter of nervous energy in the pit of my stomach. I couldn't believe I was actually here and looking like I just came from a damn church picnic or something. I smoothed down my navy-blue shirt sleeved button-up shirt and looked at my black leggings and ankle boots grimacing. I was going to fuck Faxx up for taking me here before I could change.

A door ahead of us opened and a man with a black and gold bird-like face mask stepped out. His chest was bare and his brown skin fucking shined. The multiple tattoos that covered his upper chest and arms were hot as fuck. The neatly trimmed beard was long, but you could tell he took care of that by the way it glistened in the low lights. I looked down as he held a leash in his hand. He stared in our direction as he yanked on the gold chain. I saw an arm first before the woman crawled out the door on hands and knees. She wore an entire black leather body suit that crisscrossed over her body, except her face. The only thing covering her face was a thick gold cloth tied over her eyes. She stopped by the man and rubbed her cheek against his leg.

"Mistress, I didn't know you would be here tonight," he said, lowering his head slightly. The small smile that played on Shantel's lips schooled into a line.

"Not long, Jose. Just like your assignment. Not too much longer," she said cryptically. He raised his head slightly and I saw a brow raise in surprise.

"Good to know," he bowed before pulling on the leash leading the woman down the hall following after him like a lost puppy.

"Bissh, is that the crazy shit I'm going to be seeing or what? That's your brother right? Why would he call you Mistress?" I asked tapping my lips.

"Cent, you're going to witness some wild ass shit, and when I am in this building everyone on the lower levels calls me that because that is who I am," she stated and continued walking.

"Well, yes Mistress," I said.

"Hmm, you're learning," she laughed.

Damn, that's some boss ass shit but I was trying to do the mental math in my head. How big was *MYTH* in the first place? The more I thought about it the dimensions from the front of the club and the upstairs part don't seem like it could be this large.

As we approached a discreet door at the end of the hall, Shantel turned to me with a mischievous glint in her eye.

"Are you ready for this, Crescent?" she asked, her voice tinged with excitement.

I looked both ways down each end of the halls not seeing a soul. Where the fuck was Tali and Henny? I knew they were here, but I guess they were already inside. I nodded, my heart pounding in my chest. It was happening! I honestly thought I would never get down in these rooms to see what it was all about, so I was hyped. I had never been to a place like this before, but I knew for a fact that this would be an unforgettable experience. I know Tali is trippin' right now.

Shantel opened the door and a woman wearing an all-black fitted dress with gold heels ushered us into a small, opulently decorated room. By the smile on her face and bright eyes, you could see the confident and elegantly dressed woman was at home. She handed me a bag containing something black. I was guessing it was an outfit like hers, but I would find out soon.

"The bathroom is over there with everything you need to shower and moisturize. Then change into what's inside the bag," Shantel pointed. I looked toward a closed door and took a deep breath. This was some serious shit.

"Why change?" I asked reaching for the handle.

"Ease of access," she taunted. I looked over my shoulder and laughed. One thing I wasn't worried about was no one accessing me unless it was Faxx. His ass would shut this damn club down and no one needed that mess. Shantel's smile widened, and I rolled my eyes opening the door.

After I finished, I reached into the bag pulling out two pieces of clothing. I pulled the pieces apart and it revealed a gold and black cropped bustier made of velvet and lurex lace with foam-lined half-moon cups. It had adjustable halter chain straps, a jewelry clasp closure, and a removable gold multi-chain with a tassel. Bustier and G-string that both featured wide velvet straps with gold buckle loop connectors with a see-through skirt. A fucking skirt for what because you could still see all my shit. I didn't know if this was a joke or if Shantel was serious about this shit. I reached for the door, pulling it open slightly.

"Shantel?"

"Yes, I'm serious and yes this is the attire for tonight. Could you put it on, girl? You know that shit is going to look sexy as fuck, especially with that collar," she said, pushing the door closed.

"This mind-reading bitch," I mumbled. This was sexy as fuck, but it was barely fucking clothes. I was way too thick for this little shit. Shantel must have my shit mixed up with someone else cause ain't no fucking way. I shook my head but slipped into the bustier and G-string with ease. I stared in the mirror and decided to pull my braids into a low ponytail so the detail in the chain could be seen. The shit was hot, and it fit like the shit was made for me. I frowned at myself in the mirror because was it? I shook my head as I felt a surge of empowerment and anticipation. The fabric clung to my skin in all the right places, and I couldn't help but feel a sense of confidence with or without the fucking shirt.

"Yass, bissh, yass," I said turning around to look at myself from the back. I swallowed as I saw the intricate colorful butterfly with the broken wing on my right cheek. The burn mark I received from Roman's bitch ass was under it. I blinked and shoved those thoughts to the side as a knock sounded on the door.

"Stop procrastinating and bring your ass out here girl," Shantel shouted.

I opened the door and stepped out as the woman who greeted us held out a hand for the bag. I handed it over, knowing I didn't need to worry about my belongings. Shantel looked me over before she smirked. She stepped forward, still dressed in a pair of wide-legged dress pants and a high-collared white shirt without sleeves. She handed me a consent form, her eyes serious and unwavering. I scanned through the document, my gaze flitting over the bolded headings and the detailed clauses. It outlined the nature of the activities that may take place within the club, emphasizing the importance of clear communication, boundaries, and the right to withdraw consent at any time. I understood the gravity of the form and the significance of the commitments I was about to make. At the bottom, there was an added clause that everything that happens behind the curtain stays behind the curtain. Everything that is done or will be done happens between the agreed guests, and it will only happen inside 'Behind the Curtain.' All partners must consent and abide by the rules.

I sucked in a breath as I flipped the page still trying to process the last bit of what it would mean. As I flipped the page my heart pounded because I legit had to sign a fucking contract.

"I know you're fucking lying right now. Who printed my name and I...I don't...oh shit, oh shit. Why is he fucking with me," I murmured. "And how the fuck is he the emergency contact? This...do I really need to—"

I looked up when I heard the door open, and Faxx stepped inside. I watched as he approached me with a smile while his eyes burned through my skin. It was like I was completely naked as he stared at me. I hadn't even noticed that the woman and Shantel had left the damn room. These niggas were crazy as shit and always on one fucking with people. I knew for sure Tali's eyes would probably fall out of her head if she got this same thing.

"Fransisco, I know you read this because you're crazy ass put yourself down as the damn emergency contact like that's not a problem in itself, but you know damn well none of what's in this will happen. Y'all play, but ain't none of y'all niggas letting nobody touch us. Negative captain," I laughed.

"*Mi Amor*," he began his voice gentle yet firm.

"I want you to understand why signing this form isn't crucial, but it ensures that you're fully aware of what you're consenting to. You have boundaries, and you know I fucking have boundaries, but none of that shit matters as long as you trust me. You said you trust me to know what you want, and when you can handle it. The contract is more for your understanding than anything," he smirked.

I could feel his hands on my waist pulling me closer to him with the consent form between us. He hadn't looked away from me while I stared at him trying to figure out the game. I knew clubs like this did have these types of forms, but something said this was more.

"Did Tali sign this already?"

Faxx chuckled as his hands gripped my ass and squeezed while pressing against him. His hard dick pressed against my stomach making my pussy slick and my breathing increase.

"She's already sitting in the room having a drink and watching the show," he shrugged. This bitch probably just signed it because she knew like I knew, we were here to have fun. Watch some kink-ass show, get drunk, and try to forget people were trying to murder us. It wasn't like I didn't trust Faxx, or any of them because one thing for sure and two things for certain, I knew they wouldn't let shit happen to me.

I looked into his eyes, and I could see that he knew I trusted him with my whole being. Fuck it, what would happen? I get spanked again which was a possibility, but I could handle Daddy Dom Oz. Faxx stepped back and I moved to the small table, picked up the gold pen, and signed the form. I had a surge of empowerment as I did it, proving I wasn't scared of all this smoke and mirrors shit. Faxx took the form out of hand before grabbing it and leading me out of the room.

We made our way towards the room called 'BEHIND THE CURTAIN,' and I felt a mix of emotions swirling within me—excitement, anticipation, and a deep sense of being unsure if I was ready to see this side of life. I had no idea why because it wasn't like I hadn't done some questionable shit with Faxx or seen some wild things already but this...this felt different. We came to the end of a hall with two large black double doors trimmed in emerald-green with the engraved words Don't Look Behind the Curtain across it.

"Oz is wild as fuck for this shit," I said as Faxx opened the doors.

I stepped through the doorway into the room, and a wave of sensations washed over me. The room was dimly lit, the ambient lighting casting an alluring golden glow that danced across the walls. The air was heavy with the scent of incense, mingling with the faint aroma of leather and polished wood. It was intoxicating and strangely comforting. I swore if Tali didn't have some freak shit on I was going to be hot.

I saw the table further toward the back almost in shadow and I squinted slightly trying to see who all was up in here. I didn't trust Oz's ass not to pop up out of nowhere and try to punish me for that good bullshit.

"Cent, it's about time," Tali said, standing. I relaxed slightly looking at her as she walked across the room to me. Faxx stepped beside me when Oz and Dea came out of a side door.

"I'm going to holla at Oz real quick," he said, his hand leaving the middle of my back. As Tali got closer, Faxx must have said something because she pushed his shoulder as he made his way over toward Oz.

"Girl, if Seyra wasn't sitting over there in some kind of see-through one-piece, I would have lost my shit. I haven't been to one of these kinds of clubs in a minute and I'm damn sure not used to going with them," she said, looking over her shoulder. Tali had on a black Bavarian corset dress with a push-up zipper lace-up. If someone pulled that string, the entire outfit was coming apart.

"Tali, they got you out here looking like the slut on a pirate ship," I choked.

"Bissh, let me tell you how I threatened Henny if you weren't wearing something equal, I was leaving all y'all asses here. But you're cute girl, yass," she laughed walking around me.

"Why, who else is here?" I asked as she started walking. The music was playing, but it was almost more like you could feel it instead of hearing it.

"Seyra, Sanchez, Dea, and Oz were the only ones here when we arrived. I haven't seen anyone else. I'm waiting for the show for real. They got this stage with a bed and shit set up over there," Tali answered.

The room itself was spacious and exuded an aura of opulence. Rich, dark green curtains adorned the walls, creating an intimate and private atmosphere. The center of the room held an imposing structure—a St. Andrew's Cross, its dark wood gleaming in the soft light. My heart pounded thinking about the shit Dea's ass be saying. Did she actually get up there? Was she serious about fucking with me because yes, I called them Doms, but it was only because of their personalities. I never saw that side, not really. I guess I knew Link for certain was a Dom because his ass was the Black Wolf. As we passed by, I saw the chains and cuffs dangling from its sturdy frame, the promise of thrilling experiences lingering in the air. The sight sent a shiver of anticipation down my spine, and I couldn't help but marvel at the craftsmanship and the potent symbolism it held.

To one side of the room, a collection of meticulously arranged implements caught my eye.

"What kind of show will it be?" I asked.

I couldn't help but stare at the whips, floggers, and paddles hung from hooks, their supple leather and polished wood gleaming in the subdued lighting. It was a display of exquisite craftsmanship, each item seemingly whispering tales of pleasure and pain, of trust and surrender.

"I have no idea. Sanchez said that this was Oz's private section and only special performances would happen behind these doors for privacy," Tali said, unsure. I looked to the left and in the corner. A low, plush chaise lounge beckoned invitingly. Its gold upholstery looked almost black, a stark contrast to the dark surroundings. It seemed to exude an air of comfort and luxury, a place for rest and reflection amidst the intensity of the room's purpose. The room was a carefully curated blend of sensuality and safety, a sanctuary where desires could be explored, and boundaries respected. It was a place where trust reigned supreme, where the interplay of power and submission was honored and revered.

We made it to the table and Sanchez stood up holding out his arms.

"Cent, it's about time. What took you so long?" he asked kissing my cheek. I pulled away, his black dress shirt fit his frame perfectly much like his tailored black pants. I was so used to seeing him at the hospital I forgot this nigga was paid, paid. He was one of three of the only black architects in Union City and his work stood out more than most. He'd told me about building the Casino and redoing the hospital, while also drawing up the plans for the Women's Center before his sight began to fail him.

"I mean it takes time to come out here looking this fucking good," I said twirling around to the music. Seyra sat on the long sofa sipping on some wine as she danced in her seat. That's when I realized you could hear the lyrics to the music better in this section. Sanchez's face was pained when Dea walked up holding her belly laughing at his face.

"Crescent, don't do that. I do not feel like fucking with your crazy ass husband. Definitely not now," Sanchez chuckled.

"Oh my God will everybody stop," I laughed.

"Cent, don't hurt him out here chile. He just got his vision back," Dea laughed.

"Seyra, come get your man," Tali shook her head. Sanchez kissed Dea before picking Tali's ass up and tossing her on the couch next to Seyra.

"Seyra," Tali shouted.

"Sanchez, leave her alone. You know she trying to keep down that little ass dress before her whole pussy is out on display," Seyra laughed as Tali pushed her before taking her cup. Dea stood in front of me smiling like a lunatic as I stood there, taking in the sights and sounds of the room. I knew we just had that whole fight scene, but this was one of the more normal days I've had. I felt a flutter of excitement within these walls, and also a little fear when I saw something that looked like a web. I tilted my head to the side trying to figure out how you used it. I blinked seeing Dea step to the side and I looked at her.

"Why the hell are you looking like you just ate twenty pounds of peanut butter?" I asked.

The look on Dea's face confused me for a second until I smelled that unique scent that I associated with Dr. Sexy. And then I heard a slow deep chuckle behind me that had my heart about to leap out of my chest. I was freefalling for one second and the next, my back was firmly pressed against the cold, thin chains of that fucking web.

I let out a small breath of air, looking around, but I still didn't have time to react before Faxx was all up in my space. My heart was pounding erratically as Faxx pinned me onto the black spider-web-like metal contraption.

"Fransisco, what the fuck? This is a trap," I said quickly, glaring at Dea. She laughed so hard she was bent over the table. Tali's face was in shock as Sanchez laid against the couch putting his arm over top of it. His slow sexy-ass smile had me wanting to throw hot grease at him to blind his ass all over again. That nigga knew what was up and so did that damn Shandea!

Faxx seized my wrists first and secured down my right wrist with the dark green leather handcuffs. I gasped, my mind quickly catching up as he worked on securing the other wrist before I could object. I saw the barely held-back laughter and narrowed my eyes on his ass before turning my head to see Henny standing there. He stood feet apart right hand on his left elbow while he rubbed along his goatee.

"W-what are y'all doing? Y'all really taking this shit too damn far," I hissed, wiggling and pulling against the restraints while Faxx continued to bound me down, using his body to force me onto the stupid gear. I was stunned and astounded at the way he worked in perfect sync with Oz while Henny just smirked at me.

"It's over Dr. Sexy. Over, for helping them. I was punished enough already," I said, glaring.

"Aww Cent don't say that. Who said it was enough? Did anyone say Cent learned her lesson, because I didn't hear it," Henny deadpanned. Shit. This was the psycho Henny looking at me and Tali punk ass sitting on the sidelines. All I could hear close to my ear was Oz chuckling like this shit was hilarious.

Henny moved, stepping closer, grabbing onto my bad ankle gently, but he forced my legs apart, and I felt it being confined onto the stupid contraption. Then, the other one, Faxx my ex-husband, caught my other ankle and did the same thing, so I was entirely immobile.

Standing in a spread-eagle position for all to see, all I could hear was cheers and laughter as a large warm hand rubbed my lower back. It was so messed up and just so fucking wrong because my core throbbed at the small touch, and I had no idea which one it was. The yelling crowd of Tali, Dea Sanchez, and that damn Seyra screaming *'pin her up'* had me pissed. Those bitches weren't shit sitting there laughing. Tali wiggled her brows at me, her gray eyes laughing at my position. This bitch thought this was funny. I narrowed my eyes on Dea because I knew for sure she set this shit up. Her manic-ass smile and that Annabelle baby was doing a number on her mental.

Talking about taking her place!

This was some bullshit but all I had to do was take a few spankings, get a quick nut out of it, and go the fuck home.

"You set me up!" I screamed at Dea. She held a hand to her belly with wide eyes like she was innocent. All this was wild. These niggas were wild and the only reason Faxx punk ass was going along was because I kept asking if the Black Wolf would be at *MYTH* when we went, to fuck with him.

"It's for your own good Cent! All you need to do is what they say and it's over," Dea shrugged.

This bitch!

I think the only reason why I was outraged at this mess was because I was wet as hell at the thought. Was it wrong? What will happen tomorrow when this was all over and shit went back to normal. They were already a little liquored up, except for Dea, but I could blame this on her hormones. Not to mention I was married with a whole child. I thought back on the consent and the verbiage it used and what I could do if I really wasn't comfortable with any of this. I sucked in a breath as Fransisco's words floated through my mind like a highlighted sticky note.

'Do you trust me to give you everything you need?'

He'd been prepping my ass this entire time.

HE WAS CALCULATED.

This was a calculated and coordinated attack on all of us.

"Come on Cent, you've been asking to see MYTH. The real MYTH, so here we are," Sanchez smirked with his hands up. He knew this entire time what was going to happen, and I was sure it was planned. Even my big dick bestie was down with the bullshit. I just couldn't understand why it was just me. Tali let that bitch ass nigga Tremont touch her arm, but I don't see no spanking brigade coming for her.

"Fuck you too with your seeing eye dog needing ass," I snapped, and they laughed. Bastards.

My breath came out in little pants, my nipples beading inside my laced corset. Instinctively, I wanted to press my thighs together as the growing sensation between my legs spread at the rapacious eyes on me and the multiple hands on me.

I felt just like the butterfly on my ass. Trapped there forever and my ankle was the broken damn wing. They had me as the butterfly, artfully pinned down, *immortalized,* and spread for all to see, completely entangled in the spider web for these predatory psycho-ass niggas.

Fuck.

I struggled and writhed around the cuffs, scowling like a cornered animal because—last I checked—

I freaking was.

"You're fucking crazy. You're all fucking crazy. Why is Tali not up here? She was the one letting another man touch her," I squeaked when I felt a slap on my ass.

"Shut up Cent!" Tali yelled.

The club's light shined at us putting on a little show for those traitors to all witness as Faxx, Oz, and Henny circled me, watching with an almost maniacal tension I've never seen before. I knew damn well Oz wouldn't even consider helping me because he's been threatening me since he first saw me. Henny was always the safest bet because Faxx had that look. I knew that look and he was holding his Glock.

"Dr. Sexy you don't have to do this. I promise that I learned my lesson and—"

SMACK. SMACK. SMACK.

My mouth went dry as I struggled to draw in a breath when I felt lips at my ear and a beard tickled the side of my neck. I was staring at Henny, and I could see Faxx on the side of me, so I knew exactly who this was, and I shivered. Fucking Shandea. I was starting to believe she's the biggest freak of us all because when I glanced in her direction the intensity of her gaze and quick smirk told me she knew exactly what was about to happen. I closed my eyes feeling the warm breath on my skin as he breathed so close to me.

"No Crescent," Oz said switching to my other ear, "your Dr. Sexy is not helping you out of this, not when you're in my house, my room, and my web. You should've thought about that shit before you had niggas trippin' and worried about you. I don't like that shit Cent," Oz said, against my ear.

"Oh my God. Crazy and deranged," I gasped. They were insane if they thought they could make this work. But I wanted to know 'how' so bad I bit down on my tongue. I knew they were fucking with me and Tali and Dea were letting this shit happen. The thought crossed my mind that maybe they hadn't even realized how we were slowly introduced, never judged on what we liked, and given extreme amounts of leeway even when it didn't seem like it. But only with them. I could still feel Oz close, his front pressed against my back and his dick pushed against my ass. I shuddered but forced my eyes open and stared into eyes so dark my pussy jumped and then throbbed.

Faxx only chuckled, tilting his head to the side as he watched reading my expressions and seeing everything.

"*Mi Amor*, you ain't seen crazy just yet," Faxx stated as he stepped to the side. His Glock slid along the exposed skin on my stomach and my nipple tightened more.

"Crazy was when we thought we had lost you. That's a fucked up feeling Cent," Henny added, stepping closer. His platinum grills flashed as he unbuttoned his sleeves and started to roll them up to his elbows. The tattoos that crawled up his arms disappeared at his elbow under his sleeve but since his top buttons were undone, I saw the large tattoo peeking out. My gaze traveled up his chest and to his eyes and I saw the wickedness in them like he was relieved in what he was doing.

"I've been punished already. Why am I—"

Henny looked over his shoulder then back to me and smiled.

"Sanchez, hold Tali's hands to the table and don't let her play with herself," he said staring at me. My mouth fell open, and he smiled wider damn near blinding me. I clamped it closed as Sanchez maneuvered Tali into his lap slamming her hand to the table and caging her between him and the table. Seyra leaned back sipping a drink while trying not to laugh and Dea was fucking loving it. He's turning her into some kind of dominatrix or something.

"Sanchez! Hold up, wait," Tali screamed, but Sanchez whispered something in her ear that had her shaking.

"See Crescent, you haven't seen motherfucking crazy yet," Oz agreed as Henny moved so he'd stand right in front of my bounded body. "Which begs the question, shouldn't you take *responsibility* then, for making us feel that way about you? The niggas that did it will be, or have been dealt with so..."

My mouth parted, ready to just beg because it wasn't as if *I* meant to be abducted when suddenly, Oz grabbed the front of my corset. I was pulled in both directions, hating how much I was enjoying the pain of the bonds around my wrists while straining. A glisten caught my eyes, and I turned my head to see Faxx with his tactical knife. He brought the blade to the center of my chest trailing it between my breast making my nipples bead, and my folds slick with wetness as I stood there while he cut every piece of clothing off me. Oh. My. God. I didn't know what to think or if I wanted it to stop. I was completely naked now and I stared at Faxx, Oz, and Henny as they stared straight into my eyes before they took me in from head to toe. The only thing that stayed in place was the chains that had held my corset together. I could hear my pulse in my ears. I tried not to flinch as they stood there, not giving me any idea what was going to come next.

Their eyes drink me up and Faxx lets out a low, dangerous chuckle that almost sounds predatory.

Maybe more like unhinged.

"If I didn't know any better, I would have thought you came to *MYTH expecting* this," Faxx murmured as Oz stepped back and Faxx stood in front of me, blade grazing over my hard nipples.

"Who? I never said that—"

"What do you want? You can tell me wh—"

"I thought I was supposed to trust that you knew exactly what I wanted," I interjected then widened my eyes.

"It's a setup Cen— don't ans—" Tali shouted but was cut off. My eye flicked over Faxx shoulder and I saw Dea covering Tali's mouth as Seyra damn near fell out on the floor. I clamped my mouth shut, but I knew it was too late. The moment I opened my smart-ass mouth I had fucked up. He was giving me an out and I went headfirst in the opposite direction.

Faxx chuckled as his grin spread wider while the blade slid further down and slapped my clit with the flat side.

"Oh shit," I moaned.

I wasn't going to fool anyone if I tried saying, naw, not with the way my nipples were so hard and swollen. My head spun as Faxx ran his tatted hands over my body, and slowly roamed up until his thumb ran across my parched lips.

Instinctively, I licked my lips, and before I could close them, he slowly pushed it into my mouth. He was so close, I knew no one else could hear him as his other hand came up my body and his blade was at my neck. He pulled out his thumb and licked my lips.

"Crescent, I suggest you keep that smart ass mouth closed unless you're begging and moaning," he rasped. I shuddered violently as he ran his thumb over my lips, and I opened them.

"Still opening your mouth but you know I like that shit," he said, dropping his hand. Faxx removed his knife and threw it to the floor. The loud thud seemed to echo in my head as he raised his other hand, now holding his Glock again. The lemon smell had me inhaling and my clit throbbing at the same time. I opened my mouth, and he slid his Glock between my lips and down my throat.

"Oh fuck," Dea gasped.

I gagged, my throat tightening around it as he slid it back and forth, and I felt my juices running down my leg.

"Did they know that you like to suck on my Glock like you suck on my dick, *Mi Amor*?"

I knew and he knew I couldn't reply, but the needy moan had my eyes closing.

"Naw, Cent. Keep them open and look at me. What's your safe word?" Faxx demanded. His other hand squeezed and twisted at my nipples as he moved faster with the Glock. In and out, back and forth, he moved and the twist and pull at my nipples began to get harder and harder until the next moment, he pulled the Glock back.

"What do you say, *Mi Amor*?"

"Mango, mango, Papi," I panted as his fingers that were torturing my nipples moved up and gripped my chin, forcing me to look up at him. The way his focus on me sharpened is a tangible thing, similar to a cord drawn tightly around my neck with him holding the leash. The club seemed to feel suspended from everything else around us for a moment.

I'm too captivated by his attention to feel the passage of time ticking by.

With a look of obsession written over his face, Faxx slid his other hand up to rest behind my head, then pulled me into a deep, and heavy kiss. I thought he'd kissed me before, but this was like he was taking and pouring life into my body at the same time. If not for being tied up on the web, I might have fallen from how weak my knees had gotten. I couldn't stop the shaking and I hated it because they could all see it. They could see how crazy he had me and made me. Faxx pulled away and went back in licking my lips and his way back into my mouth. As our lips brushed together, I felt my eyes shut this time, and a soft moan tumble from my mouth.

"*Mm.*"

Faxx pulled me closer as he forcibly tilted my head back by my low ponytail and nipped hard on my lower lip causing me to gasp. He wasted no time in sliding his tongue in, and the wet sound of our growing kiss was more than audible throughout the club, or so I believed. It was probably all in my head. He pulled away as his tongue trailed down my chin to suck a nipple into his hot mouth as I trembled, gasping for air.

"Papi," I moaned forgetting everything and what was happening as he bit down on one nipple and pinched the other. He pulled away from my nipples and licked his way back to my lips.

"Fuck," I gasped against him, and he smiled.

My body jolted when I felt another pair of hands from behind the spider web's mechanism, and warm oil spread across my back, ass, and legs before those hands reached through the web and palmed my breasts. Squeezing and plucking my nipples made my body writhe. My eyes opened, and Faxx watched me. I could see Henny standing in front of me, looking down. So, the deranged person who was tormenting my body had to be no one other than Oz. Mother fucking Daddy Dom Oz, and I was about to cry. I was so worked up. Then I felt familiar clamps around my aching nipples, followed by a short chuckle when I moaned. Faxx was still pulling on my ponytail as Oz's lips traveled to my ear.

"You like the way that feels Crescent," Oz grunted. I opened my mouth as Faxx traveled his teeth over my throat.

"I can't hear you Cent. I asked you a question," Oz said. I felt him step back, and then a crack sounded across my butt, making me cry and then moan. The sensations of Faxx's mouth on me and the next hit had me needing to cum.

"Yes! Yes," I cried.

I felt Oz on the other side of me, lips pressed against my ear, his hand rubbing at the area where he had just spanked me.

"Yes. What?" he gritted. I shook. I fucking shook as whatever he was holding slid down the crack of my ass.

"Yes, it feels good,"

"Did you forget my name Crescent?"

I sucked in a breath and my eyes flew open when Oz licked the shell of my ear before he leaned away, and I felt another smack.

"Yes, yes, Daddy Dom Oz," I panted. Oh, my damn, this was so wrong and when I looked at Dea, she was leaning forward biting the tip of a nail. Fucking enjoying my torture.

"Good girl Cent," Oz praised.

Faxx pulled my hair harder, tilting my head back further to where I couldn't see anyone else.

"Dea, this...I've seen things...but this is," Tali trailed off.

"I know," Dea answered as Sanchez chuckled.

"Y'all don't let Crescent think this is it. She still has a ways to go," Seyra said.

I closed my eyes as I felt Oz move and his arm grazed my body as he connected a chain to each nipple clamp. He pulled the chain making the ache intensify and my nipples harden further from the weight of the chain. But it felt so fucking good I cried out, but it turned into a long moan as the vibrators attached made it feel like someone was tugging my sensitive nipples. The bullet vibrators attached to its clamps were thumping against my chest, making my head spin. I whimpered, trying not to move my hips because when I did, I rubbed along Oz's hard dick. It didn't matter though, because his hand landed on my hip as he held me still and pressed me against his length holding me in place, like a butterfly pinned down.

The leather whip Oz was using began to slap at my thighs, first on the back and then the front, causing me to grind against him seeking friction as he laughed. I opened my eyes and Faxx was standing over me watching my face and I couldn't hide how badly I was turned the fuck on. He smirked at me just as I felt another pair of hands coming from nowhere, slowly parting my drenched slits even more and spreading my arousal around as the finger circled my clit.

"Oh shit," I cried. Faxx slowly reached my ponytail inch by inch, letting my neck get used to the position.

SMACK. SMACK. SMACK.

I felt my thighs trembling but the squelching noises and Henny's hands running around the back of my calves made me tremble and shake.

Slowly.

Almost...meanderingly gentle, from the way they were touching me, was giving me the false sense that this was going to be the extent of it. It was enough to cum, the way they played with me like a possession.

I knew that I was wrong as soon as the thought came into my mind. I knew these niggas didn't do half-assessed shit. They were the type to have you turnt up and turned the fuck out. My face twisted to the side as Faxx sealed his mouth over mine sucking my tongue into his mouth.

His other hand slowly slipped from my hair and came to rest on my waist down to my peachy ass, palming it hard. I whined because he lifted my ass cheek making Oz's covered dick slide between my cheeks. His hard, tented length nudged against my entrance.

"Mmm, mmm," I moaned into Faxx's mouth as Henny spread my lips open.

Yes, yes, yes—this was what my body had been craving.

"I'm sure you already know the only way I'm going to stop is if you scream platinum," Henny said against my clit. I wanted to cry, scream, beg, and run at the same time.

"Oh, shit, shit, shit. Oh my God," I panted into the breathless kiss.

The long swipe of Henny's tongue would have made me collapse if I wasn't strapped to this fucking web.

"Damn. Fuck, Sanchez, let me go, please," Tali cried.

Faxx's hand came around my neck and I opened my eyes just as Henny's tongue circled my clit again. He sucked and slurped while his tongue felt like a blanket over my entire pussy. Faxx squeezed and I swear I saw the pearly gate.

"Keep your eyes open *Mi Amor*," Faxx ordered. I snapped them open just as Oz pulled on the chain. I gasped, trying to suck in air that Faxx wasn't allowing me to get.

"Mmm, please, I, I—"

I knew I was mumbling but when Henny used his finger to spread my lips and his tongue dipped into my core everything went white. I felt like I was blind as Faxx eased the pressure on my neck but when Oz bit down on the side of my neck before he slapped my ass, I knew I died. There was no way I was in control of my body as I came. I felt Henny's hand clamp around my calves tightly as his tongue flicked over my clit faster and faster.

"Mmm, I can tell by the way you're making a face like you're dying to be dicked down. You want to ride my dick while you watch me give Tali that mango treatment," Faxx asked.

"Ahh...God...shit...fuck...oh shit damn Papi," I cried.

Henny bit my clit and I jerked trying to move my hips, but Oz had me pinned. I pushed back and he chuckled before I felt another slap.

"That's what you want to see Crescent? What do you say Cent?"

SMACK.

"Please, please, I need, oh God, I need," I mumbled.

Henny's tongue slid so deep inside me my walls tried to hold onto his tongue as he wiggled it.

"What? I couldn't hear you," Faxx grunted. His hand resting around my neck tightened without warning forcing me to face him and I stared into his eyes wanting to cry at the sensations. I could feel my orgasms building into a rogue wave as Henny licked at my clit, Oz pulled at the chain connected to the nipple clamps, and Faxx pushed his finger into my mouth. Faxx pulled his fingers out abruptly and wrapped them around my neck forcing me to look at him.

"She's practically begging to cum with all that moaning, but I ain't hear her ask permission," Oz rumbled. I felt Oz step back leaving my back cold, but I felt his fingers against the side of my face as he leaned into the back of my neck. The stroking of my swollen clit in gentle, agonizingly slow motions had tears sliding down my cheeks. I was free to move my hips and I tried rotating to get the extra friction, but my rhythm was off as I gasped. Faxx let go and leaned in, kissing me as I moaned in his mouth. I didn't even know Oz moved because Henny began to suck on my clit while sliding his hand up the back of my legs. My body was shaking like an old woman with bad knees. Faxx pulled back letting my neck pull at the clamps causing a reaction that had my hips moving against Henny's face faster.

SMACK. SMACK. SMACK.

The three smacks came on each cheek and my thighs just as Henny pulled back slapping my clit as my juices poured from me.

"Please! I need to cum. Please let me cum please," I cried.

Oz's hands rubbed at the area where he hit and pressed up against my heart and I could feel his bare chest on my back.

"You cum when we fucking tell you to cum," Oz rumbled.

Oh.

My.

God.

I couldn't hold it back and Oz knew it by the way he was kneading my ass and licking my shoulder. Oz chuckled darkly, smacking my breasts as they bounced and Faxx pulled at the chain.

"Nah, not until she understands her place. She knows what she needs to say," Faxx said. The slurping and splashing sound as Henny hummed into my pussy tugged at what little sanity I had left.

"Pwease, please, pl, plea, platinum. PLATINUM!" I screamed. I sank my teeth against my lower lip as the orgasm I was holding came rushing over me.

"Cum for me, *Mi Amor*, let them see how you look for me when you cum," Faxx demanded. And I did while whimpering pathetically against Faxx's lips as he sucked my tongue and Henny slid a finger into my core causing my walls to and then the smack at the underside of my buttock with Oz's open palm in perfect timing with the suck on my clit.

"Oh my God please let me go. I need to walk this shit off. I...fuck," Tali panted.

I could barely hear because everything felt like it was underwater, but the groans from my mouth echoed around the room, exciting me more than I knew I was being watched.

It's wild. This entire situation was wild.

"Oh, she thinks we're done," Oz chuckled.

"Wh—what? No, I can't, I can't," I panted. Henny kissed my pussy and I shuttered.

"You aren't done until we fucking say you're done," Oz laughed.

WHAT?

How in the hell weren't we done? I couldn't—

Faxx then tugged me back into a deep, knee-trembling, and ground-shaking kiss. From the way he was kissing me, his tongue rubbing inside of my caverns so damn thoroughly, I was surely going to taste nothing but him for the next few days. All the while the spanking and rubbing on my ass was beginning to make my clit throb and my core clench. My head was spinning and the shouts and comments from the assholes watching were lost in my overstimulated state.

"Lennox, I think...I think...I need you to take me back into the o-ffice...because...mmm, please," I heard Shandea's voice closer than before.

"You see how my wife still wants to help you Cent? It doesn't mean it's over," Oz whispered against my ear before pulling away. I shivered at his words and the way his mouth moved against my ear while his beard tickled my neck. My ass, thighs, and calves were on fire for one minute, but then I felt a cooling sensation as an oil was rubbed into my skin. I blinked as Faxx rubbed a thumb over my lips before pulling the bottom one down. The hands rubbing my body went away leaving me feeling drugged and drunk all at once. Faxx leaned back down licking my lips and pushing his tongue into my mouth. I opened my eyes breathing harshly in between our kisses as Faxx urged me to press harder onto the web. His fingers moved between my breasts as he pulled on the chain making me hiss before he kept moving over my stomach until he was between my thighs while Henny used his index and middle fingers to spread me open. It allowed Faxx to rub his fingers in circles on my swollen bundle of nerves without any barriers as three fingers slowly nudged into my opening.

"Fuck, fuck, I can't...Papi please," I moaned. It provided some relief in that instant as I started to grind my hips to the rhythm they set.

"Yes, you can and you will. It's what you wanted right, so you will take all that shit, *Mi Amor*," Faxx chuckled. I shook as my core was clamping on the emptiness that was begging to be filled. My arousal was leaking and making a mess all over Henny's finger before he pulled away once more. Faxx's fingers never stopped moving but I could feel the restraint loosening on my right arm, then my right and left leg. A strong hand rubbed at my ankles before trailing up my body as Henny stood facing me. One of his hands pulled the chain as he stared me in the eyes. The honey brown flashed when I cried out just his he reached up releasing my other hand. Fax moved away as I fell forward into Henny's chest. My legs were shaking as I stepped forward. Henny's arms came around me to hold me up as Faxx came up behind me. I felt his arms snake up over my chest as one anchored me to his body. Henny let go and my shaking body fell against Faxx. Henny's head tilted as he licked his lips and smiled at me. I knew I was slowly blinking and I felt like time was standing still.

"You got my dick hard Cent with that wet ass pussy. You think Tali going to be able to take this dick tonight?"

"I...oh shit," I panted. My eyes slid to Tali, who sat with her chest pressed against the table as she struggled to move. Her eyes grew wide with that remark, and I could see her breaths pick up. Faxx turned me to face him as Henny walked away. I swayed but he gripped my waist lifting me and I instinctively wrapped my legs around his waist. I hadn't noticed when his shirt came off, but my hands roamed over his body as my lips met his collarbone, neck, and then his ear.

"F-Faxx...please. Ha...ha-ah, I want...want more," I moaned.

The gleam in Faxx's eye turned into something predatory, his mouth ticking upward into a smile as he moved over to a sitting area. The long couches surrounded a long black platform.

"*Mi Amor*, what you are about to do is ride this dick, but I want your eyes open. Can you keep them open for me Cent?" Faxx asked with a look resembling someone planning a murder. The victim was me, because I could tell by the grip he had on my ass and the way his length pressed into me, there would be no slow stroking. I knew he wasn't done with me and even though I didn't think I could take it, I would take it. As we got closer, I saw Henny with Tali wrapped around him. His finger slid up her crease, getting closer to the area we were heading.

"What do you say to me Crescent?" Faxx gritted against my neck. I sucked in my breath and moaned when his tongue touched my skin.

"Yes, Papi," I said quickly.

He smiled liking to see me needing what he could give me. Faxx liked to see me cry and beg for it to be harder. He seemed to like to see me hoarse and edged until the time he slid into my wet heat because he knew I would already be *gone*.

"Yeah? You want that shit. Just like you want to cum for me while I eat Tali's tight-ass pussy," he said huskily. I fucking shuddered because no I shouldn't want to see it, but I wanted to fucking see it so fucking bad. I wanted to watch Henny fuck her while Faxx made me cum so hard I would go blind.

"Oh my God," I whispered. I felt Faxx step up as we got to the platform and he turned his back on Henny while pulling at my braids. My head tilted back as he leaned against the platform. My body slid down his and when my feet touched the floor I noticed that my body never stopped shaking.

"Take off my pants Cent," he commanded letting go of my hair.

"Hendrix, please, I just need...fuck me," Tali begged.

My hands fumbled with his belt and button but all he did was watch as I did what I was told. I pulled at his jeans pushing them down along with his boxers. He pulled me closer to him by my neck as he positioned himself on the platform. His hands slid down my neck and over my shoulders before resting on my hips. The breathy moan that left my throat scared me as he helped me onto the platform. My knees settled on each side of his hips and my pussy hovered over his stiff dick. He leaned back on the platform and pulled me closer to him by the chain of the nipple clamps.

"Fuck," I moaned.

I was filled with nothing but desperation and a breathless moan like a withdrawn drug addict would make, willing to do anything for their next little hit. This nigga had me *gone* and when I looked up Henny smirked at me because he knew it too. He had a hand wrapped tightly in Tali's locs as her head lolled to the side lethargically in complete submission as he slowly licked the side of her neck.

"Hendrix, please," Tali whispered right as Faxx slowly pushed his fingers deep into my tightness until he was halfway in.

"You might be wet as fuck *Mi Amor* but this pussy stays fucking tight," he groaned.

I licked my dry lips when he squeezed my hips as the head of his dick pushed into me in one stroke.

"*Papi.*"

My attention was caught when Henny moved chuckling against Tali's neck. But Faxx's finger began to move and stretch as my breathing increased.

"You want to cum Tali?" Henny asked.

"Yes, I need to Hendrix you know I do," she panted.

"Then be a good girl and suck this dick, *Thickness*. Did you watch how Cent sucked on that Glock? That's what I want. I want you to gag on it when I hit the back," he gritted.

"Oh fuck," I moaned while Faxx's fingers lazily moved pushing deeper while rubbing his dick along my other hole. I let out a loud groan that made my head spin when Henny stepped forward lifting Tali off the platform. Faxx pulled his hands from my pussy and grabbed my neck causing me to look down as he pushed his dick inside my pussy in one stroke.

"Fuck! Papi," I cried. My back arched and I leaned back just as Henny sat Tali on Faxx's face.

What? Oh shit, oh shit!

Faxx's dick jerked and his hand flexed as he pushed me down harder his he pushed upward.

"Baby, shit right there," I screamed but I could take my eyes off the scene in front of me

I'M. A. HOE.

"Oh fuck! Shit," Tali groaned as her body froze. Henny's hand came to the back of her neck as he slowly lowered her body forward. He stared at me as I rock and Faxx's hand came down on my ass urging me to move faster while grinding into me.

"F...fuc..fuck," I cried. Henny smiled as Faxx's other hand on my neck slowly tightened. It was something about the weight around my neck and the pressure that had my eyes rolling.

"You clearly don't want it enough if you're not sucking this dick Tali," Henny taunted before stroking his length. He pushed Tali down and her mouth wrapped around the head before she sucked it in while moaning. She put a hand on the table, and it shook as her hips moved.

"Yeah just like that *Thickness*," Henny grunted. Henny released the back of her neck as she licked around the head and he reached over slapping her ass.

"Mmm," Faxx groaned and my pussy spasmed. Faxx's upward thrust and the forceful way he slammed me down had me trying to pull in air. He released my throat and I gasped and moaned practically burning up inside at how Henny leaned forward pushing deeper into Tali's mouth and reached out to grab the chain between my breasts and pulled.

"Oh! Ahh shit, Frans—shit," I moaned and moved faster. Faxx reached up to Tali's hip while the other grasped mine. The tattoos moved as he pushed Tali down harder. His grip on my hip loosened but only for him to slap my ass while he brought up his leg for a better angle.

It felt like they wanted us crazy and were making us lose all semblance of what should be and what it is. I was quivering feeling myself growing warm all over. I didn't even know my eyes were closed until a hand covered my throat yanking me forward. They popped open only to stare at Henny whose gaze roamed over my face.

My nails dug into my palm, and my toes curled as Henny swiped his tongue over my neck before shoving his fingers into my panting, parted mouth.

"That's right Crescent. Keep your eyes open and suck them like you sucked that Glock. I didn't know I liked that shit until those lips were wrapped around it. Are you going to cum for me again? You can fuck him while you scream PLATINUM. Let me hear you work wife," he smirked.

There was something so erotic and hot in the way he spoke when it was absolutely fucked up. My walls tightened causing Faxx to grind into me as he made slurping noises. Tali pulled back slightly moaning around Henny's dick.

"Fuck, Faxx, shit, I'm going to cum, shit," she mumbled. Instinctively, I moaned and suck his digits like my favorite lollipop—like it was Faxx's G lock.

Lemon fucking fresh.

"You look like you're hoping to be fucked stupid," Henny rumbled. My entire body flinched when I felt his breath fanning over my cheek. He pulled his fingers out of my mouth and trailed them down my cheek and then gripped my chin. Faxx flexed and released Tali's hip and both his hands landed on my ass. I felt my cheeks spread as he raised me up and slammed me back down.

"Oh, shit. Fuck, fuck, fuck," I cried. I felt Henny's firm grip and my eyes focused on him as he pulled his hips back and then pushed back into Tali's mouth making her gag but she didn't stop. Her small hand wrapped around his length as she began to stroke.

"Fuck *Thickness*, show Daddy how bad you want me to fuck you," he whispered.

"Oh shit, fuck," I moaned.

I screamed while rotating my hips. My walls tighten as I gush of wetness had to be sliding over Faxx's dick as he thrusted faster slamming into my walls over and over until my eyes rolled.

"I know that pussy is dripping. It's probably dripping just as much when I stuck my tongue inside. All that nut sliding down my throat tasted so good Cent," Henny chuckled.

Faxx's dick pumped into my wet pussy hitting that spot that had me trembling and moaning as I increased my speed.

Henny's words rolled around in my head as Faxx pushed up hitting my G-spot. Henny let my chin go and I threw my head back rocking as I rode the wave of that movement. I was drenched but I flexed my hip and rolled greedily for more. Henny's hand was back in Tali's locs, fisting them as he moved her head like he wanted. His other hand caressed her jawline as he pushed in and out.

"Mmmm, mmmm," Tali moaned.

Faxx slapped my ass as he moved me up and down but when I felt the tug of the chain giving me the sting I needed I cried out. My eyes cracked open slightly seeing Sanchez. Seyra stood behind him licking her lips at the entire scene.

"San—"

My words cut off when his tongue licked around my nipple before he pulled the chain again.

So good.

So fucking good.

"Eyes on me, Cent," Henny ordered and I obeyed.

My eyes snapped open at the command, head lolling back to see the whole scene for what it was.

Sexy. Hot and fucking insane. I felt Faxx's dick jerk inside me when Tali raised slightly trying to chase Henny's dick. I saw his long tongue cover her pussy as he flicked her clit.

What the fuck was wrong with me?

"Shit! I'm cumming," Tali screamed.

"Mmm shit Tali. I like that dark Chocolate. Let that shit slide down my throat," Faxx rasped.

My hand came down on Sanchez's head pressing him closer as his teeth grazed over my flesh while my brain broke. I stared at Henny as he leaned his head back the tattoos covering his body making him as a product of the street and a Union City King.

His arms were crossed, a look crossing his face I didn't know if I wanted to know what he was thinking. He stepped forward again as Tali cried and moved her hips faster. Sanchez pulled back kissing up the side of my neck and to my ear.

"I think Henny is right Cent because the way I want to watch my dick slide down your throat got my shit rock fucking hard," Sanchez whispered.

"Oh my God," I wheezed. Faxx pushed me down and I rotated my hips as I held onto his forearms as Sanchez's words sent me over.

It's so fucking wrong.

It should go against everything I am, and yet...and yet...

I found myself moaning and writhing for more because the incentive was so damn rewarding as Henny walked forward sliding his fingers over my throat and squeezing.

"Cum for me Crescent. Let me see you cum," he gritted. Faxx was pushed deep into my core now, pumping into me his mouth open as his beard glinted. His dark eyes were on me and he licked his lips. I had no clue where Tali was or if this shit was real. All I knew was the rush coming that was starting at my toes. Henny squeezed tighter cutting off my oxygen making me lightheaded as a black spot danced at the edges of my vision. Faxx's hand released my butt and I felt him drag his nails over my skin before his fingers pinched the sweet, nerve-ending that short-circuited my entire body.

"Cum," Henny commanded and I did. I came all over Faxx's dick as he kept up his stroke never stopping as he fucked me through one of the biggest and longest orgasms I'd ever had. Henny let go as tears rolled down my face and I screamed.

"Oh fuck Papi! Shit, yes, yes! Fuck yes, PLATINUM, fuck" I repeated until my voice was hoarse.

Henny moved as Faxx sat up and lifted me off his dick and stood. My legs felt fake like they could snap at any time. He spun me around and pushed my chest onto the platform while kicking my feet apart. Then he slammed back inside of me, gripping my braids and raising my head up.

"Papi! Fuck," I screamed.

"That's right *Mi Amor*, give Papi that pussy and look at your friend Cent. Scream louder so she can hear you take this dick," Faxx said slamming hard as my ass bounced back. His hand in my hair pulled then angled my face toward Tali. Henny sat on the couch as he had Tali in between his legs, bouncing on his dick, but my pussy squeezed Faxx so tight he groaned.

"You like that shit don't you?" Faxx grunted.

Tali's hand slid down Sanchez's chest as he slide his dick between her lips. He threw his head back but when he did Seyra wrapped her delicate hand over his throat and dragged her nails over the tattoos covering his neck. Seyra leaned over licking Sanchez's nipple before pulling back as he stroked deeper into Tali's mouth. Sanchez angled his head down taking Seyra's lips shoving his tongue down her throat before she pulled away and slapped the fuck out of him.

"You didn't ask my permission for that Sans," he grinned.

Oh my God, I was losing it because I did like it. I felt my walls clench as Faxx slammed harder and leaned over my back biting my ear when the doors opened.

My eyes widened when Link walked in frown on his face as he looked around with Mala behind him. His gaze found mine and narrowed. The black cloak he wore and nothing else except something on his head had my entire body shaking.

"Fuck," I moaned, wanting to close my eyes but wanting to be a good girl for Faxx and keep my eyes open. He wanted me to see everything. He wanted to show me exactly what I could and couldn't have, and I got it. He would be the only nigga fucking me but that didn't mean the only one that would make me cum.

"You wanted the Black Wolf, right? You wanted to see," he whispered in my ear. He pushed deep before pulling out.

"Oh! Fuck, fuck," I said legs shaking barely able to hold myself up. I didn't have time to wonder where the fuck Faxx went as Link climbed onto the platform staring down at me.

"So you're here with them but you asked for me first. Mmm, I don't like that Cent," Link chuckled.

"I...I didn't kno...kno what—"

I felt something cold yet familiar run over my skin. Sweat was running down my body, my body glistening from massage oil, and sweat as Link suddenly curled his finger under my chin to make me look at him.

I felt the Glock ran along my skin and over my ass until he tapped it against my clit.

"Shhh, it's too late for all that now. Open your mouth and lick the tip of my dick to apologize. That's what you should do, right Mala?" he grinned. Faxx tapped my clit again before sliding it lower rubbing the Glock against my opening. My heart was pounding and my breaths came out in hot pants as my eyes found Mala's. She smirked at me as she climbed on the platform and pulled the wolf down to cover his face.

"All you need to do is breathe through it, Cent," she said, biting her lip as Link pushed his head between my lips exactly as Faxx pushed the Glock inside me. My eyes opened my jaws slackened as a pool of wetness poured out of me.

"Take that shit and suck this dick Crescent," Link ordered as he pushed my head down. The small, bumpy spot was grazed and I cried while the Glock slid in and out.

What the fuck was wrong with me because Jesus Jerome Christ, I was going to cum again.

"Oh...fuck, there, there. There, Hen...Henny. Fuck me harder, harder please, please," Tali cried.

"If you keep teasing me like that, I'm not going to be able to control myself, *Dove*," Link chuckled as Mala pulled at his locs while her tongue ran over his body. I opened my mouth wider trying to figure out how to fucking breathe! Faxx pulled his Glock out and tapped it against my clit twice making me jump and jerk seeking something my walls could grab on.

"I can't let my Glock feel all that cum *Mi Amor*. I need that shit coating my dick," he said before slamming inside me. His hand kneaded my ass while the other held the wet Glock on the top of my ass as he thrusted. I ran my tongue up from the very bottom to the tip before sucking Link's dick back in my mouth. My eyes were closed as my swollen clit jumped with each thrust and slide of Link's dick across my tongue.

"Mmm, mmmm, shi...shit," I mumbled before Link resumed his oral *obsession*.

"Henny!"

"Fuck," Henny growled.

"Make her gag on it Sans. What did I tell you before? If you die, you fucking die," Seyra moaned as slurping noises followed.

I tried turning my head but Link's hand tightened. He pulled my head back the tip of his dick sitting on my lips. Faxx leaned over me licking up my spine causing me to shiver.

"Look at that. Look what you did Cent," Link said. My eyes darted down as I moaned using the sturdiness of the platform to hold me up as Faxx pulled out and slammed in hard.

"Fuck! Papi! Papi, please, oh shit, right there, Papi. Harder please, faster please," I cried. My eyes opened again and looked up to the black wolf-shaped mask with red fur weaving through it on the sides. Then I looked down at the cum on the tip of Link's dick. I screamed again when Faxx slapped my ass and pulled me back as I bounced.

"Lick it Cent. Stick out that tongue so I can push my nut down your throat. Are you going to let me titty fuck you before I cum?" Link asked.

My pussy spasmed and my walls clamped down on Faxx so badly his hand slapped onto the platform as he leaned over me.

"Fuck Cent, Fuck baby. Grip that shit just like that. That's right fuck Papi just like that," Faxx groaned. His words along with Link pushed the envelope and I was done. I came again hard because I could feel myself squirting as Faxx pushed deeper grinding his dick into me.

"Ahh, oh, oh, shit fuck, ahh," I screamed. Then Link pushed his dick to the back of my throat making me gag but I swallowed around it tasting his cum before he pulled back and slid back inside while stroking my cheek.

"That's right Cent, take that shit. You can handle it. Breathe with me but you better keep sucking baby," Link gritted. I let my teeth graze over his head and he groaned throwing his head back. I was dizzy as fuck and I felt my body trying to shut the fuck down. I felt Faxx's hands on my hips pulling me back up as he pressed harder into my body holding me in place. His fast short stroke grew faster and harder. The tighter his grip got meant he was close. I felt him raise my butt cheek before he leaned away slightly on an upstroke. I swallowed Link's thick pre-cum and sucked the tip letting go with a pop.

"Oh shit! Papi," I screamed. That was enough for him to slam hard inside as his dick pumped his nut deeper inside as he groaned.

"Crescent! Fuck," he grunted.

I raised a shaky hand wrapped it around Link's length and twisted.

"Hmm, shit Cent. Suck it," he gasped. My eyes flicked up as my legs trembled seeing Mala standing over him her hand wrapped tightly around his neck as she whispered in his ear.

"Fuck! Shit, *Dove*, fuck," Link gritted. As soon as she let go of his neck he sucked in a breath and I felt hot thick cum on my tongue and his hand pushing my face down as he pumped in and out.

"Mmm fuck! Now let me see if those pillows you call titties so they can wake my dick back up. You owe me that Crescent," Link growled.

I clenched hard feeling more cum and juices pour from my body leaving me feeling fatigued and dehydrated.

"Shit, fuck," Faxx moaned giving one last thrust and pulling out. I felt him behind me and his hands spread my cheeks I felt his tongue lick from my clit to my ass before his tongue pushed into the tight ring and I screamed. My mind went blank when his finger pushed into my pussy.

"I can't...No more...please....more," I moaned before my legs gave out.

I felt Faxx catch me but I couldn't open my eyes as my body shuddered.

"Seyra! Seyra! It's Dea! I think she's in labor," Oz shouted.

That was the last thing I heard.

CHAPTER FOURTEEN

RODNEY 'ROE' GATES

I woke up to the blaring sound of Channel 7 News morning anchors talking about the recent activity happening in Union City. The raid that happened at *MYTH* was now old news. Now the news got fucking U.C.K. was out here looking like fucking saints after that so-called doctor Malone gave her two cents. I groaned as I rubbed my eyes looking out of the window of my second-story apartment on another day, another step closer to having my promotion. I was through fucking with Charles and if Dmar-Clap Productions getting blown up wasn't enough for him to be worried about Theodore, then maybe the threat of federal jail time would do it. I still had all the files and evidence from that weapons charge

I could bring into play. I used the bathroom and did what I needed to do before looking at the time. I yanked a white dress shirt from the hanger and grabbed a black pair of pants before pulling on the black suit jacket and stumbled into the kitchen. I poured myself a cup of hot coffee, no cream. The aroma filled the air as I pondered my next move in taking down the Union City Kings as a show that I could get shit done. I checked my phone to see the four missed calls from my Sienna. I smoothed a hand over my goatee before sucking my teeth and hitting the callback button.

"Where in the hell have you been Gates?"

"Getting some rest Sienna. I've been doing double time since Higgins is MIA," he grunted.

"MIA! Do you think he went MIA? Are you this fucking stupid Rodney?"

"I am sure I can find him. He's probably just lying low right now. I'll contact him and figure this shit out," I said quickly. Where the fuck was Higgins?

"This is becoming entirely too hot Roe. You have no idea the position you just put me in. I'm backing off, whatever resources you have now is what you can keep. Everything else I'm pulling and if Thomas is not found or found dead this will be on you," Sienna said quickly. I pulled at my tie and frowned, not knowing what she was talking about. Yeah, it was taking longer than I wanted, but I had a plan, and I was close.

"I will find Higgins, but I have a doctor willing to testify about the hospital and its unethical practices, intimidation, and blackmail," he said quickly.

"You don't get it, Roe," she sighed.

"Baby, listen once I take them down, everything that I will uncover what they're connected to will shine a light on others. This is a win-win," I grunted. I had to keep her on board with this because I couldn't fuck this up. Powerful people wanted them taken care of and since I was very loosely affiliated with them back in college, I was the go-to because Oz, Hendrix,

Link, and Faxx were just that fucking good for some reason. People higher than Administrator Sienna Barnes wanted them put down. It wasn't that easy without help.

"Rodney, I want you to listen to me. I cannot have this blowback. And I cannot allow my husband to find out we've been fucking from the morning news! They have recordings, pictures, and files on me. On us! Are you catching what I am saying? I will not go down because you couldn't handle some thugs that like to play in suits!"

I swallowed at her words thinking rapidly at the meaning of it. How the fuck had they known about her? About us? What more did they have and what else did them niggas know? I knew I had to use any means necessary to climb the ranks. The Union City Kings were my ticket to the top, once I was tapped, and I was willing to get my hands dirty to bring them down. I had been gathering evidence on them for months, biding my time until I had enough to make a move. I was close! I needed her dumbass to believe that shit as well.

"I have a body. I for sure have a body connecting them to a high-profile murder. Just give me seventy-two hours baby. Have I ever let you down?" I asked. I looked down at my lukewarm coffee and grimaced. Sienna was quiet for a minute before I heard a long sigh.

"You have seventy-two hours but this...this shit with us is over, Agent Gates. Whatever shit you stepped us both into is beginning to track back to me. Seventy-two hours Gates or clear out all of your shit," she spat. I looked at the blacked-out screen and placed my phone down as my jaw worked. I picked up the coffee cup and looked into it before throwing it at the pale blue wall.

"Fuck! Fuck!" I shouted.

Deputy Mayor Charles Morgan better have the information I needed, or he could kiss his bid for Mayor of Union City goodbye. I had dirt on Theodore Banks, and it was enough to make him think twice about playing his little fucking games. I knew what could ruin them both, and I was ready to exploit it for my own gain. Ever since Pamela's ass fell off the grid everything with the hospital except Tremont was falling apart. If I could find her bitch ass brother that may also help with the charges, I would bring forth that will stick. I knew Henny was running Big Pharma and Oz sold shit out of his club that was more than just pussy and a fantasy. I ran a hand over my face before fixing my jacket into place calming myself down. Charles was my ticket to what needed to be done. Either he would talk, or I would go public with all that I know about him. While also submitting my findings on his man. I grabbed my keys and stormed out of my apartment trying to regain control of my temper before the doors of the elevator opened.

"Fuck," I gritted as the doors slide open.

I made my way to City Hall, my mind racing with the possibilities. I parked in the underground parking lot, checking my surroundings before jumping out of my SUV. I made my way to his floor, hoping that it would still be fairly empty, so I could get my point across to his ass. The doors opened and I stepped off the elevators noticing that no one was at his administrative assistant's desk. Good. The floor was quiet as I picked up speed. The tracker I put on his car had stayed in the same place for days, so I knew he'd found it. But I knew Charles had to be here today because of the bullshit ass Blackbay debacle. When nobody turned up and all the eyes looked at me, I saw the hate and panic in Charles' eyes. Whatever else he was hiding wasn't going in his favor as well. Maybe this exchange would be beneficial for both of us now.

No more games and no more bullshit.

I found Charles in his office, his brow furrowed as he looked up at me with a mix of fear, defiance, then anger. I smirked, knowing I had him right where I wanted him whether he knew it or not.

"Rodney, what the hell do you want?" Charles spat. His voice was tinged with anger as he stared at me. I stepped inside, closing the door behind me before leaning against it.

"I think you know exactly what I want, Charles. I want your help in taking down the Union City Kings. It's not like you don't know what the fuck I want," I answered. I unbuttoned my suit jacket and stuck my hands into my pants pockets as I watched him.

Charles stared at me for a long minute, realizing that he knew I hadn't forgotten about our little conversation. He sighed heavily, leaning back into his leather chair.

"What do you need from me? I got you help with the police department. I did everything you wanted, but you still found nothing," he accused.

"I want you to lead me to a body, Charles. You said that you know where a body is and that you could take me to it. I want that, and I want your sworn testimony that you saw who murdered the person," I said, my eyes narrowing.

"I know you've got something on one of the Kings, and I want it."

Charles hesitated, but then he nodded.

"I can lead you to a body. I witnessed one of the Kings, kill a man. I'm willing to testify if—"

"If what? I'm done with the bullshit Charles, ain't shit you can say this time. Give me the body and testify, then we're done or—"

"I'm going to need you to calm the fuck down. Just because you believe that you've got me in a tough position don't get it fucked up Rodney. I'm willing to give you the body and the person who murdered Mayor Holmes," he smiled. I knew my eyes were wide as that little piece of knowledge slipped out. I felt a rush of triumph surge through me. This was it, my ticket to where I belonged, and the ordered favor completed. I had the leverage that I needed to take down the Kings or at least one of them. Once I got one of them, the rest would follow because I would get all the available resources.

"Who? Which one of those bitches was it?"

"Does it really matter? The person I want you to arrest for the murder is Lakyn Moore. Call your contact in the department and make sure it's kept under wraps. Tell them all they need to do is drain the pond in Union City Park," Charles said, standing. He held out his hand, his face sat in a firm line as his jaw flexed. I pushed from the door taking his hand before turning and exiting his office.

I had what I needed, and I wasn't about to waste time in getting shit started. I left City Hall, my mind was already racing with plans. I would use Charles' testimony to make my move, and who wouldn't believe the new Mayoral candidate who has done nothing but serve this city? U.C.K. was about to fall, and I was going to be there watching all four of those niggas fall. I texted Sienna with the information while sending out emails and alerts for what was about to happen. We needed every agency on board for this because when they fell, I wanted them to get whatever the max is. I just hoped that was enough.

My phone buzzed with a text, and I glanced down to see a message from my Sienna.

> **Sienna: Seventy-two hours.**

I smiled to myself, knowing that I was one step closer to the power and success I craved. And I was one step closer to showing Shandea how wrong she'd chosen. Even though she was having that niggas baby I could get over that. Once Oz was dead or locked up, I would make it a point to raise his child as mine.

Malikita 'Mala' Samuels

After all the shit at *MYTH* went down and then the whole Dea going into labor, my mind was whirling. I was panicked because I knew she was in labor way too early, but Seyra was on it. I was still dressed, so I went with her and Oz to the hospital. Once there, it only took about an hour and a half before everyone else began to show up. We knew she would have to have a C-section, but none of us were expecting two babies. Two girls were born at four-thirty in the morning, one at five and a half pounds and the other at four pounds and two ounces. The larger one was hiding the other, so surprise, surprise. It was a bittersweet moment because, at the end of the day, they still lost one of the triplets. When Oz stepped out of the

OR looking stunned, shocked, and terrified, I almost lost it when he held his chest. Once he uttered the words two girls, then damn near fell out, I knew he was replaying Cece's first years. Every last one of them watched her like she could get up and walk away. Lucky for his big ass, Henny was next to him. That happening made everything we had to do more apparent. They were both in the NICU for now, but Seyra assured us all they were stro ng.

I blew out a breath as the replay of that night re-winded to when we opened the door to '*BEHIND THE CURTAIN.*' The entire scene at *MYTH* unfolded because the sensuality of it was firmly imprinted at the forefront of my mind because it was so...so fucking sexy. I wanted to see it again. It was weird because for the most part, my eyes hadn't left Link's face but that was all I needed to see anyway. I shivered at the knowledge that I knew that shit would happen again. It wasn't my first time witnessing some shit like that, and it wasn't like we never spoke about it. I've always known from the first moment I met Lakyn, and everyone else, our dynamic was completely different. Our entire way of thinking bordered on insane, if not fully crossing the line. I let out my breath because I knew we had erased that fucking line a long time ago.

I stared at my face in the mirror of my Mercedes trying to get up the courage to walk through the doors of my mother's house. Her midnight blue Bentley SUV sat in the circle driveway with a baby pink two-door BMW M8 convertible behind it.

"Fuck, not Stephanie too," I sighed.

My mother was enough, but the two of them together was like a ball of hellfire aimed down on you. It didn't matter how old we were, it was ingrained in us to respect and protect our family, especially our parents. We've lost enough of them already and we refused to lose another until old age came and claimed their souls. I sucked in a breath before I let out a scream. I had to do this, and the best time was now before more shit popped off. I wanted to catch her before she went to the hospital. My phone buzzed and I looked at the name and smiled.

"Yes," I answered.

"Mala, do you think Link will let us really use the yacht? I told Tali I would take over while she's with Dea," Crescent yawned.

"Yes, I do, and if he says no I would do it anyway," I laughed.

"I think since the babies are early, which I still can't believe it's more Andersons running around, we may have to postpone," she said clearing her throat. I leaned back in my seat and closed the visor.

"Let's see how it plays out. The babies will be in the NICU for a little while. Shandea will need a break and we will arrange something, so she has it. It will be good for her. But *MYTH* though," I smirked. I heard her whine in the background as the movement came over the line.

"Why? Why would you bring that up? My pussy and nipples still hurt and...and—"

"Your throat hurts," I laughed.

"Bissh fuck you! I give it to you because listen...listen ain't no way you didn't gag on that shit. I can't...I can't talk to you about this," she stammered, and I laughed harder.

"It's not funny Mala. That fucking mask had me. I'm done I can't," Crescent huffed. "Ain't none of this shit right," she sighed.

"Baby, ain't none of us right in the fucking head. Just own it and it won't bother you, but let me go. I need to handle a few things before going back to the hospital. I will deal with Lakyn, but I should warn you," I stated.

"Warn me about what? Because I have paid my debt at this point," she laughed.

"Ahh, I agree, but your Master Zaddy is highly upset he didn't get to play with his pillo—"

I fell out when the call disconnected. Crescent was so easy to fuck with and I needed that shit before dealing with the rest of my day. I grabbed my purse and opened the door. I stepped out and smoothed down my tan and black long-sleeved crew neck geometric print split hem top. I ran my fingers over the slim necklace of a dove and released any pent-up stress. I closed the door and made my way over to the house. The guard that stood outside of the door nodded at me as he opened it allowing me inside the three-story mini mansion a far cry from how we used to live. The heels of my knee boots clicked on the floor as I followed the sound of two voices arguing over which one of them was going to go into the NICU first to see the babies. I stood in the archway to the dining room looking at all of the gifts spread out on the large glass table. My mother noticed me first before Stephanie. Stephanie stopped speaking and followed my mother's line of sight.

"Oh! And there she is. Miss Malikita herself. It's about time you brought your ass here to explain your bullshit," Stephanie said crossing her arms over her chest. The black turtleneck sweater dress screamed elegance, but the light pink tipped curls and sculpted eyebrows that were raised to the ceiling screamed, 'Yeah, *I still look fucking good*'.

"Hey Mommy, hey Aunt Stephanie," I said in a voice that belonged to a child.

"Don't just stand there Malikita, come and sit your ass down," Vanessa said straight-faced. I let out a breath, but slowed it before one of them said I was huffing and puffing.

"Yes, ma'am," I said quickly.

I sat down feeling like it was a sweltering summer night as the air filled with thick tension. I sat across from my mother, and Stephanie. The silence between us was suffocating, and I could feel their piercing gazes boring into me, demanding an explanation for the web of lies I had spun over the years. Thank you, Hendrix, for this bullshit.

"Mom, I... I need to tell you everything from the beginning," I began, my voice barely above a whisper. Vanessa's eyes narrowed, and I could see the disappointment etched into her features because she knew some of it.

I was sure Henny told her enough just to understand what happened the night of the dinner.

"Tell me what, Mala? I hope it's a damn good explanation for why you've been parading around for eight years with that fake engagement ring," she snapped, her usually warm brown eyes now filled with a mix of anger and hurt.

"Mmm humm, that's what I'm saying. Get her V," Stephanie replied, with a look like I better start talking fast.

Fuck, I was grown and felt like I was sixteen years old again getting caught sneaking out with Lakyn. I took a deep breath, steeling myself for what was to come.

"Well, you know it's about Charles, but what you might not know is that he's been blackmailing me since the day I turned eighteen. Honestly, it started a week before then, but I had to wait until I was legal to leave on my own," I confessed, my voice sardonic.

"I told you I never liked that nigga. It was the eyes," Stephanie sneered.

"Mmmm you're right Steph it was always something, but I couldn't place it. You were good Mala," Vanessa scoffed. I swallowed and just kept it moving. If I address that last statement, it will open doors that weren't important.

"He has evidence of a crime done by U.C.K., and he's been using it to force me into this fake engagement with him," I said quickly. I didn't want to get into what it was exactly because they didn't need to know those details. The less they knew the better the chance of them not being implicated.

My mother and Stephanie's expressions softened slightly, but the disbelief of me not saying a word remained a problem.

"Blackmail? What crime? And why didn't you come to us for help, Mala? Your family is here for you, always," Vanessa said shaking her head.

I held her gaze and the weight of her disappointment crushed me.

"I couldn't, Mom. You'll understand why if you think about it logically. U.C.K. is everything to our family and more importantly, they are our family. The worst part of it is that...it implicated Link the most. I can't let them go down, especially not Link and you of all people know I would never let anything happen to him. Not while I could prevent it," I pleaded.

The desperation crept into my voice as I spoke. Venessa and Stephanie looked at each other with tight closed lips before turning back to stare at me. I clamped my jaws shut waiting to see what they would say or ask. I would tell them what was needed and nothing more. The silence was suffocating, and I could feel the tension crackling between us like electricity.

"Mom, Aunt Stephanie I know you're upset," I began, my voice barely above a whisper. "I understand why you're angry, and I'm sorry for lying to you. But I had to do it. I had to protect them."

Vanessa's eyes bore into mine, her expression a mixture of frustration and concern. At the same time, Stephanie sucked in a breath before releasing it in frustration. I could see the pain in her gaze when she looked up at me.

"Protect who, Mala? Charles and his lies have no hold over us. You could have come to us, to your family, for help. We would have found a way to handle this without you having to endure it alone. I can see your thought process and how the boys would've reacted but us. We taught you to always think first," Stephanie protested.

"Exactly Steph, exactly what I was thinking," my mother said sighing loudly.

I shook my head, my heart aching at the pain I had caused them.

"It's not about Charles. It's about U.C.K. and the people I care about. They're my family too, you know that. Without U.C.K. there would be no hospital, no order, and no one to look out for those who were disenfranchised. Hendrix, Lennox, Fransisco, and Lakyn had a plan and I refused to let one person destroy what they would become. I couldn't bear the thought of Link or any of them suffering because I couldn't do what was needed to make sure U.C.K. became what we are now. Every one of us pays a price for this family and this was mine," I stated.

My mother and Stephanie's features softened slightly, but the hurt still lingered in their eyes.

"I understand that, Mala. But you didn't have to bear these burdens alone. We're in this together, always. I wish you had trusted us to help you through this."

Tears welled up in my eyes as I struggled to find the right words to convey the depth of my feelings.

"I know, trust me, I know but it's done, and I would've done it again. The only thing I regret is having to keep this from you all, but I didn't see any other way. It's U.C.K. for life and at that time we had been through so much. Shantel was snatched, and Kreed was arrested then sentenced, all the while they all were working so hard to build us up. I saw what happened to Kreed and I refused to let that shit happen to the rest of them. I couldn't let it all crumble because of a bitch ass nigga who thought I would be a weak link. Charles is a monster and a master manipulator, but he didn't realize he had a bigger one sleeping under the same roof," I gritted. "I just had to bide my time and wait for the right moment before chopping off his dick and shoving it down his throat. Knowing him, he would like it," I shrugged.

My mother reached out and took my hands in hers, her touch, a soothing balm to my troubled soul.

"Mala, I want you to know that I'm not condoning what you did. I'm upset, and I won't pretend otherwise. But I understand. I see the love and loyalty you have for this family, and I know that you made this choice out of that love. You made a necessary sacrifice that I wish was never placed on your shoulders," she sighed heavily.

I nodded, the tears now flowing freely down my cheeks at finally getting that shit off my chest.

"I never meant to hurt you, either of you. I hope y'all know that. I just… I couldn't bear the thought of losing anyone else," I said, holding her eyes.

Stephanie closed her eyes, and I could tell she was fighting back tears of anger. She stood up and rounded the table placing both hands on my shoulders and leaning down to kiss the crown of my head before her grip tightened. My eyes went wide as my mother's hands tightened on mine.

"We know, baby. We understand but I want you to understand if something like this ever, ever happened again, I will beat your ass up and down this fucking house. Do you understand me, Malikita Samuels," she gritted through clenched teeth. Her voice filled with a mixture of sadness, understanding, and a deadly serious note I wasn't going to mess with.

"We'll figure this out together, Mala. We'll find a way to untangle this mess and make sure this nigga knows fucking with U.C.K. can only end in four ways. The FARM, RANGE, BUTCHER SHOP, and the CLINIC. We're a family, and we face our challenges together. End of fucking story," Stephanie said before letting me go.

I breathed a sigh of relief at getting off this easily. I didn't want to mention that she should've added another one to that list. I refused to risk my life telling them that the ASYLUM had been reopened and was currently taking on new patients.

I sat there letting each of them fuss over me and allowed them to go on and on about my planning a wedding I didn't know I was having but whatever. My mother was on the phone with Mrs. Laverne like shit was set in stone when Lakyn hadn't even asked the question. I felt my phone buzz in my purse next to me, and I reached over, pulling it out to see Link's name crossing the screen.

> **Black Wolf: I can still feel your hand around my neck and taste your pussy on my tongue.**

I swallowed hard and pressed my legs together under the table. My black leather pants suddenly felt way too tight around my body.

> **Mala: And I still feel that long tongue in my pussy. Other than making me cum through text messages, what did you need?**

> **Black Wolf: What I always need *Dove*, you. I've only always needed you. The way you got me in this chokehold keeps my dick consistently hard. Your presence is so suffocating that I figured out a way to live without breathing. All I need to live is you and nothing else.**

My heart pounded and I felt the air slowly being sucked out of the room as I stared at his words. My field of vision narrowed down to nothing else but the screen.

> **Black Wolf: Breathe *Dove*, always breathe for me.**

I sucked in a breath before I ran my hand over the tattoo on the back of my neck of a dove with wings covering a black wolf like a blanket. I knew he could tell I wasn't breathing because he was monitoring me through the tattoo. His possessiveness and obsessiveness of me felt like an iron grip around my throat. And it felt so fucking good.

> **Mala: There will never be a day where I wouldn't choose to breathe through anything for you Lakyn.**

> **Black Wolf: I don't understand your need to say that because I already know. There was never any choice after you came to me, *Dove*. All that you are, I alone possess, and you can feel it.**

My body trembled slightly, as my breathing picked up, I closed my eyes until I felt another buzz. I opened my eyes to read his next text.

> **Black Wolf: It's time to get to work, *Dove*.**

I frowned for a second when an alert flashed on my phone that Kami was being the idiot, I knew she would be. At least now no one could say I killed her out of a fit of jealousy.

Mala: I love you.

Black Wolf: We've established these feelings, *Dove*. There is no need to reiterate it constantly when it's clearly shown.

I smiled at the text and gave it a minute to process.

Black Wolf: I love you too.

I stood up, reaching for my purse as my mother screamed that she was able to get an appointment with one of the most exclusive black wedding designers in the country.

"And she has an opening at the store out in Southgriffin in three weeks! This is perfect," Vanessa shouted.

I sent a quick text to Konceited, sending him the location to where I needed him to meet me.

Green Eyes: I'm outside Beautiful.

I rolled my eyes because I knew Link had probably sent his ass or this nigga was stalking me for Link. Either scenario was possible, but crazy because of their long-running feud.

"Mom, I need to run. I have a few things I need to take care of today, I'll call you later," I said, walking toward her.

"Malikita, please be careful and think about what you want your wedding colors to be," she said, kissing my cheek. I kissed her back and smiled with a nod. She turned around, putting the phone back to her ear. I wasn't worried about the colors because I was sure they already had it chosen.

"Laverne, did you just say Meridian and Noelani are back in town? Is he still sexy as—"

I rushed out of the door refusing to hear the rest of that conversation. I didn't want to know if my mama was doing half of what Link's parents were into. The guard knocked on the door and it opened for me to step through. A sleek white on white Rolls-Royce Phantom sedan sat idling as Konceited stood leaning against it.

"There is one of the most beautiful women I have ever had the pleasure to work for. I've come so you can ride me, I apologize, ride with me to whatever destination you need. I hope it's a long ride because I seem to be only capable of those," he grinned.

I tried not to laugh, but the closer I got to him and his flashing green eyes, I couldn't help it.

"I still need you as my muscle Konceited. Please do not tempt Link into shooting you because you know just as well as I do, he can hear whatever he wants with these cars," I laughed.

"Fuck him, it's me and you forever," he smirked as he opened the back door.

"Forever and always Green Eyes at least before you leave me for bigger and better things," I smiled, climbing inside. The black leather interior felt like sliding across a bed of silk. Konceited leaned down with a sexy ass smile, but I saw the excitement in his eyes.

"But I know you're going to make this shit so much fun until then," he chuckled with a deep rumble that rolled over my body. He closed the door, sliding in the front, catching my eyes in the mirror and smirked. I let out a laugh raising my legs to prepare for the ride. Konceited was definitely one nigga that needed to stay away from BEHIND THE CURTAIN.

As I stepped out of the sleek white Rolls-Royce Phantom and into the neon-lit chaos of downtown Union City, the stench of stupidity and privilege hung heavy in the air. Tonight I was determined to tie up the loose ends that had been haunting my Casino long enough. The email I opened in the car confused me and then shocked me after I finished reading. I had no idea that Lakyn had me down as co-owner of the Casino since it had been built. We all had shares, but I had no idea that I received more than anyone else except him. I blew out a breath pushing my happiness to the side as Konceited joined me on the sidewalk after he parked the car on the opposite side of the street. I looked down at my phone waiting for the numbers to change into a name to see what was being sent.

> **Ma:** Boss, she is making her move and trying to get her father out of the country. I wanted to see what she would do if I pulled the men off her and it's confirmed. Her little act was just that.

> **Mala:** Bet.

I put my phone into the pocket of my leather pants as Konceited began to roll up the sleeves of his sky-blue dress shirt. He dug into his pocket pulling out a pair of black leather gloves and pulled them on. I was surprised that he left the tan suit jacket in the car, but I got a look at how that shirt just clung to his chest like it was made to fit him. It probably was, and I wasn't asking because he would use that shit as an in to start fucking with me. The day was alive with the pulsating beat of the city, and I could feel the weight of my decision as I made my way through the throngs of people. My senses were on high alert, every click of my heels was a calculated move in the game I had been forced to play. All she had to do was sit the fuck down and shut the fuck up. And she couldn't even do that shit right. I adjusted the papers under my arm before I tapped on the small earpiece in my right ear.

My first move was to tap into the listening device that I implanted in Kami's bloodstream. The streets had ears, and they had sung for me when she brought her ass here. As I listened to the details of her conversation with her father I heard the fear in their voices, and I knew shivers were running down their spines. It wasn't like Kami hadn't known U.C.K. was coming for her father, and she knew why—the Cartel.

Indigo had been playing a dangerous game, and now it was time for him to face the consequences of his actions.

Indigo Gaming Technology's building stood as a towering symbol of modern elegance and sophistication, its sleek glass façade reflected the surrounding cityscape. It was located in the heart of Union City and was an architectural marvel with its impressive height and imposing presence. It would look even better once it was under new ownership. As Konceited and I entered the building, we were greeted by a grand lobby adorned with luxurious materials and exquisite contemporary art, creating an atmosphere of opulence and refinement.

"Humm, I can say she has good taste," I acquiesced.

"The security is suboptimal compared to mine or Link's, but high quality to others. I probably could hack it using one of those TV sticks that plug into the USB port, a landline phone, and a monitor," Konceited said. His tone was light, but that nigga was dead-ass serious when he said it. His eyes scanned every inch of the building taking note of it all just as I was.

"I wouldn't doubt it Green Eyes," I said.

The interior design of the building was a seamless fusion of functionality and extravagance, featuring high ceilings, polished marble floors, and intricate lighting fixtures that exude a warm, inviting glow. The common areas are adorned with lavish furnishings, including plush leather sofas, ornate coffee tables, and meticulously curated décor that reflects a sense of timeless sophistication.

Their so-called state-of-the-art technology was integrated throughout the building, providing a seamless and modern experience for their employees. Smart climate control systems, high-speed elevators, and security features ensure that the building not only meets but exceeds the highest standards of convenience, and safety. Perfect. It was less work Nia would need to do once it belonged to the Union City Kings.

Once we stepped into the elevator, I pulled my Sig from my waist holster. Konceited hit the button for the top floor where the main offices for Kami and her father were located. He pressed a few different buttons to bypass the security code. The elevator shot up fast not stopping on any of the other floors and didn't stop until we reached the top. The doors opened and we stepped off my feet landing on plush tanned carpet. The air was thick with tension as we made our way through the outer office and down the hall towards large white doors. I tapped my ear turning off the sound of Kami's irritating voice because I could clearly hear her speaking through the cracked doors. Konceited stepped up beside me and leaned against the wall. His gaze traveled over me taking note of my Sig in my hand before he winked at me.

"Don't start," I smirked. Konceited shrugged his shoulders with an innocent look on his face that would have fooled the majority of women.

"I didn't say anything, Beautiful. I'm just here to watch you work, I can't help that you turn me on when you get violent," he whispered.

"Lawd be with me," I said rolling my eyes. I tuned back into the family drama behind the doors when their voices increased. I could tell by the empty office they had sent their assistants home as well as their bodyguards. Kami didn't want anyone to know what their plans were or where she was sending her father.

"Tell me it's not true, Dad," Kami demanded, her voice trembling with barely contained rage.

"Tell me you didn't help the Cartel rig the gaming systems for Blackbay Casino," she seethed.

I pushed the door slightly and I could see the two, standing next to his desk. Indigo had his hand on his desk while Kami paced back and forth in front of him.

Indigo's expression remained stoic, but a flicker of guilt danced in his eyes.

"Kami, you don't understand. I had no choice in the matter. You took what choice I had the day you thought it was best for me to *take a step back*' in the company I built from the ground up," he argued.

"No choice?" Kami retorted, her voice rising.

"Yes! No damn choice!" Indigo shouted right back.

"You had every choice, and you chose to betray Lakyn and U.C.K. You chose to put innocent lives at risk for your own gain. You chose to put my life at risk for one of your stupid lessons," she hissed.

Indigo sighed heavily, running a hand through his long graying locs.

"You think I did this for personal gain? You really think I did this to teach you some kind of lesson. You have no idea what you've done, Kami. When you stole the company from under my feet, you put us in a position where I had to do something, so we survived," Indigo growled.

I tilted my head to the side, raising my brows waiting for the conversation to continue.

Kami's eyes blazed with fury as she shook her head.

"Survive? Is that what you call it? You endangered the lives of our family just because you couldn't handle being bested by your own daughter. You taught me the game Dad and all I did was follow in your footsteps. Because let's be honest, there would be no gaming company if you hadn't stolen your father's textile company from your sisters when he died. It runs in the family," she snapped.

Indigo's façade cracked, and for a moment, a look of regret flashed across his features.

"I know mistakes have been made on both sides, Kami. But the Cartel had me in their grip, and I was working on a way out. The newest heads of the Cartel gave me a deal I couldn't refuse, and it was at the same time you did your little power play," he huffed.

"You should've come to me," Kami shot back, her voice raw with emotion.

"We could've found a solution together. Instead, you chose to become a pawn in their game, with the most powerful people in Union City! Not only did they believe I had something to do with it but now U.C.K. is coming for you."

Indigo's eyes widened in alarm as he looked around before moving around his desk. He typed on his computer with shaking hands.

"How do you know U.C.K. knows I had anything to do with this?"

Kami's gaze hardened as she folded her arms across her chest letting out a sigh.

"Why the hell do you think I had to see a plastic surgeon? Look at my face, Dad. You need to leave the country. U.C.K. won't stop until they've made you pay for what you've done. I won't let you die because of your mistakes. And I refuse to let my company fall because of it either," she fumed.

Indigo's shoulders sagged, and for the first time, he looked over the screen. I knew he was probably checking the camera footage but that had been on repeat for the past thirty minutes or so.

"I can't just leave everything behind, Kami. This is my life's work we're talking about."

"It's not worth your life, Dad, I don't want to keep going over this" Kami insisted, her voice softening.

"You have to go into hiding, at least until we can figure out a way to deal with this mess," she said her stance loosening.

"I'll leave tonight. But Kami, promise me you'll find a way to make things right. I never wanted any of this to happen. Since you have a relationship with...with that Lakyn maybe he will take care of the Cartel problem for us. And whatever we learn we could take the rest of it to the authorities and get rid of them as well. It's at least a thought," Indigo spluttered.

"I'll do whatever it takes, Dad. I'll take care of this company, even if it's the last thing I do. No one threatens our business without some action being taken. I just need time," Kami's resolve hardened as she looked at her father with a mix of love and disappointment in her eyes. I pushed the door open wider and stepped into the large office that would rival some of the ones at Casino. The long expanse of the windows let in enough light that you didn't even need artificial lighting. I could see across Union City at this height, and it was beautiful.

"Indigo," I said, my voice cutting through the silence like a knife. "It's time to settle our accounts," I smiled.

When I finally came face to face with Kami and Indigo, the air crackled with the promise of retribution and the anticipation of death. He looked at me with a sly grin, but I could see the fear lurking behind his eyes.

"You must be Mala, my dear, what a surprise. To what do I owe the pleasure?"

My eyes narrowed at his fake ass smile like we were fucking friends. I approached Indigo and Kami. I saw Kami flinch as I walked toward them while my heart pounded against my chest with anger that they still thought they could fuck over U.C.K. like we couldn't figure it out. I knew they could feel the air crackle with tension as I took a deep breath, ready to get to the fucking point. I stopped a few feet away from the two tapping my Sig against my thigh while staring at them as a slow smile crossed my face.

"Indigo, Kami, let me start over so you don't think this visit is a friendly one," I began, my voice firm.

"I need to know the truth. How long have you been working for the Cartel to corrupt the machines at the Casino?"

Indigo's eyes darted nervously, while Kami's gaze dropped, betraying the unease that simmered beneath the surface.

"We don't know what you're talking about, Mala," Indigo stammered, his voice strained with feigned innocence.

"We have nothing to do with the Cartel. I was just explaining to my daughter that this all had to be some misunderstanding. If...if I could just speak to Mr. Moore, I'm sure we can figure this out," Indigo chuckled. I blinked at him and stared at him as if he was the dumbest nigga on earth.

"What you can do is speak to me. Because we all know who is in fucking charge, isn't that right Kamille?" I asked as I locked eyes with Kami. I saw the flicker of guilt dancing in her gaze. She knew the terms and what I had said before I let her go. Do not attempt to help your father.

"Kami, by you being here you are now involved in this too. You can't keep lying to me," I pressed, my voice tinged with urgency.

"What was I supposed to do? I—"

Kami's words died on her tongue as I raised a brow along with my Sig. Her lips trembled, but before she could say another word, I shot a quick glance at Konceited, signaling him to step forward. Konceited's towering figure and expressionless face as he came closer were suffused with an unspoken warning.

"Listen, Mala, we don't want any trouble," Indigo stammered, his voice faltering as he took a step back.

"We were just trying to live like anyone that owns a business such as ours. We had to do things none of us wanted. The Cartel, they... they made us an offer we couldn't refuse," Indigo said quickly.

"You chose to betray us, to put our entire company at risk to lose billions. You know the consequences of crossing U.C.K., Indigo. We can't have disloyalty with the people we do business with. I explained that to your daughter, but it seems she is more like her father than she realized," I said holding his gaze, my expression unyielding. I could see the fear flicker in Indigo's eyes as he realized the gravity of the situation.

"Please, Mala, we didn't mean to cause any harm. I can...I can pay you whatever is owed. We'll stop, we'll do whatever you ask," he pleaded, desperation creeping into his voice.

Konceited took a step closer, his presence looming over them at the desk.

"You've already done enough, Indigo. The money doesn't matter because we've gotten that back. It's the principle of it all. We gave your daughter an out she didn't take it. You've endangered everything you built by fucking with the wrong people. There are consequences for your actions," Konceited intoned while holding out his hand. I placed the documents under my arm in his outstretched hand while I still held my gun on them.

Konceited's words hung in the air, as a heavy silence settled over the room, punctuated only by the shallow breaths of Indigo and Kami. The weight of their betrayal, and actions lingered, casting a shadow over their faces.

"Konceited, make sure they understand the gravity of their actions," I instructed, my voice firm.

I watched as Konceited grabbed Indigo in a flash making Kami scream and step back as he pulled her father over to the large desk slamming his head into it.

"Ahh! No...no...wait please," Indigo wailed.

"Shut the fuck up and stop crying like a bitch. All you need to do is sign where the X is," I shouted over their cries. Konceited's hand clamped around the back of Indigo's neck forcing his face into the papers. Indigo was a large man but age and laziness work to his disadvantage. His arms flailed as he tried to grab hold of something to help his predicament. I stepped forward rolling a pen across the desk and it hit his hand.

"You can't do this! This is my company! You can't do this! Kamille!"

"Just sign the fucking papers, Daddy! Please," Kami cried with her back pressed against the large window. I waited as Indigo grabbed onto the pen and quickly signed the bottom.

"It's done! Now let us go. You have what you want," he hissed.

"Nope, you need to flip the page and initial. You as well Kami. We need to be sure this is all legitimate, you know. For taxes," I smiled.

Kami's trembling frame stumbled over to the desk, and she snatched the pen from her father quickly signing and initialing each page. She threw down the pen looking back up at me with rage and hate in her gaze.

Konceited pulled Indigo the rest of the way over the desk and then slammed him into it harder, causing blood to spray over the tan carpet.

"Shhhhit! You...ahhh—" he screamed. Konceited collected the documents and stepped back looking them over as he moved. Indigo placed a hand on his desk shakily pushing himself to his feet.

"See, Kami, that look you're giving me only leaves me with one course of action. I don't like thinking I have someone plotting to stab me in the back," I smiled. Before either of them could say another word, I lunged at Indigo, my fists a whirlwind of vengeance as each punch to his stomach, face, and chest forced him back to his knees.

"Tell me the truth, Indigo," I hissed, my voice laced with fury. "What else did the Cartel want from you?! What did they promise you to make that fucking deal?" I gritted.

His eyes widened in fear as the truth dawned on him. We knew about the ports already, but there was more to it than that. It all felt...it felt personal.

"I... I had no choice," he stammered, his voice a desperate plea. "They will kill me."

"Bitch I will fucking kill you," I giggled.

"Oh God, oh God, it wasn't supposed to go this way. If...If—"

"You made your fucking bed, Indigo, and now you'll lie in it. What. Do. They. Want!"

"Revenge! They want revenge!"

My face scrunched up in confusion and disbelief because the only beef we had with the Cartel started because of them and that bitch Jakobe. And it couldn't be because of the *Silk* warehouse. I pushed my Sig under Indigo's chin with my finger on the trigger.

"Aht! Don't fucking move little girl. Adults are speaking," Konceited ordered.

I pushed harder into the fleshy part of his chin and leaned in close so he could see his death in my eyes.

"Speak!" I shouted in his face.

"Because U.C.K. took something that belonged to them! And...and before they take it back, they want all of you to suffer. They want all of you to watch as Union City is taken right out from under you," he cried.

As I turned to confront Kami, I saw the fire in her eyes, a reflection of the fury burning within me.

"You knew," I said, my voice cold and unyielding. I dropped Indigo and stood to my feet. I saw Konceited move as Indigo cried in pain. I kept my eyes on Kami as I moved forward. She pressed her body against the glass like she could escape out of it.

"I...I don't know why...what you're—"

Blood and spit flew out of her mouth as my Sig came across her face. I reached out grabbing her lavender blouse to pull her back up to look at me. Her bloodshot eyes found mine as I slammed her against the window.

"What did we take? I know you know because you look like you're the kind of woman willing to do anything to save her life. So, tell me what the fuck you know and maybe that could work out in your favor once again," I hissed.

"He...he...never used names. He...only said that...that U.C.K. had to pay. They had to pay for taking his possession, and his favorite pet," she whispered.

"I was trying to save his life and mine, Mala. He's my father, and despite everything, I couldn't bear to see him pay for his mistakes with his life. So, I told him about every person who had access to the top levels of the Casino. That's...that's why I was so mad that I was restricted. I had no more information to give once you came," she gritted. Tears welled up in her eyes, but her voice was resolute.

"Well, I can understand doing what you need to do for your family. But your father's choices have consequences, Kami. And so does yours," I said, slamming her head hard against the glass. Blood smeared down the glass as she slumped to the floor holding her head.

"Ahh, ahhh, oh, oh, ahhh—" she cried.

"Kami! Kami! She's done nothing. All of this is on me. It was all me," Indigo pleaded.

I nodded, knowing that the time for mercy had long passed.

"Make sure he watches this Green Eyes. He needs to see the consequence of his actions before he dies," I commanded, my tone leaving no room for argument. I leaned over and grabbed Kami by her hair as she screamed. I dragged her across the floor making sure Indigo had a full view of what was about to happen.

"No! Let me go! You said you'd let me go!" Kami screamed and twisted in my grip. I slammed my gun on the top of her head twice, making her hand fall away.

"See, one of my best friends told me a story a few days ago. And I wished I could have seen it in person. He told me it was a rush with instant satisfaction," I smiled. Indigo twisted in Konceited's grasp, but I wasn't worried.

"Ooouu Beautiful, I think I heard this story. The insanity of your mind just...it gets my dick rock-hard. I probably should make a therapy appointment because of this, but use this gun instead," Konceited chuckled holding out his hand. I turned to him, taking the gun out of his hand and aimed it at Kami before holstering my Sig. Then I switched hands, raising my arm and aimed. I pulled the trigger until I saw the cracks begin to appear in the reinforced window.

"What...what the hell are you doing?" Indigo screamed.

I dragged Kami to her feet and pushed her in front of me. Blood marred her face and clothes as she held the back of her head. I stepped forward and she stepped backward. I stepped forward again as she moved around the desk. I took another step, my thighs hitting the solid wood of the large desk.

"I had to do what I had to do for my family. At least I was providing Lakyn with a good fuck before he died," she rasped. I raised my brows before I smiled.

"I completely understand. At least you've given me the perfect opportunity to use you as a story to stay the fuck away from what belongs to me. So, fuck this," I smirked as I pulled the trigger hitting her in each shoulder, chest, stomach, and pussy pushing her backward enough to crash through the window.

"Oh, that shit cold as fuck," Konceited chuckled.

"No! Kamille! You fucking bitc—"

I turned to face Konceited just as he gripped Indigo's throat.

"Gun, Beautiful," he said holding out his gloved hand. I used my shirt to wipe off my fingerprints before handing him the gun. I watched as he gripped Indigo's left hand, forcing the gun into it.

"No! No! Stop, please we can—"

Konceited used Indigo's hand to put the muzzle of the gun under his chin and made him pull the trigger. Blood, brain tissue, and bone matter splattered the white wall behind Indigo. Konceited stepped back as the older man fell backward against the wall and slid sideways to the floor.

"This will need to be remodeled and cleaned. I shouted, as the wind whipped through the room.

"Will do, Boss. Let's move," he said, holding out a hand. I grabbed it just as my normal phone beeped in my pocket. I allowed Konceited to pull me out of the office while I holstered my Sig and reached for the phone.

"Emails dismissing everyone in the company have gone out. Severance package documents are included," Konceited stated. I stepped into the outer offices and hit the screen.

"Thank you, Green Eyes. Let's get out of here," I answered.

I pulled up the message and it was from Charles.

> Charles: Dinner has been moved up. You will be here at six tonight or you know the consequences.

My jaw clenched as my hand flexed around the phone. Not only was I trying to figure out this shit about the Cartel, but now I had this shit to deal with. I blew out a breath before hitting reply.

> **Mala: I will meet you there or you know the consequences, unless you want to explain more injuries to your person.**

> Charles: Live it up now because all of this is about to come to an end. Tell your family to save the date. We're getting married in two weeks.

"Konceited?"

"Yes," he answered while strolling down the carpeted hall.

"We need to make a stop. I need to find something to wear for dinner," I instructed.

I stared at my phone waiting for a text back from Link when I saw Charles's car pass by on the road leading up to his grandparent's estate. I blew out a sigh, mentally preparing myself for the bullshit, and more than likely threats.

> Black Wolf: What the fuck you mean you're having dinner with that bitch ass nigga?

> **Mala: It's at the Astor estate and you know why I have to be here baby.**

> **Black Wolf: Earpiece on Malikita. I want constant contact, no matter what. I will be there before it's over, because if that nigga thinks you're going anywhere but back to me, he's fucking crazy.**

I blew out a breath as my heart began to race because I knew if anything, anything said wrong Link would come in that mansion guns blazing, and not giving a fuck.

"Pull to the gate Konceited," I said, before looking back at my phone.

> **Mala: There was never any doubt that you would be here. If you hear me say *Dove* that's when I need you to come inside. Not before Link.**

> **Black Wolf: Nothing will stop me if they touch you, Mala, nothing at all.**

I figured that was the best that I was going to get from him. As we pulled to the front gate, we stopped at the small guard building. The security guard stepped out dressed in an all-black suit with a white silk tie. I immediately rolled down my window so they could see my face. Even though I hadn't been here in over seven years I knew they knew who I was.

"Miss Samuels, I hope your evening is well," the man nodded, before stepping back. I pressed my lips together rolling up the window as the gates opened. We drove up the long drive and an old-style mansion stood as a grand testament to a bygone era. Its imposing silhouette cast a regal presence against the backdrop of the estate. Just by the look of it, you could see the old money.

"Are you going to be good Mala? We've known who his people were for a while, but nothing really about them until now. I don't like this,"

Konceited grunted. His serious look and tone had me reaching forward placing a hand on his shoulder.

"I'll be good. Trust me, I'm still strapped, and if need be, I will shoot my way out of this bitch," I smiled. He stared at me for a long moment before opening the door and stepping out. As Konceited opened the door for me, I grabbed my purse and tapped the earpiece twice to ensure it was transmitting. I stepped out of the Phantom dressed as would be expected. The elegant pantsuit exuded sophistication and modern flair, perfectly tailored to command attention and respect. I knew they would hate it and Charles would lose it because it wasn't something he'd allowed me to buy. The ensemble was crafted from a luxurious fabric that draped elegantly, accentuating my silhouette. The pants were a sleek, high-waisted style in a deep, midnight blue hue, that possessed a subtle sheen that caught the light from the fading sun as I moved.

The blazer was in a matching shade of midnight blue, and the lapels were adorned with delicate, gold-toned buttons, adding a touch of understated glamour to the ensemble. Beneath the blazer, I wore a pristine, ivory silk blouse with a delicately ruffled neckline, adding a touch of femininity adding a soft, ethereal quality to the look. I made sure to wear a pair of pointed-toe stiletto heels in a coordinating shade of midnight blue, that would have me standing close to Charles's height. He would hate that shit so much my smile grew wider when I placed a finger on the gold dove necklace.

"It's all good. You don't need to stay. I have a ride home."

"I will stay until I know that ride is here," Konceited said, opening the driver's side door.

I could tell he wasn't happy about me walking straight into the enemy's home, but there was no choice. Not until we found Theodore. The mansion's façade boasted intricate architectural details, with ornate carvings adorning the stone columns that framed the entrance. The front steps, weathered by centuries of use, led to a pair of towering, mahogany doors, the polished surfaces reflecting the sunlight that filtered through the surrounding trees. I took a deep breath as the door opened revealing the grand foyer.

"Good evening, Miss Samuels, dinner will be in the main dining hall. Please follow me," the butler, whose name I never knew, said.

"Good evening," I replied, as he gestured for me to enter before he turned on his heel.

I followed him as I took in the majestic chandeliers, adorned with glittering crystals, hanging from the ceiling. The walls were lined with portraits of stern-faced ancestors, their watchful eyes following my every move as I traversed the expansive space. I had money. We all had money, but these people had a wealth that went on so long that I was sure they had owned slaves.

The interior was a labyrinth of richly adorned rooms, each one steeped in history and tradition. The parlor beckoned with its plush velvet armchairs and intricately carved wooden furnishings. At the same time, the library boasted towering shelves of leather-bound tomes, their spines bearing the weight of centuries of knowledge. I couldn't wait until all this shit burned to the ground.

"Malikita, it is always lovely to see you. I don't get to see you that often. My son sure takes up a lot of your time," Kenneth smiled. I passed on a polite smile as I air-kissed his cheeks and pulled away quickly.

"Grandfather said it is time for dinner," Charles stated as he entered behind me. I raised my brows at him as he looked me over and sneered at me once he stood in front of me. He did do an excellent job on his face though, because you could barely see the discoloration.

"It's about fucking time," Priscilla hissed. She swallowed the contents of the glass and slammed it back onto the table. Kenneth held out his arm and she shoved it around him as he led her from the room.

"I told you about that city girl hair and this outfit isn't anything I approved of Kita. It looks...cheap," he smirked. I walked to within inches of him looking him in the eyes. I could see that he hated it, and it messed with his need to feel like he was in power. I leaned in close to his ear, causing him to stiffen slightly.

"Not as cheap as you look with all that foundation on," I hissed. I ran my finger across his face causing him to step back and move to the mirror. I smirked as I left his dumbass checking his makeup.

I sat at the dinner table, keeping my mouth closed as the clinking of silverware and polite conversation filled the air. But my mind was elsewhere thinking of where was that Teddy nigga and where the fuck was this original file. It was all we needed, but I could feel we were getting close to the answers we needed. I glanced at Charles and this new rock that sat on my finger. It was ugly as fuck and nothing I would've wanted. He wore a strained smile as he engaged in small talk with his relatives.

"Grandfather, Malikita and I would like to thank you for allowing us to use the rings. But, I have a request," Charles said, his voice tinged with urgency.

"And what is it, Charles, spit it out," Cornelius said.

"Since the Mayoral race is heating up, I believe it would look good for optics if we got married a little sooner. I was thinking in maybe two weeks or so," Charles stated.

Cornelius looked at his grandson for what felt like hours as he chewed on a piece of his filet mignon. I could tell by Charles's actions and the nervous knee bounce under the table that his granddaddy didn't know he had a problem. I had no idea what conditions he was under for the family or why he couldn't ask for help to find Teddy, but I knew Teddy's disappearance wasn't something that he wanted Cornelius to know about.

"I think it will be an excellent idea if you do Charles. You have yet to let me down," he smiled.

"Wonderful idea son! If I could marry your mother all over again I would," Kenneth smiled. Priscilla rolled her eyes as she sipped her wine and looked at her slim Rolex.

"Wonderful! Don't you think so Dove," Charles grinned.

"I'm going to cut his fucking tongue out of his mouth." Link seethed in my ear.

I took a sip of water and nodded so I didn't have to answer. I didn't want to give him the satisfaction of seeing my rage at him using that fucking word. Charles's phone began to ring and he pushed his chair back.

"Excuse me for a moment, everyone. I need to take this," he said standing.

As Charles left the table, I felt a sense of unease settle over me. His sudden need to move up the wedding date and his frantic demeanor didn't bode well.

"Malikita," he began, his tone heavy with authority. "I trust you understand the gravity of the situation and that you still understand your place. What my grandson wants will happen."

I blinked, realizing we were alone at the table. I nodded, trying to maintain composure while my heart pounded in my chest.

"Slow your heart rate down—none of what he says matters because we will get them before they ever get us. Trust me," Link promised.

"I don't think you do," he continued, his voice taking on a menacing edge. "You see, my family has a long-standing tradition of protecting our interests at any cost. And if you want to protect your family you'll do well to remember that," Cornelius said slamming his fist.

"Oh, good Lord," Madaline jumped. Cornelius's eyes never left mine as he comforted his wife and promised it was a mistake. The way he spoke was more like a master to his favorite pet but to each his own.

The old man turned back to me his eyes narrowing as he leaned in closer, his gaze unwavering.

"You will do as we say, without question. The wedding will take place in less than two weeks, and you will be expected to adhere to our family's code of conduct."

Play it smart, Mala. Just like you always have. They will die. We will kill them all.

"Nice and quiet like a good girl," he began, his voice deceptively calm. "You are about to become a part of this family, and there are certain expectations that come with that."

I bristled at the implication, my hands clenching into fists under the table.

"I won't be a pawn in your sick games," I gritted before I could bite my tongue.

A cruel smile tugged at the corners of his mouth.

"Oh, my dear, you have no choice but to play our game. You see, we have a long memory and long assets. And all of us will take care of our own. Your family and that young man you care so much about will be safe as long as you fulfill your duties. We have no problem letting this little...U.C.K. run as long as it's controlled," he smiled. "You will be expected to devote yourself entirely to this family, to serve without question, and to uphold our customs."

I struggled to maintain my composure, the weight of my knowledge knowing what he was talking about pressed down on me like a suffocating blanket. As he detailed the unspeakable acts, I would be required to perform to ensure the safety of my loved ones, a cold deadly rage simmered within me, threatening to boil over.

"I won't let you turn me into a slave to satisfy your twisted desires."

"You will, Malikita, or you will watch as your mother is torn apart and cut into pieces, suffering for your disobedience. You will watch as all of the men you love are condemned and Lakyn suffers a fate worse than death."

The weight of his threat settled over me, suffocating me with its cruel inevitability. I could see that he thought he was invincible, just like his grandson, believing no one could be smarter than him. I wondered if Cornelius and Charles wouldn't mind putting their invincibility to the test very soon.

"I'll play your game," I intoned pushing my chair back.

I stood up to my full height and turned on my heel, heading for the door. With each step I took, the flames of determination flickered brighter within me. If we didn't manage to find Theodore or the file, this wedding would go down in Union City's history as a bloody fucking massacre.

CHAPTER SIXTEEN

LAKYN 'LINK' MOORE

I stared at the wall intensely in my room at my penthouse inside of the Casino. Then swung my legs onto the side of the bed and stood. I moved to stand in front of the large TV that was playing several news stations reporting on everything that was happening throughout Union City. It seemed that having Mena go on Channel 7 News worked in our favor. No one was really focusing on us anymore, but wondering who the other fractions were disrupting the peace of our city. Things were beginning to fall into place as we took the time to lie low and line shit up. The real reason was that we wanted Oz to be with Shandea as much as possible. It had been a week since the birth of their daughters *Onnyx and*

Soleil and they've been at the hospital ever since. We were finally able to convince Shandea to get out for a few hours so Tali, Cent, and the rest could surprise her with a baby shower. It was important that I kept her mind off the bullshit and focused on what really mattered. Oz. And also the family, but that was a given. I looked in the right corner of the screen and pointed the remote, turning the volume up just enough to hear, so I wouldn't wake Mala yet.

UNION CITY'S WBJ: CHANNEL 12 NEWS

Good morning Union City, this is Jane Smith of WBJL Channel 12 News reporting live from downtown Union City. We bring you breaking news where a tragic incident has occurred at the headquarters of Indigo Gaming Technology. We have new reports coming in that a father and daughter who were found dead on the company's premises seemed to have been in a bitter battle over said company. Back to you, Vince.

I looked down at my watch seeing the update from Justice about gaining custody of Dylan. We should be getting an answer sometime today or tomorrow. If legal doesn't work out in our favor, I would do what was necessary. Shit was a lot easier done legally when it came to things like this. I looked back up as Jane continued talking.

That's right, Jane. According to the initial reports, the deceased individuals have been identified as Kamille Indigo, CEO of Indigo Gaming Technology, and her father, Leonard Indigo who had to step down when he nearly had a fatal heart attack last year. Am I right, Jane?

Yes, Vince, you are correct as usual with your facts. The circumstances surrounding their deaths are still unclear, but authorities have indicated that it appears to be a murder-suicide. The Union City Police Department has launched a full investigation into the matter. Close sources to the case have told me that it was Indigo who took the life of his only daughter Kamille. This was once a prominent family-owned company that was built from the ground up. Underneath, it seems that they have been having financial difficulty. I just received a report stating that the privately owned Indigo Gaming Technology had just recently sold the company to Kalm Horizon National Credit Union for an undisclosed amount.

Wow, Jane, great sources. This is a truly tragic turn of events when it seemed their financial troubles may have been over. What could have driven a father to commit such a heinous act against his own daughter?

It's hard to say at this point, but some sources are speculating that there may have been underlying tensions within the family that led to this devastating outcome, Vince.

Jane, have your sources said anything about there being more to this story than meets the eye? Could there have been external factors at play that pushed Indigo to take such drastic measures?

I stood waiting for the remote aimed at the TV waiting for the answer.

Vince, we'll have to wait for the official statement from the authorities to shed more light on this heartbreaking incident. But from what my sources tell me this looks like a cut-and-dry case. It is a very sad day for many people, I'm sure. In the meantime, our thoughts and prayers are with the friends and colleagues of the deceased.

I hit the mute button and tossed the remote to the bed. The investigation seemed to be heading in the direction we wanted it to. I wasn't worried about the police because Konceited was tapped into that for monitoring. Ever since Henny had found out niggas been moving secretly in the department by keeping things offline, he made moves to slide shit in place. We also had Sam's contacts keeping their ears to the ground. I was still skeptical about this nigga Cortez, but Henny said he had it handled. I didn't think we could trust a nigga with a sneaky grown-ass son fucking with my baby. I sucked in a breath thinking that I had more kids now I had to worry about. If they turned out to be anything like their father, we all would probably die of stress. I decided to get dressed and made my way down to my office, still not wanting to wake Mala.

I looked over the program that was going through all Monica's files and stopped on a folder that was listed as Denton House. I remembered what that nigga Jimmy had said before he took his flight. There was a Burrow in Puafton called Denton. I opened the folder, and a list of locations filled my screen. I set the program to focus on this file to weigh out the probabilities of where Roman was located. My phone buzzed in my pocket, and when I pulled it out, Whisper's name flashed across the screen.

"Yo," I answered.

"Link, I think Tarryn has found something. I was watching her, and I saw her freeze before she rapidly began typing. I stopped her," Whisper said, without preamble.

I immediately knew that she had found something on Teddy and was going to try and cover it up. Tarryn wasn't stupid by far, and she was very street-smart. She knew if she held the information, it would keep her alive. Apparently, she wasn't smart enough not to think that shit would matter. We would get it out of her either way.

"I'll be there," I said, disconnecting.

I didn't waste any time and stood up from my desk after securing my laptop. I made my way into the outer office nodding at Mallory sitting where Monica once sat.

"Do me a favor," I said, pulling the white gold Cuban chain from under my black shirt.

"Sure Boss, what's up," she asked, typing.

"I need you to follow someone for me."

"Okay, tell me what I need to know," she frowned as she stopped typing. Ma turned her head and looked at me confused. I knew she was wondering why I wanted her to do it when there were so many others, and technically she was Mala's assistant, but she was good at what she did.

"I want you to follow a woman named Danita James. I'll send over all the details in a few hours on her. This is important, but if you feel like some dangerous shit is about to pop off, just bounce," I said, raising a brow. I didn't know what type of bullshit Danita was into, but looking over her life, shit was spotty. I wasn't feelin' it.

"Boss, I'm U.C.K., I'm sure I can handle whatever the fuck comes at me," she pursed her lips. I chuckled and headed towards the elevator.

"Get on it once you receive the files. I'll let Mala know," I said, hitting the button. The doors slid open, and I stepped inside.

I slid into the driver's seat of my SUV and revved the engine. I pulled out of the garage and headed towards the CLINIC. That had me thinking about that agent that was working with Rodney. I needed to check into whatever Oz and Henny found out about Rodney after they tortured him. The city lights blurred past as I raced toward the CLINIC feeling like I needed to get this information ASAP.

I pulled up to the warehouse and the doors began to open, revealing Whisper as she stepped to the side. I pulled inside and as soon as the truck cleared the doors, they were already closing. I was preparing myself for the bullshit I knew was coming, but looking at the time, I had to make this shit quick. I wasn't about to be late to this fucking party because I didn't trust niggas on my shit when I wasn't around. I hopped out of the SUV and nodded to Whisper as she pointed toward the back.

"I put her in one of the lower rooms. She's in the very last room before the stairs," Whisper called out. I made my way to the room and stood outside the door watching her on the monitor as she paced the floor muttering to herself. I punched the code into the panel on the side of the door and waited as it slid open. The room was cold with a twin bed, table, and chair.

Usually at the very minimum, I liked them in the pool room, but she wasn't necessarily the problem. I looked over my shoulder as Faxx made his way toward me. I turned back to Tarryn, and she eyed me warily as I entered the dimly lit room, her gaze guarded and her body tense.

"I got a message that someone found something we were looking for?" Faxx stepped inside behind me. I tilted my head staring at her intently watching her shake as she pushed her glasses up her nose.

"Yeah, apparently, Tarryn was about to try and hide something. I am sick of people hiding shit from me. I don't like it. And I always find out the truth and then I have to do shit to punish those who hide things from me. You should ask my wife," I smirked. Tarryn's eyes widened, and her lips trembled as she drew in a shaky breath.

"You proposed and got married? Since when? Mala ain't tell me nothing and I just saw her ass," Faxx inquired.

"From what I was told our parents are planning the wedding already. I think they have it set like eight months out or something. I don't know the details," I answered. My gaze never left Tarryn, and I knew it unnerved her by the way she flinched. I sometimes wondered how Mala could look into them the way she did because I knew how flat they looked. I never understood when people said I looked like I had no soul until I met Faxx. Then I saw it. I could see what they were talking about, but I didn't see the problem with it.

"Nigga. That doesn't mean that you don't fucking propose to her. You have to at least ask her to marry you my nigga," Faxx chuckled. My brows pulled together because what sense did it make? Legally she was already my wife anyway. The day she signed those papers to take the job was the day she signed her life to me. She's been mine since the day she walked away even if she didn't know it.

"Did you?"

"Yes. I told Crescent we were getting married, and she signed the papers," he shrugged.

"So, you didn't ask her, you told her," I confirmed.

"Technically, I did. It wouldn't matter anyway because it was inevitable," Faxx replied. I pulled out my phone, hit Mala's name, and waited.

"Yes? Is everything good Lakyn?" she asked.

"We're getting married."

"What?"

"We are getting married," I repeated.

"This nigga is wild! Link are you serious?" Faxx boomed.

"Baby, I don't have time for this," Mala sighed.

"Faxx said I had to tell you that we were getting married."

"Lakyn, our parents are already planning the wedding, so this conversation is unnecessary," Mala stated.

"Why? Did you expect me not to ask because of my lack of social cues or something?" I asked. I needed to know because if that was the case, I had to work on it. Be normal and act normal and all that bull shit Faxx said.

"Okay, baby listen to me. Do I know you?"

"Yes," I answered without hesitation.

"Then know that I found all your shit. I've seen the papers and the marriage certificate you conveniently never mentioned over the weeks," Mala deadpanned. My eyes widened and it caused Tarryn to whimper slightly.

"And you called me fucking crazy! Naw, you got me beat my nigga," Faxx laughed.

"*Dove*, if you thought another nigga was going to marry you then you've lost your fucking mind," I affirmed.

"Yes Link, I know, but Faxx is right. You still should ask me, but if you don't, so what because I'm still walking down the aisle. Before you start over-analyzing shit or trying to figure out the best way to do it, just do what your father would do. That's it. That's all baby, but I need to go. I'll see you when you get back," Mala rushed out before disconnecting.

"Take my advice and do that shit in private," Faxx said, walking to the side and leaning against the wall. I put my phone back into my jeans pocket and tilted my to the other side, eyes still on Tarryn.

"Alright, Tarryn," I said my voice commanding attention. "Tell me everything you know about Banks."

Tarryn hesitated, her eyes flickering with a mix of fear and a little defiance. She glanced at Faxx, but brought her gaze back to mine. She tried to play it cool, but I could see the cracks, so I leaned in closer, my presence looming over her like a shadow.

"Tarryn," I said, my voice low. "You know why I'm here. Tell me where Theodore is hiding."

Tarryn's eyes narrowed, as she crossed her arms, taking a step backward.

"I...I don't know what you're talking about. I haven't found anything yet, I tried telling that big bitch out there, but she wouldn't listen," she said, her voice tinged with false bravado.

I took a step closer, my gaze piercing through her façade.

"Don't play games with me, Tarryn. You found him or at least you think you did. You're probably thinking how do I know right? It's been written all over your face since you hesitated this morning in your keystrokes. It was off by two point five seconds," I confirmed.

She hesitated, her eyes flitting around the room as she weighed her options. I could tell my words had shocked her and I could see the fear lurking in her brown gaze. So knew the dangerous line she was walking. When she didn't respond, I moved closer, my patience wearing thin.

"Speak, Tarryn," I pressed, my voice taking on an edge.

"She probably believes you don't kill women since she's still alive," Faxx shrugged. I raised my brows letting a smile cross my face. I knew it changed it because I saw her relax slightly.

"That would be the most idiotic thing she could believe considering I had a woman that worked for me for years stare into my eyes while I hypnotized her to let a bomb be strapped to her chest and then to blow herself up. It would be very unintelligent to think I couldn't do the same and you aren't stupid right, Tarryn?" I finished.

Tarryn's façade began to crumble, and desperation flickered in her eyes while she tried to control the shaking of her body.

"If...if I...tell you, you're going to kill me," she whispered. I moved grabbing her by the throat and slamming her into the steel wall behind her.

"If you don't fucking open your mouth and tell me, I will make that shit hurt. Now speak," I commanded.

"He's on the yacht!"

"He isn't on his yacht because I would've known that Tarryn. See..."

"No...no... no... just... listen...he's on the yacht belonging to Yung D-Mar. It was put up for sale but hasn't been sold yet. The last destination that was filed was for Ppp...P-Town! He's docked in Puafton Harbor and hasn't moved," she squeaked as I squeezed tighter. I looked over my shoulder at Faxx as Tarryn's hands wrapped around my wrist trying to pull me away. Her attempts were getting weaker.

"I'll let Oz know we are having a destination baby shower," Faxx declared, pulling out his phone.

I loosened my grip when I turned back to Tarryn as she weakly slapped me against my arms. She sucked in a breath and began to cough. I stepped back and she leaned over on her knees as tears streamed down her face. I squatted down in front of her as she sucked in breath after breath.

"Pl...plea...please don't kk...kk...kill me," she wheezed.

"Tell me something," I said softly.

"An...anything," she gasped.

"In any of those accounts were there any for a Crescent Johnson," I asked quietly.

"Yyy...yes. All of Crescent's money is deposited first into Mr. Banks accounts and then into Roman. But...but I did what you said and transferred all the money in those accounts to the banking information you gave me," she answered quickly.

"Okay, good. Did you know Crescent at all, or you didn't?"

"Sh...she was Roman's girl. That's about all I know," she stated. Her chest rose in fell in rapid motions as she shook slightly.

"Don't lie to me Tarryn. Did she ever come to you for help? Remember, I'm asking you to not hide shit from me. Don't do that," I said calmly.

"Once! It was only once, and I couldn't do anything to help her. Whatever I did would've gotten us both killed," she said quickly. I nodded understanding what she was saying just as Faxx came to stand beside us.

"Okay, next one and this is the last. What's the name of the yacht Banks is using?" I asked.

"The Intrepid," she said, looking up. I looked at Faxx as he typed in his phone and stood.

We began making our way toward the door, but I turned around.

"Tarryn. You told her, and I quote 'not to fuck things up for the rest of us and that she should lay down and deal with it', after she told you her age and what was happening to her," I said. Tarryn's eye bulged out of her head as her mouth fell open.

"It was in another file," I said, before unholstering my pistol and shooting her in the forehead. Faxx looked at me and then at Tarryn as her body hit the floor.

"You're still mad about the *MYTH* thing?" he asked. I holstered my pistol and screwed my face up.

"You're fucking right I'm still mad. You were trying to keep me out of *'BEHIND THE CURTAIN.'* So, I feel like taking your kill was payment," I shrugged.

"Bet. Aight, you got it. You got that, but don't say shit when you're chaperoning Cece's playdate with Travis," he chuckled, before walking o ut.

"Don't fucking play with me Fransisco. That nigga ain't getting in my fucking car! He grown enough to drive as it is," I shouted, letting the door shut tight behind me.

I stood on the deck of my yacht, surrounded by friends and family. I looked at my watch trying to make sure none of these niggas fucked up my shit.

"Lakyn, it's a party, hunny. Whatever happens, it can be cleaned or fixed," my mother said calmly. I swallowed as I looked out at the bay as we headed toward Puafton.

"Yes, Mother. You're right, I'm good," I smiled.

"Very practiced, but very good," she patted my shoulder before walking back over to my Godmother Noelani. I closed my eyes trying my hardest to erase that memory from my head. Mala came toward me and stopped in front of me looking up.

"Did my mother send you over here? I said I was good," I said, leaning against the railing.

"Nope, I told her you'd be fine. You can fuck me on the sundeck later," she laughed.

"Bet. If I knew having a party would get you up there more, I would have been suggesting it more often," I chuckled. I reached out, turning her around, so she could lean against my chest.

"Teddy?" she asked sipping her wine.

"That nigga is still exactly where he was an hour ago. I'm watching him," I said.

"Good, because it's getting way too close," she said, rubbing my fore-arm.

"*Dove*, fuck them, people. I got us. We got us," I affirmed. Mala pressed harder against me as the sun began to set, casting a warm, golden glow over the tranquil waters, creating the perfect atmosphere for the celebration that was about to unfold. I couldn't wait to shoot a nigga.

I glanced over at Faxx, Henny, and Sanchez, who were all chatting and laughing as Cece punched Konceited in the back of the knee. Now that was worth this whole party. As the yacht gently swayed with the rhythm of the waves, I couldn't help but feel a sense of contentment wash over me while holding Mala.

"Finally, she opened the presents," Mala clapped.

I sometimes wondered how her ass could act so normal when she was crazy as fuck, but she was related to Henny. I guess that said it all. His ass could call me whatever he wanted, but what's psycho was a nigga who could be three different people at one time. And functioning like that shit was normal.

Shandea was glowing with happiness, and I could tell she had no idea. We moved closer to ensure Shandea saw all of us close by. She always took the time to seek us all out like she had to know if we were alive. Mala and I stood together, watching as Shandea opened each present, her eyes lit up with delight as she unwrapped gifts for her twin girls. After she finished opening the last of the gifts, she turned to me with a grateful smile.

"Link, you really let all these people on your yacht for me?"

"Of course. You don't need to thank me for anything. If I got it, you got it," I said, kissing Dea's cheek.

"See Oz, I told you he is so sweet," Shandea laughed.

"That nigga is phony as fuck right now. He's probably counting how many people bumped into a table," he chuckled. It was twenty-seven, but so the fuck what. It would have been twenty-eight, but he slipped over the side. He was lucky Ace got his dumbass out. I think it was someone from the Boys and Girls Club.

"You can even have a bachelorette party at the Casino. Anything you want," I smiled over her shoulder at Oz. I hugged Shandea making sure to rub her lower back.

"I'm going to fucking kill his high-functioning ass," Oz gritted.

Shandea pulled back looking up at me and I could see the genuine appreciation in her eyes along with affection. But little did she know that the surprises were far from over. I could see in Oz's face how uncomfortable he was in his classic three-piece navy-blue tailored suit with a blue and white striped tie. He pulled at the diamond blue sapphire cufflinks as he approached. We all knew when he said this shit that he didn't want to do it. But after Tali cussed him out, and ran so he couldn't beat her ass, he folded. It was something Shandea wanted, and whatever Dea wanted, she got.

Shandea turned around and came practically face to face with Oz. Her expression shifted from gratitude to sheer astonishment, then fear.

"Oz, what the hell are you doing? I am not going to ride your face in front of these people," she hissed through clenched teeth. Oz was down on one knee, but when he pulled out a ring Shandea froze. The entire deck fell silent as everyone, including Mala and I, watched as this big ass nigga actually went through with it.

"Shandea," Oz began, his voice steady. "From the moment I met you, I knew you were the one, so I purposefully inserted myself into your life. You've brought so much love and light into my life, and I can't imagine a future without you by my side.

Oz took Shandea's hands in his, his eyes filled with a deep, sincere love that seemed to radiate from his very being. His voice was confident yet tender as he began to speak, and I could feel the emotions in every word he uttered.

"Shandea, you have captivated my heart and soul in a way I never thought possible. You are my light, my joy, and my inspiration. I cannot imagine my life without you by my side."

He paused, and I could see the intensity of his crazy coming through.

"I am completely obsessed with you, and our children."

Shandea's eyes filled with tears, and I could see how deeply his words were touching her. And I could tell she was praying he wouldn't confess to how many niggas he'd killed because of his obsession. She clutched his hands tightly, holding her breath.

"Shandea Saunders, will you do me the honor of becoming my wife, my partner, and my forever?"

Tali wrote this shit for his ass. It was her or Cent. Because ain't no way this nigga came up with that shit.

A smile spread across her face, and she nodded, unable to speak through her tears.

The deck erupted into cheers and applause as Shandea threw her arms around Oz, holding him tightly as tears of happiness streamed down her face. The medicine Henny gave her for the pain after having a c-section must've been working well.

"He better have said it right," Mala grumbled.

"I knew y'all wrote that shit," I chuckled.

"No, he did it on his own, but it was heavily edited," Mala smiled as she moved over to hug Shandea.

"I'm just happy I can fit it. My other one is still too small," Shandea cried.

Oz came to stand next to me fixing his collar and clearing his throat.

"How long until I can chop niggas head off?"

I raised my arm to look at my watch before looking out at the bay.

"Another forty minutes and we're there," I answered. I tilted my head from side to side in anticipation of finally getting to someone I wanted. Theodore Banks wasn't innocent in any of this shit. Not only did he know what fuck shit Roman was on, but he had to know exactly what Charles had been doing to Mala. And for that alone wanted this nigga to run because he would only die slow and tired.

The bay air filled my lungs as I stood on the deck of our yacht, slowly making my way to the stern. Each of us slipped away to change so we blended in with the darkening sky and black waters. We were pulling close to the docks, but I knew my four-hundred-foot yacht couldn't be anchored in Puafton Harbor because of its size. Ace came along as Faxx then Henny and finally Oz joined me. We crossed over to the sleek burgundy cigarette boat. The man I pushed overboard sat curled up and passed out.

"What the fuck happened?"

"Pressure point. He wouldn't shut the fuck up," Ace replied. As soon as Faxx jumped into the boat, Ace pulled away. We had to sneak away from the baby shower to be sure everyone was a witness. We were there the entire time. That was why I didn't want to dock for deniability when *The Intrepid* blows the fuck up.

As we approached the luxurious two-hundred-foot super yacht where Banks was hiding, I scanned the lower and upper decks. My gaze settled on the sleek lines of the vessel as I scanned the best way to board. And I knew that tonight would be a game-changer. D-Mar looked like he was actually doing nice for himself if he truly owned *The Intrepid*. Faxx stepped forward, looking over the boat with a quick glance before turning to us.

"We need to make this shit quick fast and hard. Too many other yachts and smaller boats are around for this to go on long. I don't see anyone patrolling because more than likely they believe they are safe. Or they believe ain't nobody looking for Teddy. We go from the stern," Faxx said, looking at Ace.

"We get in and out. No witnesses and take Teddy bitch ass with us and get the answers we need," Henny stated.

"Let's get this shit done so me and Shandea can get back to the hospital. I can tell even though Vanessa and Stephanie are there, she's getting impatient," Oz grunted.

The dim lights of *The Intrepid* beckoned us, and with a silent nod, we slipped on board, our footsteps muffled by the plush carpeting. Faxx was on point, and then Oz, Henny, and I moved with the fluidity of shadows behind him. We found ourselves in the opulent lounge, where the chime of glasses and the low murmur of voices filled the air. There he was, Teddy, lounging on a red velvet couch, staring at a large screen wearing leather chaps with an open front and a shoulder harness. He held out his arms as Charles stared at him angrily.

"Where the fuck are you?"

"Listen, I called because I thought you needed to see that I'm alive. I'm wearing this for you," Teddy stressed.

"Theodore, where the fuck are you? Do you understand what this means if you're caught?" Charles shouted.

"Jesus Christ Charles! I'm alive and no one, not Alex, not Roman, or the fucking U.C.K. people know where I am! You don't even know where I am. And you shouldn't know until it's safe. I've been MIA for weeks now. I know, I know I fucked up trusting Roman with the copy, but I had no choice at the time. Rodney was breathing down my fucking neck. From what I know Alex, Roman, and U.C.K., might just take themselves out of the picture and we're golden," Teddy explained.

Charles's jaw firmed as he wiped a hand over his face before shaking his head.

"I need this plan to stay in place, you know how Cornelius is and I don't need him looking over my shoulder. It was my job to find an organization that could take the fall for the family if shit ever went left. And that fell into my hands that night I saw Lakyn killing the mayor. There is no way I will be able to keep them under my thumb if other people have what only we should know about. You need to disappear Theodore and I can make it happen. Just tell me where you are," Charles suggested.

I looked at Henny and his frown said what I was thinking. Charles was looking for Teddy because he was going to kill him or have him killed. Teddy was quiet for a moment as he leaned forward.

"I think... I should stay where I am. Let's just let this mess die off and when it does, I will tell you where I am. It's best if no one knows right now," Teddy said. "This was a mistake in calling."

"No! It wasn't a mistake. We'll figure this out in person like we do everything else. I've got your location and I'm coming to you," Charles stated. Teddy stood quickly alarm rising on his face as he pointed a remote and disconnected the call.

"Fuck!" he screamed. I couldn't tell if this nigga was just scared or if he was thinking the same as we were. It didn't matter because as of now we knew that there was not another file floating around and all we needed to do was destroy the original. Faxx turned to face us counting down from three on his gloved hand.

"Move," he mouthed and stood.

Without another word, we made our move. We stepped into the room just as Teddy turned to face us. The alarm was written across his face. When his eyes landed on me, I saw the instant recognition that he knew who I was. And if Theodore Banks knew who I was, then he had to know what Mala meant to me. Teddy was in this shit just as deep as Charles.

"Teddy, it seems like everyone is catching up with you tonight," I said before the room erupted into chaos. Two men rounded the corner shocked looks on their faces, but their reaction time was fast.

"We've been infiltra—"

The guard started to yell before a cleaver landed in the center of his forehead. As he fell, he must have pulled the trigger because shots went flying everywhere. I sprinted for cover as bullets whizzed past my head, the staccato rhythm of gunfire echoing in my ears. Henny, Faxx, and Oz were right beside me, their faces set in grim determination to take these niggas out and get Teddy. I saw Teddy's punk ass run toward a door his ass hanging out as he shouted.

"It's them! It's him," he screamed. The other guard screamed into his wrist.

"Attack! Butcher! Butcher!"

"Naw fuck that shit. I need a name 'cause this is ridiculous," Henny shouted.

"It isn't my fault my name rings bells in this bitch," Oz gritted as he let off three shots. The smell of gun smoke hung heavy in the air, mixing with the smell of the bay. More guards came from each direction, and it was more than I thought. When I flew over the drone, I had picked up maybe eight, but no more unless Teddy called in more.

We returned fire, our weapons spitting hot lead as we pressed forward, inch by inch. The guards were everywhere, their shouts blending with the waves crashing against the dock. We ducked and weaved, using every scrap of cover we could find, but the odds were stacked against us. I came upon one guard firing in the direction of Faxx. I reached out, putting my pistol to his temple and pulled the trigger. I was closer to the door where I saw Teddy had disappeared a few minutes ago.

"Keep moving!" I yelled over the cacophony of fire, my heart pounding in my chest. We were outnumbered and outgunned, but we weren't out-skilled.

"I see an opening to the left!" Henny shouted. I followed his lead, lying down suppressing fire as we moved to the door while Faxx and Oz kept the other at bay. The guards were relentless, but so were we. I felt a searing pain in my shoulder, but there was no time to dwell on it. By the burn, I knew it was a graze.

"Fuck," I gritted my teeth and kept moving.

"You good?" Henny asked as he kicked the door open and stepped inside.

"I'm good," I called out the pain fueling my adrenaline.

I leaned back out of the door while Henny pressed forward, giving off a headshot to one—a shot to the leg, then the chest to another. Faxx had thrown a tactical knife into someone's throat before shooting another man on the ground in the head. I kept returning fire with everything we had, forcing them to take cover as we stormed the gangway. Faxx moved using the short break to lay down fire so Oz could run into the room while I reloaded.

"Henny?" Oz panted.

"Through there," I nodded, and he moved. As soon as Faxx rolled through the door we were moving. The yacht was large, and these niggas kept coming.

"Get him out of here! Get him out—"

Oz kicked the man in the chest before shooting him in the chest and then head. We kept moving as the battle raged on. We pushed out onto the deck taking shots in the vest but giving them back leaving the deck slick with blood.

"Fuck!" Faxx shouted before he unloaded his Glock into a guard that came up from the rear.

"Nigga you straight?" I asked the air thick with the smell of death.

"Keep moving! Time! Time!" Faxx shouted.

We kept moving until we saw six guards pushing Teddy toward the bow and I wondered what the fuck they were thinking. It didn't matter because we need to make this shit quick. It seemed like it had been hours when in reality it had only been five minutes but even that was too long. Our shots were suppressed but not theirs.

I raised my pistol aiming for one of them shooting a guard in the back of the head. Henny shot at another hitting him in the shoulder and spinning him around before a bullet went through his eye.

"Get me out of here! Now!" Teddy screamed bolting for cover, but we were faster. While they kept the other guard busy I lunged and tackled Teddy to the deck. I gripped him by his hair and slammed his head into the deck as bullets whizzed through the air. I rolled diving for cover, the staccato of gunfire echoing in my ears. I aimed and took out the bitch that shot at me my round slamming into his chest knocking him overboard. I looked back at Teddy as he stumbled to his feet trying to run. With a swift movement, I ran at him, our bodies colliding with a resounding thud as I slammed him to the ground.

"Bitch you better stay the fuck down," I gritted.

"Ahh...ahhh," Teddy screamed as I slammed his head repeatedly until he stopped screaming. I looked up and saw Henny casually moving from body to body, giving headshots to those who were still moving.

"We need to move. Now," Faxx shouted as he dropped something to the deck.

"Sink this shit so we can get the fuck out of here. Hopefully, they didn't hear anything at the party," Oz said. I stood up gripping the leather holster Teddy wore and pulled him with me. Oz was looking over the side. I threw Teddy over my shoulder following Oz.

"Faster! We need to be off this boat now!" Faxx shouted.

Oz went over the side first, then it was Henny. I looked over, seeing them come to the surface as Faxx vaulted over the rail and into the water. I hit the button on my watch sending an alert to the drones to start the show. Bright lights lit up the sky as I threw Teddy bitch ass over before swinging my legs over the rail and jumping into the water as the yacht exploded.

It didn't take long to get back to the yacht and to get cleaned up. The bruise spreading over Faxx's side was visible through his tattoos. Henny wrapped him saying he more than likely had some broken ribs. We returned to the party, and I gave word to the Captain to depart back to Union City. I caught Mala's eyes and nodded, letting her know that we had him. She made her way over to me along with Faxx and Crescent who was looking at Faxx strangely by the way he was moving. Once we made it on board I had gotten an alert that the files I had the program running had come up with three possible locations. Shit was coming together and it was time to hit all these niggas at once.

"What the fuck happened?" Cent asked as soon as we were away from the guest.

"It's fine, *Mi Amor*. Just bumps and bruises. We got that nigga Teddy though and three locations of where Roman's ass is hiding," he said quickly. I lead them to the lower compartments of the yacht to the room I had customized for shit like this.

"Fuck Teddy, and Roman, Fransisco. You're moving like something is broken," Cent snapped. She reached out to touch his side, but he caught her hand, and pulled it into his side.

"Later Crescent. We need to narrow this shit down while Link and Mala do what they need to do," Faxx said, looking at me. I pushed open a door leading into a small office.

"Pull up the file named Denton on the watch and cast it to the screen," I said, tipping my chin. I could see the concern and hope flashing in Cent's eyes. She swallowed hard clamping her mouth shut probably waiting for the right time to dig into Faxx's shit.

"Bet, handle that shit. Because if we get the location tonight I'm hitting that bitch," Faxx grunted. I only nodded before closing the door and turning toward the one we were holding Teddy in.

"Don't...don't kill him Lakyn. I need Charles to watch as I do it," Mala said with false calm.

"Anything you want *Dove*," I said pushing open the cabin door.

I opened the door to the dimly lit room, as Mala followed closely behind me. Her face set in determined expression while also filled with hate. I understood because even though it was Charles who put her in this position Theodore was a willing participant in the bullshit. In the center of the room, Teddy sat bound to a chair, a haunted look in his eyes. He took a deep breath when Mala entered the room and for me, that was a sign of his guilt.

"Where is it, Teddy?" Mala demanded, her voice cutting through the tense silence.

"I...I... I don't know wh...what this is about. I...don't—"

"Stop the fucking bullshit, Teddy," I boomed. "We now know all about you and fucking Charles. And we know you know all about us, so don't play pussy. Where the fuck is Charles keeping the file, and how many other copies are there," I demanded. Teddy's eyes went wide, and his wet body shivered in the steel chair.

"Co...copies? Original? I...I don't know anything," he stammered.

Teddy's eyes darted between us, his jaw clenched.

"I don't know what you're talking about. I don't know who you are," Teddy muttered, his voice barely above a whisper.

Mala moved stepping in front of Teddy and leaning forward, her gaze fixed on his.

"You know exactly what we are talking about, and who the fuck I am. The original files' location, now," Mala spat.

I stepped forward shaking my head as I went over to the wall and placed my hand on a panel. The locks disengaged as the wall opened revealing different types of cords, robes, chains, plastic, and more.

"You better start talking, Teddy. We won't hesitate to make you fucking speak. Let's be real, do you really believe Charles wouldn't give you up in a second if it was to save his ass?" I spoke. I reached for the black paracord rope before turning to face him.

I saw as Teddy's resolve seemed to waver for a moment, but then he shook his head. Mala hadn't moved as she began to laugh in his face.

"I don't have anything to tell you," he spat, his voice tinged with hesitation when he saw what I had.

"Okay, bet. Perhaps this will jog your memory," I said, placing the cord in Mala's outstretched hand. Mala stood up straight as she began to unravel the cord before wrapping it tightly around her hands. My dick was hard as fuck as I watched her strain off the cord. Mala turned slightly looking me up and down and stopped at my dick. She licked her lips before pulling, testing the strength. Mala smirked before turning back to Teddy whose eyes widened at the sight of the cord, but then he shook his head.

"You wouldn't! There's no way you could because you know what will happen. I won't betray Charles," he muttered, his voice filled with uncertainty.

Mala took a step forward, her expression hard and unimpressed.

"You've made a mistake, Teddy. I'm not sure what the fuck Charles has told you about me, but trust me when I say I will strangle you, cut off your dick, and shove that shit so far down your throat you'll taste it in Hell. We can make this easy for you, or we can make it very, very difficult. I prefe r difficult," Mala attested.

Before Teddy could respond, I lunged forward, grabbing him by the chest holster. His arms strained against the chains, keeping him bound to the chair as I pulled him forward. Mala moved around the chair to the back of him. Teddy's eyes were wild as his breathing picked up.

"Tell us where it is, Teddy! We won't ask again!"

Teddy struggled against the chains, but then he let out a pained grunt.

"Ahh, fuck—"

Mala put the chord around his neck and yanked him backward. I let go as his back slammed against the metal frame of the chair. He struggled, but there was nothing he could do as his face turned beat red, and tears streamed from his widened eyes.

"Whoever thought of using the fireworks along with the explosion was a genius," Mala smiled.

"You are," I chuckled as she let go. Teddy dragged in a long inhale as he choked. We waited for a second for him to catch his breath as drool rolled down his chin. Mala began to pull back, but he screamed.

"Ooo...pleas...okay, okay," he gasped, his eyes filled with fear. "It's at Charles's grandparents' estate. There's an old cellphone. I know there is some kind of vault hidden there somewhere on the property. It's in a hidden room but I don't...I don't know where, but I know it's there," he wheezed.

"Are you sure, Teddy?" I asked, my voice low. "Is that the only copy or is it more?"

Teddy nodded, his eyes pleading. "I swear, that's all I know. I had a copy, but it was stolen. I...I don't know if there are more. Charles could've, but I have no idea. Please, you have to believe me," he panicked. "If I know Charles the way I believe, I don't think he would keep another file," Teddy shook.

"That estate is heavily guarded Link, and we wouldn't even know where to begin," Mala gritted.

I knew she was right just like I knew the best way to get on that property was on the day of that fucking wedding. But how would I find a room that was meant to be hidden? I pulled out my phone staring into Mala's eyes and I could see the complete trust that we would figure this shit out. I dialed a number placing the phone in my head waiting for the line to pick up.

"This is Dr. McQueen," Seyra answered.

"Seyra, it's Link," I said.

"Oh, oh okay, it came up restricted. What's up?" Seyra asked.

I wasn't worried about her phone because there was no way anyone could even pick up on this call. If anyone ever looked at her phone records it would be like there was never a call placed.

"Do you have Kenneth's complete loyalty?" I asked.

"He is in love, of course," she confirmed. Of course, that nigga was. We've noticed his type, and every one of them had a close resemblance to each other.

"Good. Then Kenny will do what's needed when you tell him you're being watched," I said, looking at Mala. We all knew about what Oz's mother went through before she died and now about Ian's. If Seyra says something of that nature, Kenneth will automatically know what's up.

"By who?"

"You believe it's a stalker, but he will know differently," I said.

"And he will tell me what he knows because?"

"He's in love, and when you step on his neck and twist his balls, he will fold. He will tell you all about the others and promise it won't happen to you. You were taught domination by Oz, so that means you were taught by the best, just like I was," I chuckled, staring at Mala. A slow smile crossed Mala's face as she began to see where this was going.

"I can do that," she said.

"And when he tells you, make sure Kenny tells you where all of Astor's family secrets would be hiding. Words like vault or hidden rooms are key," I instructed.

"It can be done. Hopefully, I can move on from this shit," Seyra sucked her teeth.

"It's possible, but make sure he believes that if he can gain access, it would ensure your relationship could never be touched by them like the others were," I said.

"Done," Seyra said, disconnecting the call.

CHAPTER SEVENTEEN

Fransisco 'Faxx' Wellington

After reviewing the files about Roman with Cent, I thought one location might stand out to her. Crescent did manage to point out three locations that seemed vaguely familiar to her from when he used to drag her along with him to different locations. I typed a few keywords into Link's program to narrow it down because the addresses on two of them looked familiar to me. It reminded me of something I saw in a file on Alex. Being that they were working together on this bullshit was another clue. I left my home gym and stopped at the door where I built the studio for Crescent. I looked through the viewing window, watching Crescent and Cece. I stared at my daughter as she noted everything Cent was doing.

Cece's eyes never strayed away from Crescent's face while she bobbed her head. Travis's ass wasn't far away from her and was sitting in the other rolling chair next to them.

I was glad to see Crescent finally step into the studio, just like it was good to know she wanted to attend the rest of her classes on campus. With knowing that information, I needed Roman's ass to be put down. I already knew he had to be panicking and going fucking crazy after all the money in those accounts was either frozen or transferred. All the money he'd taken from other artists and what he stole from Crescent went to exactly where that shit belonged. I pushed open the door, and Crescent looked up at me with her mouth open, trying not to laugh as a beat played. I heard Cece's voice.

'So, shout out to Travis, my Good Guy, and my boyfriend.

He's my best buddy and my friend until the very end.

He said we'll stick together through thick and thin.

Forever and ever, he'll be my best friend til the end!'

Cece turned around and smiled when she saw me.

"Papi! Papi, Mommy let me make a song, and she said it was the best she's ever heard," Cece said, jumping off Crescent's lap. I stared at Crescent while she tried not to laugh. I reached out and fixed her black and red taekwondo uniform before lifting her into my arms.

"It...it was something. Never heard anything like it. Do you want to know what I think?"

"Yes," she nodded seriously.

"When Uncle Link picks you up for class, you should let him hear it. I think he will lose his mind. But you need to finish getting ready because he'll be here," I stated.

"Yes, Papi! I gotta call Uncle Henny and Uncle Oz too, so they can hear it. Mommy, can you put it on my tablet?" Cece asked as she bounced from side to side.

"Ahh, yes, I will, once I finish cleaning it up. But listen to Papi and get your bag ready," Cent smiled. I waited until I heard Cece's feet hit the stairs before saying a word.

"First of all, I did not tell her to say any of that, and your ass is dead fucking wrong. You know damn well Link is going to have a fucking heart attack," she laughed.

"It's not funny, Crescent, but Link deserves what's coming," I chuckled. I stepped closer as she spun around in the chair to face me. Cent leaned forward and reached out to wrap her arms around my waist.

"It's so funny. Travis and Cece are just children, Papi. Francesca had a wonderful session with Mena. She also seemed to manage a way to keep the door closed on the others," she said, pulling back. I grabbed her arm and raised her hand to look at her finger.

"Good. I wanted to be there this morning but had to deal with a few shipments. We will take Cece to the next appointment together. I don't like missing those if I don't have to," I rubbed the light bruise on her skin.

She didn't flinch away in pain, and the swelling had reduced faster than I thought it would.

"I know that Papi. I made another appointment in two weeks. But you do remember mine is coming up. The day before that funky ass wedding," Cent fumed. None of us were happy that the shit was still going on, but until we had the location on that file, there was no choice. But honestly, the only way we would gain access to the estate would be that day.

"Fuck that wedding. That shit will never fucking happen. Let's talk about how you're going to make it up to me for helping Cece make that song. I think fucking that mouth might help you make better decisions," I said, my hand wrapping to the back of her neck.

"You're...fuck," she shivered, but reached for the string on my sweats.

As soon as she tugged on the string, my watch vibrated. I glanced down and saw the information of the locations Link's program had pulled from Monica's files, and what I entered about Alex showed it was complete.

"Shit," I said, releasing Crescent. She looked up with a frown on her face as her hands slid up my abs.

"What? Can it wait for a little bit because—"

I tapped the screen, and I felt my body go taught as I read the information that was gathered.

"As much as I want those thick lips wrapped around my dick, *Mi Amor*, this can't wait," I said as she sat back. Her frown turned to concern as she retied the string.

"What's going on? Is it another shipment Alex tried to fuck up or," she trailed off when I looked up at her. I felt my teeth clench together, and I knew my cold gaze screamed murder. It was a mix of excitement, thrill, anticipation, and rage. It felt good.

"Nope. I know where that nigga Roman is hiding, and he's about to understand what true fear and pain feels like," I stated. Crescent stood up, and a trace of apprehension and trust radiated from her eyes. I felt her hands slide across the skin on my waist and to my back as she hugged me.

"So...so this shit can be over soon, is what you're saying to me," she whispered. I wrapped my arms around her as she shook against my chest. I pulled back so I could look in her face while trying to control my expression if she was crying because of that nigga. But when she looked up, I could see the pure hate and rage as his nails dug into my skin. That shit made my dick hard as fuck.

"It will be over soon, *Mi Amor*, bet on that shit," I promised.

"Good, because I want to see him explode from the inside out," she seethed. I tilted my head to the side, my dick getting harder because I could actually give her just that.

"*MiAmor*, you should be very careful with your choice of words because you know I will find a way to give you exactly what you want," I smirked as her brows raised higher.

I already knew that the place would be heavily guarded, but I wanted to be sure about this information. I sent out a quick text to Echo telling him to get a drone in the air so we could get eyes on the spot. I wanted to know who was going and coming. I also wanted confirmation that Roman was there hiding like a little bitch. I walked into my garage and pulled the rest of the information on my phone. From what the files revealed, Roman's whereabouts were in a large warehouse on the outskirts of Puafton. It was hard to trace who owned the large building because of so many shell companies attached to it. But, when it got down to it, it was first owned by Tilderman incorporated before it was sold over a year ago. It wasn't sold directly to Roman but to another one of his shell companies. Apparently, he was also trying to take that city because he was trying to create a little empire. The familiar surge of adrenaline coursed through my veins as I absorbed the details, knowing that this could be the moment I'd been waiting for.

Echo: Done.

When the door opened, I stopped at my blacked-out Escalade, and Damari stepped inside.

"Where are you going?" he asked, walking toward the back.

"If this info is legit, and I'm sure it is, then we about to hit Roman's warehouse and drag his bitch ass out along with whoever else is there," I answered.

Damari nodded as he placed a hand on the panel that you wouldn't know is there unless you were told.

"Good, I need to release some tension," he laughed as a false panel on the wall slid to the side. Row after row after row of weapons line the walls, along with dozens of crates and shelves containing enough to take over a small country. At the back, there were duffle bags prepared for shit like this, depending on what you wanted to do. Each bag had a different color tag attached, telling me what was in them.

"Tension? Not getting enough rest because of little Julian?"

Damari grabbed two Glock G21 semi-automatics before moving toward the bags.

"Naw, he's good. Just still not over the whole Milo situation," he answered.

I completely understood where he was coming from because, technically, I hadn't either, and that was another reason Roman needed to be put the fuck down.

"Grab the green tags, and let's go. I want to be on my way there when Echo hits us," I said, opening the driver's side door. I looked at my phone, hitting up Henny because I knew Link was consumed, making sure everything was in place when shit got crazy at the fucking wedding.

Faxx: Are you at the hospital or dealing with your patient?

Henny: I am finished with all of my patients for the day. What's up?

Faxx: I'll be at the CLINIC in the next twenty minutes.

Henny: Say less.

The truck opened and closed after Damari put the gear inside. I hit the button to raise the garage doors just as Damari slid into the passenger seat.

It didn't take long to get to the CLINIC, and it took even less time once we got on the highway heading toward Puafton.

"Where the fuck are we going? It looks like you have enough shit that would start a war," Henny inquired.

"If I'm not mistaken, that bitch nigga Roman is held up on the outskirts of Puafton in a warehouse where I think he's making that *Silk* shit," I answered. Henny turned to face the front after looking through the bag in the back. He rubbed a hand over his goatee as he nodded. He sucked his teeth, his grill flashing as he clenched his jaw. Roman's name sat everybody on edge, and none of them knew the worst except Link. But Roman was not only fucking with my wife, but that nigga was involved somewhere down the line in Milo's murder. My phone rang through the truck's speakers, and I wasted no time hitting the answer button.

"Yo," I answered. I pressed on the gas a little harder as the feeling of confirmation settled over me. I knew before Echo would speak that the mutha fucka Roman was there. He's been right there this entire time, and I was getting closer.

"You may need backup. The place is packed and secured like shit. Whisper and I are already en route to the location. We brought some special shit for these niggas. But it seems some of them aren't armed and just workers. But it's confirmed that Roman is there," Echo stated.

I felt my blood heat up as I gripped the steering wheel tighter, thinking it was the trigger.

"It was the same when we hit the warehouse Jakobe was operating. I'm sure he probably runs it the same, especially if the Cartel has anything to do with it, and we know they do," Henny declared.

"We get in and find that nigga take out whoever is in the fucking way. Echo, I will leave it up to you and Whisper to make some noise once you arrive," I ordered.

"And it will be loud, and trust the shit we got coming will leave that building leveled," Echoed thundered.

I cracked my neck as a calm settled over me. The gloves were off with all these niggas. Ain't no more trying to keep things quiet. When this nigga fall, so will that other fucking tower in Clapton taking away his last remaining property. I wanted that nigga running scared, broke, and alone because once niggas find out you can't pay, it's over. He has no more loyal niggas rockin' with him because he wasn't shit and would never be shit. I looked into the rearview mirror, seeing the same flat, distant stare in Henny's eyes that I knew was in mine. This nigga was about to see what the fuck a Union City King was all about. He should feel privileged that two Horsemen of the U.C.K. were here to show him what the hell looked like.

As we approached the warehouse, a sense of foreboding washed over me, and I always took that shit to heart. The building loomed large and imposing, its darkened windows like eyes peering out at us from the shadows. We intentionally waited until the sunset as we watched the building and studied their movements. They weren't sloppy and had some kind of training, at least in security. But there was always an opening. Someone usually slips up or begins to get lazy, and I could tell which guard would be doing the perimeter check. We geared up just as the sun lowered behind the trees, and I saw that same guard again, and he was constantly one minute later than the others.

I pointed at the door on the side of the building. We had that one minute to enter the door before that guard spotted us and sent out an all-call. I hit a few things on my watch, pulling up a program that should easily override the locking system. I held up my fisted hand and began to count down in my head. I stood, knowing Henny and Damari were behind me when I took the step. I stepped forward, but it was like an invisible string pulling my leg backward. I stopped and waited. If I'd moved, we would have been lit up by the spotlight that suddenly appeared directly in our path.

"Shits changed. Stay on me because we're moving fast. We might go in the opposite direction in less than a minute, but we have no choice. We going to need to take niggas out and drag them inside," I commanded. I turned back around and faced the building, counting under my breath as the prompter guard passed by. When the light blinded him, we moved, slipping into the treeline.

We slipped through the perimeter, taking out two guards with precision and silence. Damari dragged the body of one guard, and Henny had the other while I gained access to the door. I counted under my breath, and when I got to ten, the light turned green, and the locks disengaged. I pulled the door open, holding my Glock up in case someone was standing there. From the blueprints of this warehouse, I knew this entered into a smal l office. From what I could tell from the drone, nothing was in it.

I stepped inside, Henny and Damari on my heels, as he dragged the two men inside, closing the door lightly. I stood still until I heard the lock reengage. Henny pulled the body. He had the collar dragging him into a corner. I saw Damari do the same as I crept to the door, listening for any voices or noise. I heard no one and grabbed the handle, turning it slightly while easing the door open. I stepped out into the darkness. The only light seen was at the end of the narrow hallway. I knew at the end of this hall it would lead us right into the central area of the warehouse. I knew a n office space was upstairs, and part of the warehouse had been made into apartments. If Roman weren't on the floor checking over his shit, he would be up there. Either way, I would find that nigga before the drones dropped their packages.

"We have forty minutes to find this nigga. If we don't, we must be out before the first drone hits the building," I said.

"That's enough time. Most of these people are unarmed and will probably run, as for everyone else, fuckem'," Henny said, checking his clip. I nodded, hitting the button on my watch to start the countdown. I moved silently and quickly down the hall toward the lit area. The inner parts of the warehouse were a hive of activity, with crates of the drug *Silk* being loaded and unloaded by women and men from different races. We moved cautiously, sticking to the shadows as we made our way deeper into the warehouse, trying to locate the stairs that would lead us upstairs.

We crept through the maze of crates and corridors, our senses on high alert. I stopped looking out of the area at the syringes being loaded into boxes and placed on trucks. I scanned the area to see if I saw any guards or Roman. I stepped around the corner, keeping close to the wall when two loud voices rose in an argument. I stopped behind a large crate, listening to what they were saying. One of the men was Roman, but the other sounded familiar as fuck. I looked at Henny, and a sneer accompanied by the tightening grip on his gun said all I needed. I leaned out, first catching sight of the Roman, then the other man I knew, Marvin.

Roman paced back and forth, rubbing a hand over his head before cracking his neck. He pulled at his wrinkled dark gray suit jacket before stopping in front of Marvin. His jaw clenched, and I could tell Roman was fucking losing it. I checked my watch settings, and he must have gotten the alert an hour ago. We still had two minutes before Echo made the call to him. I knew that would rattle him because no one except two people could have narrowed that signal down.

Marvin cleared his throat before removing his tinted glasses and pushing them into his pocket.

"Roman, we need to talk. Carmelo ain't so happy about the money you owe us again. This looks like it's becoming an unhealthy pattern, Roman. And we don't like those kinds," Marvin smiled. I saw a vehicle drive into the warehouse, but we couldn't get a visual inside the sedan. I shifted when Roman folded his arms across his chest. He looked at the men that had come with Marvin. I could tell he was thinking about taking this nigga out, but he knew the Cartel would come at him full throttle. It wouldn't matter, though, because they would never find him.

Roman forced a confident smile as he shrugged.

"Marvin, my friend, I assure you, I'm working tirelessly to resolve our financial matters. But we've encountered an unforeseen problem, and it's left us in a bit of a bind. I just need more time," Roman grunted.

Marvin's face screwed up before he chuckled, shaking his head to Roman.

"Nigga let's cut all this formal bullshit. This isn't a fucking 'we' problem. It's your problem. You're saying an unforeseen problem, but let's be one hundred. It's a U.C.K. problem, and we don't care about your problems, Roman. Carmelo wants his money, and he wants it now. You know what happens to those who can't pay up. You can easily be replaced," Marvin finished.

Roman tilted his head back, bringing his fingers to his chin.

"Okay, okay fuck it. Look, my nigga, I understand the gravity of the situation, but I don't know what the fuck happened to our money. Y'all niggas can threaten me all you want, but the fact remains that them bitch niggas stole our shit! A dead man can't repay anything, but I know I can get the money just like before. I just need more time," Roman fumed.

Marvin stepped closer, causing both their men to tense.

"Time is something we can't afford to give, Roman. You better have a plan to get our money. Killing you isn't the only way to make up for your incompetence. The Rojas brothers have ways of breaking a nigga down. I've seen others bigger than you broken," Marvin snorted.

I looked back at Henny as he aimed at Marvin, but one of his men stood in the way. He caught my glance, nodding at what Marvin was hinting at. Did they have something to do with what we saw at that mansion?

"What the fuck is that shit supposed to mean, my nigga? Don't fucking threaten m—"

Roman stopped speaking as a phone on the wall rang loudly. Some workers stopped a second but quickly put their heads back down and continued.

"Who the fuck...nigga don't fucking stand there, answer that shit," Roman stiffened. The man standing closer to the phone moved to pick it up.

"You better find that fucking money, Roman. And this ain't no fucking threat, so let's not act like you don't know what's up," Marvin said gruffly. Roman opened his mouth, but the man with the phone pulled it away from his ear and looked at it.

"Ahh Boss...it... there's no one on the line," he said, before his cell phone rang. Standing to my full height, I smirked as he answered the video call.

"Roman Sharpe," Echo boomed.

"Who the fuck is this?" Roman asked.

One of his men stepped beside him, holding his weapon on Marvin as Marvin's guards tensed.

"Who I am doesn't matter. I'm only delivering a message. You can try to hide from a Horseman, but death will always find you," Echo chuckled. Then, I could hear the explosion that destroyed Roman's last remaining property.

I stepped out from behind the crate, aiming my Glock and pulling the trigger. My first round slammed into the head of the guard next to him and the other at the man on the catwalk above where Roman stood.

Suddenly, the sound of footsteps echoed through the warehouse as shouts and screams filled the space.

"Move, move," I shouted as bullets flew, and the acrid scent of gunpowder filled the air as we engaged. The crack of gunfire reverberated off the walls, and the adrenaline surged through my veins as I fought my way toward Roman. Marvin dove behind a table when the first shot was fired. The blare of alarms was drowned out by the shouts of people trying to find a way out.

Bullets flew, and the air as we dodged and ducked, taking whoever out that got in our way. Our training and instincts guided us through the unorganized chaos. The warehouse became a battleground, each corner hiding a new threat as we pushed forward. Damari hit one man in the chest, then side-kicked another as he reloaded.

I rounded a table, reloading when someone stood up, aiming for my chest. I slammed the magazine in and reached for the knife to my chest, throwing it at his neck. I racked the slide, giving him a headshot as I kept moving.

I caught sight of Roman, his cold eyes locking onto mine from across the warehouse.

"Naw, don't run now nigga," I shouted.

Roman's expression was a cruel sneer as he raised his own weapon.

"Y'all niggas in my house! And—"

We both knew what this was, so I didn't know why this nigga was talking. I moved his guard and began pushing him back until I shot that nigga in the face. Roman aimed his two pistols when his guard fell to the ground. The air crackled with tension as we exchanged fire, each shot bringing us closer so I could make this shit personal.

"You killed my fucking seed nigga!" Marvin shouted as more gunfire sounded. I could hear the cough of a rifle, and I knew it was Whisper up high.

"That fake ass nigga body danced before it hit the ground," Henny taunted.

"That nigga went out looking like one of the zombies from Thriller," Damari laughed.

Everything faded as I counted Roman's shots and knew it was his last round. Before he could reload, I holstered my Glock, grabbed a discarded chair, and threw it. The metallic clang of the chair slamming into his raised arm echoed through the space. Before he could recover, I already had my booted foot in his chest. Roman hit the concrete wall hard.

"Okay nigga," he grunted. We circled each other without a word, our movements calculated and precise. Roman's eyes darted to the left, where his gun lay after the chair knocked it out of her hand.

"Do it! Go for that shit," I urged. I could feel the burn of anticipation in my muscles, my every instinct honed to beat this nigga down.

"Y'all U.C.K. niggas think you're untouchable. But every nigga got a weakness," Roman sneered, his voice dripping with contempt. "Crescent was the first of mine to break and mold as I plea—"

I wasn't for all the monologue bullshit. We circled as soon as he reached the corner of the table, and I moved. I reached out and grabbed his collar, pulling him down so fast that his face slammed into the metal table it dented.

"Keep running that shit nigga," I grunted, throwing a punch that caught him in the side of the head. He blocked the next one and then shoved the table into my midsection. I grunted, but I kept moving.

With every blow exchanged, his taunts grew more malicious, more insidious, each word a calculated attack designed to rattle me. This nigga didn't know me because my mind could only focus on one thing, and that was the wedding gift for Cent.

"Crescent will still be slu—"

The words died on Roman's lips as I launched myself at him with a ferocity to shut him the fuck up.

"Nigga you talk too much," I gritted as I slammed palm strikes one after another. The knee into his stomach had him gasping, but he swung out, managing to hit me in my broken ribs. I grunted and stumbled slightly when I felt the punch to the other side. I shifted, catching Roman on the side of his head. I rained down blow after blow on Roman, each fueled by his knowledge of what he's done.

Every strike and parry were met with a counter, our movements a blur of calculated violence. I slammed his face into the wall and dragged him to the end of it. Roman stumbled, which gave him an advantage I let him take, and he used it precisely. The punch to my side and his low leg sweep dropped me. I rolled over backward, moving just in time as his foot came down where my head would've been. I moved, ramming my shoulder into the chest.

Don't kill him. Don't kill him. Don't kill him.

I repeated so I wouldn't slip up and fuck up my gift. The fight took us across the warehouse, crashing through crates and sending debris flying in our wake. Crushed syringes of Silk lay scattered over the floor. Every move and strike was calculated as I moved him closer to the large doors.

I managed to land a solid blow to Roman's midsection, staggering him for a moment. My surroundings faded into a haze of adrenaline and focus. Instinct and training took over, and I deflected his attack, countering with a swift strike that sent him reeling. Roman hit hard, blood pouring from his torn cheek and his mouth. But Roman had some speed on him as he ran toward me. His rage was put off control, leaving a perfect opening. I reached for my second Glock strapped to my leg and hit him in the right bicep and left hip. I wanted him in pain and hurt in the places Crescent suffered the most. Roman staggered, crumbling to the ground as he screamed.

"Ahhhh...ahhhh fuck!" he screamed.

I dropped to my knees over him as the world faded. I rained blow after blow on him, each strike fueled by pent-up rage and revenge. I raised his head, slamming it into the ground twice before pulling my tactical knife from my vest. I stabbed Roman in the right side of his chest before I peeled the flesh that hung on the side of his face.

I pulled back, my breathing ragged just as the beeping on my watch sounded.

As I rose to my feet, my heart pounded with urgency. I grabbed an unconscious Roman by the ankle, dragging him to the large doors.

"Henny! Damari! We need to go now," I roared. It was like the haze was lifted all at once, and every sound returned to full volume. Intermittent gunfire still filled the space, but I pushed open the door. I heard footsteps and turned my Glock aimed, but it was Henny with Damari covering them from behind.

"Echo said we got seconds," Henny shouted. I turned around, dragging Roman's bleeding body behind me, when a loud whooshing sound came from everywhere. I felt my body being lifted as the heat of the flames licked at my back. I saw Roman's body hit the ground hard as he rolled several feet away from me. I pushed to my feet, grabbing Damari by the collar because he was the closest. I knew it wasn't over, and we had to get further away.

"Henny!" I shouted over the noise.

"I'm good! Go, go," he yelled. I saw him out of the corner of my eye as he approached me. I heard the buzzing overhead just as we got to a still-unconscious Roman. I pushed Damari toward Henny and grabbed Roman when everything turned white.

We stumbled out of the burning woods to where the truck, Echo, and Whisper should've been waiting. Damari was hurt, but it was nothing fatal because he shook it off as we ran. It was dark as fuck, and going through the wooded area while we dragged Roman was irritating but necessary to my wife's healing. She needed to see this nigga die for herself so she could let go and know this nigga would never fuck with her again. My ears were still ringing from the explosion, and I only knew that when Henny punched my shoulder to gain my attention.

"Yo!"

"We need to get his ass to the *CLINIC* if you want him alive," Henny shouted. Damari moved forward, flashing a small light to let Echo and Whisper know that it was us approaching. I was sure that we were screaming, and they knew it already.

"Bet. I need this nigga alive long enough to see tomorrow morning," I shouted as bright headlights came on in our direction. Once we made it to the road, Henny and I dropped Roman's body to the ground. I looked down at him while grabbing my side, where he landed some good ass punches. Roman lay on the ground, bloodied, broken, and fucked up. I had finally caught up to this nigga after weeks of chasing him down. Not only did I strip him of everything he owned, but now I get to hold his life in my hands as he did to Crescent. It was also time to see if we could get the answers about Alex.

"I got you my nigga. We need to move," Henny yelled. Echo came over as Dmari slid into the Escalade and started the vehicle.

"Echo, get this nigga to the *CLINIC* asap. Slap a pouch on that nigga so he'll make it," I ordered.

"We got it," he nodded, and I helped him hoist Roman up and dragged him toward a blacked-out van. The back doors swung opened as Whisper reached out, gripping under Roman's shoulders, and helped Echo pull him inside. I moved carefully back over to the S.U.V. but as fast as I could because the fire was beginning to spread. I looked toward where the warehouse would still be, but all I saw were ashes that swirled around like a sandstorm. I climbed into the back seat, knowing this shit was almost over, and these past weeks I was sure niggas learn not to fuck with shit that belongs to U.C.K. I slammed the door shut just as Damari pulled off, leaving the chaos and destruction behind us.

We drove through the darkened city streets, and the only sound was the engine of the S.U.V. Henny sat up front, his eyes fixed on his phone, but I could see the tightness in his jaw. Whatever the fuck was going on, I knew it had to have something to do with Tali. That being said, I knew it had to be that nigga Tremont.

"Nigga, what is it? I didn't get any alerts, so this is some other shit," I groaned. I leaned over, reaching under the driver's seat to pull out one of the emergency cases.

"Tremont. You already know what it is. This nigga is really trying to play in a nigga face, but that shit is about to be dead. Link's program just finished going over the files he managed to get from Rodney. This nigga is really trying to fuck up my hospital," he chuckled. "First Joint Commission, and now this nigga trying to set me up," Henny seethed.

"We're out right now. Might as well pick this nigga up on the fucking way to the *CLINIC*," I suggested. I leaned over with a grunt and pulled my phone out of my back pocket.

"Who do you have on him right now?" Henny asked.

"A few little niggas. Enough to make sure his bitch didn't leave Union. I was hoping he tried, but now I see why he stayed. Right now, that nigga is staying in an Airbnb on Hawks Avenue and thirty-third street," I answered. I texted to make sure his ass was still in the house before looking back up.

"We're making a stop, Damari. Take us to Hawks Avenue and Thirty-third Street," Henny ordered. I popped four ibuprofens before leaning back into the leather seats. If we were cleaning up, we might as well get rid of all these trash ass niggas in our city. Henny knew exactly what needed to be done when he called for bodies to fall.

Damari pulled onto Hawks Avenue, and I sent a text for them little niggas to bounce. None of them needed to be seen around her after we took this nigga. Henny pulled out his personal phone, sending off a quick text as we turned onto Thirty-third Street. We pulled up to a nondescript modern two-story house in a quiet neighborhood. The residences surrounding the house were spaced nicely apart but close enough that someone could hear a scream. My watch vibrated as we pulled to a stop, letting me know Echo and Whisper had made it back to the *CLINIC*. We had to make this run quickly and as quietly as possible. I tuned slightly, reaching in the back and pulling open a navy-blue bag that was tied to the side panel. I reached inside, grabbing two masks, not looking to see what they were.

"We get in and out with this nigga. Tremont has an appointment that can't be missed," Henny stated.

All Tremont had to do was finish out his fucking contract and take the fucking money. The nigga had a slight pass because he saved Tali and Dea's mother, but that shit was dead. We had too much other shit going on than to be worried about this bitch made nigga snitching on shit that he knows nothing about. Tremont fucked up by not only trying to get Henny locked, but he kept fucking with Tali. That's what got that nigga dead tonight while another would get a second chance at life.

"Nigga, I'm just going to put this shit out there, and you take how you want to take it," I said as we exchanged a silent nod before donning our masks.

I pulled the black strap over my head and pulled the ice rink raider mask, the old school white hockey goalie mask with blood splatters on it. Meanwhile, Henny's was a stylized skull that emphasized the seriousness of our purpose. We stepped out of the car and made our way to Tremont's front door. The night was still, and the only sound was the distant hum of traffic a block over from the silent neighborhood. I looked the door over, seeing that it was one of the smart locks making shit easier. I hit the small button on the side of my watch and held it up to the screen. The lock beeped, so I pulled my hand away and then pulled on my black leather gloves. Henny was staring at me as he flexed his black latex gloves while I turned the knob. I slowly pushed the door open and looked at the wall. The security system was already disengaged when I overrode the lock.

"The fact that you even brought up some random shit right now tells me it's about Link. And since it's about Link, then it must be about Mala," he deduced as usual. But I knew even he wouldn't see this shit coming.

"Do you know this nigga married her ass? Had her sign some shit when she started working at the Casino," I said quietly. Henny stared at me for a long minute before closing the door softly. Once inside the house, we moved quickly and quietly, navigating the darkened hallway until we reached Tremont's bedroom. It wasn't hard to find by the light snores coming from the end of the hall. I grimaced at the pain on my side, knowing full well Henny would need to rewrap this shit.

The door creaked open, and we stepped inside, our masks casting eerie shadows in the dim light. Tremont lay in bed as Henny moved closer to it. Henny kicked the fuck out of the bed, causing Tremont to shout as his eyes widened in terror as he realized he was not alone.

"W-what the fuck! Who are you? What do you want?" Tremont stammered, his voice quivering.

"You know exactly why we're here, Tremont. You think you can come into my city and try to put heat on me nigga? I gave you a pass because of who you were in the field, and you also saved Tali's mother. But what I didn't do is tell you to touch what the fuck is mine nigga. All that other shit is whatever a part of the business, but you just don't fucking learn," Henny said. His tone was cold and commanding as he spoke, stepping closer and closer.

Tremont's eyes darted back and forth between us, but he remained silent, refusing to admit his wrongdoing. The clench in his jaw and the way the sweat beaded on his temples gave it all away, even if we didn't know.

"I don't know what kind of gang shit this is, but I will be pressing charg—"

"Fuck this nigga! We don't have time for his bullshit," I grunted. I pulled out my Glock and aimed it at his head, waiting for the same reaction. "At least you're holding it this time, Pissy T," I scowled.

"You've been telling the authorities, mainly that bitch nigga agent Rodney Gates that you will testify in court that I'm selling medication from my hospital. You got me fucked up, my nigga. I know Rodney, and I'm sure he didn't explain the shit you just stepped in. It doesn't matter though, because we have an appointment to get to. So, get the fuck up," Henny demanded, his voice growing more insistent.

Tremont's shocked silence wasn't a surprise for us, but to him, us knowing that information just fucked up his world.

"Nigga did you hear me?" Henny asked, lunging forward and grabbing Tremont by his white tee shirt. Henny's masked face was inches from Tremont's.

Tremont's eyes widened in shock as Henny's grip tightened, and I could see the fear in his expression. It was clear that he had underestimated just how far Henny was willing to go or just who we were.

"Get the fuck up nigga! Normally mutha fuckas don't get chances, but you did, and you chose to fuck over U.C.K., and we can't have that shit. Now, get. The. Fuck. Up!" I shouted as Henny dragged him out of the bed. Henny pulled Tremont to his feet as he struggled to get away. Henny shoved Tremont into the wall, making a loud thudding sound. Then he turned to me, his eyes blazing with intensity.

"Grab his shit. Where this bitch is going ain't nobody going to find him," Henny said as he slammed Tremont's head into the wall. I moved around the room, quickly grabbing his luggage bag and wallet. Henny grabbed him by the neck and threw him out of the door and into the hall.

"Get the fuck up nigga. Walk that shit off like a man. You like touching shit that you were told to stay the fuck away from, and you thought I would let that ride?" Henny taunted.

"Fuck! Fuck, this is not...I... I'll leave! I'll leave, and you won't see me again," Tremont stammered, pushing to his feet. I followed Henny out of the room as he stalked Tremont, who tripped over nothing. Tremont held out his hand like it would keep niggas off his ass.

"Hen...Hendrix, this...this can all...all be fixed," Tremont shuddered. Henny stopped moving as Tremont bumped into the couch, feeling around so he could get further away. Henny tilted his head to the side and then looked at his watch.

"Okay, okay, bet," Henny nodded.

"Okay! I will leave tonight, and you will never hear from me again," Tremont rushed out. Henny dropped his hand to his side and nodded for me to head out.

"I like that idea, my nigga, but I'm going to need your word on that," Henny said, holding out his hand. I opened the door but turned back around to see the shocked but nervous look on Tremont's face as he stepped closer.

"That's all we got these days is our...ahh...ahh...ahhh—"

Tremont screamed as Henny sliced through Tremont's wrist like butter. Blood sprayed over the couch and onto the carpeted floor.

I made my way to the S.U.V. and opened the back door just as Henny shoved Tremont outside, making him miss the small step as he fell to the ground. Tremont's once-white tee shirt was now red and wrapped around his stump. Henny leaned over the skull mask as shining light from the moon hit it.

"Once we get somewhere a little more sterile, I'm going to need that other one, my nigga," Henny grunted. Tremont screamed and screamed while lights from the surrounding houses began to turn on. I tossed his shit in the truck and left it open so we could put his ass back there too.

I walked back over to Henny as he reached down, gripping Tremont by the back of his neck, and yanked until Tremont stumbled to his feet.

"I need a hospital, I need a hospital, I need—"

His words cut off when I slammed my Glock into his temple knocking his ass out. Henny caught him and dragged his ass over toward the truck. We pushed him inside and slammed it closed.

"My problem is that I am sure Mala read all of those papers and still signed anyway," Henny said as we slid inside the back seats. Before the doors were closed, Damari had pulled off just as I heard sirens in the distance.

We arrived at the *CLINIC*, the nondescript building loom*ing* large in the dark. There were no lights until the large doors began to rise to let us inside. Damari pulled inside, cutting the ignition as the doors began to lower. Henny opened the door and slid out, tossing the mask on the back seat. I saw Tali come out of a room, running her hands through her locs as she rushed over to him.

"Faxx, anything else? What will we need to do about Roman once you're finished?" Damari asked. He looked over his shoulder, and for one second, I saw Milo. I blinked and shook myself as I opened the back door.

"Get cleaned up and checked over by Echo or Whisper unless you need Henny to handle it," I replied.

"Bet, I'm good, just sore, but I'll get one of them to stitch this gash up," he responded.

"When I get what I need from this nigga Roman and Henny finishes with him, I want him at the *RANGE*. I want him on the south end of the property where the container is set up," I ordered. I looked in the back as moans filled the space, and I saw Echo heading toward us.

"I got you. Roman will be exactly where you want him," Damari said as I stepped out. Echo rounded the S.U.V., looking me over quickly before turning his attention to the truck.

"You're all good, or did you take another hit?" he smirked.

"Fuck you, nigga. Grab that bitch nigga and bring him to surgery," I said, holding my side. Tali's eyes were wide as Henny spoke. Her gray gaze slid to me with a frown as I started to limp more and groan.

"Oh, my God, Faxx! Henny, you didn't say he was hurt," Tali said, brushing him off and coming over to me.

"He's fine," Henny sucked his teeth.

"I'm good chocolate, just some pain," I groaned. Tali moved and wrapped her arms around my waist, so I could lean on her short ass. I looked at Henny over her head as I pulled her close.

"Tali! Ain't nothing wrong with that fake ass nigga. If he needed a hand, that's all he needed to say," he shouted.

"Hendrix! He is in pain, don't act like that. Just get the room set up while I take care of my baby. Look at him. He can barely walk," Tali argued. My arm dropped to her lower back, and I felt something hit me in the back of my head. When I turned around, I saw Tremont's severed hand on the ground.

"That will be your hand next. No funeral repeats," Henny announced as we stepped through the doors.

After Tali wrapped my ribs again, we joined Henny in the operating room. Roman lay on the table, his eyes open and alert. His arms and legs were strapped down to the metal table, but his head moved back and forth. Tali went to stand next to Henny, but her narrowed eyes stared at Tremont on the table beside Roman. His head was strapped down to the table, facing us in horror. Tali shook her head as she pulled on a pair of gloves and started to prepare a tray. I watched as she picked up a scalpel, and then she stabbed Roman in the inner thigh close to his dick but just barely missing his femoral artery.

"Ahh! Ahhh...you...you stu...dumb bitch," Roman hissed. Tali pulled the scalpel out and looked at it before dropping it into a waste basket. Henny moved, gripping Roman's face with his gloved hand and squeezing until he began to scream from the pressure.

"It wasn't sharp enough," Tali shrugged.

"It's all good, *Thickness*. You know how I like my shit," Henny reassured.

"Jesus... Jesus, pl...please...somebody help me," Tremont cried.

"Somebody help me," I mocked. "I don't know what the fuck you saw in that nigga," I chuckled.

"Can we just say that I was young and impressionable at the time," Tali sighed. I chuckled before looking back at Roman. Henny let go of his face, pushing it to the side.

"You ...fuck...fuck U.C.K. and that bitch Crescent," Roman hissed through bloody lips.

"Who the fuck told Two-Face he could speak?" Henny asked.

Tali shook her head, trying not to laugh when she looked at Roman's peeled face.

I stared down at Roman, my eyes cold and unyielding. His voice, using Crescent's name, echoed in my head. I refused to let his attempts at using her name faze me. I didn't want to kill him before I was ready intentionally. I had to ensure my wedding gift made it safely to its destination. My focus remained unwavering, fixed solely on the one task at hand—finding Alex. Not only was this nigga one of the last remaining threats to Crescent, but this nigga had it in his head that he would fucking touch Mala.

"Where in the hell is Alex?" I demanded, my voice cutting through the sterile air. "You can waste your breath on insults and bullshit, Roman, but it won't change anything. I will still kill you, but I will make sure if you don't, I take my time peeling the rest of the skin off your face," I gritted.

Roman's eyes narrowed as he tried to grin. The skin there pulled at the corners of his mouth, causing bloody drool to roll down the side of his face.

"I'm from Clapton nigga. Y'all Union City boys ain't shit. You can't intimidate me, Faxx. Your obsession with Crescent blinds you so much that you can't see the bigger picture of what's at play."

I resisted the urge to react, refusing to let his jabs get under my skin.

"You don't understand how obsessed I truly am with my wife. I could be so obsessive that I tracked down every person who touched, hurt, or refused to help her. My obsession is what helps me to see clearly my objective. You have no idea what I'm capable of, Roman. Now, the location of Alex—tell me," I demanded.

Roman's defiance faltered for a moment, a flicker of uncertainty crossing his features. He stared into the black pits of my gaze, and I knew what he saw. Roman may have believed he was hard, a tough ass nigga that made it out of Clapton's hoods, but he wasn't me. Roman has killed and would kill if he has to. But I knew he saw that everyone saw in me before they died. They saw the pleasure I got from it as they took their last breath.

"You're too late, Faxx. Alex has people behind him that y'all niggas could never compare to."

"That's what you believe? That's what he believes, Henny. This nigga acting like he knows us and shit," I chuckled.

"Y'all have no idea wh—"

I slammed my fist into his mouth twice before I pulled back to look at him. Roman sneered at me, blood trickling from the corner of his mouth. I nodded to Henny, who injected the serum into Roman's arm. The effect was almost immediate. Roman's eyes widened, and he began to squirm in his restraints.

"You can do whatever you want to me, but I won't help you. Fuck you, nigg—"

Henny moved to Roman's side, preparing to extract his kidney. I watched as Roman's resolve began to crumble, the concoction Henny perfected working faster than the first trials. Roman's eyes rolled as pain clouded his eyes, but he couldn't move to see what was happening.

"Where is Alex?" I demanded, my voice low.

"Oh my God! Are you...oh God...no...no...no—" Tremont cried as he watched Tali assist Henny in the removal of a kidney while the patient was still awake. I guess it was a little fucked up.

Roman's breath came in ragged gasps as Henny began his work.

"Where is Alex?"

Roman shook his head, his brows furrowed as his mouth opened without his permission. It always worked differently for each person.

"He's... he's...heee'sss," he hissed as tears rolled down his face mixing with the blood pooling beneath him.

"Where is Alex Tilderman?" I boomed.

"He's at the Astor estate," he gasped. "In the catacombs beneath the main house. That's where he's hiding. That's where he is...oh God...Ah-hhh...Astor, Astor....make it stop....ahhh," he screamed. The sound bounced off the walls, and it made Tremont begin to thrash against his restraints, begging for his life.

I nodded, satisfied with the information.

"Thank you, Roman. You've been very helpful. Once the surgery is over, the Doc will make sure you are ready to go for the main event. You don't know how long I've waited for this shit. It'll...it will be—"

"Therapeutic!" Tali shouted over the screaming.

"Exactly! See, Tali knows her baby, Henny," I chuckled. I couldn't see his face behind the mask, but his eyes said it all. Tali couldn't stop laughing until he cut his eyes at her, and she held her breath.

"I'm going to need both of y'all to shut the fuck up," Henny warned. Tali couldn't stop laughing as she helped Henny. I stared at Roman's face the entire time as he screamed.

"Roman, this is nothing. You can take that shit and work through the pain," I chuckled. Henny pulled away, raising the kidney in the air. I grabbed Roman's face and made him turn to look.

"Wha—wh...what the fuck? Whh...ahhh—"

Tremont began to pray as Henny placed the organ in a sealed cold container. He turned back and began closing up the surgical area while Tali pushed in a medication that knocked Roman out. Henny finished his work, patching up Roman's wound. We left him there, still bound and now weakened. The next time his ass will wake up, he will be trapped just like my wife had been with him.

Henny and Tali left the room to change for another surgery that might take longer. I walked over to Tremont. His eyes were wide, as his breathing increased to the point I thought he would pass the fuck out.

"It's all good, Tremont. You're in one of the best hands that ever did it," I laughed. I laughed harder the more he struggled when Tali and Henny approached him. Henny leaned over Tali's shoulder and stared at Tremont. He reached up, pulled down his mask, and smirked at him.

"Ignacio, thank you for saving my mother, but you had an out. It would've been best if you had taken it," Tali said as she began to prepare the tray.

"Tali, Tali...Tali don... don't do this...don't let them do this. This isn't you, Tali. What has he done to you?" he hissed.

"What I've done to her? It's funny because I thought the same thing at one point until I realized it was the other way around. But, that doesn't matter now, does it, my nigga? How about we focus on your last act as a doctor?"

"You're fucking insane...you're all fucking crazy," Tremont heaved.

"Hey, you should calm down. You will have managed to save five more people. Look at this nigga Faxx, going above and beyond for the community," Henny chuckled as Tali injected a syringe filled with a liquid that had yellowish-green tint.

"No! No! No, please, no—"

Tremont's scream lasted about five seconds until he fell still. I pulled over the large mirror, setting it in front of his face. The only thing left on his body that he could move was his eyes. He tried to close them, but Tali moved, placing tape on each lid. Tremont watched in horror as each organ was harvested for as long as his body could hold out.

"I'm thinking we need to let Link, Mala, and Seyra know about those catacombs. What if that's where the phone is hidden," I considered.

"Hit them up because if anyone were able to find out for certain, it would be Link or Seyra," Henny concluded as he placed each lung inside a cooler. I headed for the door so I could make sure I was home before Crescent and Francesca would wake up. All I needed to do was find that nigga Eric, but Stax said he would handle it while I dealt with the important shit. If he didn't find him when I finished with these other niggas, he was at the top of my niggas to kill list. I didn't give a shit where that nigga was hiding. It will never be good enough because I would find that nigga, and the next broken thing on his body will be his neck.

CHAPTER
EIGHTEEN

CRESCENT 'CENT' WELLINGTON

I moaned as I was turned over and onto my back. I opened my eyes, blinking slowly as Faxx settled his large, warm body between my legs. It had gotten easier to lay on my side or stomach now that the scar wasn't so tender. I reached down and ran my fingers along his scalp, realizing he must have washed his hair because it was out.

"Everything good, Papi," I yawned. I looked over to the clock, seeing it was still early, and I was actually surprised he made it home this early. I was worried about the bandage I could feel wrapped around his ribs while, at the same time, I wanted him to tell me what the fuck happened tonight.

"Yeah, we good, *Mi Amor*," he grumbled against the skin on my stomach. I felt his hands slide up my sides, pushing my sleep tank up until he reached my nipples. He pinched them, and my clit jumped, causing me to inhale sharply and flex my fingers in his hair.

"Papi," I moaned. Then I noticed something was off when I moved my hand. My finger had healed at the same rate as my ankle, but it was still a little sore. Whatever shit Dr. Sexy was coming up with for healing needed to be on the fucking market.

"I know it's early, but do you feel up to going somewhere with me?"

I pulled my hands out of his hair and leaned over to the bedside table. Faxx's grip tightened so I couldn't fall off while trying to grab the remote for the lights. My hand was shaking slightly, but I reached it and hit the button. I settled back into the pillows and looked down at him. I reached out for his face, turning it so I could see the bruises forming on his lower jaw and the bandage that covered his bicep.

"Papi, what the fuck happened? Did you get shot? Who shot you," I demanded.

When I reached to touch his arm, I stopped halfway, seeing a ring on my hand. It wasn't the wedding set that I had before, but something entirely different.

"Don't worry about me, Cent, I'm good. It's a scratch, that's all. I'm more worried about my dick not being in your pussy, *Mi Amor*," he deflected.

I heard him, but I couldn't answer his dumb ass at the moment. I could feel his dark eyes watching me while his fingers stroked up and down my sides.

"Wh—when did you...what happened to my other ring?" I whispered.

"I don't want you wearing something that bitch touched. Too much negativity surrounding it," he reasoned. I opened my mouth and closed it as I stared at the ring. I could feel tears at the back of my eyes, but I was not about to fucking cry.

"It's so... beautiful. Oh my God, who made this or designed it? It's—"

"There is only one person we use for our jewelry. I drew it one night while looking at your tattoos because it hit me and made sense. I don't know how I missed it at first, but...it came out to ten carats. Does it need more?" he answered.

"Hell no," I shouted as I stared at my wedding ring.

The diamond butterfly sat surrounded by smaller diamonds that amounted to up to ten karats on a white-gold band. I stared at the heart of the ring, the breathtaking butterfly, its form frozen in eternal flight like the one on my chest. The butterfly's wings had my chest tightening because each one was meticulously adorned with a scattering of diamonds. The stones had to be carefully selected for their exceptional clarity because dayum! It sparkled in the light like captured stardust, casting a mesmerizing array of shimmering reflections with every movement. How the fuck had he remembered this? It had been one fucking conversation before we even called what we had anything. All I said was that I wanted my ring to reflect my body, but it was just in passing. We didn't even elaborate or stick to the subject. I didn't think this nigga would put that together. When we actually happened, I didn't give a shit what my ring looked like.

"Crescent, you already know that I can recall every word you've spoken to me. Sometimes it comes together later. But fuck all that—"

"I love you, Fransisco," I said, staring into his eyes. They were dark as fuck, even with the lights on. I could tell in his gaze that some shit went down tonight, and I was afraid to ask if they found him. His dark look, which was normally cold, felt like it was burning my skin as it traveled over my face.

"I was told tonight that my obsession for you blinds me. And I found it funny because it does nothing but focus me. *Mi Amor*, you already know how obsessive I am over you, just like you know how possessive I am of you. But my fixation with you, Crescent, gets more dangerous by the day," he whispered.

"You're fucking crazy, Fransisco," I exhaled. My chest was tight, and my core ached. I knew damn well that the words he used were not good. He was so unwell that I should really be afraid of his severe mental problems. His brows came down as he pushed up and leaned over me, licking at my lips until I opened them.

"*Mi Amor*, that's the kind of shit that get that pussy wet. You already know every thought, and every breath is mine. I've said I love you since the day I realized my fixated obsession with you was going to consume me. So, I took calculated steps to ensure I would always possess you."

"Are you sure it's not an infatuation? How can you tell the difference between the two?" I panted. His body pressed against mine as he grinded down on me. His dick pressed against my clit, giving it enough pressure that I rolled my hips, trying to get more. I exhaled trying not to fall under the spell of the dick because I wanted to hear his answer.

"Cent, I was infatuated when you rubbed that thick ass on my dick at *MYTH*. I became obsessed when you let me rub my Glock between your breasts. But I was in love the moment you covered me when those niggas blew the VIP doors open. Just don't do that shit again," he chuckled before kissing me. I felt his tongue at the roof of my mouth before he sucked my soul out. Faxx pulled back while raising my tank top and pulling my shorts down. I refused to tell him that I would do it again because I knew if I did he would stop what he was doing.

"Fuck," I breathed.

"Hmmm, let me slide in that wet ass pussy wife," he said, low and demanding.

I whined, and my head lolled to the side as he worked his dick into my tightness. His hand slid over my breasts and squeezed.

"Fuck," I moaned. I felt his other hand move as he pushed my right thigh down to the bed and slowly pulled back out to the tip. Faxx pushed slowly back into my core, moving in and out of me, drawing it out as he watched me. I couldn't control my breathing, my eyes, or my mouth as I begged for him to fuck me harder.

"Papi, Papi, please," I gasped as the stretch in my thigh that he held down burned with a pleasurable pain that made me addicted. My pussy stretched around him, and my walls held his dick so tightly he groaned as he pulled out.

"Naw, *Mi Amor*, I want this shit slow. I want to feel every inch of this pussy sliding along my dick. Can you handle that for Papi?" he grunted in my ear. Faxx pushed in slowly, sinking deep and grinding against me. I circled my hips as his hand moved from my leg, and he reached above me. He leaned down, licking my lips before moving his tongue in my mouth to the pace of his strokes.

"I didn't hear you, Cent," he said against my lips. I could barely as he thrusted and rotated his hips, making me spread my legs wider apart.

"Yes, Papi, yes," I moaned. I was willing to say anything because I needed it. I wanted it, and I loved the fullness.

"Do you want more, *Mi Amor*? Because it looks like you want me to pound that little pussy out,"

Faxx asked, pulling away from my lips.

"Oh my...oh fuck," I panted. Just the thought had my walls clamping down on Faxx's length so tight he groaned.

"Damn, Cent," he gritted.

My eyelids were heavy as the slow drag against his dick in my pussy. I wrapped a leg around his hip just as he pulled me up and got to his knees. He grunted, a momentary flash of pain crossing his face.

"Fransis—"

I started, but he rolled to the side, holding me tightly until I was straddling him. Faxx's hand slid up my chest until his finger wrapped around my neck. He used his other hand to push down on his length as he squeezed tight. My eyes rolled back as I seated myself on him, beginning to circle and rotate on him.

"Oh fuck," I panted. The up-and-down motion and Faxx's grip on my ass slammed me down harder.

"You wanted it harder? Take all that dick so I can feel that pussy jumping for me," he grunted. The grip on me and his words had me moving faster as I pressed my legs into his sides. He hissed, and I remembered his ribs, but I felt his legs bend, lifting me slightly as he stroked upward and used my neck to push me back down. I opened my eyes, and Faxx's dark eyes looked over my face and down my body.

"Papi," I gasped as his grip loosened. His hand moved to the back of my neck as I rose slightly and rocked my hip when I came back down.

"That's right, Cent. Take that shit how you want it," he grunted as he pulled me onto his chest. I felt his tongue on my ear as I moaned with each rough thrust slamming into me. I felt a smack on my ass, making me cry out and move faster, circling and bouncing as I took more of him.

I clawed mindlessly at the sheets and pillows, with each upward stroke stretching me out. I felt a finger run down my butt, moving lower and circling my hole. I was wet as fuck, and with each deep stroke, more and more of my juices slid down Faxx's dick. He used my wetness and slid it over my hole, pushing in slightly.

"Oh God! Please. Papi, I...shit, I'm going to cum," I groan in his shoulder. I felt his tongue on my neck as he pushed his finger on deeper and used his other hand to slam my ass down repeatedly. His last upward thrust, his finger pushed past his knuckle, moving in and out as he held me on his dick, pushing every single inch of his length inside. His finger pressed down when he pushed upward and moved his hips, hitting that spot that made me see stars. The press on that spot and the pressure in my ass had me convulsing atop of him cumming so hard I couldn't breathe.

"Hmmm. Shit, *Mi Amor*. Fuck," he shouted as he grinded into me. I pushed down harder, trying to ride both his dick and his finger, when his tongue pushed into my mouth, fucking it like he was fucking me through my orgasm. Faxx's firm grasp held me down on top of him while he bucked up into me, using his legs for leverage. He hit that spot every single time until I pulled away and screamed as my toes curled while another orgasm ripped through my body.

"Fuck!" I screamed.

"That pussy is so tight, Crescent, and it's so wet. That's right, cum all over Papi's dick. Make me nut Cent. Give it to me," he ordered.

Faxx snapped his hips while pumping into me and pushing to insanity as I gasped.

I raised my hips and pushed back down, moving at the pace he had set. My thighs and body shook around his length as he pounded into me, filling my entire core. Faxx moved his hand from my hip as I rocked against him and brought it to my neck, tightening his grasp and causing my eyes to roll.

"No! Keep your eyes on me so you can see how crazy this pussy makes me. Cum for me again, *Mi Amor*. Let me see it," he ordered.

My pussy clenched around him, and his grip on my neck increased with each bounce.

"Fuck Crescent! Give that pussy, baby. That's right, make your husband cum. Show me you can take it. Can you take it?" he asked.

I could barely speak as I opened my mouth. The grip lessened as black spots danced at the edges. I mumbled a string of words as Faxx's dick jerked, and he slammed harder.

"I said can you take it? Can you handle this obsession I have with you? With this pussy?"

"Ye...yes, Papi! Yes, I can," I cried, tears rolling down my face as I repeated the same words over and over. I felt his last thrust slam into me as his finger slid deeper into my ass, pressing down as his cum filled me.

"Shit! Damn, fuck, Cent," he gritted as his dick pulsated between my wet folds.

"Oh shit, shit, Papi," I gasped. My vision faded in and out. I felt his hand caressing my neck as I tried to catch my breath. He pulled me down until I was hovering over him.

"That's it, *Mi Amor*. Grip that dick and take all the cum," he whispered against my lips. I saw my tears falling on his face, and he leaned forward, licking my face before kissing back down until his lips met mine. I clasped on his chest as he pulled his finger out of my hole. I tried to keep my eyes open, but it was getting too hard.

"Fuck," I breathed.

"Hmmm, let me slide in that wet ass pussy wife," he said, low and demanding.

"Just an hour, Fransisco. I just need some sleep for an hour," I sighed. Faxx chuckled against my neck before biting it quickly. My fucking clit jumped like that bitch could do something again.

"You can sleep in the truck, *Mi Amor*. I have to take you to your wedding present," he rasped. His low rumble against my neck made my hips move.

"If it's *MYTH*, I'm not ready yet," I yawned while he laughed at my exhaustion.

"Crescent, it's a surprise. Trust me, when we next go to *MYTH*, you'll know it," he said, his voice filled with excitement. I just nodded with my eyes closed, but I noticed his excitement, and that in itself was scary as fuck. I barely moved when I felt him sitting up except for wrapping my arms around his neck.

I stretched in the seat when I felt the road change from smooth to bumpy and rough. It wasn't like that the entire way to the *RANGE*, but it told me when we had arrived. Faxx's hand on my thigh flexed slightly before he removed it to grip the steering wheel. This time, instead of going straight to the house, he turned onto a narrow road where the trees seemed closer than before.

"Is this it? Is this where you gut me like a fish for my insurance money," I yawned. Faxx looked at his watch before cutting his eyes to me.

"I really think you do believe one day I'm going to snap and take you out," he chuckled.

"Nigga, have you met yourself? Clearly, you're insane, not crazy, even though I say it. You should be happy that I just like living dangerously and shit," I replied. I leaned forward, tapping the screen so my seat would adjust to a sitting position.

"What I find hilarious is it's you who are actually the insane one," he answered. I blinked a few times as we approached a tall gate. Faxx's window went down as he held out his arm to a scanner on a wooden pole.

"How so? I really want to understand your logic on this shit," I laughed.

With the window down, I could feel the chilly, misty air as Faxx smirked once he leaned back inside. The window went up, and he leaned his head on the headrest and looked at me.

"Your husband is diagnosed with antisocial personality disorder, but this is what's insane. Your work husband has the same issue on top of multiple personalities. So again, which one of us is the crazy one?" he asked. The gate slid open, and he hit the gas, leaving me to glare at the smirk on his face.

The RANGE was a vast expanse of woodland that I wouldn't have ever known existed on the outskirts of Union City. It was a private place where chaos, murder, and torture knew no limit. And I knew all of this and was still in the fucking truck. I hated when this nigga was right.

"I don't like you, Fransisco," I said, leaning forward.

"I don't need you to like me. I need more than that, *Mi Amor*. I need you barely able to think straight when you don't say my name for a period of time," he said, making a right.

"Obsessed?" I laughed.

"Completely," he said as we ventured deeper into the woods. The sun began to peek through the dense canopy, casting dappled light on the forest floor. I could feel my anticipation, curiosity, and paranoia growing the longer we drove. I prayed this nigga wouldn't have me out here running a damn marathon after fucking me like that. Because this bitch will sit in this fucking truck while he hunted himself. Eventually, we arrived at the far part of the property that I'd never been to. It felt different, almost ominous, and I began to sense we were about to do something too much for this early in the morning.

"Faxx, what's going on? Why are we here?" I asked, looking around.

"Trust me, Crescent. Just a little further, but we need to get out. Let's go," Faxx reassured me as he opened the door. I slid my feet into my sneakers, and he opened the door, gripping my hand to help me out. Faxx held onto my hand tightly, lacing our fingers as he went off the dirt road and into the woods.

"Is this is some wrong turn type of shit?" I huffed.

He didn't answer me, but I saw the serious look on his face as we stepped out into a clearing. It reminded me of the area where Tony was buried in the ground, but this was in the middle of nowhere while we were in the middle of nowhere. My heart skipped a beat when I saw him—

"Roman," I whispered. I stared at the man who had held me captive for two and a half years. I knew I had frozen in shock because Faxx stopped walking. My breath caught in my throat as memory after memory of beatings, mental torture, starvation, stabbings, and grazes from the bullets from being shot at. Everything replayed in my mind like a record of the worst mistake I could've made in my life.

"*Mi Amor*, it ain't shit that nigga can do to you now. All of that shit in your head happened to Crescent Johnson. You're Crescent Wellington, and your husband found a way to bury your past so you can focus on the future you want," he said.

Faxx stood in front of me, blocking my view of Roman. I felt his tatted hand grip my jaw and lift my face, so I looked up at him. The two quick cornrows I put in his hair hung down his shoulders. I blinked, and I looked into his eyes, seeing exactly what I needed to see. A cold dead-eye stare that should have had me made my instincts to run turn on, but all it did was get my nipples hard and my pussy wet. I closed my eyes because this nigga was right. He had me turnt out, obsessed, and fucking pressed over him, knowing what I knew about him. I was completely insane.

"How? Is...is that where you got the bruises?" I demanded, my voice rising with a mix of emotions—fear, anger, and disbelief. Disbelief because he'd gotten hurt, and that should've never been able to happen.

"Crescent, you need closure. So, whatever I need to do to make sure you have what you need will be done. If I need to take a few hits, I will. Because if I didn't hold back, I would've killed that nigga," he seethed. His eyes were filled with so much hate, rage, and death I would have taken a step back. But I didn't move and waited until his eyes focused back on me. When he did, if you were looking, you could see the slight change in them.

"Don't fucking get hurt again, Fransisco. I don't care what the reason is."

"Naw, all that shit was worth it so that I could see this. Don't freeze. Just do what you need to do, say what you need to say, and let me know when you're ready," Faxx encouraged. I wasn't sure if that meant ready for a gun or a grenade, but I guess time would tell. Faxx pulled away his hand, sliding it over my chin and down my neck before turning around. He stepped to the side, and this time, I saw what I didn't see at first. Roman looked...he looked terrible. His usually light brown skin looked gray, and his brown eyes that glared at me looked washed out and filled with pain. But his appearance wasn't what had my attention. It was the fact that Faxx had this man in some kind of container that looked like it was made of glass, but even from this distance, I could tell it wasn't. I could only see him from the shoulders up because my crazy ass husband buried this nigga alive in a sealed fucking container.

I took a step forward, my gaze locked with Roman's. The memories flooded back again—the fear, the pain, and the years of my life stolen from me. Instead of freezing, I could feel burning rage building up inside me, boiling over into a fury that I had never felt before. I felt Faxx at my back, his arm snaking around my waist as he wrapped the other around my chest.

His touch was possessive, suffocating, and obsessive. It was what I needed while I stared at a man who took so much pride in his looks buried in dirt with half of his face.

"Why? All you needed to do was leave me the fuck alone," I demanded, my voice shaking with a mix of rage and hurt. "You took so much from me. You stole my freedom and my sense of safety and tried to destroy me. But I refuse to let you hold power over me, and you know that. You hated me for it."

Roman's cold, uncaring, flat, pained stare met mine, and a bitter laugh escaped his lips.

"Why, Crescent? Because I could and because no one else wanted you. Not your mother and definitely not your father. And because you were mine to control, to break. You were nothing but a pawn in a game you knew nothing about and a toy for my amusement," he spat, his words like venom. He wrinkled his nose as she shifted in the packed dirt.

The weight of his callous confession turned the simmering anger into searing rage. I felt Faxx behind me, his body pressed tightly to my back, and his arms squeezed tighter around me. I glared at Roman, my fists clenched at my sides.

"At least your face finally resembles the fucking monster you really are," I seethed. "I tried to control me. You tried to break me, but you couldn't manage to do either one. You made my life feel like I was buried alive under piles of shit. You dumped that on me because you weren't shit and will never be shit," I laughed.

"Remember, in the beginning, you used to like that shit. You wanted to take the shit I dished out because you weren't shi—"

"He's buried in a pile of shit. Isn't that right, Roman?" Faxx snapped. "Take a deep fucking breath and take in all that bullshit you tried to bury my wife in. You talk so much shit, then came into my fucking city and thought you could take what's mine. That is what put you where you are right now," Faxx seethed.

"That's shit?" I laughed lightly. The grimaced pain on Roman's face as he gagged told me what I wanted to know.

"Shit, and the ashes of the niggas that rode with him on this suicide mission. Y'all niggas came at U.C.K. and thought you were going to walk out. Naw, my nigga that isn't the way it works," Faxx chuckled.

"He's going to use you. He's going to do exactly what I did. Think Cent! That nigga ain't no different," Roman screamed. I clenched my hand into a fist, wishing I could finish ripping the skin off the rest of his face. I tried to take a step forward, but Faxx stopped me.

"NO Papi! He doesn't get to say that shit. My husband will never be anything close to the sick, demented pedophile that you are. Fuck you," I shouted. Faxx pulled me closer, and I wished he would let me go so I could pull out Rose.

"Shh, shh, *Mi Amor*. Calm down and look at him. Look at him, Crescent. He's weak, pathetic, and a bitch ass nigga who needed help from people who would have killed you when it was over," Faxx raged. I could feel his body vibrating from anger the longer he stared at Roman.

"Fuck you! What else can you do to me? I'm dead if I get out of here and dead if I sit here. You destroyed me, but I refuse to let you hold power over me any longer," I said, releasing a breath. What in the hell was I doing? Why did I feel like I needed to know his reasons for what he did? I wanted to confront him for so long, but now that I can, there's no point. I didn't need to hear or see this nigga anymore. I didn't need explanations because I already knew how this world was, and it was full of people like him, ready to do whatever it took for money. Roman was right, and I was just a pawn in a game between sick ass people who don't deserve my words.

I took a deep breath and released it. I let my body fall still against Faxx as I stared at Roman, who still had a little smile on his face. I knew it was because me continuing to ask him why I was just handing him power, and I refused to let that shit go on any longer.

"You may have haunted my past, Roman, but you will never define my future," I declared, my voice unwavering. "I'm ready, Papi," I insisted.

"Did you get what you need from it?" Faxx asked as he pulled away. I could hear the concern in his voice, but it wasn't needed. I was holding on to shit because I didn't know how to let go.

"Yes, Fransisco. It's good, so can I shoot him now," I asked. I stared at Roman while I said it, not moving my glare away from him.

"What? Naw, *Mi Amor*. It ain't no shooting this nigga. He isn't worth the round it would take to kill him. I need him to feel that shit when it happens, painfully and slowly."

I turned to look up at him, wondering what kind of crazy shit he was about to have me do.

"Tell me what I need to do," I stated with my hand out. Faxx looked at my hand and back to my face as a deranged smile formed on his lips. The little brown I saw earlier was gone, and a cold intensity blanketed them. He reached out, took my hand, and faced me toward Roman.

"Press right here, but make sure you watch him. I want you to see what I fucking do to niggas who think fucking with me, and mine, is a game," he grunted. I looked down at his watch, actually seeing what was on it for the first time. The black screen lit up with a blue dot in the middle of waves flowing across the screen. I swallowed, not sure what in the hell this shit would do, but I was pretty sure it had to do with a bomb. I pressed the center of the dot and then stared at Roman.

"Www...wha...ahhh.ahhh...wh...is....wha....ahhh—"

Roman screamed, but to me, it sounded muffled. I watched as his eyes widened, and the top of his head turned a bright red. Sweat began to pour down his face as he began to foam at the mouth. My breath caught as blood began to run from his eyes, his ears, and his nose. Roman's blood-covered eyes rolled in his head as his body shook uncontrollably, and red and pinkish fluid poured out of his mouth.

"What in the fuck is happening?" I asked. I wanted to look away, but at the same time, I was fascinated by the sight. Faxx drew in a deep breath before answering his face in lines of enjoyment as he watched.

"Link designed this container for me when I told him I wanted a person's organs to explode and liquify inside their body slowly. It's very painful because it's not all at once but one at a time. Certain frequencies can accomplish it, and that container can withstand a blast, as well as the vibration needed for this.

"Jesus Jerome Christ. Somebody needs to get Link's ass off the mutha fuckin' streets. But what happens after? Does he just die? That's...that's anticlimactic," I finished, still watching as Roman's body moved, but it was weakened.

"Nope. The brain is the last to go, and it explodes." Faxx chuckled as a muffled pop sounded, and Roman's head was gone, blown apart. All that was left to show was his tattooed neck and a body buried in the pile of shit that he tried to make my life.

"I have to say that this is at least the top five best wedding presents I received," I whispered. The relief I felt, and the knowledge that this nigga couldn't do what he did to me to another young girl had me releasing a breath that I felt I'd been holding for years.

"What's number one?" Faxx asked. I turned around, looking up into his confused and narrowed black eyes. He tilted his head from side to side with a smile that made him look like that clown, the *Terrifier*. I didn't know if he realized that shit, but it was not normal.

"Cece becoming legally mine. And dick, most definitely the dick," I laughed. Faxx looked me over before raising a brow. His real smile crossed his face as he smoothed a hand over his bread.

"You still have time before you need to be at the center. How about you let me slide my dick down your throat so you can blow his head off."

I felt the slickness between my thighs as he stepped closer. I married a sexy, psycho, deranged, and unhinged man, and I saw no problem with it.

FUCK, HE WAS RIGHT, I WAS THE MORE INSANE ONE.

I walked into the Women's Center slowly still sore as hell from fucking with Faxx. My plan was to drive today because I was going to be spending some time with Dylan after my shift. But, this mornings events kind of derailed things with that and also put us both into some shit. Instead of going back to the house I ended up showering again at the house on the *RANGE*. From there Faxx took me to work and went back home for Cece. I held the phone to my ear while my baby whined about Papi not fixing her hair right and she had to get Aunt Nia to do it so she could be cute for her boyfriend.

"Mommy, you didn't help me with my morning afformations," Cece sighed.

"Affirmations, and I'm sorry. Can Papi help you this morning with them?" I said, dropping my bag on the desk and waving to the new receptionist.

"Yes, be normal, act normal. I got it. But Mommy, I didn't see you before you left. It's not fair because Papi did. I can only see you on my tablet," she sighed. I looked up at the camera and smiled, trying not to laugh as Faxx grumbled in the background, '*It's not boyfriend, its friend, just a friend.*'

"How about I tell Papi to bring you here after school? You get out early today and you can come and help me with all these patients," I bargained.

"Yes! I can be Nurse Cece! Does anybody need a needle?"

"Ahh, we'll see. Give Papi the phone and you finish getting ready. Love you," I said, shaking my head.

"Te amo!"

I heard the phone shuffle like she dropped it to the floor before Faxx came over the line.

"*Mi Amor*, this is what I mean. I'm starting to think Link is right about this shit. She always loved my hairstyles. I took a class for this shit," he said sucking his teeth. I held in my laugh because I knew his ass just like I knew Cece. I was sure he was looking at me.

"Papi, its normal. Don't you want her to be normal and experience normal things?" I urged.

"You better have a fucking boy because I can't handle this shit again," he ranted. I rolled my eyes because I had no idea why he thought I was pregnant, but whatever. The more I thought about it, the more I figured I should just make an appointment with Seyra. If I was, I wanted to be sure, sure about it. Because I was pretty sure the way he fucks me, he probably knocked my IUD into my cervix. If not, I'll just get it removed.

"Whatever you say Papi. Listen bring Cece here when she gets out of school. I said she could chill with me for the rest of the day," I said. I turned my badge around and made my way towards Tali's office.

"Bet. I need to make a few moves so Damari will be bringing y'all home," he decided.

"Okay, let me go find Tali's ass so I can see what I need to do today," I said. We disconnected as I knocked lightly on Tali's office door.

"Yes," she answered wearily. I pushed the door open and stepped inside the large space. I pushed the door shut behind me as the scent of mangoes filled my nose.

"What in the hell is wrong with you?" I said walking closer. Tali was leaning back in her chair with her hands in her lap. When I got to the desk that was separating us, I saw her holding an ice pack. My eyes widened and I burst out laughing.

"Shut up Crescent. This shit isn't funny first of all," she groaned.

"What in the hell did Dr. Sexy do to you? It looks like he broke something down there because bissh," I laughed.

"You're fired," Tali muttered. I laughed even harder as she squeezed her eyes shut.

"I...I'm sorry. For real, I am, because I think I need one too. I don't know what time they on but—"

Tali opened her gray eyes and raised her hand in the air.

"It was because of last night bissh. I'm sure you know by now," she ventured.

"If you are referring to that dick-riding bald-ass nigga then yes. He had a...a mind-blowing revelation this morning," I smiled. Tali's eyes stayed on me as she nodded.

"Yeah well, I stabbed him in his thigh. I should have stabbed him in his dick but that would have raised his pressure even more, so there's that," she shrugged.

"Bissh, I know you lying! I wish I was there. Why the fuck didn't you call me?" I said slamming my hand on the desk.

"Girl bye, I had no idea what was going on. I was in bed asleep when Henny texted that he needed me. At that time of night and he wasn't home that only meant one thing. So, I went. I just wasn't expecting to see...Tremont or Roman," she stated. She stared at me for a long moment and I couldn't tell what the hell she was seeing.

"Well, we won't see him again. How about Tre? Did Dr. Dickhead get the message this time?" I asked.

"Yes, everything went successful, and I even learned a new technique. I never thought of being this interested in actual surgery. Fuck," she moaned when she moved.

"Okay bissh, give me the details because you look...pained," I winced.

"I started to let him do this training shit, and…I…may have asked for him to fuck me harder the deeper the toy was in there. He was saying all kinds of shit because it was right after surgery, and he gets—"

"If it's anything like that night…I…ahh—"

"Bissh fuck my beat-up pussy. Freaking *Myth*! Bissh, I've been to some places and have done some things, but…that was intense. I think because it's—"

"Bissh because it's us! I wasn't—"

I stopped and looked around the office like somebody was going to overhear me or some shit. I wasn't worried about Cece because there were no cameras in the offices.

"I wasn't expecting any of that…I swear to God I didn't know…bissh…bitch platinum," I dropped my head feeling fucked up.

"Crescent, fucking mango," she deadpanned. I snorted, and she threw a pen at me. I looked up, trying to hold back, but I needed to know.

"Sanchez?"

"Awwww God, that nigga. Listen, I was wrong. Completely fucking wrong because a soda can didn't do that thick-ass dick no justice. I was trying to figure out how Seyra was taking that shit."

"Oh shit, not the soda ain't do justice," I groaned.

"When it came at me, I was like, ain't no way that bullet train going to fit," she huffed.

"Trust me, I don't know if you saw when the Black wolf entered, but this nigga told me I had to breathe through it. How do you breathe through a fucking horse dick being shoved down your throat?" I rasped.

"Oh my God! Please…please, I can't…my pu…stop," Tali laughed.

"It was one thing to be told by your work husband to fucking cum for him, but then I got a nigga with a wolf mask saying *'Lick it, Cent. Stick out that tongue so I can push my nut down your throat.'* Like bissh, what the fuck," I shuddered.

"Exactly! Seyra was telling that three-legged nigga to make me gag on—"

Tali closed her mouth as the door opened. Her eyes widened slightly as the familiar scent of Henny filled the room. I pressed my lips together and took a deep breath to chill the hell out.

"So, what else did you need me to do today?" I asked. I knew my breath had picked up as Henny stepped behind me.

"Mmm, I really need you to help Stax with the orientation. I would, but—"

"I got it! No problem," I said before looking over my shoulder. "Hey, Dr. Sexy, what's up?" I gasped.

"Work wife, I don't get a hug now," he grinned. I turned fully around and looked at him, really seeing the difference this time. The black framed glasses, the suit, and the tie hid every tattoo on his body. I wrapped my arms around his waist, and he kissed my forehead. I heard something drop on Tali's desk as he folded his arms around me.

"Why do you always smell like this? This why them bitches be trippin'," I noted.

"Fuck them. But if you want to know what it's called, the name of it is Platinum," he grinned, rubbing his hand on my back. I fucking shuddered and tried to pull back, but he just turned me around and wrapped his arm across my chest. Tali's punk ass was trying not to laugh at my face.

"Hendrix, stop messing with Cent. She needs to get to work and not be walking around with wet panties," Tali shifted, then grimaced. I felt when Henny pulled away, but I knew it had nothing to do with giving me a reprieve.

"*Thickness*, stand up," Henny ordered. I looked at the file folder that he put down that said my name. I frowned, picking it up and looking it over.

"Come here and sit down, baby. Do you need me to kiss that pussy so it can feel better?" he asked.

"I mean, I'm not going to say no," Tali moaned. She laid her head on his chest as he leaned back in the chair.

"Hmmm, you got that *Thickness*. Cent, Justice dropped that in my office earlier when she came through," Henny stated.

"Okay, thanks. Let me head out so I can help Stax, and y'all can be office hoes," I smiled. I backed out of the office, locking the door behind me. I was slightly nervous because I knew that this envelope was the decision about Dylan. I grabbed my purse and headed for the main hospital. I tore open the envelope as I navigated through people, looking through the papers feeling relieved, sad, and tired. I already knew Jacinda would be on some good bullshit once she found out, but it was what it was. She wasn't looking out for Dylan's best interest, and once she figured out she wouldn't be getting that money, Jacinda would leave that girl like she had done me. Except this time, my grandmother wouldn't be there to save her like she did me .

I kept walking, dodging through the bustling hospital corridors. My mind raced with everything that had happened over the past few months. It was hard to believe that I wouldn't need to look over my shoulder for Roman anymore, but that still didn't mean I could get complacent. Being kidnapped proved that to me in full color. A threat could come from anywhere and anyone at this point. Especially now that I'm married and connected to people that were dangerous as fuck. Enemies could come from everywhere because when you are at the top, everybody wants to take your spot.

This would be the first time I worked with Stax, and I was curious to see how he would conduct the orientation for new staff members. He was very laid back in the kind of way he could blend into the background. That was, until he stood up or spoke, but it was always a few words. He didn't have the same dark brown eyes as Faxx. They were more of a warm brown, just like his skin tone. When we were at his house, I normally saw him in a man bun. I was actually excited about chilling with Stax today because he just gave off the older brother, 'I'll protect you' vibe. I got it, though, because he had to raise three children on his own.

I made my way to the designated meeting room, and my thoughts were suddenly interrupted by a familiar voice calling my name.

"Crescent!"

My breath caught in my throat, and the shame for how I pushed the person who was there for me away, had my eyes tearing. I turned around, forcing a smile on my face as Cressida stopped in front of me. I looked her over and smiled, loving how she had become exactly what she had set out to be. Her long white coat covered her pale green blouse with her name embroidered on the front of it. Cressida smoothed a hand down her tan, wide-legged dress pants, and looked back up at me.

"Too much? I wanted to look professional, but approachable," she stammered.

I blinked and shook my head, reaching out to soothe her nerves. Her eyes lit up at my ring, and she grabbed my hand. I only pushed Cressida away so she and her family wouldn't get hurt. I repeated in my head. But I could tell her that now—at least the reason why.

"It's not too much, girl. You look great," I said.

"Forget about me! You! Is this why you've been M.I.A. because you got engaged?" she grinned.

"Oh...oh no, I was...sick, but I'm better now. That's what I wanted to talk to you about before. This is very new. I still can't believe you're here," I choked.

Cressida dropped my hand as she smiled slightly, but I could see the hurt in her eyes. She bushed her hair over her shoulder and nodded.

"I am, and congratulations," she smiled. "Crescent, it's been years! I know you said we would talk, but then you disappeared again. I never expected to run into you here, of all places, when I came that day, but I have to believe there's a reason. What the crap is going on, and how have you really been?" she asked.

I could hear the anger in her voice, but it was mainly full of concern for me. Cressida had always been compassionate and loved to help others to the detriment of herself. She deserved to know what I couldn't tell her back then.

"I've been...okay. Things have been tough, but I'm getting through it, and life is better. How about you?" I sighed.

"I've been good, but busy as heck with work and life. But Cent, that isn't important. Why did you stop contacting me? Why did you push your family away like that? You know my parents loved you like you were their own child. They were devastated, but there was nothing they could do. They even went as far as contacting Jacinda, but of course, that didn't go anywhere. That was another reason I was surprised when she showed up in church, but I wanted to believe she'd changed. We used to be so close, and then you just disappeared," she finished. Cressida was taller than me. Even in flats, I still had to look up. She threw her head back, and I could tell she was trying not to cry.

"Cress, don't cry and mess up your make-up. You look too good for all that," I smiled. And she laughed.

"Seriously, Cent, what the heck?" she exhaled.

"I know, I know, and I'm truly sorry. It's just... after everything with Roman, I felt like I couldn't burden anyone with my problems. I was ashamed, and I didn't want to drag you or your parents into my mess. Roman...he was dangerous, just like you said, and I should've listened. I know that," I finished. I felt tears burning at the back of my eyes again, but I refused to cry here.

"Roman? That...that...butthole. He was no good at all. Did he...what happened, Crescent? You can tell me," she stepped closer. I looked around, and even though this area wasn't as busy, I knew it wasn't the place for this conversation. But I would give her the highlights because she deserved that much.

"It's hard to talk about, but the short version is that he was abusive. I didn't realize it at first, but it got worse over time. I burned all my bridges by then, and my mother, of course, wasn't shit. I felt trapped, and it took a long time for me to break free. It's been a difficult journey since then, but worth it in the end," I smiled.

Cressida sucked in a breath and clenched her teeth together. If her dark brown skin could turn red, I was sure she would be. I reached for her hand, and she took it as she exhaled.

"I knew it. I freaking knew that son of a...ahh. Crescent, I'm so sorry you had to go through that. I wish you had reached out to me for help or even when you managed to escape. I would've... would've done something. At the very least, been there for you," she whispered.

"I knew you would have, but...time. So much time had passed, and so much happened. But I know you would have, and I regret not confiding in you. That's why I want you to come with me to a therapy session. I need to explain everything in detail, and I want you to understand why I kept it all hidden. If you can't or don't want to, I understand," I said quickly.

"Give me a minute to process everything because I'm upset that you didn't tell me sooner, but I understand why you felt that way. Therapy is a good option, and you, of all people, should understand how much it's needed after something like this. I'll come. I will come to the therapy session with you, Cent," she nodded.

"I want to make things right between us. It's been too long, and I'm ready for this shit to come to a close," I said, squeezing Cressida's hand. She stared at me, trying to look stern, but the smile trembling on her lips fucked it up.

"Still cursing, I see. I value our friendship, too, Crescent. I may need some time to process all of this, but I'll be there for you. Anytime and every time," she sighed.

"This is heavy," Tali sighed.

"It is, but at least there's one good thing to come out of it," she shrugged.

"What?" I frowned.

"Roman is out of the picture, and Jacinda has apparently moved on to another scheme," she pointed out.

"True, that is very true. Jacinda is...she will always land on her feet, I guess. As for Roman, he's definitely out of the picture and probably knee-deep in some shit somewhere," I laughed.

Cressida laughed with me, shaking her head, but I could still see the mixture of concern and sadness in her gaze. Before our conversation could continue, a call for all attendees of the orientation that was about to begin, sounded over the intercom.

"Oh shit, I need to go," I said, excusing myself.

"I guess we both do because that's exactly where I'm going," Cressida said on my heels.

I pushed through the large hospital conference room doors, opening them as Cressida and I rushed in, scanning the room filled with new employees. Cressida quickly took a seat up at the front, her expression a mix of surprise, shock, curiosity, and...lust as I made my way to the front to join Dr. Wellington.

"Hey, Stax," I smiled, still concerned at Cressida's look.

"Little sister, how are you feeling? Is my brother treating you like a Queen?" He turned to smile at me. I caught his eyes looking to the side of me and widened slightly, but he closed his face down as he looked back in my direction.

"He better. Fransisco knows what's up and that I have no problem shooting him to make his ass comply," I joked. Stax chuckled as he stood to his six-foot and four-inch height. His muscular chest was barely fucking hidden under his white dress shirt, and his hair was neatly pulled into a braided style, so it was off his shoulders.

"I'm not sure if he wouldn't actually like that, so just be careful, and tell him I said don't fuck up," he said softly. I've never heard Stax so much as raise his voice, but the shit was...smooth, deep, and commanding.

"I do all the time," I said, looking over the presentation. I sat my things down next to the long table at the front and waited for Stax to get things started.

The presentation began, and I assisted Stax as he guided the new staff through the orientation session. His expertise, smooth tone, and charisma held the room's attention, and the atmosphere was one of eager anticipation as we delved into the details of hospital protocols and best practices.

The presentation reached the section on C.P.R. instruction in no time. Stax suddenly pointed to Cressida, who was sitting up front, and asked her to join him as his assistant. To my surprise, Cressida appeared...flustered, or was it terrified by request? I watched as she swallowed hard and shakily stood to her feet. She cast quick glances at me while she hesitantly made her way to the front. I sensed an underlying tension, or was it sexual frustration? Hell, I didn't even know if she'd lost her virginity yet. Cressida stood there, her eyes wide as she stared at Stax with a 'what the fuck' expression.

We waited while Stax paired people together to start the hands-on portion of the class, and as the room filled with the sound of shuffling chairs and murmured conversations, I couldn't help but notice the way Stax positioned himself in front of Cressida. He was looking down at her with an expression I couldn't place. It was a look someone gave to a person they never thought they would see again. The way he licked his lips as his lips pulled into a smile had me clutching my fucking pearls. What the hell? I watched the interaction unfold like this shit was a live T.V. show streaming just for me. Ahh, shit now, but did she know...who he was? Naw, naw, she couldn't have had an idea who she was talking to right now.

I moved around the room, sticking close, so I could eavesdrop. I wanted to send Faxx a text, but my phone was in my purse. I watched Cressida's nervous movements as she stood next to Stax. I moved around to the other side of the table to mess with some papers, so I could hear what the hell they were saying. This shit was wild because ain't no way in hell Cress would fuck with a U.C.K. man.

"Cressida, it's been quite some time. How have you been?" Stax asked. His gaze traveled over her before going back to her eyes. I could see the moment Cressida almost ran the fuck out. She put a hand to her chest as she met his gaze.

"I've been well, Dr. Wellington, thank you," she replied, her voice betraying a hint of nervousness. Jesus, she was still a virgin! She's had to be.

"Santino. You know better, Cressida."

"It's good to see you again, Santino," she smiled. I saw her eyes flick over to me, but she adjusted and stood straighter.

A subtle smile played at the corners of Stax's lips before he chuckled. He knew damn well he was way, way too much for that girl.

"I'm pleased to see you, Cressida. I didn't think you were ever going to return to Union City. From what I remember, Briggerton General in Cape Cliffs was where you saw yourself," he smiled.

"I was offered an opportunity that I couldn't pass up. Union has always been home to me, and…I'm glad that I decided to move back," she said, glancing at me. I knew I looked like a spectator watching a match as Stax listened to every word, his eyes lingering on her, and were filled with an undeniable attraction. More like a need or…fuck. Ahh shit, no, it was like she was a possession. Maybe I was way too into this shit and projecting my own relationship craziness onto them. Stax wasn't Faxx. And he, clearly, was the stable one out of the group. He was here to make sure they stayed alive if it got serious. I put down the papers and began to make my way back over to people who might need help. You could see they were the only two people in their room, lost in their own private exchange.

I stood up from showing a team the proper placement for their hands when, before I could process the situation, a strong grip wrapped around my arm, pulling me forcefully around to face them. Eric, the nigga that seemed to never learn his fucking lesson. I thought a broken wrist would have been enough to remind him not to go around touching people. His bitch ass had the nerve to fucking be here like shit was sweet. I glanced around, but luckily, no one was paying attention. I twisted and yanked down, breaking his hold on me.

"What the hell are you doing here, Eric?" I hissed.

"Crescent," Eric spat, his voice laced with accusation. "You're the reason my sister is gone. What the fuck did you do to her?" he gritted.

My heart raced as anger and disbelief mingled within me. This nigga was bugged the fuck out. He couldn't be serious.

"I don't know what the hell you're talking about, Eric. If anything, I should be demanding answers from you. You know exactly what happened, and you know it," I shot back, my voice trembling with rage.

Eric stepped closer, getting into my personal space, and I raised my brow. I didn't give a fuck who was here. If this nigga moved wrong, Rose would be the last bitch he sees.

"If you would have stopped and thought about the slut shit you were doing, we wouldn't be here now. My sister understands that all I want to do is save you from yourself. I would've in Clapton, but that nigga made you quit going to classes before I could. You need to come with me, Crescent. You can't say we didn't have something between us."

"You're fucking delusional. I wouldn't have gone with you anywhere, Eric. That's not what this was, and you knew that. Stop this bullshit and leave. Fuck you and your sister's crazy stalking asses," I said in a low forceful tone.

"That nigga ain't here this time Cent," he spat, reaching out for me again. I had my hand at my back when Stax stepped in between us. His imposing presence seemed to fill up the space and air surrounding us. It felt...it felt dangerous as fuck. I've never seen Stax look at anyone the way he was staring down at Eric. I didn't even know how he saw us because we were partially behind a half-wall separating stations for the next portion of the class. Stax's dead-eyed stare fixed on Eric, who visibly faltered under the intensity of it.

"This doesn't have anything...to do with you. It's between me and my girl," Eric humbled.

Stax's unwavering glare felt heavy, but it was his silence that had my breathing increasing.

"Eric Manning, correct?" Stax asked in a monotone voice. Eric's lips pressed together, his eyes glancing toward me, but Stax leaned in the way.

"That's none of your business, man. I can deal with this shit later," Eric said, turning away.

Mistake. That was a fucking mistake to turn your back on a predator, and no matter what, I thought this Stax was just that. He reached out, gripping the back of Eric's neck tightly, almost making it look like a bro hug or some shit.

"My fucking sister is my fucking problem, nigga. I guess you couldn't resist that text, could you? You and I have something to discuss about your procedure," Stax grumbled.

"Stax? It's way too many people—"

I sucked in a breath when Bryson walked inside through the back entrance and frowned. His thick brows pulled down as he made his way over to us. I knew him only because he used to do all of Mrs. Naomi's X-rays, and he was cool as shit.

"You good Dr. Wellington?" Bryson asked. His voice was deep, but you wouldn't think so at how tall and skinny he was, but his body was toned as fuck. Bryson folded his arms across his chest, his biceps flexing.

"Yeah, we're good. Thanks for coming up. I got a call that some equipment was needed that wasn't in the emergency room. I need you to take Crescent and pick it up from the other main imaging center," Stax said. He never took his eyes off Eric, and it was like Eric was paralyzed.

"Stax, I can't go with—"

Stax glanced at me quickly and put his gaze back on Eric.

"It's fine, Cent, he's family," Stax answered. Bryson raised his brows and then nodded, pushing up his sleeve, revealing a crown and the letters U.C.K. on his arm.

"But—"

"Grab your things, Crescent. Shantel will be here in an hour with Francesca," Stax ordered. I swallowed, my eyes glancing at Eric, who apparently could not move or speak.

"Now, Crescent," he gritted. I wanted to know what Stax had done, but at the same time, my feet moved to obey him, and I followed Bryson out of the door.

We walked silently over to his car, and I raised my brows.

"Ooouu, this is nice," I said as he hit the key fob to unlock the doors.

"Thanks, this is my baby, because I am not having children," Bryson laughed. He opened the door, and I climbed inside of the Lexus. I buckled up as he slid in the driver's seat, starting the engine.

"Is this a convertible?" I asked, looking around. I might have to tell Faxx that I need this shit.

"Yeah, it's a Lexus LC 500 Convertible hardtop. You like this shit, huh?" he chuckled. The imaging center wasn't far, but it would be faster if we drove. I figured Stax just wanted me far away from Eric, and I was not trying to argue with Big Brother.

"Yeah, I'm feeling it," I smiled.

"So...so when the hell your ass hook up with U.C.K. because I ain't never think...well, word around the hospital is—"

"Don't fucking start! I am not fucking Dr. Sexy," I snapped.

"Dr. Sexy? I mean that shit right there is a dead giveaway. I don't know, Cent," Bryson glanced at me, grinning.

"It's not funny, man. He stays fucking with me, but it's...not..." I trailed off as I leaned forward to look in the side mirror at this big ass black Ford F-250 or 450. I didn't know which, but that bitch was moving.

"He stays fucking with...what the fuck? What the fuck is wrong with this nigga?" Bryson grunted, reaching down to the side of his door.

"I don't know, they—"

The truck had to press on the gas as it got into the other lane and passed us.

"What the fuck!" Bryson roared. The truck spun around, doing a full three-sixty, causing us to slam on brakes.

"Oh my God—" I screamed as Bryson swerved slightly as the huge truck faced us. We weren't going fast, but this shit was fucking insane.

"Ahh fuck this shit. What the fuck is wrong with them," Bryson gritted as he swung the door open. I saw the gun in his hand as he stepped out of the car. I fumbled with my seatbelt when the passenger door to the truck swung open.

"Oh no. Oh, shit," I screamed, jumping out of the car as Faxx moved up on Bryson.

"What the fuck I tell you, Cent? Who the fuck is this nigga? It's like you want niggas to die," Faxx shouted. Bryson had stopped moving, but that shit didn't mean anything because Faxx was already on him, knocking the gun out of his hand as cars blew their horns zooming by.

"Faxx! Faxx, stop! He's..."

"Yo, yo, yo, Faxx, hold up," Bryson said, his hands up. I came around the front of the car, vaguely hearing another door slam shut.

"Papi! Please stop it. We were just going to pick up equipment," I said, pulling at his shirt. It was wet, and when I looked at my hand, it had a tinge of red. "Papi!"

"What the fuck did I say Crescent?" Faxx asked. His Glock was at Bryson's head, and I was about to panic.

"He's U.C.K. Faxx. He isn't random and—"

"You think I give a fuck?" he asked, looking at me.

"Shit, Faxx, it's me! It's Bryson. Cent, why didn't you say you were with this crazy ass nigga?"

I felt a hand on my shoulder and saw Link frowning, but then it cleared.

"Fransisco, let that man go. You know who he is, my nigga," Link chuckled.

"I don't know this mot—"

"Gabe. Gabriel's husband," Link said, laughing.

"I don't give a fuck who husband he is when he rides with my fucking wife in the car," Faxx gritted. But he moved the Glock and stepped back slightly.

"Ahh, hell naw. Nope. Fuck this shit. Crescent, girl, I like you, but never again. I need to—"

Bryson shook his head as he pulled out his phone and hit a button on the side.

"Yes?"

"Babe! I'm done. I can't do this U.C.K. shit anymore. Look at this," he said, turning the phone around. Link was on my shoulder shaking as Faxx stared at Bryson like he was figuring out the best way to dispose of him.

"Baby, you are U.C.K. What are you talking about?" Gabriel asked, confused.

"This nigga Faxx tried to kill me," he shouted.

"Did he hit you? Shoot you?" he asked.

"No! But—"

"Then you all good. He's not going to kill you," Gabriel sighed.

"No, he isn't!" I shouted, pushing Faxx. "Nigga, you got to stop showing the crazy out in the open. Stax said it was fine and—

"Stax told you to go with him?" Faxx asked quietly. My face screwed up, and I nodded.

"Yes...he said."

"Oh, well, that's all you needed to say, *Mi Amor*. Let's not tell him about this little incident," Faxx smiled before kissing my forehead. He and Link jogged back to the truck, and I looked over at Bryson. This nigga Faxx was more worried about Stax, than someone calling the police!

"I know you fucking lying!" Bryson scoffed.

The elevator doors dinged, and I grabbed Cece's hand as I stepped into the sterile, fluorescent-lit hallway of the Pediatric Intensive Care Unit. She held Travis under her arm as she followed silently beside me. She'd visited Dylan before doing a big sister job, as she said, and watched out for her. My heart sat heavy with a mix of emotions as we made our way to the room. The news I had received this morning had turned my world upside down but corrected itself because I knew it was the right decision. My baby sister lay in the PICU on life support, and I still felt like it was my fault. I knew that it wasn't, but I felt like I should have done more to save her.

Now that I had been granted full custody over her, the responsibility weighed heavily on my shoulders, but I knew I had to be there for her, no matter what.

"Mommy, can I read Dylan a story on my tablet," Cece asked.

"I think that will be really nice. Which story is it?" I asked. We turned down the hall, and I prayed Jacinda's ass didn't show up. She was always here in the morning checking the updates on Dylan like she was a concerned parent. But we both knew why she was doing it, and it wasn't because she gave a fuck.

"Travis put a book on there for me. It gotta be really, really good because he wrote it. It's about a boy named Leon, and he's a detective. Leon solves all his crimes from the computer because you can do anything with a computer, even if you have to make one. That's what Uncle Kode and Uncle Link say," Cece giggled. I laughed and shook my head because I thought Link had a whole baby out there in them streets, and he's fakin'.

"Oh, okay. I think you should start it with Dylan, and we can read it together later," I smiled.

"Yes," she whispered. She leaned over, brought Travis to her face, and whispered into his ear.

We approached the door to Dylan's room, and I saw Jacinda sitting in the corner. Her eyes red and puffy when she looked up as we entered. I could see the anger and resentment simmering beneath the surface, and I braced myself for what was to come. There she goes with the bullshit, but it didn't matter.

"Crescent, what the fuck is this shit?" Jacinda hissed as I closed the door behind me.

"Francesca," I spoke slowly. Cece brought her dark eyes back to me. Her small lips pressed firmly together as her little face turned red.

"Yes, Mommy?" she answered softly.

"I want you to sit next to Dylan and put on your headphones, okay?"

"How dare you serve me with those court papers? You can't just take my daughter away from me!" Jacinda interrupted. I said nothing, quickly moving Cece to the couch and lifting her onto it. I pulled her tablet and headphones out and made sure they were on and her music was playing, before I stood. I took a deep breath, trying to keep my composure as I turned to face Jacinda.

"Dylan needs stability, Jacinda, and you know that. You know as well as I do that you've been using her for a payday and nothing more. This...this is for her own good," I gestured to Dylan.

"For her own good?" Jacinda scoffed. "You have no idea what it's like to raise a child on your own. You think you're so much better than me, don't you, because you're living it up after you fucked your way there? At least you learned this time," she sneered. Her gaze traveled to Cece, and I stepped in front of her.

"You keep your eyes on me, not her. And anyway, I learned from the best, right? Just go, Jacinda. You have a chance to leave Union City and find another rich man to fund your life. You're not old, and you're still snatched. I'm sure you still know what to do. As for me and my little sister, we'll be good. Go," I said, pointing toward the door.

Jacinda stared at me. The tension in the room was palpable, and I could feel my patience wearing thin.

"You and the little demon child can get the fuck out of my daughter's room," she shouted at the end. My jaw clenched, and I glanced over my shoulder to see Cece still looking at her tablet. I motioned for Jacinda to step outside with me, so that I could get this bitch away from my child. She pushed me, and I looked at Cece as she raised her head.

"Stay here and watch Dylan for Mommy, okay?" I said as I grabbed my phone from my purse. I sent a quick text to Faxx, telling him that she would become a problem. I stuck my phone into the pocket of my scrub pants and looked at Cece.

"Yes, Mommy," she frowned.

"Good," I said, while waiting as she put her headphones back over her ears.

I stepped into the hall as Jacinda paced outside the door.

"You need to fucking leave Jacinda because if you say one more fucking word about mine—"

A nurse looked around the corner and dipped back into a room. I looked at each end of thc hall and then started to move.

"Yours? That child is not yours no matter what the fuck you claim, and neither is Dylan," she snapped.

We entered the stairwell, and I could feel the heat of Jacinda's anger radiating off her as she glared at me. She was seething, her eyes blazing with hate.

"You have no right to do this to me, Crescent. I've been taking care of Dylan all these months, and now you want to swoop in and play Mommy? You don't know the first thing about being a mother," she spat.

I clenched my fists, trying to keep my voice steady and control my anger.

"Bitch, and you think that you do? You ain't never been a mother to either one of us! I honestly don't understand how you turned out this way. My grandmother, who is my true mother, died over two and a half years ago. And she's still a better mother than you could ever be, and you're still alive. So, miss me with that shit," I gritted.

"Ha! Really? Do you really think I give a fuck who you call your mother? I think the fuck not. But what I do know is that you are the one who put my baby in that bed. So no, I'm not leaving, and you can't have her," she retorted.

"Me? Are you fucking serious right now? You're the one who put her in this situation, Jacinda. You've made your choices, and now you have to face the consequences. If you think you will win this shit, you're fucking delusional," I laughed.

"You're new to this game, Cent, because you don't know shit. If I can't do it, trust and believe Alex, y'all father, will," she smirked. I shifted my stance and leaned away from her, looking over as I shook my head.

"It's almost like you forgot. Like you forgot the man I married, you know, the one that placed that bomb around your neck. If you believe Alex will be a factor in any of this, then you are just as fucking stupid as I was, believing you would help me escape Roman. Ain't no money coming, Jacinda, so pick up your shit and leave my city. This is it, the last time I tell you," I promised.

"You...you fucking fat bitch," she hissed.

Before I could say another word, Jacinda lunged at me, her nails clawing at my skin. I stumbled backward, trying to block her from scratching my face, but she was relentless. I grabbed her hands and pushed her away.

"Jacinda cut the shit!" I shouted, my voice echoing off the cold concrete walls.

It was then that I felt a tug on my arm. I turned to see Cece standing there with her Chucky doll clutched tightly in her small arm. Her eyes were wide with fury, and I knew I had to end this shit.

"Go! We're done here," I said, dismissing her. Jacinda stood there, her eyes filled with hate and desperation. She started for the door as I looked down at Cece, moving her out of the way. But Jacinda lashed out and tried to hit me again. Cece swung the doll with all her might, hitting Jacinda on the arm hard.

"Don't touch her," Cece gritted. Jacinda recoiled but then snatched the doll from Cece's grasp as she stumbled backward.

"Ahh naw bitch! Cece, stay back," I said, my heart racing.

I reached for Rose, who was resting on my back, while keeping my eyes on Jacinda. I felt the holster as her eyes blazed with a ferocity I had never seen before. She raised the doll to strike, but before she would hit my baby, I would fucking kill her. I grabbed Rose, but before I unholstered, Cece screamed.

"Cece!" I shouted.

"You don't touch my Mommy! She's mine, and you don't ever touch Travis," she screamed. Then she kicked Jacinda in the knee, causing her to drop the doll as she leaned over.

"You little b—"

While she was unsteady, Cece punched her in the chest, and I watched in horror as Jacinda tumbled backward down the stairs. Her head hit every other step with a loud cracking sound before slamming hard on the landing below us. It all happened in a matter of seconds. I blinked once, then twice before snapping out of it. Cece stood shaking, and I moved, lifting her into my arms.

"Don't you ever touch my Mommy," Cece mumbled into my neck. I held her tightly as I stared in disbelief at Jacinda's twisted body. The pool of blood began to spread out.

"Are you okay, baby?" I panted. I fumbled for the phone in my pocket as I looked around. Lawd, I hope no one came in here.

"Yes, I didn't like her. Travis didn't either," Cece said against my neck.

I dialed Faxx but got voicemail, and I remembered he said he had something to do. I quickly dialed Shantel. She could tell me what to do or how to handle this.

"Hey, Cent, what's up?"

"Are you still at the hospital?"

"I am. I just finished helping Stax. Why, what's wrong?" she said, her voice becoming serious.

I swallowed as I looked at the numbers on the door beside me.

"Ahh, we have a situation, and I'm not quite sure what I'm supposed to do," I finished.

"Where are you?" she asked. I could hear the click of her heels as she moved down a hall.

"In the stairwell on the seventh floor, but...you should come in on the sixth floor," I said slowly.

"Two minutes," she said, ending the call.

I had no idea what I would feel if this moment ever happened. I think I was sadder at the fact that I felt absolutely nothing. The only feeling I had was, worry, for Cece and how we were going to deal with this situation. I rubbed Cece's back as she hummed her rap song in my ear when the door below opened. I stepped back and to the side until I saw Shantel's head poke inside.

"Damn, I didn't have death by fall on my bingo card for her," she said, stepping inside. Shantel looked up with her phone to her ear.

"She...tripped," I said.

"Clean up. My location and make that shit quick. All stairwells need to be locked down," Shantel said rapidly. She went over to the body, looking her over, shaking her head. "You sure this witch of the east is dead?" Shantel asked while kicking Jacinda's body and shrugged.

"No way she was coming out of this alive," I huffed. Cece raised her head and turned to Shantel.

"Auntie Shantel, I really tried to be nice, but she touched Mommy and threw Travis," Cece said. Shantel met my eyes, and I nodded while she placed another call.

"Mena? Yeah...we need to talk."

CHAPTER NINETEEN

MALIKITA 'MALA' SAMUELS

I held Link's hand as we drove toward Mena's office for Crescent's appointment. I was still wondering how in the hell she had gotten Link to come to this. This man had refused to even step foot into one of these offices since I'd known him. From what Mama Laverne told me, one day, they took him to one man who ended up trying to study him and not help him. From that day forward, she and Mr. Elijah decided they would handle it on their own. For all intents and purposes, it worked out well for him. Link grew up in a stable home that maintained a strict routine while instilling respect into him as much as possible. They showed him what love was, even if that only extended to a very small number of people.

I knew me focusing on Link was my own way of trying to get that fucking wedding out of my mind. I ignored it for as long as I could, but seeing that it was tomorrow, my time was over.

"Talk to me, *Dove*, you're too quiet," he insisted.

I breathed out a sigh as we took the exit for downtown. I had no clue how we were going to pull this shit off, but we had to because if not, a lot of people might die, including us.

"The catacombs, how sure are we that it's a real thing? Can we really trust Kenneth to get the location of the entrance to this so-called place?" I asked. Link squeezed my hand before bringing it to his lips. I turned to look at his profile, making sure I remembered every detail. His locs were pulled away from his face and into two barrels that hung down his back. The red tips were dyed to a more of a crimson now. His beard was trimmed shorter than usual, but it was still full.

"*Dove*, I wasn't expecting to find any kind of map in the underground tunnels. I'm sure that Roman wasn't lying when he said that because Union City is full of them. They were here before the city because the city was built on top of them. So, do I think some old, extremely wealthy people wouldn't find a way to use them to their advantage? I am sure they would because it makes perfect sense. Even if Charles were to turn that phone on, it wouldn't get any signal to track. Seyra will get the answer out of Kenny," Link attested. He made a right on Glen Dale and then turned into the parking garage that was connected to the large modern-styled building where Mena was located. I exhaled, letting go of my doubts that we would figure this shit out. Either way, we had to get on that property, and the wedding was the only way to do it. Link and Ian did concede that if the entrance were anywhere, it would be on the east end of the estate.

"Okay, but have we all just put that nigga Rodney on the back burner? He's been too fucking quiet, and I don't like that shit. I don't like that we can't get to that fucking body without being noticed," I huffed. Link pulled into a parking spot before turning to look at me. His eyes seemed to see everything about me, in me, and even what I thought when he looked at me like this.

"I want them to find the body."

"What?" I asked incredulously.

"I feel like if the body is found, that is one less thing Charles has. They drag it up out of the water, and if there was any evidence on that body, it would be destroyed by now. I know that there isn't, but having that hanging over my head is getting annoying. It's all good, *Dove*. All we need to do is get the fucking phone check it, destroy it, and nothing will matter," Link insisted.

"One more day and it's either we get it or—"

"Or we get the shit. These people believe that they are on top, and I give to them because they have been. They've hid in the shadows, playing their little games until a few got greedy. Alex got greedy, and Charles just overplayed his hand. Even with this threat of the person who killed Ian and Oz's mothers hanging over us, it doesn't matter. What would be the reason this person comes at us if his employer was dead? This is Union City," Link started.

"And U.C.K. runs Union City," I finished.

"Now, let's get this shit over with," he huffed.

"Why the hell are you going anyway? You hate therapy," I laughed.

I stepped out of the car and wrapped my long sweater around me as he headed for the entrance. Link came up beside me and wrapped his arm around my waist.

"I took Cece a few times before. Yesterday, after her...incident, I went in with her, Faxx, and Crescent. I wanted to tell her she did a good job because that woman deserved more than that, but I knew that wasn't the correct time to say it," he said, pulling open the door.

"Baby, when the hell do you think the correct time to tell her job well done after...after she takes a life," I whispered. The sound of our feet hitting the tiled floors made it seem like a hoard of people was running through there. We stopped at the elevators, and I hit the button while waiting for his answer because I had to know.

"I don't think that six years old is appropriate for that. Cece needs to be at least, at minimum, ten or twelve. I think twelve is right. That's when—"

"Stop right there. We will not be telling Francesca anything like that at all. This is why she needs to have normalcy in her life, Lakyn. I hate that she was so young for her first, but if we're being technical about it, it was self-defense," I protested. The doors slid open, and we stepped on. I hit the button for the tenth floor, hoping he would just let me decide this one.

"Hmmm. I'll let you decide on this one," Link stated. I closed my eyes, remembering that he was Cece at one point in time, but not exactly the same. They had a lot of the same traits.

"Thank you, baby," I said, looking up at him. Link frowned, but said nothing as he leaned over to kiss me. The elevator came to a stop, and the doors opened to a large waiting area.

I saw Crescent sitting next to Faxx, holding his hand as she stared blankly at the wall.

"And to answer your question, I'm here because I like Cent. When she asked for us to be here, I said I would do it. By the look on Faxx's face, he thought I was lying," Link shook his head. I said nothing, just smiled because even if he didn't realize it, that was a major step for him. He cared about someone else's well-being beyond family. My gaze landed on Cent, and I could see her pulse racing as she turned to face us. She smiled like she had just realized we were all here. I hoped she felt surrounded by the supportive faces of her new family. She fidgeted with the hem of her dress, displaying some anxiety, even knowing that Roman wouldn't be able to hurt her anymore.

"Hey, Master Zaddy," Cent said, standing. Link hugged her before Faxx snatched her ass back.

"This nigga always trippin'. I know my place, Fransisco. I'm just the sneaky link," he smirked. Crescent burst out laughing while Tali and Dea tried holding it in. Shantel stood up with her hands on her hips, breathing deeply.

"This is what I mean. Niggas take shit as a fucking joke until they can't find their boats where they left them," Faxx sucked his teeth.

"Papi, he's fucking with you," Crescent said as she discreetly pointed between her and Link.

"Oh my God, I can't," Tali said, covering her face. Henny stood up and came to kiss my cheek before dapping up Link.

"Can we all get serious for a minute? All of this is something we need to take seriously right now. Crescent, when did you plan on telling us about your side nigga?" Henny questioned.

"That's it! We're done. Where the hell is Mena?" Dea said, standing.

"Really, Dr. Sexy? I know damn well you can't be serious right now," Cent asked, her mouth open. The sad part was that I think he was entirely serious while breaking her out of her own thoughts at the same time.

"Completely," Henny said, crossing his arms. Crescent looked at me, and I just shook my head. I was not about to get into that shit. Then she looked up at Faxx. I saw her friend Cressida, and she looked completely confused, shocked, and horrified that Crescent might actually be in a relationship with all three of them. But she didn't leave and just closed her mouth, leaning back into her chair.

"Papi?"

"Naw, I'm trying to hear the answer to this question," Faxx said.

"Nope. Just hell no, y'all are not going to fuck with me today," Crescent shouted, squeezing through them. Oz stood, opening his arms with a smile.

"Come on home to Daddy Dom," he chuckled.

"Dea!" Crescent cried.

"Y'all leave Cent alone. Come here, baby," Dea said, holding out her hand. Tali was hanging off Shantel's shoulder as they laughed at the dumbasses.

"Thank you. Shantel and Tali fuck you. Mala, you're really classy, letting your man blow up my spot. Everybody wants to be a fucking comedian today," Cent huffed.

"I didn't even do anything," I choked.

"Exactly," Crescent pointed, and I lost it.

Dr. Mena, a compassionate and experienced therapist, welcomed us into her office with a warm smile. The U.C.K tattoo visible on her upper arm was to exude a sense of safety and trust. It wasn't for us because we'd known Mena before the doctor was attached to her name. As we settled into the comfortable chairs, Mena began the session by setting the tone for an open and honest conversation, emphasizing the importance of creating a safe space for Crescent to share her story.

Crescent took a deep breath and started at the beginning, recounting how she'd met Roman and how our relationship had begun. I was already thirty-eight hot because she was a fucking baby. I could tell Faxx was listening and, at the same time, probably replaying Roman's murder in his head. Faxx held her hand in his lap, but from my point of view, I could see his other clenched into a fist. Henny was next to Crescent, and she leaned against him, his face blank. But anyone who knew him knows that he was worse than him, showing you that he was mad.

Crescent explained how things had quickly spiraled into a nightmare of manipulation, control, and abuse on the day she turned eighteen.

"It escalated into physical violence where nothing was off the fucking table, and the emotional trauma left scars that cut deeper than any bruise, burn, or stab wound," Crescent said. I saw her look over at her friend Cressida. She sat on Tali's opposite side with her hand over her mouth and tears in her eyes. I turned slightly and looked at Link. His jaw was tight, and when he flicked his gaze to me, I understood a few things more clearly. First, the way Crescent explained the style of abuse was reminiscent of Shantel. The second reason was that I knew it reminded him of the way that the therapist tried to use him the way Roman did with Cent's talent. I looked in Shantel's direction, where she sat with her legs crossed, looking at her nails. She sat on Oz's side, pressing against him, but I saw the slight shaking in her frame. Tali scooted forward on her seat to look at Crescent. I could tell she knew some of what happened by the anger on her face.

"Crescent, I want you to know that whatever you went through, you don't have to face it alone. We're here for you, always," Tali said, her voice filled with determination. Tali's eyes cut to Cressida, and she pressed her lips together, holding back from saying anything else.

"Thanks, Tali, but you know that I know that. This was the reason why I wanted to get it out there all at once. I didn't want y'all wondering or trying to tiptoe around me. I can assure y'all that is not what I need," Crescent said, her eyes firm.

I nodded to myself, realizing the reasons why they did fuck with her so much. Faxx, I was sure, probably picked up on something. He might not have known what caused her trauma, but he could tell she needed something to help her deal with it. More than likely, it brushed off on everyone else except Henny. He already liked Cent from the beginning without knowing a damn thing. His intuition, or whatever it was to see potential in others, was what sealed their connection. Cressida dropped her hand and took a deep breath.

"I'm sorry, Crescent. I've known you for so long that it feels like it was practically all our lives, and you didn't deserve any of it. You're strong, and you're so much more than what he made you feel. I should've—"

"No. There would have been nothing you or your parents could have done. Your support means everything to me now," Crescent said, shaking her head and cutting Cressida off from whatever she was about to say. Cressida nodded, but I could still see the guilt in her eyes from thinking she hadn't done enough.

"Does anyone else need to say anything? Crescent, is there more you need to share that we haven't heard?" Mena asked. She sat her tablet down and waited for an answer from Cent. I could tell by her foot tapping she was ready to go off, and I think she would have if Cressida weren't present.

Shantel stood abruptly, rubbing her hands down a pair of loose-fitting sweatpants.

"How the hell did she get my sweats? Again," Link grumbled.

Shantel looked at Crescent with fierce determination in her eyes as she walked closer to her. Shantel knelt in front of her, taking her hand.

"You're not alone, Crescent. Whatever you went through, we're here for you, and we'll kill— fight for you."

"Shantel, you don—"

Shantel leaned in, her gaze filled with so much anger I knew this had thrown her back into memories she'd locked away.

"I want you to know that I'm here to help you reclaim your strength, your independence, and your sense of self-worth. You are on your way there, but trust me when I say, I know it comes back when you least expect it. We'll train. I'll train her," Shantel said, standing.

"Oh God," Henny groaned.

Crescent smiled and just nodded yes, not realizing what the hell she was getting into with that. I knew we'd said that we would train them, but I had a feeling Shantel meant more than the standard way.

Mena took a deep breath before looking at all of us, then settled on Crescent.

"Crescent, this is your time, and you can say what you want or not. Is there anything else you need to get off your chest?" Mena asked. I could tell, and I knew the guys could see that Mena knew something no one else did. Faxx slowly looked at Crescent as she sat there with her eyes closed.

"*Mi Amor*, you don't need to say shit if you're not ready. Whatever it is, you already know we'll deal with the issue like the others," Faxx stated.

"Explosively," Oz rumbled. I had a feeling after this session, a lot of random ass people would end up in the *Butcher's Shop*.

"Cent, you're a part of our family now, and your pain is our pain. Whatever it is, when you're ready to say it, we're here," Dea said with deep understanding in her eyes. Crescent opened her eyes and turned to look at Dea for a long moment. I knew Dea, Tali, and Crescent had a bond that went deep for the little time they'd known each other. So whatever Crescent saw in Shandea's eyes must have given her what she needed.

"I know that Faxx has seen recordings of the shit that happened to me. I also know that Link more than likely saw it as well," she sighed. Link's hand flexed in mine when Cent looked in our direction. "I know they saw the forced burns, the physical beatings, names, or just random shit being carved into my skin. That's the reason for the tattoos. But I know that no one else saw it because it wasn't recorded. I never stopped fighting no matter what the fuck would happen, and this one particular time must have been the wrong time to say fuck you. I refused to produce anything for Roman, and I refused to react to any of his shit anymore. I made up my mind that I just wasn't going to live this way any longer. But before I had a chance even to try to do anything, he took me to one of those warehouses. That's how I recognized a few of them. He took me to a fucking auction, like a real fucking stand on a stage auction, and told me that I thought I had it bad," she finished.

Crescent wiped a tear away before shaking her head and breathing in deeply. Crescent took another deep breath and began to recount the shit she had seen. And it all aligned too well for it to be a coincidence from what little I did know about the time Shantel was taken. She would describe rooms in a large space with little to no windows.

Henny, Link, and Oz's clenched jaws revealed the thin string was about to snap, and I could tell Mena noticed it. Hell, I was about to lose it because how long had this shit been happening?

"But, one thing I knew was that he wanted my skill because it was making him money, and if there was one thing he loved, it was money. Money, power, and submission, so that's what I did until I got the opportunity to run," Crescent finished. The long sigh she released seemed to drain the tension out of her body. It was quiet for a moment, then Mena leaned forward, taking control before someone said something wild as fuck.

"Crescent, you did well. I feel like you managed to remove that weight you've been carrying around. If you feel like this is needed again, or you need to bring it up in our private sessions, it's completely up to you. Does anyone need to say anything else?" Mena asked. Her eyes flicked to each person but held longer on Henny, Link, Oz, and Faxx.

"I think I'm good for now, Doc Mena," Crescent nodded.

Faxx pulled Cent closer to him and whispered something into her ear. It had her nodding while Henny, Oz, and Link stared at each other. Link stood up, making me stand with him since I was holding his hand.

"Cent, I don't do this therapy shit, but if you need to do this again, you know how to reach me. Use the same sixty-nine text you always send out," Link smirked.

"*Mi Amor*, let's go before this nigga find out what it's like to be on a sinking ship," Faxx gritted.

I could tell that Mena's guidance and understanding presence allowed Cent to unpack the trauma, but seeing that nigga Roman die was what released her. I followed everyone out the door, surprised at how quiet Henny and Oz were throughout the session. I knew it had a lot to do with that chick Cressida, so when Cent said goodbye and then joined us, shit went left.

"Crescent, if that nigga wasn't already dead, I would have taken his fucking head off. But I want to know what kind of fuck shit has been going on? These niggas are moving in and out of this city on some slick shit?" Oz boomed.

"My thought was that we ended that shit here in Union once we got Shantel, but apparently, it just shifted. If we're being honest, this shit had to be going on before U.C.K. was even on the scene," Henny grunted. He moved and pulled Crescent into a hug, looking over her head at Faxx.

"Exactly. Do the words 'we don't know who we are fucking with' make sense now?" Faxx asked.

"I don't give a fuck what makes sense. I want to know who is behind it, kill them, and clean this fucking city out. We know it's larger than Union, but if we're doing this expansion, we can't have this shit at our backs," Oz raged. Henny let Cent go and looked toward Shantel, who was leaning against a wall. She looked up from her phone before sticking it into her pocket.

"I'm good. I feel like if we handle this shit with Charles, things will begin to reveal themselves. We know that it is still happening. Let's not stand here and think we are doing some kind of service because I'm not. This is about revenge for me and now for Cent. It's about telling whoever they are that we run this shit and no one else," Shantel stated.

"Bet. I'll start digging into what data I have from everyone because there is a pattern and commonality in all of this shit. But it's agreed that Charles's situation needs to end tomorrow. Either fucking way, that shit is dead," Link finalized. The silent understanding passed between us as we turned to walk out the doors. Link laced his fingers with mine, hitting the button for the elevators. We all rode down in silence, mentally preparing for whatever bullshit would come after. The doors slid open, and we stepped out into the lobby. Standing in front of us were a shit load of police with guns drawn. I saw the hesitation with everyone reaching when the man from the basketball game stepped forward. Why would an interim Chief be here?

"This nigga," Link grunted.

"LAKYN MOORE, YOU ARE UNDER ARREST FOR THE MURDER OF MAYOR RICHARD HOLMES," Cortez announced.

My eyes widened, and my grip tightened around his hand. I felt him loosening my grip as Cortez stepped forward. The look on Cortez's face looked enraged. His eyes flicked to the side, and I followed his line of vision. Rodney stood leaning against the wall with a smirk on his face before pushing off and walking away.

I always had this consistent feeling that I could barely breathe when around Lakyn or just thinking about him. But this feeling of suffocation was almost crippling. This wasn't something I couldn't breathe through, no matter how much I tried. Link was first my best fucking friend, a person that we did everything together. Someone who I completely understood and who understood me. It had been like that since day one with us. It was never anything other than that, but what we did know was that we would be together. That was it, he was it, and I knew I was the same for him. And now everything that I tried to avoid was fucking happening.

"What the fuck does Justice mean they have him on suspicion of murder? Shouldn't he get bail?" I shouted.

"Mala, there is no bail set yet. There won't be until tomorrow, so right now, we need to continue. We have everything that Link has so far, and I'm looking it over," Henny grumbled. I was sitting on the couch at his place, rocking back and forth, my anger building.

"He knew. Link knew this was going to happen, but he said there's no evidence," I said quickly.

"There is no evidence, but from what Justice has gathered, they say there is," Henny said, reading. I felt someone sit next to me, and I looked at Oz. He opened his arms, and I laid my head against his chest.

"Lakyn isn't stupid, Mala. There is no evidence, just a witch hunt. What does it say about Rodney?" Oz asked.

"It was in his files that he had strong evidence confirming that Link was the killer. Someone made it possible for him to push that shit through," Henny said, looking up.

"Someone above him?" I asked. The door opened to an enraged face. Shantel and I had always been close and best friends, but she, Link, and I understood each other.

"I know where he is, and I want him dead now," she fumed. I sat up, looking her in the eyes, and I could see the hurt and the fury.

Henny sat Link's laptop down and looked at us. He checked his watch before taking in a deep breath. His quick glance at Oz lasted for about a second, and probably all they needed for them to read each other.

"It was definitely someone above him, and we gave her a warning. Shantel, send Sienna's family photos of her and Roe along with the video footage of the two. Once you confirm that they saw it, then please send it out to all the stations in Union City. I want that nigga on edge and running. Oz, send Sienna pieces of Agent Higgins's body to her office. He isn't needed anymore. Also, put Sam on Rodney because he's a runner," Henny stated.

"Bet it's done," Oz grumbled.

"After Faxx finishes setting shit up with Echo, Ace, and Whisper for tomorrow, I'll have him place a bomb on Sienna's car. Since the bitch can't get the fucking picture and sit the fuck down. I want this shit done before tomorrow," Henny gritted. Shantel moved to do what she needed to do, and Oz grinned, already on his phone.

"Rodney? He did this. He took Cent, and now he's fucked with Link," I gritted. Henny stared at me, his honey-brown eyes flashing with an intensity I hadn't seen for a minute.

"Before tonight is over with, Rodney's career and character will be destroyed. And after that," he shrugged.

"Good. I want answers because there is only one way he would know where to find that body," I seethed. The only people who knew were us,

528 PRODUCT OF THE STREET

Teddy, and Charles, where that body was hidden. Henny leaned back in the chair, looking at his phone before he smirked.

"I asked Konceited to run back all of the footage from Charles's office. It seems he liked to keep a camera inside of there, probably for blackmail purposes. It was probably a way to hold Rodney off if it was needed. Let's just say it's about to be a breaking news moment. Rodney's character and methods will be in question. Everything that Roe has had his hands on, from *MYTH* to the hospital, and now Link, will be worthless," Henny smirked.

"Just let me know when we can go. I don't give a fuck what we need to do, but I will break Lakyn out if I have to," I said, standing. I left the living room, needing a minute to myself as everything that's happened up until this point raced through my mind. I walked into the bathroom and closed the door before walking over to the sink. I put both hands on the vanity and leaned over, letting out a silent scream. I didn't know what kind of game Charles thought he was playing, but I refused to let this bastard win. I don't give a fuck who his family is or who they know. If they were all fucking dead, it wouldn't matter, and as soon as we got that fucking phone, the first person getting a headshot was Cornelius. I turned on the sink and splashed some cold water on my face. After I dried off, I went back out into the living room.

Since Link wasn't here, we had to go off the files he had on the underground tunnels. He refused to call catacombs. He was right about the east side of the house once Seyra called with the information.

"Kenneth admitted there was no way for him to get in there without being seen. He also said access had been restricted, and Charles has been quietly enraged about it. But the location has been confirmed. There is a vault down there, and Kenneth is sure that's where they would be keeping anything on me and dirt on other people. But what he can do is make sure no one is watching that side of the house tomorrow for a certain period of time. I told him to do it and not worry about the rest," Seyra sighed.

"Bet. When this is over, you're done. After we have what we need, Kenny will no longer be your concern. Oz will handle it from there," Henny stated.

"Great! I will see y'all tomorrow," Seyra said, disconnecting.

Shantel sat down beside me, taking my hand in hers before looking at Henny.

"It should be all happening now as we speak. When I spoke with Ian, he told me that he and Link had a way to scan the device to see how many copies have been made," she said. I wondered if Charles would have made another copy by now and hidden it, but it looked like it wasn't possible.

Shantel was right, and it didn't take long for all that shit to leak. Not only had she sent it to the news stations, but she had Ian leak everything on every social media platform there was. I was sure this shit would be all across the country before the night was over. I turned my head toward Oz when his phone rang. I could tell he was getting impatient and probably wanted to be with his family.

"Yo?" Oz answered. He nodded his head a few times as he stood. "And he's still there? Good."

Oz looked at us and then at me and smiled.

"Looks like Rodney was walked out of his office with pending charges of extortion, blackmail, witness tampering, and the list continues. Sam said he looked paranoid and didn't go back to the apartment he was staying in. Like you said, he's hiding, so let's go find his ass," Oz said, walking toward the door. I was already on my feet, and Shantel was behind me. If all that was true, then it was just a matter of time before Link could be released.

I never thought I'd find myself in a situation like this, but life has a funny way of leading you down unexpected paths. My heart was pounding as we pulled up to the run-down motel where Rodney was hiding out. It was dark, and the air was heavy with tension as I glanced at Oz, Shantel, and Henny, and my stomach churned with anger that this nigga thought he could get away with this shit. Rodney, of all people, should've known fucking with U.C.K. wasn't good for his retirement plan.

A black truck pulled up as Faxx jumped out, rubbing his hands together in anticipation of fucking that nigga up. Rodney had the attention of U.C.K. and its Horsemen, so he had to feel the chill of death around him.

"Sienna is...alive, but barely. She was too close to the car when she unlocked it," Faxx chuckled.

"You didn't want to wait until she got inside?" I asked.

"Naw, I want her to feel how badly she fucked up. It's not like she didn't have a chance to save her life. She chose not to, and has to suffer those consequences," he stated.

"Bet, let's move," Henny said, taking a step forward.

Rodney's involvement in the kidnapping of Crescent and his part in framing my Link had anger and frustration simmering inside me. All I needed to know was where he'd gotten the information and how much of it he really knew.

As we approached the door to Rodney's room, I felt a surge of adrenaline. We weren't here to intimidate but to make Rodney feel the fear and helplessness that he had inflicted on Crescent and to answer for his part in having Link locked up.

We weren't worried about cameras in this part of Union City, but Konceited did a sweep to ensure nothing was looking this way. Neither were we worried about the people at this spot. Everyone here would know to keep their mouths closed.

Oz got to the door, and without stopping, kicked it in. The door folded like cardboard as he stepped through.

"Naw, nigga don't run. Remember all that fucking mouth you had?" Oz boomed.

Rodney's eyes widened in terror as he realized what was happening.

"Fuck! Shit, fuck," he shouted as he reached for his gun on the bedside table. Rodney jerked his hand back when a knife embedded itself in the wood of the table.

"Shit! What the fuck? Y'all don't know how big of a mistake you're making. I am a Federal—"

Faxx moved, ripping his tactical knife from the table, and stabbing it into Rodney's shoulder.

"Nigga shut the fuck up. You thought we wouldn't come for you? Did you think you could skate after you helped that bitch take my wife?"

"Ahhhh...fuck!" Rodney screamed as Faxx jerked his knife back. He used it and his fist and began to rain down punches as Rodney tried to deflect.

"Don't kill him, Faxx. I want him to be able to feel when my cleaver chops up his body," Oz chuckled.

Rodney's attempts to escape had come to an abrupt halt when Faxx grabbed him by the back of the neck and slammed his head on the table. I felt Henny move, not wasting any time, as he grabbed Rodney by the collar, dragged him out of the bed, and slammed him against the wall.

"Who. Told. You. About. The. Body?" Henny's voice reverberated through the room, and I could see the fear in Rodney's eyes, his tough façade crumbling, but Rodney was stubborn. He fixed his face into a glare and clamped his mouth shut in defiance, which only fueled the fire. I moved forward as Shantel stood by the door, looking outside in case someone was that stupid to call the police.

"You think you're so clever, Rodney," I seethed, my voice trembling with a mix of fury and hate. "You didn't stumble upon the location of the mayor's body by accident. Someone told you, and I want to know for sure who it was."

Rodney's eyes darted around the room, his expression a mix of defiance and fear.

"I don't know what you're talking about," he spat, his voice laced with bitterness. Henny pressed his thumb into the wound on his shoulder, making Rodney scream in pain.

"You don't know. Then I don't know how this happened," Faxx chuckled. He grabbed one of Rodney's arms and pressed it against the wall. He put his Glock against the palm of his hand and pulled the trigger.

"Ahhhh! You...bit...you...ahhh...fuck," Rodney screamed.

"I know you didn't expect us to believe that?" I shot back, taking a step closer to him. "You were involved in Crescent's kidnapping, and you chose Link out of all people. Someone helped you, and I want a name," I hissed.

"I don't owe you any explanations. I had to do it! I had to find something...I had no choice. Do you think I wanted to come back here? I had no choice," he snapped, but his voice betrayed his inner turmoil.

Henny got closer, his figure casting a shadow over Rodney as he squinted.

"You seem to have a little more information than we initially came for," Henny growled, his voice like thunder in the confined space of the motel room. "You're going to tell us who the fuck gave you the location."

Oz stepped closer as he played with the tip of his cleaver. Rodney's eyes grew wider, and I took it from Oz and slammed it on the arm Faxx was still holding. His bloody hand dropped to the dirty floor.

"Ahhhh!! Sto....ahhh...ahhh—"

Rodney screamed until I put the cleaver under his chin and stared him in the eyes.

"Ooouuu, that had to hurt like a bitch," Shantel laughed.

"Are you sure you aren't pregnant? Because that rage looks familiar," Oz surmised. I glared at him until he shrugged.

Rodney's resolve crumbled. He shifted uncomfortably, his gaze darting between each of us.

"Speak nigga! You want to live, right?" Henny shouted.

"Okay....o...okay, okay," he gasped, his voice strained. "It was... it was Charles. He's the one who told me about the body and where to find it. He's willing to testify," Rodney heaved.

"Thank you for being honest, Rodney," I said, my voice steady despite the storm of emotions raging within me. "You've made the right choice. You get to live," I stated, stepping backward.

"Ples....pl....I ne....med...medi...help," he rasped. Henny tilted his head to the side while Faxx grabbed a pillowcase and covered his bleeding stump.

"You shouldn't have come back here, Roe. Now you know something you probably shouldn't, and I want to know what it is. I'm sure some time at the *BUTCHER SHOP* will help you remember why you ran the first time," Henny gritted. Henny let Rodney's body drop to the ground as Oz squatted down, gripping his head and making him look at his face.

"My wife has been asking for heads in a box. I can't wait to fulfill that request again," Oz smiled before slamming his face into the blood-stained floor.

I turned away so I could prepare myself for a wedding and a funeral.

We approached the large old-styled mansion estate, and the grandeur of the occasion became immediately evident. The estate was surrounded by meticulously manicured gardens adorned with colorful blooms and ornate topiaries.

"So, this is that money, money shit," Crescent said in the back seat.

"More money than people like them should have," Tali huffed.

"Tali is right on that one. These are the kinds of people that should not have unlimited resources," I sighed.

The mansion itself is a display of timeless elegance, constructed from weathered stone and adorned with elaborate carvings and intricate architectural details. It was decorated with shades of tans and whites.

I saw the guests being greeted by a team of uniformed staff who ushered them inside. I didn't know any of these people, but something about them just looked off. Yes, it was a wedding, but everyone wore just about the same thing. The men were all older or middle-aged. They had on dark tuxes or suits, and the women all had on shades of tan.

"Anybody else seeing this shit?" Seyra asked. I stopped my car at the front entrance and took a deep breath, trying to get ready for the day. All I needed to do was play the part until I heard what was needed over the earpiece. Everything and everyone was in place. My mother and Stephanie would be arriving because shit would be off if they didn't.

"I'm sure we all see the weird ass shit that's happening," Shantel muttered.

I stepped out of Link's truck and was immediately greeted by the staff. I handed over the keys as everyone gathered what we needed to make this shit look real. My dress was already here hand, picked my Charles. I began walking toward the doors, and once we stepped inside the grand foyer, I looked toward the cascading staircase adorned with garlands of fresh flowers that led to the upper levels of the mansion. The air is filled with the sweet fragrance of floral arrangements, and the soft strains of classical music provide a sophisticated backdrop to the festivities. Charles stood there speaking urgently to one of the staff when he caught sight of me. He descended the stairs quickly, a fake smile in place as people moved from room to room.

"Kita, it's about time, and you've brought guests," he grimaced.

"Cut the shit, Charles. You already know this will be it for me after today. You've taken everything else from me. Can I at least have this?" I rebutted. Charles's face went through a range of emotions before he smiled.

"What? Are you upset about your little boyfriend?" He taunted me like I did him. Charles stepped closer, grabbing my arm until we were a breath away from each other. I already knew it was taking Shantel every ounce of willpower not to knock this nigga the fuck out.

"Why? What the fuck was the purpose of giving up the body now?" I hissed.

"Insurance."

"There is no reason to go through any of this if he goes down for this shit, Charles," I mumbled.

Charles smiled as his eyes roamed over me. I could tell he was feeling himself again, thinking he was in control of shit.

"Once this is finished, I will recant my story. No harm, no foul," he sighed, pleased with himself.

"And I should believe that?"

"You got me there, Kita. You are always so smart, and you're right not to believe it. But what if I told you with the added footage of that night, all of them would go down? This way, everyone gets something. I get you, and U.C.K. stays out of my business. The police get a killer, my father and I can use it in the campaign, and the rest of your family can live peacefully. Someone had to take the fall," he smiled.

"You really did have all of this planned out. All from the day you first approached me," I said, shaking my head.

"As soon as I saw Link with you, I knew what I had to do. I followed him for days as he held your hand, bought you things, took you out on dates, and gave you whatever you wanted. But what sealed the deal for me was the way you looked at him and watched him when he wasn't looking. Young, dumb, and pathetically easy, but less so than Monica. You had family in

U.C.K. and another that loved you. You were the perfect target, and by the looks of things, their weakest link," Charles smirked.

I blinked as I reeled in my rage and then pulled away from him. Once the wedding started, before I could step foot down the aisle, his face would be all over the news being linked to Rodney.

"I need a room on the east end. It's where the most natural light is," I stated loudly.

"We've prepared a room already, and I have people to help—"

"East end Charles and I have my own people. I can ask your grandfather if you like. And while I'm at it, we can chat about Teddy and his fumbling hands," I said softly. Charles's jaw clenched, and then he adjusted his bowtie as he exhaled. He snapped his fingers at a passing staff member.

"Take my soon-to-be wife to a room on the east end of the estate and have her dress brought to her," he ordered. He looked at me for one more moment and held up a finger. "Oh, I forgot, my grandfather will be giving you away since you don't have a father," Charles smirked and turned away.

"Bitch," I fumed.

CHAPTER

TWENTY

LAKYN 'LINK' MOORE

I never thought I'd be sitting in a cold, sterile interrogation room, staring at the harsh fluorescent lights overhead with my hands cuffed to a fucking table. None of us had been in a position like this before, except for Kreed. I wasn't surprised that the police would pick me up. I just wasn't expecting that shit to happen at Mena's. Another reason why I don't go to those types of places is that I saw it coming, and I did everything I could to prepare. Henny had everything he needed to find the vault in the mansion's underground tunnels. I was sure that's where it would be because it made sense.

I leaned back in this hard, uneven seat, waiting for Justice to see about this fucking bail. They had a body, but I hadn't heard what evidence I was being held on. It was bullshit, and I wouldn't be stressing this shit if that fucking wedding wasn't today.

The door opened, and that nigga Cortez walked in, looking like this was the last place he wanted to be.

"Missed one, I take it," he asked, kicking his chair. "Let's start from the beginning, Link," Cortez sighed, his voice low and steady. "Walk me through the events of that night, step by step."

I took a deep breath, trying to gather my thoughts as I recounted the events of that night.

"What night?" I asked.

"The night you coldly murdered Mayor Holmes," he stated.

"How can I tell you about a night I have no idea about? That was what, seven or eight years ago?" I tilted my head to the side. Cortez leaned back, the look on his face displaying aggravation.

"Eight years ago. Listen, we have the body. We have the statement. Just make the shit easy. Where were you on the night of the murder? Why were you at city hall?"

"Cortez, right? See, I don't need to say shit because I have no idea what you're talking about. Have y'all done your jobs and looked into this 'person' who's an eyewitness to a murder over eight years ago? I mean, they wait this long to talk. That sounds...a little suspicious to me," I shrugged. Cortez looked down, a small smile on his face before he schooled it and looked back up. His eyes were drawn to the camera in the corner before going back to me.

"It shouldn't even be me in here questioning you. Below my pay grade and all, but my officers seem to have a real fear of you. A...Casino owner. Let's not play this game, Link. You killed a mayor. This is serious," Cortez said, raising a brow.

"It's the truth, Chief. I have witnesses who can vouch for my presence. I couldn't have been at the scene of the crime, but I will let my attorney handle all that," I said as I held his gaze, my jaw set.

Cortez leaned forward, his hands clasped together on the table. His eyes narrowed, and he leaned in closer, his voice taking on a steely edge.

"I'm not convinced. There's an eyewitness who places you at the scene of the crime. You can't talk your way out of that."

"Then there's no need for me to talk. Do whatever you need to do, but make sure you keep that Travis nigga away from my child," I smirked.

"Do not bring my son into this conversation," he gritted.

"Then stop placing me at places I've never been, my nigga," I replied.

I felt the walls closing in around me as the tension in the room shifted. We stared at each other for a long moment, each of us knowing damn well I fucking did it. Or, in Cortez's case, he probably thought I did. I raised a brow when Cortez's phone buzzed, and a message appeared on the screen. He took his hard gaze off mine and glanced down. His eyes widened at whatever he saw, and I wanted to know what it was. As Cortez looked up from his phone, I could see the suspicion and humor creeping into his eyes. For the first time since the interrogation began, I saw what Konceited was talking about in his steely gaze. He wouldn't fuck with us as long as we weren't dropping bodies all over the streets. At least it wasn't many since he'd been here.

"Wait here. I need to check on some things. Some...new information has come to light," Cortez chuckled. Cortez pushed to his feet just as the door swung open again.

"Sorry, sir, but Mr. Moore's lawyer is here," an officer announced.

"It's fine. I was finished here anyway," Cortez said.

"As you should be. No one, including you, Interim Chief, will speak to my client again without representation. Cut the cameras on your way out," Justice snapped. She slammed her black leather briefcase on the small table and raised a brow at the men until they left. Justice waited a minute and looked at the camera to be sure the light was off. Before she opened her mouth again, she hit a button on the side of her watch just to be on the safe side.

Justice's grim expression shifted when she got a beep.

"There was an eyewitness, Charles. Apparently, Charles made a deal with Rodney to testify against you. I'm more than certain it was all orchestrated to ensure you were locked up on the day of the wedding.

"I'm sure it was. But Cortez got something on his phone just now before walking out."

"You think it's the same shit I got anonymously in my email with you at a Robotics competition on the night of said murder. Your face was clearly visible at the time it took place because you were there all day and night until you won first place."

I already knew where I was and that my professor would have marked me present that day. But video? The only people who had video were my parents, and I definitely wasn't there the entire night.

"Really?"

"But fuck that. Everything about Rodney and Charles just hit the media like a wave. Whatever cases Rodney was working on or involved in are up for question. My argument will be: *how do we know if Charles isn't the one who murdered the old Mayor?* Just give me ten minutes," Justice said, walking to the door. I looked at the clock and mentally tried to slow down time so I would make it there before shit went down. I knew Ian and his team could handle the other shit with the phone, but I needed to watch that fucking place crumble to the fucking ground.

It took three minutes with Justice for them to realize that they had nothing to hold me on, but I had everything to sue the fuck out of them. I stepped out of the police station and immediately put on my watch to see what the fuck was happening. It was still early, and I knew the wedding hadn't started yet. I was going to be cutting it close, but none of that shit mattered as long as I made it. If that nigga Charles that he had this shit in the bag, that nigga was big trippin'. The cool air offered a welcome respite from the suffocating atmosphere inside. I didn't know how niggas could do that shit. That's why I had so much respect for Kreed. Hopefully, when he got out in the next couple of weeks, all this shit would be put to bed. Justice fell into step beside me, her expression calculating as she typed away on her phone. I was pretty sure she was going to slap the station and city with a major lawsuit so they wouldn't repeat the same mistake.

"Ace should be here in a few minutes," she said as she made her way to the waiting car.

"I see him on the tracking. Thanks, Justice, as always," I said. I didn't have time to run down the information on the Robotics shit, but I definitely would be looking into it because who would know that? Who would know to send it directly to Cortez and Justice? I knew it wasn't Konceited because Justice would have known that.

Before Justice could respond, a familiar little figure caught my eye. This nigga Travis. He closed the door to a green SUV and began walking up the steps.

"Travis, slow down, please," the lady called out as she locked up the car.

"Yes, ma'am," he said over his shoulder.

"Oh, is that Cece's little friend?" Justice smiled. Travis glanced at her and then smiled politely.

"Yes, ma'am. My name is Travis," he said, holding out a hand. Justice reached out and took it, and I almost smacked her hand. I didn't know what this little nigga thought he was doing, but I didn't trust it.

"Well, Cece has good taste in friends, very polite," Justice smiled. Travis looked over his shoulder again as the older woman made her way to him and back to me.

"Hello, Mr. Moore," he said, a sly smile tugging at the corner of his lips. "It seems like it's a pattern with you, always being late to things, like when Francesca was born. So, when Francesca called me upset, I really had to think, what else would he be late for?"

"What are you?" I gritted, and Justice elbowed me.

I narrowed my eyes at this grown man. Who the fuck did he think he was?

Travis's expression turned serious, his eyes locking onto mine with an intensity that a child shouldn't have.

"Francesca told me about your win at the semi-annual Robotics competition back in ancient times and how it was an all-day event. I go next month, and I'm pretty sure I'll win. Just remember you owe me, and I suggest you stay out of my way when it comes to Francesca, Unc. Bye!"

"Travis, let's go. You know your father doesn't like to be late," the woman said, taking his hand.

As he walked away, I looked at Justice.

"He's a little fucking psychopath," I hissed. I wasn't his fucking uncle, but I couldn't help but be slightly impressed. Even without the recording, I would've gotten out, but it pushed things to go faster. Fuck, he got me. I saw Ace turning into the station while Justice stared with her mouth open.

"Link, are you sure you don't have a child you didn't know about? Because if he was saying what I swear he was saying and he looks—"

"That little nigga ain't mine," I said, cutting her off. "Answer the phone when I need a witness to keep him away from Cece," I shouted and ran to the truck.

I jumped in the back seat, managing to close the door before Ace pulled off. He handed me my phone and earpiece. I immediately put that in before reaching for the black duffle bag.

"Link?" Faxx questioned.

"Where the fuck is Mala?" I asked while changing clothes.

"Mala and the others are inside now. Vanessa and Stephanie just arrived and are being directed to the gardens where the wedding will take place. We have no contact with them while they are on the east end of the estate. Cornelius wasn't playing when he locked it down. Everything else is in place for us to run up in this shit as soon *as Shantel says she's got it. Ian is in the sky for overwatch," Faxx explained.*

"Bet. So that means Shantel won't be able to contact anyone until she's on the other side? What do you see? Is Alex visible?" I asked.

I reached back into the bag and pulled out my holster and pistol, gearing up.

"Yeah, that's true, but it's what has to happen. Alex hasn't been seen, but that bitch will show. But he isn't even the real problem. How the fuck were the Cartel invited to this shit? Not just some regular niggas either. The two that met up with Astor are the heads of the Cartel, I'm sure of it. Ain't no way this shit isn't a coincidence. Fuck the Silk. Them niggas been involved in all of this at every angle," Faxx grunted.

"Fuck it. Even better. They can get got just like the rest of them," I chuckled.

"They came deep as fuck, and brought a lot of guests that aren't dressed for a wedding. All wearing some kind of tan clothing," Henny jumped in.

"Like that party with Milford. Say less. I'm less than twenty minutes out. Just get Mala out of that shit asap. If the Cartel is there, it's going to make shit more difficult. How are you sure it's them? Because we've never managed to get a visual on who they were," I asked.

"Because that's bitch nigga Marvin is with them. That nigga threw every guard he could in his path to make it out that night. A roach just like his fucking son," Henny conceded.

I sat up straight, trying to fit the pieces together. Everyone was out to get something from us, and it was mainly control over the ports. In the beginning, I would have thought it was to move that *Silk* shit in and out. I wasn't completely pushing that shit to the side, but it wasn't the main reason. What sold the most in this fucked ass world? People. Alex and his family had connections to trafficking. Then you had Jakobe, but he was just the in or disorganizer to destabilize us with the *Silk* shit. You had

Monica with files on the *Silk* businesses and warehouses. Roman, for all intents and purposes, was given Crescent. It all circled back around to these niggas and their ease of getting the product these people wanted. And it wasn't just here, but in Del Mar, Clapton, and I was sure Puafton. And then you had Charles trying to secure his family's role in this bullshit. I tapped my earpiece, needing to know the answer to one question I'd never asked. At the time, it didn't matter because we found Shantel and got her b ack.

"*Oz!*"

"*Yeah, I will be able to see Mala when she walks out. I'm not letting her out of my sight nigga,*" he answered.

"*Nigga, who told you where to find Shantel?*" I asked. It was quiet for a second before I heard the noise again.

"*Sinclair. He said he'd gotten information about missing women and men from Wes Wilmont,*" Oz finished.

Wilmont was in that world deep as fuck, but he wasn't one of the families not like Alex, Charles, or Milford.

"*Are you sure he got it from Wes, or did he know because he was a part of it?*" I asked.

"*If he knew about that fuck shit back then, okay. But what does that have to do with now?*" Oz questioned.

"*Look at the people in front of you. Y'all niggas said tan, right? Same shit as when we ran up in that mansion. We even said it while we were there. We know Shantel was wearing the exact same shit.*"

"I don't think those niggas were Cartel. I would have noticed the skull-neck tattoos on them back then like we do now."

"*Not if they weren't the Cartel yet,*" I grunted.

The earpiece went completely silent because it made complete sense, and they knew it.

"*Fuck! It's starting. Where the fuck are you?*" Faxx demanded.

Ace slowed down as we came up on the treeline that would lead straight toward the gardens and Mala.

"About to meet my wife at the alter," I answered before jumping out.

"Nigga we ain't at church," Oz laughed.

CHAPTER
TWENTY- ONE

SHANTEL JENSON WATERS

Throughout the estate, every room has been transformed into a breathtaking display of luxury and extravagance. The ballroom is adorned with shimmering chandeliers and draped in cascades of silk fabric. At the same time, the dining hall is set with gleaming silverware, crystal stemware, and towering centerpieces of roses and peonies. The walls are adorned with gilded mirrors and intricate tapestries, adding to the sense of grandeur and sophistication. A whole lot of bullshit is what it was.

We gathered in the room given to Mala, waiting for the maids and staff to sit everything down and leave the room. We stared at the flowing gown, which was all white except the tan silk that wrapped around the waist. We didn't waste time as Dea, Tali, and Crescent helped Mala into the gown as I walked around the room. I tapped my ear, but I couldn't hear anyone. As Seyra had said, this side of the estate was on lockdown, and I guess it meant that everything was locked, even the signal. I moved to the window and looked out over the expanse of the grounds. I stepped out onto the small balcony and leaned over to see the area where the wedding would be held. Outside, beneath a canopy a man stood in all black speaking urgently to another man before he moved off. I kept scanning the area and looked over the lush garden that had been transformed into an enchanting outdoor reception area. Canopied tables draped in fine linens are surrounded by towering floral arrangements and flickering candlelight, creating an intimate and romantic atmosphere for the wedding celebration. I stepped back inside, not noticing anyone walking around patrolling the grounds on this side, so I guessed Kenny's punk ass was good for something.

The air in the room was filled with a sense of urgency and determination. I turned and looked at Mala's face, and you could see the sadness in contrast to how radiant she looked in her wedding gown. It was her eyes that betrayed the fear... Anger and resolve shined through. I took her hands in mine, squeezing them gently but firmly until she focused on me.

"We'll get through this together, Mala. I will find it, and we will take every person out that gets in the way," I reassured her, my voice filled with determination.

"Even if you don't, there isn't any way I can go back. It's all out there, and I...I refuse to let him go again. I promised that I would never do that again. So yeah, they are going to have to kill me if we can't—"

"Naw, you know that shit isn't happening. Shantel comes through every single time, Mala, you know that," Crescent interjected.

"Y'all right. I'm just...I want this shit over and this nigga Charles where he belongs," she sighed. I stepped away and moved to the door, cracking it open to look each way down the long hall. I looked over my shoulder at Seyra and nodded.

"We can't waste any more time. Seyra and I are going to find a way into the tunnels, and I will come back with what we need. If anyone comes and starts asking questions, just say we went down to the gardens," I said.

I stepped out of the door with Seyra behind me. Since Mala was able to get us to the east wing of the mansion, things should move faster. As long as Tali, Dea, and Crescent remained with Mala, keeping up appearances and ensuring no one suspected anything, we should be in and out.

"Where did Kenneth say to look?" I asked as we moved further toward the east end. You could tell this was an older side and hadn't really been updated, but it was still maintained. Since I could see that, I knew it wouldn't be long before people would come back to this end of the mansion.

"He kept talking about this particular symbol, pattern, and object that covers the entire room. He said it would be closer toward the end. It would look like we would run into the wall. But the pattern on the wallpaper won't be the same as this. The color is the same, but the pattern isn't," Seyra finished.

We kept moving quickly down the hall, getting closer to the end. I was on high alert for any signs that matched the description, but each hall looked exactly the same. We navigated through the mansion, and it felt like it was taking too fucking long. I almost stopped thinking Kenny's ass was fucking with us until I saw it. I stopped and stepped backward, almost running into Seyra.

"Shit, my bad, but did you see that?" I asked.

I took another step forward, and I saw the change. It was subtle, something you would not notice unless you were looking for it. The lines on the wallpaper the entire way to this point had been horizontal. Now, they were vertical. The lines were so pale in color against the pale green of the wallpaper that it was hard to notice.

"I see it. Shit, I would've missed that," Seyra said, looking closer. I looked around, trying to see if anything else was out of the ordinary or should we keep moving forward.

"They slick with it, I can tell you that," I said, looking at my watch. Time was running out, and we had to figure this shit out in the next few minutes or risk it all and go back. I kept my eyes on the lines of the wallpaper while I took a step forward, and I saw it.

"What the fuck?" I whispered.

"What?"

I put my hand on the wall, took a step beside it, and ended up in an entirely different room.

"Oh, shit, this...this is crazy?" Seyra panted.

"There has to be something that opens around here. Did Kenneth say anything else as to how to get down there?" I asked, moving forward. It was dark, so I used the flashlight on my phone to look around the narrow room.

"He said it's all about the patterns and the game. That's all he really knew about it because he wasn't permitted here. He only got that information because Priscilla was always drinking," Seyra laughed. I said nothing as I swept the room, not seeing anything but old pictures and toys that could probably be collector's items. Game boards and chess sets sat on a table, still set up like someone was in the middle of a game. I blinked and then frowned as I brought the light closer. Each piece was in identical spots except for one. One that didn't follow that pattern. I moved around the table and stood in front of the game, flashing my light at the wall across from it.

"It's like the wall. I can see it," Seyra said, stepping forward. I moved to follow her and ended up in a small hall facing a large door.

"If you want to hide some shit, this is how you do it," I said, feeling along the door. I pushed, and it swung open. I stepped forward and then turned to Seyra.

"You stay here and make sure no one can come behind me. If I'm not back in less than twenty minutes, leave and get to the other side where you can hear the signal and tell them to blow this bitch up," I stated.

"Shantel? You know damn well that shit ain't happening. I'll go and tell everyone what's going on, and then I will be back for your ass. Just fucking be careful," she said, stepping back around the false wall. I made my way through the dark and winding stairs until I hit the bottom. You could feel the difference in pressure telling me that I was beneath the Astor estate. My heart pounded with anticipation and trepidation as I pressed forward. We were all pressed for time, and I knew the longer it would take, the worse off we would be. My flashlight cast eerie shadows on the damp stone walls, and the air was heavy with the scent of age and decay. I was so focused on finding the end that I didn't notice the faint sound of approaching footsteps until it was almost too late.

"Who the fuck are you?" The man asked in confusion.

My instincts kicked into high gear, and without a word, the guard moved to block my path. Why was he down here? His hands tightened around the grips of his weapon, and it was clear to me that he was prepared to kill and worry about who the fuck I was later.

I dropped my phone to the ground, and the glinting steel of his weapon flashed as he brought his arm up. I pulled two knives and threw them where his neck should be. I dropped to the ground just in case he managed to let off a shot. I grabbed my phone when I heard choking noises. I stood up, holding the light in the direction of the man. He held his throat, and the side of his neck where my blades stuck out.

"Can't have no gunfire this early in the game," I said, stepping over his body as it slumped to the floor. I reached down, pulling my knives from his neck. The gurgling sound was even too loud in my ears, causing memories I wanted to be buried, to rise. I leaned over, slitting his throat to stop the noise. Adrenaline surged through my veins as I focused on the task at hand. My senses were heightened now, and I moved faster down the narrow stone hal lway,

As I made my way through the tunnel only lit by my phone, my senses stayed on high alert after that guard because where did he come from? It only made me more certain that the vault was down here, and I couldn't shake the feeling that I was getting closer. Then I saw a light, and the closer I got, the brighter it got. I slowed my pace and cut my flashlight off as I moved. I put my knives away more in favor of my Sig. I was deep enough underground that no one should hear a shot. I stopped at a large metal-style bank vault door that sat open. The light coming from inside was bright, lighting up the space. The red carpet and red walls made the light look like it was a club setting. I walked forward, stepping into the room, not seeing anyone, but it was large. I stepped forward again, looking around for what I had come for. All I had to do was get in and get out. I started at the tables and shelves, looking for anything resembling an old phone. I turned in a circle facing the plush red couches that faced each other. The table beside one of the couches had a lamp and leather books stacked on top of each other.

The other table just had a half-empty glass and a bottle of whisky from the 1920s, and the other table had an older laptop with a cell phone on top of it. I moved over to it, lifting it to find the power button. I hit it, but nothing happened. I looked at my watch and held it for a minute longer than what Ian said to be on the safe side. The phone powered up, and I saw the battery symbol at the top with two bars. The make of the phone flashed across the screen before it went black, and then a home screen popped up. I holstered my Sig and began looking through the phone's gallery to see if I could find the video. I scrolled through tons of videos on how to write a proper speech and self-help videos on making people believe you are better than what you actually are.

"What the fuck?" I whispered.

Then, at the very end, I saw it, and hit the play button. The video began to play when my senses kicked in, and I could feel someone behind me. I turned around and pushed the phone into a pocket as I faced Alex Tilderman.

"Shantel," Alex sneered, his voice dripping with contempt. "You shouldn't know about this place. How did you get down here?"

I met his gaze and raised a brow. My jaw set as I sized him up. I searched for any sign of weakness or vulnerability.

"I definitely wasn't looking for you. But most creatures reside underground," I smiled. I kept an eye on my surroundings, making sure it was just us down here.

Alex licked his lips as his gaze traveled over me, making me want to throw up. I hated it when he came into the restaurant because I knew what he was. You could always tell the ones that liked to hurt you for their pleasure.

"You should know that better than anyone, right? Did it feel like years when you were kept in the dark, not knowing who was touching you? I saw what he saw in you, Shantel," Alex chuckled. I stared at him, stunned at his words. How the fuck had he known that? How did he...no...no. My mind went blank for a brief second, just a fucking second, when he lunged at me. Alex was a bigger man, and he came at me with a ferocity that left me no choice but to defend myself with everything I had. I felt his fist on my side, but I managed to block it with my arm and sent a palm strike to his throat. He swung, but I leaned back, picking up the bottle and smashing it over his head.

"Fucking little bitch. That's what I liked about you. Why did you think I would come to Emerald every night?" He taunted. Alex stepped backward, keeping me in his sight. I had to block out his words because I knew they were designed as blows.

"You won't make it off these grounds. Not today," Alex smiled. I knew I had to act decisively to gain the advantage. I could go for my Sig, but it would give him too much of an opening. I could take my chance and run, but that wasn't something I did. With lightning speed, I drew my slim knives, their razor-sharp edges glinting in the red light as Alex attacked. I knew what he thought and what he was used to, but that wasn't me any longer. His large body crashed into mine, moving me backward as I stabbed him with skilled precision. We hit the metal wall, and my head slammed against it as my hand gripped my wrist. The hit to the metal had my head spinning as it echoed through the vault-like room. I felt his nose on my neck as his fingers dug into my wrist.

"You're not getting out this time, Shantel. I could probably gain a lot of access if I bring you back to him," Alex grunted in my ear.

In a determined moment, I twisted, throwing my hip into his groin before I pushed my head upward, slamming it into his chin.

"Fuck!" He screamed, releasing me, and stepping back. I took that opening and pulled my Sig from behind my back. I aimed at his knees and pulled the trigger, dropping his big ass down to my level.

"What the fuck is his name?" I gritted. I shoved my gun under his chin while stepping on one of his legs.

"Aahhh...fu....fuc—"

"Naw, it's all good. You don't need to tell me because I will find out. I'll make sure your trust fund goes to your children," I sneered. I used the gun and rained down punches until he was down on the floor, covered in blood. I stood up, panting, wiping the blood from my face as I tried to catch my breath. Alex's gasps of air were strained and weak. I grabbed the half-empty glass and tossed back the contents, letting the burn push away the cold I felt in my veins. I dropped the glass, reached for the phone, and held it to my watch again. I waited as it read the phone and its files. It beeped, and I pulled the phone away to look at my watch. It was green, confirming copies had been made. I waited a second longer when it changed into a number. Two. I exhaled hard but stuck the phone into my pocket before looking at Alex.

"I remember you now," I panted and then shot him in his dick before hitting his forehead. I turned to leave out of the room, but I hesitated, looking back at the laptop. Without thinking about it too much, I grabbed it and started to jog my way back toward the stairs.

With my heart racing and adrenaline coursing through my veins, I took the stairs two at a time. I got to the landing and rounded the wall, not seeing Seyra anywhere. I looked at the time release she had left ten minutes ago. I clutched the laptop as I ran from behind the other wall and down the hallway leading back to the room where we helped Mala get dressed. I kept moving, pushing forward, trying to get out of the dead zone. I pressed my earpiece, and still nothing. I saw a man in black walking toward me, and as he reached for his weapon, I aimed and fired. My round slammed into his chest, knocking him back and to the ground. I kept moving, pushing harder, knowing damn well Mala was probably in that garden. I pressed my earpiece again, connecting with Ian.

"Ian! I got it. I found it," I said, my voice taut with urgency.

"Were there copies?" Ian asked.

"Two, and we have those. Did everyone hear that? Move now," I shouted. *I flung myself down the staircase, pushing the flowers that twined up the banister off as I moved.*

"Dea, Tali, Cent, get the fuck out of there now," Faxx shouted.

I went outside toward the gardens as gunfire sounded from every direction. I saw Mala aiming her gun at Cornelius's head. Charles screamed as she pulled the trigger. The older man dropped, crashing to the ground as his daughter began to scream. There were way more people than there was originally, but I pushed through them, and anyone that looked like they were reaching caught a bullet.

"Shantel, get out of here! Leave now," Oz boomed.

I searched the crowd to make sure everyone had gotten out. My eyes connected with my mother's as she slammed a man's head against the table. I started in her direction, needing to get her the fuck out of there. I saw Link and Mala shooting at some men on the far right. I knew they weren't the security from the estate by the tattoos showing on their necks. Cartel?

"The Cartel? What the fuck is happening?" I screamed, so the earpiece could pick it up.

I saw a man crawling on the ground, dragging a struggling girl with him as she screamed. I kicked him in his back, flipping him over, and shot him in the chest.

"Get out of here," I shouted when I felt something slam into my back. The laptop flew forward, sliding across the stone walkway leading to the side of the house. I rolled over onto my back with my Sig aimed and saw my mother beating some man with a plate until it broke. Then she stabbed him in the neck with it before rushing to me. Stephanie Jenson was crazy as hell, so it was never a question of where I got it from.

"Get your ass up, girl, and come on," she urged. "And the next time you try and tell me to leave, I will beat the living hell out of you."

I pushed to my feet using my mother's hand for help.

"Is that why you hit me?"

"Yes and no. That bastard was aiming at my baby," she huffed. I pulled my mother around the side, where I saw the laptop slide when I saw Link kick a man and stomp in his face as he shot someone else. I scanned the area and saw Mala dragging Charles across the stage, slamming his face into it and screaming. The white linens were all stained with blood while people crawled away. I saw Faxx laying down cover fire as they tried to make it in their direction.

"Shantel, we need to go. They will make it," my mom said, pulling my arm. I could hear sirens getting closer, and I knew it was a matter of time before the police would be here.

"Time! Time! Time!" Ian shouted.

"Ian, can you hit the northwest side?" I shouted.

"Whatever you need, Sweet Angel," he answered.

"Sweet Angel? You mean tart demon," Oz gritted.

I shook my head, trying not to laugh, when I turned around to get my mother out of there.

"Let's go—"

"See, Alejandro, I told you I saw her. Have you lost your manners? What do you need to say to your Master," he grinned. I stared at the scar on his face, remembering the night I put it there. I felt like I couldn't fucking breathe as all sound faded except the voice in my ear.

"Shantel!" Ian screamed repeatedly.

Large, scarred, and tattooed hands were wrapped around my mother's throat, and I couldn't move.

"Carmelo, we need to go. Marvin has the chopper ready. Just take her even though it looks like she's broken already," the other man said. I knew his voice, too, because he said those same words.

"Remind me to thank Marvin, instead of killing him, for bringing us here," Carmelo smirked as he stabbed my mother in the chest, letting her body fall from his arms as he stepped forward. "Come to your MASTER," he smirked as he reached for me.

Move. Move. Move. Move.

I shouted that one word in my head, but what made me move was the hail of gunfire raining down from the sky. I dropped to the ground, and I could hear Alejandro screaming and dragging his brother with him. But I could still feel his eyes on me as I crawled to my mother.

"Mama? No...no...get up. Get up! Mama, Mama, please! Mama!" I screamed, pulling her into my lap as blood covered my hands.

"Shantel! Shantel!" Ian roared in my ear.

MALIKITA 'MALA' SAMUELS

UNION CITY'S CHANNEL 7 NEWS

Good evening, Union City. I'm John Goodwin here with my colleague, Natalie Bass of Channel 7 News, and we're bringing you the latest on the shocking scandal involving former Deputy Mayor Charles Morgan, rogue DEA agent Rodney Gates, and the disappearance of Roman Sharpe, the beloved Humanitarian against gun violence out of the city of Clapton. Devastating events have been taking place all over.

That's right, John. The shocking disappearance of Roman Sharpe has stunned not only the city of Clapton but also us. My sources tell me there is more to the story, as wild allegations about Sharpe's business dealings are coming to light. We should have more on that at 11. But let's talk about the scandal that has rocked Union City to its core. Reports have surfaced alleging that Charles Morgan and Rodney Gates were involved in an illicit affair, and that's just the tip of the iceberg. Channel 7 News has these shocking scenes, and we'll play it tonight at eleven. As always, viewer discretion is advised.

Absolutely, Natalie. It's been revealed that Charles Morgan is suspected of the murder of former Mayor Holmes over eight years ago. My sources from Union City's police department has confirmed that Charles knew the location of former Mayor Holmes's body. Former Deputy Mayor Charles Morgan tried to frame a prominent business owner in Union City. Lakyn Moore, the owner of Blackbay Casino, was cleared immediately as more evidence became available. This revelation has sent shockwaves through our community. Lakyn Moore has done so much for Union City's youth and has provided much-needed job opportunities to Union City's communities.

It's such a shame, but I'm glad the authorities cleared Mr. Moore's name quickly. But, the plot thickens, John. Just yesterday, police attempted to arrest Charles Morgan during his wedding to an unnamed woman at the Astor Estate. It hasn't been confirmed if it had been his long-term girlfriend or not. But authorities found themselves embroiled in a violent and deadly confrontation.

That's right, Natalie. Tragically, the grandparents, Cornelius Astor, and his wife, as well as their daughter Priscilla, mother of Charles, were found dead at the scene, along with many other guests attending the affair. It's a truly horrific turn of events. The only survivor of this event was Kenneth Morgan, the father of Charles and husband to Priscilla Astor Morgan. The candidate for the next Governor, Kenneth Morgan, is hospitalized at this time. We hope to get an update on his condition. Our thoughts and prayers are going out to him.

John, to make matters worse, Charles Morgan is now missing and presumed to be on the run. Police believe that this entire ordeal was an elaborate setup orchestrated by Charles to seize control of his family's fortune, which is estimated to be in the hundreds of billions. It's a devastating situation, Natalie. Our thoughts are with the victims and their families during this difficult time.

Absolutely, John. We will keep you updated as this story continues to unfold. For now, Natalie Bass and John Goldwin are reporting live on this developing scandal.

BREAKING NEWS

This is John Goldwin with Channel 7 News. I'm here with my colleague, Natalie, and we're bringing you a shocking update on the scandal involving former Deputy Mayor Charles Morgan and rogue DEA agent Rodney Gates.

That's right, John. In a chilling turn of events, the body of Rodney Gates has been discovered outside Union City's DEA headquarters with a cleaver buried in its chest moments ago. What's even more disturbing is that his head is nowhere to be found.

This development has sent shockwaves through the city once again, Natalie. It's a gruesome and perplexing twist in an already harrowing saga.

Absolutely, John. The circumstances surrounding Rodney Gates' death only add to the mystery and intrigue of this unfolding story.

It's clear that there are still many unanswered questions, Natalie. Our investigative teams will be working tirelessly to uncover the truth behind these shocking events.

The speculation surrounding the possible involvement of the Union City Butcher in this case is understandable, given the gruesome nature of the crime and the similarities to previous incidents associated with the infamous Butcher. However, it's important to remember that, at this stage, these reports are purely speculative. Union City's law enforcement, along with other authorities, will undoubtedly conduct a thorough investigation to determine the true circumstances behind Rodney Gates' tragic demise.

We'll continue to keep you updated as more information becomes available. Until eleven this has been, Natalie Bass and John Goldwin are reporting live on this breaking news. Don't forget to join us at eleven as we are bringing Dr. Mena Malone tonight to analyze this shocking footage of Charles Morgan and former DEA agent Rodney Gates. In other news, ROAD RAGE *is becoming a problem in Union City—*

I cut the T.V. off and turned around to face Charles. I looked down at my phone to see if Shantel had called, but there was still nothing. I looked at Link, and he shook his head before putting his phone back into his pocket. I released a sigh, but my jaw hardened as I focused on Charles. For eight fucking years, this nigga literally made my life hell. He stole those years from me and Link, but now I get to make sure he knew how I felt all those years.

"What have you...ddd...done?" Charles gasped. Link sat in a leather chair a few feet away from the metal table Charles was strapped down to. Half of his naked body was covered in a sheen of sweat, while part of the other side was nothing more than bloody flesh that I had been slowly cutting away.

"What have we done? Noo, the question is, what have you all done? I want you to tell me about that laptop. How many more of you sick bitches are there in our city? What else of ours do they want because they will never get the ports?" I snapped.

"Y...you...you don't understand. To be at the top, you have to do what is asked of you. Even us," Charles cried.

"Who is above you?" I asked, stepping closer.

Charles was quiet, closing his mouth and squeezing his one remaining good eye closed. I felt an arm wrap around my waist, and I was pulled down to sit in Link's lap. His black dress shirt had the first two buttons undone, and his sleeves were rolled up to his elbows, revealing the tattoo on his inner forearm that read Union City Kings. On the opposite arm, in the same location, was the *FOUR HORSEMEN* looking like they were riding their horses up his arm. I rubbed my hands along dark brown skin and over the tattoos. I caressed the one running along his ring finger that was newly added. It was of the date and time, to the very second, that I came back to him.

"Whoever it is, I hope they fucking kill every last one of you," Charles hissed. Spit flew from his lips as tears streamed down his swelling face. "I don't know!" Charles screamed. His voice was hoarse and broken after I took my time with the Machete and peeled his skin.

"I don't think he knows *Dove*. If he did, he would have told us by now, but it's all good. We'll hack it in time. Then we will find out what's on there," Link said along my neck. I tilted my head to the side and drew in a long breath before exhaling.

"You're right," I sighed and stood to my feet. I moved over to Charles, placed the blade on his left peck, and sliced.

"Ahhh...ff...you're fucking insane," Charles cried. I blinked and pulled the Sickle Machete away from his skin.

"And you're right as well," I nodded and hit the button on the side of the table. It began to move as I stepped away, walking to stand next to Link. Charles was still strapped down to the table that was now in an upright position, facing us.

I was trying to keep my head focused, and off of Shantel and everything she was going through, but it wasn't easy. Her pain tore away a piece of my soul, making me hate Charles even more for keeping me from being at her side. Even though I wanted eight long fucking days with this piece of shit, I had to cut it short so we could be with Shantel. Hypnosis would have been good, but we had something that would work better. It would also give me more satisfaction. No matter that Charles would have taken Teddy out if needed, I knew how much he actually cared for him. I put the Machete down on the table and clasped my hands together.

"Fuck it. Let's get this shit started then. I hope you're ready, Charles. We have a surprise guest for you," I said, clapping. Link stood up and moved over to the door and the next room.

"I...I don't know anything...mistake...it was all a mistake...I...it...you had to be done, Kita! Kita! Please, Kita, don't do this...I...I can leav—"

Charles's words died on his tongue in mid-sentence as Link rolled a metal chair into the room. Teddy was strapped down to it, thrashing and gagging around the ball gag jammed between his teeth.

"See, Charles! At least I let you see who you've been searching for all this time. You know the man you were fucking? The man who also knew the bitch shit you were doing to me," I shouted. I didn't know I had picked up the Machete again until Charles began to scream.

"Nooo! Ahhh...pl....ahhh...wait! No, hold on, just wait a minute. He...he doesn't—"

I put the blade to Charles's skin, which caused him to suck in a deep breath, cutting off his words.

"You might be right," I sighed as I withdrew the blade from his skin. I moved around Charles and went to stand in front of Teddy. His red-rimmed eyes were wide with fear as tears flowed down his cheeks. I looked over my shoulder at Charles, who stared at Teddy like he couldn't believe he was still alive. I raised the Sickle Machete in the air as Charles began to beg. The ball gag shoved into Teddy's mouth prevented his screams, but it was all in the eyes.

"Malikita! Mala! Mala, please!" Charles begged. I slowly turned around to face him, stepping to the side and moving enough for him to see Teddy. Link unhooked the buckle, releasing the gag from Teddy's mouth.

"Ahh...oh God...I don't know anything else. I swear," Teddy croaked. I looked at Link, and he began to chuckle before reaching into his waistband. He pulled out his pistol and slammed it across the back of Teddy's head.

"Ahh! Ahh! Oh...ah—"

"He doesn't know anything! Mala! Mala, Please lea—"

"Tell me about the laptop," I demanded as I cut my eyes at a battered Teddy.

"I told you th—"

Charles let out a loud scream when Link aimed and pulled the trigger. Blood oozed from Charles's right shoulder as he screamed.

"I just remembered that little *Dove* bullshit. You're lucky you still need that tongue right now," Link chuckled.

"Charles! Oh my God, Charles! He can't tell what he doesn't know," Teddy screamed.

"Shut. The. Fuck. Up. It's like all of y'all are broken fucking records. It's always I don't know anything, I swear," Link mocked. "Who the fuck asked if you knew anything, my nigga?"

I moved closer to Teddy and leaned over slightly so he could see my eyes. Link grabbed Teddy's head and pulled it back, making him look at me.

"See, Theodore, I believe you," I said softly. I stood up straight, walked over to Charles, and leaned against the metal table with my arms across my chest. I stared at Teddy, his eyes darting between me and Charles. I waited for a long moment before raising my arm, putting the Machete across Charles's throat, and slowly dragging it across.

"No! No, no, no, no! He doesn't know! He doesn't know because it's mine!"

"What's the password?" Link boomed.

"I don't know! I don't know! Wait," Teddy screamed as I slid further.

"Speak nigga! Ya' man ain't got all day," Link ordered.

"I don't know because it changes constantly. The log-in only appears when it's time for the next sale, and it could be months away!"

"How do you know when to look," Link pressed. Teddy closed his eyes, and I slid the blade deeper.

"Agg...ag—" Charles gurgled.

"Fuck! Stop, just fucking stop! Every third Tuesday...every third Tuesday I need to be at the laptop. It's voice and thumbprint recognition," Teddy gritted with his eyes firmly on Charles.

"Nigga, Charles is going to bleed out during all your stalling. Now, catch your breath and say that shit correctly," Link demanded.

"Listen, assemblage, vivification," Teddy dropped his head. Link's eyes darted down and looked back up at me. I stopped what I was doing, moved quickly to the table, grabbed the bandage, and slapped it to Charles's throat. I held it as the pad began to heat and form around his neck to seal the wound and stop the bleeding. Charles's eyes were barely open, but his lips were moving. He stared at Teddy, trying to move his head, but it was to o much.

"Is that what this tattoo means?" Link asked, tapping the back of Teddy's neck with his pistol.

"Yes, LAV. We all have it. Charles has one under his upper lip. Just help hi—"

"Nigga, you're not commanding shit, and you're not done. What is it?" Link grunted.

"It's connected to the system where all the money for the proceeds are bb...being held. My job is to move the money. That is what my family does. We move all the money that's made from the sales, after Union, into the account that is listed at that time. All I did was move money after those people were sol—"

Link placed his pistol on Teddy's neck and pulled the trigger. Charles keened as he tried and failed to scream. The pain of it must have been too much, causing him to pass out.

I lay on a stiff mattress, my arm wrapped securely around a bandaged neck. It was nothing for Link to patch Charles up as good as new for us to finish our time together. His body was covered in white bandages, with his hands cuffed together and his feet tied down. I knew at any moment, he would wake up, and I couldn't wait. His body shook, and I could feel him trying to move, so I tightened my biceps.

"Hold the fuck still, Charles," I gritted into his ear.

"Mali—"

I tightened my arm again, and he stiffened.

"I don't need you to talk. I want you to listen. You fucked me over for eight fucking years. Eight damn years, took me away from everyone, and everything I loved. You fucked me over while fucking other people for your sick little game. Do you feel that?" I asked. "I said, do you feel that?" I screamed into his ear.

"Yesss, yes," he hissed.

"Good, because I think it's about time that you know how it feels to get fucked," I sneered.

"Wai...wait—"

Charles fucked me over long, hard, and dry. So, this nigga gets no lube. I rammed an enlarged, self-lengthening spiked dildo into his ass repeatedly until his voice gave out, and I couldn't hear his screams anymore.

"No...no...ah—"

CATHARTIC.

I stepped out of the en suite and into our room at the farmhouse. Link sat in the chair in the small living room area with his laptop on the table. It had been an hour since my rendezvous with Charles.

"It's about time, *Dove*. I thought I would need to rewind this shit for you. Echo just dropped this nigga off," he said, looking up. I moved over to him, a weight I'd felt for eight years lifted off of my shoulders. Link held out his arms for me to sit in his lap. I straddled him, reverse cowgirl style, and leaned back against his chest. Link's arms wrapped tightly around my body, pressing me into him.

"Breathe for me, *Dove*," he whispered against my ear. I automatically inhaled, finally able to breathe now that I had my air.

"No way I would miss this," I sighed. Link's lips pressed against the side of my neck while he held me. He leaned over, tapping a button to bring up a view of a bandaged naked Charles hobbling down the street, screaming. The large dildo was still lodged in his ass as he screamed with each step.

"Help! Someone help me!"

Charles screamed as people stopped and stared, shocked at what they saw.

"This is so fucked up! I can't believe you left that shit in that nigga. You're wild as fuck for that," Link laughed.

"You're damn right. I left that shit there. I didn't want it," I snorted.

Charles limped through downtown Union City streets and straight to the police station.

"Shit! How are we going to see inside? No way the drone can get in without being seen, and I really need to see what your ass got planned," I laughed.

"It's all good. You know damn well I'm deeply tapped into every police station's systems. All I had to do was find which station Cortez bitch ass was at today. We need to make sure that nigga understands who runs this city," Link smirked. I rolled my eyes because this nigga was still worried about this shit with Travis and taking it out on his fine-ass daddy.

"Ooouu! Look, look," I pointed. Charles stumbled inside the station and up to the desk as people moved away from the crazy naked nigga. He was bleeding through the bandages, making his appearance more hideous, just like his soul.

"Help! Please help me! She fucked me! She fucked me in the ass!"

"Excuse me? Sir, you need to back the hell up," the desk Sergeant stated firmly.

The desk Sergeant was already unholstered with his gun in his hand.

"You're not listening! She's going to fuck me and kill me! She kidnapped me. Please help me. Why won't anyone help me?" he cried in a hoarse, scratchy voice.

"You need to calm down! Do you have an I.D.? What is your name?"

"Charles Morgan!" Charles screamed as the station went silent.

Charles stood alone in the middle of a quiet waiting area with people as far away from him as possible.

"Charles Morgan? You're telling me that you are Charles Morgan?"

"YES! They are going to kill me U—"

"In that case, Charles Morgan, you are under arrest for the murders of—"

Link twisted his wrist and pressed down on his watch, and Charles's body exploded from the inside out. It left nothing but a red mist hanging in the air.

SANCHEZ BUTLER

I watched Kaleb stroll confidently into the *WEST BRIDGE INSTITUTE FOR TALENTED YOUTH,* which Cece also attended, for gifted children. I had to enroll him under our alias for added precaution. It'd been a few weeks, and I still felt a surge of pride mixed with anxiousness. Kaleb smacked hands with Travis, or as we call him, Link's son. I didn't give a fuck what he said because that boy was his. Kaleb threw his arm over Cece's shoulder as all three walked toward the school together. The decision to move him to this new school was not taken lightly. This hiding shit was getting to him and me. But my first priority was to ensure Kaleb's safety and show him every day that I loved him while providing him with the best education possible. I glanced at Damari as he pulled up beside me. I put the window down as he leaned over. His reassuring nod eased some of my tension as I nodded back. I turned back to look one more time, making sure they were inside. The kid Travis looked back at me, and I pointed to my eyes and then at Cece and shook my head no. Travis smirked as he opened the door for them to walk inside. I turned back to Damari, who was dying laughing.

"All of y'all niggas is trippin'. But is everything good at the spot?" he said, sobering.

"Fuck you nigga, and yeah, we're good," I answered. I moved us as far as possible without having to disrupt Kaleb's life.

"Bet," he nodded. Damari leaned back against the seat before pulling out into traffic. I drove away after him, leaving the kids in the capable hands of the school.

Back at the house, we were using it as our temporary residence. I found Seyra waiting for me in the large, contemporary-styled living room. Seyra was standing with one high black heeled foot on the coffee table, butt ass naked. My dick was instantly hard as fuck just looking at her. I let my eyes roam over her smooth brown skin, thick hips, and round ass that bounced when she wasn't even trying. I kept looking until I got to the nipple rings she had gotten a few weeks ago. Seyra was someone I had grown interested in quickly, and her presence offered a welcomed distraction from all the bullshit going on.

"Why are you standing there, Sanchez? Come to me, now," she commanded. Seyra knew how to talk me into doing whatever the fuck she wanted. I moved, keeping my eyes on hers until her brows rose. I fought off the need to bend her over the couch and fuck her until she would cum for me.

"Did I ask you to look me in the eye?" she snapped.

My dick throbbed at her tone and the way her tongue licked her bottom lip when she saw what she was doing to me. The hand on her hip reached out, grabbed my dick and squeezed as soon as I stood in front of her. I lowered my eyes, which was all good for many reasons. The thin strip of hair on her pussy was calling me. I already knew when I slid my tongue between her slit she would be wet as fuck and dripping down my throat.

"No DOMINA Seyra. I apologize," I groaned. I flicked my gaze to the lit candle she held in her other hand. She removed her hand slowly, and I could feel the heat of her gaze on me.

"I thought so. Now, take off your shirt and get on your fucking knees," Seyra ordered. I did what she asked, and as I lowered to the floor, her hand came to my shoulder. Then it moved to the back of my neck, and I could feel her nails digging into my skin as she pushed my face into her waiting pussy. I felt hot wax begin to drip onto my skin as I took a long lick up her slit, flicking her clit until she moaned.

"Mmm. Suck my clit until I tell you when to stop, and you better keep that same fucking rhythm," Seyra ordered, and I had no fucking problem. All this just promised to take my mind off everything, from the bullshit with Tye, what happened with Crescent, and whatever was going on that had everyone on edge.

"Shit, oh fuck, Sans," she moaned, causing my attention to focus where it should be. Seyra's hips began to move as the pressure of her hand on my neck increased. The sting of her sharp nails had my dick throbbing, and I knew my tip was leaking. The splash of the wax had me growling into her pussy, not able to control my movements. I grabbed her thick ass and pushed her closer to me. My mouth attached to her clit like it was the only thing that would give me what I needed to quench my thirst.

"Fuck," she screamed.

Just as she bucked her hips and began to moan my name on repeat, my phone rang. The loud sound shattered the atmosphere, causing my eyes to snap open.

"Fuck that phone," Seyra groaned.

I pulled away, kissing her thigh as I reached into my pocket.

"I can't *Yaura*. It's the school ringtone," I grunted.

"Stop saying that," she sighed.

I knew I was getting feelings for her from the way I needed her. She was becoming exactly what I nicknamed her. *My hearts desire*. Because she possessed everything I needed. Except when she would pull back and go silent on a nigga. I heard her put the candle down before she sat down on the floor in front of me. Her hand was still on my neck, and it slid to the side of my face as I glanced at the caller I.D., making sure I was right.

"Hello, this is Mr. Butler," I said, clearing my throat.

My brows dropped low as the office assistant informed me that Kaleb was not in class, and they wanted to know if he was sick. I took a deep breath, trying to gather my thoughts before responding.

"Kaleb should be in class. I dropped him off myself this morning and watched him enter the school with his sister, Francesca Wellington," I replied, my mind racing to understand what could have gone wrong. Seyra scooted closer, but she released me to grab something off the couch beside us.

"Yes. I'm completely sure that neither Kaleb nor apparently Francesca is in their homeroom. They have been marked as absent," the assistant assured me. I knew Seyra heard the woman as she pulled on her dress, frowning.

"The teacher needs to look again, and they need to lock down the school," Seyra rushed out while reaching for her phone on the table.

"You need to check again! This is impossible because I saw them go into the school," I shouted, getting to my feet. I reached for my shirt, pulling it over my head as the woman promised they were looking into the matter, when a loud alarm sounded, accompanied by gunshots.

"Lock the—"

"Hello! Hello," I roared into the phone, which was now dead silent.

UNTIL NEXT TIME

Deear Reader,

Thank You For Reading This Far!
Product of the Street is a series that will span at least five books. When I do epilogues, they are not used to give you a happily-ever-after ending. They are used to progress the story's plot and develop characters in this universe. Product of the Street is a series. Every character will still be a part of the storyline, and you will always see how their relationships progress. Those of you who have read my paranormal series already know. Once this series concludes, you will have an epilogue telling the futures of each character. I hope you stick along for the ride and know that just because the story moves on does not mean it is the end of the story for your favorite character.

This is it! one more book to go!

I would love to hear from you, so please consider joining the Product Of the Street book group on Facebook!

http://www.fb://group/558629379526942?ref=share&mibextid=NSM WBT

I Hope You're Ready For Book Five! (Date TBA)

RECIPE

Mango Cheesecake

Ingredients
Yield: 8 To 10 Servings
For The Cheesecake Base

- 8ounces (About 15 2½-By-5-Inch) Graham Crackers

- 3tablespoons Dark Brown Sugar

- 1stick Butter, Softened and Cut Into Pieces

For The Filling

- 4 small Mangoes (To Make Approximately 2 Cups Purée)

- 1½Pounds Cream Cheese

- 1cup Superfine Sugar

- 6large Eggs

- Juice of half a lime

Step 1

Prepare cheesecake base: Place graham crackers in the bowl of a food processor. Process until they are almost fine crumbs. Add dark brown sugar and butter. Process until the mixture clumps together like damp sand. Press the mixture evenly into the bottom of a 9-inch springform pan and refrigerate while preparing the filling.

Step 2

Prepare filling: Heat oven to 325 degrees. Bring a kettle of water to boil. Peel and cut flesh from mangoes and purée in a food processor until smooth. Add cream cheese and process until smooth. Add superfine sugar, and with the motor running, add eggs one at a time through the processor's feed tube. Add lime juice, and process until blended.

Step 3

Place the springform pan on a double layer of strong foil. Crimp edges up around the pan to make a waterproof nest. Place foil-covered pan in a deep roasting pan. Scrape the filling into the pan and pour boiling water into the roasting pan to come about halfway up the sides of the cake pan.

Step 4

Bake until the filling is set and wobbles slightly in the center (it will continue to cook as it cools), about 1 hour and 45 minutes. Remove the springform pan from the water bath. Discard the foil and place the pan on a cooling rack. When cool, refrigerate overnight. To serve, remove from pan and place on a serving platter before slicing.

https://cooking.nytimes.com/recipes/1018799-mango-cheesecake

POEM

FOOD PLAY BY INDIGO EUPHORIA

FOOD PLAY: IS THE ACT OF BRINGING FOODS INTO THE BEDROOM THAT CAN ELEVATE YOUR SENSES AND HEIGHTEN YOUR AROUSAL FOR THE BEDROOM, TO USE DURING SEX AND FOREPLAY, ACCORDING TO KINKILY.

HE MAKES MY MOUTH SQUINCH UP

LIKE, I'M EATING SOUR SKITTLES

HE CAN BE CARAMEL

AND POUR HIMSELF ALL OVER ME

HE CAN ALSO BE MY BANANA-SPLIT

WITH STRAWBERRIES ON TOP

LIKE A CHERRY LOLLIPOP

HE LICKED ME

LIKE I'M ICE CREAM WITH SPRINKLES

WHILE EATING PRINGLES

OOH, I COULDN'T TELL HIM TO STOP

BECAUSE I'M HAVING TOO MUCH FUN

HE WORKED HIS WAY TO THE MIDDLE OF THE THIGHS

AND TORE ME UP LIKE CHECKERS FRIES

HE SUCKED MY CLIT IN BETWEEN THE SHEETS

AND TOLD ME IT TASTED SO SWEET

MY TITTIES WERE HIS CARAMEL APPLES

NOW, THAT WAS THE FOREPLAY

LET'S GET THIS PARTY STARTED

FOR THE REST OF THE FOOD FEST

FOR THE SEX PLAY
HTTPS://MYBOOK.TO/LHQGGD

FROM THE PAGES OF LICENTIOUS (EROTIC TALES BOOK 1)

ABOUT THE AUTHOR

E. BOWSER IS AN AUTHOR OF PARANORMAL ROMANCE, FANTASY, URBAN, AND HORROR FICTION. SHE WRITES WHATEVER STORIES HER IMAGINATION CAN CONCEIVE. E. BOWSER HAS ALWAYS WANTED TO WRITE A STORY THAT PEOPLE WOULD LIKE TO READ AND WOULD FALL IN LOVE WITH THE CHARACTERS. SHE LOVES IT WHEN READERS GIVE THEIR FEEDBACK SO SHE CAN MAKE HER NEXT BOOK BETTER. E. BOWSER LOVES TO READ HERSELF AND TAKES GREAT PLEASURE IN DOING SO WHENEVER SHE HAS THE CHANCE. E. BOWSER STARTED WRITING SHORT STORIES ABOUT LIFE, ANYTHING HORROR OR PARA-NORMAL, WHEN SHE WAS IN MIDDLE SCHOOL AND STILL HAS NOT STOPPED. E. BOWSER HAS BEEN AN INDEPENDENT SELF-PUBLISHED

AUTHOR SINCE 2015 AND HAS NO PLANS TO STOP AS LONG AS HER CHARACTERS KEEP TALKING.

THANK YOU FOR READING. I HOPE YOU ENJOY THE SERIES SO FAR! PLEASE REVIEW. I LOVE THEM, OR FEEL FREE TO CONTACT ME ON FACEBOOK, TWITTER, INSTAGRAM, GOOD READS, BOOK BUB, OR THROUGH MY WEBSITE. THANK YOU AGAIN FOR READING, AND KEEP LOOKING FOR MORE DEADLY SECRETS SERIES, THE RAYNE PACK SERIES SPIN-OFF, DREAM WALKER, AND PRODUCT OF THE STREET UNION CITY SERIES!

FOLLOW OR CONTACT ME AT THE LINKS BELOW TO SEE WHAT IS COMING UP NEXT!

WWW.EBOWSERBOOKS.COM

WWW.FACEBOOK.COM/AUTHORE.BOWSER

HTTPS://WWW.TIKTOK.COM/@EBOWSERAUTHOR

HTTPS://WWW.INSTAGRAM.COM/E.BOWSERBOOKS/

HTTPS://WWW.BOOKBUB.COM/AUTHORS/E-BOWSER

HTTPS://WWW.GOODREADS.COM/EBOWSER

BOOKS BY THE AUTHOR

Deadly Secrets Brothers That Bite Books 1-5

The Deadly Secrets is an exciting series focused on Taria, Michael Quinn, and LaToya are friends and lovers fighting against evil forces.

Deadly Secrets Awakening Book 1
Deadly Secrets Revealed Book 2
Deadly Secrets Consequences Book 3
Deadly Secrets Consequences Book 4
Deadly Secrets Royalty Book 5

Deadly Secrets Novellas/Novelettes

This collection of stories will give you a glimpse into the lives of Taria, Michael, LaToya, and Quinn, along with many others. Sit back and fall back into the paranormal world of Deadly Secrets.

Desires of the Harvest Moon
Twice Marked Witches and Wolves
Rise of the Phoenix
A Vampire and His Alpha Mate
A Hunter Touched My Soul
Brothers That Bite Chronicles Volume 1
Trick Or Treat The Babysitters From Hell: Deadly Secrets Halloween
Rescued By Fire: Gio & Selena's Story
Scorched By Desire: Sire & Lydia's Story
Trick Or Treat A Night From Hell: Deadly Secrets Halloween

The Crown Series Books 1-3 On-Going series
This series would be best read if you start with the Deadly Secrets Series Brothers That Bite books 1-5 and other novellas.

Taria, LaToya, Michael, and Quinn are back together again in Deadly Secrets Hunters Regin: The Crown Series. Taria Cross was turned into a Vampire by Michael Vaughn, and she became his Queen. Not only does she have to figure out this new part of her life, but she is a Hunter as well, and that is a whole other list of duties.

Deadly Secrets Hunters Reign Book 1
Their Sirenian Queen Deadly Secrets Story
Deadly Secrets A Vampire's Temptation Book 2
Deadly Secrets When Queens Are Crowned Book 3
Twice Marked A True Alpha And His Witch Deadly Secrets Story

Shades Of Passion Deadly Secrets Story Book 1

The Rayne Pack Series On-Going

Follow the Rayne Brothers as they find their Mates and fight the forces of evil. See how Dax, Max, Malic, Alex, Jarod, and Thomas fight for those they love while being attacked on all sides.

An Alpha's Claim Book 1
Submission To An Alpha Book 2

Dream Walker: Visions of the Dead On-Going Series.

What if you had the ability to see things before, they happened? Saw a zombie outbreak unfold before your very eyes? Could you embrace visions of the dead coming back to life? For Kaylee, who has been chosen to receive this gift, these visions are the beginning of a nightmare.

Dream Walker: Visions of the Dead Book 1
Dream Walker: Visions of the Dead Book 2
Dream Walker: Visions of the Dead Book 3
Dream Walker: Visions of the Dead Novella (Collection of short stories)

Product Of The Street: Union City On-Going Series.

In a single night, soul ties were created that bonded these two couples in ways they'd never planned or imagined. But will betrayal, jealousy, and death make them second guess their connections being destiny or tear them apart?
This book contains explicit language, graphic violence, and strong sexual content. It is intended for adults.

Product Of The Street: Union City Book 1
Product Of The Street: Union City Book 2

Product Of The Street: Union City Book 3
Product Of The Street: Union City Book 4
Product Of The Street: Union City Book 5 Finale (TBA)

Made in the USA
Middletown, DE
31 August 2024

60084212R00331